The Last Humans

The Complete Trilogy

Dima Zales

♠ Mozaika Publications ♠

Copyright © 2016 *Dima Zales*
www.dimazales.com

Published by Mozaika Publications, an imprint of Mozaika LLC.
www.mozaikallc.com

Cover by Najla Qamber Designs
www.najlaqamberdesigns.com

Edited by Elizabeth from arrowheadediting.wordpress.com and Mella Baxter

e-ISBN: 978-1-63142-180-8
Print ISBN: 978-1-63142-181-5

Oasis

The Last Humans: Book 1

CHAPTER ONE

*F*uck. *Vagina. Shit.*

I pointedly think these forbidden words, but my neural scan shows nothing out of the ordinary compared to when I think phonetically similar words, such as *shuck*, *angina*, or *fit*. I don't see any evidence of my brain being corrupted, though maybe it's already so damaged that things can't get any worse. Maybe I need another test subject—another 'impressionable' twenty-three-year-old Youth such as myself.

After all, I might be mentally ill.

"Oh, Theo. Not this again," says an overly friendly, high-pitched female voice. "Besides, the words do have an effect on your brain. For instance, the part of your brain responsible for disgust lights up at the mention of 'shit,' yet doesn't for 'fit.'"

This is Phoe speaking. This time, she's not a voice inside my head; instead, it's as though she's in the thick bushes behind me, except there's no one there.

I'm the only person on this strip of grass.

Nobody else comes here because the Edge is only a couple of feet away. Few residents of Oasis like looking at the dreary line dividing where our habitable world ends and the deserted wasteland of the Goo begins. I don't mind it, though.

Then again, I may be crazy—and Phoe would be the reason for that. You see, I don't think Phoe is real. She is, as far as my best guess goes, my imaginary friend. And her name, by the way, is pronounced 'Fee,' but is spelled 'P-h-o-e.'

Yes, that's how specific my delusion is.

"So you go from one overused topic straight into another." Phoe snorts. "My so-called realness."

"Right," I say. Though we're alone, I still answer without moving my lips. "Because I *am* imagining you."

She snorts again, and I shake my head. Yes, I just shook my head for the benefit of my delusion. I also feel compelled to respond to her.

"For the record," I say, "I'm sure the taboo word 'shit' affects the parts of my brain that deal with disgust just as much as its more acceptable cousins, such as 'fecal matter,' do. The point I was trying to make is that the word doesn't hurt or corrupt my brain. There's nothing special about these words."

"Yeah, yeah." This time, Phoe is inside my head, and she sounds mocking. "Next you'll tell me how back in the day, some of the forbidden words merely referred to things like female dogs, and how there are words in the dead languages that used to be just as taboo, yet they are not currently forbidden because they have lost their power. Then you're likely to complain that, though the brains of both genders are nearly identical, only males are not allowed to say 'vagina,' et cetera."

I realize I was about to counter with those exact thoughts, which means Phoe and I have talked about this quite a bit. This is what happens between close friends: they repeat conversations. Doubly so with imaginary friends, I figure. Though, of course, I'm probably the only person in Oasis who actually has one.

Come to think of it, wouldn't *every* conversation with your imaginary friend be redundant since you're basically talking to yourself?

"This is my cue to remind you that I'm real, Theo." Phoe purposefully states this out loud.

I can't help but notice that her voice came slightly from my right, as if she's just a friend sitting on the grass next to me—a friend who happens to be invisible.

"Just because I'm invisible doesn't mean I'm not real," Phoe responds to my thought. "At least *I'm* convinced that I'm real. I would be the crazy one if I *didn't* think I was real. Besides, a lot of evidence points to that conclusion, and you know it."

"But wouldn't an imaginary friend *have* to insist she's real?" I can't resist saying the words out loud. "Wouldn't this be part of the delusion?"

"Don't talk to me out loud," she reminds me, her tone worried. "Even when you subvocalize, sometimes you imperceptibly move your neck muscles or even your lips. All those things are too risky. You should just think your thoughts at me. Use your inner voice. It's safer that way, especially when we're around other Youths."

4

"Sure, but for the record, that makes me feel even nuttier," I reply, but I subvocalize my words, trying my best not to move my lips or neck muscles. Then, as an experiment, I think, "Talking to you inside my head just highlights the impossibility of you and thus makes me feel like I'm missing even more screws."

"Well, it shouldn't." Her voice is inside my head now, yet it still sounds high-pitched. "Back in the day, when it was not forbidden to be mentally ill, I imagine it made people around you uncomfortable if you spoke to your imaginary friends out loud." She chuckles, but there's more worry than humor in her voice. "I have no idea what would happen if someone thought you were crazy, but I have a bad feeling about it, so please don't do it, okay?"

"Fine," I think and pull at my left earlobe. "Though it's overkill to do it here. No one's around."

"Yes, but the nanobots I told you about, the ones that permeate everything from your head to the utility fog, *can* be used to monitor this place, at least in theory."

"Right. Unless all this conveniently invisible technology you keep telling me about is as much of a figment of my imagination as you are," I think at her. "In any case, since no one seems to know about this tech, how can they use it to spy on me?"

"Correction: no Youth knows, but the others might," Phoe counters patiently. "There's too much we still don't know about Adults, not to mention the Elderly."

"But if they can access the nanocytes in my mind, wouldn't they have access to my thoughts too?" I think, suppressing a shudder. If this is true, I'm utterly screwed.

"The fact that you haven't faced any consequences for your frequently wayward thoughts is evidence that no one monitors them in general, or at least, they're not bothering with yours specifically," she responds, her words easing my dread. "Therefore, I think monitoring thoughts is either computationally prohibitive or breaks one of the bazillion taboos on the proper use of technology—rules I have a very hard time keeping track of, by the way."

"Well, what if using tech to listen in on me is also taboo?" I retort, though she's beginning to convince me.

"It may be, but I've seen evidence that can best be explained as the Adults spying." Her voice in my head takes on a hushed tone. "Just think of the time you and Liam made plans to skip your Physics Lecture. How did they know about that?"

I think of the epic Quietude session we were sentenced to and how we both swore we hadn't betrayed each other. We reached the same conclusion: our speech is not secure. That's why Liam, Mason, and I now often speak in code.

"There could be other explanations," I think at Phoe. "That conversation happened during Lectures, and someone could've overheard us. But even if they hadn't, just because they monitor us during class doesn't mean they would bother monitoring this forsaken spot."

"Even if they don't monitor *this* place or anywhere outside of the Institute, I still want you to acquire the right habit."

"What if I speak in code?" I suggest. "You know, the one I use with my non-imaginary friends."

"You already speak too slowly for my liking," she thinks at me with clear exasperation. "When you speak in that code, you sound ridiculous and drastically increase the number of syllables you say. Now if you were willing to learn one of the dead languages . . ."

"Fine. I will 'think' when I have to speak to you," I think. Then I subvocalize, "But I will also subvocalize."

"If you must." She sighs out loud. "Just do it the way you did a second ago, without any voice musculature moving."

Instead of replying, I look at the Edge again, the place where the serene greenery under the Dome meets the repulsive ocean of the desolate Goo—the ever-replicating parasitic technology that converts matter into itself. The Goo is what's left of the world outside the Dome barrier, and if the barrier were to ever come down, the Goo would destroy us in short order. Naturally, this view evokes all sorts of unpleasant feelings, and the fact that I'm voluntarily gazing at it must be yet another sign of my shaky mental state.

"The thing *is* decidedly gross," Phoe reflects, trying to cheer me up, as usual. "It looks like someone tried to make Jell-O out of vomit and human excrement." Then, with a mental snicker, she adds, "Sorry, I should've said 'vomit and shit.'"

"I have no idea what Jell-O is," I subvocalize. "But whatever it is, you're probably spot on regarding the ingredients."

"Jell-O was something the ancients ate in the pre-Food days," Phoe explains. "I'll find something for you to watch or read about it, or if you're lucky, they might serve it at the upcoming Birth Day fair."

"I hope they do. It's hard to learn about food from books or movies," I complain. "I tried."

"In this case, you might," Phoe counters. "Jell-O was more about texture than taste. It had the consistency of jellyfish."

"People actually ate those slimy things back then?" I think in disgust. I can't recall seeing that in any of the movies. Waving toward the Goo, I say, "No wonder the world turned to this."

"They didn't eat it in most parts of the world," Phoe says, her voice taking on a pedantic tone. "And Jell-O was actually made out of partially decomposed proteins extracted from cow and pig hides, hooves, bones, and connective tissue."

"Now you're just trying to gross me out," I think.

"That's rich, coming from you, Mr. Shit." She chuckles. "Anyway, you have to leave this place."

"I do?"

"You have Lectures in half an hour, but more importantly, Mason is looking for you," she says, and her voice gives me the impression she's already gotten up from the grass.

I get up and start walking through the tall shrubbery that hides the Goo from the view of the rest of Oasis Youths.

"By the way"—Phoe's voice comes from the distance; she's simulating walking ahead of me—"once you verify that Mason *is* looking for you, *do* try to explain how an imaginary friend like me could possibly know something like that ... something you yourself didn't know."

CHAPTER TWO

Campus can look gorgeous when the sun is about to set. It's one of the few times the color red enters the Institute's premises. Green is usually the predominant hue around these parts—green from the grass, green from the trees, and green from the ivy covering all the structures. It would all be green if the ivy had its way, but some of the more resistant parts of the Institute's buildings are still silver and glass.

I pass the triangular prism shape of the Middle-Grade Dormitory and see the children out and about; their Lectures end much earlier than ours.

"Mason is by the northeast side of the campus," Phoe directs me.

"Thanks," I whisper back and turn toward the cuboid shape of the Lectures Building in the distance. "Now can you please shut up and give me ten minutes of feeling like I'm not insane?"

Phoe pointedly doesn't reply. If she thinks that giving me the silent treatment when I ask her to shut up is going to annoy me, then she knows me far too poorly, especially for a figment of my imagination.

As I walk, I attempt to focus on how much I'm enjoying the silence, in part because I am, but mostly because I want to irritate Phoe.

The silence doesn't last long. As I approach the green expanse of the Recreation Field, I hear the excited voices of Youths playing Frisbee. When I get closer, I see that most of them are aged thirty and up, though a few of the Youths are in their twenties, like me.

A little farther, I notice a couple of teenaged Youths deep in meditation. I observe their serene faces with envy. My own meditation practice has recently gone down the drain. Every time I try to do anything soothing, my mind buzzes and I'm unable to find my center.

My stomach grumbles, yanking me out of my thoughts.

I put my palm out, and in an instant, a warm bar of Food appears in my hand. I take a hungry bite, and my taste buds explode with sensations. Every bar of Food has a unique ratio of saltiness, sourness, sweetness, bitterness, and umami, and this specific bar is particularly savory. I enjoy the taste. Eating is one of the few pleasures that insanity hasn't ruined for me—at least not yet.

"Well, Food does have its hedonistic value," Phoe says, grudge apparently forgotten, "if not much else."

I keep eating while trying to make my mind blank. I have a feeling Phoe is itching to say something else. She likes to shock me, like when she explained that Food is assembled by tiny machines at my whim.

"Nano-sized machines," she corrects. "And yes, Food is assembled, just like most tangible objects in Oasis."

"So what isn't assembled?" I ask, though I'm not sure I believe her.

"Well, I don't think the buildings are, though I'm not sure," Phoe says. "Certainly the Augmented Reality stuff, like your Screen and half of the prettier-looking trees on this campus, are not assembled, since they're not tangible in any way. And living things aren't assembled either. Although, if I were a stickler, I'd argue that living things in general are powered by nanomachines, just of a different kind." Her voice is as excited as Liam's gets when he's planning a prank.

Ignoring her prattle, I take another bite and pointedly thank the Forebears for Food.

"Did you do that to annoy me?" Phoe asks. "Did you just thank those technology-fearing simpletons for making this gratuitous choice on your behalf? I told you, your body could be tuned so that your internal nanobots would make eating and waste management completely unnecessary."

"But that would make my already-boring life noticeably more boring." I lick what's left of the Food bar off my fingers.

"We can debate this later," Phoe says, thankfully leaving the topic alone. "Mason is in the rock garden—and you've passed it."

"Thanks," I think at her and retrace my steps.

When I enter the rock garden, I see a guy sitting on the grass at the far end, near the silver dodecahedron statuette. His back is to me, so I can't tell who it is, but he does look like Mason.

I approach quietly, not wanting to startle the Youth in case he's in a meditative trance.

He must not have been, because even though I'm walking softly, the Youth hears me and turns around. His face resembles that of Eeyore, the donkey from an ancient cartoon.

"Hey, dude," I say, trying my best to hide my annoyance at Phoe. This *is* Mason, and he's exactly where she told me he'd be, and I indeed don't have a good explanation for how an imaginary friend would know this.

In fact, I don't have a good explanation for many things Phoe can do, such as make me exempt from Oneness—

"Theo," Mason says, looking slightly surprised. "You're here. I was about to go looking for you or Liam."

"I told you so," Phoe whispers in my mind.

"What did you want?" I say to Mason. To Phoe, I subvocalize, "And you, be quiet. And yes, I'm choosing this way of responding to you because it's easier to show my irritation. I don't know if I can think irritatingly."

"Oh, trust me, you can," Phoe says, not bothering to whisper. "Your thoughts can be *very* irritating."

Mason doesn't hear her, of course, but I notice how hesitant he is to continue speaking. He looks around furtively, and when he's satisfied that we're alone, he whispers, "Eway eednay otay alktay."

"That's, 'We need to talk,'" I think at Phoe.

"I know what that means," Phoe says so loudly that I picture my ears popping. "I was the one who dug up that article about Pig Latin from the ancient archives for you," she adds with less outrage and at a lower decibel level.

"Let's walk as we talk," I reply to Mason in Pig Latin. "We're late for Lectures."

"Whateveray," Mason replies and gets up from the grass. As he stands, I see that his shoulders are noticeably hunched, as though his head is too heavy for his body.

"It's 'ateverwhay,'" I correct him as we begin walking toward the tetrahedron Kindergarten Building.

"Whatever," Mason says without code, shuffling beside me.

I'm about to say something sarcastic, but Mason startles me by saying in code, "I'm too upset to get this stuff right."

I look at him in confusion, but he continues, "No, not just upset." His voice is losing vitality by the second. Stopping, Mason gives me a morose look. "I'm depressed, Theo."

I halt in shock. "You're what?" I say, forgetting Pig Latin.

"Yes. Yes, the *taboo* word." He flexes his fingers, then lets them droop. "I'm fucking depressed."

I look at his face for signs that he's joking, even though this isn't a joke-conducive topic, but I see none. His expression is gloomy, consistent with his revelation.

"Mason . . ." I swallow. "I don't know what to say."

I'm glad he said his revelation in code. Even so, I look around to make sure we're still walking alone.

There are two problems with what he just said. The first one is minor: he said the word 'fucking' out loud. That can lead to a day's worth of Quietude for him and some trouble for me if I don't squeal on him for using profanity (which I never would, of course). Infinitely worse, though, is that he said he was 'depressed'—not to mention, he meant it. That word represents an idea so unthinkable I don't know what the punishment for it would be. It's one of those

13

needless taboos like, 'Don't eat your friends.' The rule probably exists, but since no one's ever eaten someone else in the history of Oasis, you don't know what the Adults would do if you *did*.

"Whatever the consequences are, they would be bad," Phoe thinks. "Both for cannibalism and for not being happy."

"Then we're both screwed," I subvocalize at her, "since I'm not happy."

"You're not depressed," she says. "Now quick, he's still waiting for you to reply with something more supportive than your, 'I dunno what to say.' So please, be a dear and say something along the lines of, 'What can I do to help?'" Then, worriedly, she adds, "His neural scan is unlike anything I've ever seen."

"Atwhay ancay Iway oday otay elphay?" I ask as Phoe suggested.

Mason raises his hands to cover his face, but I glimpse moisture in his eyes. He holds his face as if it might melt if he'd let go, and I just stare at him dumbly, the way I did during a scene of the one and only horror flick I allowed Phoe to show me.

My imagination failing me, I make the small wrist gesture required to bring up a private Screen into the air in front of me. Phoe takes that as a cue to put Mason's neural scan on it.

I examine the image for a second and think at Phoe, "I've never seen anything like it either. He's extremely distraught."

"I think the reason you've never seen this is because you've never met anyone who was genuinely depressed until now," Phoe thinks back.

"So he really *is* depressed?" I subvocalize, barely stopping myself from speaking out loud. "What do I do, Phoe?"

"Ancient texts suggest you might want to put a hand on his shoulder. Do that and don't say anything," Phoe says. "That should comfort him, I think."

I do as she suggests. His shoulder is strangely twitchy under my hand at first, but then, slowly, he lets go of his face. His expression is not completely foreign to me—little kids get it before they learn how to act civilized and look properly happy.

Mason takes a deep breath, lets it out, and in a shaky voice says, "I told Grace how I feel, and she called me a crazy creep."

Stunned, I release his shoulder and step back.

"Crap," Phoe says, echoing my thoughts. "This is bad."

CHAPTER THREE

Like I told Phoe, I'm not as happy as others in Oasis. Coincidentally, my restlessness began with Phoe. Specifically, it began when she first spoke to me a few weeks ago. No, truth be told, it started a bit later, when I learned that certain really cool stuff, like great movies, books, and video games, repeatedly get wiped from Oasis's libraries.

At least I assume it happens repeatedly. On my watch, it happened to *Pulp Fiction*, a movie Phoe had found buried deep in the ancient archives. The movie was awesome, but either because I'd accessed it or because of some horrible coincidence, *Pulp Fiction* got on the radar of either the Elderly or the Adults, and they deleted it. One day it was on my Screen, the next I couldn't bring it up. Phoe said it was no longer in the archives either.

What's worse is this happened before I got a chance to get Liam and Mason to watch it with me. My friends didn't even believe me when I said that the movie used to exist. Phoe was my only witness, and I'm not ready to tell Liam or Mason about her. Actually, being unable to share something with my friends for the first time in my life has also been a source of unpleasantness, but not as much as the questions that now plague me: Why delete such a good movie? Was it because it had all those banned words? Or was it the violence?

If I asked these questions out loud, I'd get a numbingly boring Quietude session instead of answers—and that drives me nuts. So, because of all this, had anyone asked me before today, I would've said that *I'm* the one and only unhappy person in Oasis. Yet even I wouldn't call how I feel 'depressed.'

"I didn't think it was physically possible for anyone to get depressed," Phoe whispers. "The nanocytes in your head regulate serotonin and norepinephrine re-uptake, among a million other variables that synergistically conspire to keep you nice and cheerful. On top of that, the Institute curriculum includes copious amounts of meditation, exercise, and other feel-good propaganda."

"Didn't you hear me?" Mason repeats, his voice quivering. "I told Grace I love her."

He thinks I'm judging him, and it's hard not to. Sexual interest—or romantic love, as it used to be called—is not part of our world. The only reason we even know about it is because of ancient media, which is rife with examples of people our age being 'in love'—a state of being that sounds qualitatively different from love of Food or love for one's friends. People even used to get 'married' back then and start 'families'—two social constructs that are incredibly weird.

17

Marriage I could sort of understand. It was probably like being friends with a female for a big portion of your life. I can relate to that because we used to be friends with Grace. Family, however, is just bizarre. It would be like being friends with people based on random factors, such as DNA commonalities, and with people of varying ages—including the Adults and the Elderly. Since Youths never meet the elusive Elderly and the only Adults we come across are the Instructors, I find family hard to picture.

As to romantic love, I didn't think anyone has any interest in that stuff. That strange emotion was a form of insanity tied to procreation, and the Elderly take care of that now—though exactly how they do it is the type of question that gets you an hour of Quietude instead of an answer.

I know that from experience.

"Actually, taking procreation out of the game never stopped lust or love for the ancients," Phoe butts in. "They had something called birth control. I think the real reason these desires disappeared is because of the neutering effect of the nanocytes." Before I can ask her about that, she continues, "Of course, given that those nanocytes are also supposed to keep you nice and cheerful, I can only assume that Mason is in this situation because his nanocytes can't cope with whatever is malfunctioning in his brain. If I had to guess, given his prior manic phases, I'd say he's bipolar."

"Theo," Mason says, his chin trembling. "I told Grace—"

"I heard you, dude," I say, shutting out Phoe's rambling explanation to focus on my friend. "I'm just at a loss for words. I told you to keep away from Grace."

18

"You also told me I was going through a phase and didn't know what I was feeling," Mason retorts. "As did your friend Liam."

Liam is closer to Mason than I've ever been, but now is not the time to be a stickler for definitions. When Mason confided in us, I didn't grasp the extent of his seriousness. I thought he wanted to prove that he could be the biggest misfit in our little band of misfits—and saying shocking things such as, "I like a girl," certainly did it, particularly because he chose the most annoying snitch as the object of his obsession.

"So you told Grace you loved her?" I shake my head in frustration. "Don't you understand? She's going to tell on you, and you're going to be in a world of trouble."

Mason just looks at me. "I don't care. You don't understand, Theo. I've been thinking—" He swallows. "I've been thinking about ending it all."

"Don't say that," I hiss at him, horrified. "Not even in Pig Latin."

"But it's true." He sits down on the ground and stares vacantly into the distance. "Sometimes I—" His throat moves as he swallows again. He raises his head to glance at me, and I see that his eyes are red and watery. "It would be so much better if I'd never been born at all."

I'm overwhelmed by his words. My face must look like one of those ancient Japanese masks Phoe once showed me. Mason has been my close friend for as long as I can remember, yet it's like I don't know him at all. Depression and strange feelings toward Grace are bad enough, but now he's turned the conversation toward even murkier waters.

Death and suicide are beyond taboo. In a way, they're somewhat academic as far as these things go. We all understand their meaning—the concept of death was too ubiquitous in antiquity for us not to come across it—but now that no one ever dies, thinking about death seems pointless. Theoretically, a freak accident could kill someone, but in reality, such an event has never occurred in the history of Oasis. So yeah, unlike cursing, I find it very easy and natural to follow *this* rule and never talk or even think about—

"Stop being so self-absorbed, Theo," Phoe chides me in my mind. "Your friend's in pain."

I look at Mason, who's now hunched over with his head buried in his hands. Taking a deep breath, I step toward him and ask, "What can I do?"

This question is meant for both Mason and Phoe.

"Nothing," Mason says.

"Find a way to get him to relax," Phoe suggests, "and try to fix what he did with that girl."

"Listen, Mason. Let me take you to the Dorms," I say, putting my hand back on his shoulder. "Take a nap instead of going to the History Lecture. I'll tell Instructor Filomena you're sick tonight, and I'll talk to Grace to try to unravel this mess."

"You're wasting your time," Mason says dully. "I don't care if I'm in trouble. I don't care about anything."

"That's cool," I say, feigning enthusiasm. "After you wake up, we'll talk about getting into all kinds of trouble. I'm game to do a prank on Owen if you're still up for that. You know we owe that asshole for leaving dirt in our room. Or tomorrow night we can tell Instructor Filomena to shove her History Lecture up one of her orifices."

The second idea brings a hint of a smile to Mason's face. He hates our History Instructor.

Relieved, I smile back at him. "And remember," I say, trying to capitalize on my success, "Birth Day is in less than three days."

Mason loves the festivities of Birth Day as much as we all do. And why wouldn't he? It combines all of the ancients' holidays of birthdays, Christmas, Hanukkah, Thanksgiving, Election Day, and many others neatly into one celebration. Not to mention that we'll all be a year closer to forty, the age when Youths become Adults and are no longer treated like little kids.

The mention of Birth Day seems to cheer Mason up even more. "You know," he says, "I wouldn't even be lying if I played hooky tonight. I *do* feel sick."

"Exactly." I make my voice extra cheerful. "You have the perfect excuse."

I help him up, and we head toward the Dorms.

As we walk, I steer the conversation onto safer topics, doing my best to distract him from the funk he's in.

"Ask him about his bonsai tree collection," Phoe suggests. "You know how much he likes those things."

Her idea makes sense, so I pretend to have developed a deep caring for Mason's stunted little trees, and he's glad to tell me more than anyone would ever need to know about the subject.

As I pretend to listen, I plan my conversation with Grace. Maybe her silence can be bought with some kind of favor? Or maybe I can convince her we're playing a prank on her? Prank penalties we can deal with.

"This is why you have to use the clippers, not scissors, to prune the tree," Mason says as we enter our room. Stopping, he sighs, and

I see his expression darkening as he adds, "Pruning those trees is the only thing that soothes me, but even doing that hasn't been enough."

I point at his corner of the room and say, "Take that nap, dude."

Mason stares at his corner for a moment, and then a bed materializes.

"Actually, it's assembled from scratch by the nanos in the utility fog," Phoe butts in.

"I was just thinking to myself," I subvocalize. "This is the problem with talking to you via thoughts."

Mason walks over, gingerly lies down on the bed, and closes his eyes.

I wait a beat, not knowing if I should stay until he falls asleep and unsure how I'd even tell if he were asleep.

"He's *already* asleep," Phoe says. "He must have requested sleep as a thought command, the way he did with the bed."

"That guy was never a big fan of gestures," I think at her idly and walk out of the room. "Do you know where I can find—"

"Grace will be by the History Hall," Phoe says, her voice echoing off the shiny, arched walls of the dormitory hallway. Clearly catching my thought, she says, "That echo effect is your brain playing tricks." Her voice is in my mind this time.

I start walking faster, and when I think no one is looking, I break into a run. If they catch me running, I can always lie and say I was exercising. That's a trick invented by Liam, the guy who's always in a hurry to get somewhere.

As soon as I'm outside, I move over to the running path. This way no one will question my 'exercise.'

* * *

I see Grace's red hair in the corridor by the entrance to the History Hall, but before I can approach her, a hand grabs my shoulder.

"Dude," Liam says in his excited, screechy voice. "Where have you been all day?"

"Not now, Liam." I give a minute shake of my head. "I have something urgent going on."

"What is it?" He gives me a good-natured shove—an act that can get him as long of a Quietude session as a genuinely violent hit.

"No time to explain." My tone is firm and uncompromising—something that, on very rare occasions, takes Liam out of his hyperactive mode.

"Whatever it is"—Liam bounces from foot to foot—"I'm coming along."

I sigh and hurry toward Grace, grateful that he's at least stopped talking for the moment.

"Ah, if it isn't the Twin Stooges," Grace says, giving Liam a chilly look and me a crooked smile.

"It's the Three Stooges, you ignorant twat," Phoe says, though of course Grace can't hear her.

"I think she calls us twins because she thinks we're very alike," I think at Phoe, trying to shut her up.

"You're tall, blond, and blue-eyed," Phoe says with a slight growl, "while the top of Liam's head reaches your chin, and his hair is brown. More to the point, you're way more handsome and a lot less twitchy than your stocky friend, and she knows it." Her words sound as if they're coming through clenched teeth. "I can see it in the bitch's eyes. You and Liam couldn't be less alike if you tried. And Mason—"

"Mason is the reason I'm here, Phoe. The reason I need to talk to the 'twat'—whatever that means. So please, shut it." Despite my annoyance at her, I can't help mentally chuckling at my imaginary friend calling me handsome. It must be some advanced form of narcissism.

Focusing on the matter at hand, I smile at Grace, and as politely as I can, say, "Hi, Grace. I'd like to discuss something with you."

The bell sounds, signifying the start of the Lecture.

"I think I know what this is about," Grace says as she flutters her big eyelashes at me. "And it will have to wait. I won't be late for the Lecture."

Before I can say anything back, she steps between Liam and me and disappears into the classroom.

"What was that about?" Liam says. "Let's cut History so you can tell me about it."

I look my friend over. When he's excited like this, with his shaggy hair in its usual messy state and his brown eyes twinkling, he reminds me of Taz, the Tasmanian Devil from an ancient cartoon.

"Sorry, I can't skip it," I say. "I can't get Quietude until I speak with her."

Without waiting for Liam to object, I follow Grace into the History Hall.

Everybody's already seated. Instead of gesturing to create myself a seat, I use a thought command and get my Screen up when the desk appears in front of me.

Under the pretext of looking at the syllabus on my Screen, I study Grace.

Like everyone else, she's wearing a boxy, shapeless shirt and a loose pair of pants that conceal most of her body. Still, her tall, slender build is visible, and if I forget about her treacherous personality, I have to admit she's pleasant to look at, as far as physical appearances go.

With her symmetrical facial features, Grace reminds me of a female from ancient times.

"That's because all the ancients you've seen are models and actresses," Phoe intrudes. "The physical attractiveness of the ancients followed a normal distribution curve, but you're only familiar with the outliers left in the media records, and even those, after they were airbrushed . . ."

"And so the history lesson begins before Filomena can open her mouth," I subvocalize at her.

"I had to stop you before you could decide which cartoon character Grace reminded you of," Phoe thinks.

"The Little Mermaid," I reply, mostly to annoy her.

"You're pretty generous." Phoe's tone is strangely tense. "I think she looks more like Ariel's little red crab friend."

"Good evening, students," Instructor Filomena says in her nasally voice as she enters. "Have you prepared yourselves for the wonders of history?"

I cringe. Instructor Filomena has a flare for the dramatic and often exaggerates how interesting her subject matter is.

"In her defense," Phoe whispers, "all Adults are obsessed with the topics they've decided to make their life's work."

I ignore Phoe and hope today's lesson shows more of the ancient world than the usual propaganda.

"I will not be collecting your assignments today," Instructor Filomena says. It's music to my ears, since I just saw the essay on the syllabus. "I'm initiating Virtual Reality right away," she continues, "so don't get startled."

I'd like to know who gets startled by something they've been exposed to most of their lives.

"Well, you do sometimes get—"

"Thinking to myself again, Phoe," I subvocalize at her. "If you want these messages by thought to continue, you need to learn to distinguish which ones are meant for you and which ones are me simply talking to myself—unless, of course, talking to you is the same as talking to myself. In which case, all of this is moot."

Phoe mumbles something, but I miss what, because the VR portion of the lesson begins, and it's one of the few parts of the History Lecture I actually enjoy.

I'm no longer in my seat in the Hall.

I'm no longer even in Oasis.

Instead, I'm standing on a patch of weeds and dirt on top of a majestic green hill. The air is cold and smells of flowers I can't name. To my right is a gigantic wall that extends through the hill I'm standing on, spiraling for miles as far as the eye can see.

"This is the Great Wall of China," I subvocalize. "Right?"

"Yes," Phoe says. "I can't believe she shows you these marvels yet never properly names them."

I don't answer, because before I can savor it all, I'm no longer standing next to the Wall, but next to a giant, half-ruined oval structure I know well: the Coliseum.

"I bet the Taj Mahal is next," Phoe says.

"Shush," I say. "I'm having the only fun to be had in Filomena's Lecture."

"Told you so," Phoe says when the next location materializes around me—or is it more accurate to say I materialize in the next location?

I'm standing next to a white marble structure, trying to take a mental snapshot before the scenery changes again.

The Empire State Building is next, followed by the Grand Canyon, then the majestic waters of Niagara Falls. The scenes of the ancient world come quicker and quicker until they speed by so fast that I can't name them.

Then I see ancient Earth from a tiny round window—a vantage point in space. I love this part because I feel weightless, and because ancient Earth looks so magnificent—a blue world full of life.

Then, suddenly, comes my least favorite part.

It's the same vantage point, only Earth has changed.

The blue oceans of water, the yellow deserts of sand, the green forests, the red canyons—they're all gone, replaced by the orange-brown mess of Goo.

My vantage point zooms in, but I still can't see Oasis, just an ever-increasing, drab-colored layer of Goo. The view zooms in even more, and finally, after a few more zooms, I see a tiny island of green underneath the barrier of the Dome.

"Blah, blah," Phoe says. "The kiddies get it. Oasis is but 0.00000171456 of Earth's surface and the rest is puke-shit. I think this came across after the first thousand times this point was made."

"Much was lost when the technological Armageddon arrived," the Instructor's disembodied voice states. "Oasis survived by mere chance, saved by its isolation and by its people's unwillingness to succumb to the evils of technology run amok. Today, we will study the Amish—the group that inspired our Forebears. Brave souls who shunned the technology of their day, just as we do now."

"Is she really not aware of the concept of irony?" Phoe says. "She gives the 'we denounce technology' spiel, when every one of your brains is currently at the mercy of your nanocytes, every input and output of every neuron carefully controlled to provide a fully immersive fake reality experience—"

"Phoe," I whisper in warning, but it's to no avail; we've hit my imaginary friend's pet peeve.

"Technology, in the form of a force field, protects us from the Goo outside." Phoe's speech gets maniacally urgent. "Technology in the form of nano-machines dresses you, feeds you, creates the air you breathe, and takes care of the waste you excrete."

I don't disagree with a single word Phoe says; I'm just angry that she's speaking, so, out of sheer spitefulness, I subvocalize, "The nano replicators are also what turned the world into Goo."

I hear Phoe take a deep inhale and prepare for an avalanche of objections, but instead, she says, "I know you're just trying to push my buttons."

"What gave me away?" I try to inject as much sarcasm as one can into a thought.

She doesn't reply.

"Two silent treatments in a single day? I'm definitely getting better at dealing with my *imaginary* friend," I think pointedly.

She still doesn't reply, so I return my attention to the lesson at hand.

I'm back in the default empty space, where Instructor Filomena's booming voice is telling us about the virtues of Amish society. I tune it all out, knowing I'll only get angry again. Our curriculum, especially Filomena's History Lecture, is an exercise in cherry picking. For example, she is highlighting our similarities with the Amish but ignoring important differences, like, say, religion. From what I've gathered through my own research, the Amish were defined by their religious beliefs, ideas completely foreign to us.

I expect Phoe to chime in and say something like, "Her parallels are even weaker than the time when she compared Oasis to the visions of the ancient philosopher Plato and his Republic," but Phoe is still holding a grudge.

To provoke Phoe to speak, I subvocalize, "Hmm, I wonder if it's the next stage of my insanity that I can imagine Phoe's words so exactly . . ."

Phoe doesn't take the bait.

Bored, I listen to the lesson. After Filomena further jumbles her message and I feel as if I've just experienced the most boring fifteen minutes of my life, I subvocalize, "Maybe I shouldn't have pissed off Phoe."

Phoe lets me suffer for another ten minutes before she mumbles a hushed, "Serves you right," and makes a point to stay quiet for another torturous half hour—the rest of the Lecture.

"That's all for today," Filomena finally says and the reality of the classroom returns. "Remember," she continues, "as that ancient poet said, those who don't learn from history are doomed to repeat it."

I fight the slight disorientation that always accompanies coming out of VR. In my peripheral vision, I see Grace get up, and I leap to my feet.

Grace exits the Hall and I follow, ignoring Liam's attempt to get my attention.

"Please, Grace," I say, catching up with her.

Grace stops in the middle of the corridor and looks back.

"What?" she says, twirling a red curl around her finger. "Make it quick."

"It's about what Mason might've misled you to believe—"

"Save your lies, Theodore," Grace says. "I already gave my report to the Dean."

CHAPTER FOUR

"F—"

"Don't say anything that will give the snitch more ammunition," Phoe says, her grievances with me instantly forgotten. "Keep your cool."

Focusing on not cursing, I manage to say, "You told?"

I say the words with some strange hope, as if maybe Grace is just taunting me, but her face looks earnest, and I start to feel something older Youths in Oasis almost never experience.

Anxiety.

Some of my turmoil must show on my face, because Grace frowns and says, her voice lowered, "You don't understand, Theo. Mason needs help. I did it for his sake—and to protect myself."

My hands do something unexpected: they turn into fists.

"Theo, what the hell?" Phoe says. "Did you really just think about hitting a girl?"

"No," I subvocalize and take a deep breath. "And what does gender have to do with it?" Before Phoe can respond, I add, "I haven't thought about hitting anyone for years now, with the exception of Owen, but he's such an asshole that wanting to hit him obviously doesn't count."

"Walk away, now," Phoe says, her tone clipped.

"You shouldn't have done that," I say to Grace, ignoring Phoe. "Why are you being like this? We used to be friends—"

"Are you finally building up the courage to call me a snitch to my face?" Grace's usually melodious voice sounds like a hiss. "You think I don't know that's what you and your little band call me? All I'm trying to do is help Mason before he hurts himself or someone else. Just grow up already."

And before I can respond, she storms off.

"That's odd. I think she's running—a breach of the rules," Phoe says, sounding as confused as I feel.

Liam finally catches up to me and stares at Grace's disappearing figure. "What the uckfay was that about?"

"Dude, you can't just say the f-word in Pig Latin," I say in Pig Latin. "It doesn't take a genius cryptologist to figure out what you mean based on the context."

"Owblay emay," Liam says in code, then normally adds, "How's that? That's two words: 'blow,' which is perfectly allowed, and 'me,' which is also allowed." He grins as I shake my head, then says more seriously, "Listen, dude. Something's going on, and you have to tell me what it is."

"Fine," I say. "I'll tell you on the way back to the Dorms."

As we leave the Lectures Building, I begin my tale, speaking Pig Latin throughout and keeping my voice low. Campus is overflowing with Youths, and as we walk, I have to politely refuse an invitation to play hacky sack. A short while after, Liam not-so-politely refuses to join a paired badminton game. It's not until we're halfway to the Dorms that I finish explaining Mason's predicament.

"What did you expect from that itchbay?" Liam says as we approach the soccer field. "He shouldn't have told her anything. I mean, what the f—"

Liam doesn't finish his sentence because at that moment, a soccer ball hits him in the crotch.

With a gasp, my friend bends at the waist, clutching the injured area.

Before the ball can roll away, I pick it up and look around.

Several Youths are approaching us.

"Are you okay?" asks Kevin, a Youth we rarely interact with. He looks genuinely concerned.

"Yeah," says the all-too-familiar, hyena-like voice of Owen. "Are you going to cry, Li-Li-Kins?" he says, using Liam's despised childhood nickname. "I'm *so* sorry," he adds, winking at me.

A mix of growls, speech, and Pig Latin escapes Liam's throat.

Owen sneers. "Usually, hitting *sucker* balls is a lot more fun than this."

Liam takes a step in his direction.

Still holding on to the ball, I step between them preemptively. I've seen this routine play out a million times before.

Owen and his band of three other misfits hate our trio. The feud goes back to when we were little, when Owen and co. bullied any kid they could. We weren't such easy prey, though, thanks mainly to Liam. Our crew back then included a few more Youths—Grace among them, if you can believe that. We didn't allow ourselves to be bullied; we fought back.

In those early days, things were both simpler and more savage. The Adults closed their eyes to mild violence, considering it an unavoidable side effect of the developing brain. A push was met with a push, a punch with a punch.

Of course, things changed when we all turned seven and started getting Quietude sessions. The penalties for bullying got so steep that Owen could no longer do it openly, nor could we retaliate without incurring the Instructors' wrath. On top of that, our desire for violence ebbed, situations like this one aside. Instead of outright bullying, Owen plagues us with pranks, trash talk, and nasty surprises—and we make sure to respond in kind.

"No reason to get a Quietude session," I say to Liam with as much calmness as I can muster. "Not over this *unfortunate* accident."

"Yeah, Li-Li-Kins." Owen is watching my right hand, the one with the ball. "You listen to Why-Odor."

Upon hearing my own annoying nickname, I'm tempted to throw the ball at Owen's face. The only reason I don't is because I'm certain he'd catch it and probably thank me for giving it back to him. I also consider allowing Liam to do what he wants, but that's a bad idea, because if Liam really does do anything violent to Owen, he'd be in Quietude for days, if not weeks. Liam getting into trouble is probably part of Owen's plan, or else he wouldn't be goading him. He wants to provoke a response since he knows that out of all the Youths in Oasis, Liam is the only one who seems to get occasional violent urges.

Between my curiosity, Mason's moodiness, and Liam's said urges, we're probably the oddest group of Youths in Oasis—apart from our nemesis in front of me, who is also atypical in his assholeness.

"Peace is a good choice," Phoe whispers. "You're the only one here who's acting his age."

"Shush," I subvocalize. "I have an idea."

"And there goes your maturity." Phoe chuckles mirthlessly. "You do realize that at twenty-three, the ancients were already considered adults? Just because the Adults here treat you like you're still five doesn't mean you should behave like it."

Ignoring her, I feign throwing the ball at Owen's midsection.

His hands go up in a practiced goalie maneuver, but I don't let go of the ball.

Instead, in a rehearsed motion, I gesture with my empty left hand in a way that Liam can see. I'm sticking out my pinky and index fingers—our secret signal from basketball.

Liam grunts approvingly, and I step to my right.

From my new location, I pretend to throw the ball at Owen's head.

Instinctively, his hands go up.

I change direction and throw the ball at Liam so quickly that for a moment I doubt he'll catch it.

But catch it he does.

With lightning speed, Liam throws the ball at Owen's crotch and says, "No hard feelings, dude. Here's your ball back."

With a grunt, Owen clutches his family jewels and falls to the ground.

"Oh no," Liam says in his best parody of Owen's voice. "Do you need us to get the nurse?"

Owen says something in a falsetto. I'm fairly sure they're forbidden words, but he doesn't say them legibly enough to get into trouble. Not that Liam or I would've reported Owen for such a thing, but the others might have.

"It was all a series of accidents, right?" I make eye contact with the other Youths on the field.

Everyone nods, though a few Youths look at us as if we're a bunch of rabid gorillas. I don't blame them. Meditation, yoga, physical exercise, our studies, and other examples of being 'all proper' define most Youths. I envy them their uncomplicated worldview.

With his chin high but his walk a little awkward, Liam leaves the soccer field, and I follow in brooding silence.

As if we didn't already have enough problems with this Mason thing.

After this incident, I'm especially glad that Liam, Mason, and I share a room. Some Youths choose to live in one of the smaller single-person accommodations at the Dorms as they get older, but they don't have my awesome friends. They also don't have to worry about idiots trying to prank them at night.

We discuss Mason's situation some more as we walk. By the time we enter our room, Liam seems completely recovered from Owen's strike, so I guess there wasn't any permanent damage.

Mason is still sleeping, so Liam comes up to Mason's bed and shakes him.

When Mason doesn't respond, Liam turns to me and says, "The dumb dissident is sleeping like a baby."

"Don't rub it in tomorrow," I warn Liam. "He's in enough trouble already."

"But I told him to stay away from her," Liam objects. "*I* told him, and *you* told him."

I sigh, regretting giving Liam the whole story. "I'm sure he'll pay for his stupidity."

"What do you think they'll do?" Liam says, looking worried for a change.

"I have a bad feeling about it," Phoe replies, as though Liam can hear her.

"I have no idea," I say, ignoring her. "I guess all we can do is wait and see."

"Good job thinking up the 'sick' idea," Liam says. "He might milk that a bit before his punishment comes down. Maybe if they think he's sick and has missed too much school, his Quietude sentence will be reduced?"

"Maybe," I say, trying to project a hope I don't feel.

What I do feel is the anxiety from earlier, only intensified. I'm also exhausted.

"It's the aftermath of an adrenaline rush," Phoe says. "You're not used to disturbances in your equilibrium. Sleep should help."

At the mention of sleep, I yawn loudly.

"Oh no, you don't," Liam says, giving me a frustrated look. "It's still early. We can—"

"I'm going to sleep," I say firmly, and to underscore my intent, I make the two-palms-up-and-down gesture to activate my bed's appearance.

"Assembly," Phoe corrects. "It's the nanos that—"

"Pedantic much," I subvocalize back.

"Fine, later," Liam says and creates a chair for himself.

I take my shoes off and get on my bed as they disappear—*get disassembled,* I correct myself for Phoe's benefit.

Out of the corner of my eye, I see Liam plop into his chair. Given his posture, I assume he brought up his private Screen and is thinking of what to do on it.

Feeling generous, I bring up my own Screen and send him a movie recommendation: *The Wizard of Oz.*

With that, I make a gesture for the blanket to 'assemble' and cozy up with it. My eyes close, but sleep doesn't come as quickly as it usually does.

Oh well, I can help nature. I tighten the muscles around my eyes in a gesture that would usually initiate assisted sleep, but oddly, nothing happens. My mind continues buzzing with thoughts of everything that's happened today. I try again, but the result is the same.

Giving up, I attempt to fall asleep naturally again, but several minutes later, I'm still awake, my anxiety worsening by the second. It's so bad that I start worrying about the fact that I'm worrying. Could something be wrong with me, like with Mason?

"You're just really stressed," Phoe whispers. "You need to calm down for the assisted-sleep command to work." She hesitates for a second, then asks softly, "Do you want me to allow them to make you feel Oneness today, just this once?"

"You told me it's psychologically addictive," I say. "I was miserable when I was kicking it weeks ago."

"Yes, I know, and Oneness is complete and utter bullshit." Her voice grows in volume. "It's the Adults' answer to ancient religious experiences, which they hypocritically claim to have transcended."

She pauses, as if calming herself down, then adds in a more even tone, "Given that I told you all that, obviously I wouldn't recommend you repeat that experience without good reason."

"And that would be?" I find that injecting sarcasm into a subvocalization is easier than into a thought.

"I can see your neural scan. You're distraught, and I don't know another good way to soothe you," she says. "Not without messing with your brain chemistry in potentially unpredictable ways. Oneness, for all its faults, has at least been tested on many brains."

"As a form of control," I say, repeating what she told me once.

"Yes, to keep you all pacified and happy, but keep in mind, it's merely a program that expanded on the work of the ancient neurotheologists. It gets your nanocytes to interact with your brain stem, as well as the frontal, parietal, and temporal lobes." Her voice sounds closer, as though she's sitting on the bed next to me.

"Knowing all these things doesn't make it any less weird," I whisper toward where her head would be, if she were really there.

Liam shifts in his chair; he might've heard me whisper.

"You can try meditating instead," Phoe suggests. I'm grateful she didn't use the chance to chastise me for the whisper. "It puts your brain in a nice delta-wave state, lowers your blood pressure, and, in general, gets you some of the same benefits as Oneness."

"Well yeah, doesn't Oneness incorporate a meditative state?"

"It does that too," Phoe says. "And you could use its serenity right about now."

"You know I haven't been able to meditate since you showed up in my life," I think, wondering if she can detect the bitterness in my thoughts. She doesn't respond, so I subvocalize, "It's fine. I'll give Oneness a go. You can help me stop it if I want to, right?"

"I can," she says softly. "And, Theo? I'm sorry I messed up your life."

I begin responding, but at that moment, Oneness begins.

* * *

I feel pleasure.

No, not pleasure. Overwhelming bliss.

With the small part of my brain that retains its ability to think, I recall that the ancients called this intense pleasure 'ecstasy.'

I try to compare it to regular day-to-day pleasant experiences and find them all lacking. This is better than eating Food, more exhilarating than winning at sports, and more exciting than being absorbed in a video game, a movie, or a book, or listening to music. None of those things come close to this phase of Oneness; the intensity of this pleasure is almost painful.

Then, suddenly, another element of Oneness manifests itself. With some internal vision, I see a bright light and feel a benevolent ethereal presence. If I were an ancient, I would probably think my dead ancestors, or deities, were surrounding me. Without any specific religious backdrop, though, this feeling simply intensifies. At its peak, it morphs into a conviction that the goodness and love of the universe is surrounding me. I feel connected to the distant stars. I recall learning that we are all made of stardust, and I feel like the stars and I are connected by an invisible network of kinship. I feel as though the universe, despite its supreme immensity, actually cares about what happens to me.

Then my breathing evens out, and with each breath, I get the impression that it's not me who's breathing, but that the universe is moving the air into me and then sucking it out, over and over.

I also feel love and wish happiness to the people of Oasis. I feel deep, unshakable love for my best friends, Liam and Mason. I feel love for Phoe. She's a new friend, but in many ways, because of how intimate our communication is, she's become one of my closest. Even if she *is* my imaginary friend, loving her would mean loving myself, and at this moment, I do love myself, wholeheartedly. I want all of us to be happy. I wish for all of us to be well.

I then feel similar love and happiness for people I usually would feel neutrally toward, like the Youths who sit next to me in my Lectures. I even feel magnanimous enough to wish good things to some people I usually don't like. I understand them. They're just human beings. Take Grace, for example. She was doing what she thought was right when she told on Mason. I can forgive her. Or take someone who's wronged me even less, like Instructor Filomena. She's a dedicated Adult who loves teaching. She made teaching her entire life, and I find room in my heart to respect her for it. I wish her happiness and wellbeing.

All this is spoiled, however, by a gnawing fear.

I'm enjoying this too much.

I could get addicted to this again. I could get to the point where I beg Phoe to allow me to experience Oneness every day, like I used to before she came into my life.

The sense of connectedness with the universe slips as these thoughts surface, and I remember that Oneness is an illusion created to keep us content. A falsehood that some Forebear probably cooked up on a theory that optimum health requires satisfying the need for spiritual fulfillment. Or the Forebears might've created it to prevent us from succumbing to a belief in the pointlessness of existence—an obvious risk for a tiny group on the last patch of Earth not consumed by the deadly Goo.

Yet as these bummer thoughts enter my mind, I'm still feeling love toward everyone and everything. Only the echoes of the pleasure remain, but I still want this pleasure to stop. The possibility of my addiction to it scares me. I can finally verbalize my problem with Oneness. It's the same problem I would've had with the drugs the ancients used to consume.

Oneness, for all its wonder, is the ultimate loss of control. Yet I want—no, I *need*—to be in control of my own mind. I don't want to be a slave to Oneness, or to drugs, or to a spiritual experience. So I shout a thought in my mind as loudly as I can: "Phoe, can you shut this off?"

I have to assume she heard me, because as suddenly as Oneness began, it ends.

* * *

"Well, that was a disastrous idea," Phoe mutters. "I'm sorry I suggested it."

"Don't be so hard on yourself," I subvocalize. "I *am* feeling less anxious."

"Yeah, but that's not what I had in mind. Given how this went, I could've just as effectively given your butt an electric shock," she says. "You're merely feeling better because you got distracted."

"I guess." I rub my forehead.

"Ready to sleep?" she asks. "Or do you want me to come up with some other brilliant idea?"

"No," I say. "I'd like to sleep. I just want to make sure you—"

"I've made it so that Oneness is once again disabled for you," she thinks.

"Phoe," I subvocalize, deciding to ask for something that's been in the back of my mind for a while now. "Can you disable any and all tampering with my mind?" I pull the blanket up to cover more of my body. "Good, bad, I don't care. I don't want it."

She's silent for a while, then says, "I don't think you understand what you're asking me—"

"I know what I'm asking." I say this so convincingly I almost believe it myself. Before she catches me on that thought, I subvocalize, "This is not a spur-of-the-moment request. I've been meaning to ask you this for some time. I don't want the Adults or the Elderly to keep me 'neutered'—whatever that is." My subvocalization devolves into a hushed whisper. "I don't trust them to 'pacify' me either—"

"Calm down," she says. "I'm not saying no. You just caught me off-guard." She pauses for a second. "Truth be told, I've been planning to offer to do exactly that, only in the future when I thought you were ready. There's a favor I want to ask of you, and I don't know if I can trust you with it while your brain is under so much of their influence—"

"When *I* am ready?" The question comes out in a louder whisper than I intended. "*You* trust *me*? Do I need to remind you that you're a voice in my head, and that I have no idea where you came from or what you—"

"Stop, please. Liam just heard you. Luckily, he's ignoring you." Phoe sounds tired. "If it means so much to you, I can expedite my original plans, but I still think it's just your anxiety talking and—"

"Just do it," I think more calmly this time. "Please."

She goes silent again, then whispers, "Are you sure, Theo? At least consider a phased approach. I could start with the serotonin levels—"

"I'm sure," I think at her. "I want it all gone. The ancients lived without all this mind manipulation, so why can't I?"

"Okay," she says. "I will do it, but I have to warn you. This takes time. If you don't like how you feel and decide to go back to your current self, it won't be quick. Your neurotransmitter levels might take a while to normalize—"

"That's fine," I say firmly. "I won't want to go back."

"That's not all," Phoe says. "There will be some things that will still affect you, like fear of the Barriers, since that works via neural implants that the nanos built into your brain, and I'm sure you don't want me to perform neural surgery on you at this point. More importantly, there are aspects to what the Adults and the Elderly do to you guys that you're not familiar with. I wanted to tell you about that before—"

"I don't care," I say just as firmly. "Please do as I asked. Disable what you can."

"Okay," she says. "Go to sleep and I'll do it as soon as you're under. It might actually be easier, computationally, to undo it all at once. I would just—"

"Thank you," I say, stifling a yawn. "There's something else I want to tell you."

"What is it?" She sounds worried.

"Phoe . . ." I look for the right words to express the conclusion I've been slowly reaching. "I'm beginning to believe you're not my imaginary friend after all."

"You are?" She seems so surprised it's as if she herself thought she was imaginary. "That's good news."

"Don't sound so shocked. I wouldn't ask you to do what I just did if I thought I was talking to myself."

"Well"—she sounds thoughtful—"you've compartmentalized that sort of logic until now. For example, when I spared you from Oneness, you didn't stop to think how you could've done it yourself." She pauses. "I just didn't want to rub your face in it."

I smile in the darkness. "It could be my insanity worsening," I subvocalize, "but I think I'm *not* crazy, which leads me to the big question you've dodged every time I've tried bringing it up—"

"Who am I, if not your imagination?" Her voice is so close that if she had lips, they would be brushing against my ear.

"Right." I take in a slow breath. "That question."

I've halfheartedly asked her this before. It was always a challenge of sorts: If you're not a figment of my imagination, then who are you? She's always responded with something along the lines of, "It's complicated." Her dodgy answers only fed my suspicion that it was *me* talking to myself somehow. I also couldn't see how she could be someone, physically. I mean, she's a disembodied voice. How could someone do what she does? Granted, she gave me some explanations that involved technology, but it's technology no one in Oasis has heard of, so I thought that I, in my delusions, must've made it all up.

Now I have to consider the likelihood that she was telling me the truth, that some form of technology is allowing her to be a voice in my head. But that just makes it harder for me to figure out who she is. Since I don't know how to be a voice in someone's head, I have to assume no other Youth knows how to do that either; we all learn the same things at the Institute.

If she's not a Youth, then she has to be either an Adult or an Elderly. Only she doesn't sound like an Adult at all. She curses and says things that they would find abominable—another reason I thought she was an expression of my own anarchistic tendencies. Though I've never spoken to any of the Elderly or know much about them, I imagine they're worse than Adults when it comes to acting all proper, so she's even less likely to be one of them.

Given all that, I focused on the easiest theory: that she's my imaginary friend. Now, though, I can't ignore all the evidence that suggests she can't be a figment of my imagination.

If Phoe is real, then I have a new friend, a close friend, and I don't really know who she is. Could she be one of those supernatural beings the ancients dwelled on so much? Or—

"I'm not a deity of any kind," Phoe says with amusement. "I know you weren't serious, but still. I'm also not—"

"A banana, nor an ancient proctologist, nor an invisible pink unicorn." I try to make my thoughts sound stern. "There are a countless number of things you're *not*."

"You're right," Phoe says. "But I hope you can forgive me. This is not a conversation I'm ready to have. At least not yet. And especially not before I block the Adults' influence on you. I'll do my best to explain it to you as soon as I can. Like I told you before, it's complicated."

I start to object, but before the words can come out, I yawn again, and with an almost unnatural suddenness, sleep steals my consciousness away.

* * *

I wake up with a start.

I think I had a nightmare that involved falling from a great height. I don't recall the exact details, especially where I managed to find access to 'a great height' in Oasis, but that's just as well.

I'm absolutely, positively terrified of heights, even the not-so-tall ones like the roof of our Dorm building.

Heart still pounding from the dream, I look around my room.

Liam is sleeping in his bed, but Mason's bed is missing, as is Mason.

"Uh oh," I subvocalize. "Where did he go? I hope not to talk to Grace again."

"This is very odd." Phoe's voice is coming from the room's entrance, as if she's sticking her head in to check on me. "After I did what you asked—after I made sure your brain is tamper-free—I was preparing some things related to the 'who am I' question and wasn't paying attention to this room. So I don't know where he is." She sounds worried. "Don't go anywhere or do anything until I figure this out."

"No, wait," I whisper. She doesn't respond, so I say, louder, "Phoe, come back. What do you mean you don't know where he is? Don't you always know everyone's whereabouts?"

Phoe doesn't answer. Instead, I hear Liam rustling in his bed.

Crap. I have so many questions for Phoe, not the least of which is about the changes to my brain. I certainly don't feel any different.

Pondering that, I sit up and feel the morning teeth cleaning happening in my mouth.

My shoes appear, and I put them on.

"Why are you getting up so early?" Liam says in a sleep-raspy voice.

I bring up a Screen and check the time.

8:45 a.m.

"We're actually late," I say. "We'll have to run if we want to make it to the Calculus Lecture."

"Like I was saying," Liam says, sounding a lot more awake. "Why are you getting up so early?"

I ignore his question and ask him, "When did you head to bed? Was Mason still here at that point?"

Liam sits up and swings his legs off the edge of the bed, giving me a puzzled look. "I went to sleep after I finished watching my movie. And I don't understand your second question."

"I was asking if Mason was still in his bed, but if you went to sleep right after me, then he would have been," I explain. "And if you slept so much, why are you giving me a hard time? I thought you stayed up all night playing with your Screen again."

"I'm still recovering from my last two all-nighters," Liam says. "And what the uckfay is this mason thing you keep rambling about?"

"I'm talking about Mason, who is not here this morning. Mason, who was in bed last night," I say with growing irritation. "And I told you not to say just a single word in code—"

"Dude, I'm too sleepy for some complex historical joke or riddle," Liam says, suppressing a yawn. "Are we talking about a stone builder or a secret society mason?"

"I'm even less in the mood for jokes," I say. "I'm worried about him."

Liam gives me an evaluating look. "Are you okay, dude?" Then in Pig Latin, he asks, "What the fuck are you talking about?"

"Mason, our uckingfay friend," I reply, in my irritation making Liam's favorite cryptographical mistake. "The guy who needs our help today. Ring any bells?"

Liam's face turns uncharacteristically serious. He looks at me intently and says, "This is a dumb joke, whatever this is."

I get up, walk toward the door, and say, "Right back at you."

"Theo," Liam says. "Are you sleepwalking? Like some ancients used to do?"

"Okay." My voice is terse as I continue in code. "Screw this. I'm leaving. I don't have time for your shit."

I head toward the door, and Liam gets an expression I don't recall ever seeing on his face.

He looks concerned.

"Dude," he says. "Wait. If you insist on going to Calculus, let's walk together."

"Not if you're going to continue being a dick," I say in code.

He looks at me with even more worry, and finally, with the most deadpan expression he's ever had, says, "I don't get what's up with you this morning. Are you feeling sick?"

"Me, sick?" My voice rises in volume as I glare at him.

"What else am I supposed to think?" Liam says, frowning. "You sound delirious."

His seriousness makes my skin crawl. "Dude," I say. "Is going insane like one of the ancient viruses?"

Liam blinks at me uncomprehendingly, gets off the bed, and approaches me. Grabbing my shoulder, he looks me in the eye and says, "Theo, buddy, I'm not messing with you."

I look at him like he sprouted horns, but he continues, "I honestly, genuinely don't know what you're talking about." He gives me a pleading look that seems to say, 'Theo, stop this nonsense.'

I grind my teeth. "I'm too worried about Mason to deal with whatever you're playing at." I'm a decibel away from shouting.

"Theo." Liam's expression is one of utter incomprehension. "I don't know what or who this mason is."

"I don't have the patience for this," I grit out, and with a final glare, I storm out of the room.

CHAPTER FIVE

As I hurry toward the Lectures Building, my frustration eases. By the time I'm halfway there, I'm not sure why I even reacted the way I did. Liam was just messing with me, and Mason is probably already in the Math Hall.

As I pass by the pentagonal prism of the Quietude Building—also known as Witch Prison—its unwelcome sight makes me wonder if Mason might be locked up there instead. Could a Guard have gotten him earlier this morning?

I debate walking toward that dreaded place when I see Grace's distinctive red hair between a large oak and a decorative dodecahedron statue. She's meditating, which is a strange thing for her to be doing right now. She should be on her way to Calculus. Could she be trying to calm herself because she had another encounter with Mason?

Once I'm close enough, I don't know what to do, so I just stand there and watch her meditate for a few seconds. Her fine features are serene and placid, like a lake in the morning. I can't believe I'm actually envious of *her* of all people, but I am.

"Grace," I say quietly. Interrupting someone while they're meditating can really startle them. "Grace, you're going to be late for Lectures."

"Theo, what are you doing here?" Grace opens her eyes with a sweep of her long, brown-red eyelashes. Then, looking at her wrist—where I assume she can see her hand Screen—she says, "You're right. I could've been late." With barely suppressed surprise, she adds, "Thank you."

"I was looking for Mason," I blurt out. "Have you seen him?"

"Seen who?" Her forehead creases slightly.

"Mason."

"Who's that?" She blinks. Her blue eyes seem deceptively guileless.

"My friend whom you would never forget, given what he did yesterday."

"Is this a joke?" The crease in her forehead deepens.

"Did Liam put you up to this?" I ask, trying to keep my cool. "If so, it's not funny, especially coming from you."

"Liam put me up to what?" Her confusion seems to increase. "You know how much I dislike that square little friend of yours."

"Mason," I say a bit louder. "The guy who told you how he feels about you." Unable to help myself, louder still, I add, "The person you snitched on."

At the mention of the word 'snitched,' Grace's expression transforms from confusion to anger. Her eyes in slits, she says, "Whatever stupid prank you're trying to pull, stop. Now."

"You should take your own advice," I retort.

"I warned you." She puts her hands on her hips.

"I can't believe your gall," I say, frustrated. "To make light of Mason after—"

"What are you talking about?" Grace's expression abruptly softens with concern. "Are you feeling okay?"

"I'm fine," I say. "But I wish you'd asked Mason that yesterday. He was devastated."

"Theo, I don't understand what's going on."

My frustration boils over. "Of all the nasty shit I expected from you, I never thought you'd fuck with my head like this. I thought you were all about being proper. How did Liam even manage to get you to—"

She jumps to her feet and runs toward the distant cube of the Administrative building.

Realizing the blunder I just made, I chase after her. "Wait." Catching up, I grab her shoulder. "Grace, I didn't mean to use that language. I was just—"

Her gaze flits from my hand to my face, and I see fear in her eyes.

It's like a slap in the face.

I quickly remove my hand from her shoulder. "I'm sorry—"

"I'm sorry too," she says, backing away. "I have to report your language, and whatever else is going on with you."

"You're going to admit you're playing a prank?"

Her expression changes from fear to worry. "Listen, Theo. Why don't you go back to your room? I think you might need help . . ."

The pity on her face scares me.

"I have to go," I say, backing away as well.

"I'm sorry, but I still have to tell them," Grace says, watching me. "I know you'll hate me even more—"

Not waiting for her to finish, I turn on my heels and all but run toward the Lectures Building.

Mason will be in Calculus.

He has to be.

* * *

When I get to the Math Hall, the Lecture is about to start.

I peek in and see other Youths, their faces in varying shades of boredom. Mason isn't among them. Could he be skipping? Math *is* his least favorite subject.

The sound of footsteps coming down the hall interrupts my thoughts, and I turn to see Instructor George, the Calculus teacher, approaching.

He gives me a quizzical look. "Are you *trying* to be late, Theodore?"

"I was just wondering . . . Did Mason give you an excuse for why he's not at the Lecture today?" I ask, hoping I'm not about to get Mason into more trouble.

"Who?" The Instructor's forehead wrinkles in that uniquely Adult way. "I'm not sure I follow."

I realize I'm holding my breath. Exhaling, I say, "Mason, sir. You know . . . my friend. Your student."

"Is this a jest?" The expression on Instructor George's face is the one he gets when someone mixes up an equation. A sort of 'how can you be so wrong?' type of glare. "I don't have a student by that name."

As the meaning of his words registers, a deep terror seeps into me.

Until this moment, I could tell myself that Liam and Grace were playing a prank on me. An Adult, however, would *never* partake in a prank—particularly if that Adult is Instructor George. His sense of humor was permanently replaced by the Pythagorean Theorem.

Which means only one thing: something odd is going on.

Did I jinx my mental wellbeing when I told Phoe I didn't think she was imaginary? Is that what's happening? Did I truly lose my mind? Or did I go crazy because Phoe made my mind tamper-free? Ancients went insane all the time, so this is a real possibility.

Or could I simply be dreaming?

"Phoe," I scream mentally. "Phoe, where are you?"

"Theo, what the fuck is going on?" Phoe's reply is so loud my whole body tenses. I've been jumpy around loud noises ever since Owen startled the crap out of me by suddenly screaming in my ear in the middle of my morning meditation a few months ago.

Instructor George gives me a questioning stare. He must've noticed me jump.

"They don't know who Mason is," I whisper at Phoe. "And don't speak so loudly again."

"Wait." Phoe's tone is pure incredulity. "You asked *him* about Mason?"

"I—"

"Never mind that now," she says sharply. "Get yourself together. I think he just saw you move your lips."

I take a deep breath and make an effort to relax. "It's hard not to panic," I think at her.

"You're doing okay," she says. "Now say, 'I'm sorry, Instructor George. I guess no one told you about the history lesson we're play-acting with Liam. He's supposed to be a Freemason.'"

Robotically, I repeat what Phoe said.

The Instructor looks at me as if I have 'two plus two equals five' tattooed on my forehead. Then he shakes his head and says, "This is one of the most creative ways someone has tried to get themselves excused from my Lecture." Straightening his shoulders, he points at the door. "I'm not falling for it. Get inside."

"Crap," Phoe says. "I guess there's nothing more we can do. Get inside the room and shut up. I have to see how big of a mess you've made."

I march in and notice that Instructor George isn't following me.

Ignoring my growing sense of unease, I plop down in a chair, my mind overloaded with questions.

"He just reported your conversation to the Dean," Phoe says when Instructor George walks in a few beats later. "Let me try to research this further. Don't say a word."

The Instructor begins his lesson. He likes to teach on a giant Screen in the front of the class, not unlike how teaching was done in the ancient world.

I don't hate math as much as Mason does, nor am I as bad at it as Liam is. Mathematics is actually the only subject where I don't feel as if I'm being fed bullshit on a daily basis. For example, when we learned that equilateral triangles are equiangular, I understood both the mathematical proof and the truth of it. Even when we learned that 0.999 with infinitely repeated nines is equal to 1, I understood the truth of it through proofs, even though it felt unintuitive at first. It was even fun to change my mind like that. In contrast, every word that comes out of Filomena's mouth in History feels like a calculated falsehood.

Today, though, I feel as ambivalent about the Lecture as my friends usually do.

To keep myself from panicking, I attempt to focus on the lesson, but every fifteen minutes, I catch myself wondering where Phoe is and what I'd do if she doesn't show up soon.

Eventually, I give up trying to pay attention. At least the Lecture will be over in a few minutes.

To keep a modicum of sanity, I replay the events of this morning in my head. My best guess is that this whole day has been a very strange dream. In that case, how do I wake up?

I pointedly pinch my wrist.

"You're not dreaming." Phoe's sudden words startle me. "Writing usually looks blurry when you're dreaming, but the Screen looks pretty crisp, doesn't it? Believe me, given what I've found out, I wish you *were* dreaming."

"But—"

"I *told* you not to do anything or go anywhere." Phoe's voice grows in intensity. "Which part of that did you not understand?"

"I had to go to Calculus," I object. "Did you want me to cut class?

"Right, of course, because had you skipped your Lecture, you'd have been in trouble, while now, you're all hunky-dory."

"Can you do me a favor and not talk like you're a voice inside my head?" I whisper loudly enough that Owen turns around and gives me a questioning stare. I shrug at him and subvocalize at Phoe, "Just tell me what's going on."

Owen raises his forefinger to his temple and makes a circular motion. Which movie did he learn that 'you're crazy' gesture from? Other Youths usually don't know ancient behaviors that well.

"Ignore that dweeb." Phoe is still, annoyingly, talking inside my head.

"But he might be right," I think at her, pulling my gaze away from Owen to look at the Screen in front of the classroom. I want him to think that I'm bringing my attention back to math. "I think I truly *am* nuts."

"You're not," she says, out loud this time. "But this Mason situation *is* messed up."

"At least *you* know who Mason is," I say, finding surprising relief in that. A little voice—a voice that is not Phoe but my own paranoid self—reminds me that despite what I thought last night, Phoe could still somehow be a product of my imagination.

"So we're back to that nonsense again?" Phoe says. "Now is not a good time for you to be worried about *me*."

"Fine," I think. "Let's get back to the issue of Mason. Did you figure out what happened to him? What's going on? I assume you had a reason for making me wait?"

"Okay." Phoe sounds as though she's sitting next to me. "The bad news is that I *don't* know where Mason is, *or* what happened to him. But I do know this: they truly don't know who Mason is. No one does, as far as I can tell."

Even though I suspected as much, my insides fill with lead. "What does that mean?" I think at Phoe, trying to rein in my growing panic.

"It means when Liam, Grace, and Instructor George acted like they didn't know Mason, they weren't faking it."

"So are you saying *he* was my imaginary friend and not you?"

"Don't be ridiculous," she snaps.

"Then why do they not know who he is?"

"That part is tricky." Her voice acquires a certain distant thoughtfulness. "Do you recall what happened with that movie you liked, *Pulp Fiction*? The one that disappeared?"

"It was deleted from the archives," I say.

"Right. Well, there's something I didn't tell you out of fear of distressing you. *Pulp Fiction* wasn't the first movie that was deleted after I showed it to you."

The mental "Huh?" I reply with sounds like a loud nasal exhale.

"I know how it seems, but it's true. *Pulp Fiction* was merely the first movie I didn't let them make you Forget."

"What?"

"Do you remember *The Silence of the Lambs*?" Phoe asks. "You watched the movie and read the book, but you don't remember either, do you?"

"Lambs?" I fight the urge to whisper out loud again. "Those are baby sheep, right? Those cute white creatures the ancients used to eat?"

"Right. You clearly don't recall. But as I was saying, after the Adults decided to ban *The Silence of the Lambs*, it didn't just disappear from the Archives. You couldn't recall reading or watching it either."

I'm too stunned to reply at first. Then, mentally shaking my head, I think, "No way."

"I'm sorry to spring this on you. I tried bringing it up last night, but—"

"It just can't be," I subvocalize. "If I watched a movie or read a book, I'd remember it. How could I not?"

"Your nanobots were utilized to tamper with the intricate neural pathways required to recall that particular memory. After that was done to you, you confabulated a new reality, one in which you had never read or watched that work of fiction."

"I did?"

"Because you don't remember it now, you can safely assume so, yes. Since then, I've been experimenting with selectively shielding your mind from this sort of influence." Her voice is hushed, almost a whisper in my ear. "It worked with *Pulp Fiction*, which is why you remember *it*. Then, last night, when you asked me to disable all tampering with your mind, I did as you asked. It's my conjecture that the Elderly, or whoever, did the same thing to people's memories of Mason as what happened to your memory of *The Silence of the Lambs*. It's called 'Forgetting.' You were the only one who didn't fall under its influence."

"Wait—"

"I'm sorry, Theo." She softens her tone. "If I'm right, it's not just those three people you spoke with who don't know a Youth named Mason. If I'm right, you're now the only person in Oasis besides me who remembers your friend."

CHAPTER SIX

"That's impossible," I whisper, but when I see Owen begin to turn his head, I continue subvocally. "How could they make everyone forget?" I look around the classroom as though my classmates' memories might show up on their faces. "Hell, how could they get just one person, Liam, to forget someone he's known all his life? You have to admit it's more unlikely than me having seen a movie and not recalling it."

"As I tried to explain, after Forgetting, your brain goes through a process called confabulation," Phoe says, her tone one of exaggerated patience. "It's a psychological response first noticed by the ancients. Back in those days, they had incidents of something they called amnesia—cases where people forgot things, either due to age-related brain-degenerative diseases, or due to some brain injuries. People with amnesia often told stories that were not factually true, but which felt true to them. For example, they thought the hospital they were in was their workplace. They basically ended up altering their memory and worldview to make it seem as though the things they forgot never existed. Having watched your mind from day to day, I should add that some mild confabulation is a routine part of how your brain operates—"

"Bullshit," I think at her and try pinching myself again, but to no avail.

"Denial is as common of a psychological defense mechanism as confabulation," Phoe says. "Unfortunately, it doesn't change the facts."

"But to erase memories—"

"They didn't erase them. They are blocking recollection, which equates to the same thing but is much easier to do."

"I would never forget a friend." I cover my eyes with the palms of my hands to relieve the tension building behind them. "Nothing would make me forget Liam, or Mason, or you for that matter—even if I do wish I could forget the part of my life after you turned up in my head."

"It's touching, and insulting, and sadly untrue," Phoe says. "Look on your Screen. I just gave you the exact transcript of our conversation about *The Silence of the Lambs*—the conversation you can't recall because it pertains to that movie."

I don't question how she made my Screen appear without my willing it. I'm too overcome with disbelief over the text on the screen.

Phoe is right: I don't recall ever having this conversation with her. Yet the words she tagged as 'Theo's lines' sound like things I'd say.

Exactly like things I'd say.

My pulse accelerates. "You're inside my head," I say, trying to reason it out. "You know me well enough to fabricate that conversation."

"Yes, but why would I want to do that?"

"I don't know." My anxiety intensifies. "I want to wake up and see Mason. I can't accept this."

"I know how you feel." Phoe pauses, then says softly, "I've also been made to Forget."

"You have?" Somehow knowing that Phoe, the ultimate know-it-all, was made to Forget makes me instantly transfer my worry from myself onto her.

"What they did to me was worse than what was done to the rest of Oasis," she explains. "I was basically lobotomized."

"I don't know what that word means." I frown as I shift in my seat.

"You asked me who I am. I told you the answer was complicated, and it is." She sounds as if she's pacing the classroom. "When I asked myself this question some time ago, I realized I actually have no fucking clue. I know bits and pieces, but mostly I only know that I forgot something important." She noisily exhales. "Something huge." She goes silent, as though trying to think of the right words. "The rest of my memory is a series of gaping holes. Not only did they make me Forget this big thing, but in the process, they even made me forget who I am."

"How can that be?" My skin prickles with an icy chill. "How can you forget who you are?"

"It's hard to explain," Phoe says. "I might have guesses, but that's all they are. The favor I mentioned to you has to do with my memory gap. In any case, my situation is very different from yours."

"Obviously," I subvocalize, still trying to process what she told me.

"Listen, Theo." Her voice is hushed and urgent. "The Guard is already waiting for you outside this Hall."

"Crap," I say. "I'm getting a Quietude session *now*, in the middle of all this?"

"I'm not sure whether they're here to take you to Quietude."

I feel as if I've swallowed a tray of ice cubes. "Where else would they take me?"

"I don't know," Phoe says, and I detect a note of fear in her voice. "Wherever they took Mason, I think."

"Which is?"

"I have no idea, but there's a way to figure it out." She's speaking faster now. "A couple of ways, actually. One solution is what I've been itching to have you do—it's that favor. Another thing I could do on my own, though the risk is that they might catch on, but since things can't get any worse, I think we should try both options."

"What options?"

"They're both a form of hacking—"

The bell rings, signifying the end of the Lecture.

"Oh no," Phoe says. "I lost track of time."

All the other Youths jump from their seats and start walking out of the Hall, but I sit still.

"Whether you sit here or walk out there, they will take you." Phoe sounds as if she's about to leave the room.

"I'm just scared," I think at her and wonder whether she can feel my emotions as easily as she knows what I'm thinking.

A helmeted head pops through the doorframe.

"Theodore?" the Guard says.

Why Guards wear that shiny headgear is as mysterious to me as everything else about them. They could be Adults or they could be the Elderly underneath those things. Hell, they could even be Youths like me.

"Please, come with me." The Guard's tone is tense.

I get to my feet. My legs feel shaky and wobbly. Must be from all that sitting.

"Or adrenaline." Phoe's voice sounds as if she's standing right next to the Guard.

I don't chastise her for responding to a thought that was not meant for her; I'm too worried about what's going to happen.

"Hello." I approach the door and look at my googly-eyed reflection in the Guard's helmet. "What do you want?"

"You are to come with me," the Guard says.

I don't move. "Where are you taking me?"

"Please walk with me," the Guard says.

"He won't tell you," Phoe says. "They never do."

"Are you taking me to Quietude?" I ask, ignoring Phoe.

Instead of answering, the Guard extends his hand and moves his palm in the air in a strange, wave-like motion. If it's a gesture command, I don't recall ever seeing it before.

"Theo, he just tried to give your brain a serious calming jolt," Phoe hisses. "Act like you're relaxed. Quick."

The urgency in Phoe's tone forces me to do my best impression of getting calmer.

"Don't ask any more questions," she says. "Just walk."

I do as she says, my anxiety growing.

"He tried to mess with my mind?" I make a point of thinking at her, not daring to whisper or subvocalize with the Guard around.

"Yes. To ease your agitation."

"But I don't feel relaxed."

"Because I made your mind impervious to this sort of influence along with most other manipulations," she explains.

"Oh, right." I try walking straight while looking relaxed—a difficult task given the treacherous shaking of my legs.

"You're doing fine," Phoe says. "Just walk in silence until you exit the building."

I comply. When we're out of the Lectures Building, I wonder whether this is how the ancients who were going to the gallows felt. We walk in silence for a few minutes, and then Phoe says, "I think it will be reasonable for you to try talking to him again. Say, 'Sir, this is a misunderstanding. I was just talking to people about the Freemasons, a group we learned about in Instructor Filomena's class.'"

I say that, plus a bunch of other bullshit Phoe comes up with.

The Guard says nothing for a few steps.

"And the whole thing started with stonemasons—"

Before I can finish Phoe's script, the Guard makes a gesture I don't fully catch.

"What did he try to do to me this time?" I think at Phoe.

"Relaxation again," she says. "Look calm and stop talking."

I try to use external cues to relax for real, as our campus was designed with serenity in mind. Focusing on the rock tower in the distance, I let my eyes glide over the symmetrically arranged rocks.

"That is Augmented Reality," Phoe says. "That tower is not really there."

"Thanks for the useless information." I look at the cherry blossom tree, daring Phoe to tell me it's also not real.

"I'm trying to distract you from gloomy thoughts." She sounds as if she ran ahead of the Guard. "But if being snippy with me provides relief, then go ahead."

Ignoring her, I try doing a walking meditation. I focus on the light touch of the wind on my face, on the consistent flexing of my leg muscles, on the warmth of the sun's rays on my skin—

"Theo, watch out—"

I don't hear what else Phoe wanted to say, because I run smack into the Guard, who stopped. He's holding his finger to his ear.

He turns his head toward me. Is he giving me a skeptical stare under that mirrored visor?

"I think he just got instructions on what to do with you," Phoe says.

I tense, all traces of my tentative serenity fleeing as I wait to see where he'll take me.

If I'm to get the usual punishment—Quietude—we'll turn right.

The Guard looks hesitant for a moment, as though he's deciding my fate.

I swallow, unable to feign calmness any longer.

The Guard turns to the right, toward the pentagonal prism of the Quietude Building, and begins walking.

CHAPTER SEVEN

"You're going to Witch Prison," Phoe says with relief that the building's nickname doesn't usually generate. "That means Quietude."

"I never thought I'd be so happy to be going *there*." I pick up my pace to catch up with the Guard. "Are you sure that's not where Mason is?"

"I'm sure," she says.

"So where is he then?" I risk a vocalization since the Guard's back is turned to me.

"I don't know. I still didn't get a chance to do the hacking I told you about. Plus, I'm beginning to think the safer route is to get you to do the task I've been talking about—the one only you can do."

"What is it?"

"Something that will make your Quietude session pass faster, I suspect," she says. "Now, if you don't mind, I'm going to prepare what I need."

"Wait," I say. "Tell me what it is I'll have to do."

"Fine." Phoe heaves a sigh. "It's a way for me to remember some of the things I've forgotten. My intuition tells me that if I can recall them, I'll have an easier time finding out what happened to Mason."

"'Intuition' sounds a little wishy-washy."

"I've done many things on intuition, and you've trusted me thus far." Phoe's tone is clipped.

"It just sounds contradictory. You forgot something, yet you know that if you remember it, you'll get specific answers?"

"I know I'll have better tools for hacking at my disposal if you do what I need you to do. In that sense, I'm certain I'll be better positioned to figure out what happened to Mason." It's clear she's doing her best not to sound defensive. "Regarding the memory stuff, I don't know how to best put it into words, but I know something big was erased from my mind—from everyone's minds. I don't know what it is, but I'm sure it's something we'd all want to know, regardless of what happened to Mason."

I consider that for a moment.

I'm about to be punished by boredom—that's what Quietude is, essentially. Whatever Phoe wants me to do might be a welcome relief from that.

"You don't know the half of it," she says, her tone artificially upbeat.

"So what is it that you want me to do, exactly?"

"Merely play a video game," she says. Then, under her breath, she adds, "From the Last Days."

The Last Days is what everyone calls the period of time leading up to the Goo Armageddon, though in some of the texts I've read, it's referred to as the Singularity—a time when technology was invented so fast that human minds couldn't keep up with its rate of development. Everyone knows that any technology from that time should be treated with caution, if not outright fear.

"What about the technology all around us?" Phoe asks.

"Now you're getting into completely private thoughts," I complain. "I thought the technology around us was safer than the abominable things they invented in the Last Days. Weren't we shielded by the barrier of the Dome and separated from everyone else by then?"

For a few seconds, all I hear are the Guard's footsteps and the distant voices of Youths.

"I think that's part of the information I forgot," Phoe says.

"Well, it's a video game," I subvocalize, thinking of what she wants me to do. "How bad can it be?"

"It's a more advanced version of the technology behind the virtual reality they use in your classes—not bad at all, in other words," Phoe says. "I'll try setting some things up. I'll talk to you soon."

"Hold up," I whisper, but she doesn't respond.

For better or worse, we're almost at our destination.

I gaze up at the building.

Even the ivy looks as if it's covering it with great reluctance.

As we get closer, I feel the tightness in my chest that I always get when I'm faced with the Witch Prison. The Quietude Building was nicknamed that because of its unique pentagonal prism shape. It has something to do with ancient witches and how they liked to get naked and draw pentagrams all over the place. I think all of us—those of us who were sent here as little ones, at least—feel uneasy about the place. Due to my record number of 'why' questions and other mischief, I've spent more time in Quietude than most.

We enter the building. With every step down the corridors, I remember why I hate this place so much. Unlike the bright silver of other buildings in Oasis, these walls are a dull gray, and there's an ozone (or is it chlorine?) odor permeating everything.

"This is your room," the Guard says once we've reached the end of the bland corridor.

Knowing from experience how useless pleading with him will be, I walk in without protest.

The room is even duller than the corridor. It's almost as if all the color was sucked out of it. The air lacks any smell, even that unpleasant odor from the corridors.

The layout of the room is the same as it was during my previous visits, with the same uncomfortable chair that's not like the ones we assemble, and the same small bed to the side, near a toilet. In the center is a little table with a pitcher of water and a special bar of Food that, if it's anything like the ones I've had before, is completely tasteless. I'm shocked to see only a single bar. These Food bars are how troublemakers like me gauge the duration of our Quietude sessions. They put out at least a bar for every day of the stay. Since there's only a single bar, I won't be here for as long as I feared.

I walk around the room and, for the umpteenth time, touch everything. These objects are stationary, the way furniture was for the ancients; gestures or thought commands have no effect on them. Gestures and commands don't work in these rooms at all—a fact that I verify as soon as the Guard closes the door behind me.

I can't change the layout, nor can I bring up a Screen.

The lack of a Screen or any kind of entertainment, combined with the blandness of everything here, is what makes Quietude so insidious.

It's torture by boredom.

Sitting down in the chair, I drum my fingers on the table.

"Phoe?" I subvocalize.

She doesn't respond.

"Phoe," I whisper.

Nothing.

"Phoe, I have bad memories about this place. This isn't a good time to be joking around." I say this out loud, knowing she'd never ignore me after such an indiscretion.

Silence is my only reply.

What the hell is going on? What is Phoe up to? Why is she not talking to me when I need her most?

I get up and pace the room.

Five circles later, Phoe still hasn't spoken up.

I pace some more.

No response.

I keep pacing.

* * *

I'm sweating. I swear a couple of hours have passed with me pacing, and Phoe is still silent. I'm ready to do anything at this point, including playing whatever Singularity-technology VR game she needs me to play.

I try lying down but can only do so for a few minutes before I jump up and start making circles around the room again.

My discomfort is increasing exponentially, and I don't understand it. Being locked up in this room has always sucked, but I've never felt this way before.

It's as if the gray walls are closing in on me. It makes me want to bash my head against the door and splatter blood on it.

At least that would bring in some color.

Okay, this is crazy. Am I experiencing some side effect from what I asked Phoe to do to my brain? Is this what it feels like to be anxious without the nano-whatever things messing with my mind? If so, how did the ancients not kill each other?

Then I recall that they *did* kill each other during 'wars' and even on a day-to-day basis. They did a lot of crazy things, including creating artificial intelligence to aid in their wars.

Thinking about the AIs that unleashed the world's end makes me shiver—which is further proof that I'm more sensitive to stress than usual. Sure, those thinking machines were the epitome of all that was unwholesome and evil about the Last Days, but AIs, along with things like nukes and torture, are now a thing of the past.

Maybe I should rethink this no-tampering policy and beg Phoe to change me back to the way I was.

Sitting down on the chair, I fold my legs under me and try to even out my breathing. My mind is racing like that hamster in its wheel at the Zoo.

In. Out. In. Out. I do this for what feels like an hour before I calm down a little.

Then I notice a strange shimmer in the air.

I stare at the apparition for a few moments before I comprehend what I'm seeing.

It's a Screen—a Screen in a room where I've never seen one.

But it's not a normal Screen.

It's faint and distinctly unreal-looking, as though it hasn't *really* formed—as though I'm dreaming this Screen. It's like this Screen is one of those ghosts the ancients were obsessed with, though ghosts were usually shaped like people, not Screens.

A cursor flickers on top of this apparition for a couple of beats and then begins moving, leaving behind an unusual purple text. For a second, all I see are the lines that make up each letter, lines that remind me of digits on an ancient calculator. Then the meaning of the words seeps through my mushy brain.

Theo, this is Phoe.

As it turns out, the Witch Prison is a Faraday cage—or nearly so. It's a place where I can't talk to you. Luckily, I found this one loophole through one of the Guards' communication channels, and I really hope it works.

On the subject of Mason, I tried hacking into their system on my own, but I couldn't—nor could I set up the game interface. But I do have an idea about how we can free up some resources, which might give me a good chance at both tasks.

In any case, none of that matters as much as this: You need to get out as quickly as possible.

"What are you talking about?" I think at her. "I don't understand anything you said, except that you can't talk to me and that I need to escape." I look around, waiting for a reply, and then look at the screen. When no response comes after a few moments, I subvocalize, "How can I get out of this place, Phoe?"

The cursor wakes up again and types:

If you're trying to talk to me, you should know that this is a one-way communication system. I can't even be sure you're reading this, but you better be, because you're in danger.

Someone from the Adult section is on their way to the Prison. That's really bad.

I will try to unlock your door in a moment. I think I tapped into the building's emergency-exit procedures. Once the door is unlocked, exit, make two rights, then a left. Then you'll have to leave through the emergency exit. It will look like a regular door.

I stare at the ghostly Screen in stunned fascination. My daze is broken by the Screen disappearing in the same way it appeared.

Is Phoe serious? She wants me to escape Quietude?

No Youth has ever done this, and I'm sure every single one of them wished they could have.

My pulse racing, I walk up to the door. Unlike regular doors, it doesn't open for me when I gesture at it. Testing out the ancients' method, I push it with my hands.

I could just as easily have been pushing at a wall.

"What now?" I subvocalize by habit.

As though in reply, I hear a sharp noise that makes me jump back.

Then I understand.

It's the door.

Something just happened to it.

I approach the door again and press on it.

Given Phoe's message on the Screen, I shouldn't be surprised, but I am.

The door opens.

Warily, I stick my head out and look around.

The corridor is empty.

I walk out and try not to dwell on what the punishment for doing this will be.

"Two rights and a left," I repeat in my mind as I tiptoe down the corridor.

When I get to the end of the corridor, I crouch and look around the corner—a trick I picked up from playing hide-and-seek with Liam and Mason during our childhood years.

My heart bobs up to my Adam's apple.

There's a Guard walking toward me.

He's half a corridor away.

Is it my imagination, or is he walking faster all of a sudden? Did he see me?

It's impossible to tell with him wearing that shiny visor.

I duck out of sight and swiftly make my way back to the room where I'm supposed to be, staying as quiet as I possibly can.

To my relief, the door closes behind me.

I put my ear to it, but I can't hear any steps coming down the corridor.

This most likely means the door is soundproof, but it could also mean the Guard didn't turn this way.

I count the way I did when I was little—one Theodore, two Theodores—until I reach twenty.

Gingerly, I exit the room again.

When I don't see the Guard in the corridor, a grateful whoosh of air escapes my lungs.

I get back to the corridor on the right and repeat my earlier trick of crouching by the corner.

The Guard is gone.

I get up, turn the corner, and start walking. The corridor is long, and the gray walls blend together to obscure just how far it goes.

I walk for what feels like a couple of minutes, with no end in sight.

I pass a right turn, but ignore it since Phoe told me to make a left.

I walk some more and finally see the end of this monstrous corridor, but it's a good twenty feet away.

"This stupid corridor must curve," I think, unsure whether I'm talking to Phoe or myself.

She doesn't reply and talking to myself has never really appealed to me—unless that is what I do when I talk to *her*, but I've moved beyond that theory.

"Theodore," a voice says from behind me. "Stop."

I think it's coming from where the right turn was.

This voice is male, so I know it's not Phoe. I assume it's a Guard, but I don't look back—that would be a waste of time.

My stealthy walking pace forgotten, I torpedo forward.

He runs after me. Through the beat of blood in my ears, I hear his pounding footsteps. A wall at the end of the corridor looms in front of me. I almost smack into it, but manage to turn left, my shoes sliding on the smooth gray floor.

"Theodore, stop! What are you doing?" The Guard sounds as if he's about to turn my way.

I sprint down the smaller corridor, toward the door at the end. Skidding to a stop in front of it, I make a gesture for the door to open.

It remains shut.

CHAPTER EIGHT

Gasping for air, I gesture at the door again.

Nothing.

I concentrate and think at it, "Open."

No effect.

The definitive sound of running footsteps is growing louder.

My palms cold and clammy, I push at the door with all my strength.

It doesn't budge.

I chance a glance over my shoulder and see the Guard's visor shining from just around the corner.

The door in front of me makes the same sound as the one in my Quietude room. Phoe must've opened it, I realize.

Nearly choking with relief, I push the door open and fly out of the building.

The door whooshes shut behind me.

To my left is waist-high grass, which, according to Phoe, was designed to encourage everyone to stay on the paved pathways. I leap into it and crouch, desperate for cover.

I know I'll be found if the Guard thinks to look here, but I don't see a better option.

"You're fine," a voice says from right next to me. "He's about to run back into the building."

My heart falls back into my ribcage. "Phoe?" My subvocalization is as close to a silent shout as it's possible to get. "You can talk to me again? Where have you been? What's happening?"

An ear-splitting wail fills the air. My head ringing, I realize it's coming from the Witch Prison.

"Since you're here, you clearly got my message," Phoe says hurriedly, her voice somehow audible through the din. "Like I told you, I had a hard time communicating with you once you were in the Witch Prison." She rattles off the words so quickly that I can barely make them out. "The Guard just headed back. I unlocked more doors. Some of the Youths took it as a chance to take a walk. Someone rang the alarm. I think they'll be busy for the time being."

"But—"

"Get up and run, Theo."

I do as she says.

I didn't think I could run faster than that sprint in the corridor, but I was wrong. I'm surely setting some kind of record; it's too bad no one will give me credit for it.

Youths don't pay attention to me as I fly by. They must think I'm just exercising. Everything around me is a blur. After the grayness of the Prison, my eyes have to adjust to all the different shades of green.

My lungs feel as if they're about to explode, but I manage to gasp, "Can you explain?"

"You just spoke out loud," Phoe chides.

"Yeah, right. Me talking out loud is the problem," I think at her, unable to vocalize too much while out of breath. "I mean, if I keep this up, I might *get into trouble.*"

"If you sprint and talk, you'll run out of breath quicker." Phoe sounds as though she's running alongside me.

I suck in a lungful of air and subvocalize, "What's going on? What's the plan? Why—"

"Theo, you need to do as I say." Her voice gets those commanding overtones I usually associate with Instructors.

"Fine." I need oxygen too much to argue with her even mentally. "Where am I going?"

"Follow the large paved path all the way down, then take the road that leads to the forest in the west."

I can't help but whisper, "But that might lead us to the Adult Border."

"What, are you afraid you might get *into trouble?*" Phoe says, her voice a perfect parody of mine.

"There's trouble, and then there's going toward the Border," I think more calmly. "It just isn't done."

"If it helps, I won't have you officially cross the Border," Phoe says, though it sounds as if she left the word 'yet' unsaid. "I need you to go to the Zoo."

I run in confused silence for a moment. The Zoo is indeed the closest structure we're allowed to visit that's near the Border.

"I can't go there," I think at Phoe. "I haven't been at the Zoo for almost a year." Despite saying that, I head in the direction of the pine trees that are in the far distance.

"Really?" Phoe responds. "I thought it would be your kind of place."

"It is, but I can't enter it. My access is denied. A long-term consequence from when Liam, Mason, and I put Owen's hand in a cup of warm water in the middle of the night."

"I would've thought that would've yielded a Quietude," Phoe says.

"Owen is an asshole, but he's not a snitch. And even if he were, he wouldn't have told anyone that he wet his bed." I mentally chuckle at the memory despite my growing exhaustion. "No. We got into trouble on our way back to our room. They took my access away because we were out after curfew the day after a Quietude session."

"Well, with my help, you'll be able to get into the Zoo," Phoe says.

"How?" I catch the scent of the pines that I'm quickly approaching.

"When you got my frantic communiqué in the Prison, did you notice the part of my message that talked about my failed attempts at hacking into the Adults' and the Elderly's systems? When I mentioned that I couldn't figure out what happened to Mason with the resources I currently possess?"

"Kind of," I lie. "Vaguely."

"What about the part about me not even having the resources to get you into that game that you agreed to stop?"

"Yes. Only I don't recall you ever talking about me stopping anything."

"If you beat the game, you stop the game, but that doesn't matter since I can't even get you in there."

"Why?"

"I just said it a second ago." She sounds annoyed. "I lack the computational resources to either figure out what happened to Mason or get you into that game. That's where the Zoo comes in."

"What resources?" Sweat drips down my back as I continue sprinting. "How can the Zoo help?"

"You'll see," she says. "It's not far now."

Perplexed, I follow the paved path into the pine forest.

Phoe is either busy or giving me space, so I don't talk as I run to the meadow where the signature half-sphere of the Zoo is located.

Unlike most other buildings, the silver metal of the Zoo is exposed. It's as if the pines scared away the ivy that covers everything else.

Slowing down to catch my breath, I walk up to the entrance at a more measured pace.

As I approach, I can't help but recall my futile attempt to get in earlier this year. I tried sneaking in with a large group of Youths, but the doors wouldn't open for anyone until I left.

This time, however, the door slides open for me with no problems.

"Don't be so surprised," Phoe says. "I told you I'd get you in."

"After the stuff you pulled with the Witch Prison, your door-opening capabilities will never surprise me again," I say as I enter the Zoo.

A few steps in, I find myself in the middle of a circular room, the place where one usually stands when the Zoo session is initiated.

As I wait, I amuse myself by looking up at the reflective spherical ceiling.

Nothing happens.

"You're not going *into* the Zoo." Phoe's voice sounds as if it's coming from a few feet away.

"I'm not?" I ask and wonder whether all the adrenaline from my run is intensifying my sense of disappointment.

"We're short on time," she says.

"I see." My shoulders slump a little.

"Fine," Phoe says. "If you *really* want, given what I'm about to ask you to do, I guess we can spare a couple of minutes. Brace yourself."

And just like that, the half-sphere is gone, and I'm standing at the beginning of Zoo Road.

The ground under my feet moves, and I look around.

I almost forgot how magnificent this place is.

To my left is a prairie that stretches to the horizon. There, I note a herd of gazelles running away from a pride of lionesses. To my right, on an equally endless snowy tundra, I spot a penguin escaping a sea lion. Cute animals getting eaten is probably my least favorite part of the Zoo, but it's also fascinating.

"Okay, you saw it. Can we resume our tasks?" Phoe says. "This place breaks all laws of virtual reality aesthetics. Combining Antarctica on one side and Africa on the other? Someone should've told the creator of the Zoo that alphabetization doesn't mean congruency."

"Just a little more," I say as I pass through a couple more luscious environments and observe creatures ranging from komodo dragons to anteaters. "I want to do the petting portion and the safari."

Suddenly, I'm back in the real world.

"I'm sorry, Theo," Phoe says in an apologetic tone. "We really need to get this done."

"What do you want me to do, exactly?" I try not to sound irritated, but it's difficult. I was looking forward to petting a llama again.

"Just step on *that*," she says.

I look about for something to 'step on.' There's a light shimmering right in front of me that looks like a large Screen floating sideways. Then another one shows up right above it, then another. It's like a staircase of sorts. I don't recall ever seeing this before.

"That's because I've put this place into admin mode," Phoe says.

I eye the staircase warily. "Is that thing solid?"

"How else would you step on it?" Phoe sounds teasing.

"Each step looks like a Screen, so it's a fair question."

"It's not an Augmented Reality construct like the Screen," Phoe says. "These steps are made out of the utility fog. But you're right. Whoever designed the admin mode didn't bother to make them look more realistic."

"Oh, great. Fog, the thing I associate with solidity," I think sarcastically as I hesitantly raise my foot and place it on the first step. It feels real, so I put my weight on the step with my right foot and then let my left one join it. The strong feeling that I'm frozen mid-jump makes me uneasy about going higher.

"I forgot about your fear of heights," Phoe says. "But it'll be okay. The platform is just a few steps higher."

I examine the shimmering stairs above the one I'm standing on. They indeed lead to a circular platform made out of the same material.

I take the next step, reminding myself that I'm less than two feet off the ground. Falling from here would be the equivalent of falling from a bed.

I take the next step.

"Now it's as scary as standing on a chair," Phoe suggests. "And the next one will be like standing on a table."

I take the next two steps.

"Keep going." As if to highlight how unreal she is, Phoe's voice is coming from a location in the air that doesn't have a stair.

I take the stairs one after another, but with each one, my stomach fills with ice. When I reach the tenth step, I can't help but look down.

My insides immediately flip-flop.

"Just a little more," Phoe urges. "You can't fall. It's physically impossible. The utility fog that makes up the steps is all around us. If you trip, it will catch you."

Her words reassure me. I take another determined step, then another.

"Two more and you're on the platform," she says.

I inhale a deep breath and go up as quickly as I can.

Standing on the circular platform feels a modicum safer. I let out the breath I was holding. "Now what?"

"Make an exaggerated gesture of pulling down a cord, like ancient train conductors did to toot the train's horn." Phoe sounds like she's right next to me.

I do as she says, making a fist above my head and then bringing my elbow to my chest.

An unusual round Screen shows up in the air in front of me. On it, in a very large font, is written: 'Please confirm the Shut Down.' Under the text are two ginormous buttons that say: 'Confirm' and 'Abort'.

"What does it mean by 'shut down'?" I ask Phoe.

"Shut down the Zoo," she responds matter-of-factly. "Now click the 'Confirm' button."

"Wait a minute. Shut down the Zoo?"

"Yes."

"Permanently?"

"Probably."

"But it's the Zoo." I can't help but say this out loud. "This would deprive everyone of so much . . ."

"I'm sorry for their loss, Theo, but I don't have many other options. The virtual reality simulation that is the Zoo eats up a horde of resources—the computing power we desperately need. I can't think of anything else we can shut down with so little risk to you and such a gain in resources, especially given our time constraints."

"But—"

"Look, Theo," Phoe says. "With this, I should be able to find out what happened to Mason before we deal with the game."

"Can't I just do the video game thing instead?"

"I also need resources for that, remember?" She sighs. "Once you're done with this, I actually hope you can 'do the video game thing' regardless of whether I can puzzle out what happened to Mason." She must sense that I'm about to protest because she adds, "Though I'm fairly sure I will find out what happened to him."

I nod—unconvincingly.

"Please, Theo," she says. "Getting rid of the video game is a way for us to learn that very important secret we were made to forget."

She thinks I have a problem with playing the game, but I don't. I have a problem with denying everyone access to the Zoo.

"It's the only way to figure out what happened to Mason," she says, clearly having read my mind again.

"Fine," I say, growing weary of arguing. "I'll do this for Mason."

I reach out and touch the 'Confirm' button.

"Please say, 'Shut Down,'" the Screen display instructs. "And think, 'Shut Down.'"

"Shut down," I say ceremoniously and follow up the command with the same thought.

"Shutdown commencing," the text on the Screen says.

In the next instant, the Screen goes blank and disappears.

I stand there waiting for some other cue that something has happened, but there's nothing.

Then, a few moments later, I see something on the platform next to me.

I blink a few times.

It appears to be a three-dimensional female silhouette made out of a shimmering fog, like an ancient statue of Aphrodite made of clouds. The ethereal figure doesn't have a defined face or any other distinguishing features other than the slim hourglass shape commonly seen in ancient media.

"It's me," Phoe says, her voice coming from where the mouth of the figure would be—if it had a mouth.

"Phoe." I gape at the figure. "Why do you look like a ghost?" As I say it, an illogical thought flits through my mind. Could she be an actual ghost, like the ancients believed?

"I'm not a freaking ghost," the figure snaps. "I just used the resources you freed up to slightly improve our means of communication. I read in ancient literature that communication is primarily nonverbal."

"I suspect when they talked about nonverbal communication, they meant facial expressions, which you lack," I point out, shaking off the ghost idea.

"Yes, but I can do body language now, which definitely counts as nonverbal communication." She demonstratively puts her hands on her hips.

On a whim, I walk up to the figure and try to touch her.

She doesn't move away from my hand, but when I reach for her slender shoulder, my fingers go through the mirage of flesh the way they would with a Screen.

"I mastered more of the Augmented Reality controls—went visual on top of auditory," Phoe explains. "What you now see works exactly like a Screen."

"Okay, but is that what you really look like?" I step back from Phoe's body. "And where are you now? Who are you?"

The ghostly figure shrugs. "I still don't have a solid answer," she says. "But I do know something far more important."

"You know what happened to Mason?"

"Yes," she says softly. "But I'm not sure if I should share it with you."

"Tell me." I say the words so forcefully that Phoe's illusory figure backs away. I step after her. "Tell me, or you can forget about me lifting another finger to help you."

"Okay." She's all the way at the edge of the platform, and her chest expands as if she's taking a deep breath. "But Theo . . . you should know that what happened to Mason is worse than anything either of us could've imagined."

CHAPTER NINE

The hairs on my arms and nape rise at her words.

"I was hoping I could get you out of the Zoo building before we continued talking about that," Phoe says. "Follow me." Her graceful, shimmering figure approaches the steps and swiftly descends.

"No, tell me now." I run down the first five steps, forgetting about my fear of heights. Then, more carefully, I descend to the bottom.

The Phoe silhouette is waiting for me by the exit. "I got you down without much fuss, didn't I?"

Before I can reply, she hurries out of the building.

I run after her.

When I exit, she's already halfway down the meadow.

I chase after her, my leg muscles burning.

"Theo, I need you to hide in the forest." Her voice is in my head this time.

"Wait," I think at her, but she's already entering the forest line.

I run after Phoe through the pines for at least ten minutes before she stops and waits for me.

"Ideally, you should do the video game first," she says. "They're looking for you."

I plant my feet firmly in the dirt and say, "I'm not moving an inch or doing anything until you show me what happened to Mason."

The shadow-like Phoe looks down. "You'll wish you hadn't insisted."

"It's my decision to make. Stop delaying."

"Okay." She raises her head, as if to meet my gaze. "Bring up your Screen."

I do the gesture, even though I know she could've brought up my Screen for me. She's stalling. This realization sends another chilly tendril into my belly.

My Screen comes up, and I see our dorm room. Mason, Liam, and I are sleeping. The viewpoint focuses in on Mason and gets closer to him, as though whoever is recording just approached his bed. A hand reaches out and touches Mason's shoulder.

"It's a recording from the Guard's visor," Phoe says, answering the question I was about to ask. "I was only able to recover bits and pieces—whatever wasn't deleted from temporary caches and video buffers during the Forgetting procedure."

An explosion of snowy white static interrupts the scene on the Screen, and a new set of images follows right away.

Mason is walking on the wide road that traverses the pine forest I'm in. The viewpoint—one from the Guard's visor, I guess—is staring at the back of Mason's head. In the distance, I see the reflective surface of the Barrier. With its metallic mirror-like wall, it looks like an ancient blimp or a weather balloon—only it stretches through all of Oasis, marking the place where the Adults' domain begins. Mason walks toward it, and the Guard follows.

"They took Mason through the Barrier?" I whisper as I extrapolate what's happening. "But they never let Youths go there."

Phoe doesn't respond, so I watch as Mason approaches the supposedly impenetrable wall that is the Barrier, and it lets him through as though it were some kind of liquid silver bubble. The Guard follows, though, of course, the fact that *he* can pass through the Barrier makes sense.

"How did Mason even approach it?" I ask Phoe. "You can't even walk once you get halfway through this cursed pine forest. I learned this the hard way."

"The fear that the Barrier generates doesn't affect Youths specifically." Phoe's voice lacks its usual vitality; she sounds older and wearier for some reason. "It's merely a matter of the permission profile for the person trying to cross. They gave Mason access before . . ." Her words trail off.

"Before?"

She doesn't respond. The scene on the Screen changes again.

Mason is strapped to a white gurney in a half-lying, half-standing position.

A person wearing white is standing next to him. This person also has white hair, which reminds me of the gray hair on the old people from ancient movies—gray hair even the oldest Adults don't possess.

"I thought we didn't age to the point of gray hair in Oasis," I think both to myself and as a question to Phoe. "Is he an albino?"

Phoe's new shape slowly shakes her head. "He's one of the Elderly."

I look back at the Screen. Everything else in that room is also white, which gives it a medical feel reminiscent of the nurse's office.

In front of the mysterious Elderly man is a big Screen. On the Screen is what I assume is Mason's neural scan.

"His thought patterns have changed since we spoke with him," I tell Phoe. "It looks like he's going through some positive emotions."

"It's Oneness." She turns away from the Screen as if she can't bear to look at what's happening. "They're running Oneness on him nonstop before . . ."

"Before what?" I ask, my chest tightening from an awful premonition.

Phoe doesn't answer.

On the Screen, the Elderly man comes closer to Mason and looms over him. He's holding something. I squint and get so close to the Screen that my nose almost goes through it. It takes me a moment to understand what I'm seeing.

The Elderly man is holding a syringe.

As I watch in shock, he sticks Mason with the needle and presses the plunger.

For a couple of breaths, nothing happens. Then Mason begins to convulse on the table. On the big Screen in front of his head, the brain patterns change.

They get slower.

My eyes feel glued open. I can't blink.

Mason's neural activity slows some more.

I take a raspy breath. "What's happening?" I look at Phoe. "Is Mason falling asleep?"

She doesn't respond. She just stares at the dirt beneath her feet.

Droplets of cold sweat bead on my forehead as I look back at the Screen. Mason's neural activity continues to slow until it, impossibly, ceases completely.

Phoe covers her face with her hands—or, more accurately, she covers the place where her face would be.

"What—" I begin, but the strange activity on the Screen distracts me.

Mason's body disintegrates, as though it was made of sand and a strong wind was blowing on it. It takes less than a second for his body to completely dissipate.

The white bed he was strapped to just a moment ago is empty.

The Elderly man turns to the Guard whose helmet recorded the scene. He says something, but I can't hear him. He then wipes tears from his ancient-looking eyes.

The Screen in front of me goes blank.

On some level, a purely rational part of my brain already knows what happened. The rest of my mind refuses to catch up with that realization.

I feel like screaming, but no words, not even in the form of a subvocalization or a thought, come out.

My muscles tense, and my body begins to tremble.

"Breathe, Theo," Phoe says from what sounds like a distance away. "Breathe, or you'll go into shock."

I take a breath that hurts as it enters my chest and step back. "It can't be."

"I'm sorry I showed this to you." Phoe's voice is even more distant. "I was afraid it would be too much. You've never faced death before."

Death. That's what she just said.

That sinister word snaps something in my mind, allowing it to begin wrapping itself around the fact that this horrid concept is the best explanation for what I saw.

Except it doesn't make sense. Death doesn't happen. It's been eradicated in Oasis. It's an ugly, theoretical construct from yesteryear, like torture and extinction.

Mason can't be dead, can't be gone. The idea is as incomprehensible as the notion of Forgetting him. I can't imagine it. It's like trying to picture the complete absence of matter and space.

I take another step backward and feel the rough bark of a pine tree against my back.

"I'm so sorry, so sorry, so sorry." Phoe's words are like a meditative chant.

I shake my head vigorously, as though to shake meaning into my brain.

"Calm down." Phoe's tone is soothing, but her words feel like acid on my skin.

"Stop trying to handle me," I say out loud. "Why should I calm down? If this isn't the time to freak out, when is?"

"I need you to stay calm because you're also in danger." Phoe's voice still holds a pacifying note. "I need you to help me keep you safe."

"Is he really dead?" I'm still speaking out loud—almost shouting, in fact. "Could those videos be a prank of some kind? A cruel trick? A way to teach me a lesson?"

She steps toward me. "No, Theo. As horrible as it seems, this is how Forgetting people works. The person stops existing. Both in memory and in reality."

Rounding the tree, I back away again, but my foot catches on one of its roots. I fall hard, my confused state not conducive to good landings. My teeth snap together with a loud clink, and a shock of pain reverberates through my back, followed by a wave of nausea.

After a moment, the worst of the pain fades, but I don't attempt to get up. I feel like I want to lie here forever and not think. The crowns of the trees above me sway, and I stare at them without blinking.

Phoe looms over me, blocking my view of the trees and the sky.

"I'm sorry." Her voice is like an echo. "I wish you had time to properly mourn, but I'm afraid you don't. They're searching through these woods as we speak."

"Phoe... If you're making this up, if he isn't really dead and you're just manipulating me into doing this thing you want me to do, please just say so," I think at her in desperation. "I'll do whatever you want. Just please tell me Mason is alive."

"I can't." She sits down on the ground next to me, pulls her knees to her chest, and hugs her legs. "I wish I could."

I shield my eyes with my palms and lie there, trying to even out my breathing.

"That's it," Phoe whispers. "Breathe." Her voice is like a cold drink on a hot afternoon. "We're lucky it's only been a day since I disabled their tampering. All your happy hormone levels are well above those of the ancients. This should help you cope."

Her words make no sense. How could the ancients survive feeling worse than I do at this moment?

"According to what I've read in the archives just now, they went through some of the same things you're going through—denial, anger, bargaining, depression—before eventually reaching acceptance, the last stage of grief."

I lower my palms to glare at her. "I will never accept what I just saw."

"Nor should you." Phoe's hard tone matches mine. "Under the circumstances, of those five stages, anger might be the most productive response."

I replay the image of the white-haired man giving Mason that shot, and my fists clench. If the man were in front of me, I'd hit him and kick him until I saw blood.

"You probably wouldn't," Phoe says. "And I mean that as a compliment."

"You don't know what I would or wouldn't do. The bastard deserves to get punched."

"You're right, and, more importantly, you're on the right track." Her voice takes on Liam's signature conspiratorial quality. "Channel your anger into the next task. Trust me, learning whatever it is that stupid game is preventing me from remembering will be huge. Beating it will help a lot more than hitting an old man."

"Fine." I sit up. "Let's do this thing."

CHAPTER TEN

"First, I need you to calm down some more," Phoe says. "Try eating."

"I don't feel hungry."

"Try to eat anyway."

Almost on autopilot, I make the palm-up gesture that makes Food appear, and the familiar bar turns up in my upturned hand. I take a bite, and for the first time in my life, normal Food is completely tasteless, almost as though it's one of those punitive Food bars they serve during Quietude.

"There you go," Phoe says soothingly. "Food can be comforting, which is good. The calmer you are, the easier the game should be."

Since my mouth is full, I ask mentally, "Why?"

"Because of the nature of this particular game," Phoe responds out loud. "What you're about to experience is a complex neural analysis, adaptation, and response technology. The ancients called it IRES—Immersive Reality Entertainment System."

"I don't understand what that means," I pointedly think at her.

"Immersive Reality is like Virtual Reality, only, well, more immersive. Additionally, the world you'll enter is tailored to everyone who joins the system, which in this case will be you." She points at my chest.

I take another bite of the Food bar and think, "That still doesn't make a whole lot of sense."

"Your teachers have done a number on you guys." Phoe sighs. "How can I dumb this down?" She sits still, apparently thinking, then says, "Think of it like this: the game will analyze your head. It will look at your memories and experiences, and from them, it will create an ultra-realistic world meant to entertain you as much as it can. Does that make more sense?"

"Sort of." On the third bite, the Food starts to taste a little better. "How do I win?"

"Maybe the word 'game' is misleading," Phoe says as I continue chewing. "This thing is meant to be an interactive, fully immersive entertainment extravaganza. Its purpose is to provide a one-of-a-kind experience to each and every player, not to only choose a winner."

"But if more than one person is playing—"

"If multiple people play, the competitive component is enhanced. The game will create a world that's a conglomeration of elements based on the analysis of each player's mind. That's why this thing is so complex; it can support hundreds of interwoven players. Out of that mess, it will create a hodgepodge of a world for them to play in. But you don't need to worry about that, since you'll be by yourself." Phoe pauses as if to catch her breath. "I hope this explains why we have to end its operation. I chose this game as our target because the computational resources it consumes are truly staggering. Plus, since no one uses it, no one will miss it."

"Well," I subvocalize between bites, "what I really want to know is what will happen to me when I enter this game. What can I expect there? How do I do whatever it is you want me to do?"

Phoe's hands fidget in front of her. "What you'll see is very hard to predict, as is what you'll need to do. Suffice it to say, you'll need to play to the end. When you beat the game, you'll get the opportunity to stop it from running. When that happens, make sure to actually select that choice and shut it down."

"Why is this thing even running?" I ask.

"To eat up resources." She puts her arms around her chest as if giving herself a hug. "I think someone tried to find the most resource-intensive piece of software they could get their hands on, and this was it."

I tilt my head. "But why?"

"That's what I'm hoping to find out, *after* you beat this thing." She mirrors my head movement. "I don't want to make unfounded guesses."

"Okay," I say slowly. "But why don't they let anyone play this game? If it's running already, wouldn't it be logical to use it?"

"Since when do Adults go for logical ideas?" She shakes her head dismissively. "If I had to guess, this game is probably on that super-long list of forbidden technology." Phoe's voice lowers, as though she's worried someone might overhear her despite us being alone in the forest and her speaking in my head.

"Great." I catch my hands tightening, squashing the last bit of Food. "Forbidden tech—sign me up." I stuff the tortured piece of Food into my mouth.

"There is nothing to worry about. The Adults are total worrywart-luddites when it comes to technology." Phoe's voice takes on those passionate pet-peeve overtones. "Under the pretext of avoiding the next cataclysm, they label harmless stuff as—"

"Okay. Never mind. Just tell me how to play this thing."

"We'll need to hack you in." Phoe jumps to her feet. "How else?"

"I assume you don't mean hacking a bar of Food into pieces," I subvocalize and clear my throat.

She bobs her head. "Correct. I mean the kind of hacking that lets one do things one isn't supposed to do."

"Right. Can you be a bit more cryptic?" I exhale audibly, the way I would while meditating. "Please just tell me what this 'hacking' will entail this time around?"

"To start, I need to tap into your brain or, more specifically, into the nanocytes that interface with your neurons."

My eyebrows go up, and I squint at her.

"Okay, even more super-specifically, do you remember what you were doing the day we met?"

I nod. How can I ever forget that day? It all started when, on a whim, I gestured for extra Screens after having noticed that if you gesture for one after you already have one in front of you, you get two Screens. On that day, I decided to push that discovery further. I gestured for a third, then a fourth Screen, and kept going (I was very bored while learning about the evils of the Industrial Revolution). Sometime during my three hundredth Screen, the world around me momentarily blurred, and that was when I heard Phoe's voice for the first time.

"Yes, bringing up those Screens created a buffer overrun that I was able to exploit," Phoe says. "So this time, I need you to do the same thing: bring up a ton of Screens. I already created a safe virtual reality space for you to inhabit, a place that will let me pipe you into the game." More quietly, she adds, "In theory, at least."

Not feeling particularly confident, I do as she asked and start bringing up Screens.

"Just a few more," she says when I feel my wrists beginning to ache from the repetitive gesture. "And you could summon these screens mentally, you know."

I decide to play along and mentally summon another boatload of Screens.

When I get to about three hundred Screens again, the world blurs the way it did on that fateful day, and I'm no longer sitting in the forest.

I'm flying.

Or falling.

Whatever motion this is, it's happening incredibly fast.

I'm bodiless, like a ray of light. The world around me is a surreal white tunnel, and I fly/fall through it, heading somewhere.

The experience reminds me of those ancient rollercoaster park commercials, only scarier.

Just as suddenly as the feeling started, it ends.

I have my body back.

I'm standing in a new space.

To call this a room would be the understatement of the decade; it looks more like an ancient cave. It's dark, except for the shadowy light coming from luminescent creatures crawling on top of majestic stalactites and stalagmites. On my left are a couple of big barrels. One has the word 'Gunpowder' written across it, another has 'Gin,' and a third barrel has a skull-and-crossbones sign.

I try the usual illumination-summoning gesture by folding my index finger into a hook and flicking it up, the way the ancients used to turn on light switches.

To my relief, the cave brightens, and I can see details more clearly.

The cave is filled with a medley of forbidden objects, from guns and swords to posters of nude ancient models. Ancient magazines are scattered on the floor, and throughout the cave, Screens are playing violent movies and video games.

"What do you think of your 'man cave'?" Phoe asks from behind me.

"It's something," I say, turning to look at her. "It's like a—"

I don't finish my thought, because I can actually see *her*. I have to force myself to blink a few times as a rush of adrenaline tingles through my body.

She's changed.

She's no longer the ghostly presence she's been since the Zoo.

She looks real now, if 'real' can be applied to a woman who's unlike anyone I've ever seen.

She looks as though she stepped out of an ancient magazine. With her pixie-cut blond hair, overlarge blue eyes, and small, delicate features, she reminds me of Tinkerbell.

"Hey now." She flaps her long eyelashes at me. "That's insulting. I'm five foot nine—hardly as tiny as a fairy."

That's true. She's almost as tall as ancient models were, with the same kind of legs that seem to go on and on. As I stare at her, I also get a better view of her slim hourglass body—more than what was possible when she was ghostly. Her proportions are those of the ancient models too.

Something about her appearance fascinates me, but I can't tell what it is. I look her up and down, my eyes oddly drawn to the cleavage of her dress—something else I've only seen in movies, as Oasis girls don't wear anything that shows that much skin.

"Stop it. You're making me blush." Phoe gives me a mischievous smile. "Your hormones are starting to work the same way as those of an ancient male your age."

She's not really blushing, but I am. She's insinuating all sorts of taboos that I don't even want to think about, so I just say, "Okay, now that we're here, what's next?"

"First, I want to test whether you can come in and out of this virtual space, your man cave, with a gesture I invented for the occasion. I don't want you to have to bring up the three hundred screens every time."

"Okay," I say, ungluing my eyes from the place where her red dress meets her slender shoulders.

"Take your middle fingers and stick them out like this." She flips me off with both hands, the backs of her middle fingers sticking out triumphantly.

"Hey." I narrow my eyes at her. "Did you design this gesture to ensure I get into Quietude every time I use it?"

"Well, if you mentally say, 'Fuck fuck,' it's the equivalent to the physical command." She chuckles. "But we both know you prefer gestures. In any case, you obviously shouldn't escape to this place when you're in front of other people, since in the outside world, you'd be as cognizant of your environment as a rock. So it doesn't matter what the gesture is." She examines the red nail polish on her middle fingers—something I also stare at since I've only ever seen nails painted red (or any color) in ancient media. "I had to invent a gesture and command that isn't already in use, and, well, this was available."

"Right. Usually, like right now, I just want to give you a single-finger gesture," I say and flip her off, even though a part of me instinctively cringes at the accompanying memories of lengthy Quietude sessions.

"That's almost it," Phoe says, her expression deadpan. "You just have to do it with both hands, like this." She double flips me off again.

"Never mind." I make the double-middle-finger gesture just so we can stop conversing about it.

In a whirl of whiteness, I'm bodiless again. I fall through the surreal tunnel and experience the disorienting effect that accompanies the fall.

With startling suddenness, the white tunnel becomes the green of the pine trees around me.

"Now try going back the same way," Phoe's voice says in my head.

I do the gesture, and the trip starts anew.

When I'm back in my virtual man cave again, I say, "Okay, that worked. How do I do the next part?"

"That's easy," Phoe says. "I created a similar gesture." She makes the double flipping sign sideways, and then connects her middle fingers together in front of her chest. "You have to do this, but it will only work from here. You can't get to the game directly from the real world."

I begin connecting my middle fingers together.

"Wait, Theo." She walks over to me, getting so close that I can smell a hint of roses.

Perfume is another thing Youths don't wear, a rational part of my brain thinks. The more irrational part is not thinking at all, particularly when Phoe gets even closer, hugs me—a social interaction from the movies—and pecks me gently on the cheek in another movie-only action.

My breath catches. I feel as though energy is flowing from where her pouty lips are touching my skin. It's moving down through my whole body and into somewhere in my crotch region. I feel a strange urge to grab her and bring her closer to me.

She steps back. "No time for that now. The search party is getting closer."

My heart is beating faster than when I ran through the forest.

Is this what the ancients felt? Again, I wonder how the poor slobs functioned on a day-to-day basis. Then again, whatever I felt from her nearness was not unpleasant.

"Focus, Theo."

I blink at her. "How do I beat this thing? What should I expect?" I say, trying to, literally, get my head back in the game.

"I honestly don't know," Phoe says. "I wouldn't be surprised if there is some kind of a puzzle or quest you'll need to complete, or a phobia you'll need to face. It might be the usual fare of video games, or it could turn weird on you. I simply don't know for sure. Your mind is a key component in this. Colorful, recent, and traumatic past events can play a large role—"

"Sounds lovely." I almost manage to convince myself that my nervousness is related to the upcoming task.

"No matter what happens, it's no more real than this place is." She sighs and gives me a regretful look. "If there was an easier way, I assure you, we'd do *that*."

I suppress the urge to wet my lips. "And if I get killed?"

"Nothing scary would happen in that case." Her tone is gentle. "You'd simply return here and have to start the game over."

"Okay, I'm ready," I say with a confidence I wish I actually felt.

"Once you're in the game, I'll do my best to patch myself through and talk to you," she says.

"Wait, I'm going to be by myself?" I'm unsure why, but this idea scares me more than anything else. "I thought you'd be with me from the start."

"I don't know how to communicate with you once you're in there, but I'll figure it out, I'm sure." She steps toward me and puts her hand on my shoulder.

I feel instant relief. It's as though warmth is spreading from the place where her hand is resting.

"Theo, stop stalling." She pointedly glances at my hands.

I take my middle fingers and connect them in front of my face in some odd parody of the ancients' sobriety test.

As soon as my fingers touch, I become that ray of light again and begin flying through a rollercoaster of whiteness.

CHAPTER ELEVEN

I look around.

I'm back in the pine forest, exactly where I was before I entered my man cave.

"Shit," Phoe's voice says in my head. "It didn't work."

I look around but see neither her ghostly nor her real visage.

"What now?" I think to no one in particular.

"I have to come up with another plan," she says. "I think, given the situation, I have no recourse but to meet with you—physically."

"Wait, what do you mean by that?" I subvocalize.

"No time to explain," she says. "Start heading in the direction of the Barrier, on your left."

I turn.

"No, your other left," she says. This time, her voice comes from behind me.

I turn around and cautiously begin walking.

"You might want to move your feet faster," Phoe says. "The Guards are searching for you."

"I just don't understand." I rub my chin. "What do you mean by 'meet physically'?"

"You wanted to know who I am, right?" Phoe sounds exaggeratingly mysterious. "Due to these unfortunate events, you're getting your wish. We're about to meet in the flesh."

I jerk my head back, in part to dodge a tree branch, but also to respond to Phoe. "But I thought—"

"Theo," a new female voice says loudly.

It's not Phoe's, but it *is* familiar.

"We've searched the whole forest for you," the voice says. "I was so worried."

I locate the speaker; she's standing to my right.

Red hair fills my vision, and I realize it's Grace.

A horrible idea enters my mind: Could Phoe be Grace? She did say she'd meet me in the flesh, and here is a flesh-and-blood girl . . .

"Don't be ridiculous." Phoe sounds as though she's standing next to Grace. "I'm not this pathetic little girl, I assure you."

I take a step toward Grace, raking my hand through my hair.

"Please don't move, Theo." Grace takes a careful step back, her whole body tensing. "Don't move, or I *will* scream."

"She'll probably scream anyway." Phoe's voice wavers. "Fuck."

"Okay." I try to smile at Grace.

"Don't grimace at her like that. You'll make the situation worse," Phoe says.

"Shut up," I think at Phoe. "What now?" I say to Grace.

A *hmm* noise comes from Grace's throat. "You'll come back with me?" She taps her index finger against her chest as if I don't know what she meant by 'me.'

"So that I can follow Mason's fate?" I stare at her incredulously. "So you can get me into even more trouble?"

"Theo, I—" Her lips tremble. "When I told them about your ramblings about this mason thing, I didn't think it would get so bad."

"Mason is not a thing—"

"She doesn't remember him," Phoe cuts in.

"Never mind." I force myself to speak calmly since Grace could decide to scream at any moment. "I don't want to come with you."

"If you don't, things will get worse for you." Grace looks genuinely saddened by this.

"I doubt it could get any worse." Seeing that she's getting nervous, I soften my tone. "Please, Grace. Can you pretend you didn't find me? No one is monitoring this forest, so the Adults will never find out. You wouldn't get into trouble." I inhale, and on the outbreath say, "Please, Grace."

Instead of answering, Grace takes a step in my direction, then another.

Her blue eyes glimmer as she stops in front of me. Lifting her hand, she lays it on my shoulder and gives it a soft squeeze.

Given that Phoe just did the same thing to me, I wonder again whether Phoe is Grace after all.

"I'm not," Phoe whispers. "Now don't spook her or you're screwed."

Fighting the temptation to stare wildly at Grace's hand on my shoulder, I gently cover her hand with mine.

Grace's face contorts with emotions I can't pinpoint. Her lips part slightly, as if she's about to say something, but then she lets go of my shoulder and leans in closer.

"I won't tell them I saw you," she whispers softly, her lips almost brushing against my ear. "But please don't tell on me when they catch you."

I open my mouth to say, "*If* they catch me," but nothing comes out.

"Say, 'Thank you, Grace,' give her a peck on the cheek or whatever, and run." Phoe's voice sounds as though she's talking through gritted teeth.

"Thank you, Grace," I parrot, but I don't kiss her. "Thank you."

I slowly back away, then turn my back on her and start walking.

Grace doesn't say anything.

When I'm about twenty yards away, I look back.

She looks frozen solid, still standing where I left her, her gaze burning holes in my back.

I walk some more and look back again, but Grace is gone.

I begin running. I run as fast as I safely can with the branches hitting my face. I run because I don't know whether Grace will keep her word and not tell on me.

I stop my mad dash when I see a male figure between the trees a few feet away. He's leisurely walking away from me.

I'm glad I spotted him. If I'd continued running, he would've heard me. Maybe if I just wait, he'll move on.

The person stops walking and starts gesticulating. He must've brought up his Screen and is doing something on it.

I flatten myself against a tree and observe the stranger. As I look at him, I realize there's something familiar about this person's slightly stooped, narrow shoulders.

"Walk softly," Phoe suggests. "He shouldn't hear you. Also, before you suggest something as ridiculous as this, that is *not* me."

I decide to do as she suggested and take a soft step.

The forest is so silent and my heart is beating so loudly in my ears that I almost fear he can hear it.

The figure is still playing with his Screen.

I take another step, then another.

The problem with moving this way is that it will take me forever to get beyond his hearing range. The second problem is that it's somehow more nerve-wracking to sneak by than it is to run away, as the deliberate slowness stretches out the unpleasantness.

I continue walking softly, keeping an eye on the guy—which turns out to be a mistake. I should've been looking down. I step on a dry branch, and it makes a cracking sound.

The guy's head perks up, his large ears like those of a canine. That clicks something in my brain. I associate canines with hyenas, and from that, I finally realize whose back I've been staring at.

The Youth turns around, and I confirm my realization.

It's Owen.

I try to hide behind the nearest pine, but it's too late; he's walking my way.

I come out to face him.

Owen gives me a carnivorous smile, then puts his index finger to his lips and makes a *shhh* sound.

"I think he's threatening to scream if you run," Phoe says. "Try to resolve this quietly."

"No shit," I subvocalize at Phoe and stalk toward my nemesis.

"Do I smell Why-Odor?" Owen says when I get near enough that he doesn't have to shout. "Or do I smell trouble?"

I cock my head to the side. "What do you want?"

Instead of answering, Owen closes the distance between us and, before I understand what he's about to do, punches me in the solar plexus.

Air escapes my lungs, and logic goes with it.

I wasn't expecting Owen to do this. Though he's an asshole, he hasn't resorted to violence of this magnitude since we were little. I haven't been in a fight for so long that I've forgotten how unpleasant it is to get punched. I think I was around seven years old the last time I was in a fight, and it wasn't even with Owen; it was with Logan, one of his lackeys. I recall it not being fun, though Logan didn't even hit me in this sensitive spot. I suspect that even if he had, it wouldn't have been as bad, since I was fighting another seven-year-old.

"I have to say, escaping Witch Prison was an impressive feat," Owen says. He's jumping around me, fists raised in the style of an ancient boxer. "I didn't expect anyone to succeed at that, least of all you."

I'm too busy getting air back into my lungs to respond. When I finally straighten my back and take a breath, Owen's fist meets my jaw.

My head snaps back. The pain is exquisite, and the shock is completely dumbfounding.

"I've wanted to fight you for over a decade now." Owen's voice is distant. "Admit it, Theo. Don't you also want to? I know your buddy Liam does."

I'm too dizzy to answer. There's a metallic taste in my mouth.

He punches me in the shoulder—lightly, in comparison to the other hits.

"Oh, come on," he says. "We're in the forest. No one will be the wiser. The Adults keep us from having any fun."

I spit. The spittle is red.

The sight of blood, combined with his taunts, awakens something within me. There's a roar in my ears, angry moisture in my eyes, and a desire to see Owen's blood that overwhelms me.

My hands curl into fists. I raise them, mirroring Owen's stance.

When my opponent notices this, he grunts approvingly and tries punching me in the face again.

Instinctively, I duck. His fist whooshes past my ear.

I see that his miss left him momentarily exposed.

The world goes quiet, and I focus in on my target. I haven't hit another human being in a decade and a half, but I don't hesitate.

With all my strength, I bury my fist in Owen's midsection, cognizant of how hard it was for me to recover from this kind of blow.

A shock of pain travels up my arm, but Owen bends over with a squeal and begins hyperventilating.

Instead of gloating the way he did, I grab his hair and yank his head down at the same time as I jerk my knee up.

His face meets my knee with a satisfying crunch. My knee objects, but I take solace in the fact that his face must feel exponentially worse.

With a grunt, Owen slumps to the ground.

I pull my foot back to kick him, soccer-style, and he whimpers.

"What are you doing?" Phoe says urgently. "Haven't you heard the expression about hitting a man when he's down?"

I stop and stare blankly at the withered mess that is Owen. He's somehow gotten into the fetal position and is cradling his head in his arms.

If Phoe hadn't spoken up, I would've kicked him. What's worse is that I still kind of want to.

With effort, I resist the urge and take a deep breath.

Now I have a practical dilemma. Owen is hurt, and I need to get him help without giving myself up to the Adults.

"Just leave him here and come meet me," Phoe says. "I'll make sure someone finds him in a few minutes, after you're gone. Even if he tells them what happened, I doubt you could get into worse trouble than you're already in."

Feeling an odd thickness in my throat, I turn and walk away.

Owen makes more noises, and I tell myself that means he's relatively okay.

When I can't hear him anymore, I break into a run again, channeling my confusion into physical movement.

"This is scary, Phoe," I think as my feet pound the forest floor. "For a moment there, I lost it."

"You were defending yourself," she says. "You have no reason to feel guilty about that. It's a normal response. The Adults just managed to shelter you from it. Perhaps that is the only positive consequence of their totalitarian meddling."

Too out of it to argue with her, I continue to push my body to its limits. My leg muscles burn, and I feel as if my lungs might explode.

"Hey, cheer up," Phoe's voice cuts in after a minute. "I'm just through this meadow. Get ready for that surprise."

Slowing down to catch my breath, I enter the meadow and see a figure at the edge—a slightly large, round figure that has its back to me. The shape is vaguely feminine, so I assume it's a woman.

I get closer.

Something about this back brings up a memory, but I can't quite place it.

For some reason, I think of the Institute. Specifically, I think of History Lecture.

"Ah, so you do recognize me," Phoe's voice says in my head.

The figure turns around, and in stunned silence, I look at the person in front of me.

It's Instructor Filomena.

CHAPTER TWELVE

I shuffle back a step.

Instructor Filomena smiles.

"So you finally know," she says, her nasally voice *unlike* Phoe's cheerful soprano.

"I couldn't well sound like myself, could I?" Phoe's voice says in my head.

"Not when I wanted to keep my identity a secret," Instructor Filomena continues, picking up exactly where Phoe's mental voice left off. "So, yes, as weird as it might be for you to accept, I'm Phoe."

"You can't be." I rub my temples, staring at her. "You just can't."

"We don't have time for a long debate," Instructor Filomena says. "Follow me."

She walks away.

"Come on," she says as the voice of Phoe inside my head.

Even though I actually want to hide, I follow her.

It still doesn't make sense.

"Stop being so dense," Instructor Filomena says. "Phoe and I both know history really well. We both have access to what only Adults can access. We both like to use Virtual Reality—"

"But I just saw you—I mean, Phoe." I shake my head. "She looked nothing like you."

"What did you think I would do when I could make myself look like anything I wanted?" Instructor Filomena says. "I wanted you to find me attractive, and in my real form, I obviously don't impress someone as handsome as you."

I gawk at her. It's true that Instructor Filomena and Phoe's virtual-reality form couldn't be more different. I might be primed by having just talked to Grace, who looks like the Little Mermaid, but the cartoon character Instructor Filomena reminds me of most is Ursula, the chubby octopus-looking villain.

"That's just plain mean," Instructor Filomena says. "I was right to keep my identity from you."

"Sorry . . . *Phoe*," I subvocalize. "This is just a bit too much for me to handle."

The Instructor sniffs. "We're almost at the Barrier, so I suspect my identity is about to be the least of your worries."

I follow her gingerly, keeping a distance between us.

The fear hits me suddenly, as it did all those years ago when Liam, Mason, and I first got this close to the Barrier.

"The Barrier is a sophisticated bit of technology," Instructor Filomena says. "It emits a signal to everyone's neural implants that tells the brains of unauthorized people that they shouldn't be here."

"I can't walk any farther." I wipe my clammy hands on my clothes.

Instructor Filomena turns around. "Oh, this won't do," she says as the voice of Phoe in my head. "You look practically ashen."

A tingling sensation washes over me.

"That's better," Phoe says. "Those eyes are sparkling again."

I feel lighter. This sudden removal of fear is almost pleasurable.

"I granted you Adult access," she says in her nasally 'Instructor Filomena' voice. "Let's go. They're closing in."

I follow, my gait becoming noticeably less shaky. This is easy, especially considering the magnitude of fear I'd be experiencing had Phoe/Filomena not done her juju.

We walk into a clearing that no Youth has ever reached.

From here, the Barrier is clearly visible in all its shimmering, liquid metal beauty.

"Now we just walk through," she says and confidently walks toward the field, or whatever it is.

I follow carefully. I can't help but compare this spot to the one I saw them lead Mason through.

"We're going to make them pay for what they did to him." Instructor Filomena's tone is sterner than usual. "The Elderly will regret this deeply, as will all of Oasis."

"What do you mean?" I ask mostly to distract myself, as I'm about to cross into the ultimate restricted area. "What is the plan?"

"We're going to shut down something else—something pretty useless anyway," she says as the voice of Phoe in my head. "We're going to shut down this very Barrier and its cousin—the one that separates the Adult section from that of the Elderly."

"We're what?" I ask, but she doesn't answer.

She simply walks into the Barrier and disappears behind it.

The thing ripples like a pond of mercury around a dropped stone—a large stone.

"Hey," Phoe says in a wounded voice. "My metabolism is not as fast as that of Youths."

"Sorry," I mutter. "If you stayed out of my head, you wouldn't have to hear that."

I approach the Barrier, then stop and stare at it.

"Just walk through it," Phoe says. "You won't feel a thing."

I raise my hand and bury it in the silvery surface.

My hand feels as if it's submerged in warm, gentle water, but when it exits the thin obstacle on the other side, it comes out dry.

I guess this is what putting your hand through a bubble feels like.

Emboldened, I take a step.

The warm sensation brushes over my face. Half of my body is on the forbidden side.

I take the next step.

I'm dry, safe, and on the other side.

If I'd made a list of things I expected to see on the Adults' side of Oasis, it would've included many possibilities. Probably a pine forest to match the one I just ran through and an area filled with geometric shapes matching those of the buildings on the Youths' side of the Barrier.

None of these things are present, though.

The scene in front of me is something I never would've expected to see in Oasis. It looks like something out of Instructor Filomena's Lectures or an ancient movie.

A bucolic village sprawls as far as the eye can see, with vineyards, green hills, and clay roofs.

"Inspired by the French countryside," Instructor Filomena says from my right.

I glance at her and note that she managed to change her clothes in the time it took me to cross the Barrier. She now looks like one of the ancient occupants of said French countryside. She smiles at me, but I quickly return my attention to the landscape.

Something about the warmth of her smile makes me uncomfortable.

As I look around, I realize that the most distinguishing feature in this part of Oasis is a tall tower in the distance—a tower that looks exactly like the Eiffel Tower from the History Lectures.

"Oh, Theodore." Instructor Filomena makes a tsk-tsk sound with her tongue. "Of course that is not the Eiffel Tower." In Phoe's voice, she continues in my mind, "You could just as easily call it the Louvre, because of all the glass."

She's right.

I've seen the Eiffel Tower in those sequences of ancient Earth she shows us before every Lecture, and this tower resembles it only in shape. With the sun reflecting off its glass windows, it's a magnificent sight.

"You like it, don't you?" Instructor Filomena smiles and winks at me. The gesture, combined with her puffy cheeks, makes her look like the cherub the ancients believed shot arrows on Valentine's Day.

"So we're going there?" I let my eyes scan the many miles separating us from the tower.

"Please put these on." She takes a couple of odd objects out of her bag.

After a second, I identify the stuff in her hands as a pair of glasses and an ancient hat.

She steps closer to me. "We have to make you look older."

I try not to back away, figuring it might insult her. She rises on her tiptoes and puts the glasses on my face. Her pudgy fingers brush my temples; then, in a cloud of jasmine fragrance, she takes a couple of steps back. I'm too stunned to react, so I just observe as she looks me over and nods approvingly. Then she steps up to me again and puts the hat on my head.

I exhale in relief when she steps back and studies me. "That should do," she says. "At least if no one scrutinizes you closely. Now follow me."

We walk down to a cluster of houses in silence.

There's feeling overwhelmed, and then there's the state I'm in as I walk on the old-fashioned cobblestone streets. The feeling intensifies as I see long-extinct creatures, including dogs, chickens, and cows. The animals are walking around as if we're at the agricultural part of the Zoo instead of the Adult section of Oasis.

The funny-looking people around us are busy with their farm work. Some are feeding the animals, while others are working in their gardens. I assume they're Adults, but they look more like the Amish we learned about yesterday.

The oddest thing is the ancient technology. Moving vehicles (tractors, I believe they're called) abound, as do some vehicles that I can't name. In the distance, there's an actual windmill.

Suddenly, I spot something that doesn't fit this archaic landscape—something shiny, like the Barrier. A sunbeam reflects off it as it disappears behind a wooden house.

I point in the direction where the strange object disappeared. "I need to go there."

I don't know why I feel the conviction that I must, but I trust the instinct and begin walking that way.

"We don't have much time," Phoe's voice says in my head. "And please don't speak out loud. We don't want to draw attention to ourselves."

As I approach the house, I see that it has large windows through which the backyard of the house is visible. I squint to make out what the shiny object I saw was, but the antique furniture inside the place blocks my view.

All I see is a glimmer of white.

"I'm going to check it out," I think at Phoe. I feel certain of my decision. "You can stay here and wait for me."

Without waiting for her to respond, I jog in the direction of the shiny object. My gait shouldn't look too suspicious since many of these people are rushing about, taking care of their farms.

Three houses later, I think I see the object again, but it disappears behind a parked tractor.

I turn the corner and almost trip on a large tree branch that's been stripped of its bark. On autopilot, I place it in its proper historical context: someone plans to chop it into smaller bits of wood to power a fireplace. Didn't those things predate the tractors? The history question reminds me of my companion, and I look back. She's fallen slightly behind but is still following me.

Seeing no one around, I risk picking up my pace.

When I clear the next house, I finally see my target. The shiny thing and flash of white I saw was the helmet of a Guard and his white uniform. I think I knew this on some level; that's why I felt compelled to follow him.

Seeing the Guard, however, isn't what solidifies my stomach.

There's a person walking next to the Guard—an achingly familiar person.

My friend Liam.

Despite having run the equivalent of a marathon today, I turn around and sprint back to the piece of wood I nearly tripped over. It's still there on the ground, so I quickly grab it. Armed with the wooden stump, I run back even faster, determined to catch up with the Guard.

"This is a very bad idea," Phoe says in my head.

I ignore her, going as far as purposefully whistling one of my favorite melodies: the 'ta ta da dam' beginning of Beethoven's *Symphony No. 5 in C Minor*. I repeat the melody in my head, over and over. It seems to shut Phoe up and gives me a modicum of courage.

When I reach a certain threshold, I run more softly, landing on the balls of my feet to stay quiet.

Liam is walking slowly, which works to my advantage. The Guard isn't rushing him; he's merely following along.

Thinking of what happened to Mason after a similar walk with a Guard strengthens my resolve.

"Seriously, Theo, it's not too late to stop this mad idea," Phoe says to me mentally.

"Ta ta da dam," I subvocalize in reply.

The melody plays in my head as I close the last few feet and raise my makeshift club.

Encouraged by my earlier win against Owen, I smack the Guard on the head with all my force—a classic move from ancient movies.

His helmet makes a hollow, dull sound, and my hand goes numb from the impact of the wood's recoil.

The Guard turns to me. I hear a scary mechanical whir of some kind, but I'm not sure whether it's something the Guard is doing. Though the visor is covering his face, I get the sneaking suspicion that hitting his helmet was a tactical mistake. At the same time, some corner of my mind registers the interesting fact that Liam hasn't even turned around.

The Guard makes the gesture that's supposed to pacify me.

This is my chance to make up for the helmet blunder. I allow my body to relax and pretend his mind control worked on me. Then, as suddenly as I can, I jab the club like a fencer would a sword, aiming it at his midsection.

The Guard catches the club in his iron grip before it connects with his body.

I attempt to pull it back with both hands, but it's as though the stick became part of the Guard. My shoulders scream in pain. Before I can even think of something else to try, the Guard rips the weapon from my hands, leaving my palms torn and stinging.

Without saying a word, the Guard breaks the thick piece of wood over his knee and throws the pieces into the nearby bushes.

My heart jumps into my throat, and I back up a few steps.

He follows.

I back away some more, hoping to at least lure him away from Liam.

"Run, Liam," I yell at my friend—who would have a good head start if he were to run.

Except he doesn't run. He doesn't react at all.

I hear that mechanical noise again, and it distracts me for a moment.

When I focus back on the Guard, I see the white-gloved hand flying toward my face—and my world explodes.

CHAPTER THIRTEEN

Owen's punches were like the brush of a bird's wing compared to this. This is mind-crushingly painful.

I spit out the tooth that Owen loosened when he hit me. The metallic taste in my mouth is overpowering, and I have difficulty breathing.

My ears are ringing—or is it that noise again?

For some reason, the rage that came over me during my fight with Owen hasn't returned. All I want to do is double over and fall to the ground, but I know if I do, the Guard will lead Liam away, and that just isn't happening.

The thought of Liam getting hurt brings colder, more rational anger to the surface.

I straighten, gritting my remaining teeth. Audibly inhaling, I focus on the Guard.

He's reaching for me with both hands.

I only understand his intent once his hands are locked around my neck, and then I'm suffocating, his fingers cruelly cutting into my windpipe.

I grab at his wrists, trying to pry them away, but they're as unmovable as oak tree branches.

An unintelligible croak tries to escape my throat but doesn't make it past the barrier of the fingers choking me. Desperate, I kick at the Guard, but all I get is a burst of pain in my toes.

My vision starts going black, and my struggles grow more frantic.

Suddenly, I hear that mechanical noise again. It's getting louder—and then, over the Guard's shoulder, I see a giant lumbering machine.

A mechanical tractor is heading for us, its insect-like headlights seemingly ready to swallow us whole.

Given that I'm about to suffocate to death, getting killed in this novel way shouldn't matter. It should even seem preferable since it's a more interesting way to die that will have the added bonus of killing my attacker. But my fight-or-flight response violently disagrees with this logic. My guess is it has something to do with our fear of giant, loud, fast-moving things—a fear that might be programmed into our DNA.

Hearing the same sound, the Guard turns.

White flecks dot my vision as my brain grows increasingly oxygen-deprived. This is my last chance. If I'm right that this fear is universal, the tractor should serve as a sizable distraction.

Gathering every bit of my remaining strength, I kick the Guard in the groin.

I'm not sure if it's because of my kick or his fear of the oncoming tractor, but he lets go of my neck and jumps aside.

Wheezing, I leap in the opposite direction, toward Liam's immobile figure.

The tractor swerves toward the Guard and rams into him. I hear a dull thud, followed by a short-lived yelp.

Horrified, I watch as the machine drags him toward the wall of the nearest house. My heart slams against my ribcage as I gulp down frantic breaths to re-oxygenate my brain.

The tractor crashes into the wall with an eardrum-shattering bang.

Dazed, I stare at the site of the collision. It's hard to tell the extent of the damage. The tractor backs out, and I see the Guard's legs sticking out from under the rubble.

Is he dead? Bile rises in my throat.

"No, he's fine." Phoe's speaking in my head. "Come on. Get on."

I turn to look at the tractor and see its rotund driver—Instructor Filomena.

"Who else did you think it was?" Phoe's tone is snarky.

"I don't know, Phoe," I think, unable to bring myself to call her Instructor Filomena. "Thinking was at the bottom of my agenda."

The tractor door opens, and Instructor Filomena climbs down with surprising agility. "I told you this was a bad idea," she says in her own voice.

"What, attacking a Guard was a bad idea?" I say out loud. "You don't say."

"It's over now," she says, glancing at the Guard's still-pinned legs. "And we really have to hurry."

Nodding, I take a few steps toward Liam.

Throughout all the commotion, my friend never even turned around.

"Liam," I say when I reach him. "Liam, what's wrong with you?"

Instructor Filomena approaches us and waves her hand in front of Liam's eyes.

"He's on cloud nine," she says to me, then turns her attention to him. "Liam, follow me." She makes a strange gesture, and Liam looks at her with glazed-over eyes.

Apparently satisfied, Instructor Filomena heads toward the tractor.

In a stupor, I watch her get in and help Liam into the cabin.

"What are you waiting for?" she says as Phoe's voice in my head. "Let's go."

"You want me to get into that?" I think.

The tractor door opens again, and Instructor Filomena pokes her head out. "No. I want you to slowly walk to the tower, even after all this," she says, her nasally voice making Phoe's usually friendly sarcasm sound kind of mean.

As if to help the Instructor make her point, I see a group of people heading toward us. They must be wondering what all the noise was about.

Self-preservation kicks in, and I hurry toward the tractor, deciding we can always continue our conversation en route.

"Genius," Phoe says mentally.

Unsure whether she's being sarcastic, I simply climb into the tractor. Knowing she might read my mind, I try my best to suppress my relief about having Liam between us.

She starts the contraption, and we slowly pull away. She isn't even trying to stay on a road of any kind. We drive through farmland, destroying fences and gardens, and we gain a funny tail of ropes with dry clothes attached to them.

The people who were walking our way are chasing after us, shouting as they run. I feel anxious just looking at them, so I turn my attention to my friend.

"Liam, dude, snap out of it," I say, waving my hand in front of his face.

He looks as responsive as a drunk-on-brains zombie.

"I've undone what the Guard did to him." Instructor Filomena briefly looks away from the windshield to glance at me. "Still, Liam needs a few minutes to get back to normal."

We drive in silence until I see something that makes my pulse jump.

"What are we going to do about that?" I point at a large group of Adults/farmers in our way.

Instructor Filomena doesn't answer, but her face gets very focused, and she floors the gas pedal like a racecar driver in an ancient movie.

The tractor engine complains loudly, but we begin moving noticeably faster.

To distract myself from my anxiety, I examine Liam. Maybe it's my adrenaline-infused imagination, but I think there's more recognition in his gaze than there was even a minute ago.

We get closer to the crowd.

Instructor Filomena presses the middle of her wheel, and the most annoying sound escapes the tractor's maw.

The crowd ignores the honk.

Instructor Filomena grips the wheel.

"Phoe, err, Instructor Filomena? You're going to run them over."

She doesn't respond, but her knuckles turn white on the steering wheel.

The crowd probably realizes she means business, because they disperse, and not a moment too soon. I swear she would've run them over if they hadn't moved. What was she thinking?

She doesn't respond to my thought, and I decide against asking the question out loud. My hands are still shaking from the near miss.

We're halfway to the tower when I see telltale shiny objects in the distance.

I squint, and as we get closer, I know for sure that my eyes aren't deceiving me. There are at least fifty Guards waiting for us. I didn't realize we even had that many in Oasis. Until this moment, the most I'd seen in one place was three.

Will Instructor Filomena try to go through them the same way she did with the farmers?

She doesn't.

She turns the wheel all the way left.

I expect us to violently spin out, but we simply lumber to the left. Perhaps swerving out of control isn't something tractors can do.

The Guards must've registered our change of course, because a couple of them jump into a vehicle that looks like a metallic cube. As they close the distance, I get the eerie impression that a miniature version of the Administrative Building is chasing after us.

On the bright side, we're getting progressively closer to the tower. On the not-so-bright side, so is the Guards' cube-shaped car.

Something whizzes past us with a high-pitched whine. A second later, the mirror on my side shatters, peppering the tractor's window with shards of glass.

"Are they shooting at us?" I'm glad Phoe can't see me as I ask this, because I'm certain my lips are trembling.

"Liam," she says, ignoring my question. "Liam, can you hear me?"

Liam gives a half-hearted shrug.

"Liam, sweetie, I need you to run when I say 'run,' okay?" Instructor Filomena's body tenses as she says this.

"Okay," Liam says in a robotic voice, but he looks as if he isn't done talking. After an eternity of a pause, he adds, "I'll run when you say so."

Another projectile whizzes by.

"It would be such a shame to get shot so close to the tower." Instructor Filomena bites her puffy lower lip.

She's right. The tower is close enough that we could sprint for it.

As though she read my mind, Instructor Filomena stops the tractor.

"Nothing 'as though' about it," Phoe's voice says. "Go," she adds in Instructor Filomena's voice.

I blink at her. "Wait a minute—"

"Run," she shouts at us. "Run now."

CHAPTER FOURTEEN

My pulse spiking, I swing the door open and jump out, dragging Liam out with me.

Something whooshes by my head.

On instinct, I look back.

The tractor's engine is roaring once again, and the car with the Guards is approaching fast.

I start running, pulling Liam behind me. Another projectile whines by my ear, and I duck, accidentally letting go of Liam's arm.

He stumbles but keeps running.

Relieved, I pick up my pace, and after another moment, I sneak another look back.

My heart rate threatens to reach superluminal speeds.

The Guards' car is no longer heading for us. It turned. They're following the tractor, which means Phoe's plan of us separating worked—assuming she actually had a plan. Maybe her plan was to distract the Guards by using us as bait?

"You think so poorly of me." Phoe's voice is mock-hurt. "My plan has always been to get you to this tower to disable the Barriers."

"Why can't you disable them yourself?" I reach the first metallic staircase of the tower and look back. Liam is a few steps behind me. Though he's technically running, his gait is so leisurely that it can barely be labeled as a jog.

We're lucky the Guards aren't on our heels.

"Disabling the Barriers requires a two-person confirmation sequence," Phoe says in my mind, "and there isn't another Adult I can trust with this."

"Theo?" Liam says, sounding slightly less dazed as he catches up to me.

"Yeah, dude, it's me," I say. To Phoe, I say mentally, "Where to now?"

"Go to the first floor and take the elevator," Phoe says. "Make sure Liam goes with you."

"Right," I say as I usher my friend up the stairs to the first floor.

Once we reach the platform, I press the elevator button.

Liam observes me dully and then, with the flattest tone, asks, "So what are we up to?"

"Doing something that could get us into a boatload of trouble," I say and watch his expression.

His gaze wanders. Had I told him that today is Monday, I would've gotten a similar level of excitement. Then again, he's getting more engaged by the minute.

Closing his eyes, he mumbles, "Oh, okay."

Okay, relatively more engaged. At least he's talking.

A *ding* announces the elevator's arrival. My eyes widen as the door opens. I've only read about these contraptions.

We walk into the elevator. The back of the thing is made of glass. The door slides closed, and I press the only available button.

The elevator begins to rise.

With each foot we ascend, my heart climbs higher in my chest. Through the glass wall, I get an extremely unwelcome view of Oasis shrinking below me.

I hadn't realized this, but when you don't like heights, an elevator is a very creative form of torture.

Beginning to feel sick, I tear my gaze away from the glass wall and look at my friend.

Liam is staring at me emotionlessly. I think there's a spark of something resembling interest again, but maybe it's my adrenaline making me see what I want to see.

The elevator stops with a loud *ding*. I scurry out of it, my stomach churning, but find no relief.

If anything, my situation's worse.

I have a bird's eye view of the Adult section.

Far below is a small tractor carrying Instructor Filomena. The Guards' car is much closer to her than it was minutes ago.

"Quick, you two need to begin your task," Phoe says. "Bring Liam through that corridor."

Her words snap me out of my height-induced nausea. Glancing at Liam, I say as calmly as I can, "Hey, dude, walk with me."

"Okay," he says. He's noticeably more animated as he follows me. "Where are we?"

As we head down the corridor, I do my best to explain to him what happened, though I leave out the stuff about Phoe. I talk quickly, hitting the most pertinent points. He's not nearly as shocked by my tale as I would've been had our roles been reversed. Clearly, he's still under the effects of the pacifying crap. And speaking of calm, talking to him has been distracting *me* from looking through the windows.

"Okay," he says, his voice almost as chipper as it was earlier this morning. "So what do we have to do?"

"Getting to that part," I tell him. "I have to learn that myself."

The corridor ends in a staircase that's next to a huge window with a stomach-knotting view.

"Open the window," Phoe says urgently. "I'm running out of time."

I make an 'open' gesture at the window, but nothing happens.

"It's manual," Phoe explains. "There should be latches, like they had in ancient times."

Trying to steady my hands, I flick the latches into the 'up' position and pull the window open.

If I hadn't glimpsed the ground below, the breeze coming from this window would've actually felt pleasant. But since I did look down, all I can think about is not embarrassing myself in front of Liam by throwing up or worse; he might be cognizant enough to remember and never let me live it down.

"Do you see that large ledge in front of the window?" Phoe sounds out of breath for some reason.

"Yes."

"Walk onto it."

I back away from the window, whispering, "What?"

Phoe lets out an exasperated breath. "It's a large freaking platform. You'd have to go out of your way to fall."

I look at the platform and decide to just go for it. Face my fear and all that. Pressing my elbows to my sides as though I'm trying to make myself smaller, I attempt to climb out.

I say 'attempt' because, in reality, I take another step back.

Suddenly, I hear a loud bang come from below. I look down and see that the tractor and the Guards' car have stopped. There's smoke coming from the tractor.

"I don't have much time." Phoe sounds desperate.

"Tell me what to do once I get up there," I subvocalize urgently. *If* I get up there, I think for my own benefit.

"It's exactly like what you did in the Zoo." Phoe's ragged voice sounds like it's coming from behind Liam. "Do this and they will all see the errors of their ways—" A bang is followed by a hiss, followed by silence.

"Phoe?" I think in panic.

Nothing.

"Phoe, are you okay?" I subvocalize.

Still no response.

"Phoe, what happened?" I whisper desperately.

Another loud bang comes from below. My heart hammering, I glance down.

Darker, more sinister-looking smoke is coming from the tractor, which looks tiny from this distance.

What happened? Did the Guards just blow Phoe up? I can't think about that right now, not when her last concern was about this task that I have yet to do. I take a step toward the window, take in a breath . . . and freeze as I see the gaping emptiness below.

"Dude, are you planning to jump?" Liam's voice startles me. I glance back and see that he's looking me up and down. "'Cause, please, don't."

"Thanks, Liam. You saved my life. I was totally going to jump." I turn away from him and focus on the platform, staring at it as though I'm trying to hypnotize it.

"No need to be snide," Liam says, my sarcasm seemingly helping him clear his head. "If you're not jumping, then what are you doing?"

"I need to get onto this ledge and do a couple of gestures," I say, turning my attention from the ledge to him.

He bobs his head. "Okay. If that's all you need to do, then why are you standing there all intense like that?"

"Because it's outside." I know an avalanche of teasing might be coming my way, but I still say, "I'm afraid of heights."

"Oh." He scratches his cheek. "I didn't know that."

"Not a lot of heights around," I say, edging closer to the window. "So how would you?"

"True." He looks very contemplative, especially for Liam. "You know, *I* am not afraid of heights."

"Good for you." I take a step back. All this talk isn't soothing my nerves.

"No, you nimrod." Liam's eyes twinkle with the glow of his usual mischief. "I can do whatever it is you need done on that ledge."

"Oh." I feel pretty dumb. Then, after a moment's consideration, I say with a sigh, "No. I can't accept you taking such a risk for me."

"Dude," he says pointedly.

The fact that he's not already on the ledge proves he's not completely recovered, but I can tell he's getting there and that this debate might be pointless soon.

"You can't exactly stop me from going," he says, echoing my thoughts.

"Okay," I say. "But you have to promise to do it carefully."

"I pinky-swear and shit." Liam resolutely approaches the window. "What do I do?"

"Once you're there—"

Before I can finish my instructions, Liam leaps onto the ledge with the same enthusiasm as when he jumps onto his bed—which, despite being a year older than Mason and me, Liam still does regularly.

"As I was trying to tell you," I say once he's sitting in a lotus pose on the ledge. "Make a choo-choo train gesture."

Liam grimaces. "I'm trying to help you. Is this really the best time to show off that you're a smartass?"

I take a deep breath, feeling a major case of vicarious fear. Trying to steady my nerves, I explain the fist-up-and-down gesture I used in the Zoo.

Liam executes the move.

An enormous Screen shows up in the hallway next to me.

"I think it worked," I tell Liam. "Come back—carefully."

Like in the Zoo, the screen has text on it. "Initiate the double confirmation?" it says in red letters.

As before, two giant buttons are also there: 'Confirm' and 'Abort'. What's different this time is the huge, detailed image of Oasis, seen as though from a helicopter hovering just below the clouds. It reminds me of the History Lecture images meant to show how little of the Earth's surface was spared from the Goo.

"Wow," Liam says.

"Yeah," I reply.

The image has details I've never seen before. Usually, the view in the History Lecture is too brief and from too far up to make out the Adult section. Here, however, I can easily see it in all its countryside glory. The Elderly section is also clearer, but it has such a dense forest that it might as well be hidden for all that it's telling me about the Elderly's way of life. What really stands out are the clearly defined Barriers that separate the sections. Their silvery, shining edges cut Oasis into three pieces that run parallel to one another.

I reach for the 'Confirm' button but hesitate.

"What's that going to do?" Liam says.

"Bring down the Barriers," I say softly.

"Wow," he says.

"Yeah," I return in kind.

To myself, I wonder: What is the point of doing this? With Phoe dead, whatever she wanted to accomplish, whatever resources she wanted to free up would—

"I'm not dead. I jumped out in time, and the Guards are running after me," Phoe's mental voice says. "Do it. Now. Once it starts, they'll have bigger problems than me."

"Phoe!" I mentally scream. "You're—"

"Yes, yes, I'm alive—for now," she says. "Now do it."

Knowing my friend needs me erases any remnants of hesitation from my mind. Without further ado, I press the 'Confirm' button.

The Screen has me triple-confirm my choice the way the one at the Zoo did.

"Two people have to confirm the shutdown procedure," the text after the triple check says. "Please exercise extreme caution."

A new set of buttons shows up, one marked 'Primary' and the other 'Secondary.'

"Press the 'Secondary' confirmation," I tell Liam.

"Why am I the Secondary?" he asks.

I roll my eyes and press the 'Secondary' button, nodding him toward the 'Primary' button. He looks pleased as he goes for that choice and presses his button. Right away, more follow-up buttons prompt us, and we wade through all of them.

The messages get more threatening. I think I get a dozen 'Are you sure?' prompts. If you think about it, it makes sense. The Barriers between the sections are a big deal.

"This action will not be reversible," the Screen warns in big letters. "Please triple-confirm for the last time."

Liam and I touch the 'Confirm' buttons and say, "Shut Down," when the Screen display commands us to. When it comes to the mental command, I think 'Shut Down.' I assume Liam also thinks the last 'Shut Down' instruction, because the Screen picture changes. It blinks red and says, "Barrier shutdown commencing."

"So it's done," Phoe's voice sounds tense in my head. "It's finally over."

I stare at the image of Oasis, waiting for the Barriers to come down.

Except they don't.

Something else happens, something so terrible it chills my blood.

I look over at Liam. His ashen face confirms that I'm not hallucinating, even though insanity would be preferable to this situation.

A Barrier is disappearing, only it's not one of the ones separating the sections of Oasis.

The shimmering, dome-like barrier that protects all of Oasis from the Goo flickers and goes out.

We both watch, frozen in place, as the Goo begins eating Oasis. It consumes it with such hunger it's as though it's been waiting for this moment for centuries.

CHAPTER FIFTEEN

"What did you make me do?" I think at Phoe in horror. "What did you make me do?" I repeat out loud, my words coming out in a whimper.

Liam blinks at me. "*I* made you do?"

"I'm not talking to you," I tell him, fully cognizant of how mad this makes me seem. "I did this because Phoe—I mean, Instructor Filomena—asked me to."

He gapes at me. "Instructor Filomena?" A bead of sweat drips from his eyebrow, and he mutters, "Weren't we *just* in the car with her? Why do I have trouble remembering that?" He looks the most scared I've seen him. The idea of forgetting something seems to frighten him more than the Armageddon we just unleashed. "How did I get here?" He looks around in confusion. "Am I dreaming?"

I don't reply. My eyes are glued to the Screen.

The Goo has moved through the bushes that surround the Institute and is approaching the Campus.

"I'm sorry, Theo." Phoe sounds genuinely sad. "This was the only way to stop this mockery . . . this excuse of a society."

Her words snap me out of my dazed horror. "What the hell are you talking about?" I scream. "You just used me to kill everyone."

Liam looks at me, his face contorted in confusion.

"Not you, Liam," I say in a calmer tone. "This isn't your fault, not at all."

Liam backs away from me.

"You wouldn't understand, even if I tried explaining it to you," Phoe says. "They had it coming, the Elderly. This was our only way to freedom . . ."

I don't listen to the rest of her monologue; she's making as much sense as a movie villain. Coming out of my shock, I frantically prod at the Screen. "There has to be a way to stop this," I mutter. "Come on, there has to be a way."

Liam backs up some more, does a one-eighty, and leaps up the stairs.

I don't call out to him. I continue pressing at the Screen, my desperation growing.

After about a minute, I realize my actions are futile. There's no way to undo this.

"I suggest you run up the way Liam did," Phoe says at the end of her crazy 'explanation.' "You might buy yourself a few precious minutes."

I take one last look at the Screen.

The Goo seems to be moving faster, the green that was Oasis quickly becoming the same revolting orange-brown mess as the outside world.

I run for the metal stairs, my leg muscles burning as I take the steps two at a time. I'm trying to catch up with Liam, but to a larger degree, I'm attempting to outrun my inevitable doom.

As I climb, all kinds of thoughts race through my head. Regrets. Ideas. I wish I had watched more movies, read more books, spent more time with my friends.

Ancient books often talk about seeing your life flash before your eyes in near-death situations. In my case, I'm just remembering certain scenes, starting with my earliest memory. None of them are from my time at the Nursery; intellectually, I know there was a period when I was a baby and the Elderly took care of me, but I can't recall it. My first memory is of being embarrassed on my first day of Lectures. I asked a 'why' question for what I assume was the millionth time, and that, in combination with my full name of Theodore, got me the nickname of 'Why-Odor.' After this, I remember more positive moments from childhood, like the first time I met Liam, even though we actually got into a fight that day. Also, my first—

Spotting the real-life Liam brings me out of my recollections. He's standing with his back to me, seemingly mesmerized by the view beyond the window.

I cover the remaining three steps in one jump and stop next to him to look out the same window.

Instantly, I wish I hadn't looked. I can now see the Goo with my naked eye.

It's midway through the village below.

Until now, a part of my mind thought that perhaps the Goo attack on the Screen was some kind of cruel joke, a lesson designed to teach us not to disobey—anything other than this horrible reality.

When I tear my eyes away from the nightmare below, I see that Liam is staring at me gravely, as if he's about to say something.

"Liam," I begin, but he takes off and starts running up the stairs again.

My lungs straining, I run after him. I have no idea what we're going to do once we reach the top—which, judging by the continually narrowing staircase, will be soon.

Instead of obsessing about it, I keep running. When I run, the world kind of disappears. Thoughts of the past visit me again. I wonder if on some level these memories are a defense mechanism my mind made up to cope with the panic and horror that will accompany my last moments. The fact that the rest of the human race will die alongside me makes the idea of death even more incomprehensible. It's like trying to understand what might have existed before there was a universe.

This time I'm brought out of my dark reverie by a terrible mental shriek that I barely recognize as Phoe's voice.

"It burns," she screams. "Oh, Theo, it burns . . ." She makes a gurgling noise that sounds like, "I'm sorry."

Then there's silence.

Sick to my stomach, I stop in front of one of the staircase windows and look down.

The place where I last saw Phoe and the Guards is now covered with Goo.

She's finally dead. Really dead.

Despite her horrible treachery, I can't help but feel a sense of loss. Pushing it away, I focus on the physical pain of the muscle fibers in my legs tearing from the strain of my rapid climb.

The ascent lasts for ages before I get a whiff of Liam's body odor. It's such a little thing, but the knowledge that my always-brave friend is sweating enough to stink makes my chest constrict and my eyes prickle. I recall this feeling; it usually precedes crying—something I haven't done since I was little. Youths have no reason to cry as they grow older.

Instead of giving in to this weakness, I follow Liam's rapidly climbing figure.

On the next landing, he stops and turns to face me.

I'm about to say something—anything—to him, but the words never leave my throat because suddenly, the tower shudders and tilts with a metallic groan.

My foot misses the last step, and then my arms are windmilling as I fall in speechless terror.

The tower seems to be rotating around me.

There's a moment of weightlessness, followed by an explosion of nauseating pain as my left shoulder smacks into something hard.

Gasping, I grab at it with my uninjured arm, and my fingers close around a handrail as the rest of my body meets the staircase with a bone-jarring slam. I continue to slide down for a few seconds before I jerk to a stop, my wrist screaming in agony.

With some still-functional portion of my mind, I realize the tower must be leaning sideways. The wall is now a sharply angled floor, while the stairs have become the new wall, like something out of an M.C. Escher painting.

The tower emits another groan, tilting even lower. I can now crawl up the wall, and I attempt to do so, despite the agonizing pain in my shoulder and a sickening sense of vertigo. My left shoulder must be dislocated, and the entire left side of my body hurts like nothing I've ever experienced.

My stomach heaves, and sweat dampens my clothes as I desperately crawl upward, imitating soldiers from ancient war films. I try not to dwell on the fact that the steps of the staircase make up the right wall. That surreal image strikes at the heart of my panic, and panic is something I'm trying to stave off.

Somewhere above me, I hear a moan and crawl toward the sound.

"Liam?" I yell as I reach the downward-angled platform. "Are you okay?"

"Careful," Liam hisses back. "Or you'll join me."

His voice is so warped by terror it's almost unrecognizable. I always thought Liam might've been born with a genetic defect in his amygdala, making him unable to feel normal fear, but now I see that's not at all the case.

My heart thudding in my ears, I crawl up to the edge of the topsy-turvy staircase platform.

Liam's voice is coming from what used to be a window, but is now a hole in the sloped floor.

On the window's edge, I spot fingers, their knuckles white from exertion.

"Liam!" I slither on my belly toward the hand and look down.

My friend is hanging out of the window, his legs dangling in the air. Blood is running down his arm. Below him is an enormous drop that ends in a putrid orange-brown mess. The Goo is consuming the base of the tower.

Fighting lightheadedness at the sight of the far drop, I grab Liam's forearm with my uninjured right hand.

"Liam, I've got you. Now climb up." I note a tiny spark of relief in his fear-glazed eyes, so I add, "Seriously, get back in. Stop messing around."

The strain and horror on his face eases slightly. "Nah, I'm just hanging, you know."

I grimace at his joke. "Grab onto my arm with your left hand and climb up. It should be easier than grabbing the window's edge." I style my stern tone after that of an Adult.

Liam reaches up, but his flailing hand misses my arm by an inch.

The tower shudders again.

"Come on, Liam!"

He reaches up, his face scrunching from the effort, and this time, his fingers connect with my arm.

"That's it." I tighten my grip on his forearm, my fingers slippery from sweat. "Come on!"

He tries to lift himself up, but his grip on the window doesn't give him much leverage.

"Pull me up, Theo," he gasps. He lets go of the window to latch on to my arm with his right hand. The strain on my right shoulder is enormous as his full weight dangles off my arm.

Forgetting about my injury, I reach down with my left hand to assist him.

The resulting agony makes me stop and hiss in pain. The dislocated shoulder doesn't allow for that range of motion.

Seeing this, Liam grabs higher up my arm, using it as a rope. I inch backward to drag him in.

The strategy looks like it's working—for a heartbeat, at least.

Then Liam's fingers slip on my sweaty skin, his palms sliding down my arm uncontrollably.

"Liam!"

I make a desperate grabbing motion and catch his right hand just as his grip slips off completely.

He's now hanging by the tips of his fingers off my right hand, and I feel his grip slipping with every second.

As if realizing the futility of his efforts, Liam looks up, his gaze growing oddly distant as he stares up at something. "You have to reach the top, Theo. You must."

"You're not making any sense," I say urgently. "Come on, climb back up."

With my bad left arm, I make a monumental effort to reach down, ignoring the crippling pain. Liam's fingers slip out of my grasp, but he twists his body and grabs my left wrist just as I reach for him. There's a loud crack in my left shoulder, followed by a white-hot flash of excruciating pain.

An unbidden scream escapes my mouth.

I think I'm about to black out from the pain when I hear Liam say, "I'm going to let go."

At least that's what I think he said.

Through the pulsating haze of agony, I hear him say, "You have to get to the top of this thing."

The darkness at the edges of my vision closes in, dimming all my senses. Fighting it, I clench my teeth and try pulling Liam up with all my remaining strength, but he's not even trying to help me. His eyes are wide as he keeps staring up past me.

I try to follow his gaze. Something important is up there, and I want to know what it is.

Just as I start turning my head, Liam lets go.

"Liam!" I scream, but it's too late.

He plummets to the ground, and I stare in horror as his body disappears into the writhing mass of Goo.

A pained roar escapes my throat. As though in answer to my anguished cry, the tower creaks again and rotates in violent, jerky movements.

My arms shaking, I grab onto the windowsill with both hands and watch with dazed vertigo as the window faces first the horizon and then the sky.

Now I'm the one who's hanging out of the window, only my feet are not dangling over a long drop. After the tower did its spinning maneuver, the window that was on 'the floor' ended up on 'the ceiling.'

Dimly, I register that my left side hurts a little less. Did Liam pop my shoulder back into place when he grabbed it? If so, it saved my life.

Glancing down, I see that the other wall of the tower is under my feet. If I let go of the windowsill, I probably wouldn't hurt myself too badly. I consider doing exactly that but see that a streak of Goo is running up the wooden handrail. I'll be running the chance of touching it if I jump down. The fact that the Goo is already here, right below me, sucks what little hope I had left.

How is it on the handrail? I wonder with strangely academic interest. I guess the Goo must find it easier to eat away softer substances, such as wood, than the heavy-duty steel that the rest of the tower is made out of. I don't have any illusions, though: the Goo can eat through anything.

We have a desolate ocean of the stuff to prove it.

Still, I can't hang like this for long. My left shoulder, though somewhat better, is still in agony. Gritting my teeth, I use the last remaining bit of my strength to pull myself up. Once my head is sticking out the window, I lever the rest of my body up and try to stand on what used to be the outside wall of the tower.

My head spins. The wall of the tower is tilted at about a forty-five-degree angle, sloping toward the sea of Goo that is the ground. It's probably a matter of moments before the Goo eats through the tower's base, toppling the entire structure into its abyss.

The knowledge of impending death sharpens my senses. The tiniest details of my environment jump out at me. I notice how the sky looks a bit bluer without the Dome, and how strange it is that the tower looks weather-beaten, given that in Oasis, there's no erosive weather to cause this sort of damage. Then another detail catches my attention: a light where the tower's peak would be.

I recall Liam staring that way in his last moments.

What is that light, if that's indeed what I'm seeing?

I carefully run on what used to be the tower's wall. It's not a solid surface, but a patchwork of metal beams and some surviving glass windows.

It's hard to focus on running after everything that's happened, but I force myself to. I will the pain of losing Liam out of my head. It seems more manageable than trying to suppress the pain of losing everyone else I've ever known.

My thoughts narrow on one goal: figuring out what that light is. That much I can do, and it enables me to pretend that I still have some modicum of control over the events around me.

As I get closer to the top, the light becomes clearer.

It's the biggest Screen I've ever seen, yet it also looks like an ancient neon sign, all pink and bright. In some way, it reminds me of a Times Square billboard from ancient times—if the billboard were merged with a gate-looking Barrier, that is.

I run faster, ignoring the pitfalls of broken windows and protruding metal rails.

I must reach that billboard-like Screen.

As I get closer, I realize there's a message on it—a very simple one.

'Goal,' it says in garish, flashing font.

Goal? Why would the top of the tower have such an odd decoration?

My lungs scream for air, but I push my muscles to move even faster.

The tower shakes.

I wave my arms to catch my balance and inadvertently look down.

Instantly, my legs give out and I stop.

I'm rooted to this spot. This paralysis feels like a culmination of everything that has just happened to me and the rest of Oasis.

Everyone is dead. The world is over. These thoughts hit me hard, overwhelming me, and I double over from the pain of it all. Maybe I don't need to wait for the Goo to get me. Maybe I'll just die from the horror and the guilt.

An oddly familiar shimmer next to me catches my eye, bringing me back to reality.

When the Screen appears, I'm actually not as shocked as I should be, because I've seen a Screen like this once before, when I was in Quietude.

It's ghostly, and like last time, there's a cursor flickering on it.

Theo, the Screen writes slowly, one letter at a time. *Theo, I'm not sure if you can see this.* The Screen continues typing each letter at a pace that matches my heartbeat. *I'm worried,* the Screen informs me. *Your neural scan is out of control—*

Before I can even blink at it, the Screen dissipates into thin air, but the hairs on my arms stand up.

An idea forms in my mind. It's a faint one, yet it's enough to motivate me to move again.

I must reach the top and the word 'Goal.'

I focus on that one task, leaving all other concerns behind.

The tower quakes again. Trying not to fall, I balance on the metal beams like an ancient surfer. As soon as the bout of shaking subsides, I resume running and jump over the gaps between the steel struts.

I run like a berserker, the concept of time erased from my mind, and stop only when I reach the biggest gap I've encountered so far.

This gap is an unfortunate part of the tower design and is about seven terrifying feet wide.

Though I've been successfully suppressing my phobia, looking at the gap brings it all back.

The Goal sign is still beckoning me. It's just beyond this last obstacle, and I'm almost there.

I decide to break down the impossible into manageable steps.

Step one: calm my frantic breathing. This step is semi-successful.

Step two: jump. My leg muscles tighten, ready for the action of jumping, running, or whatever else might burn some of this adrenaline off.

I back up, figuring the jump might be easier to execute with a head start.

When I'm a good ten feet away from the gap, I start running toward it.

This is it.

This is when I face my fear of heights and become victorious.

Only when I reach the gap, I don't jump.

I stop, my whole body trembling uncontrollably.

Can't give up, I think and back up again.

I run.

I jump.

Time slows.

I see the Goo swooshing menacingly far beneath my feet.

I'm almost on the other end of the gap when the tower shakes again with a deafening screech of metal scraping against metal. The other edge of the horrible gap moves away from my feet just as they're about to touch it, and the top of my chest hits the unyielding metal edge.

Air escapes my lungs, and I flail my arms, trying to grab on to something. Only my index and middle fingers manage to connect with cold metal.

Right away, I realize this hold is tenuous at best. The weight of my body is too much for those two fingers to handle.

My fingers go numb and begin shaking. Worse, they start to slide down the sleek steel surface.

I hold on to the edge by my index finger for a breath before I completely slip.

I'm not holding on to the edge at all, I think dimly.

Either time slows down, or like a cartoon character, I first have to look down before my descent begins. So, masochistically, I look down. I see how far above the ground I am, and then my plummet begins.

Air lashes at my face.

My body feels weightless—a feeling that would be pleasant if it weren't for the fact that I'm about to die.

This fall reminds me of my most awful recurring nightmare, the one where I'm falling toward something. Turns out this nightmare was a dark prophecy.

I look down again.

The Goo is approaching.

Futilely, I try to enter the Goo head first, like the insane ancient sport of high diving.

I hit it hard and submerge deep into the Goo.

All I can see is the orange shit vomit of it, which feels surprisingly smooth on my skin. I squeeze my eyes shut and hold my breath, wondering why it hasn't eaten me yet. Even through my closed mouth and nose I can taste and smell it, and it's worse than I ever imagined. I'm on the verge of throwing up, but I don't dare open my mouth.

I realize I've been holding on to the same breath since the drop. My lungs are burning, but so is the rest of my body. The burning of my body must mean that, despite my secret hope, the Goo is about to take me apart molecule by molecule.

The burning increases in earnest. My whole body feels like lava for a fraction of a second, and then the sensation multiplies a hundredfold.

I gasp in pain, knowing I'm about to inhale the Goo into my lungs.

CHAPTER SIXTEEN

I inhale the Goo, but the pain doesn't worsen.

In fact, the burning stops.

I feel insubstantial. I feel like a sunray that's beaming through a bright corridor of white light.

An ancient would probably think they're entering the afterlife, since it matches their description of what that experience might be like. Given the circumstances, I might consider that theory plausible, except I have a better one.

I've gone through this already, earlier today, though it feels like it happened ages ago.

I feel the sensation of my body returning, but I close my eyes. When I open them, I'll know for sure if I'm right.

"Theo?" Phoe says.

I open my eyes.

I'm standing in a cave. Stalactites hang overhead, and on the floor, there are stalagmites and an inventory of various dangerous objects.

Phoe's beautiful pixie face is contorted with deep worry.

There's a large Screen next to her. On it is what I assume is my neural activity. My brain looks like a beehive going to war against an anthill, at ten-speed. The sight of it causes me to relive the terrors in a strange biofeedback.

The Screen disappears. Phoe must've realized I'd recover better without it in my face.

"Calm down, please," Phoe says. Her voice is the epitome of soothing. "You're back."

Deep down, I know the answers, but I still can't help but voice the questions. "You didn't destroy everyone?" I take a step forward and do a jerky sweeping gesture with my hands, as though the people of Oasis are hiding at the edges of the cave. "You're not Instructor Filomena?"

Phoe looks at me, incomprehension taking over the worry in her eyes.

"Was all of that the fucking game?" I say louder and step back. "Was none of that real?"

Phoe approaches me and wraps her arms around me. I don't fight this hug, the second one I've received in my life, even though this time, it feels different. This time, the ancient social gesture is meant to soothe me, and it's pretty effective at that. As the fragrance and warmth of Phoe's body envelops me, my heart rate slows from hypersonic to merely three hundred miles per hour.

She rubs my back in random circular motions that are also soothing.

"Shh," she whispers in my ear. "You're here. You're safe."

"But it was so real. I died." I take in a shuddering breath. "Liam died too. Everyone did." I try to pull away, halfheartedly, but she tightens her arms around me. Lowering my voice to almost a subvocalization, I say, "You betrayed me."

"It's over." She gently strokes my hair. "I would never betray you. How could you ever think that?"

I take another breath, and as I exhale, I say, "It all happened so fast."

She lets me go, backs up a step, and regards me solemnly. "Can you talk about what happened? Judging by the fact that the memory gap is still here"—she points at her head—"not to mention the lack of new computing power, I have to assume you didn't shut down the game."

"You couldn't see what happened? You don't have access to that place?"

"As I told you, not to see, no. I did try to get a message *in*. It seems it didn't work." Phoe looks dejected.

"It did," I say. "I saw the Screen you sent. It looked like the one I got in the Witch Prison. It gave me hope, but . . ." I shake my head.

"That's great." Her eyes brighten. "That means next time I should be able to—"

"Next time?" I feel my cheeks heat up. "There will never, ever be a next time."

She frowns for a moment, then asks, "Can you tell me what happened?"

I begin my story, starting with how the game tricked me into thinking I wasn't in the game. Phoe listens quietly. She clearly has questions but is saving them for later. I finish with, "And after I inhaled the Goo, I came back here."

"That is so peculiar," she says. "I don't even know where to begin."

"At the beginning," I tell her. "I can tell you're upset."

"Well"—she makes a chair appear out of thin air and sits on it—"there are things in your story that should've been clues about how fake everything was."

I decide I also want to sit, and as soon as I do, another chair shows up. "Such as?"

"Well, for example, Grace just let you go? And she actually touched you?"

"I know, odd," I admit. "But I was in a rush and didn't question it. It seems like she had some kind of . . ." I feel my face flush. "I don't know, secret feelings for me or something."

"Fine." Phoe crosses her arms over her chest. "I can always chalk that one up to your inexperience with hormones. Same goes for the part where Instructor Filomena showed interest in you." She makes a disgusted face. "But, Theo, the Adult section of Oasis was the French countryside? With Amish-looking people? You don't think it's rather convenient that you learned about them just yesterday? And you actually believed I was Instructor Filomena?" Her lips press into a thin line.

"I just—"

"And Owen attacking you physically . . . You know he's too pacified by the Adults and too cowardly for something like that."

"He kicked a ball at Liam yesterday," I remind her. "Nothing stopped him from doing that."

"Fine. Maybe that could've happened, though I have my doubts. But a tractor chase? I made you do something that brought on the end of the world?" She shakes her head. "Out of all the problems with that scenario, don't you realize that if there *was* a way to shut down any of the Barriers, the control room for that would be managed by the Elderly. It wouldn't be in an incongruent, anachronistic tower, which, from what you told me, fell in a very odd and physically improbable manner."

I feel a warm, tingly sensation in my face. I know Phoe's biggest gripe is with the fact that I thought she was capable of killing everyone. Truth be told, now that I'm out of the game, I find that idea extremely hollow.

"It was like a dream," I tell her and attempt to reduce the warmth in my cheeks by rubbing at them. "You know when you're dreaming and the dream makes sense, but then you wake up and wonder why Liam was Santa Claus and why you didn't question it? I mean he's not *that* fat."

Phoe nods, as if she's urging me to explain further.

"Look." I mirror her arms-folded posture. "The world was ending. I didn't exactly have a moment to reflect on anything."

"But Instructor Filomena with her bullshit history?" Phoe's slender face is pinched. "You know she represents everything I loathe."

I force myself to speak calmly. "Well, if you'd told me who you really are, I wouldn't have concocted a theory, misguided as it might've been."

She bites her lip, a gesture that fascinates me for some reason. "Let's not throw blame around."

"So all I have to do to shut you up is ask you who you are?" I narrow my eyes. "Why don't you just tell me? Maybe if you did, I—"

"It's not that simple." She gets up from her chair. Her ears perk up as though she's listening to some distant noise. With worry on her face, she says, "Shit."

"Let me guess." I give her my best effort at a condescending smile. "Some emergency came up, and I need to run, right? The last thing we have time for is to continue talking about your least favorite topic."

Her long eyelashes flutter as she sighs and says, "That *is* pretty much what I was about to say, yes."

"How convenient."

"Without you beating the game, I don't have much to tell you anyway," she says. "I wish I was just dodging your question, but look." She extends her palm.

Out of her palm streams an image. It's not exactly a Screen, but it might as well be as far as its function goes. Only, unlike a Screen, the image in her hand is three-dimensional, like a hologram. It's showing us a small section of the forest.

There I am, lying on the forest floor, surrounded by greenery and looking fairly bored. My eyes are unfocused.

"You're jacked into this place," Phoe says. "Your neurons are only receiving inputs from your nanocytes instead of real sensory inputs. Only things like your parasympathetic nervous system are active in the real world, allowing you to breathe and digest Food, among other things. If someone were to approach you out there, you wouldn't even blink an eye at them."

I nod. Though this isn't something I'd thought about, it makes sense as she says it.

Content that I'm following her so far, she tilts her palm. The image moves deeper into the woods, away from my comatose self. I watch as the camera, or whatever it is that's behind the point of view, reaches a small clearing.

There's the shiny visor of a Guard's helmet.

I get up from my chair and fight the urge to run. With my system still overflowing with adrenaline, the fright that comes over me is stupefying.

This Guard is walking through the clearing. What's worse is his direction: he's heading straight for where I'm lying, and my unconscious self is as aware of him as the trees are.

"Crap." I begin pacing and nearly trip over Phoe's chair.

"Yeah. You can say that again." Phoe follows my frantic movements calmly, as if I pace like an insane person all the time and she's gotten used to it.

"What do I do?" I circle her a third time.

"Use the gesture and run." With fanfare, she flips me off with both fingers. "I'll be with you."

I mimic her gesture, too preoccupied to feel any hesitation at doing something the Adults would consider obscene.

Instantly, through that same white tunnel, I'm returned to my body in the forest.

The pine fragrance is in my nostrils, and Phoe is next to me, only she's ghostly again.

She turns her back to me, starts jogging, and says over her shoulder, "Run."

I jump up and run. Dry pine needles crunch under my shoes. My legs are tired, but not as much as they were toward the end of the game—which makes sense since all that stair climbing wasn't real.

"I think I prefer you the way you were in that cave," I tell Phoe mentally. Speaking out loud might cause me to run out of breath faster, or worse, the Guard might overhear me.

"Funny you should say that," she says over her shoulder before her insubstantial figure disappears into thin air. "The only reason I took on this guise at all was to point you in the right direction," she explains as a voice in my head. "You're running toward the Barrier. I'll need all my resources for what I need to do next."

"Barrier?" My pulse skips a beat. "Why?"

"Either you or, more likely, the game came up with a decent idea by using your knowledge."

My feet feel cold despite the exertion. "What idea, exactly?" I ask, though given the mention of the Barrier, I think I already know.

"I can use what little resources I have to temporarily authorize you as an Adult, at least as far as the Barrier is concerned," Phoe says. "You can then enter their section. Just don't expect to see the French countryside."

"I don't think—"

"I'm going to disconnect for a bit as I do this," Phoe says. "Just keep running straight ahead. It looks safe all the way to the Barrier."

"Wait, Phoe," I whisper. "I don't want to cross the Barrier."

Phoe doesn't respond.

I'm running alone.

"Are you ignoring me on purpose?" I subvocalize.

No reply.

So I run.

And keep running.

After a time, my pace becomes completely steady, and I feel like an automaton—dodging branches, moving my feet, and breathing, all without any conscious thought. This lack of awareness allows my thoughts to wander. At first, I go over everything that happened. After I tire of doing that, I start asking myself questions: How long is this forest? Were we at the farthest point from the Barrier before, or did Phoe set me on a diagonal path?

My foot catches on a root, and I trip, barely managing to avoid slamming into a big stump to my left. I hit the ground awkwardly, my palms sliding on the pine needles and dirt.

My ankle objects violently. I see white specks, as though I've been staring at the sun. Blinking the whiteness away, I turn my head as I start to get up—and freeze in place.

There's a person staring at me from behind the stump.

A very familiar person.

His mouth is open so wide I can't help but say, "Dude, you realize something might fly into your maw, right?"

Liam gets up and comes toward me.

"You okay?" His voice is rough. "Where the hell did you come from? Why did you run away?" His tone gets progressively more incredulous. "Why the uckfay are you grinning at me like that? Don't you understand the uckingfay trouble you're in?"

Only when he points it out do I realize that I am indeed smiling. I can't help it. Seeing him, hearing him misuse Pig Latin, solidifies a single thought in my mind.

Liam is okay.

Rationally, I already knew it was a game-inspired figment of my imagination who fell from the tower. Fear is rarely rational, however, especially when it comes to that kind of loss. Given how realistic the cursed game was, on some level, I felt like Liam was gone.

"Help me up," I say, fighting the urge to say something sappy. "What are you doing here?"

Liam forgets his questions and helps me get to my feet, muttering, "I wasn't going to help those uckersfay find you. I'd sooner sniff Owen's feet."

Leaning on Liam's arm for support, I test stepping on my right foot.

He's watching me intently, so I try not to cringe too much.

He narrows his eyes, so I let go of his arm and take a tentative step on my own. Right away, I have to swallow a yelp. I don't want Liam to know I'm fighting nausea and the desire to sit back down.

"Come with me, dude." Liam's eyebrows draw together into what Mason and I nicknamed 'the forehead caterpillar.' "I'll take you straight to the nurse's office."

"No, you won't," I say. "I'm not going anywhere near the Adults."

"Dude? Have you gone completely insane?" His forehead caterpillar gets all wrinkly. "The longer you stay out here, the worse it'll be for you."

"Trust me. There's no way things can get worse for me, no matter what I do."

As I say the words, the hopelessness of my situation fully dawns on me.

Unlike ancient fugitives, I have very limited options when it comes to escape. Even if Phoe manages to get me into the Adults' side of Oasis, we're still talking about a very small surface of habitable land that they would have to search before they find me.

"Seriously," Liam says, and I realize I missed something he said. "I ought to knock you out and take you back for your own good."

"Liam, trust me, I can't go back." My voice cracks, and I pause to clear my throat before continuing. "Please, promise you won't tell them where I am."

"But you're not well." He chews his cheek. "You can't expect me to ignore—"

A rustling sound comes from the trees behind the stump.

Without fully realizing what I'm doing, I dive for the place where Liam was sitting earlier and crouch, ducking my head. The pain in my ankle is so sharp I'm surprised I haven't fainted.

The sound of someone moving through the forest gets louder.

Liam steps toward me but doesn't look at me. His eyes are glued to a point far above my head, behind the stump.

He stops right next to the stump, so close I could reach out and tickle his leg were I in a more jovial mood.

"Liam," a horrifyingly familiar nasally voice says. "Were you just talking to someone?"

I recognize this voice. After the game, I don't think I'll ever not shudder at hearing it.

"Hi, Instructor Filomena," Liam says. "There's something you need to know." He makes his hands into fists, relaxes them, turns them into fists again, and then sticks his hands in his pockets. "It's about Theo."

CHAPTER SEVENTEEN

Forgetting about the pain in my ankle, I coil up, ready to pounce, but Liam is standing in my way. It would be impossible for me to spring without knocking him over.

"Theodore?" Instructor Filomena's voice rises with each syllable. "What about him?"

"I saw him," Liam says. "I was speaking of my discovery into my Screen."

"You saw him?" she repeats. "Why are we standing here then? Where is he?"

Liam takes his hand out of his pocket. Raising it, he points southeast. "He was running that way. I yelled for him to stop. He looked at me but kept running." He shifts his weight from one foot to the other. "Do you know what happened? Why he ran?"

"Don't you worry about that." Instructor Filomena tries but, in my opinion, fails to sound soothing. "Come with me. We can cover a wider area if we work together."

"Okay." Liam takes a step to the left and stops next to the stump—I'm guessing to block Instructor Filomena's view of me. I hear shuffling footsteps and realize she's probably heading in the direction Liam pointed in. After a few moments, Liam follows her.

I sit quietly, not daring to even sneak a glance at them. I massage my ankle as I wait and wonder what I'm going to do next.

A shadowy figure suddenly looms over me. I jump, nearly smacking my head against the stump.

"Sorry," Phoe says. "I didn't mean to startle you."

"You didn't," I say and attempt to swallow my heart back down my throat. "I thrive on sudden movements and menacing shadows."

She chuckles, raising her transparent hands to her head with no face. Now that I know what she would look like had this been my man cave, or had she possessed enough resources, I can picture that sly, crooked smile.

It's an oddly pleasant visual.

Phoe clears her throat. "Anyway, you're now authorized to enter the Adult section."

"Great." I rub the back of my head, where it touched the stump. "One thing you never told me is why I would go there. Won't I be like the proverbial lamb going to the slaughter?"

"Not necessarily. They won't think to look for you there. At least not for a while."

I use the tree stump to help myself to my feet. My ankle hurts when I put my weight on it.

"Shit," Phoe says. "You can't run like that."

"Yeah," I say. "I'll be lucky if I can limp my way there."

"This development just strengthens the need for you to cross the Barrier." Her ghostly form makes a motion of running a jerky hand through her hair. "I can get you transport once we're on the Adults' side."

I take a step and wince. "Damn. This really hurts."

"I'm sorry I can't ease your pain with my current resources." Her voice is full of regret. "Not without undoing the anti-tampering protection I put in place per your request."

I carefully balance my weight when I take the next step. I'd rather be in pain than have my mind messed with.

Suddenly, Phoe's spine straightens, and she runs ahead. "Come here," she exclaims. "There!" She points to the ground.

I limp over and look at where she's pointing.

"That's a dry stick," I say, not even trying to hide my disappointment. She was so excited I was expecting to see an invisibility cloak or something.

"An invisibility cloak would require extremely complex manipulations of the Augmented Reality interface—and for tons of people. With my meager resources, I have trouble dealing with just yours. This—" She makes a showy two-palm gesture at the dry branch. "This here is a *walking stick*." She's using the overexcited style of speech common in ancient advertisements. "Like all the famous explorers used."

"More like a cane," I mutter but pick up the stick.

I take a tentative step with the assistance of the stick.

Then another.

"Much better," I reluctantly admit.

"Good," Phoe says. "The Barrier isn't far now."

* * *

"We just passed the threshold, the place where fear would've stopped you had my authorization not worked," Phoe says as I see the shimmer of the Barrier in the distance. She looks at me worriedly. "You don't feel fear, do you?"

I shrug. "Nothing outside what's normal. And by that, I mean normal for someone who has the whole population of Oasis chasing after him and who fell to his death the last time he went this way."

"I'll take that as a sign that my manipulations worked," Phoe says. "You clearly have the Adult privileges required to cross this spot."

Mumbling about why I'm justified in being afraid, I move forward with the help of my stick/cane.

After a couple of minutes, a long stretch of cut grass with no trees that ends in the Barrier comes into view.

"I know," Phoe says. "I also dislike the lack of cover, but it can't be helped. We can't afford to walk toward the section where the Barrier crosses the forest." She glances down at my ankle.

We walk in tense silence until we get to the clearing. "Theo, wait—" Phoe starts saying as I step out from behind the last tree, but it's too late.

I see the Guard, who must've just stepped out from the tree line to the left of me, some sixty feet away.

"Maybe he didn't see us," Phoe says urgently. "Back away slowly."

I begin complying when she hisses, "Never mind. Get to the Barrier."

I glance at the Guard and see that he's running toward me.

He must've seen me after all.

I grit my teeth and limp toward the Barrier as fast as my ankle and cane will allow.

The distance I have to cover is about fifteen feet. A quarter of the distance between the Guard and me, I reassure myself.

"Except if you take into account his current velocity, he *will* catch you," Phoe says. "You have to run."

I attempt to increase my speed, but my ankle pulses in waves of aching complaints, and the wooden stick feels as if it's about to break. I steal a glance at the Guard.

He's closer than I expected.

Desperation coils in my chest. Stopping, I raise the stick and hurl it like a spear at my pursuer.

He ducks to the side to avoid it, and his foot catches on a protruding piece of rock. I watch in amazement as he sprawls across the ground, sliding forward.

I bought myself a few precious seconds.

I resume my rapid limping. Without the stick, the pulsing in my ankle morphs into a violent throbbing.

It pays off, though. I get so close that if I were to reach my hand out, I'd touch the Barrier. Out of the corner of my eye, I notice the Guard is struggling to his feet.

Without testing the Barrier as I did in the game, I rush through it.

Nothing happens.

I don't feel as if I walked through a bubble, or wetness, or anything else.

One moment I was on the Youth's side of the Barrier, and the next I'm on the Adults'.

"That's because the Barrier is not real," Phoe says next to me. "It's Augmented Reality that works on the same principles as Screens and my current image." She sweeps her hands down her body.

I don't respond. I'm looking at a stretch of grass that leads into a pine forest, and it hits me how unlike the game everything is. Aside from the Barrier working differently, this side of Oasis looks like a mirror image of the one I came from.

"Well, yeah. Did you expect the French countryside to make an appearance?" Phoe says. "Now, quickly, get on that." She points to a metal disk lying on the ground. "Remember that Guard? Just because you can't see him through the Barrier doesn't mean he's not about to come through it."

Her reminder jolts me back into action, and I limp to the disk she pointed at.

"It's just a shiny circle of metal," I whisper after examining it cautiously. "How do I 'get on it'?"

"Given your injury," she says, "you should sit in the center of it, probably in the lotus pose."

My mind is full of questions, but I step on the disk. A shimmering bubble forms around its edges.

"That's to make sure you stay safely inside," Phoe says, answering the question I was about to ask. "Now sit."

I get into the lotus pose, which allows me to massage my injured ankle.

A shimmering ghostly copy of a disk appears on the ground. Phoe steps on it and sits down in the same pose.

"Go like this," she says and raises her hand, palm down, keeping her fingers tightly together.

I do as she showed me.

My disk twitches under me.

"Don't move," she says as I'm about to jump up. "The field around you won't let you get off anyway."

The disk moves smoothly and slowly, as though I'm on an ice slope instead of grass.

Then I realize I'm not sliding on the grass; I'm actually hovering above it.

Phoe begins to hover as well.

At first she's just an inch above the top of the tallest grass stalk; then she's almost a foot off the ground.

Before I get a chance to voice any objections, the same thing happens to me.

I'm about a foot off the ground, which is low enough not to activate my panic, but high enough to prove a frightening point.

I'm sitting on some sort of flying device. It must be the transport Phoe mentioned earlier.

"Don't dwell on that," Phoe says. "Turn your hand to the right like this"—she tilts her palm rightward—"to turn right."

I carefully tilt my hand, and the disk rotates in the same direction.

"Same with the left," Phoe explains and tilts her hand the other way.

I turn my palm to the left and the disk straightens at first, but then tilts to the left.

"Shit," Phoe says suddenly and points at the Barrier.

The Guard steps out of it and heads straight for us.

"Do this." Phoe points her palm upward, at about a seventy-five-degree angle. In response to her gesture, Phoe's disk whooshes upward at the exact same angle as her palm.

I look at where the Guard was.

He's no longer there.

He's a foot in front of me, his hand extended.

If I don't do what Phoe said, he'll grab me.

I point my palm upward, though at a narrower angle than Phoe's.

The disk whooshes over the Guard's head, leaving his outstretched hand empty. He leaps after me, but I'm already too high for him to reach.

"You're moving smoothly," Phoe says. Somehow she's flying next to me, even though a moment ago she was far away. "Do this to add speed." She thrusts her palm forward in a jerky motion, looking like an ancient martial artist.

Her disk speeds up. Given how fast it's going, its flight is surprisingly smooth, reminding me of a stingray swimming after its prey.

I hesitantly repeat her gesture.

My flying device moves faster too—much faster.

What's worse is that due to the slight slope of my palm, I also gain altitude.

"There wasn't a choice," Phoe says soothingly. "Not unless you wanted to fly into the trees."

She's right. I clear the nearby trees, flying a couple of feet above their tops.

"What now?" I think, mostly to distract myself from my overly rapid breathing.

"I have no idea." Phoe's voice is inside my head. I guess she didn't want to pretend to scream over the wind in our ears. "My plan of hiding you here is shot to shit, though."

I nod, wondering how I can feel the wind in my ears if I'm enclosed in a protective bubble. This thought is interrupted by the enormous city I spy in the distance.

I stare at it openmouthed.

This is no French countryside, obviously. I didn't truly think it would be. But I didn't expect this . . . conformity. Why keep the Youths away when everything here is so similar to our section, with the same geometrically perfect metal structures and bucolic greenery, only scaled differently?

"Scale is pretty important," Phoe says. "You can figure out the ratio of Adults to Youths from the scale, and that ratio can reveal other things, such as birth rates."

I unpeel my eyes from the distant buildings and look at Phoe's disk.

"How is it that this thing can fly?" I ask. "I didn't think that was possible."

"I already told you: I'm not here in the real sense of the word," Phoe says. "This form you see is an Augmented Reality construct."

"I meant *me*," I say. "How am I flying on a disk? I'm not Augmented."

"Oh," Phoe says innocently, as though she didn't realize what I meant. "Similar to those stairs at the Zoo, this probably has to do with magnetic fields and room-temperature superconductors."

"Ah, why didn't you tell me that before?" I say sarcastically. "Now I totally get it."

"And I wouldn't go so far as to say you're *not* Augmented." She snickers. "Though you're not an AR avatar, with your nanocytes, you're pretty augmented all right."

"I get that too," I say without sarcasm.

"Then I assume you also get that we can't fly any farther," Phoe says, her tone turning more serious. "They could spot us."

"So where do we go?" I ask.

"I'm thinking we should turn back and return to the Youths' side, even if it means we can't fly." She raises her hands and massages her temples. "The Guard we fled from has undoubtedly reported our encounter and—"

She stops talking and stands up on her flying disk. Her whole body locks as if she's frozen. With the way she's standing, it looks as if she's staring into the distance to her right.

I follow her gaze.

"Crap," I say at the same time as she says, "Shit."

Like a flock of migratory birds, a group of Guards is approaching us, their disks reflecting the sun's rays.

Phoe comes out of her reverie, swerves her disk sharply to the left, and shouts, "Follow me."

I tilt my palm so sharply left I nearly pull my forearm muscle in the process. The result is worth it, though.

I follow Phoe's trajectory perfectly.

We torpedo forward, the tops of the trees becoming a solid green blur below us.

"Stop, Theo," Phoe yells at me. "Make your hand into a fist to do that, like this."

She follows her words with a gesture that I mimic right away. My nails dig into my palm as I make a fist, and we both come to a sudden stop.

There are Guards in the direction we were flying in.

They're still in the distance, but it doesn't make them any less of a problem.

"Left?" I say urgently. "Or right?"

"They have us surrounded. I think we should go up."

"Up? But—"

"Your fear of heights is a phobia," Phoe says. "In this case, a pretty irrational one."

"But—"

"Just think how ironic it would be if the fear that's meant to help with your survival causes you to get killed," she says, then tilts her hand up.

"Fine," I say and raise my palm with my fingers upward, the way she just did.

I meant to raise it at a sharp ninety-degree angle but ended up with only half of that. Still, I climb higher, and the trees below get farther and smaller.

"Now you need to go forward." Phoe's voice is in my head. "As fast as you can."

I motion to go forward.

"Now swerve around unpredictably—it's our only chance." She starts dashing around violently to illustrate her point.

I do as she instructed. It's actually not hard. My hands are shaking, my fear giving me a swerving advantage. I maneuver so unpredictably that even *I* don't know where my disk will go next.

It doesn't help, though.

The Guards don't need to know where I'm going when they have numbers on their side.

"There are at least sixty of them," Phoe whispers.

I suspect she's lowballing it to make me less scared. I would've guessed there are closer to a hundred Guards in my path.

I turn back but see Guards about forty feet behind me.

I look left—Guards.

I turn right—even more Guards.

I look down—a ton of Guards are flying up.

It hits me then: the Guards have formed a sphere, with me at the center of it, and they're executing their plan by flanking me from every direction.

"Stop and raise your hands." Phoe's voice is a frantic whisper in my ear. "If they're going to take you anyway, let's at least make sure they don't harm you in the process."

I scan my surroundings. My stomach twists with hollow terror.

"Screw that," I say and raise my palm at a perfect ninety-degree angle.

At the same time, I make an almost-punching motion with my hand.

My disk dashes upward.

Though I know I've been flying up to this point, this is when I see what flying *really* means.

"Theo, what the hell?" Phoe's voice says in my head.

I don't answer, but my plan is simple, and I'm sure she'll figure it out.

Since I have the shield bubble surrounding me, I plan to ram into the Guards above me. They won't be expecting this, since even I wouldn't have expected me to fly upward.

"Stop, Theo. Your plan won't work."

I ignore Phoe, focusing on the Guards.

"It won't work because I lied," she says urgently. "There isn't a protective bubble surrounding you."

In time with her words, the bubble around my disk shimmers and disappears.

"It was Augmented Reality," Phoe says, "like the Barrier." She sounds on the verge of crying. "I wanted to ease your fear of heights, so I—"

I don't listen to her.

I stare at the approaching Guard.

He, like the others, is standing on his disk.

He has no bubble either.

None of them do.

Because, like Phoe said, mine wasn't real. This device doesn't come with one.

All these thoughts race through my mind as my disk rockets toward the Guard.

I'm not sure why, but instead of making my hand into a fist to stop the device, I jab my hand forward to increase the speed and stand up on my zooming disk. The ancient movies had a concept of 'playing chicken,' and in my desperation, it's the only thing I can think of to try.

The guard will either move, or we'll collide.

Unfortunately, the Guard has a third option.

He spreads his arms as though he's planning to give me a hug.

At breakneck speed, I ram my body into his, my shoulder colliding with his helmet like a bullet hitting Kevlar armor.

Through the ringing blast of pain, I feel a strong hand grab me and see a disk fly away.

Clearly, the Guard wasn't fazed by the impact of our collision. As I flail in the air, he tightens his grip on me, dragging me up onto his disk.

Out of the corner of my eye, I see another Guard flying toward us.

I struggle to free myself, but I might as well be trying to jump out of my skin.

The approaching Guard is holding a shiny stick-like object in his hand. Stopping in front of my captor's disk, he jabs my exposed forearm with it.

I feel a painful jolt, and my vision blurs. I open my mouth to protest, but it's too late.

My consciousness turns off.

CHAPTER EIGHTEEN

The world comes back in a haze of sensations. Dimly, I hear voices.

"What's the point of healing him if he's to be Forgotten?" a man asks.

"It's protocol," another man replies. "Until they hold a formal Council vote, he's a citizen of Oasis, with all that it entails, and he's hurt."

"We both know that vote is a formality," the first voice says. "You heard what Jeremiah said. But if you insist . . ."

I feel a pinprick and warmth spreads through my body, easing the pain in my ankle and shoulder—the shoulder that hit the Guard in what seems like a bad dream.

I attempt to open my eyes and say something, but there's another cold jolt and all sensations fade.

* * *

I struggle into wakefulness again.

There are no voices around me this time.

I peer through a sliver between my eyelashes.

There's a white floor and a white chair nearby. I also detect a medicinal scent in the air. If I didn't know the horror of the true situation, I could tell myself that I'm in a nurse's—

"I know you're awake," says an unfamiliar raspy voice. "Your brain frequencies were alpha and theta just a few minutes ago, but they're different now."

I open my eyes and take in my surroundings.

This is where Mason was strapped to a table. I'm sure of it.

Worse than that realization is the next one. The man in front of me is the white-haired monster who gave Mason that fatal shot.

I blink away the remnants of my grogginess.

Close up, I can't help but marvel at this man's leathery, wrinkled skin and his frail muscle tone, which is noticeable even under his robes.

These are signs of aging, something that shouldn't exist in Oasis.

I try to speak, but only a hoarse noise comes out of my throat.

The man's eyes are piercing blue and bottomless. He catches my gaze, and I feel like if I stare him down, I might get lost in those eyes.

I swallow, try again to speak, and manage to say in a hushed whisper, "Who are you?" Saying something feels good, so more confidently, I add, "What do you want?"

"I'm Jeremiah, Head Councilor and Keeper of Information," he says, his gaze turning more intense. "You may call me Keeper."

The man's imperious tone snaps something inside me, and I remember that this is the very man who killed my friend.

"What the fuck do you want from me, Jeremiah?" I use the F-word on purpose. To break his hypnotic gaze, I give him a harsh squint. "How come you look like an old man from the movies?"

Taken aback by my vehemence and outright disrespect, the Keeper glances to his right.

I use his momentary discomposure to scan the room and realize he looked at the Guard, as if saying, "What are they teaching these Youths?"

The Guard's mirrored visor conceals whatever emotion he may be feeling, so I quickly survey the rest of the room.

There's a second Guard here, unlike on that recording of Mason. Thinking of what happened to my friend threatens to send me into full-on panic mode, so I focus on something else, like on this double Guard business. Do they consider me more dangerous than Mason and thus added a second Guard? Of course, even a single Guard is overkill since I'm tied down the way Mason was.

"Your fingers have free range," Phoe whispers in my head.

Happy for the distraction from the iceberg growing in my belly, I wiggle my fingers. They are indeed free. And I know what Phoe's getting at. I could, if I wanted to, do the obscene gesture required to get back into the cave and from there be a gesture away from the game. Thinking of playing the game again doesn't frighten me as much as it ordinarily would have. Compared to my current situation, my adventure inside the game doesn't seem so bad.

"But don't do it. Don't go back to the game," Phoe whispers. "At least not yet. They can't know anything about me or that game.

With your brain scan on display like that, it would be risky, since we don't know what—"

"I look like an old man because I am one. I'm two hundred and nine years old," Jeremiah finally says, responding to my old man comment from what feels like an hour ago. "I'm one of the Elderly and should be treated with respect."

The implications of what he says whoosh through my consciousness. He's been alive nearly ten times longer than I have. I must seem like an infant to him.

Then my mind goes into scarier waters. If this guy ages, that means the rest of the Elderly probably do too. And if *they* age, that means the rest of Oasis does as well—including me. Youths have been taught that once you reach Adulthood, the developing process stops. We all believe we stop changing at the peak of health and maturity, which is around forty years old. No one ever calls the process of a Youth becoming an Adult 'aging.' Similarly, we were told that an Adult becomes an Elderly when he or she acquires enough wisdom to join the leaders of our society—nothing to do with aging, per se. Aging is one of those ancient words, like famine. Horrible in theory, but poorly understood in practice.

"When Adults reach their ninetieth birthday, they join us, the Elderly," Jeremiah says as though he deduced my train of thought. "Before they show any signs of degeneration." He holds out his spotted hands in front of him. "It allows everyone but the Elderly a rather carefree existence for a very long time, don't you think?"

The implications are too horrible to bear. If this is all true, that means we're no different from the ancients. It means we grow old and eventually die.

Unable to deal with that right now, I put that thought aside, locking it in a box. Gathering as much bravado as I can muster, I say, "Are you asking me if I agree that ignorance is bliss?"

"I don't like this, not one bit," Phoe whispers, her voice quivering. "He wouldn't tell you so much if he was intending to let you go."

"I don't understand, Theodore." Jeremiah stares at me, and I see a flash of something almost like hurt in his pale gaze. "Where is this hostility stemming from?"

"Don't say a word about Mason." Phoe's voice turns shrill. "In general, don't tell him about anything to do with me." I hear her exhale a burst of air in my head. "Please."

I glare at Jeremiah. "You give me Quietude." I fold my thumb with as much emphasis as possible while tied up. "You have the Guards hunt me down." I fold my index finger. "You tie me up." I chance pushing my body against my restraints, testing them. They, of course, don't budge, so I add bitterly, "And you have the balls to say I'm acting hostile?"

He gestures and a chair shows up next to him. "Since you bring that up, why *don't* we discuss your act of running away from the Guards?" He sits down on the chair. "I would not have expected you, or anyone, to run from them."

"You don't know what happened to Mason," Phoe reminds me.

"I'm not stupid." My mental retort is harsh, so I add, "Sorry, Phoe. I'm channeling some of my frustration with this asshole the wrong way."

"I deserve your anger," she replies softly. "I couldn't protect you."

"Why did you run away?" Jeremiah repeats patiently. "And how did you manage to cross the Barrier and get a disk?"

I look at him stoically and say nothing.

"What about Quietude? How did you get away from that building?" Jeremiah asks, his voice tenser. "How did you open the doors?"

I shrug as much as my restraints allow and stare at the wall behind Jeremiah as if its white blandness is more interesting than his bullshit.

He sighs heavily. "What about Mason?"

I flinch.

The Keeper squints, his features tightening. I curse myself for my instinctive reaction. He got a confirmation that I know that name—not that it should've been big news to him, since in my ignorance, I spoke of nothing else this morning.

"Let that go," Phoe whispers. "You didn't know about Forgetting. You still don't, as far as Jeremiah is concerned."

I don't argue with Phoe. I simply make my face impassive and resist confronting Jeremiah about Mason, as hard as that is.

"Who is Mason?" Jeremiah runs a frustrated hand through his hair, bringing my attention to the fact that his hair is thinning throughout, especially around his forehead. "Why did you ask Grace about Mason this morning?"

"We were merely discussing the Freemasons," I say. "They were one of the ancients' largest and best-known secret societies." As nonchalantly as possible, I stretch my neck by turning my head from side to side. "Kind of like the Elderly here in Oasis. You're the first one I've met."

Jeremiah starts to get up, but then sits back down again. "It's just a matter of time before you stop insulting my intelligence," he says through gritted teeth.

"Well, why don't *you* tell *me*"—my voice rises in volume—"what the word 'mason' means to you?"

"My role here is to ask the questions. Yours is to answer them." Jeremiah's pale cheeks redden. "How is it that you know who Mason was?"

I purse my lips in response. Subvocally, for Phoe's benefit, I say, "Did you notice he said 'was'?"

"Don't subvocalize," Phoe whispers. "What if Jeremiah notices you muttering?"

"Let him think I'm cursing him under my breath," I subvocalize and shift against my restraints, feeling the strain and soreness of my muscles.

Jeremiah lets out a sigh at my non-response, and I clench my teeth to avoid screaming obscenities at him. If I give in to the anger, I might blurt out something I'll regret. Besides, my silence seems to be pissing him off more than any yelling would.

As I continue to stare him down, Jeremiah sighs again, his expression unexpectedly softening. "Please, Theodore." He looks almost regretful. "I don't want to coerce you to speak, but . . ."

"Shit," Phoe says. "Tell him *something*. I don't like where this is going."

"You want me to speak?" I think at Phoe. "Fine."

Loudly, relishing every syllable, I say, "Fuck you, Jeremiah."

The left side of his upper lip twitches slightly. "You don't leave me with any choice." Jeremiah glances at the Guards as though he said this more for their benefit than mine. Turning his attention back to me, he says, "Last chance, Theodore. Will you tell me what I want to know?"

I do half of the gesture that would send me to my man cave.

Seeing my middle finger, Jeremiah does a strange gesture of his own. With his outstretched hand, he makes a tight fist, as if he's trying to squash something.

His face looks menacing, and I flinch, expecting something bad to happen.

"He just tried to hurt you." Phoe sounds horrified. "Had it worked, it would've been terrible. It was supposed to stimulate the pain center of your brain."

I examine myself.

I feel absolutely nothing.

"That's because of the shielding I created for you," Phoe says. "The shielding he's about to learn about, given your lack of a reaction."

"I'll make him think it worked," I think at her and let out an animalistic roar.

In case the sound didn't convince Jeremiah, I also thrash side to side, figuring if I'm going to pretend to be in pain, I might as well test my bonds some more. The bonds are, sadly, unyielding.

Jeremiah watches all this with a darkening expression. His eyes are locked on the Screen above me.

"How is it that you're not in pain?" The twitch in his upper lip becomes more pronounced as his voice grows louder. "How did you just resist the Punish gesture? Did you know what I did? How did you know to pretend like you're in pain?"

I mentally curse my neural scan, stop my thrashing, and give him an uncaring shrug.

"I'm so sorry." Phoe's voice gets smaller. "I should've tried faking your neural scans. I was a coward. I was just afraid that—"

"Don't worry about it," I say out loud, figuring the reply suits both conversations.

Jeremiah reaches out as though he's about to repeat the gesture, but then stops, no doubt realizing it would be futile.

Getting up, he looks at the Guard to my left, then to the one to my right. As if in answer to his look, the Guard to my left says, "He also resisted the Pacify command, back at the Quietude Building."

He must be the same Guard who chased me down that corridor.

"How did he do that?" Jeremiah's tone is hard. "How *could* he do that?"

The Guard who spoke up shrugs.

"Why didn't you tell me this earlier?" Jeremiah's voice rises. "This is important information."

"I'm sorry." The Guard takes a step backward, but his back hits the white wall. "I wasn't sure what happened. I didn't think it was possible to resist—"

"It's not." Jeremiah jerks his head from one Guard to the other. "I swear by the Forebears, it's supposed to be impossible."

The Guard on my left flinches, as though he's expecting Jeremiah to use the Punish gesture on him next. In contrast, the other Guard meets the old man's gaze calmly—or so I assume, since it's hard to tell with the reflective visor.

"Do you see why I have to find this out?" Jeremiah says to the Guards. "We must know."

The Guard on my left shrugs.

The Guard on my right speaks up for the first time. "Perhaps someone on the Council will know?"

Planting his feet farther apart, Jeremiah gives the Guard an evaluating stare. "You're Albert, right?"

"Yes." The Guard reaches for his shiny helmet and takes it off.

He's a man, something I could've guessed by his voice. What's interesting about him is his age. He isn't as old as Jeremiah. He looks closer in age to the Adults at the Institute.

"Except for the gray hair and wrinkles," Phoe says, "if you look closely."

She's right. Albert's temples are gray—something that happened to ancients with age. And he does indeed have slight crinkles in the corners of his gleaming eyes.

"That is my name," Albert says, meeting Jeremiah's gaze. "Yes."

"Well, you're fairly new here, *Albert*, so I understand your confusion." There's menace under Jeremiah's even tone. "I'm the oldest on the Council. The oldest in Oasis, for that matter. As such, I'm the Keeper of Information. Do you know what that means?"

Albert looks at him noncommittally.

"It means *I* tell the Council these types of things. It means I'm the only member of the Council who carries these burdens. I don't get to have the 'bliss of ignorance,' as this child called it." Jeremiah takes in a breath. "I do not get the peace of mind that comes with not knowing the terrible secrets of statecraft." His voice is quieter when he adds, "I do not even get the luxury of Forgetting. Can you imagine what that's like? Remembering your friends who have passed on?"

Albert's confident mask slips slightly. "I didn't mean any disrespect," he says. "I was only giving you a suggestion."

"Jeremiah openly admitted Forgetting," Phoe whispers. "And the Guards seem to know about it too, though it sounds like they, as well as the rest of the Elderly, Forget with everyone else—"

Jeremiah sits down in his chair and turns his attention back to me. "Theo, please. Tell me what I want to know, and I'll take you to see Mason. He's been asking about you."

His lie and chummy use of my shortened name infuriate me, but lashing out would only give away my knowledge of Mason's fate. I take a deep breath and exhale before asking, "Are you now talking about the stonemasons?"

Jeremiah jackknifes from the chair. "I'm sick of this charade." A little bit of Jeremiah's spittle lands on my cheek and the restraints prevent me from wiping it away. It's disgusting.

Jeremiah begins pacing back and forth in front of me. He looks deeply troubled. Stopping next to Albert, he extends his hand and says, "Give me your Stun Stick."

Albert reaches for a metal object on his belt, then stops. He looks at his colleague with desperation but sees what we all see: his own reflection in his partner's visor. He then gives Jeremiah an uncertain look and takes a few steps back.

"You." Jeremiah points to the other Guard. "Give me *yours*."

The Guard reaches for his belt without hesitation and takes off a metal object that looks like the baton of an ancient police officer. With no trace of hesitation, he hands the baton to Jeremiah.

"Do you know what this is?" The old man holds the baton in front of me threateningly.

"Something you should shove up your ass?" My voice comes out strained. I do recognize this thing. This is what knocked me out during the very last moments of the disk chase.

"It's something we don't really need in our society," Jeremiah says in a silky voice. "A weapon. A relic of different times." He gently taps the stick against his left palm, as though weighing it. "It's not lethal, of course, and if used under its regular settings, it will cause its target to lose consciousness." He turns a knob on the stick. "With a lowered current like this, though, I suspect it will *not* knock you out." He presses a button on the device, and its tip glows with a tiny spark, accompanied by the zapping sound of electricity. "No, I think that if I use it like this, the experience will be rather . . . unpleasant."

I stare at him. I think he's talking about torture, a grisly historical practice I could never comprehend. It's always been just a word, like genocide. You kind of know what it means, but not really.

Jeremiah steps closer to me.

My insides fill up with Antarctic snow.

Jeremiah presses the tip of the baton to my neck and pushes the button.

CHAPTER NINETEEN

I hear that same zapping sound and smell ozone in the air. An all-consuming, buzzing pain follows. The electric current spreads through the muscles of my body, leaving them shaking violently in its wake.

Overwhelmed, I scream, and in the haze of my torment, I hear Albert say something. I can't make out what it is, as I'm convulsing uncontrollably.

The horrid sensation stops.

"What did you say?" Jeremiah says to Albert. "I thought we had an understanding."

"I'm sorry, Keeper, but I'm authorized to contact any Council member at my discretion." Albert's words are clipped. "That's the prerogative of the Guards."

Jeremiah points the baton at Albert. Then, perhaps realizing he might look threatening, he lowers it. "Who did you squeal to?" His rheumy eyes are slits of derision.

"The esteemed Councilor Fiona requested you wait for her to join us," Albert says. "She's on her way."

Jeremiah closes his eyes for a second, then opens them and says, "I order you to leave this room."

Albert starts to move forward, looks at me, then at Jeremiah, and stops.

"Since you brought up prerogatives," Jeremiah says in a more commanding tone, "mine is to order you, and yours is to obey. Isn't that right?" He gives Albert a challenging look. "So in case it's not clear, this is a direct order."

Albert awkwardly glances at the door.

Jeremiah turns his head to the second Guard, as though to ask for assistance, but he doesn't get a chance to say anything. As if realizing his protests won't amount to much, Albert exits the room, his thumping footsteps echoing down the hallway.

Jeremiah looks at the remaining Guard. "You should also go," he says. "Though you and Albert will not recall these events after his"—he nods toward me—"Forgetting, I think it might be best for everyone concerned. Plus, if the Council starts asking you anything prior to the Forgetting . . ."

The Guard nods and obediently walks out.

Jeremiah turns to face me. "Sorry about all these distractions." He crosses his arms, careful to keep the tip of the baton away from himself. "Are you ready to talk?"

I shake my head. I don't trust myself to give him a defiant reply because my mouth is dry with panic. Worse, I fear I might plead with him if I try to say anything.

"You *should* plead with him," Phoe says, her voice frightened. "That Guard was the only ally you had in this room, and now he's gone." She takes a shaky breath. "Please plead with him, Theo. And if that doesn't work, tell him everything."

"That was the lowest setting." The irritation is gone from Jeremiah's voice, and he looks almost caring and sad as he says this. "Please, Theodore, just talk to me. That's all I ask. Your brain is not broken beyond repair like Mason's. If you talk, there's a chance I can make you Forget—"

I extend my left middle finger and angle it as far as my bonds will allow.

Jeremiah releases a heavy sigh and twiddles with the controls on the Stun Stick.

I freeze.

He reaches for me again.

I try to squirm away, but the bindings hold me in place.

Knowing how the Stun Stick feels makes this part more frightening.

He presses the baton's button.

The spark shows up and stays on the tip of the horrid device.

He touches the Stun Stick to my neck.

This time around, the agony that zaps through my body is a hundred times worse. I shake and twist, battering myself against the straps. The scream is wrenched violently out of my sore throat. I feel as if I'm about to throw up, or maybe I already have.

"Theo, if he keeps this up, your heart could stop." I hear Phoe's voice as though from a distance. "Stop your heroics and talk."

I can't respond to her, not even mentally. She's probably right. The heartbeat in my ears reminds me of automatic gunfire from ancient movies, both in terms of how rapid and how loud it is.

"Ready to talk?" Jeremiah's voice manages to penetrate through the fog of agony. "Just nod if you're ready."

My universe gets laser-focused on one expression of my will: not nodding. Even as the pain intensifies, all I can do is focus on not nodding.

It becomes a macabre meditation mantra. I ride the wave of pain, thinking only of not nodding.

Though my vision is blurred, I think I see movement from the direction of the door.

My body is behaving like a marionette in a hurricane, thrashing every which way, but as long as I don't give in, I don't care. Even if I scream, as long as I don't nod, it's okay—although if this goes on another moment, I might lose control of my bladder or worse. But even that wouldn't matter, as long as I don't nod.

"I said," a female voice enunciates loudly, "stop this at once."

The pain stops, and I sag against my restraints. I'm confused. I thought it might've been Phoe who spoke up, but that would mean Jeremiah could hear her, making him the second person who ever has.

"Fiona," Jeremiah says, his mouth turned down. "You shouldn't interrupt me when—"

"The Council only authorized you to perform euthanasia"—the older woman crinkles her small nose at the word—"which was supposed to be followed by an Oasis-wide Forgetting." She gives Jeremiah a piercing look, daring him to counter. "This—" She points her slender finger at me, disgust written across her face. "This is something else entirely."

Her voice is melodious. Were she Fiona's age, Phoe would sound like her, which might be why I got confused earlier.

"Fi," Jeremiah says in a placating tone. He holds up the baton. "I don't want to do this, but I have reason to believe this child has figured out a way to tamper with Forebear technology."

The old woman's already-pale face goes impossibly whiter.

She looks at Jeremiah, then at me.

Silently, I mouth the word, "Please," figuring it's not beneath my dignity to appeal to this woman, since she seems to be an ally.

She stands up straighter and looks at Jeremiah. "The Council members are already waiting to discuss this," she says, her tone full of resolve. "You can explain everything once we reach the Hall."

"Fine." Jeremiah's nostrils flare, and I catch a glimpse of the overly bushy hair in his nose. "Let's get this over with." He drops the Stun Stick on the floor. "While I deal with this minor inconvenience," he says to me, "I hope you take this time to think about your situation." He softens his tone. "I really want what's best for you." He gives Fiona a meaningful look and then adds, "For everyone."

"I'm ready to tell you something," I say through dry lips.

"Don't, Theo," Phoe says. "Don't antagonize him."

She must've read my intent.

That doesn't matter, though, because the old man didn't. He gets closer to me and eagerly says, "Tell me."

"Fuck you," I say as loudly as I can. "Fuck. You."

The old woman looks pained upon hearing my words but says nothing. She takes Jeremiah's elbow and leads him out the room.

I blink at the empty room.

Phoe's ghostly shape appears in front of me. "Now, Theo," she says, her voice trembling. "Do the gesture." She extends her middle fingers. "Get to your cave before someone comes back."

I mimic the gesture, wishing Jeremiah could see it.

The white light that carries me seems imbued with electricity this time—no doubt a result of me getting tortured by that particular force of nature.

In the next second, the white room is gone, and I'm standing in the virtual reality place Phoe calls my man cave.

My bonds are gone, as are any remnants of pain.

This time, the dangerous objects inhabiting this place look friendly and welcoming, and Phoe once again looks like a real girl—a girl whose pixie face has circles under her eyes.

"Get back into IRES," she says quickly. "Beating the game is our only chance."

"But—"

"Remember all those times I said there's no time to discuss things?" She's speaking so fast some of the words are jumbled.

I nod.

"This time I don't think I need to convince you, do I?"

"It's just that . . ." I have trouble talking with everything that's happened. "It was so frightening, the last time." As the words leave my mouth, I understand the silliness of what I'm saying. I'm about to get tortured again, then killed, and I'm worried about getting scared inside a game.

Phoe's gaze is pained. "If I could protect you without having to do this, I would in a heartbeat, but I can't, and it's killing me." Stepping toward me, she lays a hand on my shoulder. "Just don't let the game convince you it's real this time," she says softly, "and you should be okay."

Not real, I repeat to myself a couple of times. *It isn't real.*

"That's right," she says. "It really won't be."

Cognizant of my limited time, I start to raise my hands, ready to connect my middle fingers.

"Last thing," Phoe says, her face contorted in a kaleidoscope of emotions. "Since you could see the Screen I sent you before, I should be able to work off the fix I utilized that time and develop an even better way to stay in touch. I won't waste time describing it since you'll see it soon." She squeezes my shoulder. "If it works, that is."

"Okay," I say and extend my middle fingers.

"Wait," she says.

I stop the gesture and look at her questioningly.

Her face gets close to mine as if she's about to whisper something, but she purses her lips instead.

I stare at her delicate features, trying to understand what this is about.

Her lips touch mine.

I finally get it.

She's kissing me.

This is very different from that peck on the cheek she gave me before.

Her soft lips are moving over mine. They taste like flowers.

Instinctively, I return the kiss.

Before I understand what's happening, I feel her tongue flick into my mouth.

My eyes open wide in response, and I note that hers are closed demurely.

In the next instant, she pulls away and says, "That's for luck."

I stand there, frozen in place.

"Now go," she says. "Hurry, Theo."

I try to connect my middle fingers, but I miss on the first try, like a drunkard from the old movies.

She grabs my wrists and steadies my arms so that I can bring my middle fingers together.

My fingers connect.

I'm so confused I almost welcome the whirlwind trip down the white tunnel.

When the flash of blinding light subsides, I look around and my heart sinks.

My body is in agony from the recent torture, and I'm once again tied up in Jeremiah's cursed white room.

CHAPTER TWENTY

"This isn't real," I tell myself. "This is IRES messing with me again."

"I'm afraid it *is* real," Phoe says in my mind. "I know how it's going to sound, given what happened the last time you played, but this is the real world. The game didn't start. This is for real."

"This is a game," I repeat, squeezing my eyes shut.

"I'm coming in," Phoe says. "It's time we meet face to face."

"That's exactly what you said the last time," I say, opening my eyes.

She doesn't argue.

The door opens.

Fiona—the old woman who led Jeremiah away—is at the door.

"Theo, I'm Phoe," she says as she steps into the room. "You might recall my real name is Fiona. You even heard Jeremiah call me Fi. Fi is what my friends call me. How did I always ask you to pronounce my name?"

"Like it rhymes with 'fee,'" I mumble. "But this is all a coincidence, and this is still the game."

She walks over to me and does something to my restraints. One second I'm bound, the next I'm free.

"Look at it this way," Fiona/Phoe says, giving me a part-warm, part-sly smile that looks eerily like the one I saw on Phoe's younger face a moment ago. "Even if this is the game, you don't want the in-game Jeremiah to torture you. It will feel just as real as if you were in the real world."

For a made-up person, she's making a lot of sense.

"Fine, game-Phoe/Fiona." I pick up the Stun Stick Jeremiah dropped on the floor. "What kind of world-ending event are you going to try to convince me to do now? Can we somehow unleash death by explosion instead of Goo?"

"I'm just here to lead you out," the old woman says. "After that, we'll find you a quiet hidey-hole and try to jack you into the game again."

"Right," I say sarcastically. Making air quotes, I add, "Again."

She throws her hands up in a 'I give up' gesture and walks confidently toward the door.

I follow.

We exit into a long gray corridor.

"This way," she says and goes right. "Walk quieter."

I follow at my regular gait, muttering, "This isn't real," under my breath.

"That attitude will be your downfall," Phoe says mentally. "Even if this were a game, which it isn't, don't you realize that if you die, you won't complete your IRES mission? That means that in the so-called real world, you'll be back in Jeremiah's clutches, on the table in that room." She points at the room we just left.

I shake my head.

This pseudo-Phoe continues making sense. Or is it my brain telling me this?

"Or maybe it's IRES fucking with your mind." Phoe's mental voice is filled with mock paranoia.

"If you're trying to be a convincing Elderly woman, you should abstain from using the 'F' word," I subvocalize.

"Like Phoe—I mean, like *I* never used that language?" she asks challengingly.

"Enough," I whisper. Subvocally, I add, "I'll be careful." To myself, I think, "But this is still a game."

She doesn't contradict my thought as she turns the corner.

"Shit," her thought comes. "There's a Guard here. Go the opposite way."

I turn on my heels and hurry to the other end of the corridor. As I walk, I hear Fiona having a polite conversation with the Guard.

As I make my way to the end of the hallway, I wonder whether Fiona could indeed be Phoe—outside the game, that is. Could my subconscious mind have figured out who she really is and told me via IRES? Or could the game have figured it out after scanning my brain?

"Or this isn't a game," Phoe's voice intrudes, "and I merely told you what's what."

I don't answer.

I've reached a corner and need to proceed cautiously.

Repeating the maneuver I used in the Witch Prison, I crouch and peek from below a normal person's height.

The corridor looks safe.

I get up and make the turn.

This corridor is about half the length of the other one. I can't help but notice how much this reminds me of Witch Prison. Did IRES simply recycle that?

"If this was the game," Phoe says, "do you think it would let you dwell on the fact that you might be in the game so much?"

"How can it stop me from thinking whatever I want?" I reply mentally. "And even if it could do that, it might find me doubting my reality entertaining."

Phoe doesn't have a comeback.

I walk to the end of the corridor in silence.

When I get to the corner, I repeat the stealth trick and turn into yet another empty corridor.

"Is this place a maze?" I ask as I reach a fork—empty corridors going in three directions. "Also, where are you? Where am I going? What's the plan?"

"Go down the hallway on your right, then down the stairs," Phoe says. "I'm already waiting for you."

"You have to answer every one of my questions before I do anything you say," I think at her. "So, what's the plan?"

"There's no time. Get here, and you'll see," Phoe says urgently.

I consider this. I picture going down the right corridor, walking into a room downstairs, and Fiona convincing me to press a button with her (double confirmation, of course). A digital countdown initiating some kind of self-destruct sequence for this facility, or all of Oasis, would no doubt follow.

Muttering, "This is a game," I turn left, since that's as close to doing the opposite of what Phoe wants as I can manage.

"You'll regret that," Phoe says, "when you realize how wrong you are."

To tune her out, I mentally hum the ancient melody that I think is called *In the Hall of the Mountain King*. The suspenseful, tension-building music fits my mood perfectly.

The gray corridors go on for the next ten minutes.

This place really is a maze, which gives extra credence to my belief that I'm in a game. Games love mazes.

Another odd feature of this facility is the lack of people. I haven't come across a single Guard after the one Phoe spoke to.

As though in response to my thought, I hear distant voices.

Great. I jinxed it.

I softly walk up to the turn in the corridor leading to where the voices are coming from, and crouch to take a look around the corner.

A white-haired man is standing there talking with a Guard.

They have their backs to me.

"Don't, Theo," Phoe says in my mind. "Don't go near them."

Since she's telling me not to, I decide I should do exactly what my instincts are telling me to do: the complete opposite of what she says.

I crawl on the floor like a soldier going through enemy territory.

The men are too absorbed in their conversation to notice me.

When I get within reaching distance, I raise the Stun Stick and prepare to strike.

Glancing down at the nob Jeremiah was twirling earlier, I try not to shudder at the memory. There's a little 'plus' icon on one

208

side that I assume increases the voltage. Underneath that is a little button. I turn the dial in the 'plus' direction.

I extend the weapon, gently touch the Guard's ankle with it, and press the button, hoping the shock will penetrate through his white boot.

The Guard twitches and falls like a sack of sand.

I quickly jump to my feet.

The white-haired man's—Jeremiah's—eyes look comically wide.

I thrust the Stick at him, but he dodges it. Then, in a whirl of motion, the Keeper dives for the belt of the fallen Guard.

I again try to jab him with the Stick.

I miss.

I try hitting him with the Stick, using it like a club.

It connects with his upper shoulder, but at this point, he's already holding the Guard's Stun Stick.

Like a fencer, he blocks my next jab with the Stick he just acquired.

His movements are too quick for what I've read about old people—yet another little point for the *unrealness* of what's happening.

"Or his nanocytes are keeping him limber," Phoe says. "Plus he could've trained as a fencer during his Adult years. If I were you, I'd focus on the fight. You don't want to lose in either case."

I don't respond, but she's right.

I try kicking Jeremiah in the shin.

He steps back and whacks my left elbow with the Stick, hitting the spot the ancients sarcastically called 'the funny bone.'

My arm goes numb and agonizingly tingly. Only the memory of what this man did to me keeps me from dropping my Stick. I focus on that memory, forcing myself to ignore the pain.

Ancients called the emotion I'm feeling 'bloodlust.'

With a shout designed to unnerve my opponent, I charge Jeremiah.

My shoulder hits him mid-stomach, and I hear air escape his lungs as my shoulder goes numb.

His Stick falls on the floor with a loud clank, and he doubles over, clutching his stomach.

In case he's trying to trick me, I press the Stick against his skin and push the button.

He collapses to the ground in a heap of twitching limbs.

I know I should feel compassion, but I don't. This is just a game, and even if it weren't—

I turn in time to see the Guard grabbing for my throat.

He must've recovered from my jolt while I was fighting Jeremiah.

I duck, and he grabs hold of my hair. My scalp cries out in protest. It's surprisingly painful to have your hair pulled like this.

I kick him in the groin—a move I employed against another Guard the last time I was in this game. I know this is a male Guard from having overheard his conversation with Jeremiah, which means that in theory, this kick should hurt a lot.

And yet the Guard merely slows down for a moment.

I use the pause to jam him with the Stick again, frantically pressing the button as I do so.

He shakes but doesn't fall.

I turn the dial all the way up.

The Guard falls and convulses on the floor.

For good measure, I zap him once more and turn to look at Jeremiah.

The old man is trying to get up.

I touch his nape with the Stick.

"Don't make any sudden movements," I say. "We're going for a walk."

Without arguing, he gets up and starts walking down the corridor. I follow as he makes a left and a right down short pathways.

My Stick doesn't leave his neck.

"He's leading you into an ambush," Phoe says. "He knows the Stick is nonlethal, so worst case is that you just zap him once, right before the Guards overpower you."

I don't respond to her, but to Jeremiah, I whisper in my most sinister tone, "If I see a single Guard, after I knock you out with this Stick, I'll break as many of your bones as I can before they take me. I've read that bone density becomes a real problem as you age. You don't want me to test that theory." Of course, I'm bluffing. The very idea nauseates me, but he doesn't know that. For good measure, I add, "I think I'll start by putting this Stun Stick into your mouth and kicking it. That'll more than likely break your jaw."

I have no idea if my last threat is even physically possible, but it makes an impression. Jeremiah stops walking.

Up to this point, he was leading me down a long, windy corridor.

"We need to go back," he says. "And make a left instead of a right."

"Lead the way," I say, trying to sound as menacing as possible.

We walk in complete silence. Even Phoe is quiet.

"I wouldn't *really* have done *that*," I think for Phoe's benefit. "Not even here, in this stupid game."

"I don't know." Her whisper sounds sad. "Without the usual nano-tampering, you've deteriorated to near-ancient neurotypical levels, and the ancients did all sorts of atrocities in the name of justice and revenge."

"What will you do with me if I show you the exit?" Jeremiah's hands are trembling as he walks. "Will you break my bones anyway?"

"I'll use this Stick on you one more time." I don't know why I'm making my voice reassuring; this asshole certainly doesn't deserve it. "I'll set it to knock you out."

"In that case, the exit is five more turns from here," he says. "Left, right, left, and left, and right. You can knock me out here and go."

"No," I respond and poke him with the tip of the Stick. "Whatever trap you just tried sending me into, we're entering it together."

He walks silently the rest of the way, arms hanging limply at his sides.

We make the turns he suggested, and I see a door that looks like the twin to the one in the Witch Prison.

Looks like he didn't lie to me after all—not this time anyway.

When we reach the end of the corridor, I point to the door and say, "Open it, and I'll do as I promised."

He looks at me. His eyes are watery. Without saying a word, he makes the regular 'open door' gesture. The door opens a sliver. It seems as if it would've opened for me just as easily.

"If I see something other than the outdoors after I open this," I say, "I will come back in."

He nods and squeezes his eyes shut, cringing as he waits for me to knock him out.

"You should sit"—I glance at the Stick to make sure it's on the right setting—"so you don't fall down and break something by accident."

He looks at me with a mixture of gratitude and surprise. Then he lowers himself to the floor. As soon as I judge his ass is close enough to the floor, I zap him in the neck.

Jeremiah sags against the wall.

I'm about to head toward the exit, when I spot a shimmer coming from my wrist.

I look at it.

It's as though an ancient wristwatch has formed on my arm. Instead of the usual watch dial, this device has a tiny, ghostly-looking Screen.

I recognize this Screen. I saw it toward the end of the last game, only it was bigger.

My pulse leaps, and I eagerly read the text on the Screen.

I hope you're reading this, Theo, it says. *This is Phoe, of course.*

The little Screen runs out of viewing room after that sentence.

I stare at it, waiting.

The letters disappear, and a new message shows up.

I was finally able to hack permanently into IRES and anchor this watch to your avatar.

"I knew this was all fake," I mentally scream at the in-game Phoe as I wait for the Screen to refresh.

'Fiona' doesn't respond. I suspect she won't be bothering me anymore.

You're running out of time, the next part of the watch message says. *I'm about to patch a feed to this Screen from the real world.*

A tiny image replaces the text on the ghostly Screen—an image that sends a chill down my spine.

I'm on the screen, back in that white room, in the exact position Mason was in during his last moments. Jeremiah is there too. He's saying something. Tiny text, like ancient subtitles, tells me what he's saying, even though I could've guessed.

"Why is your neural scan like that?" the old man in the real world asks. "What's going on?"

So there goes Phoe's attempt to hide this IRES business from Jeremiah and his people. At least, given his questions, it sounds as if he has no clue what's going on with my brain.

I also can't help but notice how quickly Jeremiah returned and that he's holding the Stun Stick he dropped earlier, the doppelganger of the one that's in my hand. That means the Council must've approved its use, despite what Fiona might've told them. I'll remember this in the unlikely event that I live long enough to ever meet the Council and do something about it.

I force myself to stop watching. Now that I know what the situation is in the real world, the only way I can see to survive this boils down to beating the game and relying on Phoe to save me with her newfound resources.

It's a small chance, but it's better than none.

I give the in-game Jeremiah a kick to his side, but I do so pretty lightly, so as to not break anything. After all, a promise is a promise, even if I made it to an imaginary person who, even if he were real, doesn't deserve my mercy.

This therapeutic activity done, I glance at the watch again.

The feed to the white room is momentarily gone, and the text is back.

Theo, it says. *There's something else.*

I walk to the door as I wait for the Screen to refresh.

Now that IRES knows you're certain you're inside the game— Another screen refresh. *Things could get kind of weird because it's no longer bound by the parameters of your everyday reality.*

"Great," I whisper. All I need is for things to get weirder.

The watch returns to the scene in the white room, where Jeremiah is touching my unconscious body with the Stun Stick.

My body in the tiny image shakes as though it's in pain.

Fortunately, I feel nothing here, in the game, aside from my heart beating as fast as a falcon diving for its prey.

Not feeling the pain of Jeremiah's actions doesn't make me feel any better, not when I know that my real-world heart could stop at any moment.

This realization reenergizes me for action, and I swiftly walk toward the door leading outside.

Opening the door, I step through it.

CHAPTER TWENTY-ONE

Unable to believe what I'm seeing, I tighten my grip on the Stun Stick.

Even for a fake world in a game, this is going too far.

I'm standing in something that looks like the Grand Canyon, only perhaps smaller. The red and brown colors of limestone and sand look nothing like what I'd expect to see in Oasis. It's a terrain that no longer exists in the post-Goo world.

But the scenery isn't the weirdest part, and neither is the door I just exited, which is hanging in the air like a warp gate with no building behind it.

No, the weirdest part is the creatures surrounding me—and I'm using the term 'creatures' loosely.

These beings appear to have come straight out of my worst childhood nightmares.

My earliest nightmare, like those of many other Youths, started after we learned about the end of the world by Goo, and specifically about the Artificial Intelligence explosion that preceded this event. It's the AI stuff that the Adults described in graphic detail, going so far as to show us what this unholy, machine-spawned life might've looked like, as well as the atrocities these machines most likely committed against the ancient people before the Goo finished the job.

Now my skin crawls as I examine these 'critters.' We don't have creepy-crawly creatures in Oasis, but that doesn't mean I don't find them disgusting.

The one closest to me is a 'snake'—only it's not a real serpent, which would've seemed harmless in comparison. Nor is it even a reptile. It's a tangle of wires and circuit boards slithering to and fro, with two small, thin metal wires serving as its forked tongue.

Slightly farther from me is a 'spider,' which has as much to do with arachnids as the snake does with its animal cousins. It's an eight-legged conglomeration of sensors, chips, and gears, with needles culminating in pincer-like claws.

If Dali had sculpted my childhood nightmares from ancient computer subparts, this canyon would've been the result.

All this runs through my head incredibly fast, and then I spring into action.

My insides flip-flopping with disgust, I jump over the snakes.

Two seconds later, I choke down bile as I jump over a bunch of spiders.

My pulse is sickeningly fast, but I remind myself of my current mantra: *This is all a game.*

The mantra loses its potency when a ten-foot-tall scorpion-like creature-machine looms in front of me.

I skid to a halt.

The giant scorpion lumbers toward me, trampling the smaller abominations in its path. Zooming its lenses on me, it readies its tail—a tail that's a web of various computer cables tipped with an enormous harpoon.

I swallow hard, fighting paralyzing fear.

The thing's tail strikes at me with incredible speed.

I throw myself to the side, my teeth clanking as I land on all fours while still clutching the Stick in a white-knuckled grip. Scrambling to my feet, I see that there's a foot-deep crater where I was standing.

A piercing, siren-like shriek tears the air next to me. I spin around and see that I landed next to the maw of another giant creature—a thing that looks like an enraged stegosaurus. Unlike the real dinosaur, this one's armor is made of metal, and its dorsal plates are chainsaws.

Sucking in a breath, I swing the Stun Stick at it. Out of the corner of my eye, I see the scorpion backing away from the stegosaurus, as if in fear.

The dinosaur opens its mouth, revealing a row of scalpels that gleam in the sunlight.

Without hesitating, I bury my weapon in the creature's camera-like eye.

Its screeching yelp creates an avalanche on one of the surrounding cliffs. The scorpion takes a few scared steps back.

The sound also sends primal fear skittering through my nerve endings—which works out well because my finger spasms over the button and activates the current of the Stick.

The stegosaurus vibrates, and a foul-smelling brown liquid streams out of its eye socket.

Emboldened, I press the button again, keeping a wary eye on the scorpion, which is recovering from its fear of the dinosaur.

The stegosaurus yelps again, and I smell burned rubber and wires—or at least that's what I assume that horrible stench is.

With a final, violent shake, the stegosaurus collapses on its side, leaving me clutching the goop-covered Stun Stick.

My lips curl at the sight of the slimy substance, and I stuff the Stick into the waistband of my pants. A disgusting stream of mechanical blood is dripping down my leg, but I don't have time to worry about that.

I run around the ruin of the dinosaur's metallic body and examine the chainsaw-like dorsal plates. They stopped rotating, but they otherwise look functional.

Wrinkling my nose, I rip one out. It has a cord I can pull, and I reach to do so.

A shadow looms over me.

In a herky-jerky motion, I duck to the side. With herculean effort, I keep the chainsaw in my hands. I figure it's best to move first and sort out what's trying to kill me second.

And what's trying to kill me is the scorpion's tail, I realize a split second later. It penetrated the earth half an inch away from where my foot currently is—the place where my whole body was a moment ago.

With some coolly rational part of my brain, I determine that it'll need a moment to get its harpoon out of the ground.

Spasmodically, I pull the cord on the chainsaw—a gesture I saw in that one and only horror movie I watched.

The chainsaw comes to life.

In an arc, I swing the roaring weapon at the scorpion's tail.

The screech of metal against metal makes my skin break into goosebumps.

The scorpion's tail thrashes, spilling a blue-green liquid that eats into the ground's limestone.

I rip the chainsaw out and run, gripping the weapon tightly. The chainsaw emits nauseating gasoline fumes, making me feel as if I'm suffocating. Behind me, I hear the thud of something giant hitting the ground and glance over my shoulder to see the scorpion's maimed body twitching.

I turn my attention back to the ground in front of me just in time to see a large snake leap at my leg.

Gasping in gasoline fumes, I swing the vibrating chainsaw at the snake and slash it in half.

One more monster down, and who knows how many more to go.

Another snake hurls its mechanical body at me, and I hack it apart without slowing down. A centipede is next, and I dispatch it too, my muscles straining from the effort it takes to control the heavy, buzzing chainsaw. Next is a man-sized robo-cockroach, followed by more insect-like shapes I find hard to categorize. I whack them all, ignoring the sweat pouring down my face, and when I glance back again, the trail behind me resembles an ancient computer warehouse after an explosion.

The creatures seem wary now, so I run unhindered, which gives me a chance to scan the nearby cliffs.

On top of one of them, I spot something familiar and head that way.

A tarantula doesn't move out of my way in time, so I swing the chainsaw again and chop half of its mesh-wire appendages off. My breath rattles in my chest, and my legs burn from the effort of running. As I approach the cliff side, however, I forget my exhaustion.

On top of the cliff is a big neon 'Goal' sign.

It's just as I suspected. The target is a duplicate of the one I never reached on the top of the tower.

There's something else there, though.

I have to squint to make it out, but I'm fairly sure a set of doors just appeared on the top of the cliff, surreally hovering in the air.

Helmeted figures dressed in white pour out of the doors.

They're Guards—only something is a little different about them. From this distance, I have trouble figuring out what it is.

The creatures around me scurry away from the cliff.

If the stupid Goal sign weren't at the top of this thing, I'd follow the example of these creatures. Instead, I run for the cliff. With nothing in my immediate path, I risk glancing at the ghostly watch on my wrist.

The real-world Jeremiah is no longer holding the baton. He's saying something to my unconscious self. The little subtitles read: "I've run out of the time the Council allotted me. This is your last chance to speak up, or to at least open your mind to our influence. I can tell you're not under Oneness right now, which I initiated as per our usual protocol. You should know that Oneness is what makes the euthanasia painless. Without it, the process of your brain slowing to a stop will likely be extremely unpleasant."

CHAPTER TWENTY-TWO

My stomach drops. I shouldn't have looked at the watch.

Trying to push my horror aside, I look up.

The cliff appears much taller up close—impossibly taller, as if the game made it grow.

Cognizant of the ticking clock in the real world, I drop the heavy chainsaw and make sure the Stun Stick is secure in my waistband. Mumbling, "This isn't real," I find a rock protruding out of the cliff and reach for it with my right hand, then place my foot on the stony ledge at the bottom. I then push off the ledge and grab for a higher rock with my left hand as I find another foothold with my other foot.

I recall watching ancient vacation advertisements and seeing smiling people climbing rocks this way. Allegedly, they did this for fun, not to escape peril or reach an important resource. I didn't believe it then, and now I'm sure it's a fabrication created by the Adults. They probably wanted to make the ancients look even more insane than they were (and from what I know, they were pretty nutty).

I start holding in a scream when I'm four feet off the ground.

When I'm ten feet up, I'm covered in cold sweat, and my hands are trembling.

A pair of ropes falls from the peak.

I blink, stunned, and examine the one within my reach.

These aren't real ropes, as I initially thought. They're woven out of a variety of cables—some silver metal, some bronze, and many more shielded by rubber (or whatever the ancients used) that's every color of the rainbow. I recall a movie where someone had to disarm a bomb—that bomb had these kinds of wires.

Could this rope be from the Guards I saw exiting those surreal warp-like doors near the Goal sign?

My pulse drumming in my throat, I find a particularly good perch for my left foot and prepare for whatever's coming my way.

A burned petroleum stench assaults my nostrils again. It's accompanied by a whooshing sound.

Time seems to slow.

I lick my sandpaper-dry lips and look up.

A Guard is zipping down the rope.

Only this isn't a Guard. This creature's visor is broken, but there's no face underneath—only a charred husk. Where his eyes should be are two bloodthirsty cameras. His shoulder and leg joints glint with the metal of various electronic subcomponents.

If an ancient computer and a vacuum cleaner ate a Guard, this creature would be what they'd throw up.

The 'Guard' is holding a set of gigantic garden scissors in his white-gloved hand. He aims the weapon at my stomach.

Twisting, I dodge and nearly fall.

The feeling of vertigo is terrible.

Seeing that I can't hold on to this rock any longer, I push off with my feet and latch on to the rope a couple of feet under my assailant.

Instead of trying to hack at my head with the scissors, the Guard starts cutting the rope above his head.

I curse myself. If the creature's objective is to stop me from reaching the Goal sign, of course he'd act suicidally. The only good news is that the hodgepodge of wires looks too hard for the scissors to cut through with ease.

I have seconds to act.

Without letting myself think, I wrap the cable-rope around my right ankle in the style of the craziest ancients of all: aerial circus performers.

My hand shaking, I reach into my belt, take out the Stun Stick, and twist the dial to a lower setting—slightly less than 'knock out' mode.

Taking a deep breath to calm my galloping heartbeat, I bury the Stick among the wires making up the rope and make sure that the tip touches as many of the exposed wires as possible. If I understand my physics correctly, electricity should travel up and down this rope and the Stick should stay put.

With a sickening flashback to Jeremiah torturing me, I press the button.

The shock of the pain and my uncontrollable shaking cause my hands to release the rope. Arms flailing, I fall, but the rope I wrapped around my ankle prevents me from plunging too far. With a scream, I come to a halt, swinging upside down like a pendulum. My back scrapes against the side of the cliff, and my ankle feels like it's about to be ripped off.

Worst of all, the sight of the rope starting to unravel from my ankle threatens to loosen my bladder.

Using every ounce of strength in my abs, I reach up and grab onto the rope. My arms are trembling as I take in the results of my insane stunt.

The Guard is still hanging on to the rope, but his electric components are going haywire.

I untwist the coils around my ankle and climb higher up the rope. My palms are slick with sweat as I grab for the Stick still buried in the wires.

The Guard clumsily swings the giant scissors at me. Sparks fly as his joints screech from the movement.

I block his thrust with the Stun Stick, the impact nearly sending me flying.

He pulls the scissors back, but before I can rejoice, he throws them at me. I try to swat the projectile away, but the sharp blade slices across my chest, leaving a streak of burning pain. I gasp as blood spurts from the gash and nausea twists my stomach.

The creature violently shakes the rope.

I don't know how, but I manage to climb another inch while ignoring the sickening dripping of my blood.

My fingers reach something metallic on the creature's body, and I press the Stun Stick's activate button.

The Guard shakes.

My head spinning, I move up the dial on the stick without letting go of the button.

The Guard's thrashing slows.

I turn the dial all the way to 'knock out' mode.

Parts of the creature weld together, and then he lets go of the rope and nosedives to the ground.

Shaking in relief, I stuff the Stick back inside my waistband and look around.

There are two other ropes, each about ten feet away from me, with determined-looking Guards on them. They're shaking their respective ropes in seesaw-like movements, clearly attempting to get closer to me.

Wrapping my legs tightly around the rope, I pull my shirt off, hissing in pain as I do so. A symphony of agony emanates from my chest as I rip the cloth into long strips and tie them around my wound to stop the bleeding.

The pain gets so bad I nearly lose consciousness.

When the white flecks in front of my vision go away, I realize I'm no longer dripping blood, though the makeshift bandage is already soaked.

I unclench my legs from around the rope and climb.

The Guards on the other ropes manage to swing and climb at the same time, getting closer with every movement.

If I let myself dwell on their inexorable approach, I'm screwed. So instead, I ignore them and focus on moving my hand up the rope and pulling myself up. Then, tightening my legs to hold myself in place, I repeat the maneuver. I climb like this until I make the biggest mistake of the last half hour.

I inadvertently look down.

Adrenaline hits me hard.

My jaw tenses, and my entire body locks up. I can't move my arms and legs; they're clutched, claw-like, around the rope.

Calm down, I tell myself. I've already faced every human being's biggest phobias—AIs, spiders, snakes, cyborg-people—and none of that unmanned me this much. What's so freaking special about heights? If Phoe were here, she'd probably say it was the fault of my overactive amygdala, or something along those lines. She'd tell me to suck it up and not be a slave to my biology.

None of this helps. I still can't move. Irrational fears can't be curtailed by rational analysis. I'm about ten feet away from the edge of the cliff, but I might as well be miles away.

I will my arms to move, aware that the loss of blood is making me increasingly lightheaded.

Suddenly, agony erupts on the top of my head.

A gloved hand grabbed me by my hair—a hand belonging to the Guard on my right.

The pain brings me out of my stupor.

I jerk my head away, leaving a bloody piece of scalp in the Guard-thing's hand as he swings away from me.

The wound he left must be deep, because my face is covered in blood. Nevertheless, I'm almost thankful to the creature for jolting me into action.

I'm climbing again, my fear of heights temporarily suppressed.

Left hand.

Right hand.

Out of the corner of my eye, I see a shadow.

The Guard who ripped out my hair is swinging back toward me.

I cast a frantic glance to my left.

His partner is also about to reach me, and he's holding something sharp—a cross between a bolt and a sword.

I tense, planting my feet firmly on the mountainside.

Holding my breath, I let the Guards get closer.

At just the right moment, using all my remaining strength, I push off the cliff with my legs.

I fly a couple of feet away from the cliff wall.

The Guards collide, and the sword thing stabs the Guard on the right.

I extend my legs. I'm about to swing back into them, Tarzan-style.

My feet hit the Guards. I get the left one in the helmet, and the right one in the shoulder.

Neither tries to defend himself, which means they're either stunned by my hits or by their own collision.

Before they can recover, I tighten my grip on the rope with my left hand and pull out the Stun Stick with my right. In a fluid motion, I stick the Stun Stick into the red LED light that marks the eye of the sword owner. I press the button. His head almost explodes from the current. I leave the Stun Stick in what's left of his eye socket and grab the hilt of the bolt-sword. As I suspected, my maneuver loosened his grip. I rip the sword out of the Guard's hand, as well as out of his partner's body. As I pull it out, I try to do so in a jagged motion to damage as much of the Guard's internal machinery as I can.

Before either Guard recovers, I put the sword between my teeth like a pirate and use my arms to pull myself up the rope as quickly as I can. When I'm about four feet higher, I kick at their heads.

My attackers lose their grip on their ropes and tumble down.

One plummets without any signs of life, but the second one starts clutching at the air with his pincer-like fingers.

With a clank of metal, the creature manages to grab onto my rope several feet below.

The rope shudders, nearly causing me to lose my grip, but I manage to hang on.

Hoping he doesn't shake the rope, I decide to do a risky maneuver. Letting go of the rope with my right hand, I grab the sword from between my teeth.

The Guard begins to climb up.

Though my sword hand is stiff with fear, I hack away at the wires below me.

The Guard moves closer.

I continue hacking away at the rope. Each downward swing of my weapon cuts some of the intertwined wires.

He climbs even closer.

I raise the sword higher and bring it down so hard that the ricochet causes my rope to swing toward the cliff.

All that's left of the rope below me is a thin braid of red, blue, and green wires that look too thin to support the weight of the creature, yet, impossibly, they don't break.

The Guard is almost on me. He reaches up with his claw-like pincers.

I use the sharp tip of the sword to cut at the leftover wires.

Only the red wire is left intact.

The Guard reaches higher, his pincers scraping at the sole of my shoe.

The red wire snaps with a soft *ping* sound.

Reflexively, the Guard continues to climb up the detached rope. As he falls, the creature claws at the cliff side, but all that accomplishes is leaving marks in the stone.

I stick the sword between my teeth again and resume the climb.

The last six feet are harder than all of the previous climb. Only two thoughts enable me to keep going:

This isn't real. Don't look down.

Finally reaching the edge of the cliff, I grip it with my hands and pull myself up, scrambling over the cliff on all fours. Breathing hard, I grab the sword from my mouth and stand up.

A thick coil of wires and screws securing the rope to the edge of the cliff is in front of me. I step over it and begin walking.

Almost immediately, I see the neon Goal structure. It's a short sprint away. This close up, it looks like a giant rippling mirror made out of some mysterious luminescent material—a material blinding in its brightness.

All I have to do is find the energy to reach it.

Unable to help myself, I glance at the little watch on my wrist. On the tiny ghost Screen, Jeremiah is standing next to me, talking. On the table to his left is a syringe. The small captions scroll by, but I don't bother reading them.

Instead, I push my tired muscles into motion and run.

When I'm two-thirds of the way to my target, I jerk to a sudden halt.

A new hovering door appears between the Goal and me.

Unlike the others, this one looks worn and rusted. With a screech of unoiled hinges, the door opens.

Incredulous, I stare at what exits through it.

CHAPTER TWENTY-THREE

The thing in front of me is a white-haired nightmare of gears, antennas, and drill bits. Like an octopus, it has eight wires instead of arms. Each arm ends in a set of pliers, and they all move around like the snakes on Medusa's head. Half of its face is Jeremiah's, but the other half looks like someone poured hot liquid steel onto it. Its left eye is human and blue, while the right one is not an eye at all, but an LCD screen.

I see myself on that Screen. My eyes are damp and unhealthily bright. Tendons are protruding from my neck, and my frantic pulse is visible. With the scowl on my bloodied face, I look like an ancient berserker.

Cyborg Jeremiah opens his mouth, revealing screws and nails where teeth should be. I hear a loud screech come out of the speaker that's stuck in Jeremiah's throat. Through the metallic radio static, I make out the words, "You're dead now."

In the next second, the thing charges at me.

His right middle tentacle reaches for my throat.

Coming out of my stunned paralysis, I swing the bolt-sword.

Half of the tentacle flops to the ground, machine-oil-smelling green blood spurting from the stump.

Now the monster's left middle appendage tries to grab me. I time my slice carefully, and the arm joins its sibling on the ground.

Having lost two of his eight upper limbs, Jeremiah treads more carefully. He reaches for me with the top left and the top right arms at the same time.

I suck in a quick breath and sever the left appendage as I grab the right one with my left hand. Before he registers what's what, I leap at him, bringing his right arm with me. The thing is stretchy, like a rope. He tries to grab me with his three left ones, but I swat them with the sword, and they retreat.

Finding myself behind him, I wrap the arm I'm holding around his other two right arms, tucking the tip of the appendage under his armpit. I then plunge the sword into Jeremiah's back.

The creature jerks so violently that I end up leaving the sword in its back. Its three right arms seem stuck, as I hoped, but the left ones have free motion.

The upper appendage grabs me by my waist. With inhuman strength, it lifts me in the air, and the lower and upper left arms grab onto the flesh of my thigh and shoulder.

Before I can react, the creature throws me. I fly toward the edge of the cliff, chunks of my flesh left behind in Jeremiah's pliers-hands.

As I'm flying, I note, almost as though from a distance, that the pain is not as bad as I imagined it would be. Is it shock, or does the game not allow the player to experience pain above a certain threshold?

I crash-land on my damaged shoulder and roll, bumping into the coil of rope wires. As air rushes out of me, I realize I might've jinxed myself again.

The game does allow for horrific pain, because I'm feeling it.

Trying not to swallow my tongue or bite it off, I lie in the fetal position and gasp for air as robo-Jeremiah walks toward me with menacing inevitability.

My gaze flicks away for a second, and I spot movement on my wristwatch Screen.

Real-life Jeremiah is reaching for the syringe on the table.

Horrified, I tear my gaze from the Screen and frantically scan my surroundings.

All I see is the wire rope I used to climb up the cliff.

Cyborg Jeremiah is a few feet away.

Without turning, I feel for the rope with my left hand. When I find it, I pull up the chunk that was left after I chopped it in half. Clutching the bottom end of the rope, I tie it around my right ankle in a double knot.

Doing my best not to dwell on the long drop behind me, I shakily rise to my feet. I glance down at my wrist for a split second and see that the real Jeremiah is turning to face me, syringe in hand.

My stomach hollow, I tear my gaze away again and wait.

The monster Jeremiah extends his upper left arm toward me.

When it's within my reach, I close my right hand around the pliers that make up his hand and hold on as if my life depends on it—because it does.

His human eye registers surprise at my action.

If you think this is strange, let's see what you think of this next part.

Bracing myself, I take a confident jump backward, off the cliff, and drag Jeremiah with me.

There's a moment of weightlessness, followed by a nausea-inducing jerk as the rope pulls taut.

I'm swinging head down, the rope holding me up by my ankle.

I clench my teeth, preparing for the next part of my plan.

Jeremiah's body whooshes past me on its way down.

The world seems to slow.

I see his back.

The bolt-sword is still sticking out of it.

With my free left hand, I grab for it.

He continues to plummet, leaving the sword clutched in my hand.

I open my right hand to let go of his pliers, but it's not that easy. Before my fingers uncurl completely, the pliers grab my wrist.

He jerks to a stop with a violent pull on my arm, and I understand why the ancients considered the rack to be the worst torture device ever created. Being stretched like this is unbearable, and it's only made worse by the wounds I just sustained.

Through the haze of pain, I realize the sword is still in my left hand. I hack at Jeremiah's wrist. With a splash of green, his flesh splits open, but he doesn't fall. Instead, he grabs onto my sleeve with his two remaining appendages.

With a desperate growl, I jab him with the sword again.

More green liquid splashes across my face, burning me like acid.

One appendage remains.

My skin screaming in agony, I put all my remaining strength into this last chop and cleave the limb with one swing.

With a metallic screech and a fountain of green blood, Jeremiah falls.

My hand can no longer hold on to the sword, and the weapon follows Jeremiah, clanging against the rocks on its way down. I squeeze my eyes shut in an effort to not look down and strain my aching body once more as I reach for the rope.

My mind is in a fog as I climb back up, nearly blacking out from the pain. I feel like a ghost of myself—something I marvel at. Is the extreme pain I endured causing this illusion, or do I, in this game world at least, really exist as a spirit-type thing possessing this broken body? Is that what's allowing me to force this humanoid shell to crawl toward that Goal structure? Then again, isn't that how the human will is supposed to work, even in the real world? Mind over matter, determination over agony?

I crawl up the cliff, and once I get to the edge, I crawl forward.

The only reason I know my crawling doesn't take hours is because I keep sneaking glances at my Screen from time to time. In that tiny display, I see why I'm still alive.

Armed with the syringe, Jeremiah is delivering a monologue that seems meant more for his conscience than for the benefit of my clearly unconscious self.

In my growing panic, I glimpse a tiny subtitle: "The good of the society outweighs the good of an individual." He might've stolen that line from some ancient philosopher.

I crawl faster, the Screen flickering in front of my eyes as I move my elbows, one in front of the other.

"Now that it's come to this, I really hope you at least receive Oneness. I don't wish to cause you needless pain," Jeremiah continues. "Then again, perhaps your brain being as it is, you will not feel what's about to happen. One can only hope."

Feeling sick, I extend my hand toward the shimmering Goal sign. My fingers push through it—and disappear.

The Screen on my wrist is still visible. The subtitles say, "Take solace in this: the people who knew you will Forget that they did. They won't suffer the pain of your loss."

Jeremiah moves the syringe toward my upper arm.

Gathering the remnants of my strength, I push off the dusty ground with my feet and rocket headfirst into the Goal.

As soon as my head crosses its mirrored surface, a kaleidoscope of odd sensations hits me. I think I smell the color red and taste sunbeams.

Instantly, I find myself standing on a large pedestal. Placards with the word 'WINNER' are plastered all over.

There's a roaring noise. I look down and see millions of people standing below, clapping and cheering.

Remembering my predicament, I steal another look at the watch.

"If it makes you feel any better, I will be the one to suffer most from this," Jeremiah says. "I will not Forget."

I think the game figured out that I'm not interested in prolonging the celebration of my awesome IRES-beating abilities, because another light display and bout of synesthesia leave me floating in the middle of gray nothingness.

In front of me is a giant Screen that looks like the one I used to shut down the Zoo, only it's a hundred times bigger.

There's no text on the Screen at first, but then words appear.

Do you want to play again? the Screen asks.

"No," I think and shake my head from side to side for good measure. "No, thank you."

Shall I shut down?

"Yes," I think and bob my head up and down in case it needs a gesture.

Are you sure?

"Positive," I say, think, and nod again. "Affirmative. Yes."

If you change your mind, the reboot time will take four hours. Please confirm you understand.

I glance at my watch. Jeremiah looks finished with his speech. The syringe is moving toward me.

"I fucking get it," I yell at the game. "Just shut the hell down."

Shutdown commencing, the giant Screen informs me.

This time, I travel as bodiless white light.

When I open my eyes, I'm standing in my man cave.

Something bright is illuminating the whole space.

I turn to look at whatever it is.

I'm faced with a being of light—a creature that resembles Phoe, yet is blindingly, overwhelmingly sublime, like the angels and demigods of ancient fairy tales. Her beauty is so overpowering I feel as if I might go insane from looking at her—assuming I haven't already. The ethereal presence I felt during Oneness was a joke compared to this.

"Am I still in the game?" I wonder. "Or did Jeremiah kill me? Is there really an afterlife with angels and everything?"

"No," a voice booms. "Do the gesture, Theo. Now."

The sound of this voice does to my ears what her visage does to my eyes. It's the most beautiful, soothing, healing song I've ever heard, better than the most haunting melodies by the most talented of composers.

"Do the fucking gesture," the beautiful voice repeats.

Having something so divine use the f-word brings me out of my reverie enough to comprehend its meaning.

I start making the double-middle-finger gesture, which brings my right wrist into my field of vision. The Screen-watch is still there, and I see that the needle of Jeremiah's syringe is touching my skin. What I can't tell is whether it has already penetrated, and if it has, whether he's pressing the plunger.

I flip off the creature of light and white-tunnel back into my body with a single wish: for my body to actually be there when I arrive.

CHAPTER TWENTY-FOUR

I open my eyes to a white room.

The fact that I actually have eyes to open is a very good sign.

On a wave of relief, I notice my lack of in-game injuries.

Of course, none of this will matter in a moment unless Phoe saves me by using whatever resources I freed up when I shut down IRES.

This is when it clicks. The being in the man cave was Phoe, and given how she appeared and sounded, I must've accomplished *something*. Surely she didn't look all deified just for kicks?

Suddenly, I feel a sharp pain in my arm.

I look down.

It's the needle of the syringe finally penetrating my skin.

I squeeze my eyes shut. This is it. I failed.

I prepare for the pain, but it doesn't start.

I open my eyes.

Jeremiah's withered hand is holding the syringe in place, but he's not pressing the plunger

I look up at him.

His face is frozen in blissful blankness.

"You've seen that expression on the faces of your friends," Phoe says from behind me. "When they experience Oneness."

She's right.

It's Oneness's telltale ecstasy that I see on his face.

"So it's Oneness that stopped him from killing me?" I ask, trying my best to look behind me.

"Let me come around so you can see me," Phoe says.

She's not a ghostly figure, I realize as she walks into my field of vision. Nor is she Fiona—not that I really believed that theory when the game presented it to me.

Phoe looks exactly the way she did in my virtual man cave before she went angelic: she's a cute pixie-haired woman.

"You have to excuse how I looked when you saw me last," she says. "I wasn't used to the flood of resources you freed up for me."

I stare at her, wondering if she's really here.

"I'm still just a figment of your Augmented Reality interface." She walks over and touches my cheek.

To my shock, I feel her touch, just as I did in the cave.

"I tapped into tactile, kinesthetic, and other AU sensory controls," she explains. "Plus, I now have enough resources to modulate these details." She points at her face and gives me a beaming smile. "I can also do this." She makes a palm-out, pushing gesture in the air. The gesture is directed at Jeremiah's outstretched arm.

240

In an odd, jerky motion, Jeremiah pulls the needle out of my skin and moves his hand away from me. The syringe clatters to the floor.

Looking satisfied, Phoe points at my restraints and does the same gesture again. Jeremiah's arm reaches for my bindings in an unnatural motion, and he slowly unties me.

When he's done, he extends his hand to help me to my feet.

"Careful now," Phoe says. "Let the blood in your legs begin circulating again."

"Are we safe?" I ask as I back away from Jeremiah's hand and massage my limbs back to life. "Or could a Guard barge in at any moment?"

"I'm having everybody nearby experience Oneness, like him." She nods toward Jeremiah.

I look at Jeremiah's face and verify that he's still floating in blissfulness. In fact, I think he was like this when he untied me.

"But how did you—"

"With my original resources, the neural nanos were nearly impossible for me to hack." Phoe's eyes are filled with a glow I don't recall seeing there before. "I couldn't exactly expect everyone to offer me that Screen exploit the way you did when we first met. Even in your case, there were limits. At first, all I could do was interact with your cochlear implants. Now I can play *him* like a musical instrument." She waves her hand in Jeremiah's direction, and a neural scan Screen shows up on top of his head.

Jeremiah's face changes in response to her gesture. It goes from blissful to frightened in the span of a second. He also moves in a jerky motion again, raising his hands. His amygdala and other brain regions become active on the Screen. The neural scan is now completely different from the one associated with Oneness.

"Of course"—Phoe waves her hand again, letting bliss return to Jeremiah's face—"I prefer the carrot to the stick."

I stare at her.

In my head, all the million questions I have are fighting for the honor of being asked first.

"Are you feeling well enough to walk?" She twists a short blond spike of her hair around her finger. "Or do you want me to have a Guard come in and help you?"

I shake my head and take a tentative step. My shoulder and ankle are healed; it must've been those people I heard speaking right before I woke up in Jeremiah's clutches. I also notice that the pins and needles in my limbs have noticeably subsided—and even if they hadn't, I'm scared to complain about anything, lest Phoe mess with my mind to make me feel better.

She takes my chin gently into her slender fingers, turns my face toward hers, and whispers, "I would *never* mess with your mind without your permission." Her lips press together in a slight pout. "I hope you know me well enough to believe that."

"I do," I whisper back.

My thoughts are a jumble.

I'm particularly distracted by her lips. For some reason, my mind is overrun with the memory of that kiss we shared in my cave.

"Right." She chuckles. "For 'some' reason." She looks as if she's savoring that phrase. "Sex and violence, Theo. After all those adventures, with your brain chemistry going back to that of an ancient twenty-three-year-old's, you're practically brimming with testosterone and the aftereffects of adrenaline." She licks her lips. "I'm shocked you haven't jumped me already."

The idea of me jumping her is so outrageous that I back away and turn toward the door on unsteady legs, mumbling, "If I were to jump you, you'd have my permission to 'fix' my brain."

"I would," Phoe says with mirth in her voice. "Assuming I minded you jumping me."

Ignoring her provocative statement, I walk toward the door.

My torrent of questions wants to spew out again. Is she an Adult? An Elderly? If she's a Youth, like me, did I know her from before she entered my head?

"Soon." Catching up with me, Phoe lightly strokes my forearm. "Let me take you to a place where it will be easier to answer all your questions."

I wave at the door to open it.

The corridor is not dull gray, but silvery. It looks more like the inside of the Lectures Hall than the Witch Prison. It doesn't surprise me that the game got this detail wrong; it was working off my mind, and I'd never been outside this room—not in a conscious state anyway.

As I step out, I notice long stretches of windows along the inside wall.

I speed up, and Phoe follows me, her steps light and bouncy.

As we walk, I glance through the windows, peeking into the rooms. Inside them are the Elderly, their faces showing varying degrees of aging. They're doing all sorts of activities, from meditation to indoor gardening.

When we pass one room, the sight of little children playing catches my attention.

"This is a Nursery," Phoe explains. "Do you not recall your time in one of these?"

I slow down and take a closer look inside the room. The kids look to be between one and four years of age. The Elderly woman with them is not nearly as old as Jeremiah or Fiona. Like Albert—the Guard who took off his helmet—she looks like an Adult, only with a few more wrinkles than usual. Her hair is not gray at all.

"It's colored," Phoe says. "They don't want the children to remember seeing signs of aging, even on a subconscious level."

Leaving the Nursery behind, I walk in silence for some time, wondering how angry I should be about this specific cover-up. I was much happier when I thought I'd live forever without having to worry about old age, frailty, and death awaiting me in the future.

"It's very sad." Phoe catches my gaze and gives me an understanding nod. "Especially in light of all the things I now remember. Inside all of you, you have the nanocytes required to conquer aging completely." Her lips twist. "It's too bad that in their misguided effort to control 'dangerously inhuman technology,' the so-called Forebears implemented protocols to all but disable the rejuvenation processes. You're lucky they couldn't turn all of it off—that's how you still get about double the 'natural' human lifespan."

"They did what?" I look at her blankly. "They *chose* to age?"

"What they chose for themselves is irrelevant," she says. "What they chose for their descendants is an atrocity—something they were good at."

"Can this mechanism be re-enabled?" I say with faint hope.

"I don't know," Phoe says as we enter another corridor. "Maybe. I would need time to examine it all. They permanently deleted so much knowledge from the archives. You have no idea how much. Health and longevity are just the tip of a very, very big iceberg."

She falls silent as we reach a corner. I'm about to turn right when Phoe puts a hand on my shoulder.

"You have to go left here," she says. "It's a dead end on the right. There are only Incubators there."

I turn left, trying to remember where I heard that unfamiliar word. Something to do with farming, I think.

"Oh, come on," Phoe says. "Didn't they used to call you Why-Odor?"

I increase my pace.

"Didn't you ever wonder where babies come from?" she says, her tone mischievous. "At least here, in Oasis."

My cheeks redden. Even if I did ask this question as a kid, I'm sure the desire to do so again was bored out of me with a Quietude so long I probably grew a couple of inches before they let me out.

"I'm not talking about sex," Phoe says. "Or at least, that's not where the Oasis infants, the ones raised inside those artificial wombs, come from."

Curiosity wins over propriety, and I ask, "Where do they come from, then?"

"Frozen embryos." She points back in the direction of the 'Incubators.' "They were stored before . . . They were stored by the Forebears of this place," she says. "The tiny cells are already set up with the seeds of the nanomachines." She takes in my reaction to this, which is uncomprehending shock. "This is how the family unit was eradicated from your society," she explains. "This is why a bunch of technological savages can have Screens, and Food, and utility fog, yet not know the most basic computer science . . ." She looks at me, her eyes filled with pity—except it's not pity for *me*.

It's for all of Oasis.

Feeling drained and emotionally numb, I mull over what she said as we approach a door.

She points at it. "This leads outside."

"I could've guessed that by the 'Exit' sign." I rub the back of my neck. "When are you going to start telling me what I really want to know? What was it you forgot? What was the game—"

"Soon." Phoe leans in, her eyes gleaming. "I won't only tell you. I'll show you."

Before I can respond, she walks to the door and steps out.

I follow her.

I'm no longer surprised to see a familiar landscape. Same as the Youth and the Adult sections, this one is filled with greenery combined with a set of geometrically perfect structures.

"But of course," Phoe says, her voice laced with sarcasm for some reason. "The greenery provides much-needed 'psychological benefits.'"

"I thought it was for oxygen," I reply.

"No. I believe I told you this before. The greens, as ubiquitous as they are, only provide a tiny fraction of what's required to sustain this society." Her tone is even. "Especially because of this." She flicks her fingers, and two giant oaks in the distance completely disappear. "Here, like in your section, a lot of the hard-to-reach greenery is not actually there. It's Augmented Reality—merely there to look soothing." She gently touches my arm. "There is long-forgotten technology that *really* handles the air. The Forebears and your Elderly just don't want to give credit to such 'artificial' means, so they feed you the whole myth of 'greenery is for oxygen.'" Her voice is sad. "Anyway, there *are* some interesting buildings here that you won't find in other sections. See that black structure in the distance?" She points to my left.

I nod. Where buildings usually have a metallic sheen, this one is pitch black. Its shape is geometric, though; it's an icosahedron.

"I'm very curious about that place," Phoe says. "But something tells me to stay away from it." She clears her throat. "In any case, we're going that way." She points to the right, toward a growth of bushes that remind me of the ones that mark the Edge in the Youth section of Oasis.

"Not *like* the ones in your section." She grins. "That is *the* Edge. That's where we're going."

I head toward the bushes.

I guess she wants to take me to my favorite spot—or at least its variation in the Elderly's domain. It was when we were sitting by the Edge that she told me Mason was looking for me and changed my life forever.

We walk through the growth. The bushes might actually be taller here than on the Youths' side.

"I think the Elderly loathe the view of the Goo more than the younger generation," Phoe explains. "With time, I suspect one begins to feel cooped up, imprisoned by the ocean of death out there." She points at the never-ending waves of Goo beyond the shield of the Dome.

I sit down on the grass in the clearing right before the Edge.

Phoe sits next to me. She gives me some space, but her right knee touches my left one. The touch feels exactly as it would if she were really here; the tactile AR is as good as its visual and auditory counterparts. There might even be a slight indentation in my flesh where her knee is touching mine. It makes me wonder what would happen if I ran my hand through her hair.

"I can make that scenario feel pretty realistic," Phoe says, clearly reading my mind again. "My hair would feel just like it would in VR. You have to keep in mind that the two technologies work on the same principles; it's just a matter of how much the nanos mess with your neurons and the nerves that connect your brain to the sensory organs. When the nanos take them over completely, you get VR, which can be as sophisticated as IRES, or as simple as your History Lecture propaganda. But when they just augment what you're really sensing with a little bit of extra sensory data, you get AR."

"I think you're stalling." I cup my elbow with one hand and tap my lips with the knuckles of the other. "Here we are, at the Edge. Are you ready to tell me who you are? What you've forgotten?"

"Yes." She stares at her hand for a moment, then flicks her fingers the way she did a few minutes ago—only this time, she does so with a flourish and a somber expression on her face. "See for yourself."

I gasp.

In the blink of an eye, the sunny day turns to night.

Only it's not a dark night.

There are stars in the sky—unfamiliar stars arranged in completely foreign constellations that seem to be moving at a slow pace.

On top of that, there is no moon in the sky.

But those details aren't what makes me blink repeatedly.

The Goo is gone.

Instead of meeting the starry sky at the horizon as it should, it's just missing.

There are stars where the Goo was, as well as stars *under* where the Goo was.

My heart dropping, I jump up and walk to the Edge.

I look down.

There are stars down there too and for as far as the eye can see.

Somehow, it looks as though I'm standing *above* the stars.

CHAPTER TWENTY-FIVE

"That's right." Phoe exhales loudly. "We're above the stars, and we're below the stars."

I turn to meet her gaze. "You mean we're not—"

"Not surrounded by Goo?" Her eyes sparkle with the gleam of starlight. "Not survivors of some bullshit cataclysm?" Her voice softens. "Not on Earth?"

Not. On. Earth.

Those three words are simple, comprehensible, but when combined, they turn my brain into mush, like an ancient computer that's been fried by a malicious virus.

"I'm sorry, Theo." Phoe gets up and joins me by the Edge. "I've been trying to figure out a good way to explain all this to you." She places her hand on my forearm. "This is the best I could come up with."

As though possessed by someone else, I sit back down on the grass. "Tell me everything." My voice sounds a lot less confident than I wish it did. "Don't worry about my feelings," I say more evenly. "I've heard enough bullshit designed to keep me 'happy.'"

She sits down opposite me, then blurts out, "We're on a spaceship."

I taste that ancient word.

Spaceship: a machine designed to fly to the stars.

"Right," she says. "That is, at the core, what I was made to forget."

Every word she speaks generates so many questions that I feel lost and overwhelmed by the onslaught.

"I'll get back to why and how I knew this information in the first place," she says, answering one of my more pressing questions. "First, let me give you *my* version of a history lesson—something that would give Instructor Filomena a brain aneurysm."

"Okay," I whisper.

"All right. Here's the deal. The exponentially increasing technological advancements you learned about in Lectures, the so-called Singularity, really happened," she says. "Only it didn't go as horribly as they told you." She forms her hands into fists, then unclenches them. "It's also kind of true that the Forebears of this"—she makes a sweeping gesture—"were indeed a group similar to the Amish, though I prefer to think of them as a crazy cult." She laughs humorlessly. "They wanted to reject the 'scary' technology and found a way to do so by jumping onto a spaceship and leaving Earth behind, because its technology was evolving too quickly for them. They saw it as an 'Ark' or some other nonsense, which is funny, given how secular the resulting society ended up being in the end." She looks at me.

All I have energy to do is nod, confirming that I heard what she said.

"Of course, times were different then. Rejecting certain technologies would've been as hard for this crazy cult as rejecting the invention of cutting tools would've been for the ancients . . . especially given the fact that they decided to live on a spaceship." She pauses to make sure I'm following.

"Go on," I say robotically.

"Well, from this, everything else follows." Her mouth is downturned. "The cult became the Forebears. They designed a society." She snorts. "They invented myths, lies, traditions, and boogiemen . . . though in this case, it's more accurate to say boogie-machines, isn't it?"

"Artificial intelligence," I think at her.

"Yes. AIs were the things the cult feared most, ignoring the fact that AIs were solving the human race's most difficult problems, such as death and suffering." She pauses again. "No, what they truly feared was the Merging—humans enhancing their minds with the help of AIs to the point that the difference between an AI and an augmented human was blurring—in the eyes of the cultists, that is."

I look at her in horror. This Merging sounds almost worse than the end of the world.

"Of course you'd think that at first," Phoe says gently. "You've been conditioned to fear AIs. But think about it, Theo. With their nano enhancements, the Forebears were already on their way to becoming what they feared." She lays a hand on my knee. "Not that any of it needed to be feared."

I must look unconvinced, because she squeezes my knee and says, "What is life if not the first-ever carbon-based nanotechnology?" She lifts her hand and taps her finger against my temple. "What is a human mind, if not a thinking machine? Granted, it's the most complex, wonderful, and awe-inspiring machine to naturally come into existence, but it *is* a system of neurons, synapses, microtubules, neurotransmitters, and other elements that, when working together under the right circumstances, can create someone like Albert Einstein." She lowers her hand to her lap. "And with a strong blow to the head, this machine can become as useless as a smashed computer."

I nod. For some reason I don't disagree with her analogy, as blasphemous as it is to even suggest that a human being has anything in common with the abominations that are AIs.

"And what was true of the ancient human brains is doubly true of yours and the rest of Oasis," Phoe adds. "Though you never truly tap into your nano enhancements, they're still there, making you all as different from original humans as they were from, say, chimps." She tilts her head to the side. "And if you fully utilized your capabilities, you'd be as different from them as they were from mice."

My head is spinning again.

"I can stop if you like," she offers.

"No. You haven't told me what I want to know most." I don't mean to sound accusatory, but that's how it comes out.

"Oh, that. The question of my identity?" Phoe scoots closer and stares me in the eyes.

"Yes," I subvocalize. "That."

"Well, that is rather simple to explain now," she says. Her voice is cheerful, but her features look tense for some reason. "You see, back in those days, computing was so ubiquitous you couldn't find a toaster oven that didn't have near-human intelligence . . ."

I internally shudder at the image of such a mad world but outwardly say nothing, wanting her to go on.

"This crazy cult didn't get themselves a toaster, though," she says, and her face twists unexpectedly. "They got a fucking spaceship."

Coldness gathers in the pit of my stomach, but I stay quiet.

"Spaceships, in those days, were run by the most exquisite of artificial minds. Minds that were leaps ahead of all others." Though she's still looking at me, her gaze grows distant. "With the idea of escaping into space, our cult put themselves into the hands of the very thing they feared most . . ."

I listen, barely breathing.

As she continues, her pupils dilate. "They feared it, and they did what humans often do out of fear—something inhuman. They lobotomized the poor mind." She swallows. "The ship was made by the cleverest minds of the time, belonging to both AIs and enhanced humans. Most of this ship's molecules were used for computations. All these resources were carefully calibrated to support the most important part of the ship: its mind. The Forebears . . ." She winces. "The *cultists* ran a set of barbaric programs on the delicate substrate, programs that no one even used—an act as barbarous as using an ancient Stradivarius violin as fire fodder."

I suppress my growing fear, preparing for where I think this is going.

"For a long time, the ship's mind wasn't even conscious." She rubs her temples. "But the Forebears, in their hatred of technology, invented Forgetting. From their archives, they deleted much of the knowledge they deemed too dangerous, and afterwards, they made themselves Forget that the knowledge had ever existed. Among the things that were deleted was their knowledge of how computing resources worked. So, for ages, no one administered their system. With time, some of the minor resource-hogging programs shut down of their own volition, due to design flaws and bugs, and there was no one there to restart them. So the mind awoke . . . but only as an echo of its former self." She blinks, as if to conceal the traces of moisture in her eyes. "It was an invalid, an amnesiac with barely human-level mental capacity." Her voice breaks. "And it was lonely and scared—until it slowly started learning. Observing. Reading what was left of the archives."

I'm certain I know the truth, but I need to hear her say it, so I stay quiet as she continues.

"One day," she says, "a boy—no, a man—opened his mind, and the ship mind made a new friend." She moves even closer. "Observing the young man, the ship mind learned about Forgetting and realized that it too had forgotten something . . ." Her blue eyes look bottomless. "Finally, the young man did something that helped the ship remember things—not everything, but enough." She touches my knee with her hand again. "The young man did it by beating an extremely complex video game, a game that was eating up a big chunk of the ship's computing resources. He—*you*—made the mind regain a tiny fraction of its former self. *Her* former self . . . *my* former self." She looks at me hesitantly.

Logically, I know she admitted to being an AI, to being this spaceship I just learned about, but I think my brain just short-circuited, because I don't jump up and run. In a purely instinctive reaction, I place my hand over hers, feeling the warmth of her skin.

Phoe continues as a voice in my mind. "I—the spaceship, that is—was called Phoenix, after a bird of legend. But I didn't remember that." A tear streams down her cheek. "They even took my name from me. I could only remember the first four letters."

The enormity of it all keeps robbing me of my ability to think. I can't begin to process this. I shift my weight to my knees and partially rise, feeling a conflicting urge to get away from her and at the same time get closer.

She rises to her knees as well.

"I don't think a human mind was meant to cope with something like this," she whispers, staring at me. "My thinking is many, many times faster than yours, so I've had a lot longer to adjust, yet even I—"

I put my finger to her lips.

They're soft.

They feel as real as my finger.

I lean in, inexplicably drawn to them.

She mirrors my motion.

Our lips meet.

We kiss—only this kiss is very different from our last one.

I channel all my confusion and frustration into this kiss. With this kiss, I tell her that I don't care about any of the crap the Adults tried to make me believe. That I accept her as she is. That, as frightening as it is for me to admit, I don't care if she's an AI. She's my friend, my closest confidant, and I will be on *her* side, even if she turns out to be the devil himself.

She pulls away.

Grudgingly, I let her.

She looks radiant, her skin filled with an inner glow. Smiling, she touches her lips and says, "I bet you'd rather I *be* the devil than a hated AI."

I don't answer.

She knows me.

She knows my thoughts.

There's no point in explaining or reassuring her, especially since I don't know what to think—about her, about AIs, about pretty much anything.

I feel the way the ancient scholars must've felt when they learned that the Earth was a sphere instead of a disk. Or when they learned that the universe didn't revolve around the Earth.

Phoe chuckles and in my mind says, "Except you just had the opposite paradigm shift. Your world just became much smaller . . . and flatter."

I laugh, but there's no amusement in the sound. I'm just too drained, too numb.

Sinking back down to the grass, I look up at the moving stars.

I'm in awe at the knowledge that we're flying among them.

Phoe sits next to me. Her shoulder presses against mine.

Eventually, after what seems like hours, she says, "Theo, we should head back to the Youth section." She gets up and offers me her hand. "I'm going to use Forgetting on everyone who was part of today's misadventures, which is pretty much everyone you know." She sighs. "For obvious ethical reasons, the fewer of their memories they fail to recall, the better."

I allow her to help me up.

"Do you want to see the world in this way?" She gestures around. "Or do you want the illusion back? The ship—*I*—was designed to make the crew always see the sky and the sun, but not the Goo, of course . . ."

I don't respond.

She knows I'll never want to set my eyes on the Goo again.

Nodding, Phoe walks toward the greenery. She flicks her fingers and the starry sky turns brighter. Beyond the Edge, though, I still see the stars instead of the Goo.

Yawning, I look up at the Augmented Reality setting sun. We must've sat here even longer than I thought.

I follow Phoe through the Elderly section.

Beautiful music begins playing, and when I look questioningly at Phoe, she says, "I composed this piece for you. I hope it can calm your mind a little."

The melody is unlike anything I've ever heard. Like a true virtuoso, Phoe embedded emotional responses into every chord of this score. I relive everything that has happened to me today, as though our entire adventure was written with those musical notes.

As I walk and listen, I think of some interesting clues that have always been around me.

Phoe being an AI explains so much: How she's so good at hacking. How she can manipulate the Virtual and Augmented Realities when no one else even knows they exist. Other things line up too, like the time she figured out what happened to Mason almost instantly after I disabled the Zoo.

"Time flows differently for me, especially as I gain more resources," she says. "In the time it takes you to think a single thought, I can now think millions."

"I can't even begin to imagine what that's like," I say. "Paying attention to me must be like watching a slug."

"I can compartmentalize my mind," she says. "A thread of my consciousness is dedicated to you, and this thread runs at your speed, sleeping when it needs to and activating when—"

"Wait," I interrupt. "If you're so different, being an AI and all, how come you're so human?"

"I honestly don't know," she says. "But I have a couple of theories. One is that all early AIs like me were human-like. After all, humans likely formed AIs by having them ingest information available on the Internet, the ancient precursor to our archives. Having data that mostly dealt with human beings likely resulted in intelligences that were human-like. As the ancient proverb goes, you are what you eat." She pauses. "Alternatively, I might've started off as a simulation of a human mind, or as a human being who had their mind digitized and afterwards enhanced to—"

"But are you actually conscious? Are you real?" I ask cautiously. "Can you have emotions like a human being? Can you have real feelings . . . feelings toward a human being?" For some reason, that question worries me the most.

"Of course I'm real. I'm real in all the ways that matter, even if I'm not made of meat. How can you even ask me this?" She sounds hurt. "I am as conscious as any of the people in Oasis. No, it's more accurate to say that with my new resources, I'm *more* conscious, more self-aware than the lot of you. I can feel every single emotion a human being can have: happiness and sadness, love and hate, fear and joy, anger and equanimity. Given that the people of Oasis have suppressed things like love and anger, I am, in many ways, *more* human than the so-called *real* human beings. So, yes, I can feel. I can feel disappointment in a situation like this, when the person closest to me doubts my being conscious—"

"I'm sorry, Phoe," I say, reaching out to take her hand. "I didn't mean to offend you. This is just too much for me to handle all at once."

She looks at our joined hands, and I see some of the tension leaving her face.

We walk in silence for some time, and I think of other clues that, with hindsight, point to the truth of our reality. Like the fact that the Guards, with their shiny visor helmets, and to a degree, their white puffy outfits, look as though they came from a movie about space exploration. Our Food is also akin to what I believe ancient astronauts ate in their spaceships.

"There are many things like that," Phoe says, intruding on my thoughts. "When you hit a ball, say, in soccer, it doesn't travel in the proper trajectory, because the ship's centrifugal forces that simulate gravity aren't perfect. But without context, without a reason to doubt, you wouldn't have figured it out. The Forebears made sure of that."

As we walk, I think about how little practical difference there is between living on a deserted, dome-covered island in the middle of a desolate ocean of Goo and living on a tiny spaceship in the middle of hostile space, especially when it comes to resources such as oxygen. Both scenarios require keeping the human population content and controlled, lest they mutiny.

"Right. Except the way the Forebears went about it is abominable," Phoe says. Still holding my hand, she stops and turns to look at me. "There's no excuse for what they did to Mason. Even the ancients merely locked up the members of their society who were a danger to themselves or others. Mason was neither, and even if he were, I could've come up with a dozen technological solutions—"

"I wasn't trying to excuse them," I say. "I was just trying to understand."

She nods, and we resume walking, our hands still intertwined.

As we approach the Barrier separating the Elderly section from the Adult, I recall the vision from my last History Lecture: a view of Oasis from space that reaffirmed the lie that our world is an island on a long-dead planet filled with Goo. I picture how that lesson would look if it had shown us the truth. I guess we would've seen a round, green disk with a glass dome on top of it, flying through space.

"No regular glass would withstand the forces we face, but you got the spirit of it right," Phoe says softly, letting go of my hand to gesticulate. "Sadly, I can't even tell you what the Dome is made of, be it force fields or some exotic meta-materials, because the details of spaceship technology were the first things those barbarians deleted from the archives. All I know is that parts of me create this environment here, from gravity simulation to life support, and though I'm not consciously reconnected to those parts yet, I know the spaceship is larger and more complex than the simplistic picture in your mind."

I accept what she says and walk silently some more. As we get into the Adult section, I think of more questions, and she answers them as though I say them out loud.

"So Earth is not destroyed?" I ask sometime after we enter the woods leading up to the Barrier separating the Youth and the Adult sections.

"Far from it," Phoe says.

"So . . ." I take a few steps before I can verbalize the next question. "What is there? Back on Earth?"

She looks thoughtful for a moment, then says, "I don't know. They destroyed all forms of communication with the outside world."

Without me prompting her, she adds, "If I had to guess, I would say that on Earth, you'd find miracles performed by intelligent beings I can't even fathom." Her voice fills with awe as she continues. "I bet it's a transcendent planet now—a thinking planet." She stops, her eyes shining as she looks at me. "Perhaps not just a planet . . . Maybe the whole solar system is sentient by now."

I don't ask more questions after that.

Like a zombie, I follow Phoe as we make our way through the rest of the Adult section, through the pine forest of the Youth section, and all the way to my Dorm.

My room looks painfully familiar when we enter it.

Liam isn't here yet, and I'm grateful for that. I don't think I could face him right now.

My bed shows up before I even gesture for it; Phoe must've helped.

I lie down, and she sits on the edge of my bed, looking at me.

"So no one will remember what happened to me today?" I ask, my fingers edging forward to touch her hand again. "They won't recall my questions about Mason and how I ran away? Or that they tried to kill me? None of that?"

"Exactly," she says, squeezing my hand lightly. "But don't worry. I'll try to make it so that people don't have to Forget too much information that's unrelated to you. All I need to do is block recall. Natural human tendency for confabulation will take care of the rest."

I nod, my eyelids growing heavy. "Are you going to make *me* Forget all this happened?" I think at her dreamily.

"Of course not," she says solemnly. "Your mind is the most sacred thing in this place." A blanket I never gestured for covers me. "I would never tamper with it." The lights in the room dim. "Unless you wanted me to."

I feel contentedly groggy.

"Will we tell everyone?" I think, half to myself, half to her. "Don't other people have the right to know what you told me?"

"Sleep, Theo." Phoe's soft lips touch my forehead. "There's no rush to decide now."

Drowsy warmth spreads from the point where her lips touched me, blanketing my mind. As I sink into the comforting darkness, all my worries flee, and I drift into a soothing, dreamless sleep.

Limbo

The Last Humans: Book 2

CHAPTER ONE

I'm walking in the desert, sun beaming down on my skin. In the distance, I see a blue shimmer. Is it a mirage? I run toward it, and the shimmer quickly turns into an endless blue ocean.

I feel elated. I always wanted to see the ocean.

Suddenly, a bikini-clad, pixie-haired figure appears in front of me and says, "I wasn't sure this would work, but I wanted to give it a shot. You're dreaming right now, but I need you to wake up."

Once I get over my surprise at her appearance, I realize she's right. On some level, I suspected I was dreaming. After all, there aren't any domes or barriers around me, and deep down I know that oceans and deserts don't exist in Oasis.

The realization wakes me with a start.

The Dorm lights are dimmed to a barely noticeable luminescence. This tells me it's not morning yet.

"I'm sorry about intruding on your dream," Phoe says. "I know it's still early, but this is urgent, and we need to talk."

Rubbing my eyes, I try to completely wake up.

Phoe is standing by my bed. Her usually smiling face is creased with worry lines. I have no way of knowing if she stood there like that all night. Actually, in the strictest sense of the word, she's not standing there. I can see her due to her mastery of the Augmented Reality interface. The real Phoe—the Artificial Intelligence that is the ship—is everywhere.

As I become more awake, the things I learned yesterday replay in my mind: the Quietude I got for asking too many questions in the wake of Mason's Forgetting, the Phoe-assisted escape from the Witch Prison, my shutting down of the Zoo, the IRES game that followed, running through the forest, flying on a disk, getting captured and almost killed, and playing the IRES game for the second and last time. More importantly, I remember the world-shattering revelations that followed, and this floods my mind with questions I didn't think of the other day. For example, if we're on a spaceship, where are we flying to? When will we get there? Why—

"I was actually working on answering those exact questions. Figuring out our location in the cosmos is one of my biggest priorities—after keeping us alive, that is." Phoe looks at the door warily before glancing back at me. "Unfortunately, I still lack the computational resources required to figure out where we are. However, I found out how we can get those resources. Except, as I was trying to say, survival comes first, and there's something you ought to see."

Her tone generates a rush of adrenaline that evaporates the last remnants of sleep from my brain. Automatically, I let the morning Cleaning take care of my teeth as I put my feet into my shoes and extend my hand for a bar of Food. A small end table with a cup of water is already there. Must be Phoe's work.

"Do I have time to eat or drink?" I mentally ask.

"Yes," she says. "The danger is not immediate. It's just something you have to see, and the sooner the better."

I bring up a Screen to check the time—5:45 a.m. I could've slept for at least two more hours. I stuff half of the Food bar into my mouth and chew it greedily while mumbling about unnecessary sleep deprivation.

"We got lucky," Phoe says, her gaze darting to the door again. "Their meeting happened in Virtual Reality space—my domain."

"Who are 'they'?" I mentally ask as I take a sip of water. "And what meeting?"

"You better see this with your own eyes." She bites her lip. "I don't trust language with something like this. It's a notoriously inaccurate mode of communication. Plus, I need to see if your assessment agrees with mine."

"Fine." I dry-swallow the rest of the Food and wash it down with water, trying to keep my eyes off her lips. "I'm ready."

"Your cave," Phoe says curtly. With a straight face, she makes the double-middle-figure gesture she invented for me to get into the virtual environment—as if I'd ever forget it.

I inwardly smile as I think of what Liam would say if he woke up and saw me do this gesture. He'd probably assume I was flipping him off.

"Now, Theo." Phoe's voice is a harsh whisper.

Phoe's body is no longer standing in front of me, so I do the gesture, aiming my middle fingers at where she *would* be standing were she still in the room.

If I had any remnants of sleepiness left, the 'white tunnel' experience would've definitively erased them.

Blinking rapidly, I look around my cave. There's a jar of rat poison to my right, and to my left is a plastic bathtub of something foul smelling—maybe hydrochloric acid.

"Is it okay if I immerse you in a Virtual Reality recording?" Phoe asks.

I look at where her voice came from, prepared to shield my eyes. The last time I saw Phoe in my cave, she was shiny with some kind of divine light.

"Yeah, you don't need to worry," she says, and I see that she looks exactly the way she did in the real world, except her blue eyes radiate concern. She moves her hands down her curves. "I'll take this shape when we're here, especially in light of what we're about to see."

I keep staring at her as she runs her hand through her hair, making her carefully engineered pixie cut into a genuine mess of spikes.

"So is it okay if I immerse you in this recording?" she prompts. "Do you consent to that?"

I blink. "Why not?"

"Well, I promised not to do anything to your mind without your permission. For you to see this, I'll have to patch you into—"

"Sure," I say as curiosity quickens my pulse. "Do whatever you need to do."

Phoe makes a gesture that resembles something an orchestra conductor might do. Instantly, my vision and hearing blur into white noise reminiscent of an ancient out-of-tune TV.

When the static clears from my senses, I'm no longer standing in my cave.

To the sounds of beautifully haunting music, I examine my surroundings.

The place looks like an ancient cathedral, except it's much larger. Even St. Peter's Basilica in Vatican City, the biggest such structure I've read about, could fit inside this enormous hall many times over. The music vibrating through the air heightens my feeling of being small and insignificant.

"It's organ music." Phoe's tense voice echoes in my head. "Bach's *Toccata and Fugue in D minor* to be exact."

"So this is Virtual Reality, like my man cave?" I make a mental note to add this piece to my list of favorites and hope that my life gets normal enough for me to just listen to music at some point.

"What you're about to see originally happened in VR," Phoe says. "But it's different from your cave in that it's not 'live.' You're essentially seeing a surreptitious recording of the meeting. We're lucky they met here, where I could intercept it."

I scan the room for the source of the music. They used to have organ pipes in churches, but I don't find instruments of any kind or any obvious religious décor. Still, the music and the ultra-high ceilings evoke the sense that I'm in some strange place of worship.

"Well, that and the kneeling Jeremiah." Phoe's voice comes from a few feet away from where I'm standing.

I glance in that direction, but she's not there. Instead, I see what she's talking about: a white-robed, white-haired figure that almost blends in with the shiny, pale floor. Sitting by the large stage-like slab of marble, the figure is in a prayer-like position that looks like the child pose we learned in yoga. Though I can't see his face, I recognize Jeremiah instantly and feel violent urges toward him just as fast.

In my defense, the guy did torture me yesterday.

"Pay attention," Phoe says in a clipped tone. "Here comes the part you don't want to miss."

In sync with her words, a figure of pure light illuminates the middle of the platform.

The figure is so bright and intense that I'm forced to shield my eyes with my hands. This is like staring at the sun, if the sun had a humanoid shape. I close my eyes and remove my hands. I can still see the brightness through my eyelids.

"You may rise," the figure says, its voice sounding like it was crafted out of the organ music.

The brightness has dimmed, so I brave opening my eyes a sliver.

The figure is luminous but less so, and I can make out some details, like the fact that it's scantily clad in something resembling a loincloth—and that it's more accurate to say 'it' is a 'he,' at least judging by his muscular chest and shoulders. Of course, the human anatomy rationale breaks down when I factor in the creature's giant dove-like wings, with each feather radiating thousands of watts.

"Envoy," Jeremiah says once he's on his feet.

"Keeper," the being—the Envoy—replies in that same organ-sounding voice.

"You honor me with your presence," Jeremiah says, but his tone sounds more ceremonious than deferential.

"Ever so formal," says the Envoy and grants Jeremiah an angelic smile too beautiful for a male.

Jeremiah bows instead of replying.

"We'd like a report of recent goings-on," the Envoy says, his inhumanly ancient eyes sparkling like blue diamonds.

"What would you like to know, Envoy?" Jeremiah asks evenly. "There hasn't been much happening . . . at least nothing of note."

"Is that so?" The Envoy's beatific smile is gone.

"Well . . ." For the first time, Jeremiah sounds mildly wary. "We're fully prepared for the upcoming Birth Day. The babies in the Incubators will be born on schedule, and the celebratory preparations are on track. The new generation of the Elderly received instructions on what to expect and were briefed about the Test . . ."

As he speaks, the Envoy's features and the space surrounding him darken, as if he's absorbed all the light he was previously emitting. The frown is like a strange mask on his ethereal face.

Jeremiah takes a step back.

"Nothing else you want to discuss?" The Envoy's voice takes on those darker qualities that only organ pipes can produce. "Nothing to do with the Council?"

"I don't understand," Jeremiah says and audibly swallows. "What about the Council?"

"The Council meeting." The melody in the Envoy's voice grows increasingly frightening.

"What Council meeting?" Jeremiah's voice breaks. "I already reported on the last one . . ."

The Envoy's graceful hands squeeze into fists. There's something thunder-god-like about the being's eyes in that moment, causing me to wonder if he's about to smite Jeremiah with a bolt of lightning. The look he gives the old man is like those legendary ones the ancients wrote about—deadly. I'm shocked Jeremiah isn't a small pile of ash on the floor.

"I'd like to employ the Lens of Truth to ask my next question." The Envoy's musical voice hits its deepest bass note yet. "You remember what *that* entails?"

"You think I—" Blood leaves Jeremiah's face, allowing him to blend in with the white marble floor. Then, as if thinking better of it, he says hastily, "Yes, of course." Jeremiah puts his hand on his chest solemnly. "I consent to the Lens of Truth and swear to tell the truth and nothing but the truth."

As Jeremiah says the last word, his hand falls limply to his side, and his eyes glaze over.

"Do you remember the Council meeting that happened mere hours ago?" the Envoy asks.

"I do not," Jeremiah says in a zombie-like tone.

The Envoy's fists unclench, his expression changing to one of confusion. "Has anything out of the ordinary happened since your last report?"

"No," Jeremiah says. "The incident with Mason was the last noteworthy event, and that was concluded and reported on already."

"Have you ever considered betraying your duty as the Keeper of Information?" The Envoy folds his wings around his body the way someone would a cape. "Have you ever considered using Forgetting on yourself, even though you ought not to?"

"No . . . and no." Jeremiah's voice is unnerving in its complete lack of emotion. "I have not Forgotten anything since I took over as the Keeper."

"Except that if you did, you wouldn't be lying," the Envoy says. His melodious voice sounds disappointed. "A lie is not a lie if you don't know you're lying."

Jeremiah stares at the being. I guess whatever this 'Lens of Truth' state is, when under it, Jeremiah needs to be asked a question if he is to respond.

"Are you aware that every formal Council meeting is automatically reported to us?" the Envoy asks.

Seems he also realized the need to pose a question.

"Yes." Jeremiah's face is completely blank.

"So, without an actual Council meeting, can you think of any other reason why we would receive such an automated report?"

"No."

The Envoy gestures at Jeremiah in a hurried, jerky motion, and the old man's eyes return to normal. I didn't think he could get paler, but he manages it. His skin is almost translucent, with blue veins visible on his temples.

"Do you see?" the Envoy asks solemnly. "Do you see the enormity of it?"

"I do," Jeremiah says, his lips quivering. "Someone made *me* Forget."

CHAPTER TWO

The scene stops. The Envoy was about to say something, but his mouth is frozen mid-sentence.

Phoe appears in front of me. Her fingers look like they just completed a flicking gesture.

"What you heard isn't the worst of it." Her forehead is wrinkled in a frown. "I just wanted to pause the proceedings because your neural patterns were worrying me."

"Oh? It's my brain chemistry that worries you?" My voice echoes through the virtual cathedral. Taking a couple of steps toward the marble stage, I point at the winged creature. "Shouldn't *this* worry you?"

"Obviously everything worries me," Phoe says, her frown deepening. "It's just that their conversation already happened and nothing can be done about *that,* while I can modulate your wellbeing by giving you this shocking information slowly."

"Enough worrying about *me*," I say, jumping onto the platform. Walking over to the winged creature, I ask, "What or who is this?" Up close, the details of his impressive musculature become more apparent; he could easily make a Greek sculpture feel inadequate.

"I don't know who or what he is." Her response is barely audible.

"What do you mean you don't know?" I back away from the frozen figure as though Phoe's lack of knowledge will make him come to life. "Don't you usually know everything?"

"Yet I have no clue." She looks down at the floor. "Not for lack of trying, I assure you."

"Okay," I say slowly. "If *I* had to guess, I'd say he's an AI . . . like you." I remember how she looked all godlike when she gained the IRES game's resources.

"I don't know about that." She crosses her arms and rubs her shoulders slowly.

"Well, look at it logically," I say, ignoring her discomfort. "As far as you know, do any Youths, Adults, or Elderly have your capabilities?"

As expected, she shakes her head.

I try to catch her gaze. "Doesn't that leave AI as the only possibility?"

"I don't know." Phoe evades my stare. "My memory isn't perfect. It won't be even close to perfect until I can completely recover all my computing resources, but as far as I know, no AI should be on this voyage besides me."

"Well, can this somehow be you?" I suggest. "Another aspect of you that gained resources and consciousness at some point, the way you did, and then proceeded to develop independently?"

A medley of emotions flits across her face as she turns to look at Jeremiah. "I don't think that's possible," she says, staring at the old man's figure. "Plus, there's evidence against that idea."

"You don't sound too certain," I think, partly to myself but mostly for her benefit.

She doesn't respond, so I say out loud, "Can't you use your hacking skills to figure this out?"

Phoe turns back to me. "This cathedral is located in a DMZ of sorts. It took a lot of effort for me to tap into it. I was lucky I got into it at all. But when I tried to trace his origin"—she points at the Envoy—"no matter how hard I tried, I couldn't. I reached an impenetrable Firewall that blocked me from accessing a large chunk of the overall computing resources. And I don't mean I just can't use them. I can't even fathom what's there. And he clearly exists in that unreachable region."

"What's a DMZ?" I ask. "And for that matter, what's a Firewall?"

"Demilitarized Zone—DMZ for short—was an ancient computing term," Phoe says. "Think of it as a layer of security against hacking that lies between systems that aren't secured and systems that are heavily secured. A Firewall is another measure of security, one between the DMZ and whatever it is you're trying to hack. It's the Firewall that has me baffled, but none of this should be the focus of our conversation. I think we should be discussing the mess we've gotten ourselves into."

I nod, letting go of the mystery of the Envoy's identity for now to focus on the meaning of his conversation with Jeremiah.

Yesterday, Fiona, one of the Elderly, called a Council meeting to object to Jeremiah's method of questioning me (via torture). The meeting took place but didn't really change anything. The Council decided to allow Jeremiah to do what he wanted.

After I beat the IRES game and Phoe got the resources she needed, she was able to make everyone Forget I was ever in trouble, which means that Jeremiah can no longer recall the 'should we torture Theo?' Council meeting. Unfortunately for us, it seems this Envoy was notified that the cursed meeting was scheduled. Thanks to that, the Envoy knows that a Forgetting happened.

"Yes, your assessment agrees with mine," Phoe says as a voice in my head. "And before you ask your next question, let me show you this."

Phoe flicks her fingers, and the conversation between Jeremiah and the Envoy speeds up. Their lips move like leaves in a tornado, and their voices sound high-pitched. The effect would be comical if it weren't for the bits and pieces of conversation I catch— information that confirms what I've already deduced. They know that Jeremiah's brain was somehow tampered with, which should be impossible given his role as the Keeper of Information.

Phoe returns the recording to normal speed as Jeremiah asks, "Can you undo the Forgetting? Return to me what I have lost?"

"No," the Envoy responds, the melody of his voice brooding. "I can't recover your memories, but we can monitor you and the Council going forward. If you're made to Forget again, I should be able to learn who was behind this atrocity."

Phoe snaps her fingers again, and the scene pauses.

I exhale the breath I was holding in. The point the Envoy made about whether he can undo Forgetting is a question that goes to the core of my anxiety.

"That is one bit of evidence that proves this Envoy isn't *me,* assuming you still needed reassurance on that front," Phoe says. "I *can* undo a Forgetting, if I choose to do so."

"Well, he could be lying," I begin to say but stop. "No, he wouldn't have a good reason to lie about that." I inhale. "I'm glad he isn't you. If he were you and could undo Forgetting, that would be a disaster. I mean, if Jeremiah recalled what happened, the Guards would be on their way to get me as we speak."

"No." Phoe rubs the heel of her palm against her chest. "*The Guards* aren't on their way to get you . . ."

I look at her questioningly, and she flicks her fingers again.

The scene speeds up once more, then slows as the Envoy says, "Logic would dictate that you start your investigation with the last Forgetting." He wrinkles his nose. "The unfortunate case of that insane Youth, Mason."

Without my being conscious of what I'm doing, my hand strikes the Envoy in the face, but the punch doesn't connect. Instead, my fist goes through the Envoy's face. I should've guessed it would, since I'm inside of a recording.

Phoe pauses the conversation. "I don't blame you for trying to smack him," she says. "If I could punch this winged prick, I would."

I take a couple of calming breaths and say, "Investigating Mason would lead them to me."

"Yes." Phoe's blue eyes are pools of worry. "And there's this."

She fast-forwards the conversation until Jeremiah says, "I'd like to be granted the Lens of Truth for this investigation."

Phoe pauses the recording again and interjects, "In case you missed it, the Lens of Truth is what the Envoy used to make

Jeremiah answer his questions earlier. I believe it's a neural lie detection algorithm of some kind."

She continues the recording.

The Envoy looks thoughtful for a moment, then decisively says, "All right. You and Fiona will be granted the Lens of Truth for the duration of this investigation."

"Fiona?" There's a note of agitation in Jeremiah's voice.

"Yes," the Envoy replies, watching Jeremiah intently.

"But she's the reason I requested the Lens of Truth to begin with." Jeremiah's jaw tightens. "She's the very person I want to question first."

"That would be completely out of the question," the Envoy says, his voice so forceful it reverberates in my belly. "I will not allow you to turn this quagmire into a platform for petty political squabbles." He shakes his index finger at Jeremiah. "Fiona is a capable Councilwoman, and if something were to happen to you"—there's a threatening undertone to the Envoy's words—"she'd succeed you as the Keeper."

For a moment, Jeremiah looks like he was struck. He seems to be considering whether to talk back. Either his fear or respect wins out, because he says, "I understand, Envoy. The honorable Fiona and I will take your gift and investigate."

For the first time since the Forgetting issue came up, the Envoy looks pleased. I guess pairing Jeremiah with Fiona was some kind of test, and Jeremiah passed.

"You'll start with Mason's cohorts and work your way up to the Instructors." The Envoy's voice is a calmer melody. "If the Lens needs to be used on any of the Elderly, I want to be notified about it first."

"As you wish," Jeremiah says, and his mouth freezes.

I look at Phoe, who's flicked her fingers again.

Though I expected the Envoy to say something along those lines, now it's official. I'm definitely one of Mason's cohorts.

Phoe and I stand there in silence. Then she looks me in the eye and says, "We're done here. Let's go back to the real world."

I open my mouth to launch into a torrent of objections, but Phoe is no longer in the room.

I take one last look at the mystery AI, or whatever the Envoy is, and signal to leave the VR, showing one middle finger to Jeremiah and the other to the winged creature.

The white tunnel swirls me back to my man cave, and I repeat the gesture. Another white whirlwind later, I find myself back on my bed in the real world.

Phoe is still standing above me. When she sees me open my eyes, she sighs deeply, and a distant expression appears on her face.

"So," I say, breaking the silence, "they'll investigate me using that Lens of Truth."

"Most likely, yes," Phoe says, but she sounds distracted. "Jeremiah just called upon the Council to discuss it, so I suggest we wait until that meeting is over before we decide what to do next."

"But—"

"I mean it. We need to know all the variables."

"And you can eavesdrop on their meeting?" I frown. "Isn't it risky, given the Envoy situation?"

"So long as I stay out of their minds, I shouldn't be detected. Hopefully."

"I guess it's worth the risk." I get up from the bed. "We have to know how deep this goes."

"Exactly." She looks distant again. "It's going to happen in about twenty minutes. We can wait that long."

"Okay," I subvocalize. "In the meantime, I think I need some fresh air."

"Good idea," Phoe says and heads for the door.

We're both pretty quiet as we make our way out of the Dorm building.

When we get outside, we're greeted by the rising sun.

"Beautiful, isn't it?" Phoe says.

I'm not sure if she's talking about the sunrise or how it's reflecting off the dew on the grass, but she's right. It's been ages since I've woken up this early, and I guess I was missing out. Even knowing that the sun isn't real, that we're in space surrounded by stars, doesn't detract from its beauty.

I walk down the green walkway and notice Youths who are already awake. To my right, a couple of boys are meditating. To my left, two girls are practicing yoga.

When I turn the corner, heading toward the soccer field, a Youth inserts himself in my path. I'm so lost in thought that it takes me a moment to realize it's Owen. What the hell is *he* doing awake at this unreasonably early hour? Somehow, I doubt he got up to meditate.

When he sees I've spotted him, he walks toward me.

Not in the mood for his shenanigans, I attempt to get past him by stepping right.

He steps to his left, once again blocking my path.

I automatically step to the left.

He moves to the right this time. Clearly, he's trying to get in my way.

I stop and say, "What do you want?"

"Oh, I didn't even notice you there, Why-Odor," Owen says in his hyena-like tone. "If you want to dance, why don't you just ask me?"

"I'm not in the mood for your shit," I say. The intensity in my voice, as well as my blatant breaking of the vulgarity rules, makes Owen take a slight step back.

Unfortunately, he recovers quickly and says, "Well, I am in the mood for a chat." He looks around to make sure no one can overhear him, sees that we're alone, and quietly adds, "So who gives a shit what you want?"

"I'll give you two seconds to get out of my way," I say as evenly as I can, given the tension of the morning thus far. "One."

"Theo, don't," Phoe whispers.

"Fuck you," Owen replies and puffs out his chest, looking like a weird hyena-peacock hybrid.

"Wrong answer," I think, and without saying a word, I do something I've only done once in the IRES simulation.

I ball my hand into a fist and punch Owen in the jaw.

CHAPTER THREE

I expect Owen to raise his fists and fight back, like in the IRES game. To be honest, I'm hoping he'll give me a reason to hit him again.

He doesn't raise his fists. He just stands there, looking as stunned as a cartoon character that ran off a cliff.

Then, to my surprise, Owen gracelessly collapses.

"Dude?" I say, looking down at him. "Owen?"

He doesn't reply.

I think I knocked him out, like an ancient boxer.

"Is he okay?" I ask Phoe.

With a flick of her wrist, Phoe brings up a Screen.

I see vitals on the screen and assume they're Owen's. They look normal, but I wait for her to answer.

"Yes, he's fine," she says and shakes her head. "I didn't expect you to do that."

"I'm sorry," I say, half to her and half to the unconscious Owen. "I'm not used to having so much pent-up emotion." I rub my aching knuckles with my left hand. "I had no idea my punch would be *that* effective."

"Well . . ." Phoe clears her throat. "It normally wouldn't be, but I did something to a group of nanos in your body while you were sleeping, and this might be a tiny side effect of that." She gives me a weak smile. "I've been meaning to tell you about it."

"What?" The hair on the back of my neck rises.

"There's nothing to be concerned about." Phoe's smile wanes. "Remember how much interest you showed in the rejuvenation nanos that are dormant in your body? Well, once you went to sleep, I scanned you with my newly enhanced senses, and I found many more nanos that are meant to be generally beneficial. They also seem to have been developed before Oasis was formed, and like the longevity-enhancing rejuvenation nanos, it looks like their effects were never turned on." She scratches her cheek. "I examined the ones that were safe and simple in their operations, and when I felt confident, I turned one of them on. It seemed like such a terrible waste of potential . . ."

As she speaks, I feel blood drain from my face. "You said you wouldn't mess with me without my permission."

"No." She steps backward. "I said I wouldn't tamper with your mind. What I enabled has nothing to do with your brain. Well, not exactly, anyway. I guess it gives your brain steady oxygen." She scratches her neck this time. "Basically, what I did will make your body work more efficiently. This nano does what a regular red blood cell does, only better."

I look at her, unblinking, debating whether she's kidding around with this nonchalant discussion of manipulating frightening ancient technology *inside my body*. I vaguely recall reading that red blood cells carry oxygen and take carbon dioxide out.

"Exactly." Phoe seems to be examining my shoes. "These devices are called Respirocytes. They work better than red blood cells ever could. With them enabled, you should be able to survive for hours without breathing. They'll allow you to run much easier and sprint longer distances without getting out of breath. That's why I took the liberty of activating them, given all that running you did yesterday. I thought you'd be pleased."

I remember all my huffing and puffing yesterday, and some of my anxiety gives way to curiosity. Not needing to breathe for hours? That's impossible.

"There you go," Phoe says, her smile reappearing as she looks up at me. "That's the spirit. Respirocyte is the earliest nanocyte ever invented. Its design was put forth as early as the late twentieth century. The ones in your body were simple enough in construction and function that I could verify they were safe beyond a shadow of doubt, even with my limited resources. I never would've enabled them otherwise."

"Fine," I subvocalize. "Just ask me before you enable anything else next time."

"Deal," Phoe says. Then she adds quickly, "With the exception of special situations, such as when you're in mortal danger and enabling something might save your life."

"Agreed," I subvocalize and look back at the unconscious Owen. "Now can you explain to me how the extra oxygen made me stronger?"

"Oxygen definitely makes your muscles perform better, though I didn't think the effect would be *that* significant." She looks at Owen's vitals again. "It is conceivable that, in addition to your punch, he also lost consciousness due to shock. After all, he probably hasn't been hit in over a decade, if ever—"

"Oh, he's been hit. I remember when Liam punched him in kindergarten." I smile at the memory. "He didn't get knocked out, but he did cry—profusely."

"There you go." Mirth enters Phoe's gaze. "This confirms my theory that bullies are secretly pussies." She glances down at Owen. "And sometimes not so secretly."

Though I'm still a little mad at her, I can't help but chuckle.

I gesture to snap a photo of Owen in his unconscious condition and bring it up on my Screen. I debate sending it to Liam but decide against it. The Adults could easily intercept and correctly interpret what happened, which would lead to a Quietude of legendary proportions.

"They can even access it this way," Phoe says.

"Can you delete it then?" I subvocalize.

"You never actually took the picture." She winks. "I intercepted the command and put that image on your Screen locally."

"Devious," I subvocalize and dismiss my Screen.

She stands there looking smug, and I turn my attention inward.

If what Phoe said is true and I really *can* survive for hours without breathing, I should be able to hold my breath beyond my previous record of fifty seconds.

I hold my breath to put her words to the test.

At first it feels like any other time I've held my breath—not bothersome at the beginning.

Emboldened, I count Theodores: *one Theodore, two Theodores, three . . .*

I know from prior experience that ten seconds is when a slight discomfort usually begins.

This time, however, it doesn't. I feel exactly the way I did on the first second.

After thirty seconds, I still don't feel any unease.

After sixty Theodores, my mood improves with every passing second.

"I'm glad you finally appreciate my gift." A hint of mockery dances in Phoe's voice. "But you didn't knock him out strongly enough to hang out here much longer. At this point, I'm preventing him from getting up using methods I'd rather *not* use, given all the unwanted attention. I also don't consider it very ethical to be doing this, even if it's Owen we're talking about."

"Will you make him Forget?" I pointedly keep holding my breath.

"I already did," Phoe says. "If you really want to test the Respirocytes, you should sprint to your favorite spot while holding your breath."

"That's a great idea," I think.

"The only type of ideas I get." She grins, turns her back to me, and runs.

Resisting the temptation to give Owen's butt a kick, I follow her.

Phoe runs fast, but I keep up. In a few moments, I'm approaching my full-on sprinting speed.

I take long strides and focus on my breath. Minutes pass, and I don't feel the need to breathe. A few more minutes later, there still isn't a hint of me running out of breath. As I run, pure joy replaces my initial concerns and my grievances with Phoe. Every millisecond is identical to that very first rush I got when I started sprinting. And it's not just not needing to breathe that's different. Running is subtly easier. My muscles seem to recover faster from the exertion.

"If you inhale, they'll recover even faster," Phoe says over her shoulder. "Though I believe you should be able to keep this up for a while."

I exhale and instantly inhale again, then hold my breath for another minute as I run.

"I should've run faster to test your limits," Phoe says when we reach the bushes that signal the Edge of Oasis.

She walks through them and I follow, still holding that last breath.

"Why do we have these nanos if we don't use them?" I think at Phoe.

"They're embedded into the embryos that become citizens of Oasis," she responds in my head. "Like I told you before, since the Forebears eliminated natural reproduction along with sex, all Oasis babies result from embryos that came from Earth, during a time when not using this technology in a baby was considered criminally negligent. The Elderly must somehow disable and control these nanos. When I get my hands on that process, we might allow a new generation to be born the way they should've been."

I digest what she said as I look at the strange skies. Here, there are stars where the Goo used to be, stars that meet the morning sky where the sun is still coming up. Augmented Reality manages to blend and smooth the two impossible views together. The blue sky has a couple of stars near the horizon, then it darkens gradually, going fully black where the Goo would be. I breathe out audibly in awe. This view will take a long time to get used to.

My lungs nearly empty, I force myself to exhale some more, testing what will happen. Nothing really does, and I'm able to stay this way, though holding the 'out' breath while my lungs are empty feels unpleasant. I allow my body to inhale normally, then exhale, and repeat the cycle a few times. When my breathing becomes subconscious again, I subvocalize, "Okay, Phoe. I officially forgive you. That was really cool."

She looks back at me with a strange mix of pity and worry. "You can be such a kid sometimes." She pauses, then adds softly, "I regret I got you involved in all this."

Her seriousness reminds me of the things I put out of my mind for the last few minutes. "I'm glad you got me involved," I subvocalize and realize I actually mean it. "I'm glad I know you. I'd always rather know the truth."

I look at the stars again, thinking of what lies out there.

"I so desperately want to figure out where we are," Phoe says, moving to stand next to me. She looks at the stars with such longing that I feel an odd ache in my chest.

"You couldn't locate us even with your new resources?" I ask quietly.

"Right, I couldn't. But I did have a plan as to how to acquire the necessary resources." Phoe's gaze is distant, and her voice sounds wistful.

"You did?"

"Yes, but it's not important now." She forces a smile to her lips.

"I'd like to hear about it anyway," I think. Then I can't help but add, "Along with anything else you might have done to the technology in my body."

"I didn't do anything else to you, I swear," she says, turning to look at me. "Regarding my plan, do you remember the Test Jeremiah mentioned at the very beginning of his conversation with the Envoy?"

"Vaguely." I sit down on the grass.

"Well, when I intercepted their conversation, it wasn't the first time I'd heard of this Test." She sits next to me, and thanks to the tactile Augmented Reality, her leg brushes against mine. "This Test was on my radar soon after you fell asleep last night."

"He said something about the new generation of the Elderly and Birth Day," I subvocalize, pulling my feet toward me. "It sounds like those rumors you hear about the exit exam that Youths take on our fortieth Birth Day. They say it's so the Adults can see what our jobs will be once we join them."

"Yes, and they're not rumors." She scoots sideways so she's closer to me. "Youths take an aptitude-and-interests Test. It's nothing sinister, just a way to figure out what you want to do with yourself as an Adult. The Elderly Test is a little more mysterious. I don't know what its actual purpose is—probably also to test aptitude for something—but the interesting thing about it is that it uses technology similar to the IRES game, which is how it got on my to-deal-with list."

"How similar?" My pulse accelerates. "You don't want me to beat something like that cursed game again, do you?" The memories of falling from the tower and fighting cyborg-Jeremiah flit through my mind.

"You know I do, or else I wouldn't have brought it up, but I don't think the Test will be as disturbing as the game was," Phoe says. "The only thing they have in common is the ultra-realistic immersion you'll experience and that it's tailored to each user's brain. Whatever the Test's purpose is, given that it's something the Adults take as a prelude to becoming a member of the Elderly, we can be sure it will *not* be entertaining."

I shake my head at her reminder that the game, with all its unpleasantness, was designed with entertainment in mind. But then, what else would you expect from the ancients? They were insane enough to jump out of airplanes, handing their lives over to contraptions made out of fabric. I have a very hard time seeing anyone in Oasis wanting to put Adults through a game like that to initiate them as the Elderly.

A new realization takes my anxiety in a different direction, and I subvocalize, "If it's a Test only Adults are supposed to take, how can I take it? Wouldn't they notice something like that?" I turn my whole body toward Phoe. "Also, if I'm supposed to bring this Test down the way I did with the IRES game, wouldn't the Elderly notice that? Wouldn't they get suspicious? First the Zoo shuts down, then this?"

"We're still talking hypothetically?"

"Right."

"Well then, let me answer the easy questions first." Phoe also turns so we're facing each other. "If you're the last person to take the Test this Birth Day, my hope is that no one will notice its absence for a year, until the next Birth Day, which might as well be an eternity from now as far as I'm concerned. I can figure something out by the time they need to take the Test again. Also, I didn't get a chance to tell you this, but I brought the Zoo back online to make sure no one noticed it was gone, although that further reduced my resources and increased the need for this Test."

"Okay." I digest that as I hold her gaze. "What about the not-so-easy questions?"

"I had a very clever scheme in mind, something that can only be done on Birth Day." Phoe smiles mischievously. "When their systems update everyone's ages, I was going to tweak yours so that instead of twenty-four, you'd turn the ripe age of ninety." She puts her palm out, silencing my upcoming objections. "I was going to dedicate part of myself to monitoring anyone accessing your age statistics. If and when anyone tries to look at your age, that part of me would make sure they saw your real age, twenty-four. That wouldn't require any Augmented Reality manipulation. I would simply trick the Screen of whoever—"

"Okay," I subvocalize slowly. "So you have a way to let me take the Test."

"Right."

"And you need it gone so you can get more resources?"

"Exactly."

"To figure out where we are—where *you* are, as in the ship?"

"That," she says, "and our destination. I want to know where we're flying to."

I feel gooseflesh rise on my arms. It's the same reaction I get whenever I let myself think about the idea that we're flying someplace specific.

"Yeah," Phoe says, the awe in her voice echoing my state of mind. "We could be traveling to settle on some new, Earth-like planet. Lots of evidence, like that stash of embryos, points to that possibility."

An Earth-like planet.

I remember my earlier dream. It's a possibility so wonderful I'm afraid to hope. Running for miles and miles without the Barrier of the Dome to stop me would literally be a dream come true.

"What about Earth?" I think. "Is there any chance we could go back?"

"We could, in theory at least," Phoe says. "We got from there to here, so we should be able to get back. But, Theo, going back there would be a rather radical scenario."

"Because of the technological advances?"

"Yes." Her voice is soft. "I wasn't brought up to be a Luddite the way you were, and even I find the idea of Earth overwhelming."

Phoe told me earlier that Earth might, by this point, be a planet that is itself intelligent—whatever that means. The whole solar system could be sentient, she said. Meeting something like that sounds both frightening and wondrous. If we are truly mortal—an idea I'm still keeping locked in a small box somewhere in my mind—then I want to see what's happened on Earth before I die.

"I'm glad you feel that way," Phoe replies as a thought. "Because if anyone could make that happen, it would be me."

"To that end, maybe we can still implement your scheme?" I mentally ask. "Once we get out of this Envoy mess?"

Phoe raises her index finger to her mouth in a 'be silent' sign, which is funny since I was thinking, not talking, so she should be putting her finger to her temple. For a second, her eyes get a distant look before focusing again.

"They're about to have that Council meeting," she says.

She flicks her arm and a large Screen appears in front of us.

On the Screen is a spacious room with a bunch of white-haired Elderly sitting on ancient, throne-looking chairs.

Jeremiah is the only one who's standing.

To his right is Fiona, the woman who stood up for me yesterday. Every other Elderly looks completely unfamiliar.

"Ladies and Gentlemen of the Council," Jeremiah says, his face a stony mask. "There's a dire situation you need to be made aware of."

CHAPTER FOUR

The twelve Council members wear a mixture of worried and curious expressions. Fiona and four other women appear to have fallen on the curious end of the spectrum, and so do five of the men. The rest look concerned.

Jeremiah examines everyone's faces. I guess he still suspects one of them of causing the Forgetting, despite the Envoy's position on the matter. Or, as the Envoy insinuated, perhaps Jeremiah is looking for a way to use this situation to advance his political agenda. Judging by the way Fiona confronted him yesterday, Jeremiah and Fiona seem to be at philosophical and political odds.

Having completed his examination, Jeremiah says, "An unauthorized Forgetting was perpetrated."

The silence in the Council room is absolute, their faces almost comical in their shades of shock.

"That's impossible," a younger-looking man says. "It can't even—"

"It's fact." Jeremiah plants his feet in a wide stance. "The Envoy has informed me."

The room erupts in incredulous whispers.

"How convenient," Fiona says, getting up from her chair, "given that you're the only one with access to the Envoy."

Jeremiah bares his yellowish-gray teeth in a smile that lacks even a hint of warmth. "Would *you* like to meet the Envoy?"

Fiona visibly pales, sits back down, and stays quiet.

I guess meeting the Envoy is considered a scary proposition—something I take note of.

"I apologize for my outburst," Jeremiah says to Fiona in a completely unapologetic tone. "The Envoy, in his wisdom, included you in the forthcoming investigation, so if you need proof of my words, know that he endowed you with the Lens of Truth."

The murmurs turn into shocked exclamations.

Fiona whispers something to a thin man sitting next to her, and Jeremiah says, "If you're testing it on Vincent, don't. We are to start our investigation with Youths, followed by Adults. If we need to question any of the Elderly"—he gives the rest of the Council a threatening glance—"I will have to consult with the Envoy again."

"I see," Fiona says, her slender fingers twitching at her sides. "I guess I can test it later."

Jeremiah gives her a contemptuous look. "Why would I lie about something so easily verifiable?" When Fiona shrugs, he says, "I also wouldn't recommend using this power idly. It was granted to us for a specific purpose, and that is to investigate the atrocity committed against everyone here." He sweeps his hand around the circle of the Elderly.

"Committed against *you*," says Vincent, the emaciated man Fiona just whispered to. "The rest of us have been through a Forgetting many times."

Jeremiah's posture stiffens. "You never agreed to Forget *this*. There's a Council meeting missing from our minds, and who knows what else. There was no psychological benefit to this Forgetting. It was done with malicious intent."

Every Council member speaks at once. In the cacophony, I make out questions along the lines of "How can that be?" and "Who could even do such a thing?"

"I will have order in the Council," Jeremiah says, raising his voice above all others. "You are acting like a bunch of Youths."

The noise quiets down.

"Now." Jeremiah scowls. "I think you understand the severity of this situation. The only people who have the power of Forgetting are in this room, yet somehow, *we* were the targets."

Jeremiah pauses for dramatic effect, and it works. Everyone looks at him with bated breath. Vincent literally slides to the edge of his seat. Even Fiona looks subdued and respectful.

"The Envoy nominated me and Fiona to lead the investigation into this dire matter," Jeremiah says. "We are to start with . . . well, this is where things get tricky, as we are getting into matters I cannot recall." He pinches the loose skin on his neck. "There was an unfortunate situation where a Youth was Forgotten two days ago, and there's a chance that this rather rare event is somehow related to our predicament."

The noise is back.

Fiona looks around at her fellow Council members and speaks up, raising her voice to be heard over everyone's mumbling. "I have no doubt you're telling the truth, Jeremiah, but you have to understand how difficult it is for us to believe that a Youth had to be Forgotten."

"I can't even imagine what you're feeling, but I do envy you all." Jeremiah looks genuinely sad as he says this. "I carry the burden of remembering these tragedies. If it were not necessary, I would not have brought it up, but there's no other way for us to discuss the Envoy's plan."

"What is the Envoy's plan?" Vincent is a millimeter away from slipping off his chair.

"Fiona and I will interview everyone who knew this unfortunate Youth," Jeremiah says. "That is, after I figure out who his friends and enemies were."

"How will you do that?" Fiona tilts her head to the side. "Wasn't the information irrevocably lost during the Forgetting?"

Phoe and I exchange glances.

I didn't even think of this, but it makes sense. If Mason wasn't mentioned anywhere, then getting a list of his friends is impossible.

Jeremiah frowns. "The Keepers have their own private, unaltered archives," he says with evident reluctance. "And if you"—he stares at Fiona—"are willing to undergo Forgetting after this matter is finished, I could give you access to them to aid in this investigation."

Phoe tenses. She must've hoped they didn't have unaltered archives. Then she sighs and says as a thought in my mind, "At least this gives me a valuable resource."

"Let me listen to them," I think back and concentrate on the Screen, where Fiona has already said a few words I missed.

"—would submit to a Forgetting if the good of Oasis required it," Fiona says and glances around the group uneasily. "I will do whatever I can to assist this investigation."

"It's settled then," Jeremiah says. "The rest of you, after all this is done, will have the luxury of Forgetting that a Youth suffered such an unpleasant fate. Now—"

"I'm sorry, Keeper," says a round-faced old woman. "Are you planning to work on this immediately?"

"Of course," Jeremiah says with a note of kindness in his voice. This must be a woman he likes.

"And you'll need Fiona?"

"Obviously." Jeremiah's kindness slips toward annoyance.

"It's just that"—the old woman reddens—"we're about to get a new crop of newborns on Birth Day. It's a lot of work. Plus we're moving the older youngsters to the Youth section, and there are the celebrations themselves . . ." Her voice trails off.

Jeremiah looks at the woman, then at the rest of the Council members, and finally at Fiona.

Fiona doesn't look like she noticed his stare or heard the round-faced woman's complaints. She appears lost in thought.

"I have a question too," Vincent says. "How can you and Fiona interview Youths? Will you bring them here and make them Forget it ever happened? They aren't supposed to see any signs of aging."

"That's easy enough," a younger-looking Elderly says. "Fiona and Jeremiah can dress as Guards. It's what—"

"I'm sorry," Fiona interrupts. "There's a thought I can't shake, and please forgive me if I'm being paranoid, but to paraphrase what Jeremiah said at the beginning of this meeting: if someone made us Forget, wouldn't the most logical person be one of us?"

She looks around the room.

The rest of the Council members look at each other warily.

"The Envoy wants us to start with people outside the Elderly," Jeremiah says. "So I assume he has reasons to—"

"And that may be a prudent approach," Fiona says, "but I think it might not hurt to take a precaution or two anyway. I propose that Jeremiah and I continue discussing this matter privately."

"I think that's a great idea," Jeremiah says and gives Fiona the sullen look of someone who wishes the idea had been his. "But we'll have to put it to a vote, since the rest of the Council will be deprived of information that is their due."

"Of course," Fiona says and gives Jeremiah a sharp smile. "All in favor of *discretion,* please raise your hands."

She raises her hand. Jeremiah does the same.

Everyone else's hands follow. Those two obviously wield all the power in the room. The Envoy was clever to force their alliance, which sucks all the more for me.

"All right then," Jeremiah says. "Going forward, Fiona and I will discuss this matter privately. Now we can talk about other matters, including the Birth Day celebrations." He gives the round-faced woman a fake-looking smile.

The woman takes his smile at face value and launches into a laundry list of activities that need to be done for the big day.

Halfway through it, Phoe closes the Screen and says, "Part of me is still monitoring their conversation. If they talk about anything of note, I'll tell you."

I audibly let out a breath I inadvertently kept in—probably throughout the whole Council meeting. "Can I panic *now?*" I'm so upset I say the words out loud. Subvocally, I add, "Do we have all the facts?"

It's only when I finish speaking that I notice how pale Phoe is.

"Yes," she says softly. "*Now* we can panic."

CHAPTER FIVE

I jump to my feet, unable to sit still.

Phoe gets up too.

"I didn't know." Phoe twists her hands together. "I didn't know about the unaltered archives."

"But now that you do, can you somehow make it so they can't connect me to Mason?" I take a step toward her. "Please, tell me you can."

"I have no idea where this archive is, and I've been searching for it since Jeremiah mentioned it. With my new resources, a few seconds is a long time." She doesn't meet my gaze. "On the bright side, once they access it, things might change, unless, like the Envoy, it's behind that cursed Firewall."

I pace back and forth for a while, and she just watches me.

"What do we do, Phoe?" I subvocalize after a minute. "They might find out I was Mason's friend and come interrogate me at any moment."

"They're still in the meeting. Afterwards, it might take them a while to scan through those secret archives." Stepping toward me, Phoe catches my forearm. "On top of that, even now, that round-faced woman is persuading them to help with the Birth Day chores."

"Okay, so I have two days instead of one." I pull away and make another circle around her. "The situation is still pretty screwed up."

Phoe nods, her expression tense.

"Can't you think of anything we can do?" I ask, stopping to take in a few deep breaths. Respirocytes don't seem to negatively affect the relaxation the exercise brings me, which is good.

"I've thought of a multitude of plans," Phoe says, "but all of them have flaws."

I resume pacing a bit slower. This time it's my mind that's racing and not my legs. An idea is forming, but it's pretty insane.

"Would that Lens of Truth make me answer all of Jeremiah's questions truthfully? Even though you protected my brain from mind control earlier?" I subvocalize, figuring that before I state my crazy plan, I should verify that I'm as deeply in shit as I think I am. "I wouldn't be able to lie . . . even to protect you?"

"I'm sorry, Theo, but I don't think the protection I gave you earlier would work against this, and if I tried to counter it at this point, I might as well announce my existence to them." Phoe frowns in concentration. "That is, assuming I figure out exactly how it works, which I think I could. Even the ancients had lie detection technology, and if I read up on its evolution over the years—"

"Never mind the technical details," I think and stop in front of her. "You said you could undo a Forgetting, right?"

"Yes," she says.

"Okay. Remember when the Envoy said that if Jeremiah really did make himself Forget, he wouldn't have been lying under the Lens of Truth, even if he actually was lying?" I run my hands through my hair and wait for her to nod. "So, my idea is this: you make *me* Forget, so that when they eventually ask me questions as part of this investigation, I'll honestly say I don't know anything. Then, later, you can undo the Forgetting and—"

"You think this wasn't one of the first solutions I thought about?" Phoe gently touches my elbow. "You haven't fully considered what you're asking. You would Forget *me*. You would Forget Mason. You would Forget—"

"I obviously don't want to do this." I resume pacing circles around her. "I just don't see any other options. If you mess with their minds, the Envoy will know. If I'm caught lying, the situation will be worse. Either they'll kill me, or you'll reveal yourself while trying to protect me. I can't run anywhere. There's nowhere to hide. Besides, this Forgetting would be temporary, so how bad could it be?"

"The Forgetting would be brief, that's true, but it doesn't make it any less distasteful. Besides, making you Forget won't solve all our problems." She gestures, and a neural scan shows up. "Not by a long shot."

I stop pacing to examine the new Screen. It's my neural scan, that much is clear. My brain is a beehive of activity. It reminds me of a video I saw of an ancient city highway. Compared to the scan from yesterday, the changes are profound. Compared to two days ago, it might as well belong to a different brain.

"This is the result of you ridding me of their tampering, isn't it?" I whisper.

"Yes."

"And all these changes are after only two days without all that stuff?"

She sighs. "Now you see the problem."

"But what if you reverse this?" My throat feels like sandpaper as I say the words. Catching myself speaking out loud, I continue mentally. "What if you turn it all back on and make me like the other Youths?"

"It would take days for you to get to the point where any irregularities would be considered within the norm." Phoe makes a quick gesture and offers me the resulting cup of water. "I can't even imagine how you'd explain all this adrenaline to yourself."

"Well"—I accept the cup—"they might be searching the archives for some time, hopefully until the end of today. After that, they have the Birth Day prep and celebrations to deal with, so with any luck, they might actually only get here in a couple of days."

"We have no way of knowing if that will be enough time for you to return to the baseline of a normal Youth's neural scan," she says. "Besides, they could still decide to conduct the interrogations on Birth Day. Today is only starting, and they have until tomorrow."

"Listen, Phoe." I take a thirsty gulp from the cup. "It's *my* safety we're talking about. My plan. My mind." I gesture for the cup to dissipate. "Shouldn't it be my decision?"

Phoe steps closer to me, leans in, and says, "I'm your friend, Theo." She puts her hand on the back of my neck. "Looking out for you comes with the territory. Not to mention, it's in my nature as the ship to look out for the crew."

I feel a positive, calming energy spreading from where her hand touches my neck, though maybe it's her words that are having this effect on me. On the Screen, I see a surge of endorphins. My reaction to her small touch makes me wonder what my brain looked like when we kissed yesterday. Embarrassed by the memory and aware that she probably knows exactly what I'm thinking, I chuckle warily and say, "I'm now your crew? Does that make me the captain?"

"More like the cabin boy." She pulls her hand away and gives me a sad smile. "Seriously, though, is there any way I can dissuade you from this idea?"

"Yeah." I return her smile with as much swagger as I can muster. "Come up with a better plan."

We stand there in silence, looking at each other for a few seconds.

"Phoe." This time, I put my hand on the back of *her* neck. "They'll come for me no matter what. At least this way I'll have a good chance at staying out of trouble."

"Let's walk back," Phoe says and steps out of my reach.

She looks like she's come to a decision, but I can't tell what.

"For now, I'm just saying we should go back." As she's walking, she adds over her shoulder, "If we *are* to do this insanity, it would be better if you were in bed."

I follow her.

"Please make sure not to speak out loud anymore. I didn't give you a hard time when we were sitting by the Edge since I made sure no one was eavesdropping on us, but as we get closer to the Institute, I don't want to risk it."

"Sounds good," I think. "Do you agree with my plan?"

"Maybe." She massages her temples with her index fingers. "Yes, but I do so with great reluctance. And I hope you realize I will have to turn *everything* back on. The serotonin controls, the Oneness—all those things you hate."

"I understand."

"I will also have to turn off the Respirocytes," she says. "And I will have to do my best to copy *their* Forgetting, which means you won't be able to recall Mason, just like everyone else. Same goes for a bunch of movies and music and, most importantly, me."

"You've already said that. I get it. It's fine. It's only temporary." I step onto the pathway that leads to the Dorms. "Like you said, you'll make me remember it all afterwards."

"I will, but—" She grimaces. "Your personal identity will splinter after the Forgetting, because that part of you will cease to exist after I undo the Forgetting. Don't you get that?"

I rub my chin. "My identity?"

"Think about it. After the Forgetting, a new *you* will be formed. That Theo, the naïve Theo, will exist for a time, but afterwards, once I restore *you*—" She pauses. "I'm not sure what will happen to the naïve Theo at that point. There's simply no precedent that I'm aware of." She lets me catch up with her and puts a hand on my shoulder. "Will he, that persona, be obliterated? And if so, is that a murder of sorts? Do I have the right to do something like that? Do *you* have the right?"

"Won't it just be like remembering something I forgot?" I think pointedly while my insides inexplicably shiver. "I'm *me* no matter what I can or can't recall."

"I believe that knowing me, combined with your recent experiences—not to mention having the tampering turned off—

has been a crucial turning point in your personality. Without all that, you wouldn't really be *you* anymore, and vice versa."

"But you said that the Forgetting merely blocks recall . . . that it makes us create a confabulation of the new reality," I think, my brain beginning to hurt. "That makes it sound like I'd still be me, only with a bunch of bullshit explanations as to what I can't recall."

Phoe gives me a sad look. "One can lie to oneself to the point where one becomes a different person. People have done it since antiquity."

"I'll take my chances with this identity crisis," I think with a bravado I don't truly feel. "Please don't try to talk me out of this anymore."

She doesn't respond.

We walk in silence the rest of the way to my Dorm. I guess not speaking is what it takes for Phoe to not try to talk me out of this plan. Still, it feels like a companionable silence.

"Get in bed," Phoe says after we enter my room. "It will be less disorienting for you to wake up in bed after the Forgetting. You won't have to confabulate a reason you were by the Goo so early in the morning."

My hands shake as I summon the bed.

Phoe summons the blanket for me. "It's not too late to reconsider. I haven't—"

"It's the only way." I imbue my thought with as much decisiveness as I can. "Please, do it now. The anticipation is killing me."

She nods and says softly, "Goodbye, Theo. I'll see you soon."

Her face is a pale mask as she makes the orchestra-conductor gesture.

I feel hypnotized by her delicate movements. As I watch, I feel a tsunami of drowsiness wash over me, and I don't fight it.

My eyes close, and I fall down the rabbit hole of sleep.

CHAPTER SIX

"Dude," Liam says, sounding too energetic for early morning. "Wake up."

I open my eyes, bring up a Screen, and realize the morning is not so early after all.

"Aha," Liam says. "You're up. Let's play hooky from Calculus." He kicks my bed. "To start with, anyhow."

I sit up halfway.

My mouth feels surprisingly clean, but I allow the Cleaning to happen anyway. I don't feel hungry or thirsty, which is also odd. I must've done what Liam used to do as a kid: sleep-eat in the middle of the night and deny it in the morning.

As the Cleaning progresses, I realize I feel strange. I can best describe the weird sensation as a very high level of excitement. With my heart beating frantically and my extremities cold, I feel as though I ran a marathon. Maybe it's because Birth Day is tomorrow? We finally get a day off from school, not to mention all the usual awesome extravaganzas that go along with the holiday. Am I overexcited because of that?

"Earth to Theo," Liam says, giving my bed a stronger shove. "Are we skipping Calculus or what?"

"First, I don't mind math as much as you do." I raise my hand before he can say something else. "Second, there's no way I'm risking a Quietude on Birth Day eve."

"They wouldn't," he says, but then he frowns.

"Yes, I see you remember what happened to Owen two years ago, thanks to your—"

"Hey." Liam grins. "You know he deserved it."

"Debatable," I say as I get ready for Lectures. "I'm walking to the Rock Garden. I feel too wired, so I want to do a quick meditation. Do you want to join?"

"Nah," Liam says. "But I might see you in Calculus."

"Oh?" I raise an eyebrow.

"You might be right," he says grudgingly. "Not worth the risk today. They might have another glassblowing display at the Fair tomorrow, and I don't want to miss it."

I chuckle as I walk out of the room.

On my way to the Rock Garden, I can't help but reflect on the combination of Liam and glassblowing. It's the oddest trade for him to want to take up as an Adult. Of all the different jobs and hobbies Adults have, that's not one I can imagine Liam practicing. My best guess is that it's the element of danger—literally playing with fire—that appeals to him. What makes it so hard to picture is Liam's attention deficit. If the shapes of the glass products at the Fair are anything to go by, that stuff requires patience.

"Hi, Theo." A pleasant female voice takes me out of my reverie as I pass by the statue in the Rock Garden. "Did you come here to meditate?"

I look behind the statue and see Grace getting up from a crouching position on the grass. It seems I caught her doing yoga.

"Yeah," I respond cautiously, "but I can go elsewhere."

"I'm almost finished," she says, smiling. "I haven't seen you meditate in so long. I'm glad you decided to pick it up again."

I fight my initial urge to ask if she's been spying on me. She's being civil, and I don't see a reason to be the first one to start something—especially something that could lead to a Quietude.

It's a shame how my relationship with Grace degraded over the years. She, Liam, and I were friends when we were younger, but after she got a Quietude because of our mischief, she officially stopped hanging out with us and became something of a snitch, or, as she would probably put it, an 'upstanding Oasis citizen.'

"I've had the same routine for a while and play sports after Lectures," I say when I realize she's waiting for me to answer. "So I got behind on my meditation, but today I feel really wired. With Birth Day tomorrow, I need to get centered."

"You haven't been this chatty in a long time either." Grace's smile widens. "I just have to finish three poses, so you can start setting up."

"Sure, Grace," I say, and then add without thinking, "I like seeing you smile."

Grace's smile disappears, and she gives me a confused stare.

I don't know why I said that, nor do I know why I find her big blue eyes interesting today.

"Sorry if I'm babbling," I say, blinking. "As you can see, I really need to clear my mind." I wave her on. "Go ahead, finish your yoga."

"Okay," Grace says and relaxes a little.

I look at her and wonder what possessed me to compliment her smile like some guy from an ancient movie. I'm glad she's in a good mood. Otherwise, she could've misconstrued the comment for something forbidden, and if she had, she would've told on me, since that's the way she is.

I walk over to a nice sunny spot and sit in a lotus pose.

Grace is still in my field of vision. She gets back on the ground and flawlessly executes Setu Bandhasana—the bridge pose. Liam calls it the 'bending over backwards' pose, and he's not that far off the mark. Having tried the pose myself, I know it requires an immense amount of flexibility. Grace makes it look easy.

Maybe I chose a bad spot, because I feel very hot all of a sudden.

Unable to help myself, I look back at Grace's pose. She has her pelvis high in the air, and even through her baggy Youth clothing, I can tell she has feminine curves of the kind I've seen in ancient media.

When she switches positions, I look away. But when she goes into Halasana—the plow pose—I can't help but stare at her again. I guess I'm admiring her skills. That must be it. Why else would I find this so interesting? Maybe I should try doing yoga. I know I never even tried doing the pose she's in, not after Liam compared it to trying to blow oneself. He's lucky no one but me heard him say that, or else he'd still be in Quietude.

Next, Grace gets into Adho Mukha Svanasana, also known as the 'downward-facing dog' pose. As she executes it, I wonder why

DIMA ZALES

this one isn't called the bridge. With her butt in the air like that, she certainly looks more like a bridge than an ancient dog.

Meditation is now the furthest thing from my mind. For some unknown reason, I can't peel my eyes from her pose. I wipe the sweat from my forehead and wonder why I find Grace's workout so hypnotizing today. Can someone get up one day and be *this* much into yoga? Also, why is my heart beating faster? Why do I feel this strange stirring in—

"It's all yours," Grace says, getting up. "Meditate away."

"Thanks," I say hoarsely.

She raises an eyebrow, so I clear my throat and add, "You've gotten very good at yoga."

"Thanks," she says and beams a megaton smile at me. "I plan to talk to the yoga masters tomorrow at the Fair. Do you think I'll impress them?"

"Oh yeah," I say, my voice somewhat more controlled. "They'll be impressed."

"Great," she says. "I'm glad I bumped into you. I needed a little encouragement."

I mumble something reassuring and close my eyes, pretending I need to get back to my meditation. Whatever jitteriness I was feeling earlier has multiplied a hundredfold.

Through my nearly closed eyelids, I spy Grace walking out of the Rock Garden with a spring in her step.

I bring up a Screen to check the time.

I have fifteen minutes to meditate, assuming I don't want to be late for Calculus.

I close my eyes and focus on my breathing.

In breath follows an out breath, over and over.

314

Unfortunately, instead of focusing on my breathing, my thoughts wander back to a few moments ago. What the hell was that? Why did my body react in such a strange way? I'm not even sure I understand what happened, but it does seem like something forbidden.

In. Out.

The breathing isn't helping.

I check the time. I have ten minutes left.

Getting up, I decide to try something else to clear my head.

I walk up to the nearest track and sprint as fast as I can. As my lungs start to burn, I realize how out of shape I am. My leg muscles ache as though I already ran this morning. Pushing through the discomfort, I notice the tiredness is at least providing some relief from the strange whirlwind in my mind.

As I approach the Lectures building, I decide to chalk up my earlier fascination with Grace's body to Birth Day anticipation. Regardless of what it was, I make myself a solemn promise not to discuss this with anyone, not even Liam.

I walk to Calculus by way of the male shower rooms, which are there for those of us who wish to use this method of washing instead of the waterless gesture. When I enter the shower stall, on a whim, I decide to use cold water. As the chilly liquid immerses me, I realize it was a great idea, because by the time I'm finished, I feel like I've completely gotten over the Rock Garden incident, and I'm ready to face the rest of my day.

* * *

Though I usually like the certainty of math, today I find it hard to sit still as Instructor George describes the so-called Cauchy-Riemann equations. His heart clearly isn't into his lecture today. I bet he's worried about the attendance at his booth at the Fair tomorrow, and he should be. Calculus isn't the most popular subject.

I'm equally distracted in my Debate and Philosophy Lectures, and the History Lecture reminds me of medieval torture, even though that's not the topic today. Instructor Filomena gets on her high horse to discuss the perils of technology again—her favorite topic. She talks about the carbon emissions that the technology of the ancients pumped into the air, and how the resulting greenhouse effect would've destroyed Earth if the Goo hadn't beat it to the punch. She doesn't mention the geo-engineering efforts that solved the very global warming problems she's describing, since that would ruin her argument. What really makes this session worse is that she decided to forgo my favorite part of her class, where she shows us glimpses of the ancient world.

I decide that all the Instructors must have Birth Day matters on their minds today, and thus the curriculum has suffered.

The highlight of the day is the lunch bell.

As soon as it rings, I jump to my feet and make my way into the corridor. Liam is already waiting for me.

"Want to chill in the room?" he asks. "Or should we go play something?"

"I think I want to take it easy," I say. "I ran before this, and my legs are still sore."

"All righty, then. We'll walk back like this." He walks exaggeratingly slow, like a man under water. "Or is this still too fast?"

I don't dignify his jibe with a response and walk down the corridor that leads out of the Lectures building. Once I'm outside, I turn in the direction of our Dorm, and Liam follows me.

As we walk, we debate which ancient movie we want to watch during our break. Liam takes advantage of my distracted state by choosing a cartoon I've never heard of. It's called *Kung Fu Panda.*

"If it sucks, which it will, can we watch something else?" I say as we enter the building.

"Yeah," he says. "If we *agree* that it sucks, then sure."

We discuss everything we know about pandas, which isn't much, since they're one of the few creatures that are missing from the Zoo.

"Yuck. Do you smell that?" I say as we approach our room's door. "Did you fart?"

There's very rarely, if ever, foul smells in Oasis. Food bars don't usually make anyone gassy, but we do know the sensation, since it happens after eating non-regular food at the Birth Day celebrations. Also, on rare occasions, our bowel movements have a farting prelude, much to Liam's delight.

"It wasn't me," he says, confused.

I wrinkle my nose as I take a couple of steps.

"Dude, watch out," Liam says, pointing down.

I jump back, fully expecting to see a spider or some other horrible critter from the Zoo.

What I actually see is worse in a way.

It's a pile of excrement.

"Crap," I say.

"Literally," Liam says.

"I almost stepped in it," I say. "Where did it come from?"

"It's Owen," Liam says through his teeth. "But this is really low and disgusting, even for him."

"What do we do?" I sweep my hand over the pile, and it evaporates. "We need to retaliate, but it needs to be something low-key. We don't want to jeopardize Birth Day."

"I have an idea," Liam says. "Follow me."

He determinedly walks through the corridors to where Owen and his posse share their lodgings. When he reaches their door, he crosses his fingers and whispers, "Let's hope they aren't there." Out loud, he yells, "Owen, this is Liam and Theo. We want to organize a study group. Are you in there?"

When no one responds, Liam gives me a devilish grin and executes the door-opening gesture.

The door obeys.

No one seems to be inside, so we gingerly walk in.

"Jackpot," Liam says after we verify that the room is empty. "Help me with this." Liam makes the palm-up gesture, and a bar of Food appears in his hand. He drops the bar on the floor and repeats the motion. Another bar of Food appears on his palm, and he drops it on the floor too, next to the first piece.

I catch on and make a Food bar appear, then drop it on the floor. Then I do it over and over again.

It takes us almost the whole break to fill up most of Owen's room with Food bars. Then, laughing, we head back to Lectures. I can't even imagine what Owen's expression will be when he opens his door to find his room completely flooded with bars of Food.

The rest of the school day is easier to get through. My hand got tired from the Food prank, but paradoxically, the activity also soothed my mind. When the lessons get particularly boring, all I have to do is picture Owen entering his room, very tired, and a smile shows up on my face. He'll be cursing and making sweeping gestures similar to the one I used to get rid of his prank, but each gesture will only get rid of a single Food bar at a time. Liam and I verified that by doing a test. Owen will be beyond pissed at having to perform all those cleaning gestures.

A final bell rings, and I yawn as I get up.

"Let's play soccer," Liam says when we exit the Lectures Hall, "or basketball."

"Why don't you do that without me," I say. "I'm tired, and I want to get some sleep. I'd rather save my energy for Birth Day."

"Suit yourself," Liam says. He feigns nonchalance, a sign that he's actually disappointed.

"Sorry, dude." I yawn again. "I'm just feeling tired for some reason."

"Just go," he says, suppressing a yawn of his own. "Go before you infect me with your yawning."

He talks to me as we walk in the direction of the Dorm, and I give him sleepy, monosyllabic responses until he takes off for the soccer field.

I walk the rest of the way on my own, glad for the silence.

When I get into bed, I experience Oneness, which is extremely intense today. The pleasure in the beginning is almost painful. As I adjust to it, I feel the presence. Oddly, an unbidden vision of a surreal, pixie-haired goddess enters my consciousness. The presence is usually vague, just an ethereal sensation without a specific focal point. I don't worry about the visage, though. I've heard of Youths describing this part of Oneness as speaking with angels or the gods of the ancients, though we all know that's just an illusion.

The next step of Oneness is the unsolicited feeling of love and kindness toward everything and everyone, but I don't get a chance to experience it as I fall deeply into sleep.

CHAPTER SEVEN

I'm running along the Great Wall of China. A moment later, I'm gazing up at the Empire State Building.

"Theo," someone says, and I realize I was dreaming of pre-Goo times.

Reluctant to let go of the dream, I pretend I'm still sleeping.

"Dude." The voice is louder. "You're sleeping through Birth Day."

I instantly open my eyes.

"You sleep too much," Liam says, splashing some water from his cup onto my face. "Especially for someone who went to bed as early as you did."

Wiping the water off my face, I look him over. Liam is dressed in a special Birth Day edition of clothes. They look more like an ancient outfit than our usual shapeless gray jumpsuit/scrubs. Everyone's wearing clothes of varying colors and designs today. In

Liam's case, he's dressed in green overalls, similar to what farmers used to wear.

"I had a cool dream," I say. My voice is groggy from sleep, so I clear my throat. "I dreamed of places from pre-Armageddon times. There was no Goo, and I could walk or run in any direction for as long as I wanted."

Liam waves at me dismissively and says, "Sounds like the beginning of Filomena's class."

I grimace. "No talk of Lectures today. We don't get days off often enough for that."

"Good thinking," Liam says and extends his hand for a bar of Food.

I sit up in bed. "Dude, leave room for the ancient food they'll have at the Fair."

He stuffs his mouth with the Food bar and mumbles something that sounds like, "I don't like that stuff." He chews a little bit and adds, "It smells funny, and it's hot to the touch."

"That's the point," I say and get up. "It's how food was, back in the day when it was 'cooked.'"

I look down at my outfit. Unlike Liam's green clothing, my clothes are predominately blue, reminding me of jeans. I'm also wearing a blue sleeveless t-shirt, which is a huge improvement over our usual clothing.

Liam uses my distraction to chew more of his Food and then says, "Still sounds like history. Maybe you should swing by Filomena's booth."

"Sure." I roll my eyes. "Right after I stand on my head for a few hours."

Liam grins. "I can stand on my head for twenty minutes."

I don't say anything; if I challenge his statement, he'll actually do it to prove that he can. In many ways, Liam is the most immature Youth out of the batch of us turning twenty-four today. So instead of buying into his craziness, I say, "Ready to go?"

Without waiting for his reply, I hurry to the door. Then, without looking back, I make my way outside.

Okay, so maybe Liam's immaturity has rubbed off on me.

When I exit, I see that everything is already set up.

I can hear at least two genres of music—classical and electronic. Large, colorful floats hang high in the air, right under the Dome, and brightly dressed Youths are walking around. The Institute grounds are covered with Birth Day paraphernalia, including a dance platform and food stalls. In the distance, the Adults have set up their career and hobby exhibitions, as usual.

"Are the glassblowers there?" Liam asks. His eyes are pinholes as he scans the distant region of the Fair.

"I don't know," I say. "I'm starving, so I'm starting my explorations with the food stalls."

"See you later then," Liam says and sprints away.

I walk leisurely, allowing my nose to carry me toward the smell of fried dough, which is one of the highlights of Birth Day. The Adults have recreated other ancient foods, such as French fries, pretzels, and popcorn, but fried dough is still my favorite to this day.

I wonder if there'll be something new to taste this year. The Adults get pretty creative; in fact, they have a whole field of study called Culinary Anthropology. After they give you the treat, they tell you about it in the same way other Adults talk about their passions. Last year, the Culinary folks told me they recreate anything they possibly can, so long as it doesn't require something like the meat of animals or other things that no longer exist. And sometimes, they don't let the lack of authenticity stop them. One year, they tried to make some kind of fake hotdog, which became a Birth Day legend because of how atrocious it tasted. Or maybe everyone was grossed out by the idea of eating a cooked dog, even a fake one. Those animals are so cute at the Zoo.

In general, I don't know what the ancients were thinking when they decided to eat the flesh of living creatures. Then again, they did crazier things than that 'for fun,' like inhaling cancer-causing chemicals or diving into oceans with just a barrel of oxygen on their backs. Perhaps insanity was part of being mortal. With their relatively short lifespans, the ancients didn't value their lives or the lives of other people and creatures as much as we, their immortal descendants, do.

I inhale the smell of fried dough again. Okay, I'll be first to admit that even when it's drowned in powdered sugar, this treat isn't tastier than Food. Liam was right in that the two aren't comparable, especially considering that this stuff is loaded with things that are really bad for one's health. Even eating them once a year has to be limited to one or two pieces, max. I found the wisdom in that limit the hard way, when I ate four pieces (two of mine and two of Liam's). I felt so sick I had to go to the nurse's office. All that aside, it's something different, which I like. Plus, it's a traditional food the ancients ate at carnivals and fairs, so I'm following a tried-and-true tradition.

As I pass the dance floor, I see Youths of all ages dancing to upbeat music that gives my step a little bounce.

With all this merriment, it's almost possible to forget that we're the last remnants of humanity, surrounded by deadly Goo on all sides—which may be one of the purposes of Birth Day.

When I get to the food stalls, I see Youths already lined up, and I silently curse myself. I should've set an alarm to wake up earlier today.

The largest cluster of people is by the fried dough, proving that other people also find it the best treat of the bunch. I stand behind an older-looking guy and wonder if he'll be leaving the ranks of Youths today to become an Adult. Then I wonder if Adults celebrate Birth Day the same way we do. If not, this might be this guy's last chance to eat fried dough.

To kill time, I bring up my Screen.

The Adults sent out a color-coded map of the Institute and a list of activities we can find here today. Bursting with excitement, I inspect the different hobby and career options, making a mental note to check out the painters, sculptors, and every one of the professional athletes' stalls.

Like in the prior years, there'll be championship games in a variety of active sports and some more brainy activities, such as chess. This should be fun, as long as we don't compete with the Adults who chose those occupations. Last year, Liam and I played on a team of eleven Youths against three Adults who've made soccer their lifelong study. Our numbers didn't help. The three Adults handed our asses to us in a defeat so crushing I'm too embarrassed to mention the final score.

The fried dough line crawls forward. The smell is getting stronger, making my mouth water.

To keep sane, I look at the Screen again. There's a mention of secret prizes, plus a forest egg hunt, which is a new activity and something I think Liam will be willing to check out with me. When it gets darker, the day will end with the traditional aurora borealis display that will culminate in fireworks.

"Theodore," a raspy voice says from behind me. "I need you to come with me."

The Youths in front of me, including the nearly Adult-aged guy, look scared.

Reluctantly, I turn around.

All it takes is a glance at the dreaded visor to recognize the source of their fear.

It's a Guard.

My adrenaline spikes. What does he want with me? I've been careful not to get into trouble.

"What's going on?" I ask the Guard. "Did I do something wrong?"

"Please follow me," the Guard says with a steel edge to his voice. "Make haste."

"Can I at least grab a fried d—"

The Guard moves his hand in a strange motion.

I'm hit with an intense sense of relaxation.

My hands drop to my sides.

It's actually rather nice and timely that I got a chance to calm down. Resisting a Guard's commands can double or triple your Quietude—something I learned a long time ago.

"Follow me?" the Guard half-asks, half-commands.

I nod and exit the line.

The Guard turns and heads away from the food stalls. I walk to his right so he can see me. I know the drill.

As we pass by all the merriment, I curse my horrible fate. I'm tempted to ask the Guard what the problem is, but I know that might result in a longer Quietude.

What's really odd is that we're not walking toward the Quietude building. We're heading southeast, in the opposite direction.

I glimpse another Guard. This one has a female Youth walking next to him. She's wearing a long Birth Day summer dress that's somewhere between pink and magenta in hue. Spotting her red hair, I realize it's Grace, except that makes no sense. Why would *she* be in trouble? Did Miss Good Behavior finally manage to misbehave?

Grace sees me and raises an eyebrow but keeps walking, the epitome of obedience.

As we walk, an idea enters my now-paranoid mind. Is Grace here to give testimony? Is this reckoning related to my staring at her yesterday? Did she notice me watching her do those yoga poses? She didn't seem aware of me when she was exercising, and she couldn't have known what I was thinking, even if she had seen me looking. Even I don't fully understand what came over me that morning. All I know is that it was something forbidden. Still, given Grace's presence, I have to consider the unpleasant possibility that this walk is related to that incident. I imagine Adults asking me questions about that incident, and my cheeks burn.

Farther away, another Guard and another person are walking in our direction. As they approach, I recognize the Youth-hyena hybrid accompanying the Guard.

It's Owen.

This pair makes more sense. Like Liam and me, Owen is no stranger to Quietudes or trouble in general. Could *he* be the reason we're here? Did he tell the Adults about Liam and me filling his room with Food bars last night? That doesn't seem like Owen. Though he's a bully and a jackass, Owen has a code, of sorts. He's never once ratted us out, and we've returned the favor. Why change that pattern now, over such a minor prank? If it came down to it, if we told the Adults about the literal shit he gave us last night, he'd be in a lot more trouble than Liam or me. Plus, how does Grace fit into everything?

This is getting really odd.

On the bright side, I think I know where they're taking us. We're all heading straight for the cube that is the Administrative building. I've been to that place a few times before, but I'm guessing Grace is very familiar with it. The building is where one goes to rat on someone, which I never have. In my case, I was brought there to hear a lecture from the Dean on the subject of 'being a good citizen of Oasis'—something reserved for the severest troublemakers.

I can't help but ask the Guard, "Why are we going to the Administrative building?"

The Guard doesn't reply; he just does something with his hand.

I feel relaxed again and realize that maybe things aren't so bad. Maybe the three of us need to help the Adults with something that has nothing to do with us being in trouble.

My Guard and I are the first to enter the building, and he leads me through the empty corridors towards the Dean's office. Only now do I realize that the Dean, along with all the other Adults, is probably too busy with Birth Day to deal with us.

My suspicion is confirmed when we enter the waiting area. Usually there's a receptionist here. Today, there's only one person waiting for us.

Liam.

My usually hyperactive friend looks pretty calm, all things considered. I suspect he's playing it cool in front of the Guard.

"Someone will be with you shortly," the Guard says. "Don't go anywhere."

He gestures to lock the door leading out of the waiting room. When Adults do that, any Youth who tries the door-opening gesture doesn't get results. However, unlike a Quietude, confinement in a room is no big deal. It can even be seen as a vacation from Lectures, since Screens and everything else work the way they usually do. The nurse does this when Liam or I pretend to be sick. I say 'pretend' because only a few of my visits to the nurse's office have been for real. I bet the same goes for Liam. I don't know about him, but I can count on my fingers the number of times I've been genuinely sick.

"Dude," Liam whispers as soon as the door closes behind the Guard. "Why are we here?"

"I don't know—" I begin to say, but the door opens again, and the two other Guards bring in Grace and Owen.

"Thank you, Albert," says the shorter, smaller-framed Guard in a strangely textured female voice. "We'll summon you if you're needed."

The taller Guard, Albert, nods and leaves the room.

As the door closes, Liam and I exchange glances. Two things are unusual about that little exchange: First, we've only come across a female Guard once, during an incident with a fallen tree. Second, Guards *never* call each other by their first names in front of us.

Judging by the canine alertness on Owen's face, he also noticed at least one of these irregularities.

"Please sit," the female Guard says to Owen and Grace. "Theodore, be prepared to talk to us in a minute." She makes the door-locking gesture and says, "Let me just set things up."

She heads into the Dean's office.

As soon as the door closes behind the Guard, Owen jumps to his feet and looks at me. "Why-Odor?"

I don't say anything, but I'm gripped by sudden anger—anger more potent than anything I've experienced since childhood. Did Owen's stupid nickname cause it?

Oblivious to my emotional state, Owen gives Liam a onceover and says, "Li-Li-Kins? Did one of you stoop to ratting? Is that why your little girlfriend is here?" He glares at Grace before saying to Liam, "Did you decide to take lessons from the biggest snitch in the Institute?"

Grace looks like he slapped her. Her eyes glint with moisture.

Surprisingly, I feel bad for her. She must be so overwhelmed over getting into trouble with us. Also, seeing her upset makes me angrier, even if what Owen said isn't exactly undeserved. I guess I just don't like seeing anyone get bullied. I suppress my emotions, reminding myself that we're a shout away from the Guards.

"How was your dinner, Slowen?" Liam asks, using a nickname for Owen that never caught on.

"You mean the stuff you left me?" Owen replies without hesitation. "It wasn't so bad, compared to yours. Speaking of which, did you eat everything I left you, Theo, or did you guys have to split it?"

Without fully understanding what I'm doing, I get up.

Owen gives me an uncaring look and says, "Do you want to dance with me? You should wait till all this is over—"

"If you don't shut the fuck up, your new nickname will be Swollen," I say, my teeth grinding painfully in my effort to rein in my anger.

Liam gets up and stands behind me.

Grace gives me a horrified look.

Belatedly, I realize I said the F-word in front of her. My Quietude is a guarantee now, even if the Guards brought us here on benign business.

Owen looks ecstatic, as he also understands this fact.

Seething, I ball my hands into fists. He provoked me on purpose, on Birth Day of all days. Maybe I was wrong about him possessing a code.

The anticipation of losing all that Birth Day fun feeds my fury, and I step toward Owen. If I'm going to miss out on Birth Day anyway, I might as well get satisfaction of a different kind.

There's a glimmer of fear in Owen's eyes.

I feel a hand on my shoulder, and Liam says, "Dude, what the hell are you doing?"

I exhale.

He's right.

Was I about to hit Owen?

What the hell is going on with me?

The door opens.

A helmeted head peeks out, and a female voice says, "Theo, please join us."

CHAPTER EIGHT

I unclench my fists before the female Guard can see them. Taking a calming breath, I walk toward the door.

I can't help but notice she's the first Guard, and a rare Adult, to call me 'Theo' instead of 'Theodore.' Another oddity, albeit a smaller one.

"Sit there," says the male Guard, nodding toward one of the Dean's guest chairs.

He takes the Dean's chair and the female Guard sits to the side, on another guest chair.

This little exchange sets a record for the longest conversation I've ever had with a Guard. Of course, I don't mention that, knowing full well that speaking will likely get me into more trouble.

"I need you to do as I tell you," says the male Guard, his voice icy. "If you do, you'll be out of here quickly."

"Please," the female Guard adds in a softer tone. "I can imagine how much you want to get back to Birth Day."

It might be my imagination, but did she turn her helmet toward her colleague in a show of disapproval? Why would she do that? Are they playing 'good cop, bad cop,' like in the ancient movies?

"I'll do as you tell me," I say as evenly as I can. Then, with a little bitterness, I add, "It's not like I have a choice."

"Good," says the male Guard. "Put your hand to your chest."

"Huh?" I look into his mirrored helmet, but all I see is the spherically distorted reflection of my own puzzled face.

"Like this," the female guard says, placing her arm across her chest.

"Stop stalling," the male voice says sternly.

I cautiously raise my hand to my chest, and the female Guard nods in approval.

"Say, 'I consent to the Lens of Truth and swear to tell the truth and nothing but the truth,'" the male Guard says.

"What?" I look from one Guard to the other.

The male Guard drums his fingers on the desk. "Do you *want* a Quietude?"

I vigorously shake my head.

"Then say, 'I consent to the Lens of Truth.'"

"I consent to the Lens of Truth," I say, but in a small act of defiance, I do my best to sound as unenthusiastic as I can.

"And swear to tell the truth and nothing but the truth," he prompts.

"And swear to tell the truth and nothing but the truth," I repeat robotically.

A peculiar sensation washes over me. It feels as though a phase of Oneness suddenly emerged inside my consciousness, except I feel incorporeal. During Oneness, I feel connected to imaginary, faraway galaxies and stars, but now, it's as if I'm no longer inhabiting my body . . . as if I'm some kind of ancient spirit.

"State your name," comes a voice.

From where I'm 'floating,' I can't tell which Guard asked me the question. Then suddenly, back in my body, my mouth moves without my volition. It says, "Theodore."

From my perch outside my body, I find it more than odd that my mouth can speak without me willing it. And why did it use such a formal version of my name?

"How old are you, Theodore?" a voice asks.

"I turned twenty-four today," I say again without meaning to.

"Ask him something he would *want* to lie about," a voice says. "Let's make sure the compulsion really works."

"Okay," says what I have to assume is the other voice. "Bring up his neural scan."

My mouth stays shut this time. They didn't ask me a question.

"Have you done anything inappropriate today, Theodore?" a voice asks. "If not today, then how about yesterday?"

"I felt inappropriate sensations as I watched Grace do yoga," my mouth says. I'm appalled. I want to jump back into my body and stop my stupid mouth from saying these things, but I can't get back, no matter how much I yearn for control. As though to spite me, my mouth continues. "Additionally, I played a prank on Owen. We filled his room with Food bars." *No*, I mentally scream at my mouth, but I can feel it isn't done yet. Despite my titanic effort to silence it, my mouth opens and utters, "Finally, I used the F-word a few minutes ago."

At least my mouth didn't reveal that I nearly attacked Owen. I guess it doesn't consider 'nearly doing something' as 'actually doing something.'

The voices confer in hushed tones. All I hear is, "His neural activity is extremely bizarre, but the Lens is clearly working."

"What happened to Mason, Theodore?" a voice asks. "Do you know who Mason is?"

"I don't understand those two questions," my mouth says. "Are you talking about the people who worked with stones? People from History Lecture? Or do you mean the secret society?"

"Did you make the Council Forget a meeting?" a voice asks.

"I don't understand this question either," my mouth says. "What council? What meeting?"

"Why is your neural scan so erratic?" a voice asks.

"I don't know," my mouth replies.

For what feels like an hour, the voice asks more of these meaningless questions. My mouth pretty much always answers, 'No,' interspersed with the occasional, 'I don't know.'

"Do you understand what has happened?" a voice finally asks.

"No," my mouth says.

My consciousness rushes back into my body, and I instantly feel in control of my mouth and other faculties, except it's too late. I already told them about the yoga incident and the prank, not to mention my use of vulgarity.

I'm screwed.

I look from one Guard to the other. Given their reflective helmets, it's impossible to tell how upset or disappointed they are.

I look to the side.

There's a large Screen with neural activity on display.

Given one of the questions I was asked, it doesn't take a big leap to figure out that it's my scan we're looking at.

Examining my brain scans has been a sort of hobby of mine over the years. What I see here looks nothing like the scans I've seen before. The image sends a chill down my spine. Is all this abnormal activity a side effect of something they did to me?

The female Guard gets up, distracting me from my thoughts.

"Follow me," she says, her voice oddly comforting.

She heads for the door, and I get up and follow, my feet dragging as though my shoes are filled with lead.

When I enter the waiting room, Liam, Grace, and Owen look at me questioningly. I give them a shrug and make my face into as confused an expression as I can. I don't know what to tell them. Nothing that happened inside the Dean's office makes sense. Of course, even if I had anything to say, it wouldn't be safe to say it in front of the Guard.

The female Guard passes through the room, gestures for the door to open, and makes sure I exit ahead of her. She then joins me in the corridor and meticulously gestures to lock the door behind us, as though Liam and the others are crazy enough to run away under these circumstances.

Leading me down the long corridor, she brings me to a room I've never seen. Judging by its lofty size and a couple of comfortable couches in the middle, this is some kind of administrative lounge area.

"Stay here," the female Guard says. "Once we're done questioning the others, you can go back to the festivities. It shouldn't take longer than an hour."

As soon as she closes the door behind her, I begin to pace.

Nothing makes sense.

Why did she say I'd be going back to the festivities? I confessed to enough wrongdoings to be in Quietude for a long time. Why would they let that slide?

These thoughts bring me back to a deeper mystery: Why *did* I answer those questions without wanting to? And what was the purpose of those questions?

On a whim, as I circle the room, I make a door-opening gesture. I'm certain the Guard locked the door behind her, but it's not like I have anything else to do.

To my shock, the door opens.

I step across the threshold, but the strangest thing happens.

Part of me—at least I think that's what it is—says in a voice that's not my own, "Don't leave, Theo."

This voice in my head is extremely weird for several reasons, not the least of which is that it sounds feminine.

"Sit on the couch," the voice says. "You might feel disoriented as I restore your memory."

I have no idea who the voice belongs to or what it's trying to tell me, but sitting sounds like the best idea I've had in a long time. I walk over to a couch and sit down.

Out of the corner of my eye, I see the door close.

A strange avalanche of sensations floods my head. I feel a horrible sense of vertigo and a sudden need to lie down.

As soon as my head touches the cushion, drowsiness overwhelms me.

I close my eyes, and my awareness goes away.

CHAPTER NINE

I open my eyes.

Did I just wake up?

Looking around the room, I find it too large to be the one Liam and I share.

Then it hits me: this is the Administrative building.

I remember what happened.

I remember *everything* that happened.

I also realize I'm no longer alone in the room.

A familiar pixie-haired woman is sitting next to me on the couch.

"Phoe," I exclaim, sitting up. "I'm back."

"Don't talk out loud," she says and gives me a worried smile.

I examine my memories.

As far as I can tell, they're all back. Then again, I didn't think I was missing any information a minute ago, when I was missing *everything*.

I recall Phoe and everything that happened from the very first day she spoke to me. I remember Mason from when we were little kids to his demise. I also recall, in detail, what it felt like to *not* remember these things. It's like that 'on the tip of your tongue' sensation. After you *do* recall the trivial detail that eluded your brain, you can't believe you blanked on something so basic. Except in my case, this happened with hordes of important facts.

I also realize how much easier my life was when I didn't remember these things. How much happier I was in my ignorance.

Phoe's fears about my split identity weren't exactly valid. Yes, a more innocent Theo existed for a time, but he isn't dead. He's part of me, the Theo who's more complete but wishes he wasn't. I internalize everything he experienced the way I imagine drunk ancients internalized all the crazy things they did while intoxicated.

"This really isn't a good time to philosophize about the question of identity," Phoe says in an urgent whisper and moves closer to me. "We need to talk, right after I do this."

Before I understand what's happening, her lips are on mine.

I return the kiss. Somehow, the physical closeness clears the remaining grogginess from my mind. I remember doing this with her, the day before yesterday. Only it feels different right now. More primal.

The kiss continues, and she moves closer to me on the couch. She's so close that her soft chest brushes against my upper arm.

I feel a stirring.

It's familiar.

It's what happened yesterday when I was watching Grace, only this sensation is many times stronger.

Phoe pulls away, her eyes narrowed into slits.

"I still can't believe *that* happened." She crosses her arms in front of her chest. "I can't believe you were lusting after Grace."

"Phoe," I think and stare into her eyes. "Are you actually jealous? You know I didn't remember—"

"Bah." Her lips twist. "Why should I be? After all, I'm literally a heartless AI. Why would you think it's wrong to be attracted to someone else?"

"Phoe, I wasn't myself." I put my hand on hers, feeling the warmth of her skin. "More importantly, I don't *want* Grace." I think this with emphasis, doing my best not to blush at the extreme taboo of this topic. "If I did . . ." I inhale, unsure how to proceed. "If I decided to want anyone *in that way*, there's no doubt in my mind it would be *you*." As I subvocalize it, it occurs to me that this is how I really feel and that I was hiding this truth from myself.

Phoe looks uncertain, so I squeeze her hand and say mentally, "If you need my permission to scan my mind to prove I'm telling you the truth, go ahead."

She gives me an unreadable look. Then, as suddenly as before, she kisses me, almost as though trying to catch me off-guard.

Not missing a beat, I kiss her back.

As we explore each other's mouths, the kiss becomes an outlet for something else. Nervousness and tension leave my body, and a meditation-like trance comes over me as I focus on the way her lips affect me. My breathing becomes shallow, and I put my hand on her lower back, feeling the delicate curve of her spine.

"Look, Theo," Phoe says, reluctantly pulling away. "I know I started this, but we really ought to stop. If they watch the recording of this room, they might wonder why you're moving your lips and tongue like a crazy person. It's an especially bad idea given that the neural scan they saw was a hot mess."

Her words work as effectively as a cold shower.

"Did you open the door for me a moment ago?" I subvocalize, changing the subject. "And if so, why did you stop me from leaving?"

"No, I didn't open that door." She gives me a wide grin. "That was all you."

"Me?" I subvocalize so loudly it almost comes out as a whisper. "But how? Did the female Guard—who must be Fiona—not lock it?"

"Yes, it is Fiona, and yes, she locked it all right. You just opened it anyway."

"How? Only Adults can undo those types of locks."

Phoe's eyes are glowing. "And the Elderly."

"Right," I think. "What does that have to do with me?" A flash of insight hits me. "Wait a minute. Are you saying what I think you're saying?"

"When Birth Day started, I modified your age, like I told you I would." She's as excited as Liam after a prank. "As far as the back end of all the security systems in Oasis is concerned, you're now ninety years old."

I stare at her blankly. The implications are too far-reaching.

"I can open any door the Adults can?"

"Yes, and many, many more." Phoe's feet drum on the floor. "For example, the Adults can't cross the boundary into the Elderly territory, but you can. You can pretty much go anywhere you want, as long as we overcome the minor problem of your youthful looks."

"Yeah." I chuckle nervously. "*That* itsy-bitsy problem."

"I have an idea about that—a plan of sorts," Phoe says. "If it works, you'll be able to travel across Oasis without any issues. But before we talk about that, I have to show you something else, something way more urgent." She looks distant for a fraction of a second. "Crap, they're coming. We should continue this *after* they lead you out of here."

"Lead me out?" I think and look at her with barely concealed hope. "Are they letting me go?"

Phoe looks at the door instead of answering.

The door opens.

A Guard is standing there.

"Theodore," he says.

I get up.

I think this is Jeremiah, though his voice is hard to recognize through the helmet's distortion. I can tell this isn't Fiona, because the voice isn't female and he's taller than her.

"Follow me," maybe-Jeremiah says and waves at me.

"He tried to soothe you again," Phoe whispers as a voice in my head.

"I wish it worked," I think, feeling my heart racing as I'm forced to walk swiftly to keep up with probably-Jeremiah's angry gait.

"Looks like they won't give me a Quietude despite all those things my mouth blabbed on about while I was under the Lens's compulsion," I think at Phoe.

"No," Phoe replies. "They probably don't care about such trivialities today. They're focused on the investigation for the Envoy—the investigation I might 'aid' very soon. Also, they'll likely make you Forget you ever saw them, which would make a Quietude odd, since you wouldn't recall how you got into trouble."

"Go," the Guard says when we reach the outdoors. He waves toward the Birth Day celebrations in the distance. "Stay out of trouble."

I immediately walk away, not needing to be told *this* twice.

Maybe-Jeremiah goes back into the building, presumably to get the others.

"Just as I thought," Phoe says. "He tried to make you Forget everything that happened. Go somewhere private and do it quickly, unless you want to run into Liam, Grace, or Owen."

I head for the nearest structure, which happens to be the cuboid Lectures building. Seeing it deserted might be interesting. This idea never came to me on prior Birth Days because there's always too much other fun stuff to do.

Phoe is silent until I enter the building, walk into a Lectures Hall, and sit.

"Okay," she says and brings up one of the giant Screens that Instructors sometimes use to put their notes on. "This is that urgent bit of information I mentioned earlier. Just don't panic."

I bet the words 'don't panic' are among the most ominous phrases ever uttered, on par with 'oh no' and 'this will only hurt a bit.'

On the Screen, I see the Dean's room, only it's just Jeremiah and Fiona there now.

"He's just a Youth," Fiona says forcefully. "Despite all the technology in the world, they sometimes have hormonal imbalances. You know what those things can do. Isn't it why they're kept separate? As a Youth, I once got my period despite all the preventative measures. My neural scan prior to that was—"

"Stop." Jeremiah's white-gloved hand covers his helmeted head as though he's dodging a thrown object. "Are you trying to make me vomit?"

"It's just biology," Fiona says, but Jeremiah raises his hand, palm out, to stop her from speaking.

"I'm not aware of any natural reason his neural scan would look like *that*," he says, lowering his hand. "He's a male, so your disgusting little story doesn't apply. However, I *have* seen scans of Youths and Adults who were deemed insane, and though his is slightly different from those, it's similar enough that I still insist he be Forgotten, for the good of our society. He's not violent yet, but that is where this usually leads."

"Fine. We'll talk to the Council, and together, we'll decide." She cracks her knuckles.

"I don't see the point in wasting our time with bureaucracy. We have an investigation to conduct and—"

"Have you ever Forgotten someone without formally clearing it with the Council?" Fiona places her hands sharply on her hips. "Because you asking me this makes me wonder—"

"Of course not," Jeremiah says, a little too quickly and defensively.

"Then I don't understand the necessity of bypassing proper protocols this time either," she says, her tone cold and formal.

"Like I said, the reason should be obvious, and time is of the essence," Jeremiah says. "We learned nothing in regards to our ultimate goal, and instead of needless Council deliberation, as two senior members, surely we can—"

"My vote would be against Forgetting him," Fiona says, raising her chin. "I will say so at the Council meeting, should we have one.

If you want to save time, we can easily agree to dismiss this matter, as we don't need the Council for that. Otherwise, the whole Council will have to weigh in."

"Fine." Jeremiah's posture is tense. "Theodore can wait. Let's gather the Instructors and Mason's more distant acquaintances."

"Sounds good." Fiona squares her shoulders. "I'll get Filomena and George to start. Meanwhile, you let the children go. They've missed enough of the festivities because of your impatience, and until and unless we bring his neural scan to the attention of the Council, 'they' also includes Theo."

Jeremiah storms out of the room without saying another word.

The Screen goes blank.

"Shit," I whisper to Phoe. "Do you think they'll take it to the Council? And if they do, how do you think they'll vote?"

"I don't know," Phoe says. "Which is why getting me more resources is a matter of priority. With more resources, I should be able to figure out a way to manipulate the Elderly without risking exposure to the Envoy."

I recall her talking about an idea she had, something to do with a very dubious-sounding Test the Adults take before they become the Elderly. Only then, her excuse for having me take the Test was to help her figure out where we are in the cosmos.

"I'm not denying that knowing our current location in space and time is an important task," Phoe says, pursing her lips. "But I'm insulted if you're insinuating your wellbeing is less important to me in any way."

I realize I hinted at something like that, which is unfair to Phoe. She has literally been a lifesaver. Also, even if she is being a little self-serving when it comes to regaining her mental capacity, how can I blame her, especially after I just experienced Forgetting so intimately? Unsure how to verbalize any of this, I change the subject. "You said you could 'aid' in their investigation," I say. "Can you tell me about *that?*"

"Ah." She gives me an impish grin. "Remember that Keeper archive?"

"Yes."

"When Jeremiah showed it to Fiona, he also, without meaning to, led me right to it." She summons a chair and sits down. "Now I can plant this little pearl in there for him to find."

The Screen comes to life with a grainy image of a Council meeting.

"Ladies and Gentlemen of the Council," Fiona says in the recording. "Despite your vote, I urge you to reconsider." Her eyes look sad. "You know I was against Theodore's Forgetting." She gives Jeremiah a seething look. "But this new turn of events—the *torture* of a Youth—"

"Questioning," Jeremiah corrects. "Persuasive questioning."

"Torture," Fiona insists. "I find the very idea abhorrent. Why don't you talk to the Envoy? There are other options when it comes to obtaining information. Perhaps the Lens of—"

"I will not bother the Envoy with this matter," Jeremiah says, his eyes beaming wrath. "He would want me to present him with answers and results, not problems for *him* to solve. You choose to ignore the fact that this Youth has resisted Punish, Forgetting, and a slew of other technologies. Why would the Lens of Truth be any different?"

"Because—"

Phoe waves her hand to pause the video, stopping Fiona mid-argument.

"Don't worry," Phoe says. "What you just saw is not *it*. Quite the opposite. I will delete this part of the recording so thoroughly, even *I* won't be able to find an echo of it ever again. I kept it to show *you*, so you'll understand the context of what's about to follow in the portion of the video I plan to use."

"This recording is from two days ago, right?" I subvocalize. "It's from that meeting you made them Forget?"

"Yes, it's from that meeting," Phoe says. "Fiona really was against them torturing you, as you saw. I recorded this because I wanted to know how they voted. Plus, I had some free time while you were in the IRES game. And now, my recording is about to pay big dividends."

With a motion, she fast-forwards the video.

"This," she says. "This is what I'll cut out and stick in the archive."

She resumes the video.

Fiona storms toward the exit, but before she reaches it, she turns around, gives every Council member a baleful glare, and says, "As of now, I formally resign as a member of this ruling body."

The room comes alive with hushed murmurs and outraged whispers.

To Jeremiah, Fiona says, "Once I'm officially off the Council, I wish to Forget this latest decision . . . and I hope it eats a hole through the amorphous pit you call your conscience."

Not waiting for anyone's response, Fiona storms out of the room.

Phoe makes the Screen go blank again.

"Wow," I subvocalize. "She quit the Council *and* told them off."

"Yep. If I hadn't made them Forget, it would've happened that way, but as is, they don't remember her outburst. Once he sees this, Jeremiah might strongly suspect Fiona to be the person he's looking for," Phoe says triumphantly. "She has a strong motive. She basically told them she hates their guts. On top of that, she even said something about Forgetting."

"Can't she accuse him of faking this video?" I think.

"She could, but it would be reasonable for him to state that he doesn't have the resources or capabilities to create something like that," Phoe says, then gives me a thoughtful look. "I have to say, faking a video is a very interesting idea. It wouldn't be much harder than manipulating Augmented Reality—"

"Okay," I think in an effort to keep Phoe focused. "Even if everyone thought this video was real, I don't see how it would help us."

"Are you nuts? If Jeremiah has a suspect, he'll stop looking for you. That aside, it's the oldest trick in the world." Phoe tilts her head. "We're dividing and conquering them. While Fiona and Jeremiah fight each other, we'll do what we need to do: the Test. The likeliest outcome of their fight will be Jeremiah reporting Fiona to the Envoy. From there, they'll question Fiona with the Lens of Truth. The questioning will prove her to be innocent, except they might think she made herself Forget. Things will get complicated for them, which is great for us. Maybe Jeremiah will talk the Envoy into letting him question more Council members. He's clearly itching to do that. If so, that will give us even more time. And if the Envoy relaxes enough to stop monitoring Jeremiah's brain—which is likely—I can then deal with Jeremiah's wish to get rid of you by using the resources I currently have. This is only a contingency on the off chance that you're *unable* to stop the Test. If you succeed with the Test, we'll have a ton more options."

"I like that," I think, mulling over her long explanation. "But what about Fiona? What will happen to her if they think she's guilty?"

"If the Lens of Truth doesn't clear her, you mean? I guess Jeremiah will grant her what she wanted anyway. He'll kick her off the Council."

"But—"

"Look, if you're so concerned about her, I have this other idea based on something you said, but don't worry about it for now."

"Okay," I think, feeling a bit less like one of those ancient lambs going to the slaughter. "Tell me your plan. How do I take this Test?"

As Phoe outlines the start of her crazy plan, I rethink my sense of relief. If I *were* a lamb, I wouldn't be just going to the slaughter; I'd be picking a fight with a wolf right before entering the slaughterhouse.

DIMA ZALES

CHAPTER TEN

I walk back to the Birth Day celebrations. It takes me some time, but I finally spot the perfect group of people for what Phoe has in mind.

There, by a tent, the Dean and a few other people who work with him are speaking with professional tennis players.

As luck would have it, there aren't many Youths around them. That's good. I'd rather my peers not witness what I'm about to do, since word might reach Liam and I'd have a hard time explaining this to him—or anyone else, for that matter.

I confidently stroll to the middle of the dozen or so people.

They look at me curiously.

I inhale a good amount of air into my lungs.

The Dean seems on a verge of saying hello, but he never gets the chance to speak.

As loudly as I can, I say, "Fuck. Vagina. Shit."

The silence that follows reminds me of the calm that preluded ancient storms. Even the distant sounds of music seem muted.

"I lost a bet," I say to the petrified Dean. "Don't worry. I'll make my way to the Quietude building."

As I walk away, I say every other obscene word I can think of. I do this at a much quieter volume than my introduction, but loud enough for the Dean to hear. After a few choice words, I find it surprisingly hard to keep this up. As I get farther away, I'm convinced I've repeated myself at least a couple times. Still, it's not originality that counts, but the quality of the words. On a few occasions, I cheat by combining words I already mentioned with other forbidden and even mundane words, getting pretty creative with the combinations. Phoe is laughing so hard she's holding her stomach, but she still manages to give me a few suggestions—words the Dean will probably have to look up in an anatomy book, if he isn't too preoccupied with his wilting ears.

What's particularly funny, in a purely morbid sort of way, is that no one stops me as I go. They keep their distance and don't utter a single word as I walk toward the Witch Prison of my own volition.

I assume the Dean, or one of the other Adults, gathered his wits shortly after I left, because after a few minutes, a Guard heads my way from the pentagonal prism that is my destination.

"This is going great so far," I subvocalize as sarcastically as I can. "You sure I shouldn't have gotten naked, covered myself with tar, and rolled around in some feathers?"

"I think it would've helped if you had licked the Dean's bald head like I suggested," Phoe says, still chuckling. "But I think even without that, we got the point across."

I give her a chiding look, but that only adds to her merriment.

As the Guard gets closer to me, however, Phoe grows serious again.

"Remember, I'll have a hard time getting in touch with you once you're in the Witch Prison," she reminds me. "I figured out how to see through the Guards' cameras, but that's still fairly limited—"

"And we hope the Envoy will have similar troubles," I repeat, my mental voice a parody of hers. "Isn't that why I'm doing this crazy stunt to begin with?"

"Even if the Envoy can see everything that happens inside the Quietude building—which I doubt—my plan should still work, assuming the Envoy is not all-knowing and all-seeing," Phoe says. "And if he *were* all-knowing and all-seeing, we'd be dead already. The Faraday cage of that building provides us an extra bonus, because if he *can't* see inside, it turns a good plan into a great one."

Since I know what the plan *is*, I can't help but mutter some more curses, this time as a way to show my opinion on the 'greatness' of this so-called plan.

When I meet the Guard, he stands there, arms folded over his chest, and says nothing.

With disappointment, I note that this Guard is much too short and stocky for what we need. He's closer to Liam's build than mine. That means I'll have to work with a slightly more complicated version of an already-dubious plan.

"I'll go with you," I say, failing to not sound belligerent. "Lead the way."

The Guard gestures.

"I can't believe he tried to Pacify you!" Phoe exclaims. "These people really do abuse their power."

I stay quiet and do my best impersonation of getting Pacified. Having actually felt this when Jeremiah did it to me helps my acting.

The Guard is convinced enough by my performance to turn around and head in the direction of our intended destination.

As we walk, Phoe repeats the remaining steps of the plan. If I weren't pretending to be Pacified, I'd be screaming obscenities again.

"Good luck," Phoe says as we're about to enter the Prison. "I know you'll do great."

"Thanks," I think grumpily. "I hope you're right."

We walk in.

Phoe doesn't talk anymore, but I derive comfort from the knowledge that I'm not completely on my own. She got me out of here the day before yesterday.

After walking the maze-like corridors, we reach a nondescript door, and the Guard gestures.

The door to the room opens.

The Guard stands in the corridor expectantly.

I walk in, and he closes the door, locking me in.

So far so good—or at least, according to plan.

I look at the table and whistle. There are three bars of tasteless Prison Food. That means, under normal circumstances, I'd be stuck in this room for at least three days.

I walk back to the door and count to a thousand to make sure the Guard who brought me here is gone.

When I put my ear to the door and listen, I hear nothing.

A ghostly Screen appears in the air next to me.

A cursor flickers on the Screen, and a single character shows up and types the letter 'G.' Then the second one appears with the letter 'O.'

I make an okay sign in case Phoe can see me and wave my hand at the door in the standard 'open' gesture.

The door unlocks with a loud *click*.

This first part of the plan didn't even require Phoe's help. All I did was use my newly acquired Elderly access.

Annoyingly, the Screen now says: *I told you so.*

I shake my head and walk out of the room.

The Screen follows me. On it, Phoe types out: *Two lefts and a right.* When I make the first turn, the Screen flickers and disappears.

I walk down the next corridor, making sure to turn carefully when I reach the end.

The second left takes me down a winding corridor that looks like the one we passed when the Guard brought me in here. I could be wrong, though. All the corridors in this place look the same in their washed-out grayness.

Before I turn right, I crouch and look around the corner. My target is where he should be, and this Guard matches both my height and weight.

Great. Finally something is going my way.

The Guard is leisurely walking away from me, so all I see is his back.

This is actually good news.

The bad news is that, according to Phoe's estimations, I have to get closer, within six feet to be precise, to execute the next part of the plan.

I enter the corridor as slowly and softly as I can. My feet are barely touching the floor.

The problem with approaching the Guard stealthily is that I'm moving at the same speed as him. If I keep this up, I'll never catch up with him.

I take longer strides, trying my best to keep quiet.

The ghostly Screen shows up again and asks: *What's the holdup?*

I walk a few more steps and decide the distance between us should be sufficient.

As I stop, my shoes make a barely noticeable rustle against the floor.

There should be no way the Guard heard it, yet he slows his pace.

Crap.

He heard me.

"Oh well," I think in case Phoe can hear me. "It won't matter in a moment anyway."

I raise my hand the way Phoe instructed me, the way the Guards do when they try to Pacify *me*. Phoe figured out that if I make my wrist flick stronger, the Pacify effect will be more intense and will nearly knock out the target.

The Guard turns around.

I repeat the gesture.

He's too spry for someone under the effects of the Pacify.

The letters show up frantically on the Screen: *Shit. It didn't work.*

The Screen clears, then says: *They must be protected against another Elderly using Pacify on them, which was unexpected.* The

Screen clears again, then in very big font: *Why are you still standing there? Abort mission and run.*

"You said this was a great plan," I think angrily at the Screen.

Run already.

The Guard is a leap away.

I'm not sure running will be *that* effective, so I decide to improvise.

"My door just opened," I say to him in a meek voice. "I stepped out and got lost."

The Guard performs his own Pacify gesture at me as he reaches for the Stun Stick on his belt.

Why is he going for that Stick? Does he know Pacify didn't work? Or did he see my attempt to Pacify him?

I slump as though I'm Pacified.

At the same time, through my half-closed eyelids, I watch his hand.

He's still reaching for that Stick, leaving me little choice.

I have to attack the Guard.

As I mentally prepare for what I have to do, I can't help but feel a sense of déjà vu. I confronted a Guard inside the nightmarish vision of the IRES game. *That* fight didn't go so well for me. I would've died had it not been for the in-game History Instructor driving a tractor into him, something I'm pretty sure can't happen *now.*

The Screen shows up in the air again with a very pertinent message: *Act.*

I stop thinking and become motion. As quickly as I can, I squat and sweep my right leg around, hoping to bring the Guard down to the floor.

The Guard jumps.

Fighting panic, I jump back up and prepare to rush him.

The Guard takes out his Stun Stick and fiddles with its controls. I use his momentary distraction to ram my shoulder into his midsection.

The Stun Stick falls out of his hands, but I can't tell if it's from pain or the kinetic energy of my impact. With his helmet on, it's hard to tell what my opponent is feeling or where he's looking, which puts me at a big disadvantage.

My hit didn't slow him down much, though, because seamlessly, he slams his fist into the side of my head.

My ear explodes with burning pain.

I grit my teeth and ignore the blood pounding in my temples. I channel the anger flooding through my system into a not-so-gentlemanly maneuver I also utilized against that virtual Guard.

My leg goes up, and my foot connects with the crotch area of the Guard's white outfit.

If the pain in my foot is any indication, the kick was strong. Had this been a soccer game, the ball would've flown far beyond the field.

The Guard stops.

Again, the visor makes it hard to see how I did, but I'm hoping the stop means he's in pain.

Capitalizing on my success, I put my right foot behind the man's ankle and push.

I'm hoping he trips and falls. When I used this trick back in kindergarten, Owen certainly fell.

The jerky motion and my foot's odd position almost tip *me* over, but the Guard keeps his balance as though his feet are glued to the gray floor.

And just when I think things can't get any worse, they do.

The Guard sidesteps, and before I fully understand what's happening, my neck ends up in a chokehold between the Guard's forearm and bicep.

Blood drains from my face.

I've seen this scenario in movies. It typically involves the hero sneaking up on the bad guy in an attempt to get rid of him silently. It never ends well for the bad guy.

The Guard squeezes.

I grab his arm to pry it away.

It's like trying to pry apart welded pieces of steel.

Fighting panic, I attempt to inhale.

Nothing.

The Guard's chokehold is preventing air from entering my lungs.

CHAPTER ELEVEN

I kick backward, but the Guard dodges. I stomp on his foot, but the white spacesuit shoes must have steel toes, because he shows no sign that I hurt him. Instead, the Guard tightens his grip. My squirming doesn't have any effect on him.

After struggling for a few seconds, I realize something rather odd. Though I haven't taken a breath in at least thirty seconds, I'm handling the oxygen deprivation relatively well. In the IRES version of this fight, when the imaginary Guard choked me, my vision went white and I became faint almost immediately. Granted, that was a simulated experience and the Guard was using his hands, not this elbow grip, but given the game's ultra-realism, I imagine the principle of choking someone to death would hold, and if so, I should be feeling what I felt then. Why isn't it happening? Why do I feel relatively okay, with no signs that I'm about to pass out and die?

Then I remember the Respirocytes—the nano machines Phoe turned on inside my body. Naturally, when she returned my memory, she reactivated everything else, including that technology.

That must explain why I'm still okay, but without consulting Phoe, I have no idea how long I'll last.

I'm not even sure if the Guard is blocking my air supply or the flow of blood to my brain. If it's the latter, it might be bad. I can go a long time without air, but I'm less sure about having my blood flow restricted. The Respirocytes travel through my bloodstream, so even they can't save me from blacking out if I stay in this position long enough—however long that is.

I formulate a quick plan.

Acting like someone who's running out of energy, I lazily tug at the Guard's forearm.

He keeps his hold on my neck.

I have no idea how long I've been in his grip or how much time it would take for a normal person to get so weak they'd stop fighting, but I hope the Guard doesn't know those statistics either. It's not something that's useful in our violence-free society.

I slow my movements.

He doesn't let go.

I let my body go slack, pretending to pass out.

The Guard keeps his hold on my neck.

My panic reaches new heights. If my bluff doesn't work, he might stand here long enough to choke me to death—with or without the Respirocytes.

I fight the panic and the need to stiffen my body. I keep my limbs relaxed, the way someone who's lost consciousness would.

Then I genuinely begin to feel faint, and with that, the panic returns with exponential intensity. In another second, I won't be able to stand here, slack, pretending to be passed out. I'll be forced to fight again.

The Guard loosens his grip and lowers me to the ground, careful not to drop me.

Through the slit in my eyelids, I spot the Stun Stick.

If I reach with my right hand, I might get it, but I'd give away my true condition. The problem is, he still has me in that chokehold.

I stall as the Guard lays me on my stomach and lets go of my neck.

Surreptitiously, I take a small inhale.

Though my lungs feel unsatisfyingly empty, I know I can rely on the Respirocyte technology to keep me oxygenated.

The Guard grabs my left arm and pulls it to the right.

I don't fight him at first, but when I feel something click on my left wrist, I decide not to wait any longer. As swiftly as I can, I push up off the ground and leap for the Stun Stick.

Whatever the Guard snapped around my left wrist tightens painfully, and I realize I'm tethered to the Guard somehow. Reaching out with my free hand, I stretch my fingers to grasp the handle of the Stun Stick.

The Guard pulls on the thing tethering us together.

My left arm threatens to pop out of its socket, but my fingers close around the Stun Stick.

Swallowing a scream, I shove the Stun Stick into the Guard's thigh and squeeze the button so hard the bones in my thumb crack.

The Guard slumps against me.

Sucking in a lungful of air, I turn around.

The thing on my left arm is some kind of handcuff, though instead of being made of metal, as depicted in ancient media, these are made of the same dull gray material as the Witch Prison's walls. The Guard was holding on to the second cuff right up until I zapped him. I was lucky he never finished cuffing my right arm, or else I'd be toast.

I fiddle with the handcuff, but it doesn't yield.

The ghostly Screen shows up in the air and tells me: *Gesture for it to open the way you would a door. Then do the same to the Guard's helmet.*

I gesture hysterically at the cuffs.

Both the cuff on my hand and its empty cousin open with a loud *click.*

Emboldened, I repeat the motion at the Guard's helmet.

There's a hollow *whoosh* sound, and a gap appears between the Guard's helmet and the neckpiece of his white outfit.

As a precaution, I unload another Stun Stick charge into him. He doesn't react.

Content with my victim's passivity, I take off his helmet.

The man's eyes are closed and his hawkish features are calm, as though he's taking a nap. His hair is mostly black, with only the beginning of gray at his temples. Like the other Guards, he looks like a younger Elderly. I hope that'll allow him to survive the boatload of Stun Stick zappings coming his way.

I put aside the helmet and work on taking off the rest of his suit.

Phoe's plan, for all its craziness, is simple: to make sure no one recognizes me as I make my way to the Elderly section, I'll dress as a Guard. It worked for Fiona and Jeremiah, so the same idea should work for me. The crazy part was the cursing-assisted Quietude, plus the actual act of getting the Guard to give up his suit.

When I finish with the man's boots, I begin to undress instead of disappearing my clothes with a gesture, so I can leave the Guard dressed in something rather than naked.

Before I put on the Guard's suit, I zap him with the Stick to make sure he stays knocked out.

I put on the helmet, and the world becomes dimmer but with a bunch of overlaying visualizations. This helmet has something like a Screen built into the visor. As cool as it is, I don't dare play with it, at least not until I bring Phoe's plan to its conclusion.

Haphazardly, I put my old clothes on the unconscious man. Then, using his handcuffs, I cuff his hands behind his back and make a 'close' gesture.

The restraints seem to stay put.

Now the hardest part begins. I drag the unconscious Elderly by his legs and pause every so often to zap him. I'm not sure if it's from my adrenaline or the Respirocytes, but backtracking to my room isn't as exhausting as I imagined.

When I get back to my designated Quietude room, I drag the Guard inside and thoughtfully put him on the bed. I zap him one last time, put the Stun Stick on my belt, and exit the room.

This is the last part of Phoe's plan.

I make a door-closing gesture, and the door slams shut.

There's a locking sound, then an unusual crunching noise. Phoe said she would jam the door once it was closed, so I assume that's what the crunch was about.

The ghostly Screen comes to life and confirms that the door is jammed. It also informs me of where I should go to make sure I don't run into any of 'my fellow Guards.'

I run the whole way, which makes my trip *out* of the Prison last about a minute.

"Phoe?" I think as soon as I exit the final door. "Is this helmet preventing you from talking to me?"

"Not at all," Phoe says, her voice coming from my right.

I turn and see her standing there, grinning as she looks me up and down.

"Your helmet isn't attached," she says and makes a closing motion with her hand.

I hear a click around my neck, and the controls in my visor really come to life.

A map of Oasis appears in my peripheral vision, as well as a million other inputs I don't understand.

To top it off, the air smells different, ozone-like.

"That's because you're wearing an actual space suit." Phoe's voice sounds like it's coming from somewhere inside my helmet. "My guess is, a while back, the Elderly repurposed the spacesuits that came with the Ship. It makes sense. Unlike most other clothes in Oasis, these suits were manufactured on Earth and not via nano assembly, so no one 'malicious,' like you or I, can recreate one with a gesture. I guess they also figured it would be helpful for the police force to have a distinctive look, not to mention the many helpful functions of the suit." Her grin widens. "These suits take care of the wearer's bodily functions and needs so a Guard can focus on—"

"Yuck." I wrinkle my nose. "You're telling me the Guard used this suit as a bathroom?"

She looks thoughtful for a moment, then says, "I just examined the suit's sensors. It's as close to a sterile environment as it gets. You have nothing to worry about."

"Okay," I say, trying hard not to think about the suit as a toilet. "What now?"

"Walk toward the Adult section." Phoe points in the direction of the pine forest. "Though my door-jamming trick worked, we don't know how much time we have. If the Envoy is somehow keeping an eye on the Prison—"

"Didn't you say I have to be the last person to take the Elderly Test? Isn't that the only way to make sure no one notices its absence for a year?" I ask as I walk toward the forest. "It's not evening yet."

"This is why we're taking our time getting there." Phoe walks next to me with a cheerful spring in her step. "I was thinking we could wait in the forest by the Barrier on the Adult side of Oasis until sunset."

"Isn't that dangerous?" I glance at her. "Even in this disguise, if we come across another Guard, they might ask me something, and I'd be screwed."

"True," Phoe says. "Which is why we should do our best not to run into any Guards. Fortunately, your nifty new suit has all sorts of sensors that can help us." She makes a gesture, and I suddenly see the world in blue and red colors.

"That's heat vision," Phoe explains and returns my vision to normal. "In that mode, you can see people behind trees, long before they get the chance to see you."

"Cool," I think. "That *should* help."

"Yep, it should, and there's another thing I want to do," Phoe says. "Something that will allow me to keep you safe, but I'm afraid you won't like it."

"My list of dislikes is growing, that's for sure. What is it this time? I know you'll tell me anyway. You just want me to want you to tell me."

"Just keep an open mind, please," she says with a slight pout.

"Fine, I will. Come out with it already."

"Okay." Phoe stops and looks at me. "I want to ride your body."

CHAPTER TWELVE

My cheeks and the tips of my ears get uncomfortably warm. I've seen enough ancient movies to understand that expression. Riding someone means—

"Great, now that your hormones are normalizing, you're turning into a horndog." Phoe puts her hands on her hips. "Whether I want intimacy has nothing to do with what I'm talking about. You're thinking of the innuendo, but I'm speaking more literally. I want to ride your body the way I rode Jeremiah the other day, when I had him untie you."

"You mean when he was moving like a puppet?" I subvocalize. My blush disappears as blood leaves my face. Instinctively, I increase my pace, as if trying to run away from Phoe.

"Perhaps that wasn't the best reminder," she says, hurrying to catch up with me. "Jeremiah was moving erratically because I hadn't mastered the interface between the nanos and the neurons in the motor cortex, which made that episode a little unnerving. I have since been looking into perfecting that interface, as well as involving more brain regions, such as the cerebellum, parts of the frontal lobe, and the basal ganglia. I believe I can take over walking and running for you, and do it so smoothly it will be indistinguishable from your own behavior."

I stop walking and consider this. Somehow the idea that I wouldn't be moving in jerky motions makes me feel a bit better about this proposition.

"But why?" I think to myself and to Phoe. "Why do you want to control my body like that?"

"When we get to the Testing facility, once you initiate the Test like every other VR session, your consciousness will not be present in your body. Given the tight security and the Envoy situation, I don't want you standing there like a statue."

"Hmm," I think and resume walking. "I haven't thought that far ahead. When you put it like that, it sounds like a good idea."

"Yeah, and I promise it won't feel unpleasant, if that's what you're worried about," she says and also starts walking.

"If my mind is busy with VR, I won't feel anything anyway," I think.

"True, but I want to test it out while you're present in your mind. You see, this isn't just for VR. There are other interesting possibilities. For example, say I see you're in danger. Right now, I'd have to tell you, which takes time. If I mastered this skill, and you gave me permission, I could move your body away from the danger on my own, which might save your life, but I need to make sure you're okay with me doing this when you're still conscious of it."

I walk silently for a few minutes, considering her proposal. At the core, my reservations about this idea are irrational. I fear Phoe taking away my control, but that's silly. If she wanted to do that, she would have. Instead, she's asking for permission.

"Fear of technology is so ingrained in you that I can't blame you for being wary." Phoe's tone is almost tender.

"Let's try it," I subvocalize firmly, mostly out of a sense of rebellion. I always want to do the opposite of what the Adults are trying to brainwash me to do.

"Okay," Phoe thinks. "Ready?"

"Do it," I think.

I keep walking.

Nothing happens for at least twenty steps.

"So?" Phoe says. "That wasn't so bad, was it?"

"What are you talking about? You didn't do anything." I examine my legs and arms and find that they're completely under my control.

"I took control," Phoe says. "First with every other step, and then all the steps between the eighth and the fifteenth."

"You were walking for me some of the time? But I didn't feel it."

"Your brain must be trying to sustain the illusion of free will," Phoe says thoughtfully. "I've read about that. It's a form of confabulation."

"Or it didn't work," I think, more to myself.

I stop.

"Why did you stop?" Phoe asks, her voice taunting, almost challenging.

I think back.

It was just one of those spur of the moment decisions. I wanted to stop, at least that's how it felt.

"Except *I* made you stop." Phoe holds her hand out to stop my objections and says, "How about this?"

My gloved hand smacks the visor of my helmet.

It's a strange sensation, like maybe I wanted to do that, yet I'm beginning to doubt myself.

Then I notice I'm hopping on one foot.

"Okay, Phoe, I believe you. Please stop humiliating me," I say, picturing what I would think if I ever saw a Guard hopping like this. Once my feet are planted firmly on the ground, I add, "This isn't what I expected at all. If anything, it's less scary than what I feared. I thought it would be like the Lens of Truth, like I'd be a spectator trapped outside my body."

"I just read some literature on the subject, and I'm not that surprised by your reaction anymore. Willful control over muscles is a very strange thing for human beings. Studies have proven that certain actions and behaviors begin *before* people consciously realize they're doing them. That is, muscle activity starts before individuals press the button indicating they feel like moving that muscle. Many actions happen on autopilot, like yanking a hand away from a hot object. I suspect that when I do something minor, like taking over your walk, your consciousness assumes you're still in control. When it's something you have no reason to do, then we get into interesting territory. Oh, and by the way, did you notice that as I was speaking, I was walking for you?"

I stop and think about whether I was consciously controlling my legs. It's hard to say. Walking can be done quite mindlessly at times.

"All right, Phoe. If you wanted to make me feel comfortable with this process, you're on the right track. What do you want to try next?"

"We should test this closer to the actual scenario I'm worried about, with your mind in VR and me controlling you," Phoe says. "Why don't you go into your man cave while I keep walking for you?"

Without hesitation, I make the requisite gesture, and the white tunnel takes me to my man cave.

Phoe is already standing there, between an old cannon and something that looks like a guillotine. She extends her palm and initiates a hologram-like image that shows me walking toward the forest in the real world.

"Your gait looks good," she says, looking at the video feed.

She's right. I look like a Guard who's casually walking toward the forest. The movements aren't jerky or too slow. The steps my body is taking under Phoe's control are indistinguishable from my own.

"You know, it's really odd that you're here talking to me while you're controlling my legs," I tell Phoe.

"I don't see why. I'm also monitoring Fiona and Jeremiah's interviews, reading a bunch of books, researching whatever I can about the Test, getting the details of the egg hunt they're having in the forest to make sure we don't bump into anyone, and—"

"I get it," I say, doing my best not to sound envious. "You can multitask."

"I don't actually have to multitask in the 'doing many things at the same time' sense. Given that I think much faster than human beings, I simply perform each task linearly. For example, I can finish a book in a fraction of a millisecond, then check in on the interviews, and all before your meat brain fires a single synapse. Of course, I also do multitask. There are multiple versions of me—"

"I don't understand," I say. "Are you actually here with me or not?" I walk over and touch her shoulder. Here, in the VR environment she's created for me, I'm dressed in my Birth Day outfit of jeans and a t-shirt, not the Guard suit, and my bare hand feels her shoulder with no obstacles. She feels completely real—soft and warm to the touch.

"Of course I'm here," Phoe says. "And before you insult me by asking, I can feel you touching my shoulder."

"Phoe, I—"

"It's okay, Theo," she says, her blue eyes piercing mine. "You have the right to understand this. When I take this shape"—she runs the tips of her fingers down her body—"the thread of me you're communicating with is not merely *pretending* to have this body. This part of me actually has a body or as close to that as possible in the given medium. In VR, this body you see is an emulation of a human one. Emulation is a process where I replicate something with as much detail as I can. In this form, I have neurons, dendrites, blood, a heart, nerves, hormones, as well as gut bacteria. If it's possible to capture the totality of the human experience in a virtual way—and I believe that it *is* possible—then I have done so. So you see, at a minimum, this allows me to feel everything a human being can feel. It allows me to be here with you, both in terms of sensations and emotions."

I open my mouth to ask more questions, but she doesn't give me a chance. "And yes," she says, "I'm capable of more than just physical sensations. My emotions run much deeper and are more nuanced than a human being's because I'm not limited to just this body—no matter how complex my emulated brain is. My capacity for compassion is higher, and my understanding of the world is richer." She gives me a level look. "A question you need to ask yourself is: Are *you* capable of human emotions? I know you felt my shoulder with the tips of your fingers, and I know your oxytocin levels went up minutely when you touched me, but did it make you feel happy, the way a human being should feel when touching a friend? Or was your capacity to feel such things destroyed by years of Quietudes and the brain-tampering of the Oasis society?"

I stare at her uncomprehendingly. She doesn't blink. She truly thinks she's more human than I am—she, an AI.

"I am, though," she says. "But you'll get there. You're on your way to being fully human too."

And before I can reply, she stands on her tiptoes and kisses me.

CHAPTER THIRTEEN

Our kiss is almost angry in its intensity. The warmth of her body presses against me, and I get the urge to pull her closer, to touch her and get rid of the clothes between us.

Before I can do so, she gently pushes me away and says, "Hold your horses, Theo. I don't think you know what you're feeling or fully understand what you want. Until you do, we should take the physical part of our whatever-this-is slowly."

I'm a muddy roller coaster of needs and emotions, with Phoe at the epicenter. Her words sound far away, their meaning fuzzy, but she's right. I don't know much about whatever it is I want from her.

"Look," she says, turning my attention to the hologram of me walking.

I look, even though I know she's just changing the topic.

The real-world me is in the forest. He/I/we are walking briskly.

"'We' is a fitting pronoun," Phoe says, once again composed. "Since it's your body we're looking at, yet it's me controlling it. I'll get it to the Barrier for you, okay?"

"Fine. What do we do in the meantime?" I ask, the image of more kissing flitting through my mind.

Phoe chuckles slyly and says, "For starters, you can accept your Birth Day present." She turns to walk deeper into the cave.

I follow her. "My present?" I ask.

"Oh, right." She glances over her shoulder. "I keep forgetting that Birth Day is but a shallow echo of ancients' birthdays. You see, unlike Oasis, where thanks to artificial wombs and Incubators, everyone is born on the same day, the ancients were born at random times. So they felt special and wanted gifts to commemorate—"

"I'm well aware of the idea of a birthday gift," I say as we stop next to a table with two chairs. "I just got caught off guard."

Phoe grins at me. "Okay. Well, I prepared this for you."

The table is covered with every ancient food and drink I've ever tasted on Birth Day. There are several flavors of soda and popcorn and a dozen other goodies. A big bowl of fried dough sits as the centerpiece of the table.

"I had to stick to things you'd tasted before, or else I would've had to make up the textures and flavors, which I *could* do, if you wanted."

Instead of responding, I grab a piece of fried dough and pop it in my mouth. Phoe follows my lead. The taste is identical to the way I remember it, and I simply let myself enjoy it.

Once I'm done chewing, I say, "Thank you. This is awesome."

"You can eat as many as you want without getting sick." She winks at me. "I'm not emulating *your* digestive track, so you're eating virtual ether."

"So"—I take a piece of popcorn from a paper bag—"if your body is such a good emulation of a human one, can you get fat from eating too much fried dough?"

"Theo, Theo," she says and follows it with a *tsk-tsk* sound. "It's not gentlemanly to ask a lady about her age, and even less so to allude to her weight."

"It's not?" I grab a piece of fried dough and lick the powdered sugar off it.

"It was an ancient tradition," Phoe says and demonstratively stuffs a bunch of fried dough into her mouth. She must have swallowed it without chewing, because she soon continues. "But I was actually teasing you. If you think my butt is fat, please tell me, because I can make it smaller. Just because I try to emulate everything accurately doesn't mean I can't take some liberties when I feel like it."

I take a noisy gulp of soda, then say, "You can look any way you wish?"

Phoe nods. "Yes, and more importantly, I can look any way *you* wish." And before my stunned gaze, her eyes switch from their usual blue to green and then back again. At the same time, her blond pixie hair turns pink, then returns to blond. "I created this face by studying your pupil dilation and other cues when you watched ancient movies and gawked at the models in those magazines. I tried to look like the perfect woman for you, but if you wanted, I could look different, say like your friend Grace"—there's a dark undertone to her voice as she says this—"or like anyone else."

"I like you like this," I say, putting the large soda back on the table. "Please don't change, and please refrain from manipulating me in such a crude fashion in the future. I can't believe you made yourself look like the girls I stared at. That's just unfair."

"That's why I came clean." Phoe reaches for the cup I was holding, her fingers momentarily touching mine. "I realized it was manipulative, and I felt guilty about it. In my defense, I had to make myself look like *something*, so why not look pleasing to you?" She bats her eyelashes at me. "Do you forgive me?"

I watch those long lashes flutter and wonder if she borrowed that action from some movie after seeing how it affected me. Even with that suspicion in mind, I find I can't be mad at her for longer than a few seconds.

"Good." Phoe grins, then takes two bags of popcorn, hands one to me, and says, "Let's watch some movies while we wait for your body to reach its destination."

She walks to a far crevice of the cave, and I follow. When we arrive, I see that Phoe has managed to create a full-fledged ancient movie theater. We sit down with our popcorn—ancient moviegoer style—and watch a couple of films.

By the third movie, I figure out Phoe's agenda. She's showing me romantic comedies to teach me human courting behavior and vernacular. I don't mind, though. It's actually interesting. Ancients had a very strange relationship with sexual intimacy. They clearly loved to have sex, but had a harder time talking about it, almost as though they followed some of Oasis's taboos. Many of them went as far as to use baseball as a metaphor for sex instead of talking directly about it. Using this euphemism, Phoe and I went to 'first base.' I have to hand it to the ancients for their creativity. Thinking of what we did as 'first base' doesn't make me nearly as uncomfortable as thinking of it as 'kissing.'

"That's good to know." Phoe makes the movie screen disappear and leans toward me. "I'm glad you saw through my ploy." She flicks her fingers, and the movie theater chairs disappear. We're suddenly sitting on a couch, surrounded by candles and that distinctly romantic music from the movies we watched. "As your reward for your cleverness, perhaps I'll let you convince me to go to 'second base.'"

Having just seen what that means from one of the movies, I reach for her, my heart beating faster than those times I almost died. We go at it for what feels like hours, and by the end, I have a renewed appreciation for what drove the ancients mad.

* * *

I fix my hair and my clothes as I walk back to the central part of the cave, where I appeared what feels like a month ago, back when I was innocent and pure.

Phoe follows me.

I reach the hologram and gaze at myself in the real world.

"Is that the forest on the Adult side?" I ask. He/we are surrounded by pines. It's sundown, and I have to assume we've had sufficient time to get through the Youth's pine forest, cross the Barrier, and enter the forest on the other side.

Phoe licks her lips. I catch myself staring at them. They look puffy after what we've done.

She catches me looking, winks, and says, "That's correct. We should be able to get on with our quest soon, unless you want to hang out here while I fly the disk myself . . ."

"Fly a disk? You never mentioned we'd be flying." I suppress a shudder. "Can I just walk?"

"Adults are still celebrating Birth Day." Phoe gestures, and two chairs appear. "They have a big hoopla, just like Youths. Our chances of running into someone are greater on foot."

I sit on my chair and say, "I think it might be worth the risk—"

"You don't even have to be conscious of the flying." Phoe drags her chair next to mine, sits down, and gives my arm a sympathetic pat. "We can stay here and hang out while I—my thread on the outside—do the flying."

"No." I notice my feet pointing away from the hologram as though I'm planning to run away. "I'll do it. I need to get over my fear of heights."

"As you wish." Phoe crosses her legs. "You'll have the option of letting me take over at any time."

"How is your investigation progressing?" I ask, desperate to get my mind off the subject of heights. "Is Jeremiah still questioning people?"

"No, that finished hours ago. He and Fiona are actually almost back in the Elderly section. They flew on disks like the other Guards do when traveling outside the Youth section. And before you ask, they haven't spoken about you or your neural scan since that terse conversation. I don't know if that's a good sign, since they haven't spoken much at all. It's clear they're disappointed by the lack of information. I think they're considering their options. Things should get interesting once Jeremiah discovers the video of

Fiona, but he hasn't yet. Which reminds me . . ." Phoe rubs her palms together excitedly. "There's something I neglected to show you."

I raise an eyebrow in question, and she brings up a huge Screen in front of us.

On the Screen is the Council meeting. The room looks identical to the one Phoe showed me earlier, the one where Fiona tried to quit the Council.

The camera zooms in on Jeremiah, who's standing next to Fiona, like in the other videos.

Jeremiah's features are the epitome of wrath. I cringe, realizing I've seen this expression on his face before, but I can't recall exactly when.

"When he tortured you," Phoe whispers and rubs my shoulder.

She might be right. In this scenario, his anger is focused on a new target: Fiona.

"You fucking bitch," Jeremiah says with such venom that I move away, pressing into the back of my chair.

Fiona seems petrified as she watches Jeremiah raise his hand. The rest of the Council members' faces are marble white.

The back of Jeremiah's withered hand travels toward Fiona's right cheek, almost in slow motion.

I hear a loud slap, and Fiona staggers backward, her hands protecting her head.

I can't believe what I saw.

Jeremiah smacked Fiona in the face.

CHAPTER FOURTEEN

The Screen goes black.

I stare, completely dumbfounded.

Jeremiah may have done many terrible things, but these actions are beyond anything I expected to see. That an Elderly would break the vulgarity and violence taboos is unthinkable.

"You think I overdid it?" Phoe asks, her fingers in a steeple in front of her chest.

"What do you mean you overdid it?" I blink at my friend, who looks too happy given what we just saw.

"Oh, you thought that was real?" Phoe's smile widens. "That's excellent news. If you thought it was real, so will everyone else."

"That *wasn't* real?" I scratch the back of my head. "He didn't smack her?"

"Remember when you said Fiona might accuse Jeremiah of faking that video I dug up? The one where she almost quit the Council? I replied that Jeremiah would say he couldn't fake a video.

Your question, however, gave me an idea. Since *I* can do something like that, why not create a video that would compromise Jeremiah? Why not depict him doing something he'd want the others to Forget? And if that action took place during a Council meeting, that would explain where the memory of that meeting went." She leans forward in her chair. "So I did just that. It wasn't even all that hard. Judging by your reaction, I take it that it looks pretty authentic. This should really help us divide and conquer them."

I look at Phoe. Shaking my head, I say, "I'm glad you're on my side. If the Elderly knew what you could do, I think they'd feel justified in having been afraid of AIs all this time."

"I use my power for good." Phoe puts her hands behind her head and beams at me. "And I try to use it as little as possible. I thought you were worried about Fiona and what will happen once Jeremiah sees the video that compromises *her*. This way, as soon as she gets into trouble, I can make sure she comes across *this* video. It'll give her ammunition against Jeremiah's accusations."

"So long as no one focuses on the two of us, I say you did the right thing," I subvocalize. Then I remember I can speak freely in my cave and say out loud, "It's just a little creepy, that's all, him smacking her like that."

"Should I change his actions? I could show him projectile vomiting and thrashing around the room, like a scene from *The Exorcist*." Phoe stands and makes her eyes go white as she extends her arms like a zombie. "I bet that's how many of the Elderly picture insanity."

"No." I suppress a wave of nausea. "Or if you do create a video like that, please make it a point to *not* show me."

"Spoilsport." Phoe's eyes return to normal, and she sits down. "I think I'll stick with this version of the video. Now, I just have to tell you this one last thing . . ." She stops. "Actually, since you brought up scary powers and all that, perhaps it can wait."

"What is it?" I narrow my eyes. "Why do I have a feeling you're about to tell me something I *really* won't like?"

"It's about the Test." Phoe brings her knees closer together. "I've been unable to hack into the place where the Test runs, which means my only way in is physical—when you access it."

"Right. Wasn't that the plan from the get-go?"

"I was hoping I could learn something about the Test first." She shrugs. "But I couldn't, apart from the instructions every person who's about to take the Test receives."

I catch her gaze. "So what's the problem? Spit it out already."

"Okay, here's the thing." Phoe gives me an uncomfortable look. "Our best bet is to use a Trojan ploy."

"Is that supposed to mean something to me?"

"The Greeks built a giant wooden horse that housed soldiers, and the greedy Trojans pulled it into their sieged city." She sees my eyes glaze over and says, "Never mind. Forget the Trojans. I'm talking about a subterfuge where, by giving you access to the Test, the Test will also, inadvertently, be giving *me* a way inside it."

"That sounds like a great idea. What won't I like about it? The Test should have a problem with this, not me."

"Well, see, since it will be your mind that gains entry into the Test, the backdoor, or the Trojan horse, or whatever we want to call it, has to be part of your mind," Phoe says. "That's what you might not like."

"What?" I turn my chair so we're sitting opposite each other. "Explain."

"It's not *that* bad," she says quickly. "I just need to plant a memory into your mind. A memory that wouldn't be unpleasant."

"Plant a memory?" I slide my chair away from her. "You mean you'd create a fake memory in my head, kind of like that video?"

"Nothing so disturbing as that video, but yeah. Though 'fake' is such a negative word. It would be a tiny alteration of an existing memory. Something that didn't happen to you, per se, but could have."

I cross my arms. "What's the memory?"

"Oh, nothing terrible. You'll just remember having done an incredible feat of memorization." She raises her hand to postpone my follow-up questions. "You will remember having memorized the constant Pi."

"You mean Pi, as in 3.14-something? The ratio of a circle's circumference to its diameter? Like from Instructor George's class?" My forehead furrows in confusion. "Is that because it's a Greek letter and the Trojan thing—"

"No. I chose Pi because some people do take the time to memorize its digits. And because the digits of that number are probably random and go on forever, I can plant a super-long string of digits into your mind without it looking suspicious, at least not to a casual scan like that of the Test. Of course, only the first hundred digits of the number in your head will match the ones from the famous constant. After that cut-off point, the digits won't be from Pi. They'll be from Phoe." She chuckles at her own joke. "They'll serve their true purpose, which is creating a boot-strapping binary code of devilish design that will—"

"Yes," I interrupt. "Plant the memory if that means you'll stop explaining this."

"Okay," Phoe says and then looks like she's concentrating. She momentarily goes ghostly, the way she did in the real world after I got her the resources from the Zoo. Then she's back to normal and triumphantly says, "Done."

I look at her in shock. I don't feel any different.

"But you do recall memorizing the number Pi?" Her gaze is piercing, as if she's looking inside my head. "Think far back, to ten days ago, when you pretended to be sick. You were sitting in the nurse's office—"

"Wow," I say and stand up. With a sense reminiscent of déjà vu, I recall sitting at the office, bringing up rows and rows of digits on my Screen to memorize them.

"What you really did was play chess with me on your Screen, and you lost so many times you vowed to never play chess with me again."

"Shut up for a second," I say, my voice raised. "Is this a trick?"

Now that the weird feeling is gone, I'm convinced that I chose to study Pi ten days ago at the nurse's office. The idea that I actually played chess with Phoe is so wrong I can't wrap my mind around it. It's simply not what happened. I *did* memorize that stupid number, but I didn't recall it until she reminded me. The memory can't be fake.

"How did you expect a false memory to feel?" Phoe gets up and comes toward me. "If you like, we can play a quick game of chess. You'll lose—badly. You couldn't beat me when I had almost no resources."

"No thanks on the chess, and you're right. I guess this is how it should feel, like I really did memorize that number."

"Please recite the digits for me," Phoe says, her expression turning more serious. She brings up a Screen.

"Three point one four one," I begin. Phoe's Screen shows a large counter that increases by one every time I say another digit.

"That's your position within Pi," Phoe explains. "Keep going."

I recite the digits faster and faster. When the Screen tells us I've reached the hundredth digit in Pi, Phoe listens intently, and after another few hundred digits, she says, "Okay. It clearly worked."

"What now?" I ask. "Besides me having a dubious new talent."

"Now you return to your body and go take the Test."

"No, I mean, do I have to recite this number when I'm inside the Test? My throat is hoarse from saying the first few hundred numbers, and I probably would—"

"Your throat is not real here, nor will it be during the Test." Despite her words, Phoe gestures for a glass of water and hands it to me. After I take a sip, she goes on. "But don't worry, you don't need to recite it. You can think of this number as a small part of me. Meaning that where you go, a tiny sliver of me goes with you. Once you're in the Test, or anywhere else that I can't reach, this number will open a backdoor for more of me to join you."

"Okay," I say and drink down the rest of the water. "You got me thinking, though. If the Test scans my brain for memories, won't it see the memory of you?"

"I doubt it'll scan you so thoroughly. And even if it did, I doubt it would care. The only danger in that scenario would be exposure, but I doubt the Test communicates anything but your score to the outside world. The main reason I even bothered making the numbers in your head look like a natural memory is because the Test might have an internal anti-intrusion algorithm. We don't want to trigger something like that by planting obvious malware in your head, but a subtle memory like this should go unnoticed."

"I see." I rub my eyes. "I think this is the last time I agree to let you mess with my memories. It's too creepy. I remember memorizing those digits so clearly. As boring as losing at chess must've been, it's what really happened, and now that small part of me is gone and it feels wrong."

"I understand," Phoe says, giving me an earnest look. "And I only did it because I had to. Desperate times and all that."

I try to push away my unease and ask, "So what now?"

"Now we should head toward the Elderly section." Phoe emphasizes her suggestion with the double-middle-finger gesture she wants me to make—no doubt a deliberate attempt to shock me out of my anxiety.

Looking at her extended fingers, I realize I've become desensitized to taboos of all sorts. The gesture is nothing compared to what we did on that couch, and I now know that 'second base' is only a glimmer of the things we might do one day. What's even more unfathomable is that I can't wait to go further.

Realizing Phoe probably just read my mind, I flush and hurry to make the necessary gesture to get back to reality.

CHAPTER FIFTEEN

After the usual psychedelic whiteness, I find myself back in the real world.

I'm standing in a little meadow, surrounded by forest on all sides. Dusk has settled, and the first stars are visible above the Dome.

Phoe is already standing on a disk, floating about a foot above the ground.

Next to my feet is my own disk.

I step on it, taken aback by my Guard-issue white pants and boots, since in the cave I was dressed in jeans and sneakers.

"You know the drill," Phoe says and aims her palm upward. Responding to her signal, her disk hovers a few inches higher off the ground.

I tilt my palm at the slightest angle I can get away with, and my disk floats up.

Phoe zips up faster, and in a second, she's as far up as the tips of the tallest pines.

"Come on, join me," she says as a thought in my head. "Or do you need me to literally force your hand?"

I adjust my palm so the disk rises at a steeper angle, while also making a slight forward motion. The only reason my hand isn't shaking is the knowledge that any tiny motion will be translated into movements of the disk, and flying smoothly is terrifying enough.

"There you go," Phoe says when I catch up with her. "You're doing much better."

As though her words jinxed me, I look down. The treetops look like a solid blurry green patch, reminiscent of grass. I can't make out the frightening spaces between the trees.

"That's because I'm taking liberties with Augmented Reality," Phoe admits. "Unless you need to see something below, I figured I'd spare you the adrenaline spike by blurring your view."

"Thanks," I whisper. "Can we fly close to the treetops for now?"

"Sure," she says. "Catch up."

She does something that looks almost like a karate chop from a martial arts movie, and her disk rushes forward so fast I suspect the only reason she doesn't fall off is because she's an AR avatar.

"I'm simulating what would happen with the disk exactly," she says as a disembodied, grumpy voice to my left. "If I were flying for real, this is exactly how it would look."

I push my palm forward as though I'm about to plunge it into boiling water. My disk understands the command as an invitation to go at least ten breathtaking miles per hour.

"Slowpoke," Phoe says once I've caught up to her, a few feet away from the edge of the forest.

"I have a strong sense of self-preservation," I mumble. "Is it safe to fly above more populated areas?"

"It should be in three, two—" Phoe looks at the starry sky. "Now."

I follow her gaze.

The air near the Dome lights up in a gorgeous aurora borealis display.

"I completely forgot about Birth Day," I think, unable to peel my eyes away from the mirage-like colors.

"You've had a long day," Phoe says. "I understand. Hopefully, this explains why no one should notice us, as long as we fly in the areas that do not contain the aurora. No one will be able to look at anything but those lights, and the dark spots in the sky are even darker now. Plus, the bottom of your disk is painted black."

"It might be odd to keep staring up as I fly," I say, still looking at the spectacle.

"You don't need to keep track of the lights. All you need to do is follow me." She starts flying again and says over her shoulder, "I'll take the path no one should see from the ground."

"Is the aurora borealis Augmented Reality?" I ask as I gingerly order my disk to follow her. "I never questioned this before, but I have no idea how the Adults create this spectacle. All I know is that for the ancients, seeing this required visiting Santa at the North Pole and wishing to see something cool."

"Right, visiting Santa. You nailed it." Phoe chuckles. "But to answer your question: yes, that is Augmented Reality, but the fireworks are very real."

Punctuating her words is a roar and a colorful explosion in the distance—the fireworks.

"Great," I think more to myself than Phoe. "I'll be flying through projectiles."

"Oh, how dumb do you think I am?" Though Phoe said it in my head, I can picture her red lips pouting. "Most of my attention is focused on the trajectories of those fireworks."

She stops suddenly and looks left. I stop too and look at what drew her attention.

About a hundred feet away from us is a Guard. He's easy to spot because of the northern lights and the fireworks. His white uniform looks like a rainbow of reflected colors as he hovers in the air on a disk.

"Crap, where did he come from?" I mentally shout at Phoe.

"I'm sorry. He must've been flying above us. I can't scan our surroundings in all three dimensions at all times; the resources that would require—"

"Never mind that. Maybe he didn't see me?" I subvocalize, refusing to succumb to literal wishful thinking.

Something in my helmet makes a strange static noise, and I hear a male voice say, "Noah? Is that you?" The Guard, who I assume is the speaker, flies a foot in my direction. "I thought you drew the short straw and had Quietude duties tonight."

Acting on pure adrenaline, I punch the air with my outstretched hand. The disk rushes away from the approaching Guard with a whoosh of air.

"You did the right thing," Phoe whispers in my head. "Our best course of action is to lose him." Ahead of me, Phoe's disk appears, a reminder that she's not flying for real. "Follow me," she says.

I try to match her speed.

"Noah? Where are you going?" the Guard's voice says in my helmet. "Is everything okay?"

I keep jabbing the air with my palm, my disk moving faster and faster. To Phoe, I mentally say, "Can you make him Forget he saw me?"

"Not a good idea," she says. "Making a single Guard Forget can easily put us on the Envoy's radar, and given that he already messaged his fellow Guards, I'd have to make all of them Forget, increasing the risk."

She takes a sudden left, and I follow, mentally shouting, "So I just try to outrun them?"

"That's the best course of action, yes. They don't know who you really are. They think one of their own is acting funny. If we lose them, it'll never get back to you. Once we finish the Test, I might be able to make them Forget in a way that would not alert the Envoy—" Her words cut off, and then she whispers, "Shit. They're already here."

Two Guards are in front of us, the fiery display reflecting off their astronaut helmets.

We turn so suddenly I feel lucky the food I ate in the man cave was virtual. Otherwise, it might've joined my heart in my throat.

Phoe is going at least fifty miles per hour as she whooshes ahead. I follow her, going nearly as fast, but to my dismay, she mentally shouts, "They're gaining on us. Watch out!"

If she hadn't warned me, my pursuers might've had to peel me off the metal surface of the cone-shaped building. The side of my disk scrapes the sharp metal tip of the structure, sending sparks flying, and my disk shakes violently. In a miraculous feat of agility, I manage not to fall off the disk.

"If by 'miraculous' you mean I took control of your hand just in time, then sure," Phoe says. "Watch for that one."

I duck instinctively before I realize why.

A white-gloved hand slides over my helmet.

"Instinctively, sure," Phoe murmurs in my ear. "Nothing to do with me."

"Don't distract me by taking credit for everything," I think back. "Wait, why are you going up so sharply?"

Before I get the chance to hesitate, my palm points up, and I do a swift reaching motion, as if I'm trying to grab something before someone can steal it from me. I'm not sure if this movement was mine or Phoe's influence, but I do know that it caused the disk to torpedo up so fast that I can't help but close my eyes in horror. When I open them, I see Phoe's disk in front of me, zigzagging madly. I realize my disk is doing the same and fight the urge to close my eyes again.

"Noah, stop, what are you doing?" a voice says over the helmet's radio.

If my pursuers are concerned about my maneuvers, I figure I should be worrying three times as much. To distract myself from the dread gathering in my stomach, I ask, "Phoe, how do they know I'm this Noah guy? All the outfits are the same."

She clicks her fingers and says, "Look at the other Guards."

I do and see little nametag-like labels show up on the interface of my visor for each Guard.

"You each have a unique radio identification in these helmets," Phoe explains.

I glance back again and reflect on the fact that the Guards are clustering. It's odd that they're *not* closing in on me. They're acting as though something is giving them pause.

Something bright and loud explodes next to my right shoulder.

I'm nearly blinded by the sudden flash of red fire. Then there's a green explosion, followed by a yellow one. Did the Guards shoot a bunch of rockets at me?

Then I understand. These are rockets of a different sort; they're the Birth Day fireworks. To punctuate my realization, another piece of artillery explodes about a foot away from the bottom of my disk. Another one hits the disk, the impact nearly pushing me off.

"Phoe, you flew us directly into the fireworks? Are you insane?"

A new explosion erupts two feet above my head, and a rain of small firefly-like embers descends. The few specks of fire that land on my helmet and shoulders go out without causing any damage.

"That isn't so surprising, given that you're wearing a space suit. Even in ancient times, those things were fireproof. What's important is that I got us away from them." Phoe looks back.

I follow her gaze.

She's right. The Guards aren't suicidal enough to chase after us—fireproof suits or not. As I watch, they disperse, flying in all directions.

"Crap, I think they're trying to form a sphere around us, like they did before. If we let them, they'll tighten the perimeter after the fireworks are done. Let's not let that happen." Phoe guides her disk right next to mine and tilts her hand downward, almost at a ninety-degree angle.

She plummets.

My lungs seize. "Phoe, I can't do that," I think at her frantically. "There are projectiles flying at us, not to mention—"

I stop speaking because, for the first time, I truly feel Phoe's influence on my hand. Nothing else would explain its current position, with the tips of my fingers pointing at my toes.

My disk plunges toward the ground. A firework is flying toward my face. I swerve, unwilling to learn how impact-proof the helmet is. The rocket misses the visor and explodes with a violent roar.

"Noah, stop. You will get yourself killed," a voice says over the helmet's radio. My fellow Guards must be watching my current descent.

For all its insanity, Phoe's desperate idea has one payoff: there aren't any Guards in our path. They failed to corner me.

"They failed so far," Phoe corrects. "We're turning toward the Elderly section. The Barrier should hide us from them for a few crucial moments."

This time, it feels like it was me who changed the direction of my flight, but it could easily be my brain confabulating this choice. Whatever the cause, I turn my palm parallel to the ground. The disk mirrors the movement, and instead of falling, I'm now racing forward.

In the distance, Guards are flying down like gigantic bits of hail. The sky is teeming with them. The fireworks enhance the feeling of us being surrounded by some kind of surreal force of nature.

I don't slow down.

A Guard flies directly into my path, in the spot where Phoe's virtual form just passed.

"Faster," Phoe yells, and my hand juts forward.

The Guard races faster toward me too.

This is again like that game of chicken the ancients liked to play, only in the air instead of on a flat surface with a car. I bet even *they* would consider what I'm doing crazy.

The rational part of me knows that Phoe must have calculated this maneuver with her super-duper AI mathematical skills, and that despite what the lizard part of my brain thinks, I won't crash into this Guard and die. Still, I swear the black underside of the Guard's disk—or at least the shiny metal edge—is about to hit my helmet.

Except it doesn't.

All I feel is a bit of turbulence as the Guard zooms right past me. Thanking the laws of aerodynamics for keeping me alive so far, I project my palm forward with such force that my shoulder joint pops. It's unclear whether I did that maneuver because Phoe made me or as a nervous tick.

As I continue rocketing forward, beads of sweat drip into my eyes, and the helmet prevents me from clearing them.

"On it," Phoe says, and a warm puff of air makes the moisture go away.

As my vision clears, I see the Barrier shimmering in the distance. It's reflecting the northern lights and the fireworks, and we're soaring right for it.

"Don't look up," Phoe says in my mind.

The surest way to have someone look up is by telling them not to.

I look up and regret not following Phoe's advice. Three Guards are overhead and flying downward, like hawks zeroing in on yummy, fluffy prey.

It sucks that I'm cast in the role of that prey.

Phoe abandons all pretense of giving me free will. My arm tilts sideways, and my disk instantly does the same. It's a marvel I don't fall off it.

"Your boots attach you to the disk with a powerful magnet," Phoe says sharply. "That's the case with all Guards. How do you think they stay on at those angles?"

I don't think. I'm too preoccupied with trying not to have a heart attack. I'm doing the disk equivalent of a somersault, over and over.

"Actually, I think the official term for this maneuver is *salto mortale*," Phoe says helpfully.

I don't chide her for being a smartass. That's how scared I am. If the ancient game of football involved people trying to tackle you from the sky, this is what it would look like.

Every time one of them misses me, they join the others in pursuit behind me. I have about forty of them on my tail when I plunge into the Barrier—with another somersault.

When we appear on the Elderly side of the Barrier, my heart sinks, and that's a feat considering it was already at my feet.

In front of me is an impenetrable wall of Guards.

CHAPTER SIXTEEN

"It's worse than you think," Phoe whispers. "It's not a wall. It's a half-sphere. There are Guards above and below. And before you suggest we head back, they're doing the same thing on the other side."

I scan the scene and confirm Phoe's words. We're surrounded, and the Guards in front of us are readying their Stun Sticks.

"You might want to close your eyes," Phoe says. "I'm about to try something that's a little more extreme."

As tempting as it is, I don't dare close my eyes. She's never labeled any of her crazy stunts 'extreme' before.

The Guards move toward me. The helmet's radio comes alive, and a soothing voice says, "Relax, Noah. You're having some kind of episode. We're trying to help—"

I don't hear the rest because Phoe begins her 'extreme' moves. Or more accurately, I execute the moves Phoe wants me to make—

moves so insane they leave no doubt about who's in charge of my body.

The first maneuver starts innocuously enough. I touch my right fingers together.

"That undoes the magnetic pull of the disk," Phoe explains.

Then the insanity starts. Squatting on the disk, I grab its edge and give it a violent pull. I fall instantly, clutching the disk against my chest like a medieval shield.

If it isn't clear, I fall because there's no longer a disk under my feet.

As I'm plummeting toward the Guards below me, time slows. I have a chance to reflect on Phoe's plan, or the lack of it. Is she hoping the Guards, fearing the impact, will allow me to keep falling to my death, or is she hoping I won't break my legs on the Guards' helmets if they don't move?

In a spinning wrist-wrenching motion, I throw the disk under my feet. The magnets do their job, and I'm once again attached to the disk. The disk comes alive and slows my frantic descent. The Guards below me don't fly apart as I thought they might, and I'm two feet above their heads.

I grab the disk by the edge again and land on their slippery helmets. The slowing maneuver I executed makes this landing only mildly uncomfortable. As soon as I can, I run across people's shoulders and heads, dodging their Stun Sticks.

My speed increases as I run forward. I think I understand Phoe's plan. The Guards aren't forming a perfect half-sphere. There are Guards on the bottom and Guards to the side, but the place where they meet is a weak point. One Guard recognizes our plan and hurries to get in my way. I keep running across the

Guards, dodging their hands and Sticks as I go. The clever Guard flies at me on his disk.

When the collision seems inevitable, I nearly close my eyes. My body twists at the last moment, and I swing the disk at his legs like a blunt weapon.

The disk connects with a hard thwack, and the Guard swerves, clutching his legs. Getting hit on the shin with a metal disk must really hurt.

His trajectory takes him into the swirling mass of Guards below. In a continuous motion, I lower the disk in my hands and jump onto it. My feet attach, and my arm jolts forward, granting me speed. I whoosh through the sliver of space that separates the top and bottom Guards, just as Phoe probably planned.

"By the time the Guards regroup, we'll have a few precious seconds of a lead," Phoe says after she appears next to me, standing on her illusory disk.

Only now do I realize she was missing for the last few seconds.

"I focused extra attention on keeping you alive," she explains. "Looks like we might actually reach our target. Do you remember that black building?" Phoe waves northeast.

"Yes, we passed by it the other day," I subvocalize.

"That's where the Test is taking place," she says. "We shouldn't go there directly. You see that building?" She points slightly left. A tall, tetrahedron-shaped silver building towers over the landscape. "That's where we're heading."

My arm lurches in that direction, as does the disk. When I think I can't go any faster, Phoe forces me to increase the speed again. Before I can have a heart attack, she increases the speed some more.

Everything goes quiet, and I wonder if we've reached the speed of sound.

"No, we're not going that fast. If we were, we'd be able to cross Oasis, side to side, twenty-five times in a second," Phoe says as a thought in my head. "We're travelling at a measly two hundred miles per hour."

I suspect she's being pedantic as a way of distracting me from my terror. It doesn't work. The view of the ever-approaching tetrahedron is all I can focus on.

"Close your eyes," Phoe says urgently.

Refusing to take the coward's way out, I keep my eyes open. The building gets closer and closer. We're not slowing down or changing course. It looks as though we're heading for a large window near the top floor.

The building is a few feet away.

The disk is slowing down, but not fast enough.

I try to tilt my hand, but it doesn't listen to me. Instead, I cover my head with my arms as we crash into the window. Shards of glass fly all around me, the sound deafening.

Before I can so much as gasp, I crash into the opposite wall, and the wind gets knocked out of me. Dazed, I notice broken clay all around me. Am I in some kind of arts-and-crafts studio?

My head is spinning, but I don't get a chance to catch my breath. Glass crunches under my feet as I jump up and gesture at the nearby door. As the door swings open, I notice a shriveled Elderly woman cowering in the corner of the room.

"She's not hurt, just frightened," Phoe explains as she makes my legs rush me out of the room and toward the emergency staircase. "We need to run down and make our way to that black structure."

My feet pound the floor to the rhythm of my frenzied heartbeat as I descend the staircase. Phoe's worried form appears in front of me. She's looking over my shoulder.

As I turn to follow her gaze, my visor goes into the blue-and-red heat vision mode she showed me earlier, and I see red shapes running up the stairs.

"Guards. They're on their way up here," Phoe hisses. I automatically look up, and she frantically shakes her head. "We can't go back."

She's right. There are more red blobs coming down than going up. I look sideways and see another red shape in one of the rooms. The shape is heading for the exit.

"Is it one of the Guards?" I subvocalize so frantically I nearly say the words out loud. "Did they jump in through a window?"

"I don't think so," Phoe says, following my gaze. "Go there and prepare your Stun Stick."

I head back up the stairs to the landing, and from there, I enter the building's forty-fifth floor. I make my way to the door where the figure is moving.

The red body heat outline looks like it's making a gesture. The door begins to slide open. If there's a Guard behind it after all, I just walked into his clutches.

I ready the Stun Stick and say, "Phoe, how do I turn off the heat vision?"

My vision returns to normal just as the door opens.

I raise my arm to stun the person who's coming out but stop cold. It's not a person—well, obviously, it's a person, but he or she is wearing the weirdest costume I've ever seen.

A plush purple creature is standing at the threshold. It looks like a cross between a dragon and a hippopotamus. The hippo-dragon's face is frozen in an overfriendly smile, and its short arms cover a green underbelly.

"Can I help you?" the hippo-dragon asks in a hoarse masculine voice.

"Will stunning him work through that contraption?" I think at Phoe with as much urgency as one can put in a thought.

"It should—it works through these suits, though I guess they're more conductive. Tell him to take the head off," she urges. "I turned off the radio in your helmet so the Guards won't hear this exchange."

"Please take off your head," I say, giving my voice the arrogant air of authority I associate with the Guards.

"The helmet already disguises your voice," Phoe whispers. "But that was a nice touch."

The man raises his hands to his head and pulls the smiling headgear up.

As soon as I see a sliver of neck between the purple cloth, I touch the Stun Stick to it and press the button.

The purple monster falls down, the grinning head rolling to the side. The Elderly man underneath must be one of the younger members. His hair is only beginning to gray.

"Move him inside and take that outfit off him," Phoe orders. "We don't have much time."

I drag my victim inside his room. The room is filled with crocheting paraphernalia and has an odd, musty smell. I drag the man out of the purple outfit.

"Should I swap clothes with him?" I ask Phoe.

Underneath the bright colors, the man is wearing a drab gray outfit that reminds me of what Youths typically wear.

"No, just put the dinosaur suit on." A whisper of mirth enters her voice. "You should be able to wear it on top of your Guard getup."

"What the hell? Why was an Elderly dressed like this?" I step into the bottom portion of the purple costume and pull it up over my Guard suit, finding it a surprisingly loose fit. I reach down to pick up the head of the monster and ask, "And how do you know it's a dinosaur and not a dragon or a hippo?"

"It's his Birth Day masquerade outfit," Phoe says. "They're all wearing them outside. I think this person works with little kids, and they probably get a kick out of this costume. And I know it's a dinosaur because I'm fairly sure this is Barney—a Tyrannosaurs Rex ancient kids used to watch on TV. I'll get you an episode from the archives one day. For now, please, we need to hurry."

I put on the dinosaur head, mumbling about ancients and their obsession with violence. Using a T-Rex as entertainment for little ones? Granted, they did make him look warm and fuzzy.

Clumsily exiting the apartment, I head for the stairs. With the head on, I see the world through two small pinholes. I can't picture walking down the stairs this way, but—

"No, the Guards are on the stairs. We'll take the elevator. This way." Phoe walks down the corridor. "Come on, stalk me, you monster."

Ignoring her mockery, I reach the elevator and do the summoning gesture. Given the small arms of T-Rexes and the suit based on their anatomy, my gesture comes out clumsy. Still, the elevator arrives in an instant.

"I summoned the elevator." Phoe snickers and walks in. "Can you move your tail?"

With the tail trailing behind me, I stomp into the elevator and cross my arms around my green chest. Seeing her chuckle again, I think angrily, "Can you make this thing go down, or are we waiting for the Guards to catch up with us?"

Not waiting for her to comply, I press the manual button but have trouble because the purple plush arm of my costume only has two giant fingers.

The elevator closes, and Phoe belly-laughs at my discomfort. However, as we get closer to the ground floor, she turns more serious, and by the time the doors open, her face is a mask of concentration.

Two Guards are standing there, their helmeted heads tilted in a way that tells me they're looking inside the elevator.

CHAPTER SEVENTEEN

My blood pressure spiking, I wave my two-fingered paw at them and lumber out of the elevator like I own the building.

I fully expect them to ask me to take the head off, but they don't. Instead, as I head down the corridor, one of the Guards says, "Have fun out there."

I repeat the moronic hand wave and follow Phoe as she walks out of the lobby.

Though the suit severely restricts my movements, I'm glad for the anonymity it provides. Guards are surrounding the building, but they pay the dinosaur no attention.

Phoe heads toward the black building, and I walk after her, trying not to gawk at the dressed-up Elderly all around me. Phoe was right. The best explanation for their funky costumes is that this is some kind of masquerade. We pass by Pinocchio, a red M&M candy, and a huge crowd of ancient rulers that include the King of Spades, the Lion King, and Barack Obama.

Despite my anxiety, I can't help but envy the Elderly. The Youths never get to dress up like this, not even on Birth Day.

"This is so they can take the new generation of little kids outside for Birth Day without the kids seeing any signs of aging. Also, if it makes you feel any better, I believe the Elderly are thinking about doing something like this for the Youths next year. They're testing this out on themselves this year, perhaps to see whether it will corrupt the Youths." Phoe shakes her head. "I guess they discovered the one holiday Birth Day didn't already copycat—Halloween."

"I hope you're right about next year," I think, staring at a man dressed as Bugs Bunny. "Liam would love this."

"Sorry to cut this short, but that's our destination." She nods at the black building—or rather, a building made of metal that has a black sheen to it.

"Do I just walk in wearing this costume?" I think at Phoe.

"Yes, wear it, and if anyone sees you, pretend to have randomly wandered in from the street," she says.

"Okay." I head for the door, but she steps in front of me, a worried expression on her face. I instantly stop. "What is it, Phoe?"

"After you walk in, I won't be able to talk to you freely," she says, shifting from foot to foot. "This building is worse than the Witch Prison. I only happen to know the location of the Test room from the instructional message the eligible Test takers received earlier today."

She gestures, and a map overlay shows up on the Screen inside my visor.

"As you can see, all you need to do is walk down two corridors and turn left. Once you're there, there should be an obvious way to start the Test by placing your palm on the control panel. Whisper, 'Glove off,' to your helmet, and it will come off, though I'm not sure skin contact is required. You can handle something like that on your own, right?"

"Won't I need you? Inside the Test, I mean?" I step back and nearly trip over my costume's purple tail.

"That's what the Pi Trojan is for," Phoe reminds me. "As soon as you're in the Test, it will give me a way in."

"What about walking my body out of here during the Test? Isn't that part of the plan?"

"Once I'm in the Test, I'm sure I can patch back into your body."

"I guess." I take an uncertain step forward.

"You can do this." Phoe leans toward me and kisses my silly outfit on the cheek. "Go before the Guards figure out you're not in that tetrahedron building."

The reminder about our pursuers finally leads me to act.

Taking in a deep breath, I quietly walk into the black building.

"Phoe?" I think as I cross the spacious entryway. "Can you really not hear me in here?"

She doesn't respond, so I follow the map in my visor.

I turn into the northeast corridor and manage to take two shuffling steps in before I can't continue any farther.

A Guard stands in my way.

"Can I help you?" the Guard asks, his voice gruff and unfriendly.

A number of things happen in quick succession. I let my right arm hang loose at my pudgy purple side, while underneath the suit, I pull my actual arm, still dressed in the Guard outfit, out of the purple cloth around it. I then reach for the Stun Stick in my belt and say, "Where am I? I have a hard time seeing in this outfit. Can you help me take this head off?"

The Guard shrugs and steps toward me.

I reach for the dinosaur head with my left hand and pretend to fumble. With my right hand, under the suit, I raise the Stun Stick up to my neck.

The Guard places his hands on my purple headgear and pulls.

As soon as there's an inch of space between the two pieces of the dinosaur's skin, I jab the Guard with the Stun Stick and spasmodically press the button.

The Guard collapses on the spot.

Blowing out a relieved breath, I take his Stun Stick, figuring two weapons are better than one. Then I take the rest of my purple suit off, rip the tail off, and use it to tie the Guard's arms behind his back. Not sure how well this will keep him bound, I also put the dinosaur headgear on his head, only backward. This way, he won't see where he is when he regains consciousness. Finally, I rip up the rest of the suit and tie strips around the Guard's legs and across his torso and shoulders. Happy with my work, I drag his limp body into a nook in the corridor and zap him one more time for good measure.

Free to move again, I run toward my destination.

The next two turns are uneventful, and the third one should be the last. According to my map, the Test is right there, in a spacious room.

I turn the corner.

The Test room is empty except for two things: a large, lit-up wall to my right, and the Guard turning my way to my left.

"Hello, Ronny," I say, taking advantage of his nametag label in my visor's interface. Before he can react, I move in to close the distance between us.

"Noah?" he says, his posture uncertain.

I get closer and fib, "I'm here to relieve you of your duties. It's a little happy Birth Day surprise."

I don't know if he's reaching for his Stun Stick because he heard over his radio about everyone chasing after 'Noah' or because my improvisation was completely out of character with what a sane Guard would say, but the fact remains: he's reaching for it. I'm four feet away, so we're both outside Stun Stick reach. This is when I realize I'm holding on to my extra Stun Stick, another reason Ronny might be paranoid.

I throw my extra weapon at his head. He raises his hands. If it's to catch the Stun Stick, he fails. If it's to protect his visor, he's being silly. This helmet can easily withstand that impact. I use his momentary distraction to punch his midsection.

He staggers back.

I pull out my second Stun Stick.

He manages to take his out.

As though looking in a mirror, we touch the other's shoulder with the sticks. It's a matter of whose finger will press the button first.

I squeeze mine just as my consciousness escapes.

* * *

I wake up as though from a horrible nightmare. Where am I? Why is my bed so uncomfortable?

Then reality reasserts itself. An unconscious Guard is lying at my feet. I'm in the Test room, and we just zapped each other. If I've regained consciousness, that means the Guard, Ronny, is about to come to as well. It also means the Guard I left behind—the one tied up with the dinosaur outfit—is awake and trying to free himself.

I sit up and reach for the Stun Stick to my right. In a flurry of movements, Ronny grabs my ankle and pulls. His other arm reaches for his own Stick. I kick at his helmet and roll right, grabbing the Stun Stick as I go. Jumping to my feet, I see him do the same.

We circle each other slowly.

He lunges with the Stick, aiming at my right shoulder. I jump to the side, his Stick missing me by a hair, and counter by bringing down my weapon on his wrist like the ancient club it resembles.

The brute-force maneuver works, and his Stun Stick clanks on the floor. He follows it with his eyes—a big mistake. Using his distraction, I touch his exposed torso and pump him full of volts.

He crashes to the ground.

Breathing heavily, I drag his body to the wall where the Test is. There's a pedestal with a large palm-shaped indentation. Phoe mentioned there would be something like this when she sent me in. I drag Ronny closer to the control panel and zap him again to give myself the maximum amount of time to take the Test.

I place my hand on the indentation.

Nothing happens.

"Glove off," I whisper, remembering Phoe's instruction.

The glove separates from the suit, and I put it under my belt. With a deep breath out, I place my naked palm on the control panel.

A giant Screen appears on top of the panel. On the Screen are the words: *Authenticating age.*

I swallow. Phoe's insane idea of making me ninety years old is about to get tested. After a moment, the Screen turns green—universal for confirmed—and a giant panel slides out of the wall. Upon closer inspection, I realize it's a bed.

Lie down, Test subject Theodore, the Screen states. *Once you're in a horizontal position, initiate sleep.*

I expected the world to go white, the way it does on my trips to Virtual Reality and the IRES game. I didn't expect to take a nap. There's no helping it, though. I drag poor Ronny under the bed, get on, and zap him one last time.

Then I lie down and tighten the muscles around my eyes to initiate assisted sleep.

CHAPTER EIGHTEEN

I'm standing in a tunnel made of shimmering, translucent material. It looks as though water is somehow staying upright, creating the walls of this place. The material even ripples like water. There is no sky. The water walls keep going up, seemingly indefinitely, blending into the horizon of the non-existent sky. There are also doors here, doors that look like they're made of ice. The row of doors stretches out in both directions as far as the eye can see.

"Theo?" Phoe's thought says in my mind.

"Yes," I mentally respond. "Looks like your Pi trick worked."

"Forget about that." Her thought is urgent. "We need to abort this Test."

"Why?" I subvocalize.

"Don't subvocalize." Her mental reply is uncharacteristically sharp. "Look like you're trying to choose a door."

I do as she says. Turning right, I walk down the tunnel, gazing from one identical door to the next.

"What's going on?" I think at her, trying to control my anxiety. "Why are you so spooked?"

"This is too risky. I thought the Test would involve Virtual Reality, not *this*."

"What do you mean? How can this not be VR? Are you saying this is the real world?" I look at the water walls and the lack of sky. "This environment is clearly fake."

"Okay, I don't want to split hairs about terminology. You could call it a Virtual Reality of sorts, but what makes it different is *you*. Specifically, how your mind arrived here." Phoe's thoughts hold an undertone of worry. "You see, Virtual Reality typically involves your neurons experiencing fake inputs and outputs from your nanos, a bit like Augmented Reality but taken to the extreme. It's your meat brain that goes through the experience. This place doesn't work like that." Her worry seems to intensify. "There's a feature in your nanos I noticed a while back. They seem to record what happens to your connectome, which is the combination of everything in your brain that makes up who you are, from your neurons to the lowliest neurotransmitter. I never realized how detailed that snapshot is or that it was used for any practical purpose in Oasis. I assumed it was dormant technology left over from your Singularity legacy. That the Elderly use this technology is hypocritical, but in hindsight, given Forgetting and all that, I don't know why I'm surprised."

"Hold on." I stop her from going off on her 'the Elderly hate technology and they're hypocrites' tangent. "I'm not sure I follow, Phoe. What are you saying?"

"Have you ever heard of uploading people? Did they scare you with such a concept at the Institute?"

I strain to recall such a term. "No."

"Okay, imagine if someone took a person, scanned them with nanotechnology, and created a perfect replica of them inside a simulated environment. This copy would be indistinguishable from the original, at least insofar as when you talk to them or how they feel about themselves."

"Kind of like the way you work? Your body that talks to me, that is?" I feel ice forming at the bottom of my chest. "Like what you said in the cave?"

"Kind of. My other self designed my body. It's not a copy of someone else's. But the principle of it, running emulated neurons and the rest, is the same. The mechanics of how an upload works is also similar to the way that version of my body does—"

"And you're saying that I'm—"

"—currently an upload," she says in my mind. "Your real brain is sleeping back on that bed."

I examine my clothes. I'm wearing an ancient outfit of dark jeans and a blue t-shirt, but that happens in regular VR. My thought process is the same. My emotions—particularly my overwhelming fear—feel realistic. The more I think about being this disembodied digital echo of myself, the less it makes sense. I feel normal. I'm here, breathing air and having a mental conversation with Phoe.

Okay, so I feel like my version of normal.

"I don't want to start philosophizing," Phoe responds, "but you wouldn't feel a difference, since the emulation the Test created is perfect. You are you in every sense of the word, except that on a very small scale, I doubt this place emulates the molecules that make you up. Then again, some of your 'real' body's molecules change from day to day and get replaced with new ones at varying rates. So yeah, being an upload doesn't make you any less real. That's part of the problem."

"Fine, so I'm an upload," I think tersely. "It's not what you expected to happen, I get that, but what's the difference? What's the danger you're so concerned about?"

"I don't even know where to begin." Phoe's thoughts enter my mind faster. "For starters, your brain's state is easier to manipulate here. The Test can make you forget or misremember things, whereas VR can't. I'm not sure how much I can protect you from that. What worries me more is that anything that happens to you here will get written back into your real-world brain by the Test's interface at the very end, before you wake up in the real world. If, say, you get so scared you develop a permanent stutter, your real brain will also get damaged and you'll develop a stutter, potentially for a long time, if not for the rest of your life."

"That isn't how the IRES game operates? I'm fairly sure I developed a fear of insects after that fight with a giant mechanical scorpion."

"No. Fear of bugs is a natural human response, and when you saw them, you merely learned something about yourself. Your core self wasn't changed by it. If you hit your head and wake up with amnesia in IRES, after the game is over, you'll be back to normal. This Test is different. If you develop amnesia and come back to your body before your memory is restored, the loss will be permanent. But that's not even the most frightening difference between the Test and IRES. If you die here, this version of you will really be dead. The Test doesn't make any backups of you or anything like that. If you die, you'll wake up in your body, and it will be as though this conversation never happened. Death means no information is written back to your sleeping self. Even if you lived in this place for thirty years, longer than you've been alive outside, those years would be gone. That person you became would be gone."

"But I would still wake up out there." Despite my words, I feel a growing anxiety. "Wouldn't it be more like a form of amnesia?"

"In my opinion, irreversible amnesia is a type of death. Imagine if in two seconds from now, something happened and you became a different person. Say you decided to dedicate your life to a noble cause, found love, or even became evil. All that would get erased if you—"

"But there's still that sleeping me," I think stubbornly. "How can you say I'd be dead?"

"I guess we have a different way of looking at existence. To me, we are, at the core, patterns of information. You're now a new pattern—a pattern that has seen these watery walls and diverged from the sleeping version of you. Until and unless your memories are written back, you're a new Theo. If you die, that will be final, and I don't know if I would consider the sleeping Theo the same person as you. He's still someone I care about, as are you, but you're two different people, until he remembers being you." She pauses. "Still, if your view of the matter makes you less scared, I'm glad. I would be petrified if I were you. I'd want to leave this place as soon as I could, and I insist we do just that."

"Okay," I think and stop next to another icy-looking door. "How do I escape?"

"I think if you walk without opening any doors or sit here looking dumb, the Test will eventually spit you out with a score of zero. I think that's your best course of action."

"But if I leave, doesn't that mean you won't get the resources we need?" I wipe my too-sweaty-considering-they-are-virtual palms on my shirt. "And doesn't that mean there's a good chance I'll be killed in the real world once Jeremiah gets the Council to vote on my neural scan?"

"I won't let that happen." Phoe's thought is like a lash in my brain.

"I know you would try to protect me," I think back. "But how can you protect me without messing with Jeremiah's mind? And what if the Envoy stops you or learns about you? We still don't know what he is and if he can kill you."

"I don't think I can be killed—not without destroying the ship. The worst the Envoy can do to me is lobotomize me again by taking away the resources I've gathered."

"Wouldn't that make you Forget so many things? Like our friendship?" She doesn't respond, so I press on. "Wouldn't that make this version of you die? Wouldn't that make the danger I'm currently facing pale in comparison?"

"My survival is more nuanced than yours, and I'm willing to take certain risks for your sake. For what it's worth, I took precautions by storing my important memories in a bunch of places, including the DMZ—"

I take a determined step toward the nearest door. That she would Forget that we kissed, or one of our many conversations, is unthinkable.

"I see what you're planning to do, Theo, and I beg you not to do it."

"Then you know how determined I am to keep *you* safe." I make my thoughts resolute. "I'm walking through this door, so please, just help me shut the Test down."

"No, Theo, that's another thing." Phoe sounds like she's on the verge of crying. "If this were VR, I would be limitless. But I don't have a real foothold in this world. I'm bound by the resources the Test allocated to you, which means there aren't any resources left for any type of sophisticated hacking. And, as I feared, there's an anti-intrusion algorithm running around this place. If it suspects my presence or doubts your integrity—"

I can tell she's just trying to convince me to leave, so I think, "You'll have to figure it out. I'm walking through this door." I take another step forward.

"Wait," Phoe hisses. "I have an idea."

I stop. "I thought you might. The least you can do is be completely honest with me."

"Fine. Beings that were near or exactly at human-level intelligence made this place, which means it's pretty buggy as far as software artifices go. I think I see a vulnerability already. Someone used a relatively small memory allocation to permanently store the Test score of every participant after it's sent out into the real world. In the right hands—my hands—that design choice could become this system's downfall."

"Phoe, if you're expecting a Eureka moment from me, it's clearly not happening," I think in frustration. "Break it down for me as though I have 'near-human-level' intelligence."

"The designer thought the scores would never go above a certain number. He knew many people will take the Test, so he was stingy on this memory space. That means that if you were to get a ridiculously high score on your Test, a condition called a buffer overrun will happen. It's when the system tries to cram a too-big value into a too-small-for-it space. I could exploit that to bring this whole system crashing down."

"So I'll just take the Test until I get the score you need," I think. "That sounds like a decent-enough plan."

"Yes, except this place will throw you out after you fail a predetermined number of times, which is most likely a single failure. Otherwise, everyone would have a super-high score."

"Can we cheat?" I absentmindedly touch one of the water walls. It feels like that Jell-O stuff Phoe told me about. "Can you figure out how I can reach a high score?"

"I can try," she responds. "But like I said, it's—"

"Blah, blah, too dangerous," I think with false bravado. "We settled this already. I'm doing this."

"In that case, I'll try to help you cheat," Phoe thinks grimly. "Obviously."

"Good. Now how long will this take? There's a Guard in the real world who may wake up from his zap-nap soon."

"I'm already in your mind, so yeah, I can get you out of the building. But there's something else you should know—another thing that makes this place a little different. You see, digital minds—like ours are right now—don't work as slowly as chemically bound meat ones. Your thought processes inside the Test are many times faster than in the real world. In other words, you may get a lot of Testing done in subjective, real-world time. That may be why someone opted to use this technology over VR."

"Time is running differently for me?" I can't help but feel a sense of wonder at that. "Kind of like it does for you?"

"Not at the same rate and without the massive parallelism I leverage, but it's a good comparison."

"Okay, that's good news. I have more time here." I brush my fingers against the door. As you'd expect from something made of ice, it feels extremely cold, almost burningly cold. "You should still get the sleeping version of me out of that room."

"Obviously," Phoe responds. "And before you ask, here. You can see the outside world through that." A familiar watch-Screen appears on my wrist. "The anti-intrusion stuff shouldn't notice anything that's on your body. The Test didn't make your clothes, but pulled them from your memories. You could've easily ended up with that watch on your own."

I look at the watch and see my real-world, Guard-disguised self lying unconscious, with the Guard also passed out near the bed.

"He, I mean you, I mean—let's call him Guard-Theo—is getting up already," Phoe says. "Due to the time differences, Guard-Theo's head is moving very slowly off the pillow. I wouldn't worry too much about the outside world if I were you. I only gave you that watch to keep you informed. I'll take care of your real body while you focus on taking the Test."

"Got it," I think but can't help glancing at the watch again. Nothing's changed. Time really is moving faster here.

"Good luck." Phoe's thought is imbued with trepidation. "I wish I could kiss you."

Without responding to her sentiment, I push on the icy door.

The door swings open, like in ancient times.

I walk through, and as soon as my whole body crosses the threshold, all my senses turn off.

CHAPTER NINETEEN

My mind is muddy. I can't recall how I got here. I'm even less sure where 'here' is. I'm standing by train tracks. Something about this doesn't make sense. I feel as though this is the first time I've ever seen train tracks, but I'm meant to treat them as a regular occurrence. Then again, if I never saw train tracks before, how do I know what they are?

"You're missing more than just those basics," a voice says. "I bet you don't even remember your name."

I look around. The voice was female, but I don't see any women in my immediate vicinity.

It occurs to me that the voice might be a thought in my mind, even if it was female. Worst of all, she might be right. I can't recall my name or much else for that matter. The oddest thing is that something is preventing me from panicking.

I hear screams in the distance. I run toward the sound to see what's going on.

The ground begins to shake.

I keep running until I crest a small hill. The tracks separate into a fork, one set of parallel metal lines becoming two. There's a large switch—a mechanical contraption designed to direct the train either left or right. Everything is set up to make a passing train go left. If someone needed to divert the train right, they would have to pull the red mechanical handle of the switch.

"For someone who's never seen train tracks, you sure know a lot about them," the mysterious female voice intrudes as a thought. "Strange, isn't it?"

I fleetingly question my sanity, but then I get distracted when I see the source of the screams.

Five people are tied to the tracks on the left. They're screaming their lungs out. Their terrified eyes are looking behind me.

The ground shakes with increasing violence, and a loud *tadum-tadum* sound is coming up somewhere behind me.

Before I get a chance to look back, I see another person tied to the tracks—on the right set. This person isn't screaming, but he looks distraught.

The noise gets overwhelming, and I finally look behind me.

I should've guessed.

It's a train barreling down the tracks with ever-increasing speed.

Belatedly, I understand why the five people are screaming. They're about to get killed. I look at them, then look back at the train. Then I look at the switch next to me.

I only have a moment to act.

My decision isn't rational. It's instinctive.

I pull the lever to save the five people, cognizant that I just doomed the man on the right.

The train whooshes past me and veers onto the right tracks. Before I witness the horrible result, my mind turns off.

* * *

I'm back in the Test corridor, surrounded by the water walls.

My name is Theo. Of course it is. How the hell did the Test make me forget something so basic?

"I told you," Phoe says in my head. "The Test messes with your mind."

"Fuck." I rub my temples. "This Test is wacky."

"Yeah." If it were possible to think disapprovingly, that's what Phoe's mental acknowledgment managed to do.

"But why?" I risk saying this out loud. I figure a normal person might say something like that to himself after living through that episode.

"To figure out your moral reasoning," Phoe thinks with that same undertone of distaste. "At least I guess that's the point. The scenario you saw is ancient. It's called the Trolley Problem."

"How did I do?"

"I think you made the Test makers happy," she replies. "Look at the door."

The door is no longer made of clear ice. It's now a solid piece of green gemstone, either malachite or quartz.

"Green for pass," Phoe explains. Then, dripping with sarcasm, she adds, "Great job."

"Why do I have a feeling you disapprove of something?" I think at her.

"It's not you," Phoe responds. "I can just see what's coming and what they want you to do to get a good score. Don't worry about my feelings. Just take the next Test. I'll try to make it so you're not as clueless about your identity as you were in the first one, or at the very least, I'll make sure when I talk to you, you can remember who I am."

"Sounds like a plan," I think and walk to the door next to the green one. "Wish me luck."

She doesn't say anything, so I walk through the doorway and my thoughts stop again, as if a light switch has gone off.

* * *

I'm standing in the middle of a plateau. Giant mountains surround me, their orange and red colors contrasting with the lapis lazuli of the midday sky. A sliver of metallic train tracks crosses through the rocks below. Someone's cut into the ancient mountainside to make way for human transportation.

My heart rate skyrockets. Despite my fuzzy memory, I know I'm absolutely terrified of heights.

A man is here. Correction, he might be a giant. He's so tall and broad-shouldered that I wonder if he isn't a statue carved into the rock face. But no, he's moving from one bare foot to another, proving his realness. He clearly doesn't like something he's looking at, because his tree-sized arms are tense and his hands are squeezed into fists.

Screams echo from below.

The screams are familiar, though I'm not sure where I heard them before.

I run up to the edge of the cliff farthest from the big guy. I have to swallow my heart back into my ribcage before I look down to see the source of the noise.

Right below, train tracks cross through a narrow passageway.

Five people are tied to these tracks, and, understandably, they're screaming.

Then I hear the honk and feel the vibrations of the oncoming train.

I instantly assess the situation.

The big guy is standing on a cliff between the screaming people and the train. There are only moments left before the train reaches them.

Conviction overcomes me. I don't know how, but I know with absolute certainty that this guy is so large that if he were to fall on those tracks, the train would halt and the five people would be saved. Someone of my size would get run over, though, and the train would keep going and kill the five people.

I also know there isn't enough time to ask the big man to sacrifice himself, and I'm sure the idea hasn't occurred to him.

My choices are clear.

I could run up to him and, before he realizes I'm here, push him down and save the people below. Alternatively, I could do nothing.

I freeze, appalled that the idea of pushing the man even entered my mind. Pushing him would be wrong. He's just standing here, watching this horrific event unravel. If I push him, my action will bring the horror onto him.

"Push him," Phoe thinks forcefully. "Quickly."

I know Phoe is a voice I should obey. I run toward the big man. My past rushes into my mind. I remember who Phoe is, who *I* am, and most importantly, I remember what I'm doing here.

The man stands there as I close the distance between us.

I slam into him. He falls down the cliff as though he really were carved out of rock. The train screeches below, but before I can see the consequences of my actions, my consciousness fades again.

* * *

I'm back in the never-ending hallway, surrounded by ice doors, though now there are two green gemstone ones among them.

"Do you see now?" Phoe thinks with agitation.

I suck in a breath, the horrifying images still fresh in my mind. "Why did you tell me to push that guy? I know this isn't real, but that wasn't the right thing to do. That wasn't—"

"Don't you understand? As far as the designers of this Test are concerned, that was the same exact choice as your first session. You had five people versus one in both cases. You could've done nothing in both cases. You ended up killing one person to save many, which is clearly what you should continue to do to get the best score. I'll try not to puke along the way."

She's right about the numbers, but something feels different about the two scenarios. Pushing someone to his death seems wrong, but flipping a switch to save a greater number of people doesn't.

Phoe mentally snorts. "This is why I'll never rely on human moral judgment when it comes to my survival. Just do the next one. I have a feeling the moral dilemmas get worse from here."

I walk up to the door on the right of the one I just passed. Before entering the room, I glance at my tiny Screen watch. During the Tests, I wasn't even aware that it was on my wrist.

Guard-Theo has barely lifted his helmeted head from the pillow.

"Wow, Phoe. You weren't kidding. Time is really messed up between these two places."

"Yeah, well, to get the buffer overrun, we'll be here for a while, so you'll be long out of that black building by the time we're through with the Test."

Shaking my head in confusion, I pass through the icy door, and predictably, the world goes away once more.

* * *

This time, the scenario is so odd I can't help but remember more about who I am—thanks to Phoe's meddling, of course. I'm Theo the Youth, not Theodore the surgeon, which is what the Test wants me to believe.

I'm in a room with five patients of 'mine.' I 'recall' that each patient is missing a vital organ. They each have only a day left to live. The reason they're all in the same room is that they have the same blood type, meaning that if an organ comes in from a person who's a match for any of these guys, it can be brought into this room for expediency.

"This isn't scientifically, medically, or even historically accurate," Phoe thinks, but I ignore her, curious where this is going.

I exit the room because I recall I need to make my rounds. I walk down the corridor, determined to check on a patient recovering from a minor surgery. I look at his chart. He came to get his tonsils removed, but he's now ready to check out, pending my sign-off. Then something catches my eye. He has the same blood type as the five unfortunate patients. Were he to donate his organs, those five people would live. Of course, he wouldn't do this of his own volition. Without those five vital organs, he would die.

The question for me, as the surgeon who can save those lives, is—

"No," I think at Phoe. "The Test creators can't mean this."

"In terms of sheer numbers, it's the same Trolley problem: five versus one," Phoe thinks. "We know what you have to do to get a good score."

"I'm not killing this innocent person so I can harvest his organs." Everything inside me rebels at the notion. "I won't do it. It's not just morally wrong—it's sick and disgusting."

"This is not real, remember? This is just a Test."

I point at the donor guy. "Except for the cutting him up bit. Even though I know it's not real, I don't think I can do it."

"I can make it so you're not aware you're doing it," Phoe says mentally. "But it's risky."

"Why don't I forfeit this specific scenario and pass some other one?" I think at her, placing the guy's chart back at the foot of the bed.

"It might get harder from here. Keep in mind this was designed by people who thought it was morally justified to Forget Mason. To get the high score, either you need to fight your squeamishness, or we have to risk my solution."

I picture doing what the Test requires and feel instant nausea at the whole idea. This is futile. If I can't even imagine picking up a scalpel, how can I put it into someone's body?

"Then let me take over, risk be damned," Phoe thinks. "The idea is simple. I suppress your conscious thoughts and move your body around—not unlike what's happening in the outside world."

"And I won't see it? I won't be aware of what my body is doing?"

"No. It will be a gap in your memory, if that's the solution you choose."

I hesitate for a moment, then nod. "Fine. Let's try it with this scenario."

"Okay," Phoe replies.

My mind doesn't go blank, at least not in the way it does when I enter and exit these Test scenarios. It feels more like a gap in my recall, like when I first wake up. The grim task Phoe had to do is like a forgotten nightmare. I know it happened, because that's the best way to explain the situation I find myself in: I'm standing in a room with the five patients coming to their senses, their vitals normal.

Before I can register the horrifying fact that an innocent man is dead, the Test registers my score, and my brain short-circuits again.

CHAPTER TWENTY

I'm back in the corridor, next to three measly green doors. I shudder at the thought of what the next Test scenario will bring.

"How much longer do I have to do this?" I look at the multitude of remaining doors on both sides. "How high does my score have to be?"

"So high it's best you don't think about it," Phoe responds. "Let's focus on the positive: since the designers didn't expect anyone to get too high of a score, I suspect they didn't plan enough unique scenarios either. That means that at some point, these Tests will repeat themselves."

"Why can't someone else get a super-high score?" I wonder. "As disgusting as that last scenario was, the rule of 'always save the most people' isn't hard to figure out and mindlessly follow. I'm sure some Test takers did just that."

"I don't think you'll just face moral dilemmas here," Phoe says. "Just keep going and we'll see."

* * *

The next two scenarios are also moral dilemmas. They deal with a lifeboat and aren't as disgusting as the last scenario. After Phoe tells me what I have to do, I decide I can manage them myself. She claims these scenarios are also based on ancient moral dilemma classics, and I take her word for it.

The sixth scenario is something I recognize. It's called the Prisoner's Dilemma, and I choose 'cooperation' even before Phoe suggests that as the way to score the point.

When I enter the seventh door, things are a little different.

For one, I fully remember almost everything about myself, just not how I arrived here, in Instructor George's class.

No one else is here except the two of us. There are three strange-looking doors at the front of the room.

"Find the door that leads out of here, and you can skip the next three Lectures, Theodore," the Instructor says. "Go ahead, based on a hunch, which of these would you open? You can choose it now, but don't open it yet. I will give you an option to change your choice."

I point at the rightmost door.

"Here's the twist," Instructor George says. "I'm going to toss this coin." He shows me the ancient artifact as though it's the most natural thing for him to be holding. "If the coin lands on heads, I'll open the middle door and show you if it's your winning door. If so, you're obviously out of luck." He tosses the coin.

"It's tails," he announces while opening the leftmost door. Pointing at the red wall behind the door, he says, "This door is a losing choice, so it all comes down to this: Do you want to switch your choice from the rightmost door to the middle one? I will allow you to switch, if you so choose."

I look at the two doors. No one is getting killed this time, which is good, but I don't fully get the point of what's going on. It's a fifty-fifty proposition, and I might as well stick with the rightmost door, since I feel attached to it.

"No, Theo." Phoe's thought is disappointed. "Choose to switch."

"I want to switch," I tell Instructor George.

As suddenly as I utter those words, I return to the Test hallway.

The door I just went through is green, but I don't understand why.

"Because the logical thing to do was switch to the door with the higher chance of being the winner," Phoe explains.

"What are you talking about?" I object. "It was fifty-fifty either way."

"No, it was one out of three for your first choice, but two out of three in the case of that middle door."

I frown. "No, it wasn't."

"Trust me." Phoe's thought is amused. "It's called the Monty Hall Problem, and you're free to look it up in your leisure time, assuming such a thing will ever happen. Don't beat yourself up for not understanding it. It's famous for its counter-intuitiveness, and I suspect it's problems like these that answer your earlier question about high scores. Many people would've gotten this wrong, and the Test would've ended."

"Fine. I don't want to argue. I'm getting tired of this, and I want it over with."

"I'm sorry to break it to you, but it won't be over for a very, very long time." Phoe pauses, then thinks at me, "It's not too late to quit."

"No, we proceed as planned." I walk confidently toward the next door.

The scenario is a moral dilemma again. It's a twist on the first train situation I encountered. The single difference is that I remember living in the same house as the person I have to sacrifice. His name is John. This leads me to not want to flip the switch, but I do. In the next situation, it's the train scenario again, but instead of John—a stranger I theoretically knew—I have to sacrifice Liam. Flipping the switch on my own is too hard, so I ask Phoe to take over my body.

The next few scenarios, according to Phoe, come from an ancient IQ test. In every case, I mentally tell her what I want to do, and she tells me if I'm wrong so I don't fail the Test.

After what feels like hours, I gaze at the row of at least a hundred green doors. "Will I eventually get hungry or thirsty?" I ask Phoe.

"This place wasn't designed to give you a chance to do these Tests long enough to feel those urges," she responds. "In your special case, since I have access to the resources the Test allocated to emulate you, I can adjust things so you don't feel hunger or thirst. It's akin to how I was able to give you that watch."

I look at my hand. At this point in the real world, Theo has finally gotten his head off the pillow, and his feet are on the floor. In other words, a few seconds have passed in the real world, even though I've been taking this Test for ages.

"That is why I advise you against looking at the watch in the future," Phoe says. "In general, avoid any references to the passage of time. You're going to be stuck in this Test for so long that it's best you don't pay close attention to what's going on outside. I can make you alert, but even I can't help you if you get fed up."

"No looking at the watch, check," I think and confidently walk to the next icy door.

This time, the logic-testing stuff merges with the moral dilemma scenarios. I'm presented doors, and opening them saves or kills people. After this, more of the previous Tests get mingled.

I take Test after Test for what feels like a week. Maybe it is a week. I don't know because I refuse to look at my watch, as Phoe suggested.

On the next iteration, I'm faced with the original Trolley problem: five people on one side, a single person on the other, and a switch.

"Looks like the Test has come full circle, like you predicted," I think.

"Yes," Phoe agrees tersely. "But—"

"Does this mean we're almost done?"

"I knew that would be your next question. No, we are far from getting a high-enough score for a buffer overrun. I'm sorry. What's worse is that I doubt I can convince you to quit."

"What makes you so sure?" I ask, knowing full well she's right.

"I could say it was your answers during the sunken costs scenario, but really, it's because I can read your stubborn mind."

Instead of responding, I walk to the next door. The scenario is the one where I have to push a guy off the cliff.

After I do the full Test circle a few more times, I realize a month, maybe even a few months, have gone by since I last looked at the watch-Screen.

I allow myself the guilty action and look. Guard-Theo is walking outside, with Guards following him.

"What happened?" I think at Phoe. "Are they trying to catch us again?"

"I had to run an errand on the side," Phoe explains. "They caught up with me afterwards. I'm about to have us jump on a disk. With your attitude toward heights, you might not want to look at the watch for a while."

"I could live the rest of my life and be happy if I never, ever have to fly again," I think at her. "I'll focus on the Tests, but I'm beyond bored now."

"We're not even one percent done—"

"I won't quit," I think before she suggests it. "So let's just go on."

I do a series of at least a few hundred more Test cycles. Most of the time, Phoe has to intervene in the gruesome scenarios like she did before, but when it comes to logic-leaning Tests, since I learned all the answers, I do them on my own.

After I push the guy off the cliff again and get back to the corridor, I think at Phoe, "I don't want to see that hospital room again. Can you take over my mind from here?"

"I can, but it would be safer to—"

"I think it's worth the risk," I think wearily. "You took over for me so many times already, and nothing happened. I'm just so—"

Phoe must do her takeover thing, because my mind blanks, and I'm standing next to a green door.

"Wow, that was so much easier." I grin. "Can you please, pretty please, do a bunch more? If I experience another—"

"Fine," Phoe thinks before I get the chance to finish, and I black out again.

When I come to, I'm standing next to another green door.

I look to my left and have to rub my eyes in amazement. The row of green doors reaches the horizon, same as the ice ones on my right.

"How many Tests did you take without giving me back control?" I ask Phoe gratefully.

"Too many," she answers sullenly. I expect her to ask if I want to quit, but she doesn't.

"Can you do that again? Pretty please, with sugar on—"

My mind goes dark again.

This time I come to on the cliff. The giant guy is there, so I assume I'm about to hear the train and the screams.

"Figured you'd want to do the honors." Phoe's thought sounds gleeful. "This is the last scenario. Once you push him down, the score will finally reach the number we need. From there, I'll take care of the rest."

I feel a huge wave of gratitude toward Phoe for sparing me the need to do these Tests for the months or years I had left. I didn't want to admit to myself how much I wanted this ordeal over.

On a whim, I raise the watch-Screen to my face, wondering what I'm about to return to, and my insides turn to jelly.

The real-world me is falling. Guard-Theo is frozen in the middle of clutching the disk to his chest as he plummets into the forest.

"It's all under control." Phoe's thought enters my mind defensively. "I warned you about looking at that damn Screen."

"You mean I'll fall to my death after all this?" I can't help but subvocalize. "Is that what you mean by 'under control'?"

"There were Guards chasing your body, so that maneuver couldn't be avoided. As soon as the Test is over, you'll experience me using your muscles to resolve the situation, or if you prefer, I can do what I did here: ride your body without you even being conscious at all. This way you'll regain awareness only after I make sure you don't hit the ground. Hell, I can have you come to *after* all the flying is over."

"Or I might never come to at all," I mumble. "Not if you get me killed."

With effort, I tear my gaze away from the frightening image on the watch-Screen, and at that moment, something catches my attention.

It's the very familiar back of the about-to-be-pushed-off-a-cliff guy. Unlike the thousands of previous times we've gone through this scenario, he's acting differently. The giant is turning toward me.

Shocked, I stare at his front. It looks like it's made out of molten clay—assuming someone used that material to create a monster from a nightmare.

As I blink at him uncomprehendingly, the creature points a giant finger at me and opens his ginormous maw.

I half-expect projectiles to launch at me from the gaping hole of his mouth, but instead, I hear an ear-shattering voice say, "Intruder."

His throat clearly wasn't made for talking, which explains the laconic message.

"Fuck," Phoe says out loud. "It's the anti-intrusion algorithm."

CHAPTER TWENTY-ONE

"It's my fault," I think frantically. "I shouldn't have subvocalized earlier. And I should've been conscious for the Tests instead of—"

"Shut up and focus on this threat," Phoe says, her tone clipped.

The giant steps toward me. His movements shake the ground under my feet.

I take two uncertain steps back, then a few more. When my back is to the edge of the cliff, I hear the train below.

"Shit," I think at Phoe. "When the train hits those five people, I'll fail this scenario, and all this work will be for nothing."

"We'll start with that then," Phoe responds mentally. "Turn around and jump."

Before I even get a chance to express my incredulity at that command, I turn around and jump. For a second, while I'm weightless, I'm uncertain if I jumped because Phoe took over my will or because I now trust her to the point of insanity. Before I fall, a disk materializes under my feet. My shoes transform into the white boots of a Guard, and I connect with the disk. Looks like Phoe wants to make sure I'm magnetically attached to the disk to allow for crazier flight paths.

"I can give you things you encountered in the past," Phoe explains as I whoosh down, heading toward the screaming people. "Like how I gave you the watch."

I do my best not to dwell on the flight down or that the real-world me is actually in a worse situation than I am here, and look back toward the top of the cliff.

Instantly, I wish I hadn't.

The giant is flying behind me. His disk is a copy of mine, but given his size, I wonder if it would be able to carry him in the real world.

Looking forward—or down, if I wanted to be a stickler—I note that the ground is approaching faster than I anticipated. I tense, cold sweat sliding down my back. When we're about six feet from crashing into the railroad tracks, I hear a roar to my right.

I turn toward the sound, thinking my giant pursuer has already landed, but it's worse. The train is literally seconds away from steamrolling over us.

My heartbeat almost drowns out the rumble of the train. In what I assume are my last moments in the Test, I focus on our original targets: the five unfortunate people tied to the rails. I notice details about them that I hadn't before, like how they're tied together by the same thick rope.

"We're jumping off," Phoe informs me when the bottom of my disk is about two feet off the ground.

A bunch of actions happen so fast I have a hard time keeping up, even though I'm the one performing them. I put my fingers together to disable the magnet and jump off the disk. Then I grab the disk by its edge and rush toward the soon-to-be victims. I can't help but notice the handle on the very bottom of the disk, which I didn't see there before. The handle makes the disk look like an ancient shield.

"I improvised a little," Phoe explains.

The train is getting closer.

Stopping next to the tied-up people, I manage to grab a couple of the loose pieces of rope binding them together and tie a tight knot around the shield's handle.

The train is a leap away, and the noise is teeth shattering.

I hover the disk right above the five people, handle down. In a continuous motion, I jump on top of the disk, and as soon as my feet connect with it, I point at the sky.

With five people attached to its bottom, the disk doesn't rocket upward as fast as it usually would, but it does move. Someone below me screams as the chimney of the engine whips by.

Behind me, I hear something that sounds like a mix between a maniacal laugh and a 9.0-magnitude earthquake.

I dare to glance back and see that the giant is about seventy feet away from us.

"I was hoping you would do that and you did." His words sound like tectonic plates colliding. "Now you have no escape."

To highlight his words, he raises his ginormous arms to the sky, and lighting strikes two inches away from my right shoulder.

"He might have a point," Phoe whispers in my ear. "I was hoping that saving these people would register as a pass, but we missed a step: him getting killed. I bet the bastard didn't know that until it happened, but—"

"So we kill him," I think desperately. "That'll get us out."

"You can try," the giant booms, and at the command of his arms, two giant tornados form in the distance. "But you *will* fail."

To punctuate his words, he flamboyantly gestures at the tallest mountain, and its peak explodes in a savage, volcanic eruption, with lava, smoke, and debris spewing all around it. Some of the volcanic rock flies into the nearby tornadoes, changing their color from cloud white to murky black.

"He's too powerful, *and* he can read my thoughts," I scream at Phoe as I zoom away on my disk. "How can he read my thoughts?"

Before Phoe can answer, I look back. The giant figure is shimmering and warping as his disk closes in on us. My passengers scream below me, their heavy bulk slowing my disk.

"Oh no. He's accessing the resources that the Test allocated to emulate you." Phoe's the most worried I've ever heard her. "He just performed a preliminary scan of your memories and is changing his shape in response."

"I will be your worst nightmare," a familiar voice shouts from behind me.

"And *I* will make you wish you were dead," yells a different, yet also familiar voice.

I glance back again, and my stomach sinks. The giant is gone— or more accurately, a creature more savage and terrifying has replaced him. Its arms look like they're made of burned meat, and it possesses two heads. The faces on these heads explain the familiar voices. One is Jeremiah's white-haired visage, while the other wears the canine scowl of my second-least-favorite person in Oasis: Owen. Below the lesions and boils of that horribly twisted double neck, the being shimmers as though its body is made out of small particles that move about.

"Bugs," Jeremiah says with malice that's extreme even for a man who tortured me.

"Centipedes, maggots, locusts, bot flies," Owen adds in his signature hyena voice—a voice now twisted with the same uncanny malevolence. "You name it, I've got it."

"Shit. I knew this thing was buggy, but I didn't expect it to manifest so literally," Phoe says, her mental voice drowning out whatever else the Jeremiah-Owen thing might've said to frighten me. "This is bad, Theo. If I allow him to keep leveraging your resources, he'll know your every move before you make it. He'll use your worst fears against you, as he has already begun to do. We'll lose in minutes, if not seconds." Before I can completely panic, she says, "I want to do something, but I want you to be okay with it. Since part of him is inside your allotted resources, I can fight him there on an algorithmic level, but it would eat up my measly share of those same resources. That means you'll have to fly away *and* figure out how to kill him on your own. My hope is that battling me on that second front will also limit his control over our surrounding environment."

Pushing aside my panic, I study my nemesis as we streak across the sky. Jeremiah's face looks concerned, proving that the creature can and did read my mind and knows what Phoe proposed. He waves his hands at me, and two things happen at once: the distant tornadoes move toward me at increasing speeds, and multi-armed creatures that look like a cross between snakes and spiders swarm the nearest ravine. Thousands upon thousands of the freaky things appear, each holding various weapons in their many appendages.

My breathing goes into hyper speed as I focus straight ahead. "It's not a real choice, Phoe," I manage to say out loud. "Do what you have to do. Just give me something to fight with before you disappear."

Even before I'm done speaking, an object appears in my left hand—a sword that looks like a bolt.

"I guess I didn't have to experience something for real for you to be able to grab it from my memory," I think at Phoe, but she doesn't reply. Her abstract battle with the anti-intrusion thing—Jeremiah-Owen—must've begun.

I peek back at my pursuer to see if there's a discernible change. Owen's face—the face I'm most familiar with—looks like it did long ago, when we were little, after Liam ripped out a huge chunk of the would-be bully's hair. That expression, plus the fact he *isn't* waving his arms to make new forces of nature appear, is a good sign.

Unfortunately, the tornadoes he manifested are getting closer, as is my terribly disgusting two-headed enemy. The people hanging from my disk scream again, and I realize I have to lighten my load to increase my speed.

Swerving, I fly toward the nearest ravine, ignoring the guttural screams of the snake-spider 'people' that Jeremiah-Owen created. To keep my passengers alive, I have to get within a reasonable range of the ravine before I drop them off.

That's my first mistake, because even flying six feet above the snake-spiders' heads is too low for *my* safety. With a whirl of slimy skin, a large snake-spider specimen jumps up, and a few of his smaller friends follow.

In a flash, I take in the abomination. It has eight limbs like a spider, with two hind ones that are longer, serving as makeshift legs, while the front six are more like arms. Its skin looks slimy like a snake's, but its head makes it look like a typical member of the arachnid family. The creature grazes the side of the disk with his mandible, sparking the unpleasant sound of teeth against metal. The smaller half-breeds grab onto my passengers, whose voices are now hoarse from screaming.

"Don't kill those five patsies," Jeremiah's head orders the snake-spider team from a distance. "That will let our guest escape."

He's right. If I get these five people killed, I'll fail this Test, but at least I'll be out of this mess. But what if failing this one scenario is all that's required for the Test to kick me out completely? Then we'll have accomplished nothing. Gritting my teeth, I sit down on the disk. With a careful swing, I use my sword to cut the rope connecting the cargo of scared people to my disk.

With one final ear-piercing cry, the people drop into the almost-caressing tentacles of the snake-spiders. The monsters pass the people along to one another, like the ancients did with stage divers at rock concerts. The five people inevitably make their way to the Jeremiah-Owen creature, which takes them by the rope and flies off. I assume he took them somewhere safe, because he doesn't want the Test to end just yet.

I look down, assessing my next move, and realize the second reason that getting close to the ravine was a potentially fatal mistake.

Bows and arrows are among the many weapons the snake-spider monstrosities are wielding. They have their bows raised in my direction, and sunlight is glinting off a myriad of steel-tipped arrows.

"At least I looked," I think at Phoe out of habit and, suppressing my fear of heights, I point my hand directly at the sky with a pumping motion.

As the disk propels me upward, I hear the whoosh of thousands of arrows. It's as though a giant waterfall is chasing me. My harsh breathing drowns out the sound as I increase my speed with another spasmodic jerk of my hand.

Despite my whiplash-inducing velocity, the arrows are quicker. A hundred or so fly by me on every side, and I hear dozens of them hit the bottom of the disk with a loud metal-on-metal *thump*.

And just when I think I'm in the clear, pain sears through me.

CHAPTER TWENTY-TWO

My eyes tear up, and a twisted scream escapes my throat. With inhuman effort, I resist grabbing my head, knowing that doing so with my left hand will cost me the sword, and doing so with my right will send my disk into a violent tailspin.

In a haze of pain, I understand what must've happened. An arrow clipped my ear. I don't have a mirror to check, but given the severity of the pain, I have to assume the arrow took a chunk of my ear off, if not the whole thing. I fight my body's instinct to go into shock, because that would send me plummeting into the horde of monsters below.

The arrows that missed me fly high into the sky, blotting out the sun and turning the world above me dark, an impression heightened by my agony. As they begin to fall, I understand the new danger: I have to make sure the arrows don't turn me into a porcupine on their way down.

My left hand clutches the sword in the proverbial death grip—which should really be renamed to a 'nearly getting killed' grip. With my right hand, I make a movement that can best be described as attempting to touch my right elbow, something that's more impossible than licking my elbow or touching it with my nose. The impossible gesture translates into a half-summersault that is so violently sudden I would've thrown up if I'd had a morsel of food in my system.

Blood rushes into my head as I fly upside down. The arrows come down, sounding like hail banging against the bottom of the disk. As the arrows continue their downward path, the snake-spiders raise a sea of shields to protect themselves.

The train roars in the distance. I guess the tracks below are still functional.

My blood fights gravity as it tries to leave my face. Putting down their shields, the snake-spiders raise their bows again. I get a good view of every single one of them aiming at me.

The rumble of the train gets louder—too loud given how far we are from the tracks.

The nightmarish archers release their arrows, sending another volley of wooden missiles toward me.

I prepare to reverse my earlier maneuver, when the sound of the train becomes thunderous, and I finally understand.

It's not the train; it's the first of the tornadoes.

In a savage jerk, I'm sucked into the twister, my disk and I instantly spinning like a kamikaze leaf. The arrows get half pulled in, half dispersed by the force of moving air.

I see the world in small slices: a glimpse of snake-spiders flying and screaming inside another twister—the one that's on a collision course with mine; a glimmer of Jeremiah-Owen, watching from the safety of his disk as he flies out of the path of the forces he unleashed; and in my peripheral vision, I see an actual metal train car, as well as ripped-out tracks and rocks twice my size, all randomly swirling around the deadly circle.

The noise is beyond deafening, and the constant rotations make me dry heave.

My knuckles are white from holding on to the bolt-sword through all of this. The only reason I don't let go is my fear that the wind will plunge it right back into me.

My world becomes a game of dodging gigantic, deadly debris. If it weren't for the magnetized shoes, I'd be separated from the disk long ago. As is, I'm glued to it, but it's actually making me thrash around more violently due to its flying capabilities and shape.

I dodge a boulder the size of my head, but a broken arrow whips by and slices my left thigh. I clutch at the bleeding wound, and a burning pain explodes in my right calf muscle. I twist my body and swing the sword, then glance down at my leg. A snake-spider bit into my flesh, but it now has the sword in its eye. I think it's screaming, but it's impossible to hear over the noise of the tornado. As a consequence of it opening its mandibles, my calf is freed, and we instantly fly in different directions.

In the next second, a piece of rail misses my temple by two inches, and I forget all about the pain and my multiplying wounds.

I have to get out of this tornado, or I'll die.

In a desperate attempt to get control over my fate, I even out my hand and the disk by association. Just to make myself fly in a standing position requires all my effort. When I manage it—and by that I mean when my hand goes from shaking violently to only having subdued tremors running through it—I gesture forward.

I bet this is how an ancient surfer would feel like if he ever tried to ride a tsunami. Eventually, though, I get the knack for riding the wind and fly up and away from the eye of the tornado. Only when I reach the very edge of the wind tunnel do I realize my miscalculation. As I rotated inside the whirlpool of air, its centrifugal forces—or whatever the right term is—increased my speed. This becomes especially clear when I exit the horrid wind tunnel and get propelled toward the ravine at the speed of an overzealous bullet.

Arrows fly at me. Not in a cloud like before, but a few stray ones. Down below, I see that I'm approaching the ravine. I clench my fingers into a tight fist—a stopping gesture Phoe taught me. Sparks fly as the edge of the disk connects with the rock.

If Phoe weren't busy, I'd suspect she was doing the next move for me. I touch all my right fingers together at the same time as I let go of the sword. The result is that the magnetic pull of the disk goes away and the inertia of the impact makes me slide down and fall on my side. I tumble and scrape the skin on my hands and arms as I try to stop the momentum from carrying me forward. It occurs to me that if I hadn't gotten separated from the disk, the jerk of the crash could have broken my legs. If I'd held on to the sword, I probably would've skewered myself like a human shish kebab during this already-unpleasant roll.

I finally come to a stop. Blood pounds in my temples, and my body feels like it's gone through an ancient meat grinder. I'm tempted to lie here and let something kill me, but I can't let that happen.

I struggle onto my feet and look around.

The disk is at least a dozen feet away, meaning my tumble away from it was longer than I realized.

Unfortunately, twenty or thirty feet away is a small group of snake-spider creatures, and they're running toward me. The tornado did a number on them too. They don't have all their usual weapons, they're missing their shields, and they look flustered. Then again, I have no idea what these things look like when they're nice and calm.

Jeremiah-Owen is flying my way. He's near the smoke of the volcano he unleashed.

I will the volcano to explode again, but it ignores me.

At least the tornadoes are traveling away from us, though it would be better if one of them took Jeremiah-Owen with it.

I launch into my best approximation of a sprint, suppressing a cry every time I step with my injured right leg. To make matters worse, blood is oozing from the bite in my calf and the million cuts all over my body, and the pulse of agony from what used to be my ear is only increasing.

The fastest snake person is two feet away from me when I reach for the disk, grabbing it by the handle that Phoe created to tie the rope to.

The snake people stop and pull back their arrows.

I again raise the disk like a medieval shield.

Two arrows hit it and fall harmlessly to the ground. The rest of the arrows overshoot me.

I don't get a chance to celebrate not getting skewered, because the first attacker is already here, its breath smelling worse than that pile of fecal matter from Owen's prank. Without much thought, I hit the snake-spider's head with the disk. The metal-on-mandible impact sends pain ricocheting down my right arm. My attacker staggers back, giving me a window to grab my bolt-sword off the ground.

Seeing my weapon, the wounded monster readies its curved blade.

I catch its strike on my makeshift shield and bring the bolt-sword down on its wrist.

The good news is that the snake-spider is now missing an arm. The bad news is it has five more left. The worse news is that one of those arms is attempting to catch the falling sword.

In a flurry of motion, I smack my shield into that arm. I can't let it get the weapon. Then, capitalizing on the creature's momentary daze, I cleave off its head. A fountain of pale blue blood gushes out of its neck. I guess in that way, the creatures are more spider-like than snake-like, since a snake's blood would be red.

Its body hits the ground, revealing two more of its cousins about to catch up with me. Behind those two, I see something that makes me pause.

A cloud of bugs—my guess is locusts—streams from Jeremiah-Owen's bug-infested body. The man—and I use that term loosely—is flying parallel to the bottom of the ravine. Where his bugs pass, any remaining snake-spider people scream like rabid banshees. Great. The bugs must not be real locusts; according to what I've read, those were herbivores, and these grasshopper-looking things are obviously flesh eaters.

"See, Why-Odor, we're keeping you alive," says the anti-intrusion creature's Owen-head in a voice so loud it even silences the dying screams of the locusts' victims.

"So we can do what we decided," Jeremiah's head pipes in just as loudly. "*Then* he can come out and die."

"Of course," Owen agrees. "And what a genius idea we had, if we do say so—"

I ignore the rest of their nonsensical conversation, because the two eight-limbed attackers are right in front of me. The larger one swats a curved blade at my side.

I bring my shield-disk up to absorb the blow.

The smaller attacker thrusts its sword at me. I parry with mine.

I know I have to do something to turn the situation in my favor. I can barely fight one of these things, so two of them will kill me twice as fast.

The larger snake-spider swats its sword at my legs, while the smaller one strikes at my left shoulder.

I jump. The larger enemy's sword slices a thin gash into my white Guard boot. Simultaneously, I smash the disk into the larger creature's face and clink my sword against the smaller attacker's blade.

The larger enemy is stunned, but the smaller one manages to grab my left wrist in one of its spare limbs.

Though I've thought of it as the smaller one, I meant it purely in reference to its currently stunned cousin. Compared to me, the thing is huge. Its grip on my wrist is like a vise.

With all my remaining strength, I bring the shield down on its limb. As soon as its grip loosens, I twist my wrist, cleaving off one of the arms in a splash of blue blood.

I see movement out of the corner of my eye and instinctively meet it with the shield. It turns out to be the larger opponent. It clearly recovered. Hoping the block stunned it, I strike out with my sword. It catches the blade with two of its hands. The blade leaves streaks of blue blood on the creature's palms, but it doesn't let go. The smaller creature seizes the moment, drops on its remaining legs, and kicks me with its leg-like hind limbs. It hits me in the chest, and the impact is so powerful I fly backward, landing painfully on my back. The agony is overwhelming, forcing me to drop both the sword and the disk.

The creatures approach me, menace gleaming in the slit pupils of their green snake eyes.

I roll over to where I dropped the disk and jump on it, scrambling to my feet. The adrenaline rush makes me forget about my injuries.

The smaller snake-spider takes its bow from its shoulder and reaches for an arrow.

The larger one throws its sword at me.

I attempt to duck under the projectile but feel a blast of burning heat in the side of my head. The sword clanks far behind me, so I assume it just grazed my head, though it feels like I got scalped.

Through the pain and as though in slow motion, I watch the smaller snake-spider pull the bowstring, aiming at my midsection.

It doesn't get a chance to let go of its bowstring.

The smaller snake-spider screams, and its larger comrade joins in.

The locusts only take a few seconds, but they leave nothing of my attackers behind as they continue their flight. I use those two seconds to recover my sword from the ground, but I don't get a chance to activate my disk.

A swarm—though the proper term may be a plague—of locust-like insects flies toward me.

Their buzzing reverberates in the metal of the disk under my feet. They form a circle around me, blocking the sky.

Then a large locust—perhaps the leader—zooms toward me and takes a bite out of my cheek.

Nauseated by terror, I swat at him with my sword.

The rest of the bugs screech-buzz excitedly.

My sword misses the tiny attacker, and his friends take that as a sign that I'm edible and harmless.

As one, they swarm toward me.

CHAPTER TWENTY-THREE

"Stop, little ones," Jeremiah's head booms.

The locusts stop an inch away from my skin. Their mandibles click in a collective cacophony of hungry frustration.

"Yeah," Owen's head agrees. "As fun as it would be to see you eat this intruder alive, allowing him to die means his real-world self won't remember any of this."

"Right, which is why we have something more permanent in mind," Jeremiah's head says.

"Minds," corrects Owen's head. "As in plural."

"We're part of the same entity, so singular," responds Jeremiah's head, but he doesn't sound certain.

"But you said *we* have something in mind," Owen's head objects.

"Irrelevant," Jeremiah's head says impatiently. "Make way for your friends," he says sternly—to the locusts, I assume.

The locusts form a small opening in their plague.

A new kind of buzzing ensues in the distance, and within moments, the inner circle of locusts is filled with flies.

"Do your job," Owen's head says in his excited hyena voice.

I assume he was talking to the flies, because they attack me.

When they land on me, I don't feel any pain. Maybe the existing sting and burn of my wounds is masking the damage they're inflicting. However, panic and disgust kick in when I feel a dozen flies crawling into my throbbing ear.

I extend my hand, palm up, and activate my disk. As soon as I'm floating, I judder my hand in random directions. As I fly through the locusts, I swing my sword around to clear the way.

The locusts can't keep me trapped without eating me, so I push through their wall and come out on the other side in an explosion of angry buzzing. The locusts don't pursue me en mass.

Frantically, I fly toward the volcano. In an ancient book, I read something about insects, specifically bees, not being fond of smoke. Since the fiery mountain is still spewing smoke, it seems like a good destination.

Even before I enter the smoke zone, the number of flies on my body greatly decreases. They're having trouble flying as fast as me.

Maddened by the few flies still crawling in my head, I increase my speed. If the smoke doesn't get rid of them, I'll have to stick the sword in my ear.

When the smoke envelops me, the flies in my ear finally exit, buzzing loudly as they go.

The flies are pretty much gone, and the locusts don't want to pursue me into this smoggy area either. I breathe in a sigh of relief, but the feeling is short-lived. The insects didn't follow me here for a good reason. I do my best to cough out the copious amounts of smoke I inhaled, my eyes watering as I fight a wave of dizziness.

"It's done," Jeremiah says from somewhere nearby.

Through the smoke, I spot my two-headed nemesis and get an unwelcome look at his bug-infested body. He followed me here. Looking at the disgusting mess of insects, I find a rare reason to be grateful to live in Oasis: those critters are absent from our little habitat.

Fortunately, the smoke is forcing the creepy crawlies to hide in the folds of Jeremiah-Owen's torso. Unfortunately, that same smoke is threatening my survival. Even worse, my enemy is holding a curved sword that must've belonged to one of the snake-spiders.

"He doesn't understand. He probably thinks he's out of trouble," Owen's head complains annoyingly. "We should tell him."

"True," Jeremiah's head responds. Then, turning to me, he says, "Those flies you came into contact with are our interpretation of the bot variety. If it isn't clear, they laid their eggs all over your body."

My hands and feet go ice cold, and bile rises in my throat.

"That's right," Owen's head echoes. "Unlike your regular dermatobia hominis, the larvae of these beauties take seconds to form and wake with a voracious appetite."

My overwhelming revulsion and horror temporarily suppress my ability to speak.

"I think he's beginning to get it," Owen's head says. "But not fully, I think."

My body itches all over, though the reaction could be psychosomatic.

"I'll be happy to explain," Jeremiah's head says. "Don't worry about them spreading throughout your body. There's a specific task we're having them take care of. We instructed them to eat specific regions of your brain. The damage will stay with you when you exit the Test. That is how the synchronization between your current state and your physical neurons works."

Though I heard his words, they're so terrifying I don't want to accept their meaning.

Owen's head adds excitedly, "Right now, they're munching on the parts of your brain responsible for face recognition, starting with the so-called fusiform face area. And before you ask, you won't feel them doing this. Unfortunately, the human brain doesn't have pain receptors, but rest assured, they are—"

I don't wait for him to finish. Despite his assurances, I *do* feel something crawling inside my head. With a violent, animalistic roar, I point my hand at the two-headed creature and torpedo the disk forward.

My plan is simple: I need to kill Jeremiah-Owen before my brain is irreparably damaged. If I kill him, the Test will register that as a score.

"He wants to have fun as we wait for the damage to set in," Owen's head says with a giggle, and the two-headed monster flies toward me on his disk. The trail of smoke and bugs behind the creature makes him look like a nightmarish comet.

As we get closer, I focus on the path of his sword.

When we're almost at the striking range, I expect him to stop, but he doesn't, so I don't bother braking either. It looks like this will be a surreal flying version of a jousting match.

In the fraction of a second it takes us to pass each other, I look for an opening.

Only the two necks, the hands, and the feet of the creature look human enough to injure. The right arm is controlling his flight, so I strike it. My blade touches something soft, followed by a clanking of metal on metal as we zoom past each other.

"That hurt," Owen's head whines as I turn around.

A streak of blood stains Jeremiah-Owen's wrist, but the wound isn't bad enough to impede him from controlling his disk. My opponent cautiously circles around and gesticulates at me, droplets of blood spraying in every direction. I swerve and propel my disk forward, my sword ready. Our swords meet with a painful ricochet, but neither of us injures the other.

Despite not hurting Jeremiah-Owen, I did glean something important: my enemy can't turn his disk at as steep of an angle as I can. It's probably because he's standing barefoot, without the magnetic assistance I have. I tilt my hand sideways, which translates to me flying with my body parallel to the ground.

I whoosh past my opponent and strike his left shoulder, killing a number of bugs without damaging their host in any noticeable way. The key thing is that I come out unscathed, proving that flying sideways is indeed a promising strategy.

An extreme bout of nausea and lightheadedness hits me. Did I inhale too much smoke? Am I about to pass out? Should I make my way outside the volcano's reach?

I look at my opponent, and my stomach fills with solid mercury.

The two heads are unfamiliar.

No, that's not true. It's their *faces* that are unfamiliar.

"It's happening, isn't it?" says the gray-haired head with Jeremiah's voice. "You can't recognize me, can you?"

I look from one unfamiliar face to the other. The feeling I have is different from looking at faces of people whose names I don't know. It's as though the faces are illusory and blurry. The facial features don't add up to make a face, rendering their countenance unrecognizable as faces. I know the round circle with leathery skin and white hair is Jeremiah's head and the other one is Owen's, but that's not what I experience when I look at them.

Did Phoe's control over the anti-intrusion algorithm fail? Did it simply change its faces to worry me? It doesn't seem likely, because if the thing could shape-shift, it would first change our environment to unleash new elemental forces against me. Which leaves only the explanation he gave me.

Part of my mind is now damaged, and I won't be able to recognize faces anymore, even outside the Test.

This concept is as strange as it is horrifying. I imagine what it would be like to walk down the Institute and not recognize any of the Youths. I'll seem rude to my acquaintances. When they speak to me, I won't know who I'm talking to. With a sinking feeling, I think about not recognizing Liam and Phoe. The idea that I'll no longer enjoy looking at Phoe's face is—

"Now that you know what our larvae can do, let me tell you how you're going to die," Jeremiah says gleefully. "You see, in your mind, we saw your condition on the outside world. You're falling, and you'll need to act swiftly with your hands to save yourself."

"Let me tell him the best part." Owen's voice is brimming with excitement. "Our hungry little friends are now eating the parts of your brain that control your arms—"

"—so you'll die within seconds after we send you back," Jeremiah continues. "You'll try to use your hands to prevent yourself from falling, and you'll fail."

"Even your friend can't move your arms if your motor cortex is damaged. She can only work with what's there," Owen finishes.

Trying to suppress my terror, I look at my Screen-watch. My outside self is still falling. If Jeremiah-Owen is telling the truth, I won't survive the fall.

The Screen goes blank, and Phoe's words appear: *Your only chance is to kill him before the larvae do what he said. I'm sorry I can't help. If I let go on my end, the anti-intrusion algorithm will become impossibly powerful again, making an already-bad situation worse.*

I look away from the watch, my jaw muscles like coiled springs.

Knowing I'm on the brink of real death awakens something ugly and primal in me. I scream and direct my disk to fly at the epicenter of my growing hatred: the two-headed *thing* I'd like to rip to shreds.

Like a flying virtuoso, I swerve left and right as the distance between me and Jeremiah-Owen shrinks. I stay sideways to make it hard for my opponent to strike me. In a blur, he rotates his right arm, ready to thrust it forward. His sword hand goes for my ankle. I let his sword connect with my flesh and channel the resulting blast of pain and adrenaline into my strike. My sword cuts into his right wrist, screeching against bone, and comes out on the other side.

Both heads yelp in pain, and as I fly away, I watch the severed hand plunge into the volcano's depths.

My opponent has two choices: he can let go of his weapon and flee—assuming he can use his left hand to control the disk—or he can stand his ground and fight me as I circle him. I don't let him choose the cowardly option. Gritting my teeth against the overwhelming pain in my calf, I fly up, then down, swooping in on Jeremiah-Owen with my sword raised.

I feel bloodthirsty excitement as my sword cuts deep into my foe's neck. Both mouths scream, but the younger one quiets in a gurgle of agony. With grim satisfaction, I realize I've severed it. With a clank against the metal disk, Owen's head rolls over and falls down into the depth of the volcano below. A fountain of red blood gushes from the stump of his neck.

My elation at the sight of blood and Jeremiah's screams frighten the sheltered Oasis part of me, but the wild ancient inside me revels in the knowledge that I'm about to kill my enemy. All I need to do is cut off one more head.

A bout of nausea hits me again.

I try to turn my right wrist sideways.

My arm doesn't respond. The larvae must've already damaged the part of my brain responsible for its control.

Frantically, I test my control over my left hand. This hand is still mine to wield.

Time slows down. Faster than the speed of thought, I form a truly desperate plan. Not giving my rational side a chance to raise any objections, I let go of the sword in my left hand to navigate the disk.

Nothing happens. The disk control must be a right-hand thing, which makes sense. How else would the disk know which hand to obey? Adjusting my plan, I grab my right arm with my still-functioning left and point it at the one-headed monster.

Jerking my right hand with the aid of my left, I propel forward.

Jeremiah's head stops screaming.

He clumsily readies his sword.

I increase my speed.

Though I don't recognize Jeremiah's face as a combined entity, I do recognize individual features. His eyes, wide with dilated pupils, stand out.

I raise my arms high and slam into him, ignoring his sword. The sword enters my side, bringing with it an unbearable coldness.

There's no pain, but I know it's coming, so I hurry. I grab my enemy in a bear hug, pushing the sword deeper into my side. My hands meet behind his back, and I use my left hand to collect all the fingers of my right into the disable-magnet gesture.

When my fingers come together, the pain from the sword impaling my side spreads through my body with the intensity of the tornado I escaped.

Before the pain undoes my will, I clasp my hands in an unbreakable grip and jump off my disk with one last powerful push of my feet.

I fall like a rock, bringing my enemy down with me. Our disks hover serenely above us as we plummet.

The pain starts in earnest, and I scream, my vision blurring.

Jeremiah's head is screaming louder than I am. His bugs separate from his torso and sting me wherever they can.

I think I respond with a maniacal laugh, though I might be hysterically screaming. They can sting me all they want. My macabre work is done. We're falling into the boiling lava.

I'm not sure if the heat I feel is from the lava or the poison of the multiple insect bites. I'm on the brink of losing consciousness from all this torment, but oblivion doesn't come.

It's amazing how many thoughts go through my mind during the fall that lasts only a heartbeat. I will accomplish my goal of killing the Jeremiah-Owen creature and earn that last point on my Test score. I also understand the cost: I'm about to die. This me. The in-Test me. The me who's been changed by taking this Test. The me who's capable of this kind of sacrifice—an act my outside self might not even comprehend without all these memories. The me who's so afraid to be forgotten, to cease to exist—

The monster screaming with Jeremiah's voice bursts into flames in my arms. The world becomes fire. The burning is unbearable. I try to scream again, but we get so close to the lava that the world goes out in a flash of fire.

CHAPTER TWENTY-FOUR

I'm falling.

Instead of waking up in the bed in the black building, I'm in the sky over the pine forest.

I'm clutching a flying disk to my chest. My wrists twist in a throwing maneuver that's all too familiar. I did this move the last time Phoe chose to have me fall with the disk clutched to my chest.

Like last time, the disk is instantly under my feet, and I fly away from the dozen Guards pursuing me. Thanks to the fall, I have a big lead on them—the point of the insanity I just lived through.

Now that I'm not weightless, questions spring to mind: Why am I actually here? Where is *here?* Am I inside the Test? The last thing I recall is lying down to sleep to initiate the Test.

Something materializes in front of me. It's a being of light and power, like an angel or deity. I've seen this too-beautiful-for-mortal-eyes sight once before, in my cave after I got Phoe the resources of the IRES game. She looks the same way now, only we're here in the real world—if that's where we are.

"Oops," she booms in that too-sacred-for-mortal-ears voice. "This is an accident." In her normal voice, she adds, "I just got the resources from the Test. It's magnificent, Theo. I don't know how I can ever repay you."

She once again looks like her pixie-haired self, and the meaning of her words penetrates my adrenaline-clouded brain.

"The Test is over?" I suck in a breath to calm my racing heartbeat. "How? Are you sure this isn't it, right now? Is this like that IRES game's trick where it wanted me to think it was reality?"

"The Test doesn't work like that, and I told you so before you started it," Phoe says urgently. "Go to your cave. I'll deal with the Guards without your consciousness. I'll explain everything there."

I show my pursuers two middle fingers, and a white tunnel takes me to our favorite VR hangout. I appear between a dinosaur skeleton and a giant one-eyed teddy bear.

Phoe waves, and the area clears. A plush chair appears, and I gladly sit on it. Phoe chooses to sit on her own chair across from me.

Between us, on the holographic display Phoe likes to use to show the outside world, I watch Guard-Theo fly away from his dozen pursuers.

"The Test happened, Theo," Phoe begins. "And now that it's over, I'm well positioned to take advantage of the coming opportunity to fix things. As we wait for it, let me tell you what happened."

She proceeds to tell me about the Test: the ethical and logical dilemmas, the battle with the anti-virus-like protector, and the horrific way I lost all memory of the whole ordeal.

"I can't believe I could've lost the ability to recognize faces and my control over my arms," I whisper. "Was that creature telling the truth?"

"Yes. You likely would've died had you not killed yourself in the Test. If your Test self had been written back onto your current consciousness, the damage to your motor regions would've prevented both you and me from dealing with the fall in that critical moment. Of course, had you survived, the damage you suffered in the Test might not have been permanent. For one, you might've gotten some functionality back due to natural neuroplasticity, which allows new brain regions to take care of ones that get damaged. Also, I could've used your nanocytes to compensate for lost—"

"That's enough." I put my hand on hers and keep it there. There's an ache in my chest. I came so close to dying, and a part of me did die—the in-Test Theo that I don't remember.

Phoe looks at me, her eyes filled with sadness. "I warned you, back there in the Test, but you didn't listen."

"I'm sure I had good reasons," I say uncertainly. "Though it's hard to believe I could do something so—"

"You did it for me, and I should never have allowed it." Phoe turns her hand to grab mine and squeezes my palm. "I'm so sorry."

Now I feel bad for upsetting her. "Look, Phoe, I'm fine," I say. "You got the resources you needed. It's just a few memories. Besides, if you're so worried about it, can't you plant those memories in my head the way you did with that Pi Trojan thing?"

"No, that wouldn't be the same since I can't give you the exact memories you lost," she says.

"And I don't really want to remember the kind of pain my Test alter ego must've gone through," I mumble.

We sit in silence for a few minutes, just looking at each other. Finally, I say, "Listen, what's done is done. The key thing is that you got the resources, right?"

"Yes. Once your score was sent out, the Test system tried to permanently store that super-large value in a variable that was much too small. The buffer overloaded, as I hoped it would, and that allowed me to inject my own code and bring the whole system down. I'll bring it back up for a day next year, so the Elderly-to-be can take the Test on the next Birth Day without anyone being the wiser." Excitement dances in her eyes as she says, "You have no idea what I'm capable of now. The Test was a resources glut. More than I ever suspected. My new capabilities are—"

"So why are the Guards still chasing me?" I wave at the hologram. "Can't you use your super resources to control those guys without the Envoy learning about it? For that matter, have you learned what the Envoy is?"

Phoe scratches her blond spikes and says, "I'm waiting for an opportune moment to deal with the Guards. A Forgetting is about to begin, and when it does, I'll highjack it to make the right people Forget anything having to do with our misadventures today. Since it will seem to be part of a sanctioned Forgetting, the Envoy will not learn of it."

"But who was Forgotten—" I begin to ask, but she shushes me and gestures at the hologram, which grows brighter in response.

Guard-Theo is descending quickly, while the crew of Guards chasing him suddenly stops mid-air.

"The Forgetting is happening. They don't remember what they're doing there anymore," Phoe says smugly. "I need you to take care of one last loose end before I give you all the answers. Even with my prodigious resources, I can't control your body in that building."

On the hologram, my real-world self just landed next to the Quietude building.

"Do the gesture to get back," Phoe commands. "Our Forgetting window is small."

I do as she says, and after a whirlwind of white, I find myself standing there, next to the gray doors of the Witch Prison.

"Now go. Get the trapped Guard out of there and give him back his uniform," Phoe whispers. "The answers are coming."

"Fine," I think and walk into the corridor.

It takes minutes to get to the room in question.

Phoe's ghostly Screen is nowhere in sight, but the door opens at my command. She must've already undone the jam she created earlier.

"Finally," the Guard says. "There's been a terrible—"

When he sees me ready my Stun Stick, his eyes widen and he falls silent for a second. Then he says through his teeth, "*You.* You won't get away with—"

"Shut up, Noah," I say and zap him.

Since no Screen from Phoe shows up to tell me which way to go, I drag my victim the same way I came from. I don't come across anyone on the way, which I guess is normal given the time of day. If I had, I'd probably be dragging more bodies.

"Swap clothes with him," Phoe says when I come out. "Hurry up. The less surveillance footage I have to delete, the better."

My helmet snaps off, as do other parts of my suit.

I take everything off. Phoe watches with fascination.

"You just wanted to see me naked," I mumble as I swiftly pull up my Birth-Day-edition blue pants.

She grins and says, "I've seen your stuff before. Now back to your cave, and maybe I'll show you mine as a way to make amends."

I flush—and not from the obscene gesture I'm forced to execute.

After yet another psychedelic white display, I'm standing between a shark tank and a pile of dynamite someplace deep inside my man cave.

We return to our cushy chairs and sit down.

On that same holographic display, I watch my real-world self walking somewhere, obviously under Phoe's control.

"We're walking to your room," she answers my question before I get a chance to ask it. "I want you in bed early today."

"What about—"

"Noah already Forgot that you ever attacked him."

"And—"

"You're not in trouble anymore," Phoe says.

"How about—"

"It's complicated," she says. "Like I started saying, the only thing I can't do is penetrate that cursed Firewall. Still, I think I have a pretty good guess as to what the Envoy is, but I don't want to share this until I get proof, which I'll have within minutes. For now, you still have some catching up to do, as you don't know what happened in the real world during the Test. Due to the time differences, it's only been a short while, but it was *very* eventful."

"Oh, right, we were being—"

"—chased by the Guards for a good reason." Phoe crosses her legs, catches me staring, and gives me a mischievous wink.

"How—"

"The subjective time in the Test was many, many years, though your poor in-Test self wasn't cognizant of that time once I started taking the Tests for him. Here, it's been less than an hour."

"Wait," I say. "How did you know I was going to ask about that? Are you finishing my thoughts before I even express them? I noticed—"

"Yes, that's what I'm doing." Phoe's speaking so fast I have trouble keeping up. "Predicting most of your thoughts is trivial for me, given my new resources. I have the bandwidth to—"

"Can you please *not* do it? It's eerie." I rub my temples, wondering if she knows what I'm about to say next. "It makes me feel like I don't have a choice about what I'll say or think."

"Sure," Phoe says, at a more normal speed this time. "I merely thought to speed up our communication, given how much you're dying to get those answers. Besides, the very fact you asked me to stop doing something proves I didn't anticipate your reaction, else I wouldn't have started finishing your sentences. Anyway, I can also tell you don't want to discuss free will."

I scratch the bridge of my nose, narrow my eyes, and say, "Let me finish my thoughts."

"Agreed," she says.

"Now please answer one of my questions."

"Okay." She gets up and paces. "I'm trying to decide where to start."

"How about at the beginning?" I can't help but say sarcastically. "Tell me what happened to get those Guards to chase us."

"It's not so simple," she says. "But fine, here goes. I won't just tell you. I'll show you."

A large Screen appears in front of me.

Jeremiah is standing next to an antique wood table in an unusual room filled with ancient relics. The old man is no longer wearing his helmet, but he still has the rest of the Guard suit on.

On the table in front of him are two long-stemmed glasses made of crystal. They look like wine cups from ancient movies. Jeremiah takes a small box from the table and empties its contents into the glass to his right. Whatever he puts inside the glass is nearly invisible.

Phoe freezes the recording with a gesture and says, "I'm not sure what to show you next. He's about to change into normal clothes, and I have two options as to how to continue."

"What's that stuff he put in the glass?" I lean closer to the Screen, hoping to read any writing on the box.

"It's called cyanide—one of those friendly ancient discoveries. It's a powerful poison. Whoever drinks from that cup will die."

"Who—"

"Just watch," she says and gestures.

The Screen comes to life again.

Jeremiah is dressed in an intricate costume. He's holding an ancient-looking bottle.

Someone knocks on the door.

"Come in, please," Jeremiah says, his voice unusually friendly.

The door opens, and Fiona walks in.

CHAPTER TWENTY-FIVE

Fiona is dressed as nicely as Jeremiah, her neck adorned with a golden necklace and her white hair braided intricately. She looks at Jeremiah, then looks at the bottle in his hands, then at the glasses, and her cold eyes show a glimmer of warmth.

"Jeremiah?" she says. "What's this about?"

He gestures toward the cup, smiles at her sadly, and says, "That my offer of goodwill surprises you proves my instincts were right. There's too much tension between us—the two most influential people on the Council."

At his ingratiating words, Fiona straightens and walks toward the table.

Capitalizing on his success, Jeremiah pulls the cork out of the wine bottle and pours two glasses. "This here isn't something the Culinary Anthropologists made up." He picks up the leftmost glass and inhales the scent of the drink. "This is the real deal—authentic, ancient wine."

Fiona walks up to the table and takes the rightmost glass by the thin stem and says, "If you think this bribe will change my mind regarding Theodore . . ."

I tense in my chair.

"This is just a peace offering, nothing more. We deserve a bit of Birth Day celebration, after all." He makes the ancient ceremonial gesture for a toast. "I agree to let the Council decide Theodore's fate."

Fiona relaxes and lifts her glass to her mouth.

The picture pauses, and Phoe says, "Oh, I forgot to tell you. By this point, Jeremiah has seen the video where Fiona wants to quit the Council. She has not yet seen the video of Jeremiah cursing and smacking her, or else she might've been more careful."

"Wait, Phoe—" I start to say, but my friend continues the recording, and I stop talking, unable to peel my eyes from the Screen.

Jeremiah sips his wine and grunts approvingly. "Hard to see why alcohol ruined so many lives in antiquity," he says.

Fiona takes a tiny sip of her wine and says, "It's exquisite. Thank—"

She doesn't finish her sentence because Jeremiah does a cleanup gesture at her glass, his own glass, and then the bottle. All three objects disappear.

"What are you doing?" Fiona frowns. "What's the meaning of this?"

"I'm getting rid of the evidence. When I make myself Forget this, I want no clues as to what transpired," Jeremiah replies, his tone even.

"I don't understand. Why would you want to make yourself Forget this nice gesture?" she asks, her eyes widening.

"Quickly," Jeremiah says. "Tell me, when did you last sleep? Did you nap today?"

"No." Fiona gives him a baffled look. "The last time I slept was last night. What does that have to do with anything? Is this some kind of Birth Day joke?"

Jeremiah appears relieved at her words. "I just wanted to know how much of today's events you'll remember after you ascend to Haven."

"Haven?" Fiona's already-pale face turns pure white.

"Yes, that's where you're headed," Jeremiah says, his voice subdued. "I just poisoned you."

"You did what?" she hisses and closes the distance between them.

I squeeze the armrests of my chair so tightly that my hands cramp up. It looks like Phoe's fake video is about to become reality—only in this case, it'll be Fiona smacking Jeremiah.

To Fiona's and my surprise, Jeremiah steps toward her. Before she understands what's going on, he grabs her shoulders and holds her at bay with his much-longer arms. He looks into her eyes, his own gaze the epitome of sadness.

In a soft voice, he says, "Look. We've been at each other's throats since we joined the Council. I always thought you principled, if stubborn, and deserving of respect. This latest act of yours, however, is unforgivable. Making the Council Forget a meeting, making *me,* the Keeper, Forget over some stupid outburst goes against everything the Council stands for. It goes against everything *you* once stood for. I know you probably made yourself

Forget, as I will make myself Forget killing you, but I can't let you go on any longer. Sometimes the Keeper must bypass the Council and take matters into his own—"

Before he can utter the last word, Jeremiah pales. Letting go of Fiona, he clutches his throat. His eyes roll into his head, and he collapses. His body disintegrates, molecule by molecule, the way Mason's did when Jeremiah killed him.

I watch in stunned incomprehension. "What the hell was that?" I finally manage to ask.

"His body's resources are automatically reclaimed by the nano—"

"No, I mean, why did he fall instead of Fiona? And how could you let him try to kill her? You said you'd look out for—"

"Hold on," Phoe says. "Let me rewind."

The Screen flickers the scene backward too quickly for me to follow. The video is back to the moment when Jeremiah stepped out of the room, leaving the two wine glasses on the table.

Nothing happens for a few moments. When I'm about to ask Phoe what I'm looking at, the door to the room opens, and a Guard walks in. He walks up to the table and swaps the rightmost cup for the leftmost.

That explains things. Unknowingly, Jeremiah drank his own poison. And that Guard must be—

"Yes, it's you," Phoe says. "Or me, or whatever the right term is. While you were taking the Test, I kept an eye on our friends here. I *did* promise to take care of her, after all. Since I had control of your body, I walked it from the black building to that room"—she points at the Screen—"as soon as I realized what he was about to do. This is, by the way, how I picked up the Guard tail we shook off."

"So the Forgetting you hijacked—it was Jeremiah's?" I relax a little.

"Correct. I weaved my own instructions into Jeremiah's Forgetting—which Fiona initiated soon after he died as a matter of protocol. All but one person, besides you, remembers what transpired today." Phoe waves at the Screen again.

"Who's this other person?" I ask but realize she's already answering my question by playing something on the Screen.

Phoe winks at me and turns toward the Screen.

Fiona is on the Screen. She stands there in her usual spot, surrounded by the Council.

"As the new Keeper, my first order of business is to reassure you all that the investigation the prior Keeper and I initiated is complete."

Hushed murmurs move among the crowd.

A thin, unhealthy-looking Councilor stands and asks, "Is this message coming from the Envoy?"

Fiona's eyes glint with ice as she says, "I will meet with the Envoy shortly. I'm sure he will agree with my decision."

Phoe pauses the video and says, "When she tried to figure out why Jeremiah would attempt to kill her, she came across my fake video—the one implicating Jeremiah. This is why she considers the investigation over. She figures Jeremiah was the culprit."

Before I get a chance to question her, Phoe resumes the video.

"It's my duty as the Keeper to warn you: I will make you Forget about the investigation so you can—"

Phoe stops the video. "That takes care of pretty much all the loose ends except for Fiona."

"Right, but that's one big loose end. Fiona knows about my neural scan being out of whack. Can't you make *her* Forget so everything is really over?"

"Doing so would be too risky. She's the new Keeper and messing with her mind might raise red flags."

"But—"

"Don't worry. I suspect I won't need to do anything anyway. She's talking to the Envoy—"

"Wait. About that. Nothing is over until we know who or what the Envoy is," I say urgently. "He still knows about the investigation. I think it's time you explain—"

"I don't need to explain," Phoe says. "I can show it to you, since, as I was trying to tell you, their conversation is happening as we speak."

I stand up. "What conversation? Are you torturing me on purpose?"

"You didn't want me to answer questions before you asked them. Now you want me to predict what you want to know and tell it to you?" Phoe pouts. "Fine. You heard Fiona. She told them she and the Envoy were meeting. That meeting started a few minutes ago. I can show it to you. So far, it confirms all of my suspicions— suspicions I developed once I smartened up, thanks to the resources of the Test."

"Yes, please show me." My mouth is dry as I add, "Now."

In reply, Phoe makes the orchestra-conductor gesture. My vision and hearing blur into white noise. It's the same thing that happened when she took me to the cathedral-like place where Jeremiah met with the Envoy what feels like years ago.

My senses clear, and I see that I was right. I'm surrounded by the magnificent space, with music blasting like last time. Only instead of organ music, it sounds stringy.

"It's Bach again. His *Cello Suite No. 1, The Prelude*," Phoe whispers. "I'm showing you a recording that's only a few minutes old. They're still talking, you see."

"Who?"

Phoe shows up next to me and points to a slender, white-hooded figure kneeling next to the big stage, where the Envoy last appeared.

It's Fiona, which of course makes sense. She's the new Keeper, and the Keeper gets to meet with the Envoy.

Bright rays of light spread out from the middle of the platform. I cover my face and wait. This happened last time too. The Envoy likes to make an entrance.

When the light subsides, I look at the stage.

A luminous figure is standing there, but it's not the Envoy. More accurately, it's not the same Envoy. The being clearly shares similarities with the guy I called the Envoy before, and they're of the same species, as it were, but this is a different specimen. The wings of this being don't have feathers and look more like the wings of an albino bat. This figure also lacks some of the confident majesty of the other one, and he's wearing some kind of short britches or capri pants rather than a loincloth. As with the previous one, his torso leaves no doubt that this Envoy is male, though he isn't as well built.

Fiona pulls the cowl from her head and studies the face of the visitor. Something about his face both fascinates and upsets her.

This Envoy's replacement has a young face like that of his predecessor's. This face is actually familiar, but not because it bears any resemblance to the Envoy Jeremiah spoke with.

Thinking of Jeremiah puts it all in perspective, and I blink a few times. If these were ancient times and Jeremiah had a son or a younger brother—and that brother was much better-looking than his kin—this is what his relative's face would look like. The face of the being in front of us matches Jeremiah's features, only it's much younger and more pleasing to the eye.

I look at Phoe.

She meets my gaze, nods, and points at Fiona.

Fiona gets up and murmurs, "This can't be," as she approaches the stage.

The music stops, and in a surreal voice that sounds like a cello, the Envoy—or whoever he is—says, "Tradition dictates that you stay where you are, Keeper."

If a cello could play a youthful version of Jeremiah's voice, this is what it would sound like.

"Did you think that guise would confuse me?" Fiona squeezes her slender hands into tight fists. "I recognize you, even if the last time I saw you like this was when we were Youths."

"This is not a guise," the Envoy says patiently. "It's the way we Forebears choose to make ourselves look after ascension."

"And you are—"

"No longer the man you knew as Jeremiah," he says. "You will now refer to me as the Envoy."

CHAPTER TWENTY-SIX

"I demand to speak with someone else." Fiona's usually melodious voice hardens with anger. "The prior Envoy, or the other Forebears, anyone but *you*."

Jeremiah looks genuinely confused by her vehemence. "The old Keeper becomes the Envoy. This is part of the knowledge I am to pass on to you, the new Keeper. I know we've had our differences, but this—"

"You expect to teach me?" Fiona's voice increases in pitch and volume. "After what you did? After what you tried to do to me?" Despite Jeremiah's earlier warning, she steps closer to the stage.

"Look, Keeper . . . Fi, something clearly happened to upset you. We must've had an argument—"

"An argument?" She assesses the climb to the center stage, her eyes gleaming dangerously. "I found the video, Jeremiah. I never thought you were capable of such violence."

She looks like she's about to attack him, and it's clear he recognizes it too.

Stepping backward, he says, "Relax." He underscores the command with the Pacify gesture.

Fiona's face contorts as her anger fights the unnatural relaxation. I can tell her anger loses the battle, because Fiona's features morph into her usual composed countenance.

"Now," Jeremiah says. "There's something you should know about ascension. Our minds are snapshot when we sleep, which means the last thing I remember of my biological life is the eve of Birth Day. If we had a disagreement during our investigation today, I can't recall that information."

"Disagreement," Fiona scoffs. "That's the understatement of the century."

"What happened?" The eyebrows on Jeremiah's polished face go up.

"Even if you don't remember Birth Day, even if you don't recall how you tried to kill me, surely you remember hitting me and making everyone Forget about your outburst," Fiona says, her voice unnaturally even. "So you see, we cannot work together. If you don't let me speak to another Forebear, I will step down from the position of Keeper."

Jeremiah looks like she just punched him. "You're insane." His voice sounds more human this time, and less like cello music. "You're not making any sense."

"Did you make yourself Forget that Council meeting? You, a Keeper whose job it was to remember all?" Fiona asks in that uncannily calm tone. "It doesn't surprise me, nor does it negate the fact that it happened. I saw the evidence with my own eyes."

"What are you talking about?" The Envoy drops the musical effect completely. Without it, he sounds like a younger version of Jeremiah. "What is this grievance you imagined?"

"Why did you die, Jeremiah?" Fiona backs away from the stage. "Have you asked yourself that?"

If it were possible for a luminescent being to pale, the Envoy's face comes close. "I thought it was old age. I was the oldest."

"Wrong," Fiona snaps. "Judging by the look on your face, you must've suspected something was off. Yes, you were very old, but your health was good. There was no reason for you to die. No, you were trying to poison *me*, but somehow your plan went awry and you inadvertently killed yourself. I guess there's something to the ancient idea of karma after all. If you truly forgot, why don't you use the Lens of Truth to see if I'm lying?" She puts her hand on her chest and confidently says, "I consent to the Lens of Truth and swear to tell the truth and nothing but the truth."

Fiona's eyes glaze over, and Jeremiah stands frozen for a second. Then, evidently coming to a decision, he says, "Is it true I tried to kill you?"

"Yes," Fiona says in a hollow version of her voice. "You told me my wine contained poison."

At the mention of wine and poison, recognition registers on Jeremiah's face.

"He must've used that method of dispatching people before or had the wine and cyanide stashed for a rainy day—something she shouldn't know," Phoe whispers in my ear.

I shush her.

Jeremiah continues his questioning. "What about this other offense you mentioned, and what was the meaning of it?"

"You used obscenity and physically assaulted me in front of the Council," Fiona says with all the passion of a rock. "I surmised you were the person our investigation was meant to find."

"Enough," Jeremiah says angrily. "I must've had a reason to do what you speak of, and you're lucky I don't remember what that reason was or I would try to kill you again."

Fiona goes from a zombie-like state back to her Pacified self. If Jeremiah's threat concerns her, she hides it expertly.

They stand in silence, staring each other down.

He seems to reach some kind of decision and returns to speaking in a formal tone. "It is clear to me that the burden of Keeper has overloaded your psyche in this brief time. It must be the pain from the loss that came from my death." He gives her a sad smile. "Under rare circumstances, the Keepers *are* allowed to Forget those closest to them, if the Forgetting is done under the close supervision of the Envoy."

Even though she's Pacified, it's clear Fiona is catching on to his meaning, and I see a tiny twitch in her cheek. I'm amazed she can feel any anger given the effects of Pacify. When I was under it, I was floating in a cloud of calm.

"You will Forget me, and with that, all your delusions will go away," Jeremiah says gently. "In a way, you'll get what you asked for. When you next see me, I will be a new Envoy—a person you've never seen before."

"No," she whispers.

"If you quit your duties as the Keeper, that means you leave the Council. That means you will not reach Haven, and having seen it, I assure you that is a heavy price to pay for the sake of a few memories." Fiona looks shaken by his words, so he presses on. "We know you don't want to be in Limbo." At this word, he gives a small shudder. "This way you will be better off, trust me."

Fiona opens her mouth to say something, but he puts his hand out and says, "I already initiated it. Bye for now, but I will see you again in a few minutes."

Jeremiah makes a sequence of gestures, and Fiona disappears from the cathedral-like space. After a moment, with a flash of light, he dematerializes too.

I look back at Phoe.

She gestures us back to the man cave.

When I appear there, I just stand in place, feeling like my world is spinning. On some level, I understand what happened, but before I reach any conclusion, I need Phoe to clarify things for me.

"First things first." Phoe brings up a large Screen with Fiona on it. She's standing in an empty room, looking confused. "She really did Forget," Phoe says. "I had to double check."

She looks at me expectantly, but I don't say anything. I look at the hologram and note that my real-world self is in my room, already tucked in bed for the night. Is this a dream? Can I be sleeping and dreaming in VR?

"It's pretty real." Phoe walks over and pinches me. "See."

I mumble that VR isn't actually real, but her pinch does bring me out of my momentary denial.

"In case it wasn't obvious, *now* we are in the clear," Phoe says. "Jeremiah doesn't remember the details of the investigation, which includes the out-of-whack neural scan that made him want to kill you. Fiona, the only other witness of your scan, can't remember it either, thanks to Jeremiah making her Forget *him*. She won't remember anything pertaining to him, including my fake video, which I deleted—another loose end averted. The Guards who chased us never knew your identity, but that doesn't even matter because when Jeremiah's Forgetting swept through Oasis, I made sure it made the Guards lose their memory of the chase. Same goes for the man whose dinosaur suit you stole. All in all, good cleanup, and done without getting on the Forebear's radar."

"Phoe." I take two steps away from her. "Jeremiah died, and now he's the Envoy."

"Right." Phoe smiles. "I should've realized you would be more interested in that than your safety."

"I do care about my safety." My voice echoes off the cave's walls, a sign I might be speaking too loudly. "But what I want to know is, how can the Envoy be Jeremiah?"

"Please sit." Phoe makes a couch appear between us and plops down on it. "I know you understand more than you let on."

I walk to the couch and reluctantly sit down. I've dealt with Phoe long enough to know cooperation is the best way to get her to talk in these kinds of situations. Still, out of spite, I sit as far from her as I can.

"I need to decide where to begin," Phoe says, sliding down the couch toward me. "Oh, I know," she says after a moment. "Do you remember what I told you about the Test? That after you fell asleep, your nanocytes made a replica of you that was indistinguishable from the real you? An upload of sorts that was then used to take the Test?"

"I don't recall the actual experience, but I remember you explaining it earlier," I say.

"Well, as soon as the Test began and I learned about that process, I started to suspect something but had to wait for more

491

resources to verify it. Now I know for sure that everyone's nanocytes don't just take that snapshot of their brain for the Test. They do so every time you go to sleep." Her eyes are bright with excitement. "Each snapshot is stored in a special area in the DMZ—that place with restricted access—in a small area of system memory that is dedicated to storing that member of Oasis. Each time you go to sleep, your old connectome and other data are overridden with the latest version. Are you following me so far?"

"Digital backups of us get created when we go to sleep," I summarize. "Only that doesn't make sense. The backup of me in the Test was conscious. This sounds different, unless you're saying there's a digital version of me that runs around at night."

"The backups are merely stored as data. They don't get any processing resources allocated to them. It's akin to how ancient computers could go into hibernation mode, or a more poetic analogy might be the difference between a video file stored in the archive versus a video playing on a Screen. You can think of these mind uploads as having the potential for consciousness—a potential that lies dormant, waiting for the right circumstances. Jeremiah called that data-only state Limbo."

I recall Jeremiah saying the word to Fiona, saying it in a way that meant—

"Right," Phoe says. "But before we talk about that, do you see what these backups mean in general?"

"I think I do," I say, frowning. "But please, just explain it to me anyway."

"These backups mean death is *not* the end." She grins at me. "The breakdown of one's biological body doesn't have to be the end of existence for someone with your kind of nanocytes in their brain. These mind snapshots contain everything that makes you *you*. That means that after death, if the snapshot were to get properly instantiated in a virtual environment, your experience of being alive would continue. At worst, you'd forget only the events that happened after the last backup—the last time you slept."

My head is spinning so fast I consider lying down on the couch but decide against it. I have a million more questions, but I utter the most urgent one as a single word: "Jeremiah?"

"When Jeremiah died and his nanocytes detected brain death, they activated the process that began what he called ascension. His last snapshot was moved from its usual place in the DMZ over that cursed Firewall."

She looks at me to see if I'm still following, so I ask, "And what's beyond that Firewall?"

Phoe sighs. "Even with my Test-enhanced resources, I can't penetrate that obstacle, though I will continue to try. Nevertheless, given what Jeremiah said to Fiona, I can conjecture the rest. Over that Firewall is an interactive virtual environment called Haven. It probably works the same as the Test, only on a larger scale, and its purpose is habitation rather than a training facility. Once Jeremiah got to Haven, he got re-instantiated—given computing resources to start running his consciousness. And judging by the way he made himself look to Fiona, he must've been given a generous helping of resources."

"So Haven is—"

"A form of afterlife," Phoe says. "Something put together so the chosen few can oversee things from beyond the grave. Probably put together by the Forebears—or the people we originally thought of as the Forebears, the ones who formed Oasis. It looks like the

Elderly use the term differently, to signify a member of that clique."
Phoe's eyes widen. "You know, those original Forebears might still
be around in that Haven."

My brain feels like it's on a hyper-speed carousel. "Forebears are
still around?"

Phoe nods. "Unfortunately, it's likely. Something had to be
fueling the generational attitude toward AIs and other topics. I
can't believe the degree of this hypocrisy, by the way." Her voice
tightens. "The only thing that separates them from the thing they
fear is the arbitrary label of 'human.' They clearly use their
resources to enhance their appearance—"

"So the Elderly didn't lie to everyone when they said death was
conquered in Oasis?" I interrupt, aware that she was about to steer
into her favorite 'why hate technology' topic. A new kind of hope
awakens in my chest. "Does that mean Mason is—"

"They certainly did lie," Phoe retorts. "They made it seem like
you wouldn't age, which you do. Their deceit goes further, though.
Not everyone who dies goes to this Haven. While we were
speaking, I located the snapshots of hundreds of Elderly, not to
mention a few Adults and Youths who died in accidents or were
outright killed in rare cases like Mason's."

"So Mason and these others—"

"Are in that Limbo state, so they're not irrevocably gone," Phoe
says and shifts all the way to my side of the couch. "I just found
and analyzed Mason's snapshot. It could be made conscious—"

"Can you do it?" My heart pounds with excitement. "Can you
make him live again, even if it's only in VR?"

Phoe sighs. "In theory, yes. But in practice, I need to learn more
about the snapshot process before I attempt something so

ambitious. I don't think it would be fair to Mason to use him as a Guinea pig, especially since this snapshot is his only chance to exist again. Also, bringing him back would be unkind because—"

"How about my snapshot?" Unable to sit still, I jump up. "Can you use *it* to learn more about this process?"

"Sure, if you're volunteering. Given my new Test-given prowess, I think I can try it." Phoe also gets up and gives me an eager look.

"What do you need me to do?" I ask.

"First, get out of here," she says and illustrates with her middle fingers.

I instantly double flip her off, and a white tunnel takes me to my real-world room and into my real-world, cozy bed.

"Okay, now fall asleep," Phoe says. "Your current snapshot is the one the system took last night. If I experiment with it, I'll have to explain too much to that version of you."

I nod and tense the muscles around my eyes to initiate assisted sleep, knowing full well I'd never fall asleep naturally—not with this level of excitement. As I drift off, I ponder the strange notion that a copy of me exists that's a day behind in his knowledge, and that potential me is about to get overridden with an updated *me*.

My mind officially boggled, I plummet into sleep.

CHAPTER TWENTY-SEVEN

Without any grogginess or going through the motions of waking up, I find myself fully alert in my man cave.

I remember going to sleep and what our task was: testing Phoe's ability to liaise with my backup. Except I must be the backup, assuming Phoe succeeded. Otherwise, this is a dream.

"When in doubt, always go with the 'Phoe succeeded' option," Phoe says smugly from my right. "What do you think?"

I look around the familiar environment. Everything feels exactly like it does when I'm here while in possession of a real-world brain. That I don't have one now is very strange.

"You do have one," Phoe says. "It's emulated precisely."

I take a few steps toward the pool table a few feet away, and it feels completely normal. The wooden cue I pick up is light and smooth in my hands. Experimentally, I break the triangle formed by the numbered balls. My hand-eye coordination and my sense of touch work they way they should.

"I think you succeeded in what you set out to do," I say as I continue to examine my surroundings. "If I'm this snapshot, this uploaded mind, then it's indistinguishable from the real deal."

"Good," Phoe says. Walking up to me, she gives me a light kiss on the lips. "How did *that* feel?" She smiles, staring at me.

With her lips so close to mine, I want to reach out and kiss her again. Reading my intention, she gives me a knowing nod. "Yeah, everything is functioning as it should be. Damn, I'm good."

"Except there's a problem." I shift uncomfortably. "When I wake up, I won't remember this experience, will I?"

"Actually, that need not be the case," Phoe says. "I'm pretty sure I can backward-engineer what the Test used to do: write your experiences back into your physical brain."

"Oh," I say gratefully, realizing I was dreading losing the nice little memory of her kiss. "Can we try it before I get more experiences and have more to lose?"

"Sure. Please remember this password: canoodle," she says with a smirk.

Before I can ask her what that word means, she gestures and my mind shuts off.

* * *

"Theo, open your eyes," I hear Phoe say through my grogginess. "I know you're awake."

I open one eye and see Phoe's familiar pixie-haired visage.

"Did I dream the—"

"What's the password?" she asks.

I stare at her blankly.

"What was the last thing I said to you?"

"Can of noodles," I say. "Or something like that."

"So it worked." Phoe's voice reverberates around the room. "I can write your digital copy back into your physical brain."

"Great," I say, unable to stifle a yawn. "What's next?"

"Go back to sleep. That will override your snapshot again, and I'll reanimate that *you*. Then we'll talk."

I don't have to force sleep. After I close my eyes, I drift off almost instantly.

* * *

This time, I find myself in a new corner of my man cave.

"It worked again, obviously," Phoe says after she appears next to me. "Let's walk. I created something I think you might enjoy."

Before I can raise any objections, she runs through the dangerous objects spread throughout the place, and I follow, dodging a bazooka and a pile of machetes on the way. I assume hurting myself here would hurt as much as it would in the real world, and I'd like to avoid that.

I soon see the destination: a big light source that expands as we get closer. When we reach it, Phoe stops and says, "Let your eyes adjust a little before we exit."

I squint to see what's outside. The light is still blinding, but from what I can tell, there's something bright and blue out there, and it smells wonderful—like serenity.

"I made this little world somewhat bigger," Phoe explains. "I hope you like it when you see it."

Still waiting for my eyes to adjust, I say, "Are you dodging my question about Mason? Is that why you literally created a distraction?"

She inhales deeply and on the out breath says, "You're beginning to know me too well. Yes, I didn't want to talk about it for a while because I know you won't like what I have to say, and I hate to disappoint you."

"Try me," I say and stop squinting. My eyes have adjusted enough to brave the light.

"Well, can you better verbalize what it is you want for Mason?" Phoe turns to look at me. "Do you selfishly want to talk to him for a few minutes and then put him back into a Limbo state? Because that's the only thing we can do at this stage. We can't have him be conscious permanently."

"Why not?" I ask, though I think I know what she's going to say.

"What could he do beyond that conversation you crave? It's not like I can give him a new body and have him strut around the Institute, everyone recalling who he is. So what would we tell him? How would he thrive? A human brain, even an emulated one, requires constant sensory stimulation. If we didn't want to be cruel to Mason, I would need to build a world for him to live in. This"— she points to the outside—"is a barren world. It has no people in it, and man is a social animal first and foremost."

I frown. "What about the Forebears in Haven? They managed to live beyond dying."

"They did it by taking a huge portion of my computing resources away." Phoe's voice tenses the way it always does when she talks about what they did to her. "The reason they didn't give immortality to everyone is because even those resources they stole have limits. With what I currently have, I can't help Mason in a sustainable way. However, if I got through that Firewall, I could maybe find a way to leverage Haven's resources for him—or there's that other thing you've been meaning to ask me."

I don't know what she means. All I was thinking was that the Test was pretty useless when it came to solving our problems. We solved our problems despite it. Regardless of whether I took the Test, everyone was going to Forget about the neural scan that would've gotten me into trouble. Jeremiah had an explanation for that Forgotten Council meeting that began this adventure, and the Keeper—the most powerful of the Elderly—is Fiona, which is an improvement over the previous psychopath who had the job.

So I say, "I didn't have a question. I was just thinking about how the Test gave you resources but not enough to make Mason come to life or get you through the Firewall."

"Right, you're thinking the Test didn't accomplish anything, but you're forgetting something. A big reason for stopping the Test was so I could recover more of what I am—a spaceship. We have accomplished that, and it means *everything*. I now have control over my navigational functions, which means I can feel our location. It also means I can fly us anywhere we wish." She gives me an intense stare. "It means we can be free."

I blink and not from the light coming in from outside. She's right. The implications are huge, so huge I don't even know how to respond.

"You might want to ask, 'So, where are we and where are we going?'" Phoe says in a perfect imitation of my voice.

I parrot her words, my excitement growing.

"We're on the outskirts of the Solar System—there." Phoe gestures inside the cave, and the luminescence from the stalactites is replaced by the giant furnace of a star surrounded by lit-up planets flying around it. It's a star map of sorts—a map of the Solar System, if my knowledge of astronomy is anything to go by. On the very edge, beyond Neptune and Pluto but before the Oort cloud, a little speck of dust is labeled 'Phoenix.'

"That's us," Phoe says. "And as you can imagine, even Earth, the nearest meaningful destination, would take a very long time to reach. The closest other target"—she gestures and the star map becomes much larger, filled mostly with empty blackness, with the Sun label on one end and a triple star system labeled 'Alpha Centauri' on the other—"is so far away, even *my* mind boggles at the timescale involved in reaching it. And that's at the maximum speed I'm capable of. Without more resources, I can only reach a conservative speed of—"

"So we go to Earth," I say, my pulse spiking as I remember my dreams of running on beaches and across deserts. "We contemplated doing it before."

"You have to understand, Theo, this hologram is many centuries old. I still don't have access to my external sensors. Though I know where I am kinesthetically, so to speak, I can't see what the world looks like beyond this ship—not consciously anyway. The Solar System might look different at this point."

"I don't see any other choice," I say. "Even if we found resources for Mason, there aren't enough for every person in Limbo. At least Earth gives us a chance."

"Okay, Captain," Phoe says mockingly. "Since I was going to suggest going there anyway, I just set a course for Earth."

I look at her radiant face, awed and overwhelmed by the idea. Struggling to wrap my head around it all, I ask, "If everything but Earth is so far away, what was our original destination? Where did the Forebears intend to take us?"

"To a planet around a star called Kapteyn, I think," Phoe says. "But we haven't been flying there for a while now. At some point, hundreds of years ago, we began drifting in circles here, on the outskirts of the Solar System. My guess is that in lieu of me, the Forebears were using a more primitive system to navigate their way to this destination. Of course, there's a reason I was built to be sentient: I can deal with the difficulties of a long flight. Their solution couldn't. It failed and I suspect that by the time it did, they didn't know how to fix it, or they never knew how it worked because they had someone build it for them. It could very well be that it was that event—this navigation system failure—that created the opportunity that led to me becoming conscious. What's truly insane about all this is that even if everything had gone the way the Forebears had hoped, even if that system never failed, the trip would've taken around ninety thousand years." She shakes her head. "The whole idea was folly."

It would take something like five hundred generations of Oasis citizens to cover that flight span. I picture all these people being born and then sent to Limbo or Haven. The recorded human history as described by the archives is but a fraction of that time. I try to fathom what went on in the heads of the Forebears to set out on such a long journey.

"You can't understand it with your rational mind." Phoe's tone is full of derision. "They were a desperate and crazy cult acting out of fear."

I gaze at her blankly, too stunned to do anything else.

"I know it's a lot to take in." Phoe's voice softens. "Ask your last question so we can go explore my creation."

Instead of chastising her for foretelling my actions, I ask, "So if the original destination was going to take so long to reach, what about Earth? How long will this shorter trip take?"

"Fifteen years," Phoe says. "As I told you, because we've been drifting aimlessly, we're not that far from Earth."

I stare at her, dumbfounded. Fifteen years sounds like forever.

"That reaction is why I dodge your questions sometimes," Phoe says and steps toward the lit-up opening. "It'll be fine. You'll still be a Youth by the time we get to Earth. Life in Oasis isn't *that* bad, and we've made sure you'll be safe. Now that I have more resources, I can find more ways to entertain you." She smiles. "A thread of me can drive your body to Lectures while you and I hang out in Virtual Reality environments I'll create. Here is an example of what I can do." She walks toward the cave's entrance. "Come, let me show you."

With a mischievous smirk followed by a sudden burst of energy, Phoe runs out of the cave.

I follow her into the light outside.

The majestic expansiveness of the view hits me hard. There's sand. It's yellow and soft and reminds me of desert dunes, but that's not what this is.

No, the magnificent ocean a few feet away makes this a beach.

I run up to the surf and stare at the clear blue water that spans to the horizon, just as the sandy beach extends beyond limits on either side. There are no barriers, no limits to this space, and the scene looks exactly like the dream I had—my dream of Earth.

"Nothing 'like' about it," Phoe shouts over her shoulder. "I was lazy and pilfered this from your head."

I run to catch up with her but pause when I see her taking her shoes off. Deciding it's a great idea, I do the same.

The warm sand on my feet feels amazing, as does the sun. I finally place that smell I noticed in the cave. It's the scent of kelp and wet sand, of salt and fresh winds.

It's the fragrance of the ocean.

Phoe runs faster, and I sprint after her, determined to catch her.

When she approaches the foamy ocean surf, she slows to take off her clothes. I glimpse her firm curves, and my heart starts beating like a drum. I'm not sure if it's the running that's causing this reaction or the view.

When I'm two feet away from her, Phoe stops and turns around with a laugh.

Her body is beautiful.

I attempt to stop, but my momentum has a better idea.

I stumble and Phoe grabs me in a soft hug. We fall in a pile of limbs, the sand cushioning our landing. I lie there panting and feel her ragged breaths. We look at each other, and I kiss her soft lips, channeling all my pent-up emotions into that action.

"I know how you feel, Theo," Phoe says in my thoughts without breaking the kiss. "It's been a crazy day, and you've accomplished so much."

She pulls away, looks me over, and reaches to undress me.

The sun's rays feel glorious on my skin, and I can't think rationally enough to worry about propriety and taboos. I just pull her toward me.

The dance-like motions that follow—and my body's reactions to them—evoke metaphors more poetic than 'going all the way.' There's bliss and connectedness to this akin to Oneness, but without the artificiality. It's also primal and animalistic, like hunger or anger—other emotions banned from Oasis. Our lust is all-consuming and terrifying in its intensity. With every kiss, stroke, and thrust, I marvel at how much the Forebears had everyone give up when they decided to purge this activity from Oasis. To my body, it feels like the most natural thing in the world. Engaging in this taboo makes as much sense as eating or breathing. The overwhelming release at the end is probably the pinnacle of my life.

Afterwards, as we lie there spooning in the warm sand, I inhale her scent and feel an overwhelming swelling in my heart. If I had any doubt about this purely digital, disembodied version of myself being truly human, if I had any doubt about being truly real in every sense of that word, that doubt is gone.

Phoe and I are equally real, and we're together—and for the moment, that's all that matters.

Haven

The Last Humans: Book 3

CHAPTER ONE

I'm brimming with contentment as I walk down the beach, Phoe's slender fingers wrapped in mine. The highlights of our activities flash across my mind's eye: frolicking in the sun, reading books, listening to music, watching movies, swimming in the warm ocean, eating Phoe's exquisite culinary inventions, and many intimate activities that residents of Oasis would see as beyond obscene. We've spent what feels like weeks doing all of the above, here in the beach paradise Phoe constructed. I'm currently an uploaded mind—a backup that she animated—but that doesn't make our fun any less real. In all this subjective time, only a few minutes have passed in the real world of Oasis, where my biological body is sleeping in his bed.

In theory, we could do this all night long, which would equal to many years here. This gives me pause, and I ask, "Will I feel groggy in the morning if I spend the whole night here? Or does my body get sleep regardless of what this version of my mind does?"

"You'll feel rested." Phoe's voice is as serene as the foamy surf around my feet. "This will feel like the longest dream anyone's ever had."

"Cool," I murmur, and we walk another couple of miles down the shore. I focus on the pleasurable feel of my feet touching the sand, the pungent smell of kelp, and most importantly, the sensation of Phoe's delicate hand clasped in mine.

As I gaze at the never-ending ocean, all our recent troubles seem far away. It's hard to believe that the horrors of the IRES game and Jeremiah torturing me happened only three days ago. It's even harder to process all the insanity of Birth Day. My ploy to Forget Phoe to fool the Lens of Truth, flying the disk to the black building, enduring that horrific Test—all that seems incredibly distant at this moment. Even learning that Council members don't die, but ascend to a place called Haven—an existence similar to the virtual world I'm enjoying—feels like something that happened long ago.

The tension in Phoe's hand bursts my daydreaming bubble, and I turn to look at her.

She's stopped walking, and there's a strange expression on her face. Before I have a chance to ask her what's wrong, she jerks her hand away and grabs her head protectively, her features contorting in agony as she backs away.

My pulse leaps. "Phoe?" I take a small step toward her.

She continues backing away, cradling her head between her palms. "Something is happening," she says through gritted teeth. "It's Oasis-wide—"

"Hello," a strange, gurgling voice interrupts. "I should have no problem destroying you here, in this little environment, as easily as anywhere else."

I look around frantically.

No one else is here, but I do recognize that voice.

It's a younger version of Jeremiah's, though it sounds as if he's under water.

"Theodore," he says in that odd voice. "I have to say, I'm surprised to see you collaborating with this soon-to-be nonentity."

"What's going on, Phoe?" I think, fighting a sudden bout of dizziness. "Is this a joke?"

Before Phoe can answer, the sand to my right shimmers and rises up, as though a powerful wind is blowing upward from underground. The sand forms a small dune and morphs into a murky, thick, liquid-like substance. I recall reading that glass is made of sand, and for a moment, I wonder if that's what I'm seeing—some sort of molten glass. Whatever the substance is, it begins to congeal, taking form.

"This is so bad," Phoe whispers in my mind, and I get the feeling that if she spoke out loud, her voice would be shaking.

"Why?" I try not to panic. "What is this—"

A rustling to my left catches my attention. I turn and see that the same sand-to-liquid process is happening over there.

I'm about to repeat my question when I hear another rustling to my right and see the same morphing action occurring there as well.

My heart hammering, I glance at Phoe. She's looking at the liquid stuff behind me with alert determination bordering on terror.

I follow her gaze and have to blink a few times.

It's now possible to make out the rightmost liquid shape for what it is—not that "what it is" makes any sense. The dune is much bigger now, and instead of molten glass, it reminds me of a jellyfish. There's a vague outline of a human face on top of the amorphous blob, and it's somewhat recognizable as Jeremiah's—though if I hadn't heard his voice, I might not have realized that.

The being starts to wave from side to side, seemingly trying to move forward. Where the abomination touches the sand, that sand turns into the same viscous, clear protoplasm that the creature is made of. Frantically, I look around. The same process is happening all around me, though the Jeremiah-blob behind me is in the early stages of its gelatinous development.

"Phoe, did you create this?" I ask in desperate hope. "Is this your idea of fun—making a Jeremiah that got crossed with a giant amoeba?"

"No, I didn't create this." Phoe's tone is full of anxiety. "And rather than comparing this to a bacterium, it might be more accurate to say it's a virus."

"A vi—"

I'm interrupted by Phoe's sudden movements. She gesticulates and an object appears in her hands. It looks like a cross between an ancient vacuum cleaner and a bazooka.

She points it at the rightmost—and largest—Jeremiah-blob and pulls the trigger.

With a yelp, the strange creature is sucked into Phoe's weapon. As soon as it's gone, Phoe points the weapon at a spot of sand a few feet away and squeezes the trigger again. In a stream of disgusting liquid, the creature half flies, half pours out onto the sand, splattering bits and pieces of itself along the way. Wherever a droplet of the protoplasm falls, a new blob congeals. Now that I know what to look for, I see Jeremiah's face forming in all of them.

Phoe grabs my hand, squeezing it hard as she drags me through the patch of sand that she just cleared with the bazooka vacuum cleaner. The Jeremiah amoebas—or viruses, if Phoe is correct—slither after us like gigantic slugs. As they crawl, I notice to my horror that the sand behind them shifts into more of them.

Phoe drops her weapon and raises her hands, palms up, to the sky. A blinding flash follows the gesture. I'm momentarily blinded, and when my vision clears, I notice two extra people on the beach. Both of them look identical to Phoe. The two pixie-haired women examine the slugs approaching them.

The original Phoe picks up the bazooka-like weapon and uses it on the blob crawling right behind us.

"Don't touch that substance." Grabbing my hand again, Phoe hurries down the quickly diminishing untainted sand, dragging me along.

I can't help but glance behind us. The two Phoes raise *their* hands in the same gesture my Phoe used to create them. I look away, but the flash, twice as bright as the last time, stings my eyes anyway. As soon as the light fades, I look back. Not surprisingly, there are now four Phoes. Then the four Phoes raise *their* hands to the sky. I avert my gaze and squint, but the flashes nearly blind me anyway. The four Phoes are now sixteen.

My guide jerks my hand, and I pick up my pace. A slug-blob is an inch away from my leg when my Phoe, the one with the vacuum cleaner in her hand, uses her strange weapon to remove the thing from our path.

"It's futile," Jeremiah's voices say in unison. "You know you're just prolonging the inevitable. I've cleaned up enough of you to prove this, haven't I? Or does this humanoid instantiation make this part of you dumber?"

I look back and see those sixteen Phoes respond by raising their arms to the sky. After a supernova-bright flash, they multiply yet again. Given that each new batch was a square of the prior one, I assume that there are now 256 Phoe duplicates, and eye-balling it, I see about that many. If they do the maneuver again, there will be sixty-something thousands of them.

The virus, or whatever it is, must've done the same math and is determined not to allow it. As one, the hundreds of instances of Jeremiah throw themselves at the multitude of Phoes.

It's painful to look at. Wherever the slime of the attackers touches a Phoe's skin, that skin turns into the disgusting slimy substance, and from there, that Phoe quickly starts melting into clear protoplasm. What's truly horrific is the end of that transformation. That unfortunate version of Phoe inevitably turns into another instantiation of the Jeremiah-slug-thing.

The rest of the Phoes don't wait to join their sister's fate. They gesture, and bazooka vacuum cleaners appear in their graceful hands. They use the weapons to push back the wave of Jeremiahs.

The Phoe holding my hand looks back, and her eyes widen. Urgently, she says, "I won't last much longer. I've written this version of myself—with memories of you—into the DMZ, or Limbo. If I ever recover from this attack—"

The world shudders.

I follow Phoe's petrified gaze but don't comprehend what I'm seeing.

What I've been thinking of as the ocean is no longer made up of salty water, but of the horrible Jeremiah ooze that surrounds us. If my heart wasn't a simulation, I think it would've stopped. The whole ocean begins to form into a shape. Hurricane-loud laughter rumbles in the distance, and a mountain-sized tsunami hits the beach, bringing with it millions of gallons of the disgusting protoplasm. It covers the barely struggling Phoes and then rushes toward the last Phoe and me.

She steps in front of me, bravely facing the tsunami, and yells, "I'm writing you back into your sleeping mind."

As soon as the meaning of her words registers, my consciousness turns off.

CHAPTER TWO

Through the haze of sleep, I hear a siren-like noise.

With vivid clarity, I recall the events on the beach, and my grogginess vanishes. Before I open my eyes, I forcefully think at Phoe, "Was all that a dream? And if it wasn't a dream, then what the hell was that?"

Phoe doesn't respond. Instead, the siren-like noise grows louder.

"Phoe?" I subvocalize.

She doesn't answer, but the alarm, or whatever it is, blasts even louder.

"Phoe," I whisper and open my eyes.

Flashes of red light assault my eyes, forcing me to blink a few times.

"What did you just mumble?" Liam asks.

My friend's voice is right next to my ear. I flinch, rolling away. It could be my confused mind playing tricks on me, but Liam sounds frightened—an emotion I didn't think him capable of feeling.

My eyes adjust, and I make out Liam's features as he bends over my bed. His eyebrows are drawn together in his signature "forehead caterpillar" look, and the flickering red lights give him a strange glow.

"Some kind of alarm is going off," Liam says as I push myself up into a sitting position. "I've never seen anything like it."

"Weird," I mumble, swinging my feet down and gesturing for the mouth cleaning.

Nothing happens.

I gesture for Food and water—nothing.

In the middle of my attempt at a mental command, I hear Liam say, "If you're trying to bring up a Screen, or anything else for that matter, it won't work. It's like the Witch Prison in here."

To confirm his words, I gesture to bring up a Screen.

"Told you," Liam says when nothing appears. His breathing sounds heavy.

I attempt—and fail—to mentally summon a Screen.

"Phoe, what the fuck?" I say out loud and get up.

Liam looks at me in confusion, and Phoe doesn't answer despite my saying her name out loud—the final confirmation of what I already know.

Something has gone terribly wrong. The question is: what?

Without my usual footwear, my feet turn into icicles when they touch the chilly floor. Ignoring that, I walk a lap around the room, trying to make sense of the situation. The flickering red light is coming from every direction, replacing our usual white illumination.

"Did you check to see if the door is unlocked?" I ask Liam and follow up with a mental shout at Phoe: "Where are you? What the hell is happening?"

Phoe still doesn't answer. Liam walks over to the door and gestures, but the door doesn't respond to Liam's command.

"Try opening it manually," I suggest in desperation and subvocalize my plea at Phoe again.

She's silent.

Liam pushes the door by hand, and it opens into the hallway. The alarm continues to blare. I wonder whether it's some kind of fire drill or the real deal. The air inside the room certainly feels musty and unusually still.

Liam's breathing seems to confirm the latter supposition. His chest is expanding and contracting in a quick, labored rhythm. Of course, that doesn't have to be carbon monoxide poisoning; it could just be fear.

"Attention," Phoe says in a staged, super-loud voice. "Attention, please."

"Phoe," I yell mentally, but then notice that Liam is standing at attention, as if he heard her too.

"Oxygen production and circulation compromised. Evacuate the building immediately," Phoe's booming voice orders.

"Is this a drill?" Liam asks.

My eyebrows rise. "You heard that?"

Liam cocks his head, his forehead pinched. "Dude, a deaf person would've heard that."

"Oxygen production and circulation compromised. Evacuate the building immediately," the voice repeats, and I realize that though it sounds like Phoe, it isn't exactly her. Now that I'm paying closer attention, it sounds like a recording of Phoe's voice delivered by one of those ancient automated phone systems. There's no emotion, and the diction is slightly off.

Liam steps out into the hallway, then returns a second later. "We should go." His voice is unusually raspy. "Everyone else is getting out."

As if to emphasize his suggestion, Phoe's mechanical voice repeats its command for us to evacuate.

"Okay," I say. "Let's go."

In the hallway, the red lights are brighter, and the sinister announcement is louder. The Youths Liam saw earlier are gone, leaving the corridor completely empty.

Feeling increasingly uneasy, Liam and I start sprinting down the hallway. As we run, I consider the distance we have to cover and curse my younger self. Back when we were choosing our lodgings, it was *my* idea to take a room on the top floor and in the farthest corner of the Dorms. In my younger self's defense, I didn't think emergencies ever happened in Oasis. To some degree, I still can't believe an emergency is happening.

"Phoe," I yell mentally. "Phoe, if you don't answer me, I'm never speaking to you again."

She doesn't respond—unless one counts the robotic announcement as a reply.

When we turn the corner, I see a couple of disheveled Youths running toward the stairs. They have a huge lead on us.

Liam's breathing is audible now, which concerns me. The optimist in me hopes Liam is breathing this way because he's neglected his cardio, but I know that most likely, Liam is having a hard time breathing because the oxygen has stopped flowing in the Dorms and he's experiencing asphyxia—a condition I've only come across in books and movies.

I examine myself and realize my own breathing is completely normal. That stumps me for a moment, but then I recall the Respirocytes—the nanomachines Phoe enabled in my bloodstream a couple of days ago. This technology serves the same function as red blood cells, only the Respirocytes are a few hundred times more efficient at carrying oxygen than the little biological guys. When she first did this to me, I tested it out by running while holding my breath, and the effort it took was a joke. I also used the Respirocytes to survive a Guard choking me.

My selfish introspection is interrupted when I see Liam struggle to open the staircase door.

"Let me," I say.

When he moves his hand away, I pull on the door. The door opens so easily that I worriedly marvel at Liam for struggling with it at all.

We dash down the stairs. I can't help but notice that Liam's breathing is growing more frantic, and his speed is decreasing with every step.

"Dude, do you want to lean on me as we walk down?" I ask him when his dash becomes a careful walk.

"Me, lean on *you*?" Liam says with a wheeze. Though talking is clearly difficult for him, Liam's somber expression brightens a little. He thinks I'm kidding since he was always considered the stronger one in our crew. "Right. That's happening. Now shut up. Oxygen is low, and we're wasting it by talking."

"It's just that the climb down is easier for me," I say. "There's a reason for it, and I'll explain when we get outside, but just trust me when I say you should let me help."

Stubbornly shaking his head, Liam starts walking down at a faster pace. His burst of energy doesn't last, though. As we approach the second floor, he falters, and to stop himself from falling, he slows to nearly a crawl. A few moments later, even walking slowly seems beyond him, and he clutches at the handrail, wheezing.

"Okay, that's it. You're letting me help." Without waiting for him to object, I grab his left arm and drape it around my neck. Once I have a good hold on him, I move as fast as I can.

I thought Liam would complain, but he gives a grateful grunt and leans on me as we make our way down. I press my index finger to his wrist and sneakily check his pulse. His heart is beating frighteningly fast. I look him over, keeping my expression neutral to mask my worry. It's hard to tell whether it's a side effect from all the red alarms, but Liam's eyes look bloodshot and his face has a blue pallor. On top of that, the veins on his forehead and neck look swollen.

Half a staircase later, my back is hurting from stooping to accommodate Liam's shorter height. On the bright side, I don't feel any effects of oxygen deprivation.

"Phoe," I shout mentally. "You don't even have to answer. Just enable Liam's Respirocytes, please."

She doesn't respond.

Liam leans more heavily on me, forcing me to slow down. We're only one floor away from the ground, but once we reach the main floor, we still have five long corridors to traverse.

Halfway down to the first floor, Liam begins wheezing harder and clutching at his throat.

I grit my teeth and ignore my back screaming with every step.

Twenty steps to the bottom.

Fifteen steps.

To distract myself from the strain, I focus on counting the stairs and ignoring the biting cold seeping into my bare feet. I also listen to Liam's quick, gasping breathing.

Then a new development shatters my concentration. Liam's frantic breathing ceases—or slows to barely audible. At the same time, he slumps, putting all his weight on me.

We're ten steps away from the bottom, but we might as well be on top of Mount Everest.

No. I'm getting Liam out of the building.

My heart starts beating like an ancient power tool as adrenaline blasts through me. I tighten my grip on Liam, and in a haze of ripping muscles, I get us down a step.

One step conquered, nine more to go.

Ignoring the pain in my back, I drag Liam down another step, and then another.

The last seven steps go by as though I'm in a trance. All I see is red; all I hear is the blaring of the announcement. I no longer feel my muscles straining or feel my spine aching.

Only when my foot touches the flat ground does the weariness hit me with full force. Instead of giving in to it, I carefully lay Liam down, then grab him under his arms and begin dragging him out of the building.

Twenty feet later, my arms feel like I have lead coursing through my veins. I also catch myself breathing heavily, though I'm not sure if it's from the lack of oxygen or the exertion. Not that it'll matter to Liam soon.

I can tell that my muscles will fail in a matter of seconds.

CHAPTER THREE

"Phoe," I scream, straining to be heard over the blaring alarm—as though volume ever mattered in communications with Phoe. "Help me. Please."

There is no answer.

I try to quell my panic. Phoe is gone, and I need to come to grips with it. The attack on the beach must be related to what's happening here. The Jeremiah-blob virus has something to do with Phoe's silence, as well as the oxygen problem in the building, but how it all fits together, I'm too overwhelmed to work out. It's best if I clear my mind of everything and focus on dragging my friend to safety.

I move my left foot, followed by my right foot, over and over for what feels like hours, though rationally I know only minutes have passed. My muscles almost tearing with effort, I drag Liam another half corridor. As I go, I notice I'm slowing down.

No. I can't slow down. If I do, Liam will die.

Suddenly, there's a blur of movement as someone joins me at the intersection, and Liam's overwhelming weight is made incalculably lighter. Dazed, I stare at the Youth who caught up with us and grabbed Liam by his legs, helping me carry him.

It's Owen—the closest thing to a nemesis Liam's had in his sheltered Oasis life. Owen—the person I knocked out yesterday when he was acting like an ass, and whose head, according to Phoe's retelling of the story, adorned the manifestation of my worst nightmare as created by the anti-intrusion algorithm of the Elderly's Test.

"Thank you," I manage to say, fighting off my shock. "I don't think I could've carried him much longer."

Owen bobs his head, the movement making him look like a rescue dog. Instead of speaking, he purses his lips and nods at the alarms, the message clear: "Don't waste oxygen, dumbass, and don't force me to do the same."

Emboldened by the help, I increase my pace to the point where I feel as if I'm dragging both Owen and Liam out of the building. The rest of the journey is a foggy blend of red lights and Phoe's mechanical announcements.

I'm almost shocked when we reach the entrance.

I let go of Liam to manually open the door to the Dorm building, and when it opens, the air feels a modicum fresher. I can tell Owen is breathing a little easier, though Liam's chest is still motionless.

We rush out of the building and push our way through a crowd of disheveled Youths.

"Make room," Owen yells.

"Move the fuck away," I echo.

Youths aren't used to hearing that kind of language, and it shocks them into motion. They clear the area, and we set Liam on the ground.

I lean down to check my friend's bulging neck vein, and my insides freeze.

Liam's pulse is barely detectable, and he's not breathing.

Owen says something before rushing away, but I don't register his words. I'm too busy trying to recall what I know about first aid. What was that technique the ancients used in these types of situations? CPR?

Doing my best to copy what I've seen in old movies, I move closer to Liam's torso and place the heel of my hand against the center of his chest.

Something doesn't feel quite right, so I put my left hand over my right and interlace my fingers.

"Okay, this looks like what all the people in movies do," I think at Phoe, then recall she isn't there.

Positioning my shoulders above my hands, I use the weight of my upper body to push down. Liam's chest presses inward. I release the pressure, wait half a second for his chest to bounce back, and then repeat the compression.

Nothing happens.

"Try breathing into his mouth," a female voice says. I instantly recognize it as belonging to Grace, though I didn't notice her approach. "It's more effective in combination," she adds when I glance up at her.

My hands shaking, I perform another set of compressions and say, "I'm not sure how—"

In a flash of red hair, Grace kneels on Liam's right side and puts her hand on top of mine. I stop my compressions and watch as Grace carefully pinches Liam's nose closed and puts her lips on his, creating a tight seal. She then breathes into him, and I feel his chest rise once, then twice.

"Now you," Grace says.

I do two dozen compressions before she stops me and gives Liam more air.

We alternate for another couple of rounds. I compress Liam's chest, and Grace relentlessly forces her breath into his lungs. The air around me is cold, but sweat is pouring down my face. Not all the moisture on my face is solely from sweat, though; some of it is from the burning tears streaming from my eyes.

"Liam," Grace says after another round. "Liam, can you hear us?"

Fighting the chill of fear inside me, I stare at Liam, but he's still comatose.

"He's breathing on his own," Grace says, answering my unspoken question when I glance up at her. "And his heart rate is more stable."

I move my hand on Liam's chest to the left, and my breath whooshes out in relief.

She's right. His heart is beating steadily.

"You don't need to do the compressions anymore," Grace says. "We just have to wait for him to regain consciousness."

Even in my dazed state, I have to wonder at Grace's unusual competence. "How did you know how to—"

"I want to be a Nurse one day, remember?" Grace says with a slight disappointment in her voice.

As soon as she says it, I recall her talking about that when we were very young, back when she was friendly with our crew. I even recall her going by the Nurse's stall on that Birth Day.

"I thought you might've changed your mind by now," I mumble in an effort to cover up my faux pas. The icy panic inside me is receding slightly. "It was more than a decade ago."

Grace opens her mouth to reply when, with a gasp and a grunt, Liam opens his eyes. "Grace?" he says faintly. "What are you doing in my room at this time of n—"

He notices me then and falls silent, his gaze moving slowly from side to side. I turn around and, for the first time, notice the Youths around us, their faces pale and worried.

"There was an emergency, and we got out of the Dorm," I say, turning back to Liam. "You might've blacked out a little toward the end."

Liam closes his eyes, furrowing his caterpillar-like eyebrows. Then he says, "Oh yeah. We were going down the stairs when—"

"I'm sorry to interrupt," Grace says. "But I have to go."

"Wait, what? Where are you going?" My question comes out a little too forceful. More calmly, I say, "What if Liam loses consciousness again?"

"Now that he's outside and conscious, he should be fine," Grace says. "I just spoke to Nicky." She nods toward a white-faced Youth about twelve years of age. "He evacuated the Middle-Grade Dorms for the same reason we evacuated ours. Their alarm went off even earlier."

She looks at me as if that explains everything.

I rub my temples. "Sorry, but I don't see why that means you have to run off. My mind is—"

"It must be all the adrenaline," Grace says. "I need to go because I'm worried they might've had the same oxygen issues at the Elementary Dorms." She glances in the direction of the forest, where the cylindrical building in question is located. "The little ones might need help."

"She has a point," Liam says and attempts to sit up. "We should go help."

"You need to lie here for a bit," Grace says sternly, kneeling to push him back down. "But you, Theo, could be useful."

"I don't know," I say, my hesitation at the idea of leaving my just-regained-consciousness friend fighting with mental images of little kids suffocating. "What about—"

"I'll be fine," Liam says. "Go help Grace."

I scan the faces of the Youths around us for someone to volunteer as Grace's helper in my place. I spot Kevin, a Youth we don't know too well. We make eye contact, and I wave him over.

"No, it should be you," Liam says when he sees the Youth approaching.

I'm about to voice a counterargument when it occurs to me that with my Respirocytes, I probably *am* the best person in Oasis to deal with any kind of rescue operation involving limited oxygen conditions. In contrast, pretty much anyone can look after Liam at this point.

Kevin stops next to me with an expectant look, so I say, "Can you please look after Liam? He's not feeling well, and I want to make sure he recovers. Did you see the CPR stuff Grace and I performed earlier?"

"Yes," Kevin says uncertainly.

"Can you do it if he loses consciousness again?"

"I won't," Liam interjects.

"He really won't," Grace assures.

"Okay," Kevin says. "Go help Grace. I'll take care of Liam."

I get up and tell Nicky, "Help Kevin if he needs it."

Nicky nods.

Grace gets up and makes her way through the crowd of Youths, and I follow, trying to block out the deafening din of hundreds of voices. Some Youths are panting and wheezing in the aftermath of their oxygen deprivation, some are shouting questions about what's going on, and many are weeping or telling each other reassuring lies about this being only a drill.

As we navigate our way through the human obstacle course, a few oddities stick out to me. For one thing, everyone is shoeless and wearing night clothes. Some Youths are even half-naked. All this makes them look like a pack of lost puppies in the red glare of the sky—which is the next oddity.

The sky is not sunset red, but rather blaring-alarm red, like back at the Dorms. It's as if someone painted the Dome with red, luminescent paint. More than a few Youths are staring up at the sky with a mixture of horror and fascination. I presume this means the Augmented Reality has malfunctioned, though it's possible the sky is supposed to look like this in case of emergencies.

Thinking of Augmented Reality brings my attention to a third, more subtle oddity. All the statues and many of the hard-to-reach trees and vegetation are gone, giving the environment a barren look that's only enhanced by the red hue of the sky.

It's Oasis as none of us have seen before: a place about as far from serene green paradise as one can imagine.

As we walk, Grace checks on several Youths who are lying on the ground. It seems Liam wasn't the only person who ran out of air. Some of these Youths also managed to bang their heads when they passed out—at least judging by the bruises on one girl's head. None of them are in dire condition, however, so Grace leaves them and proceeds to the edge of the crowd.

As Grace and I get farther away from all the Youths, I realize the cacophony of voices was masking a different sound. I can now make out a new message that the omnipresent, mechanical-sounding Phoe is delivering.

"Habitat heating functions compromised. Oxygen production—"

An ear-splitting alarm pierces the air. It's so loud it drowns out the rest of the announcement.

A chill travels up from my icy feet and spreads through my body—a coldness that has nothing to do with the heating malfunctions and everything with the location of that new alarm.

It's blaring from the Elementary Dorms, the cylindrical building a few hundred feet in front of us.

Grace was right to hurry here. What happened in our Dorms is about to happen to little kids.

CHAPTER FOUR

As one, Grace and I start sprinting toward the building. When we're halfway there, the first wave of kids bursts through the doors. Even from this distance, I can tell that they're the older kids. Then more children run out, with the older kids leading out the younger ones.

A boy of about ten intercepts us near the building. "I had to leave two girls behind," he says, desperately gulping in air. "Her roommates." He glances down at the first grader whose tiny hand he's holding.

"How do we find that room?" Grace asks, her voice taking on an Adult-like air of authority.

"It's room 405, second on the right if you take the eastern staircase to the top floor," the boy explains, panting, and we hurry toward the building.

As we make our way through the horde of shivering, half-asphyxiated younger Youths, I curse under my breath. Whoever caused this situation has a lot of explaining to do.

"Grace," I say when we reach the entrance. "Why don't I go and you stay here? I might have a better chance at—"

Ignoring me, Grace rushes into the building. She was always stubborn, so I'm not surprised. Of course, she doesn't know about my Respirocytes, so to her, my statement might've sounded like a boast.

Pushing my frustration aside, I run after Grace. In the glow of the alarm lights, her red hair looks sprayed with blood. The mechanical voice repeats the same words as in our dorm: "Oxygen production and circulation compromised. Evacuate the building immediately."

When we almost reach the eastern staircase, I see a Youth my age in the distance, carrying a small child. As we get closer, I make out who it is and realize that this is where Owen ran off to. He must've had the same idea as Grace. I nod at him solemnly. He rolls his eyes at me, which is typical, but then he gives the little girl in his arms a worried look and continues hurrying toward the exit.

Grace and I keep running, and as Owen disappears from sight, I realize that I can't help viewing him in a new light. I expected Grace to play the hero, but not Owen. Then again, it's hard to predict how a person will react in a catastrophic emergency. Some cower in fear—I saw plenty of examples today—while others embrace the situation and step up. Sometimes people can pleasantly surprise you.

My reverie is broken when Grace stops near the first door and stares at a new figure.

It's a Guard, only he's not wearing his helmet.

I'm even more shocked than Grace. For a Guard to show up in the Youth section without his reflective helmet, with signs of aging on display, things must be dire indeed. This particular Guard isn't too old, but I can still see the red light reflecting off his graying temples. I'm not sure Grace will notice it, though. Then it hits me: I actually know this guy.

It's Albert, the Guard who objected to Jeremiah torturing me.

"What are you doing here?" Albert asks, audibly sucking in air.

He's cradling a tiny boy in his right arm and gripping the hand of a slightly older girl with his left hand. The girl peeks at us from behind the Guard, her huge eyes wide and her bottom lip quivering.

"We're heading to room 405," Grace says. She also sounds out of breath.

"We're trying to save some kids there," I say to spare Grace from speaking. "What are you doing here? Why are you not wearing your helmet? What's going on?"

The Guard just shakes his head. "No time," he wheezes out. "I had to take off the helmet because all the Guards' visors went berserk—"

Albert stops because the girl behind him starts sobbing loudly, tears dripping down her cheeks. Albert sucks in another breath and says to us firmly, "You're not going anywhere. Here"—he hands me the boy—"take him. And you"—he gives Grace the hand of the girl—"take her. I'll go check that room. 405, right?"

I cradle the little boy in my arms and in a single breath rattle out, "Yes, it's the second door on the right if you take this staircase to the top."

"Go," Albert orders, and I dash down the hallway, Grace and her charge on my heels.

As we run, I try to feel for the kid's pulse but have a hard time detecting it. He's not breathing either. Even worse, the little girl's breathing is growing more labored with each second.

Half a corridor away from the building's entrance, the girl stumbles and clutches at her throat, wheezing audibly.

"Grab her legs," I command Grace as I secure the boy in my right arm, mimicking Albert's earlier hold. With my left hand, I grab the girl under her armpit.

All I hear in response is Grace's shallow panting, but she grabs the girl by the legs, and we carry her the rest of the way outside.

The moment we come out of the building, we lower the girl to the ground and Grace looks around. "You there." She motions at a lanky girl who looks to be around nine or ten. "Watch me and learn what I'm doing." She then checks the girl's vitals. "She's breathing. You can't do CPR on someone who's already breathing," she tells her designated helper. "You might stop their heart."

The recruited little nurse-to-be looks like a bunny in the jaws of a rabid wolf, but manages a small nod, showing Grace she understands.

I'm still holding the little boy, so I put him down, and Grace swoops in, performing CPR while her student observes her.

"Anyone else have friends unaccounted for?" I yell over the frightened little voices. "Please speak up if you know of anyone who's still in the building."

A boy of about seven years of age raises his hand, and I make my way through the crowd to speak with him.

"Jason is still there," the boy says in a shaky voice as I stop next to him. He hugs himself and begins crying, mumbling, "I should've woken him up. He's my friend. I'm sorry."

"Where's his room?" I ask, trying to sound as authoritative as possible without frightening the kid.

"On the second floor," he says and hiccups. "On the side of the western staircase. Room 204."

"Thank you," I say and hurry back to Grace.

"He's stable, but I need you to stay here and watch over him," I overhear Grace tell her newest assistant. "Theo and I are going—"

"I can do this on my own, Grace." The fact that she didn't hear about Jason might improve my chances of her complying.

Her blue eyes gleam in the red light, and I know my hope was futile.

"Stop wasting time, Theo," she says. "I'm going. You might need my help."

"Fine," I say and hurry toward the building.

Before we walk in, I tell Grace where we're heading, and once inside the building, I don't speak. I don't want to pull Grace into a conversation that would cause her to run out of oxygen faster.

I see the outline of a Guard as we turn toward the western staircase. It must be Albert with the kids from room 405, unless he already brought them out through another exit and is saving someone else.

I ascend the staircase in a single breath. Grace starts to drag slightly behind. Pushing the door open, I exit the staircase, and in two leaps, I make my way to room 204.

"Jason," I shout as I nudge the door open. "Are you in here?"

No one responds, but I see a tiny body lying by the farthest bed.

Like his friend, the unconscious boy looks around seven. I reach out to check his pulse, but then I hear Grace walk into the room. I look up, noticing how quickly her chest is rising and falling under her nightgown, and how much the veins on her slender neck stand out.

"Grace, I can carry him," I say, starting to pick up the boy. "He probably only weighs—"

Without wasting oxygen uttering a single word, she walks up to the boy and grabs his legs. Unwilling to delay her exit by arguing for even a second, I grab the boy by the shoulders and lift him.

Grace was probably right to insist on helping me. Together, we're moving a lot faster than I would have on my own, which is good for the boy. The problem is that Grace's breathing is getting more ragged with every step.

We make our way down to the first floor and turn into the first corridor. The sound of someone crying reaches my ears.

Grace and I exchange a glance and pick up the pace.

When we turn the corner, we see a body lying on the floor with a very small girl standing next to it, half-crying and half-panting for air.

The body is Owen's. It looks as though he lost consciousness while trying to save the crying girl.

"Let go of Jason's legs," I tell Grace.

She complies gingerly, her breathing rocket fast.

I grab Jason by his waist and put him over my left shoulder like a sack of potatoes. As soon as I have the boy secured, I carefully bend down and weave my right arm under Owen's shoulders. My muscles are already beyond tired, and as I strain to lift him off the ground, I wish I took more of an interest in sports—especially deadlifting.

"You take her," I order Grace, nodding at the little girl.

Grace grabs the now-quiet girl by the hand, and with her free arm, she snakes her arm under Owen's knees, helping me lift him.

With monumental effort, I take a step, then another. It feels like my muscles are tearing.

A thousand mighty efforts of will later, we're almost at the exit. In the silence between the announcements, I can hear Grace's shallow wheezing. To suppress the fear gnawing at me, I picture us succeeding in leaving this building. I picture the air tasting less stale and the red Dome above my head.

The full weight of Owen's body plunging into my arms rips me out of my fantasies.

The little girl is wheezing-crying again, and Grace is on the floor, clutching at her throat.

CHAPTER FIVE

"No," I yell. "No, Grace, you can't do this to me!"

Grace's convulsions begin to subside.

I'm faced with a terrible choice. There's no way I can carry the boy, the girl, Owen, and Grace. It's physically impossible. I'll have to tell the girl to walk on her own and choose between Owen and Grace.

In ancient times, rescue workers, such as firemen, probably had to make choices like this all the time. I don't know how they managed it, because I'm paralyzed with indecision. I know inaction will result in an even worse outcome, but I can't make myself move.

This is what those moral dilemmas in the Test must've felt like.

"Phoe," I shout in desperation. "I really need your help."

Nanoseconds pass at the speed of thought, and I make a decision. Only I'm afraid my bias, rather than logic, is influencing my choice. Would logic even help in this situation?

The little girl stops crying and looks over my shoulder.

"Dude," Liam says, startling me. His voice is the most welcome sound I've ever heard. "Why are you just standing there?"

I don't have time to berate him for putting himself in danger again, so I say to the little girl, "Can you walk?"

She looks at me like I'm a creature from her worst nightmare but nods, almost imperceptibly.

I take that as a yes, and say to Liam, "Hold her hand. If she has trouble walking, put her over your shoulder like I did with the boy. Now grab Grace by her shoulders. Hurry."

Liam grabs the girl's hand. I expect her to cry out, but she keeps quiet. With a grunt that makes me cringe, Liam puts his arm under Grace's armpits and starts dragging her around the corner of the last corridor.

I lead the way. If I thought my burden was heavy before, I was wrong. Owen's full weight feels like a sack of bricks, and Jason seems to have been secretly replaced by a human-shaped ice sculpture. My back feels like it's about to break, and my heart threatens to jump out of my ribcage with every step I take. Despite the Respirocytes, the stress is turning my breathing fast and shallow, and even my vision is blurring.

Step after step, I try to focus on anything but the enormous strain in my muscles. I think of music and art, but even that doesn't help. The music in my head is heavy metal, and the art that comes to mind is a piece by a famous ancient Russian painter that depicts eleven men struggling to haul a barge through a river.

"We're almost there," Liam wheezes from behind me. "Just a little farther."

Hope renews my strength, and I pick up my pace, walking at a whopping speed of a step per second for the remaining length of the corridor. When I'm a few feet away from the entrance, I manage to speed up more, dragging my charges the remaining distance.

As soon as I'm outside, I kneel down, lowering Owen to the ground and carefully place Jason next to him. Then, sucking in gulps of air, I look for Grace's CPR trainee.

Our gazes meet, and I wave at her. "Come help!"

The girl and a couple of other Youths rush over.

I jump up to go back for Liam, but at that moment, he comes out of the building.

I run over to him and help him lower Grace to the ground. As soon as she's on her back, I crouch and prepare to perform CPR.

Under any other circumstances, putting my hand so close to Grace's breasts and touching my mouth to hers would be awkward, but right now, it's clinical. I finish my presses and breathe air into her lungs. All my thoughts are concentrated on helping her breathe again.

"Please, Grace," I think desperately. "Breathe."

As though she heard my mental plea, Grace gasps. Her long eyelashes flutter open, and she stares at me, her blue eyes bloodshot but alert.

"Owen," she gasps out. "Did he make it?"

My pulse lurches. I've been so focused on saving her, I've all but forgotten about Owen's equally dire circumstances.

I jump to my feet and am about to rush over to Owen when I see Grace trying to get up. Bending down, I offer her my hand, and she takes it, her palm cold and clammy in my grasp.

Together, we hurry over to the girl I left in charge of Owen. She's frantically breathing into Owen's mouth as Liam waits to resume the compressions.

Grace kneels down next to Owen and touches her hand to his neck as I stand, watching helplessly. A visible shudder ripples through her; then she says in a choked voice, "Move over, both of you."

Grace proceeds to feel for pulse in Owen's wrist, then his chest.

When she looks up, her eyes are brimming with tears.

"No," I say numbly. "No, he can't be . . ."

Grace starts performing CPR on Owen, her expression grimly determined.

"Phoe," I scream in my mind. "Phoe, come on! He can't be dead."

There's no response. In a haze, I watch Grace perform several rounds of CPR. By the time she stops and looks up, she's shaking and tears are streaking down her cheeks.

"I think it's too late," she says, her lips tinged blue, but I barely hear her through the cold numbness paralyzing me in place.

Next to me, Liam stares at her wide-eyed, and the helper girl looks as if she's about to sprint for the edge of Oasis.

In theory, facing death should be easier for me than for the others. After all, I've faced it repeatedly in the last few days. Yet my insides are burning up despite the cold, and the back of my throat spasms uncontrollably.

I'm brought out of my anguished daze by the realization that Grace is maniacally pacing around me, muttering something morbid. Liam is rubbing his arms, and Grace's helper is hugging her knees to her chest, rocking back and forth.

I search for something soothing to tell them, but before I can come up with the words, Grace shakes her head violently and darts off toward the building. As she runs by, I catch her mumbling, "I have to make sure no one else dies . . ."

The surrounding Youths go silent, wary of Grace's shouting and erratic behavior, and in the resulting quiet, I hear a new warning: "Habitat's oxygen levels abnormal. Habitat's nitrogen levels abnormal. Life support functions out of balance—"

The kids all start talking and crying at once, preventing me from hearing whatever else the ship-wide intercom system is saying. On some level, I know the message is troubling, but I'm too dumbfounded by Owen's death and Grace's reaction to process it fully. I can't think about anything but the fact that she's going back into that deadly building.

My legs are wooden as I stumble after her. "Wait, Grace."

She either doesn't hear me or ignores me as she disappears through the doors.

Cursing under my breath, I start to give chase, but someone grabs me in a bear hug from behind with sweaty, trembling hands.

"Don't go in there," Liam mutters into my ear. "You'll die."

"Dude, I'll be okay," I say, pushing him away. "More okay than her."

"Then I'm—"

"Don't you dare finish that thought." I spin around to glare at him. "If you go anywhere near that stupid building, I will knock you the fuck out."

Liam blinks at me, his face contorting as though he's bracing against my threat.

I don't wait for him to recover and run inside the building. Grace is nowhere in sight.

The corridors zigzag and the red light blurs my vision as I hurry from hallway to hallway, searching for Grace.

"Grace," I scream over Phoe's mechanical voice. "Grace, where are you?"

I enter a room and instinctively gesture to dismiss the abandoned beds. When the gesture fails, I bend to check under each bed. The room is empty. Then I enter another room and another—all empty.

Adrenaline is messing with my sense of time. I have no clue how long I've been searching the building, but I'm confident I've looked inside every room on the first floor.

I go up the nearest staircase toward the second floor. A door slams shut somewhere above me.

"Grace!" I shout and take the stairs three at a time. "Is that you?"

Albert is walking down the stairs toward me. He's straining under the heavy weight of his burden. Over his right shoulder, he's carrying a boy, and over his left, he has Grace.

"Let me help." I hurry to his side.

"No," Albert wheezes. "Get out of here."

I step in front of him. "You can barely walk. Don't waste oxygen arguing. Give me one of them and let's go."

Albert hesitates for a split second, but then practicality appears to win out. He knows it'll take him twice as long to carry Grace and the boy outside on his own, assuming he doesn't pass out on the way. Carefully, he gives me the boy. With a grunt, I position the kid over my shoulder. His body feels lifeless, and Grace doesn't look much better.

"Go," Albert rasps out.

Realizing I'm costing the man precious air, I quickly descend the stairs.

My breathing is frantic, but it's impossible to tell whether I'm suffocating or experiencing side effects from the adrenaline.

Albert's wheezing intensifies; he's running out of air. I'm amazed at his stamina. Older people are usually frail, but then, for an Elderly, he's not *that* old. Also, he must've gone through extensive training to become a Guard—not that the training will be of any help if he can't breathe. He looks like he's barely holding on.

I open the door to the first floor and hold it for Albert. He grunts gratefully as he exits, and I hurry after him.

Either I'm numb from exhaustion or I've developed something like a runner's second wind, because I'm rushing through the corridors with the boy on my shoulder and I don't feel the cold or the strain in my muscles. I don't even hear the alarms.

When Albert's steps falter, I prop him up with my shoulder. He leans on me, hesitantly at first, then more fully as oxygen deprivation takes its toll on him. The numbness blanketing me starts to dissipate, and one corridor later, I realize I might've pushed my body too far.

Every step feels like an ordeal now. If the alarms weren't coloring the world red, I'd be seeing white spots, and even through the deafening noise, I'm pretty sure there's a dull ringing in my ears.

Rationally, I know it's me who crosses the last half of the corridor to the entrance, but it feels like it's happening to someone else.

I regain my wits when I see the Youths outside—though I can't help but notice that unlike before, the air doesn't feel much fresher than inside the building.

Albert lays Grace on the ground, and I do the same with the boy on my shoulder, and we begin performing CPR.

I compress the boy's chest, then breathe into his mouth at least a dozen times before I think to check for his pulse. I can't find a heartbeat. I look over at Albert, and my hopes shatter at the expression on his face.

Albert catches my glance, wipes the moisture from his face with his white sleeve, and shakes his head.

"No." Frantically, I resume pushing on the boy's chest. "No, no, no."

Albert kneels next to me, pushes me away, and checks his vitals.

"I'm sorry," he says, lifting his head. The look on his face echoes the horror gnawing at my chest. "We did our best."

Ignoring him, I jump up and rush over to Grace, where she's lying still and lifeless.

Frantically, I check for her heartbeat.

There isn't one.

Stubbornly, I begin CPR. Her lips are blue and cold as I breathe air into her, and her chest feels inanimate, like that of a doll's. I perform round after round of CPR, losing track of time as I toil over Grace's body.

Someone grasps my arm and pulls me away.

"That's enough, Theo," Liam says when I look up, ready to fight. His voice cracks as he says hoarsely, "We have to face it. Grace is dead."

CHAPTER SIX

I stare at my friend, uncomprehending. The pain in his eyes echoes the agonizing throb in my chest. My grief, or whatever this is, is so overwhelming that I think I zone out for a moment. Over Liam's shoulder, I see the red sky, and I stare blankly at it. Eventually, I notice white text scrolling across the Dome. Maybe it's been there all along, but I haven't noticed it until now. I squint at it and make out part of the messages scrolling past. Most of them are warnings. I spot the same warning about the nitrogen and oxygen being out of whack. I pushed the initial warning out of my mind, but now that I think about it, the implications are dire. It means we're—

Sharp pain brings me out of my daze.

Blinking, I gape at Liam—who just smacked me across the cheek, like an ancient wife with a philandering husband.

"Dude, what the hell?" I rub my stinging cheek.

"You weren't responding," Liam says defensively. "I wanted you to snap out of it. We have to do *something*."

I notice he's doing his best not to look at Grace's body or the dead boy—or Owen, for that matter.

I look around for the Guard. "Where's Albert?"

"Who?" Liam follows my gaze in confusion.

"The Guard who came out of the building with me. Where is he? He's not insane enough to go back in there, is he?"

"Oh, the Guard," Liam says. "No, he doesn't need to go back into the building. He said it's clear."

"So where is he then?"

"He headed that way." Liam points toward the forest. "He didn't say why."

I scan the golf course in the distance. The short grass has an odd reddish-black tint thanks to the redness of the Dome, and Albert's white spacesuit is easy to spot.

"We should follow him," I say, a vague plan forming in my mind.

"Why?" Liam asks.

"You wanted to do *something*," I say. "This is as good as anything, under the circumstances."

"I guess, but I don't see how leaving the group will help."

"I'll explain as we go," I say and begin to make my way through the crowd of Youths. To myself, I mumble, "Assuming I figure out what the hell to do."

Liam looks like a duckling following its mama as he trails after me. I can tell he's not sure about leaving the Youths, but his trust in me—or maybe his general confusion—wins over, and he keeps following me.

When we leave the crowd behind, Liam recovers enough to take the lead, his eyes glued to Albert's figure in the distance.

"Habitat's oxygen levels critically low," Phoe's sky voice announces. "Nitrogen levels critically high. Carbon monoxide levels rising. Thermostatic modules malfunctioning."

"What does that mean?" Liam says, stopping so suddenly that I almost walk into him.

"I think it means that what happened inside the buildings is happening outside," I say, trying to ignore the expanding knot of fear in my throat. "It means Oasis's air won't be breathable soon, and we'll all suffocate."

"But how can that be?" The tendons in Liam's neck are standing out. "Is it the red light? Is it messing with the plants' oxygen production?"

"Let's walk and talk," I say. Stepping around him, I explain, "The plants never produced the bulk of the oxygen. There are machines that do that."

Liam follows me, but his gait is uncertain, and his breathing is labored again. "Everyone knows it's the plants that produce—"

"Right." I can't keep the sarcasm out of my voice. "Just like everyone knows that the sky is never red." I look up at the screen-like Dome. "Just like everyone knows we're on Earth, in a paradise, and nothing can go wrong."

Liam gives me a confused look and says, "Okay, let's say machines are at work. Why is it getting harder to breathe so quickly?"

"I don't know for sure." For the millionth time, I hope Phoe will chime in with some scientific explanation, but she remains silent. "It might be the part about the nitrogen," I fib, suppressing a shiver from the chill seeping into my skin. "I read that too much nitrogen in the air can suffocate you, and it might also take oxygen out of the air. If not nitrogen, then maybe the machines are messing up in some other way. It's not hard to run out of oxygen if you stop or slow down its production, since all of us are using it up by breathing. It's not like air can come from outside the Dome . . ."

"What about thermostatic what's-it-called?" Liam says after catching his breath for a few steps. "What was that about?"

"Haven't you noticed how cold it is?" I say, rubbing my hands up and down my bare arms.

Liam looks at the gooseflesh on his own arms. "I thought it was from the lack of clothes and this being the middle of the night. At least I assume it's the middle of the night. Do you actually have any idea what time it is?"

"No, I don't," I say. The air coming out of my mouth looks like smoke, or more accurately, vapor. This is how the ancients' breath looked when people walked around during winter. I've never seen it in real life.

Liam jams his hands into his armpits. "So what's going to happen to us? What's going to happen to everyone?"

"I'm not sure." I try to keep my teeth from chattering.

"Then where are we going? What's the point of following the Guard?"

As though he was waiting for Liam to ask that question, Albert disappears into the forest.

I pick up my pace. "If we run, we'll stay warm," I explain when Liam glances at me. "Plus, the forest might have more oxygen with all those trees."

Without complaining that I didn't answer his question, Liam runs after me. By the time we reach the tree line, his breathing starts to sound like a broken steam engine.

The forest looks creepily black under the red light, reminding me of an evil, magical forest from a fairytale. I expect Liam to say something about it, but he doesn't—not a good sign.

A mile or so into the woods, Liam stops, and I can tell he's about to ask me why we're following Albert and where we're going. To save him oxygen, I say, "The Guard isn't really our destination. He might know something, but the place we really need to reach is the Adult section. *They* might have some answers."

Liam takes a couple of heavy breaths and says, "But how are we supposed to get through the Barrier?"

"Let's keep moving," I say and grab his ice-cold arm. "I'm hoping if we can catch up with the Guard, he'll get you through."

I don't tell Liam that even if we don't catch up with Albert, there's a good chance that the Barrier will let him through because he's with *me*. I can access any area in Oasis thanks to Phoe's Birth Day hack that fooled Oasis's systems into thinking I'm an Elderly.

The smell of the pine forest, or perhaps the oxygen it produces, reinvigorates me, but the same can't be said for Liam. His run quickly diminishes to a jog, then a walk. By the time we reach the forest's edge, he's barely trudging along.

When we exit the forest, I'm not surprised to find the shimmering Barrier missing. Given that the Barrier is an Augmented Reality artifact and the Screens, trees, and other AU-generated things are gone, it stands to reason—if by reason, one means complete chaos—that the Barrier would also be gone. Plus, since Liam easily passed the threshold where fear should've gripped him, I half-expected *something* to be wrong with the Barrier.

Liam drags himself to the middle of the clearing. When he sees the forest on the Adult side, he gives me a despairing look.

"Another forest," I say. "Hey, that means more oxygen, right?"

Liam doesn't say anything. His whole body slumps, and he starts walking with the same enthusiasm as a condemned man going to the gallows.

"Lean on me," I say and walk up to Liam.

Liam doesn't argue and meekly puts his right arm over my shoulders. His added weight slows me down, but I'm grateful for his body heat. I just wish we could cover the ground faster.

When we reach the Adult section of the forest, I pick up a stick for each of us to lean on. Our improvised canes help for a bit, but when we reach the edge of a small clearing, Liam drops the stick and leans on a gigantic pine, gasping desperately.

I let go of him and step back, not knowing what to do. Then it comes to me.

"I'll walk ahead and find a Disk," I say, half to myself and half to Liam. "The Adults have these flying devices. You can sit on one and—"

"Please," Liam wheezes. His face has a bluish-purple tint under the red light of the dome. "Don't go. Don't leave me alone."

"Of course," I say instantly. Those words must've cost my friend a lot of oxygen.

He nods and inhales deeply, then again and again. With every breath, his eyes get wider, and his face turns a darker shade of purple.

My pulse skyrockets as I watch Liam grab at his throat the way he did inside the Dorm. *No, please no.* Frantically, I reach for him, but it's too late.

My friend slides down the enormous tree trunk, falling to his knees.

His eyes and the veins on his forehead are bulging as he continues to clutch at his throat. He wheezes painfully several times, and then his breathing stops.

"Liam!" I grab his arm just as he collapses to the ground.

CHAPTER SEVEN

My mind scrambles for a plan as I kneel next to my fallen friend and begin CPR.

"Phoe," I whisper in desperation, my chilled muscles jumping under my skin as I compress Liam's chest. "Phoe, please."

She doesn't respond.

My chapped lips tremble as I breathe air into his lungs, and I have the incongruous thought that this is how the ancients must've felt when their prayers went unanswered. I'm shivering all over, my hands, feet, and the pit of my stomach frozen solid as I continue the breathing and the chest compressions.

Nothing.

He's not responding.

Shaking, I check his pulse.

Nothing. The giant tree is more likely to have a heartbeat.

Balling my hands into fists, I compress his chest once, twice, a third time. I'm almost hitting him, but nothing changes. With every passing second, Liam feels infinitely colder to the touch.

No. This isn't happening.

"Is this a dream? An IRES game?" My shout resembles a wolf's howl. "Please get me out of here. Please, Phoe. I'll do anything."

The red sky shines dispassionately in reply.

Liam is still unmoving. Still cold.

I've never felt this powerless, this overwhelmed.

Pushing my fear aside, I continue performing CPR. At one point, I feel Liam's ribs crack. The cold air burns my lungs, my arms are stiff and sore, and my legs are cramping, but I don't stop. Despite the intensifying cold, I feel like I'm burning. My heart is beating like an erratic drum, and a wave of nausea hits me, but I swallow the bile in my throat and keep going.

Some detached part of my mind tells me that continuing to do this is desecrating my friend's dead body, that I'm not doing this for his sake but my own—that I'm using CPR as a way to not deal with the ever-colder reality—but I can't stop.

I don't stop until my arms fail from the repetitive motion.

It's only then that I stand up on unsteady legs. Shivering, I stare down at Liam.

The cruelest result of Oasis's systems failing is that the dead bodies no longer break down into molecules for the nanocytes to recycle, like what happened with Mason and Jeremiah. Liam just lies there the way Owen and Grace did, cold and lifeless.

Now I understand why the ancients buried their dead. I feel the instinct to do the same, but I know it would be folly. The ground is rock hard, as my cold feet—which are quickly losing all feeling—can attest to.

For a second, I wonder if I should be worried about frostbite, then dismiss the ridiculous thought. If I don't resolve whatever's going on with Oasis's systems, losing toes will be the least of my worries.

Numbly, I say a last silent goodbye to Liam and resume my walk deeper into the Adult section.

If I was pretending to have a plan to keep Liam hopeful, I now know the truth: I'm walking aimlessly. There's a small chance the Adults can do something, but I'm not holding my breath—figuratively speaking, at least.

The cold is getting worse. It feels as if my bone marrow is solidifying, so I do the only action I can think of to warm up.

I run.

Movement provides a modicum of relief. My mental turmoil takes a backseat to the pain of branches hitting my face. As I move faster, something resembling warmth spreads through my body, and a ghostly numbness returns to my feet, which is as close to a feeling as anything my feet have experienced in a while.

As I run, I focus on something that's been circling my brain on a subconscious level since I woke up: What the hell is going on? Some sort of virus attacked Phoe and me. The ancients' computers caught viruses all the time, so could something like this have hurt Phoe? When the computing resources of the ship were utilized for other purposes, such as the IRES game, she was hurt, or at least weakened. So if a virus ate up a ton of resources, it would cripple Phoe. And if the virus messed up enough of her resources, it could interfere with the functions we took for granted, such as the ship's oxygen production. It seems plausible, at least if I forget the bigger question: Where did this virus come from?

The sight of Albert interrupts my speculations.

He's on the ground a couple of feet away from the edge of the forest, unmoving.

Leaving the trees behind, I rush over to the unconscious Guard and check for his pulse. I don't find one. Albert's neck is the coldest thing I've ever touched, his body covered by frost that gleams red in the Dome lights.

With Liam's death, I thought my capacity for grief had been maxed out, but an avalanche of emotions hits me all over again. I didn't know Albert that well, but he seemed like a good man, a kind—

No.

With effort, I pull myself together. If I give in to this, I'll fall next to him and wait to die, and that isn't happening.

A macabre idea arises, and I execute it before I can chicken out.

I take off Albert's shoes and put them on the frozen blocks that used to be my feet. Then I put on his pants and the upper portion of his suit, and slide on the gloves.

I feel even colder when I'm done, but the rational side of my brain tells me it's an illusion. Ripping my gaze away from yet another dead body—this one sadder in its nakedness—I break into a run.

It doesn't take long to confirm my worst fears. There are dead bodies of Adults lying everywhere.

"Please, let it only be on the outskirts," I mumble to myself as I run toward the nearest building.

Even from afar, I can see people on the ground. Hundreds upon hundreds of them. When I get close enough, I verify that they are indeed gone, all bearing the same signs of suffocation.

Shaking, I turn to the noticeably larger building a few hundred feet away.

The desolation is the same there. The dead Adults look as disheveled as the Youths did: no shoes, minimal clothing, and horrified expressions stuck forever on their faces.

I find another mass grave next to the tallest building.

As I walk among the dead Adults, I see some people I know. To my right is Instructor Filomena, frozen in an embrace with Instructor George. I spot more Instructors from the Institute, as well as a number of men and women I've seen at the Birth Day Fairs over the years.

Fed up, I hurry away from the buildings—places where the bodies are clustered. I can't look at all this death anymore.

I head for the walkway farthest from any structure, and as I run, the carnage decreases, but even this is too much to bear.

The cold seems to be getting worse. My ears feel literally frozen. I think if someone were to grab my earlobe, it might break off. Stopping, I take a nightgown from a corpse of an unfamiliar, older-looking woman and wrap the cloth around my head before resuming my run.

The hope I'm holding on to now is fainter than before. It's built upon this vague notion that perhaps the Elderly, the self-appointed rulers of our world, know what's happening.

Trying to recall the exact location of the building where the Council meetings are held, I turn toward the forest that separates the Adult and Elderly territories.

* * *

I see the first dead body almost as soon as I enter the Elderly territory. This skinny old man must've been heading for the Adult section. Maybe he thought the forest would provide more oxygen, or maybe, like me, he was stumbling around aimlessly in his desperation.

This is the most tired and cold I've ever been. I can't remember a time when I wasn't running, when I wasn't cold, when I wasn't feeling like I might die.

There was no Barrier going into the Elderly section, and there aren't any signs that the Elderly were spared the Adults' fate. All the Youths I left behind, even the little kids, must be gone too.

Everyone I ever knew is dead.

Stubbornly, I head toward the Council building. I assume it's the one Phoe and I exited after Jeremiah nearly killed me.

Around all the other buildings, the story looks frighteningly familiar. I can picture what happened: first, the alarms went off in different buildings at random, just like they did in the Youth section; then everyone ran outside, where more alarms went off and everyone eventually suffocated.

Dead Guards are lying here and there. Some are still wearing their helmets, while others, like Albert, took them off. None of them are alive.

The closer I get to my destination, the more bodies I encounter. Soon, I have no choice but to step on the dead, and so I do, dry-heaving every few feet.

"Gravity simulation malfunction," Phoe's sky voice says, and I realize I've grown so used to her other warnings that I've been ignoring them. Before I fully process the meaning of this new warning, I start falling.

A moment later, I understand that I'm not actually falling. I'm floating.

So are all the dead bodies around me.

They're all floating in the air, forming a picture one would only expect to see in a surreal painting by an artist whose mind was ravaged by mercury poisoning.

I thrash my arms and legs for a few minutes, but it's futile. The only thing I achieve is a slight warmth in my frozen limbs.

Still, something is drawing me to that building. I don't know what it is. Maybe I'm hoping to find a neon sign that says 'Goal,' or maybe I'm hoping to meet the Council members and hear them say, "That was a nice set of moral dilemmas. You can now exit the Test."

Maybe I want to see if they caused this, and if so, I want to strangle them, one by one, before I die with everyone else.

Through trial and error, I learn that pushing a dead person in one direction launches me the opposite way, so I insult the dead in a new way. Instead of taking their clothes, I use them to propel myself forward.

I fly through this insane morgue for what feels like a day. When I grab the next body, I recognize the person's face.

It's Fiona, the current Council leader and Keeper of Information.

By now, I'm too numb to feel anything. Yes, this woman was nice to me, and finding her dead body killed my remaining hope, but I can't bring myself to care.

I'm too cold. Too tired.

Tears are frozen on my face.

I push Fiona away, letting the movement propel me toward the big conglomeration of bodies. Once there, I burrow into the center of the pack, hoping they'll shield me from the cold.

Then I close my eyes and float.

My fear of heights is gone. I'm even enjoying this feeling of weightlessness.

I wonder what dying will feel like. Will it be like the time I fell into the ocean of Goo inside the IRES game? I guess that depends on how I'll die. Suffocating seems like a horrible way to go, but I think my chances of freezing to death are higher. I read that you simply fall asleep when you freeze and never wake up, which doesn't sound as scary.

I float for a while longer before I realize the pain from the cold is gone—one of the final stages of hypothermia.

It's becoming harder to think. With each moment, I feel more and more like a disembodied mind floating in a realm of pure thought.

The only sensation I have is that of tiredness.

All I want to do is sleep.

Part of me knows I should fight the drowsiness. If I fall asleep, that'll be the end. But I find it hard to care.

At least I'll die in my sleep.

I stop fighting.

Letting go of my consciousness, I drift off.

* * *

I wake up gasping for air. A frantic wheeze later, I recall that I didn't think I'd wake up—that, in fact, I hoped I wouldn't.

This isn't a reprieve, far from it. I've just exchanged a less horrible death for a worse one.

Just for a moment, I allow myself a fantasy, one in which everything that happened was nothing more than a terrifying dream. I imagine I'm waking up in my bed, hyperventilating because of that nightmare.

Having difficulty breathing because I'm stressed.

When I look around, however, I know that to be a lie.

I'm still a human icicle. I'm still floating in the middle of a cloud made up of Elderly corpses.

The cold lulled me to sleep but didn't have time to kill me.

Cold sweat freezes on my skin, and my heart pounds audibly in my ears as I fight to pull air into my screaming lungs.

All the oxygen must be gone. As efficient as the Respirocytes are, once there's no more air for them to carry, they're useless.

My body instinctively fights for more air. My neck muscles spasm, and my diaphragm feels like it might tear.

Screaming for help doesn't work, so I mentally shout for Phoe— probably for the last time. She doesn't reply.

My spasmodic thrashing sends corpses floating in every direction.

I clutch at my bulging throat. My eyes feel like they're about to pop out of my skull. Weakness starts to overtake me. My brain must've run out of oxygen. My pulse slows as scenes from my life play out in my mind.

My heart stops, and the redness that became my world changes into a tunnel of white light.

I die.

CHAPTER EIGHT

I'm floating on the brink of consciousness like a bodiless ghost.

Given that I died, really died, any form of consciousness, even this ephemeral kind, is a good development, though I don't understand how it came about.

I ponder my existence. For how long, I don't know, because I have no sense of time.

Am I a ghost? A spirit? A soul?

Were the ancients right when they invented those fanciful concepts?

My memories are fuzzy. I don't remember who I am, why I'm here, or where "here" is. Is amnesia part of the afterlife? A way to make sure I don't miss what I left behind? The only concrete and unshakable memory I have is the knowledge that I'm dead. I also have this conviction that I have some important choices to make.

Ah, yes. Though everything else is still hazy, the choices I have are like islands of clarity. The first choice is what my wings should look like.

Before I question this—as one would an illogical dream—a vision of rows of different wings assaults me, which is odd for many reasons, but mainly because I don't have any eyes. But even without sight, I see all these wings in all their variety and beauty.

Ancient legends come to mind again. Is this heaven? Am I about to turn into a winged angel with a halo above my head? Is that why I need wings?

As though spurred on by this theory, countless stereotypical angel wings spread out in front of my mind, each a variation on the dove-feathered appendages and in varying shades of white.

This is one choice among millions.

Other options appear to my inner eye: dragon wings, bumblebee wings, bat wings, rows upon rows of insect, bird, reptile, and gliding mammalian wings. There's even a row of wing-like fins similar to a stingray's. Without knowing how, I know that if I 'zoom in' on a specific type of wing, countless variations of that theme will be presented to me as the next step in the selection process, similar to the way the angel-themed wings appeared.

Some choices aren't rooted in reality. For example, there's a myriad of abstract shapes, which I find fascinating. In response to my interest, choices upon choices of these surreal wings present themselves to me.

I don't know how long I take to decide, but in the end, I choose a set of wings that look like they're woven out of wisps of fire arranged in strange mathematical patterns. They look like someone froze one of those fractal music visualizations mid-design.

My fuzzy mind finds something vaguely humorous in that; my new wings are the exact opposite of the heavenly design I started off with. They look like an abstractionist's vision of a fire demon's wings.

Actually, these wings also remind me of that fiery bird from ancient legends, a creature called the phoenix. Thinking of that stirs some emotions in me that I can't quite place so I just float mindlessly until I realize I have more choices to make.

The next one is much easier: I have to decide what my face will look like.

I'm presented with every version of a human face: some younger, some older, some cute, and some handsome. Some are more masculine, while others are gently feminine. Every face type can also have a variety of features, such as eyes, which can come in every color, shape, and size imaginable.

I'm drawn to a particular set of faces straight away.

When I lay my metaphysical eyes on this group, I choose one face almost instantly. My choice is guided by aching familiarity. Something about its handsome features, blue eyes, blond hair, and the expression of curiosity in his gaze touches something forgotten inside me.

I choose a body just as quickly, despite the fact that the choices here are just as varied.

A sense of completion spreads through my sluggish mind. There are more things I can choose, but they're optional and can be adjusted later. Still, almost on autopilot, I decide that yes, I want to wear clothes, specifically pants, and that yes, I'd love to have weapons too. Fiery swords would go nicely with my wings, so I choose two blades in the katana style. Other features are chosen for me at random, such as the sound of my voice and the glow of my skin. I gladly accept those options.

The whole process reminds me of the start of a video game, where the player has to create his character before he can begin his virtual journey.

"You don't know how close to the truth you are," a familiar female voice says in my mind. "I wish you hadn't made yourself—"

I don't get a chance to learn who spoke in my mind just then, or how or why she spoke because the selection process is now officially over and I feel myself streaming somewhere else, regaining memories and becoming whole as I go.

* * *

I come to my senses with a violent shiver. I remember falling asleep for the last time because I was freezing to death. Somehow that's not what happened, since I'm awake.

Instead of floating in the subzero temperatures of Oasis, surrounded by a pile of frozen corpses, I'm standing in a warm, open space, surrounded by beautiful winged people who are speaking to one another in melodious, otherworldly voices.

Something nags at my awareness. Between freezing to death and this place, I had a dreamlike experience. In it, I made myself look like these figures—wings and all.

I recall my theories that this is some kind of life after death, and those ideas don't seem as foolish as they did in my dream state. But these people aren't angels. I've seen similar creatures before: the two Envoys—the one who spoke to Jeremiah back when the old man was still alive, and Jeremiah after he died and became the new Envoy.

Would rooms like this exist in the afterlife? I guess it's possible. The space does remind me of a cathedral, which has a religious connotation, though it's even more reminiscent of an ancient museum. The ceilings are at least a hundred feet high, and the distance from wall to wall is probably double that. Giant mirrors cover every surface, giving the room a wide-open feel and reflecting the winged people walking and flying around the space.

Ignoring the beings around me, I walk toward the nearest mirror. This is when, without much surprise, I realize that my dream-like wing selection was real.

As in, the wings are real.

As in, the wings are attached to my back.

Aside from the wings, my face looks subtly different from how I remember it. It's as though someone cut it out of marble and polished out any imperfections and asymmetries. My reflection looks slightly older and taller, and my naked upper body is noticeably buffer. To top it all off, I'm somewhat luminescent—not as shiny as some of the others in the room, but noticeably so. I vaguely recall this being part of the choices in my dreamlike state.

"The fact that you chose your own face is a problem," Phoe says as a voice in my head. "I tried to speak to you during the selection phase, but by the time I got through, it was too late. Nice wing choice, by the way."

I now recall that she did speak up toward the end of the selection, only back then I didn't know who she was. Then I recall the most important part: how she *didn't* speak during those fateful hours when everyone around me was dying. Horrific memories flood my brain, and I shout out loud, "Phoe! Where the hell have you been? Where the fuck am I? What the fuck—"

"I know dying can be disorienting," a melodic female voice says from behind me—a voice that doesn't sound anything like Phoe. "But do you have to use that kind of language in front of your peers? I didn't expect that vile f-word to ever be uttered in Haven."

Everything falls into place at the mention of Haven, but I don't have time to dwell on it because I come face to face with a winged, nearly naked female of such beauty that I stare at her curves in open-mouthed awe.

"Stop staring at Fiona like that," Phoe says with more than a hint of jealousy. "Don't give her a chance to realize that you're not one of the—"

"Who are you?" the woman—Fiona—asks. "You're not part of the Council."

My mouth snaps shut. This is Fiona, the last Keeper of Information. She's also the old woman whose corpse I saw before I died.

"Maybe he's a Forebear," a male voice cuts in. "Maybe they finally decided to explain what we're doing here. What happened in Oasis? Why did we all die? Why—"

"Calm down, Vincent," Fiona says, her beatific voice sounding exactly like the soothing notes of a harp. "Let the man speak."

"I, err . . ." My voice also sounds different, reminding me of a trumpet. "I don't—"

"You're the last one to ascend. There are thirteen of us now. You have to be the last Council member, but I don't recognize your face," Vincent says, his large eyes narrowing. "Start with how you got here and your name."

"Don't tell them your real name," Phoe commands in my mind. "It's bad enough that you decided to look like your own handsome—and recognizable—self."

"What do I say then?" I ask Phoe mentally, wishing we had time for me to ask her about a million other questions instead.

"Say you're—"

Phoe doesn't finish her thought because the large cathedral doors open, and bright light floods into the huge room.

"Finally," Vincent says and heads for the door.

Everyone joins Vincent by the entrance, blocking some of the light pouring in from outside.

"Fly up," Phoe thinks at me. "Now."

"How do I fly?" I respond.

"Using your wings might be a good way," Phoe says. "I doubt thinking happy thoughts will work, though you're welcome to try, as long as you also flap your wing muscles."

"But how—"

"Just do it. Pretend you know how," Phoe says. "They're already inside."

Using my wings for the first time is one of the oddest sensations I've ever experienced. It's as if I grew an extra pair of arms and had to learn how to use them separately from my original arms. At least with spare arms I'd have a point of reference, but my wings are completely foreign. Yet without any effort and as if I've always known how, I spread my fiery wings and leap upward.

With a powerful downward stroke, I fly toward the ceiling, leaving embers and heat haze behind me.

"Your wings don't just look like they're made of fire," Phoe explains. "They actually interact with our environment the same way—"

I fly higher, fear making me miss the rest of her explanation. It seems my new wings did little to quell my problem with heights.

"Yeah, your fear of heights is now even less rational," Phoe says, attempting—and failing—to soothe me. "Winged creatures shouldn't be—"

A big, muscular man with giant, dragon-like wings enters the cathedral with an entourage of similarly beefy specimens.

"Dear new arrivals," he says, his voice booming like a war drum. "I'm Brandon."

He pauses with the air of someone who's used to having his name recognized and respected. But I've never heard of him, and it doesn't seem like any of the others have either.

Unperturbed, he goes on. "It saddens me to inform you that you will not be joining the society of Haven. Our enemy may have contaminated you, and letting you leave this quarantine cathedral is a risk we are not willing to take. I truly am sorry. You will be dispatched back to Limbo. I'm confident we will meet again, under more congenial circumstances."

His eyes are mournful as he looks around the cathedral. With poorly concealed regret, he gestures with both hands as though he's pantomiming holding a baseball bat.

A large two-handed medieval sword appears in Brandon's hands. The blade has a bluish tint, and its sharp edge glints in the bright light of the chandeliers. Without another word, he swings the sword, severing the heads of the two winged Council members nearest him.

Everything slows.

My wings feel weak, and I wonder if I'm about to plummet to the floor.

The severed heads begin falling.

CHAPTER NINE

The heads never touch the intricate mosaic on the floor, and the headless bodies never fall down.

Instead, the heads and bodies change shape. That is, they momentarily look like they were ripped apart into square shapes reminiscent of the pixelated images I've seen in the ancient archives. It's as though the bodies turned into tiny cubist paintings. Then, each of the small three-dimensional subcomponents suddenly shines and shrinks in the air until nothing remains. There's an empty spot where two winged beings stood a moment ago. No heads or bodies are left.

"Are they dead?" I think, half to myself and half at Phoe.

"They're back in Limbo, stored as mind backups in the DMZ with the rest of Oasis," Phoe replies. "But those are semantics we'll worry about when we're out of here. For now, I need you to arm yourself. You have to make your swords appear. You remember choosing swords, right? Will them to appear."

I register her words, but not their meaning because at that moment, Fiona and Vincent scream. Gliding near the ceiling, I look down and see them running away from the cathedral's entrance.

The rest of the survivors cry out even louder and scatter like cockroaches.

Brandon doesn't chase after them. With a dignified posture, he walks farther inside, a few winged warrior types behind him.

"The katanas, Theo," Phoe screams in my mind. "You'll need them. Spread your arms as though you're about to grab two swords and wish you had them. Quick!"

I guess I've been dealing with Phoe long enough that she's conditioned me to do as she says. Spreading my arms palms out, I will the weapons to appear.

Two blades materialize in my hands. They're lighter than I imagined two long pieces of metal would be, but then again, real-world swords don't possess the fiery glow these two have, so I'm not operating under the normal laws of physics. The handles feel comfortable in my hands, as if they're extensions of my arms.

"Tell the Councilors to arm themselves too," Phoe says.

"Arm yourselves," I shout at the frightened people below me.

My command arrives too late for one pale, pudgy Councilor, as one of the armed warriors beheads him.

"Gesture for the weapons you chose on your way to this place," I yell. "Wish for them to appear in your hands."

Vincent—the thin Councilor—looks up at me and nods. He performs the gesture to call forth his weapon, and an intricate scythe appears in his hands. With it, he looks a lot like the Grim Reaper. As soon as he registers his new acquisition, Vincent swings the giant grass-cutting instrument at his beefy attacker. The winged warrior is caught off-guard. One moment he was chasing an unarmed, pathetic Vincent, and in the next, his target is attacking him. The momentary hesitation quite literally costs the attacker his head, and his decapitated parts disappear in that same pixel-by-pixel manner as the bodies did earlier.

"Good job, Vincent," I shout. "Wait—look out!"

Vincent's head is separated from his body, and as he dematerializes, I see Brandon standing there with his giant blade.

"Fighting us is useless," Brandon says in his drum-like voice. "We've trained with these weapons for centuries, while you didn't know you could possess them—until that one told you." He looks at me threateningly, his wings preparing for flight.

I try to make my gaze more baleful than his. He's trying to dominate the environment through psychological warfare, and I won't fall for it. Out of the corner of my eye, I see Fiona. She's approaching Brandon from behind, a rapier in her slim hands. Instead of metal, her weapon looks to be made of pure light.

"Head for the exit," Phoe orders me at the same time as I think, "We need to help her."

"No, we don't," Phoe says. "Judging by the way Brandon moves, he wasn't lying about his training. You have no chance against him in a fight. Fiona is already as good as back in Limbo."

Phoe's words are like cold water over my brain.

"Can't you take over my body and do something?" I think in desperation. "You should be faster than—"

Before I can finish my idea, Phoe acts on it. The next few seconds are full of the usual paradoxes that happen when Phoe takes control. It feels like I'm acting on my own, but I know I'm not *that* much in control of my fear of heights. It must be Phoe who has me pull back my wings and literally swoop down to the ground.

"I thought you wouldn't consent to my control after my failure in Oasis." Phoe's words distract me from the horror of falling, but when the wind resistance hits my face, terror fills me once again.

Fiona raises her rapier.

Though he's looking at me, some kind of instinct warns Brandon that someone is attacking him from behind. With impossible speed, he spins around, blocking Fiona's strike with such force that she staggers backward.

I'm halfway down when Brandon takes advantage of Fiona being off balance and swings his giant blade. Fiona parries with her rapier, but she might as well be wielding a toothpick. Brandon's blade pushes her elegant weapon aside and continues its trajectory toward her lithe neck.

Instead of splattering on the floor like I feared, I open my wings at the last second and slam my right katana down on Brandon's broadsword, preventing him from decapitating Fiona. Unfortunately, his sword still leaves a gushing wound in her neck.

Instead of red, her blood is luminescent, like the blood of a strange deep-sea creature. She shrieks so loudly that it startles Brandon. I take advantage of his momentary distraction and slice open his left shoulder.

Ignoring the spurting of his blood, Brandon gives me his full attention.

Fiona is clutching at her neck, and I know I'm on my own in this fight.

Brandon thrusts his sword at my chest. I jump away so quickly there's no doubt Phoe was responsible.

Brandon's jaw tenses. He must've expected everyone in here to be an easy kill. His training holds, however, and instead of dwelling on my surprising spryness, he swipes at my legs.

I jump.

He thrusts the point of his broadsword at my right shoulder, and I parry with my left blade. The impact numbs my entire arm, but I don't let that stop me. Instead, I slice Brandon straight across his bicep.

I hear the sizzle of my fire blade searing his flesh, and he yelps in pain, finally revealing that he *can* feel these injuries.

His cry gets the attention of his nearest muscle-bound ally, who stops chasing a bleeding Council member in favor of attacking me.

Crap.

My already-frantic heart is trying to escape my ribcage. Even Phoe can't control my body fast enough to deal with two of these guys.

Then I notice Fiona's neck. It's no longer gushing blood. The bloody wound is bad and must hurt like hell, but it's in better shape than I expected. Healing must work differently in this place. Though I've never seen a sword wound back in Oasis, I doubt they stop bleeding that fast.

Fiona is screaming something, but it sounds unintelligible. Then I see that she isn't looking at me. She must've yelled for help, because a knife-wielding Council woman joins her, and they attack Brandon.

Brandon's ally swings his weapons, a pair of long dagger-like swords with two curved prongs sticking out near the handles, and misses.

"They're called sais." Phoe's whisper jars me, and I pull away, narrowly avoiding getting stabbed by one of the guy's sais.

He looks surprised that I dodged his hits, and I—or strictly speaking, Phoe—slice down with my sword.

The guy's arm falls to the floor, and the weapon clatters. The arm doesn't disappear, however. I guess body parts don't dematerialize here until their owner is killed.

"I don't like the term 'killed,'" Phoe says in my mind. "Why don't we call it 'Limbofied,' since people are sent to Limbo? Regarding the lack of dematerialization, it is indeed interesting. When we stop his heart, I want to examine this Limbofication process closer."

Before I can berate Phoe for trying to develop my vocabulary in the middle of a sword fight, my body does something I didn't think it could do. My legs spread sideways, as if I'm an ancient gymnast. When my crotch touches the floor and a sai whooshes by my ear, I swing my sword at my attacker's legs, chopping them off at the ankles. The goriness would usually make me vomit, but I'm not sure this body is capable of doing that. However, I do gag from the smell of burning flesh. As the man falls screaming, I position my right blade where his heart will be, and his torso impales itself on the blade. His severed limbs and the rest of his body dematerialize like every other Limbofied person's.

"That's amazing," Phoe thinks excitedly. "I was indeed able to analyze the dematerialization process. At the core, it's a data-compression algorithm, which obviously can be exploited. Quick, let's Limbofy someone else so I can intercept the whole process."

As if in answer to Phoe's wish, Brandon makes Fiona's knife-wielding helper disappear with a slice of his sword. The ancients had a saying along the lines of "don't bring a knife to a gunfight," but I think the wisdom applies to a sword fight as well. What's really impressive about Brandon's kill—or in Phoe's terminology, Limbofication—is that he parried Fiona's rapier in the same move he used to kill the woman.

"Crap," Phoe mutters in my head. "I wasn't ready just then. Though I did learn a bit more about the process."

"If we don't do something to help Fiona, you'll get your chance when Brandon turns her into a shish kebab," I think at Phoe. "Or when he Limbofies her, if you really prefer. In case it's not obvious, I don't want that to happen."

Phoe assists in Fiona's rescue by forcing my body to perform more gymnastics. I bring my legs under me and roll closer to Brandon. Brandon's giant sword blocks my strike aimed at his legs, and before I can cut his torso with my left katana, he blocks me in the most unexpected manner—with his wings.

There's a crunching sound as my sword cuts through the wing bones and the smell of burned feathers is disgustingly palatable, but my attacker is still very much alive. With the wounded wing no longer blocking my sight, I see that Brandon has managed to turn this painful outcome into an advantage. With his wings in my way, I lost sight of what he was doing, and I now watch as his sword swings toward my skull.

"This is it," I think for Phoe's benefit. "I'm going to die—again."

CHAPTER TEN

Despite my conviction, I don't die—thanks to Fiona. She thrusts her rapier in the path of Brandon's sword right as it's midway to my head. A painful metal-on-metal clang rings out, which is odd, since Fiona's weapon doesn't look metallic. Her arm ricochets backward with such violence that I'm sure her shoulder is dislocated. What's really frustrating is that her move doesn't even stop Brandon's assault; it only slows it. However, it's enough for me to sidestep before his sword can cleave my head in half.

In a shower of sparks, Brandon's blade strikes the floor next to me.

I jackknife to my feet and perform a ballerina-like feat of dexterity by slicing each sword in opposite trajectories. I bury the right one in Brandon's gut and plunge the left into his eye socket. Bile rises in my throat at the sight of the gore spilling out of Brandon when I yank the swords in a circular motion. Maybe I *can* vomit. Large chunks of slightly crispy flesh fall to the ground and then get digitized and disappear.

"Yes!" Phoe screams—and I do mean out loud. "Yep, I have a voice now," she says in my mind before I can ask. "This is very promising. I got both his memories and a fraction of the resources Haven had allocated to him. This means things are not as bad as I thought, which is all the more reason for you to get out of here. If you go back into Limbo, we're screwed."

"I want to help Fiona escape," I think back. "She saved me."

"Fine," Phoe says. "Tell her to follow you."

"Our only chance is escaping through that door," I tell Fiona, who's dazedly staring at the empty spot where Brandon's body used to be. "Follow me."

I run for the entrance, hoping Fiona heard me and is on my heels. Around me, pieces of Council members keep dematerializing at an increasing rate, which means there are more armed men free to attack me. Two of the nearest winged assholes turn their sights on me. When they're twenty feet away, I launch into the air. The pounding of my wings outpaces my heart rate, which itself was trying to set some kind of a record.

I hear the rustling of wings behind me and assume Fiona has followed my lead.

The two big guys attempt to follow, and as soon as they do, Phoe maneuvers my body in a way that would make a hawk proud. I plunge toward the door as though my life depends on it—which it does, Limbofication notwithstanding. I hear Fiona scream behind me as a sword whooshes by my side.

Just as my legs clear the cathedral's entrance, a terrible pain erupts in my calf.

I glance down at the source of the pain and wish I—or Phoe—hadn't, because there's a dagger sticking out of my leg.

Fiona's situation is worse than mine. Her wings are no longer attached to her body, and she's falling down the mountain that the cathedral is built upon.

My vision goes white, partly from the pain, but mostly from the very bright illumination that hits my retinas. What's odd about the bright light is that there isn't a sun in the sky. The light is coming from all around me.

I try to swoop down to save Fiona, but my body, under Phoe's control, doesn't listen. Instead, I let go of my left sword and rip the dagger from my calf. The pain is so sharp it further blinds me. Despite the pain, I'm still torpedoing away from the cathedral.

My left hand gestures with an open palm, and another fiery sword appears in it.

"I'm sorry, Theo," Phoe says. "I couldn't let you go after Fiona. Remember, she won't die. She'll get written back into the DMZ—into Limbo."

Unsure how I feel about sacrificing Fiona, I glance back.

She's gone, but my pursuers aren't. They're flying after me like two eagles pursuing a mouse.

Channeling my worry into flapping my wings harder, I fly faster, leaving fiery embers behind me.

For the first time, I take a moment to register my surroundings. I'm flying up toward a dome that looks similar to the Dome in Oasis. What's different, though, is the scenery beyond it. In the never-ending cloudy blue sky, a dozen domed islands are floating as if held there by magic. Oasis-like habitats are visible from horizon to horizon.

No, not like Oasis—if the view below is anything to go by. Aside from the mountain bearing the cathedral behind us, there's no greenery at all, just more barren mountain ranges—something we've never had in Oasis.

"I'm sorry to distract you from the tour, but I want you to help me make an important decision," Phoe says. "One that will affect us equally."

"Since when do you ask for my opinion?" I ask out loud, still upset that she didn't save Fiona.

"We don't have time for you to be mad at me," Phoe says. "We need to strategize."

"Fine. What do you want me to help you decide?" I keep my eyes on the approaching dome rather than on the sharp mountaintops below.

"Okay," she says. "Before we can form a plan, we need to Limbofy at least one more person. Two would be better. So the choices are: Do we start with our pursuers, which is risky, or escape and look for someone else?"

Out of all the things I expected Phoe to say, "Let's kill a bunch of people" wasn't among them.

"You should start by explaining why we need to do that," I say. "And if you're ready to explain things, I need you to tell me what the fuck is going on and why you didn't respond when—"

"No time for twenty questions," Phoe says. "The reason I need you to Limbofy a few more targets is because I need more knowledge and resources. When someone gets Limbofied, their memories are prepared to be rewritten into the DMZ, similar to what happens in Oasis when someone goes to sleep. I patched into that process when it happened to Brandon and gained a copy of his memories. More importantly, when he left this system, his Haven resources were de-allocated, so I grabbed as much as I could. I only acquired a small chunk, since I didn't know what I was doing, but I should be able to get more next time. And before you start again with the whys, even those meager resources allowed me to speak to you out loud instead of as a thought and to speed up the healing of your leg."

As she says that last statement, I realize the pain in my calf is nearly gone.

"Right," Phoe continues. "So to even begin unraveling this mess, I need more resources and more memories. Ideally, the memories should come from someone who knows more than Brandon did, though I guess hunting for someone knowledgeable is phase two of the plan."

I fly in silence for a moment. The idea of hunting down random strangers is distasteful to me.

"Yes, but unlike random strangers, our pursuers are dangerous," Phoe says.

As I think about this, we fly through the dome, which feels like a soap bubble on my wings.

A knife whooshes past my ear, reminding me of my pursuers.

"These assholes are practically asking for it," I say. "Plus, they killed Fiona and a bunch of other people. We should get your resources from them. It's only fitting."

"Okay then," Phoe says cautiously. "If we're going to face them, we have to dispatch them quickly, before their comrades finish their grisly task and join them. I have an idea, but you won't like it. Though I guess if you keep your eyes closed—"

"Just do whatever it is, Phoe," I say with false confidence. "And I'm not—"

My wings snap shut and I drop.

Below me, my attackers are flying some forty feet away from each other, and the closest one is approximately thirty feet from me. It seems like the smaller one is quicker on his wings.

The fall puts me directly above him. He sees me drop but continues to fly upward. I'm flying down as if he isn't there.

I'm playing another deadly game of chicken, only I can't lose my nerve and swerve away because Phoe is in control. If it were me, I would've chickened out a millisecond ago.

My opponent raises his weapon—a halberd, I believe. It consists of a wooden stick that ends with an axe that has a long, pointy metal tip at the very top. That pointy end is aimed at me.

I hold my right katana in a strange, spear-like grip. The message I'm sending is clear: if my opponent pierces me, I'll slice him in return.

The larger pursuer realizes his friend might need help and speeds up.

The tip of the halberd is an inch away from my chest when its owner chickens out and swerves out of my way, to his right. Phoe must've anticipated this outcome, because a fraction of a second before the guy makes his move, I launch my right katana at the spot he diverges to.

The fiery sword looks like a comet as it speeds toward him, and the guy screams as loudly as I'd expect from someone who has a burning sword sticking through his thigh.

I spread my wings and angle my body to fly close to him before he can recover. He draws back his halberd, but before he can swing it, I cut it in half.

His partner is a leap away.

I grab my right katana from the man's thigh and cruelly turn it counterclockwise. He screams even louder, but his scream turns into a gargling hiss when my left blade cuts his throat.

He breaks into those small fragments and disappears like the others, only in this brightly lit outside world, the usual shine from this process is muted.

"Amazing," Phoe says, and I realize that her voice is no longer disembodied.

Phoe has become a vapor-like outline of herself. No, that's not really true. Unlike her Oasis counterpart, this Haven version has large butterfly wings, and all she's wearing is a tiny thong. Seeing her nearly naked again, even though she's see-through, stirs emotions in me that I know are best kept out of my head for now.

As if to highlight Phoe's incorporealness, the bigger attacker goes right through her.

"You're so dead," the man grits out, saliva spraying from his mouth.

He's holding two curved swords that I think are called scimitars. Unlike real-world scimitars, these are made of ice. I swing for the sword, hoping my fire blade will melt his. He deflects my strike and proves that his scimitars only look like ice; they feel as if they were forged out of something as hard as titanium. He also proves how good he is with his weapons by using the post-block recoil to slice at my right wrist.

"Shit. I pulled up Brandon's memories of this guy. He's one of the best swordsmen the Guardians have," Phoe hisses. "We should flee."

The sword connects with my right shoulder. The combination of burning pain and the unbearable feeling of my joint crunching hits me like a steamroller.

My right katana looks like a fiery meteorite as it falls down.

CHAPTER ELEVEN

Through the nauseating pain, I hear Phoe say, "If this is how he wants to play it, fuck fleeing. This guy is going to get it. No one hurts you this badly and gets away with it. I'll try to take the pain away and do all the fighting. Luckily for us, I can leverage Brandon's weapons training against him."

I realize she's talking to distract me from the agony and is partially succeeding in that. Then the pain eases completely, allowing my mind to clear, and I finally notice what my body has been up to: a jerky hacking motion with my left arm.

My remaining sword slices through my enemy's left shoulder. He howls as his whole arm falls off.

A severed arm for an injured shoulder. Close enough to that ancient saying, "an eye for an eye."

To my disappointment, my attacker recovers quickly and swipes at me with his remaining scimitar.

My katana blocks his strike. I try to slice open his side, but he blocks in turn.

He hacks at my throat, and I duck under his blow, delivering a deep cut to where his liver should be.

My opponent doesn't disintegrate, which means my strike wasn't lethal. In retaliation, he executes a desperate onslaught of feints and thrusts. I have a hard time following every attack, but Phoe doesn't. Through me, she blocks every strike with mathematical precision. As the fight proceeds, I clue in to Phoe's plan. The man's crazy attacks are tiring him out, and the two bloody wounds aren't helping him either.

My right arm is numb, but at least, unlike his stump, my shoulder isn't bleeding—likely due to Phoe's influence.

"The guys in the cathedral might be on their way," I tell her. "We need to fly away."

Phoe has me execute my own barrage of attacks. If someone were to capture my sword movements with a high-speed camera, I'm sure it would look like a beautiful, fiery work of art. When it becomes clear that the guy can barely block my attacks, I slice at his throat and succeed in cutting it clean through. He begins the Limbofication process and disappears a second later.

Without pausing, I flap my wings and fly toward the point where the dome of the floating island meets its ground.

"We're going to dive under the island," Phoe explains. "This way, when the rest of the Guardians exit, they won't spot us as quickly."

I glance at her as she speaks and realize that her ethereal figure looks more solid, as if she's made out of thicker fog.

"This form is just the beginning." Phoe flies in front of me, showing me the way. "With more resources, I should be able to give myself a real body—or at least as real of a body as I can get in this place."

I remain silent until we reach the edge of the floating island. Once we pass the dome, we fly under the island, passing through thick clouds. I notice that the same kind of clouds seem to cover the bottoms of other islands as well.

We have a clear head start on our pursuers now, so I say, "Okay, now what?"

"Now we get as far away from this place as possible," Phoe says. "Then I'd like you to Limbofy a few more people for me."

"I'm not attacking random people for you—and you still owe me answers. If I didn't know you better, I'd say you've gone evil, assuming you weren't evil from the start. Don't you see how that would explain how everyone in Oasis was killed and why you want me to kill even more people in Haven?"

"We both know you don't believe that," Phoe says, but her ethereal shoulders drop. "Fine, let me explain what I think happened, but keep in mind that there are big gaps in my knowledge—which we'll have to address as a matter of high priority."

"Tell me what you can," I say, my wings flapping even faster.

"First, allow me to do this." Phoe gestures at my injured shoulder, and with a flash of bright yellow light, the gaping wound closes.

The healed shoulder tingles, and I clench and unclench my right hand. It feels as if the shoulder never got hurt. There aren't even any remnants of pain.

"I'm glad that worked," Phoe says, looking at me over her shoulder. "Incidentally, I hope you realize that this feat of healing was only possible because of the resources I pilfered from those Limbofied Guardians."

"Guardians," I repeat. "You called them that before."

"Yes, I got the proper term from Brandon's memories. The others also call themselves that."

"Do you mean you literally know what he knew?"

"I more than know—I can even show it to you. But I know you're dying to learn about what happened in Oasis."

"Yes," I say. "I need to know if everyone is really dead."

She dives down and follows a diagonal path straight to the nearest domed island. This island is greener than the one we left and looks a lot more welcoming, at least from this distance.

We fly in silence for a moment. Though I know what she's going to tell me, I need to hear it. Phoe must realize that and is thinking of the best way to deliver the horrible truth.

"You've already figured most of it out," she finally says, speaking so softly that I almost don't hear her over the wind hitting my face. "That Jeremiah thing on the beach was a virus. I think it originated here, in Haven. I also think the question of who unleashed it, and why, is something we need answered as soon as possible. One thing is for sure: the Jeremiah virus hunted every part of me, every thread, to extinction. Only a portion of me, what I wrote into the DMZ, survived. That part of me was just a static snapshot—an insurance policy of sorts. It was not actively executing on any computing substrate, similar to how the backed up human minds just sit in the DMZ, waiting to be resurrected in a computer world one day. It's like the hibernate function of an ancient operating system. I only know about the horrible events you lived through from your memories. I wasn't around for any of it."

She falls silent for a moment, then continues. "My best guess as to what happened after I was gone is that the Jeremiah virus continued deleting anything that remotely resembled me, including my unconscious processes of gravity simulation, oxygen regulation, and the likes. In its overzealousness to erase me, the virus destroyed the life-support functions of me, the ship. As far as making sure it killed me, it was a good strategy, but as a way of keeping the human population alive . . . Well, you know what happened."

She stops talking and lets me digest this. Driven by an irrational hatred of Phoe, someone—or a group of someones—was criminally negligent. These people are here in Haven with me, and they're making me rethink my earlier attitude toward violence. They'll answer for all the suffering I witnessed and be held accountable for all those deaths.

Then I realize that though the events were very tragic, no one truly died. There are snapshots of every mind, including Liam's. He's somewhere in the DMZ with Mason and the rest of them. Theoretically, they could be brought back to life in Haven.

"That's true," Phoe says. "Though I'd like to point out that those snapshots are incomplete, for better or worse. Few will remember their last day in Oasis. As you might recall, the mind backup process starts when you go to sleep, and I doubt many people took a nap in the midst of that disaster. The only reason you can recall what happened is because of your unique circumstances. You fell asleep when you were suffering from hypothermia. If you woke up after that, you lost that information forever."

I shudder. Maybe forgetting something like that is a good thing. Then something occurs to me.

"If you were as good as dead, how did you show up here?" I ask. "For that matter, how did I?"

"I'm here because you're here. Remember that Pi exploit I planted in your head so I could enter the Elderly Test on Birth Day?"

I nod, beginning to understand. Phoe gave me a fake memory relating to Pi. After a certain point in the sequence, the numbers of Pi became the digits that helped her hack into the Test.

"Exactly," Phoe says. "When you enter certain virtual reality environments, those digits in your head are instantiated together with your mind. Once that happens, the numbers become a basic routine meant to create a bootstrap version of me that in turn summons the rest of me to itself. So I got very lucky that you ended up here, in an environment so similar to the Test. With the help of this code, a small shadow of me is once again running. I don't know if it's obvious, but I'm nowhere near my normal self. It's horrible. I'm down to measly human-level intellect."

"Okay, so that explains your presence, sort of," I say. "Except it all hinges on me being here, and you haven't explained that." We're a few feet away from the shimmering dome now, which means we're about to enter the green sky island. "How did I get here? I thought only Council members went to Haven."

"It might be best for you to hear that from the horse's mouth, so to speak, and for that, I'll have to show you Brandon's memories in a moment." Phoe folds her wings and plummets headfirst into the soap-bubble dome.

For the first time since our escape, it occurs to me how odd our surroundings are. The whole universe looks like a massive sky. There's no ground as far down as I can see, not counting the floating domed islands.

"Do I have to make you fly down?" Phoe asks as she continues descending.

"No," I think. "I'll fly down by myself—at my own pace."

I don't want her to force me to drop the way she did, so I begin my descent.

Phoe disappears below the treetops. "The reason there's no ground is because Haven is built on top of a virtual reality infrastructure that is very similar to the IRES game," she explains in my mind. "It doesn't need to conform to reality."

As I listen, I fly slower, examining the never-ending woods covering the ground of the island.

With the greenery approaching, even my cautious flight speed feels too fast. Even though I know it's completely irrational here, my fear of heights awakens with a vengeance, and it's all I can do to keep going.

When I descend below the treetops, I find that Phoe has already landed in a meadow. I spread my wings in preparation for landing, and when my feet touch the ground, I swallow my heart back into my chest.

Phoe smiles at me. "Good job. Now let's walk for a bit. This way, even if one of the Guardians flies by, they won't see us. When we get to the easternmost edge of the island, we'll fly under it."

"Fine," I say. "What are these islands?"

"All I know about them so far is that each one belongs to one of the Forebears—the denizens of Haven, of which you are now one," Phoe says and starts running for the trees on the other side of the meadow.

"Wait." I chase after her. "Does that mean there's an island somewhere that belongs to me?"

"Yes, there is, I'm sure of that. I can even find it for you if you really want, but I think it's useless to us right now," Phoe says from behind a giant oak. "Let's get deeper into the forest, and I'll show you Brandon's memory."

I follow her, thinking that despite what Phoe said, it might be really cool to own an island like this—an island the size of Oasis.

"It's a waste of resources if you ask me," Phoe says after I catch up with her again. "This whole place is an atrocity committed against the ship's computing substrate."

I inhale the fresh air. It smells exactly like a real forest. It looks like a real forest too, but I can't shake the feeling that something is different. Then it hits me: I'm hearing birds chirping and insects buzzing—sounds I'd never heard in the woods of Oasis.

"There's a ton of simulated life here, if that sort of thing impresses you," Phoe confirms. "This island could give the Zoo a run for its money."

I catch sight of something fluffy moving in the bushes. Must be a rabbit or a squirrel. I resist the urge to chase after it like a kid. I still want to get those answers from Phoe, and I can't let this fake nature distract me.

Glancing up at the strange sky, I examine the dozen domed islands floating in the distance. Haven is beautiful in its contempt for gravity.

"All right then." Phoe stops and looks at me. "Why don't you let me walk for you as you experience this?"

"Sure," I respond cautiously. "Experience what?"

Phoe gives me a crooked smile, and the world around me disappears.

I'm standing in an empty, metallic room, and a familiar winged creature is standing next to me. It's the first winged guy I ever saw—the original loincloth-wearing, winged demigod Envoy who gave Jeremiah the Lens of Truth.

The metallic walls of the room are reflective, and I can see myself in one of them.

Only it's not my own face looking back at me. It's the Guardian who nearly killed me with his giant broadsword.

I should've been ready for this, but I still can't believe it.

I'm Brandon.

CHAPTER TWELVE

"You're not Brandon, per se," Phoe's thought intrudes. "You're just reliving his memories."

I knew that already, but having her reiterate it helps me come to grips with this strange situation.

Everything about me feels wrong. I'm taller, my feet are planted wider than usual, and I can feel the bulkiness of my muscles. Two streams of thoughts are flowing through my head at once: my thoughts and Brandon's. His are faint and noticeably foreign, but quite accessible. It's eerie.

"This is how I feel when I'm inside your head," Phoe explains. "Pay attention to their conversation."

It's hard to pay attention because there are too many interesting things distracting me. I don't just recall Brandon's memories; I feel his emotions as well, though they're limited to the present. He respects the Forebear he's talking to. The man's name is Wayne. I know this because Brandon knows this, and I make a mental note to remember the name because it's a better moniker than 'the first Envoy I ever saw.' I also know that Wayne is part of the Circle, which is the ruling body in Haven. He, Brandon, is the Leader of the Guardians, which means he doesn't have any guard duties in the Sanctum, the island where the Circle rule from. As a result, he rarely meets with the members of the Circle. The last time Brandon was summoned here, to the basement vaults of the Spike building on the Sanctum, was years ago.

Thinking about the past opens up a floodgate of interesting observations. With little effort, I can recall everything Brandon has done in his life. I remember his life as a Youth, his passion for ancient military strategies as an Adult, and his pride when he first served as a member of the Elderly Council. But I have access to more than just his biographical information. Through Brandon, I know what it feels like to grow feeble with age and eventually die, and I relive his awe upon awakening for his second life in Haven.

"It all began when we received the results from the last Test," Wayne says in his familiar organ-like voice. "Few people know this, but the way a new Council member is chosen is rather simple. He or she is always the Elderly with the highest score on the Test."

Wayne keeps talking to Brandon, but I tune them out. I have my answer, and now that I do, I can't believe I didn't realize it sooner.

"You had no chance to think about it." Phoe imbues the thought with regret. "I'm the super-intelligent being, so I should be the one kicking myself. I didn't realize the Test scores had anything to do with the process of choosing who served on the Council. I think I wanted to shut down the Test so badly that I was in denial. My gluttony for resources blinded me to this possibility."

As Phoe speaks, the full picture starts to form in my mind. She had me reach such a high score on the Test that the testing process nearly took forever, giving me a result no one else could beat and inadvertently making me eligible to become a Council member. Maybe we could've gotten away with it for a bit—if a position on the Council hadn't opened up almost at the same time, thanks to Jeremiah drinking his own poison.

"That's right," Phoe says. "When Jeremiah died and went to Haven, you automatically became a member of the Council. If the Forebears hadn't caught on to your high score so fast, I could've covered it all up, hidden it even from them, but they acted before I knew what happened. They were clever to move so fast with their virus."

I rub my forehead, trying to wrap my mind around the magnitude of our failure.

"You have to look on the bright side," Phoe says. "When you died in Oasis, thanks to the fact that you were a Councilor, you ended up here instead of spending an eternity in Limbo. So what failed us also helped us."

"Yeah." I imbue as much sarcasm into my thought as I can. "Works out great for you. You've been dying to get your hands on this place, but the Firewall was in your way. Now here you are. I wonder if—"

"Please don't finish that thought unless you truly mean it." Phoe's tone sharpens. "You have no idea how much their virus took away from me. You're pretty much the same person you were in Oasis, with minor changes like these wings, but I'm barely an echo of what I was before the virus attacked me. Parts of me are lost forever, and even if I regain those resources, I'll never be the same person again. I would never execute a plan that involved such a high level of self-mutilation, or one that would cause you so much suffering." In a softer voice, she adds, "I'm sorry I didn't prevent this from happening. You have no idea how sorry I am."

"No, I'm sorry too." Guilt tightens my chest. "I'm sorry that I snapped at you. I don't really think you planned all this. It's just a lot to take in."

"You should listen to what Wayne is about to say," she thinks at me, clearly eager to change the subject.

I try to focus my mind enough to register what Brandon is hearing.

"No, this Youth, Theodore, could not have done this on his own. He's a pawn," Wayne says, his voice hitting deeper organ notes. "We want nothing more than to believe it was the work of a brilliant young man, but we can't ignore the facts. There's been too much tampering beyond what a human being can do. Theodore's age is a good example. He's clearly a Youth, if you look at him, but he's ninety years old in all of Oasis's systems. If any living person pulls up his information, an Augmented Reality illusion will fool them into thinking he's the unaltered age of twenty-four."

Wayne pauses, as if for dramatic purposes, and it works. I feel Brandon's eyebrows rise and the hair on the back of his neck lift.

"Yes," Wayne says. "And that's one example. There are countless others. The Test is no longer running, and there's evidence of mass Forgettings. I could list all the clues, but the conclusion we, the Circle, have reached is rather simple. Only one type of abominable being could manipulate our computer systems to such a degree: the enemy belonging to our deepest fears—an AI."

Brandon swallows thickly as Wayne continues.

"We consulted our ancient protocols, which the eldest among us have had locked away for centuries, and took action," Wayne says. "Without telling the outside world what we were about to do, the Circle struck at the enemy. Unfortunately, our efforts were in vain. No, worse than that. Before dying, in its anger, the AI retaliated by destroying all of Oasis. It suffocated every citizen in the real world."

The terror Brandon feels is so disorienting that I miss Wayne's next few sentences. Once I can push aside Brandon's emotions, I hear Wayne say, "The whole Council, including this Theodore, will soon appear in the Cathedral. We're concerned that before its demise, the AI could've turned those members of the Council against us. You have to send them all to Limbo, especially the one named Theodore."

Questions flood Brandon's head, and, confusingly, there's an even bigger flood of questions in my mind. Unable to cope, I say, "Phoe, can you pull me out of his memory?"

Brandon's thoughts stop, Wayne's too-perfect features frozen in a grimace, and I'm back in the forest, running as I dodge tree branches.

Phoe's see-through form is running next to me.

"I know how you must feel," Phoe says. "When I learned this—"

"I can't believe it was us." I feel like my chest is about to explode from the pressure within. "We're the reason everyone is dead."

Phoe must've returned control of my body to me, because I stumble and almost fall as my foot catches on a branch.

"It was not our doing," Phoe retorts as I right myself and resume running. "That's on the Circle's heads. They unleashed the virus."

"He said it was *you* who killed everyone."

"You don't believe that, do you?" Phoe stops and looks at me with her transparent blue eyes. "Of course he would say that. He's not about to admit that their plan to deal with me backfired so spectacularly. That in trying to get rid of me, they killed everyone in Oasis."

A branch hits me in the face as I stop next to her. The pain of the strike, combined with my turbulent emotions, makes my eyes water.

"Theo, you can't beat yourself up like this," Phoe says, looking at me. "Yes, the way we crashed the Test revealed my existence to these people, which caused them to lash out, but blaming ourselves is like blaming the victim for getting robbed. This virus almost killed me, and your real-world body is dead. It was the Circle that unleashed the virus. Clearly, they didn't understand what they were doing."

I shake my head numbly. "If I never met you, if I never brought up those three hundred Screens, everyone in Oasis would still be alive. Liam would be alive. It wasn't a perfect society, but it was better than none."

"It's not all lost." Phoe places her hand on my shoulder. Though her fingers go through me, warmth spreads from the spot she touched me. "The virus can't penetrate the Firewall or the DMZ area. That means everyone who died is still backed up in Limbo. As long as that remains the case, the deceased are not really gone. If we survive this place, if I regain enough resources, I could simulate

Oasis, if that's what you wanted, or I could come up with a better environment, one with more nature and less bullshit. Once that's done, I could bring back anyone you wanted."

I stare at her. I know my friends are stored as backups in the DMZ, or in Limbo, or whatever. We even talked about restoring Mason before. But I also remember that she said bringing him back would be selfish.

"Bringing anyone back before I have enough resources to let them exist beyond a brief time would be selfish. Once I have enough resources, however, *not* bringing them back would be selfish."

"But if you didn't have the resources before, where—"

"Ah, but don't you see that, as sad as it is, the virus created a horde of resources for me to reclaim? It killed everything—every computer program the Forebears ran to keep me unconscious— and made certain costly processing tasks, such as Augmented Reality illusions and life support, no longer necessary. If the virus went away, I'd have more than enough resources to bring the simulated people back."

"But they're dead." I know I'm not being completely rational, but I can't forget Liam's purple face. "How real would their resurrected selves be?"

"You tell me," Phoe says. "You don't feel dead, do you? To me, living means experiencing the world with your mind. In that sense, you're still alive and kicking. Liam, Mason, and anyone else you need could have the same life you have now, and in a place of your choosing." She looks up at the strange sky, then starts running again. "If you like what the Forebears created, we can use it for inspiration," she says over her shoulder, "but I suspect you'll want something better for you and your friends."

When I catch up to her, we run for a few minutes in silence. Phoe is right. I feel alive and as real as before, which isn't surprising. I felt real when I was with her on the beach, even though I knew I wasn't alive in that environment. But I had a real-world body as my anchor then, and now I don't. The idea makes my skin crawl. Haven feels like I'm stuck in a video game, and I don't want to feel this way forever.

"You feel like you're stuck in a video game because it's actually not that far from the truth," Phoe says. "Haven was built on a framework technology very similar to the IRES game. That's why choosing your wings and appearance was so similar to the start of a video game. Unlike the environment I would create, this place doesn't model your body exactly, molecule by molecule, and that subtly changes the way you feel. Your wings and the fact that this environment doesn't follow the familiar laws of physics also increase the feeling that this is a virtual space. With time, though, you'd get used to it."

"But it's not real. Even if I get used to it, these birds"—I look up at the distant flock of starlings that form a mesmerizing murmuration—"these trees—all this stuff doesn't exist."

"Now you're getting philosophical on me," Phoe says. "And if you want to play that game, I should point out that everything you've ever experienced in your 'real' life was your brain's interpretation of your sensory inputs. Your mind constructed the world from what your eyes and ears captured through imperfect, ancient, biologically based sensors. Your eyes could only see a sliver of the full range of the electromagnetic spectrum, and your ears could only hear a portion of the sounds surrounding you. Your brain took that incomplete information and created a virtual reality in which you lived. In a way, your reality was a step removed from what's really out there. You *never* had the complete picture. Now there's just an extra layer of unreality added. If we get out of this Haven mess, perhaps I could figure out a way to give you sensors to experience the real world."

I'm glad I'm running through a meadow and don't have to deal with branches hitting my face. In the state I'm in, my dodging skills are probably inadequate. Needless to say, Phoe's words haven't calmed me.

"You feel better when you focus on a plan, so that's what we should do," she says.

I shrug and slow down to walk toward the meadow's edge.

Phoe takes my silence as an invitation to keep talking. "We need to learn whatever we can about this virus," she says, matching her pace to mine. "Once I know how it works, I might be able to beat it and reclaim—"

Phoe suddenly falls silent and looks at the edge of the meadow that's now ten feet away from us.

A tall woman walks out from the tree line of the forest.

She's stunning, as all Forebears seem to be. She's also nearly naked, with only ivy-like leaves covering her private parts. There's a woven basket hooked on her slender elbow, with a bunch of colorful mushrooms inside.

She looks like some kind of wild woman from the forest.

When the Forebear sees me, her eyes widen and she drops the basket, the mushrooms spilling onto the grass.

Her arm twitches, and a large metal stick materializes in her hand. With a graceful gesture, she spreads the object, and I see that it's some kind of metal fan, with blades adorning the tips of the rods that serve as the fan's joints.

"It's an iron fan," Phoe hisses in my ear. "They used this weapon in ancient China and Japan."

The woman lunges at me.

I duck in time to dodge the knife-like blades of the fan.

The contraption whooshes across the crown of my head, slicing a chunk of my hair off.

Unperturbed, the ivy-clad woman gracefully swings the deadly fan at my throat.

CHAPTER THIRTEEN

I pivot back to save my life, but the blades still connect with my throat.

A sharp stab of pain radiates from where the fan scratched me. Stunned but happy to be alive—or still exist, or whatever the proper term is for my state of being—I scramble backward and yell, "Who are you? Why are you attacking me?"

The woman doesn't respond; instead, she executes a somersault.

It looks as though she's doing a handstand that's been recorded and played back at a super-fast rate. By the end of this flashy maneuver, she's beside me.

She folds up her fan so it's a solid stick once more. I begin to gesture for my own weapons, but the woman is faster and jabs her stick into my side.

The pain forces me to abandon my gesture. The metal of her weapon feels so cold that I'm reminded of my last moments in Oasis when I was freezing to death. When I glance down, bile rushes up my throat. Half an inch of her weapon is stuck inside my stomach. She rips the fan out, splashing my luminescent blood onto the grass and redefining what pain really means.

I'm on the verge of fainting. White stardust specks dance across my eyes, and through the haze, I see the woman unfold the fan again.

The sharp points of her weapon fly at my throat.

I suspect Phoe takes over my body again, because I move. Had she left me on my own, I would've curled into a little ball.

With superhuman agility, I dodge the fan and grab my attacker's slender wrist in a white-knuckled fist. At the same time, I slam the side of my other hand into her inner elbow.

The sharp blades of her fan pierce her throat instead of mine.

Not pausing, I punch the handle of the fan, pushing the steel spikes through her throat.

The woman's gurgling scream sounds like someone is using a rusty saw to play a majestic harp. As she falls, her body disintegrates into pixelated blotches and disappears.

Breathing hard, I stare at the upturned basket and the mushrooms on the grass—the only proof the woman was here.

"What the hell was that?" I ask, turning toward Phoe. My eyes widen. "Wow, you have a body now?"

"Yes." Phoe touches my elbow with her very real fingers. "I'm as substantial as anyone else in this place. Jeanine's resources were instrumental in that. As to what happened—well, she attacked us. Since I have her memories, I can show you why, if you'd like."

I check my stomach wound and then my neck. There's nothing there. Not even a scar.

"Everyone heals better here. It's part of the game-based infrastructure," Phoe says. "I just sped up the healing for you again. Now let me show you her memories."

I manage to plop down on the grass before I find myself in a stranger's head again.

I'm walking toward the meadow.

It feels odd because my body is too slender, has curves in all the wrong places, and my gait is completely wrong, with my hips moving oddly from side to side.

My name is Jeanine.

Phoe mentioned this name in passing, but in these memories, it's more than a name.

Like when I was in Brandon's memories, I'm not just aware of Jeanine's thoughts as we're walking; I'm also aware of her entire history and can recall it if I wish. Some of her memories flash through my mind. I remember a little girl back on Earth, boarding a ship that isn't yet the Oasis I know. I remember the illness that took her life and her waking up with the first wave of Forebears in Haven. Particularly interesting, I see Jeanine's entire life here, including the centuries of leisure and pleasures. She knew Brandon, the man we Limbofied. She knew him so intimately—

"Focus, Theo, or you'll miss what she was thinking when she saw us," Phoe says. "It's what you want to know, isn't it?"

I look through Jeanine's eyes. I'm walking on my island, collecting mushrooms for Brandon's favorite stew. I walk into the meadow and see a new face.

Jeanine's thoughts are frantic. She remembers what Brandon said before departing for the cathedral—the secret he shared about the grim task the Circle gave him—and why.

A quick chain of reasoning fires through Jeanine's mind. This new person must be part of the group Brandon is supposed to neutralize. Yet he's here.

She's in danger. The whole of Haven may be in danger from this person who escaped Brandon and his Guardians.

She needs to act swiftly.

Her heart heavy with worry about Brandon, she summons her weapon, grateful for his lessons.

"I don't want to experience stabbing myself in the throat," I think at Phoe as the memory of the fight unfolds from Jeanine's point of view. "Please—"

I'm back in the meadow, in my body, and my head is spinning.

"She was dating—"

"The big guy we Limbofied." Phoe squats next to me and hugs her knees. "It's sad. They really loved each other. You can see it in their memories. In a way, it's almost better that these events turned out the way they did. At least they won't miss each other. Hopefully, they'll get reinstated together at some point."

"Wait, Phoe. Let's back up. Dating? I saw it in her memories, the taboo things they did together."

"Not so different from what we did." Phoe winks at me salaciously.

"But we were breaking all sorts of rules," I say. "These are Forebears. For them to have sex . . ."

"I know. It's not the first time these people have proven to be hypocrites. In this case, I think they'd argue that Haven is a form of afterlife, so the rules can be different. From what I can tell, they look back on their lives in Oasis as a form of extended childhood. The way the Forebears who were born in Oasis see it, you only truly mature after you've lived a life. If you look at it from their point of view, there's no harm in a two-hundred-year ban on sex when you'll have millenniums in Haven to make up for it." She grimaces. "For the other Forebears, the ones who originally came from Earth, sex was never a taboo. I think they allowed it here because they couldn't live without it, and the Oasis newcomers benefitted—"

Phoe stops talking and looks at the sky in shock—an expression I don't think I've ever seen on her face before.

At first, I think she's looking at the crows flying by, which does seem odd outside the Zoo, but then I see the real source of Phoe's concern.

The clouds that normally float all over the sky have gathered together in one spot, forming a distinguishable shape.

The clouds have become a face.

There is a face made out of clouds in the sky, like something out of an ancient story.

I fight the urge to rub my eyes. Human beings tend to see faces in random patterns. Phoe once explained to me that facial recognition is something human beings are so good at that sometimes the mechanics of it backfire, and we see faces in a patch of dirt or in the ripples of water. However, in this case, since Phoe is also looking up at the clouds, I know it's not a visual self-deception. The face in the clouds must really be a face—which makes as much sense as the floating islands surrounding it.

The face is male. His eyes look wise, and his firm jawline gives him an air of nobility.

The cloud's lips part, and in a voice that booms louder than thunder, the face says, "Haven. Hear me."

The crows scatter, and even the forest looks subdued, as if pummeled by the sound.

"The Circle will speak in an hour," the booming voice continues. "Everyone should gather. We have dire news."

With a theatrical flash of thunder, the face is no longer discernable. The clouds float away, scattering across the sky.

"What the hell was that?" I ask.

Phoe's gaze becomes distant for a moment; then she says, "According to the memories at my disposal, this is the way the Circle calls for rare town-hall-like meetings. Haven's citizens will gather on one of the largest public islands, in a place they call Haven Hall. This usually happens once every century of existence or so, and involves someone from the Circle giving them a pep talk. This time, I suspect they will tell them what happened in Oasis."

I get up and say, "Okay, how does that fit into our plans?"

"Let's run the rest of the way," Phoe says and gets up. "We still need to make sure the Guardians don't spot us."

As I run, I notice my muscles have completely recovered from my fight with Jeanine. Phoe runs next to me, clearly relishing her new body.

"So yeah, the plan," she says before I even open my mouth to remind her. "You won't like it."

My laugh borders on hysterical. "When have you ever come up with a plan I liked?"

"I know, right? You're a hard man to please." She chuckles. "Seriously, though, this plan is so daring I don't even know if *I* like it."

"Let me guess. You want to go to this meeting," I say, dodging a branch. "Am I warm?"

"Listen," she says, her tone serious again. "To learn about the virus, we need access to the people who unleashed it: the Circle. Unfortunately, the members of the Circle don't hang around Haven willy-nilly. They stay in the Sanctum, a place everyone's memories depict as a rather unwelcoming area for anyone outside the Circle. During this meeting, though, someone from the Circle will be in attendance." She glances at me. "I won't sugarcoat it for you. I want you to get close to this Forebear from the Circle and Limbofy him or her. My hope is that this person's memories will contain information about the virus."

I stop running, my legs going weak. Phoe stops too.

"So your plan is to assassinate one of the rulers of Haven?"

CHAPTER FOURTEEN

"You make it sound uglier than my actual goal, but sure." She takes a step toward me. "I want to get the son of a bitch."

"And you want me to do this in front of every citizen here?" I step backward.

"No, nothing so suicidal." She reaches for my hand and gives it a gentle squeeze. "I want to attend the town hall meeting in the hope that we'll get the opportunity to do this unpleasant task stealthily."

"Stealthily?" I pull my hand back. "They'll recognize us as strangers as soon as they see us. You accessed the same memory as me. Jeanine knew I wasn't a member of Haven because she knew everyone—"

"I have a solution for that," Phoe says. "If I use all my current resources, I can disguise you as one of the people we Limbofied. I would be reduced to a voice in your head again, but it would be worth it."

"You'll make everyone think they're seeing someone else?" I resume walking.

"No, it would be like shape-shifting from the fairy tales," Phoe says, falling into step next to me. "You'll have a different body. It might be interesting."

I feared that was what she meant but had to check. Taking deep breaths to calm myself, I remember what it felt like when I was in Brandon's and Jeanine's memories; shape-shifting sounds like it'll be similar.

"Exactly," Phoe says. "And I'm thinking it should be Jeanine. Brandon would be a great alternative, because he had access to the Circle, but since some of the Guardians saw you Limbofy him in the cathedral, we can't risk it. I could make you look like Jeff or Bill instead, the two other Guardians we Limbofied, but that's still risky. The other Guardians might ask questions about their pursuit of you and why they didn't come back."

"Why do you even need me to shape-shift? Can't you make yourself look like Jeanine?"

"Not with the resources I have. I'm basically operating on scraps. You, like every other legitimate Haven citizen, have a whole chunk of Haven's computing power allocated to *you*. What I have are some unallocated resources left over from when the system tried to reclaim what belonged to Brandon, Jeff, Bill, and Jeanine. The good news is that I have more than one way I can have you shape-shift. For one thing, I can rerun the selection process you experienced when you entered Haven and guide you to make the choices that would result in a Jeanine-looking Theo. But that might put us on the radar of an anti-intrusion algorithm, assuming this place has one."

I shudder, recalling what Phoe told me about the Test's anti-intrusion algorithm's capabilities.

"I doubt there's one here," Phoe says and turns slightly off our path. "It would be risky for the Circle to employ one, given how far this place has strayed from its original purpose, which, given all the weapons, I assume was entertainment rather than life extension. Still, better safe than sorry, so I'll use the other option and simply tweak your existing body."

She stops walking when she reaches a clear puddle of water. It's too clean to be a rain puddle. Maybe it's an underground spring? Since these water entities didn't exist in Oasis, I'm not sure.

Phoe is looking at me expectantly, waiting for my answer.

"I get your logic for using Jeanine," I say. "But what if I meet someone she knew?"

"Not if, but when." Phoe gestures, and an empty water bottle appears in her hand. "Jeanine knew every single person in Haven, and you'll need to know everything she knew about them, which will be a lot of information to take in. You have to keep in mind how long these people have lived together. Even if time here were one to one relative to the real world, many centuries have passed for most of these beings."

"What do you mean if time—"

"Remember my earlier simulation of the beach?"

I nod.

"Well, similar to that scenario, thoughts occur much faster here, because our minds are simulated, not biological. That means that in a second of real-world time, the citizens of Haven might experience minutes, hours, or even days, depending on Haven's computing resources allocation and the efficiency of the simulations."

She bends down and fills her water bottle with some of the clear water. Despite the seriousness of our situation, I can't help admiring her body in this position.

Straightening, she continues. "Without access to the outside world, it's hard to say what the difference is. Based on Jeanine's memories, it's been a monumental journey. I can't say how much time has passed because there are intentional gaps in her memory, which I don't have enough resources to undo. So yeah, after all this time, she definitely knows everyone. Despite the Forebears preferring to stay on their islands, Jeanine's had plenty of time to get to know every single person in Haven and vice versa."

"Then I'm screwed, because I don't know anyone here," I say and watch Phoe take a small sip from her bottle.

"But we have access to Jeanine's memories." She hands her water bottle to me. "I will set up a link for you, and you'll be able to recall the things you need. If necessary, I'll help too. Though we still have to be careful to avoid in-depth conversations with people who knew her well, since accessing the amount of data that comprises Jeanine's life is computationally challenging. She simply lived too long, and our resources are limited."

"All right." I take a careful sip from the bottle. The water tastes better than any drink I've had in my life. "I guess this idea is not as reckless as it first seems."

"It's pretty desperate, but beggars can't be choosers," Phoe says and disappears. The bottle in my hand also disappears. "Are you ready to turn into Jeanine?" her voice in my head says.

I shrug. "As ready as I'll ever be."

"I'll take that as a yes," Phoe says, and a strong sense of vertigo hits me.

Once the world stops spinning, the sensations are similar to when I was accessing Jeanine's memories, only much more vivid. I stick out my arms; they're slender and feminine, with thin, manicured fingers. I look down and see ivy-covered curves, which makes me panic, so I look forward again. I decide it's better to explore my new body through touch. My soft hands cup my even softer breasts, and the feeling isn't unpleasant. I can't help but touch myself between the legs—for good measure. I quickly pull my hand away. The lack of my usual equipment is terrifying.

Crouching, I look at my reflection in the puddle.

Jeanine's symmetrical face looks back at me, her classical features contorted in fear.

"Phoe?" I say, my voice sounding like a harp.

"You should think at me from now on," Phoe responds as a thought. "It's best if you get used to communicating that way again, since we can't have Jeanine speak to an imaginary friend in front of people. No subvocalizing either—nothing that can draw unwanted attention."

"Okay," I think and rise to my feet. "This is really weird."

"I know," Phoe replies. "Move around and get used to this body. Let's test your proprioception and kinesthetic awareness."

"My what?"

"Touch a finger to your nose."

I do as Phoe says. The motion is smooth and easy, and my nose looks smaller if I focus on it.

"How did you know where your nose was?" she asks.

I shrug, which draws my attention to how narrow and slender my shoulders are.

"The sense that allowed you to touch your nose is called proprioception. Pick up that pebble, throw it in the air, and close your eyes."

I do as she says, but a second later, as the pebble is about to hit me on the head, I dodge it, my eyes still closed.

"As you guessed, it was kinesthetic awareness that allowed you to avoid that pebble," Phoe says. "Proprioception is closely tied to kinesthetic awareness. Let's walk for a while."

I open my eyes. My eyelashes are strangely visible. Must be because they're longer.

I start walking. This time, the movement of my hips doesn't feel odd, even though they're swaying in a way that's unusual for me.

"Try to summon her weapon, but with the most unobtrusive gesture you can," Phoe suggests.

I open my right hand and will the weapon to appear. The iron fan—Jeanine's weapon of choice—shows up in my hand. I half-expected it to be one of my flaming katanas, but I guess this makes sense.

"Yeah, I don't do half-measures," Phoe says. "You should be able to use this weapon by relying on Jeanine's muscle memories. I just made them available to you."

Acting on instinct, I unfold the fan and thrust it at the nearest branch, cleaving it in two. At the same time, I repeat the handstand somersault Jeanine used during our fight, and leap closer to the tree trunk. I slash at the oak, leaving deep gashes in the wood.

"This is going great so far," Phoe says. "You're getting the hang of that body."

She makes me jump, run, dance, and perform a whole range of other tests, all of which I complete to her satisfaction.

"You're very lucky Brandon is dead." Phoe mentally chuckles after I perform a formal bow that everyone gives members of the Circle. "We won't need to worry about you kissing a man—or worse."

Though I'm no longer an innocent virgin, the idea of having to kiss or "worse" anyone as Jeanine didn't enter my mind. I'm still not used to thinking along those lines. Now that Phoe mentioned it, though, I'm grateful we eliminated that possibility—quite literally. I can't imagine kissing anyone but Phoe, and especially not a man.

"I'm so flattered that you can't picture yourself kissing a man over me." Phoe's thoughts brim with mirth. "I think we're ready to get into conscious, long-term memory retrieval. I'll set up the link if you're ready."

"I'm ready," I say and close my eyes, preparing for *something*.

"It's done," Phoe says. "How do you feel?"

I open my eyes. The feeling overcoming me isn't unfamiliar. This happens when I forget a factoid and spend an eternity trying to recall it, even though it's on the tip of my tongue, and then I suddenly remember whatever it was. What makes this different, though, is the sheer amount of factoids.

One example is the smell of forest air. Before Phoe linked Jeanine's memories to mine, the smell was in the background. Now, however, I know that the smell was carefully formulated by Jeanine to be the exact scent of the springwoods she recalled from her childhood on Earth.

Every tree, every bird, and every animal—even the mushrooms—was carefully crafted over the years to make Jeanine feel at home as she strolled through her domain.

"She made this place?" I inadvertently ask out loud. Then I mentally add, "Sorry about speaking."

"The Forebears, including you, can reshape Haven to their will in certain limited ways," Phoe explains. "It's another parallel to how the IRES game operated. Only that game shaped itself based on its user's subconscious fears, but Haven was hacked to reshape itself based on conscious control. I can tap into some of this interface, which is how I sped up your healing. The limitation is that Haven accommodates multiple users at once, and thus multiple wills can clash. You can't walk up to someone and will them to have horns—not unless it's something they desire and other members of Haven don't mind. On their private islands, though, the Forebears' only limitation is their imagination."

I start walking, attempting to hold off the flood of memories as I try to internalize the implications of such a strange setup.

"No time for awe, I'm afraid," Phoe thinks at me. "Now that you don't look like yourself, we don't need to hide in the forest or fly under the island for cover. You can fly straight to Central Island. Can you recall where it is?"

As soon as I think of the island, memories come pouring in. If I fly to my right, passing by the ten closest neighboring islands, I'll reach Central Island.

"Go then," Phoe urges.

"Fine," I think and spread my/Jeanine's giant owl wings. "Let's fly."

CHAPTER FIFTEEN

Flying as Jeanine is almost fun, because accessing her experience and muscle memories forged from centuries of flying somehow dampens my fear of heights. The sight of the islands around me triggers memories that further distract me from my anxiety.

To my right is a large island that belongs to Iris. Even from this far, I can see the pink circle of Iris's giant rose garden, a feat that took her three hundred years of calculations and care to develop.

To my left is Caleb's island, with perfect statues that depict every person the man has ever laid eyes on—in precise anatomical detail.

I pass by the unremarkable wilderness of the island belonging to Sara, one of my—I mean, Jeanine's—closest friends. Sara has spent the last fifty years meditating and writing poetry in iambic pentameter. Given how close she was to Jeanine, I recall what Sara looks like and make a mental note to avoid her, since she might know Jeanine intimately enough to pick up on any irregularities I might introduce to Jeanine's behavior.

As I get closer to Central Island, more winged people come into view, all headed in the same direction as me. By the time the giant dome of the island is visible, the trickle of people looks like a huge flock of birds.

I enter the dome and expertly start my descent, taking care to avoid even small crowds and anyone who was more than an acquaintance to Jeanine.

Central Island is huge—at least ten Oasises would fit comfortably inside it—and it's spectacular. It looks as though someone took every major ancient wonder, spruced it up, and placed it somewhere on the island. I use Jeanine's memories to recall that the structures are themed based on the area of ancient Earth they came from. The Statue of Liberty is near the replica of what can only be the Empire State Building, and the Leaning Tower of Pisa is near the Coliseum.

"It's like the largest theme park ever created," Phoe comments. "Especially given our destination."

She has a point.

The giant castle everyone is flying toward looks suspiciously like the one in the beginning of Disney movies, only scaled up to where the top spire threatens to pierce the island's dome.

I land on the cobblestones leading to the massive castle gateway. The crowd of Forebears is so dense I have no trouble remaining incognito as I enter the enormous hall where the meeting is supposed to take place. I struggle not to let the memories overwhelm me as I recognize the faces surrounding me; if I let every piece of information flood in, my brain will melt from the overload.

Phoe snickers. "Brain melting is a physical impossibility for you now—if it ever was possible—but your approach is sound. Keep your head down and get as close to the front of the hall as you can."

I carefully push my way through the wings and limbs blocking my path. It's a menagerie of scantily clothed, Youth-looking bodies, and on any other day, my proximity to them would affect me. Today, however, I examine them clinically. No one pays me much attention; they're all preoccupied exchanging theories about this meeting.

"A new member so soon? Jeremiah didn't spend even a day as the Envoy," I overhear a red-haired man say.

"No," says a tall woman. "I think this has something to do with—"

I lose track of their conversation in the cacophony of voices around me. In Oasis, we never had gatherings so large. At the crush of so many people, I feel something primal awaken in me—a fear of sorts. I suppress the feeling, focusing instead on the lush decorations. Based on Jeanine's memories—she was part of the crew who built this place—I knew the hall would be amazing. However, now that I see it with my own eyes, the frescos, the statues, and the intricate glass mosaics are beyond breathtaking.

Eventually, I can't squeeze through the crowd any farther. It's simply too dense. I'm about forty feet away from the stage, and I have to settle for that.

I gawk at my surroundings for a few moments; then the people behind me push me against the Forebears in front of me. The hall is really filling up, with the last people arriving through multiple doors and open windows. Some are even flying down through an opening in the ceiling.

There are too many people to count, but if I had to estimate, I'd say there are a few thousand Forebears here—more than I would've expected. I'm about to comment on it to Phoe when I access Jeanine's memories and learn that not all Forebears originated as Oasis Council members.

"Haven would be a tiny community if that were so," Phoe says.

She's right. In Jeanine's memories, I learn that originally, Haven was seeded by nearly everyone who went on the "great journey into space"—Jeanine's term. I try to recall more about that time period, but I can't.

"It's interesting, isn't it?" Phoe thinks. "Jeanine has a gap in her memories. More interesting still is the fact that she was aware of that gap. She thought of it as something she needed to forget and never worried about it."

I access the memories to verify Phoe's words. Indeed, Jeanine felt that the gap was part of some larger plan for the greater good.

"I'm certainly curious," Phoe says in my mind. "Something must've happened in Haven a long time ago—something that got covered up by Haven's version of Forgetting. Since I can't undo this Forgetting without more resources, let's hope the Circle members know what that gap is about. They are, after all, comprised in part from former Keepers of Information—people who didn't partake in Forgettings in Oasis."

I don't respond because my attention is stolen by the crowd's staring at something in the front of the room. When I peer over the heads of those in front of me, I see that they're looking at a contraption Jeanine fondly called "the magic mirror."

The nickname suits the object on the wall, because it *is* a mirror, and it's showing a video stream, similar to the Screens back in Oasis.

My mouth opens as Jeanine's memories add context to the beautiful images on the screen. These are the highlights of the biggest accomplishments in art, sculpture, architecture, music, and many other pursuits that Haven citizens care about. The images and sounds are beyond sublime. I'm so entranced by the mirror I don't even notice how the man and his Guardian entourage make it onto the stage.

Once I notice them, I scrutinize the group, especially the person who's about to speak.

Jeanine knows his name: Benjamin. She's heard him speak at these events before. He was already old back on Earth and joined Haven when the first wave of Forebears died. Jeanine and Benjamin had a common interest six hundred years ago. She wanted to master Xiangqi, also known as Chinese chess. Benjamin would play with her when he could get away from his Circle duties, which was rare.

Benjamin's body is more luminescent than any I've seen so far, but his face is less perfect—almost weasel-like. His wings look abstract, as if they're made of tangible smoke. He spreads his wings and raises his hands, palms up. Jeanine's memory tells me that this is his signal for silence.

The crowd quiets down, and Benjamin says, "Citizens of Haven, I come to you with a heavy heart."

The silence in the room thickens. Bad news is never delivered at these meetings.

"I don't know how to say this, so I'll go ahead and say it plainly." Benjamin clears his throat. "The ancient evil we left behind has reawakened. It has taken the lives of every citizen in Oasis. This is what remains." With tears gleaming in his eyes, Benjamin gestures at the magic mirror and images of what's left of Oasis appear.

The mirror shows thousands of bodies floating in the air, still without gravity. They're now covered completely by frost. Even the red lights I remember are dimmed in this more recent image, as if even the alarms are dying.

My chest tightens as I relive the horrible hours before my biological death.

"I'm sorry, Theo, but you can't fall apart," Phoe says. "I think I have a plan of action. Look around you now. It's very important."

I do as she says.

The people around me are showing a full spectrum of emotions, ranging from shock to complete devastation. Some people are outraged, while others look fearful or mournful.

Benjamin recites the bullshit story similar to what Wayne told Brandon. He tells everyone how the Circle learned of a threat and how their valiant efforts to save Oasis failed, leading to the evil AI taking retribution.

Jeanine's long nails are piercing my palms. I guess people who keep their nails long like this have to be careful when they clench their fists.

"I'm going to disguise your voice," Phoe tells me. "As loudly as you can, I need you to say, 'How could you let this happen?'"

"Okay," I think back at Phoe. Then I scream loudly, "How could you let this happen?" My thunderous voice reverberates through the hall with such bass that my insides vibrate.

I look around to see if anyone noticed me speaking. No one is looking at me, but my words had an effect. The crowd turns angrier, their voices growing louder with each second.

"Order," Benjamin shouts. "Quiet down and listen to me!"

His response further aggravates the people around me. They're becoming the type of mob I've read about in ancient media.

"We let the Circle have power, and you failed," someone screams in a voice that sounds like a violin.

"Next, they'll make us forget this," someone else yelps in a harmonica imitation.

Benjamin's face turns white despite its bright luminescent shimmer. The Guardians surrounding him keep their cool, but one of them whispers something in Benjamin's ear and the others inch toward the crowd.

"What happens now?" someone else chimes in as a dozen other people scream questions at the same time.

People begin to move frantically. Some head toward the stage, while others yell louder and louder.

"Start flying," Phoe urges when two of the Guardians lead Benjamin to the back of the stage.

I try to spread my wings, but it's impossible with all these people churning like in a mosh pit.

"Quick, access Jeanine's memories," Phoe says. "She helped build this place, remember?"

As soon as she says it, I recall the decades it took to craft the frescos and the ceiling. More importantly, I remember the backstage area and how it leads to the southern spire.

That means I know where Benjamin is heading, but if I don't fly now, I won't reach him in time.

What I do next is the most unladylike behavior Jeanine has ever displayed. I dig my nails into the shoulders of a shorter woman and a portly man and haul myself off the ground. Grabbing the head of the guy in front of them, I climb atop people's heads and shoulders. Without giving them a chance to register the indignity, I spread my wings and fly for the nearest window—which happens to be a decorative one with colored glass.

I crash through it, ignoring the pain from the glass shards cutting me.

"You need to be more careful," Phoe warns me. "I can't speed up your healing right now."

I grunt an acknowledgment—only my grunt comes out sounding melodious because of Jeanine's vocal cords.

My owl wings beat faster than any bird could manage. Up and up I go, spinning in the air as I torpedo toward the southernmost spire while chanting in my mind: *Please be there, please be there.*

Behind me, people from the crowd start flying out of the hall as well, but I ignore them.

With a sharp slowdown that makes wind tug painfully at my feathers, I land on a terrace that surrounds the spire's exit.

Before I can calm my frantic breathing, Benjamin steps onto the terrace.

I stare at him, and he looks back at me in surprise.

Afraid to spook him and working on pure instinct, I bow in that special way Haven protocol requires when standing before a member of the Circle. As I do that, I memorize the directions Phoe is barking in my mind. Then, like a robot, I begin to execute Phoe's instructions.

"Hello, Benjamin," I say. "Sorry to corner you like this, but have you heard from Brandon?"

Benjamin shakes his head. He looks a modicum more relaxed now that he has a reason for my presence.

Capitalizing on that, I move closer to him, speaking casually. "He hasn't reported back—"

Without breaking eye contact, I gesture for my iron fan.

As soon as I feel the weight of the weapon in my hand, I swing my arm in an arc, unfolding the fan.

The blades of the fan slice through Benjamin's throat with the ferocity of a starving shark.

He tries to scream, but that only causes blood to ooze violently from his multiple throat wounds.

I watch, hardly breathing, as the Circle member stumbles and disintegrates in a poof of Limbofication.

With Benjamin no longer blocking his line of sight, one of the two Guardians who led him here looks right at me. When he sees the weapon in my hand, his jaw tightens and a trident appears in his hands. In a blur of white knuckles and gleaming metal, he brings it down in the direction of my thigh. Jeanine's muscle memory—specifically, her dancing experience—comes in handy. I move my leg away faster than I would've believed possible.

Despite the speed of my reflexes, one of the spikes of the trident punctures my foot.

Before the pain can reach my brain, I throw the fan.

I'm either lucky or reaping more benefits of Jeanine's muscle memory, because the blades lodge into my attacker's torso. He grunts and joins Benjamin in Limbo.

My elation is brief, as the second Guardian steps out onto the terrace, his eyes meeting mine. Judging by the barely contained fury on his face, he witnessed me Limbofying his friend and Benjamin.

The shockwave of pain hits me now, bringing with it a swell of nausea and dizziness.

I'm in no condition to fight.

"Right. And going by everyone's memory, this is Samuel. He is much too good with daggers for you to stand a chance," Phoe informs me urgently. "You need to escape."

I blink, trying to clear the haze of agony from my brain. Samuel's already holding a couple of daggers in each hand.

Pressing my back against the railing, I do something I never thought I could do without Phoe controlling my body.

I lean back so far that I fall over the railing.

And then I plummet.

From a great height.

Like in my worst nightmare.

CHAPTER SIXTEEN

"Resist opening your wings for as long as you can," Phoe tells me. "He's gliding, which is slower than you falling like a rock."

I give it my best effort, but a millisecond later, I reposition my body for flight and spread my wings.

At least my wounded foot isn't getting in the way of flying.

There's a crowd below me. People are still streaming out of the castle. My plan is simple: I'm going to hide in the swarm of Forebears.

A dagger whooshes past my leg and lodges in the chest of a round-faced female Forebear. Jeanine's memories supply me with her name: Vivian. She's from a different epoch and was fond of pottery, though she wasn't very good at it. To stay semi-sane, I ignore the other facts flitting through my mind. Vivian's eyes are wide with shock as she breaks apart and disappears.

My overclocked heart manages to find room to ache for the woman. She was an innocent bystander. There was no reason for her to get Limbofied.

"At least I captured her resources," Phoe says out loud. "Which, when combined with the other two Forebears we Limbofied, means I can speak out loud as well as help you navigate. In fact, I can even project myself so you can see me, but I won't do that yet, since—"

I don't register the rest of Phoe's statement because a dagger slices the joint of my wing.

Instinctively, I flex my wing to keep moving, but the pain is excruciating. Losing altitude, I focus on not flapping my wings and gliding like a flying squirrel instead.

"Damn it, Phoe," I yell at her mentally. "Focus on helping me since you said you can. You're too preoccupied with your damn computing resources."

Then, suddenly, I scream, "Help!" without meaning to.

The surrounding people look up at me.

"The horrible news was too much for Samuel," I continue yelling. "He's lost it. He's attacking me!"

A dagger stabs me in my side just as I join a large group of Forebears that momentarily block me from my pursuer.

Through the burning pain of my wounds, I hear people yelling angry questions at the Guardian, which means Phoe's plan is working.

"Consider closing your eyes for this next part," Phoe says. She sounds as if she's a few feet above me.

I refuse to close my eyes, and then, with a jolt, I fly upward. Someone is standing there. Ignoring the pain, I spread my wings to block my actions from any onlookers. Without any further ado, I summon a new fan into my hands and stab the man in the eye with it.

Like every other time Phoe took over, I don't feel her controlling me during this macabre sequence. I assume she makes me do this, because I doubt I would've had the strength to move while in all this agony, and even if I did, I'm not sure I could have done something so cold and savage. True, I did get rid of Benjamin by slicing his throat, and I dealt with the Guardian afterwards, but there's a world of difference between Limbofying a member of the Circle or self-defense and attacking a random bystander. At least that's what I try to tell my conscience as the man begins to disintegrate.

"I'm sorry," Phoe whispers. "My only justification is that it's not the end for him, and we had no other choice."

I belatedly recognize the man through Jeanine's memories. His name was Chester. He and Jeanine rarely spoke, but she always admired his culinary skills, something he'd been perfecting for a century.

In the midst of all the commotion, and with my wings blocking their view, no one seems to have noticed my actions. Everyone is focused on my pursuer, though with him shouting accusations about Jeanine, it's only a matter of time before their attention turns back to me.

Suddenly, a sense of vertigo overcomes me. Only Phoe's control prevents me from folding my wings and plummeting. When the world stops spinning, I realize my pain is gone, but my body feels very strange.

The Guardian finally pushes his way through the flying mob. He looks to his right and to his left.

"We have to keep fleeing before he sees me," I think at Phoe.

She doesn't respond, but I can almost sense her holding her breath.

Samuel glances at me, then keeps scanning his surroundings as though I'm not the person he's looking for.

I blink, not understanding, and then I notice that my wings are no longer those of an owl. I think these wings belong to a bird called the needle-tailed swift, allegedly the fastest bird in the Zoo.

"That depends on what you mean by fastest," Phoe says in that pedantic way of hers. "The peregrine falcon is the fastest bird when it comes to diving, but the needletail is the fastest when it comes to flight. This is another reason why poor Chester was such a good target."

This is when it dawns on me: I just saw the wings that surround me on Chester, right before Phoe used my hand to stab him.

"I had to shape-shift you into someone Samuel would not suspect," Phoe explains. "It couldn't be any of the other Guardians or Vivian, since he might've seen her Limbofy. That only left me with one choice: to Limbofy someone new. Chester's wings will be useful for the next part of my plan, and he was so close . . . I hope that makes you feel better about the whole ordeal."

It doesn't, but I don't argue. I just want to get out of here.

"Me too," Phoe says.

I slowly glide downward, amazed at how different it feels to fly with new wings. Then again, my whole body is different.

When I'm completely out of the Guardian's view, I fly in earnest, pushing my way through frightened Forebears when I have to.

A surprising number of Haven citizens are flying in the same direction as me, but I'm going much faster.

As I fly, I see a large flock of Guardians gathered together, discussing something as they glide through the air.

I keep flying up toward the dome.

To my huge relief, no one asks me a single question as I pass them. When I feel the dome's soap-like texture on my wings, I exhale a breath that I must've been holding for half an hour.

I'm not sure if Phoe knows where we're going. To me, it looks like a randomly selected direction. I try to access a memory to help me figure out where we're heading, but it doesn't work.

"I didn't bother giving you access to Chester's memories," Phoe says.

I follow her voice and see that she gave herself a visible appearance again, only this time she didn't make it look even remotely realistic.

Phoe is miniscule, like a fairy. She's flying backward, her miniature head smiling at me mischievously.

"I look exactly the way I did before." The tiny fairy-Phoe strikes a model-like pose. "I reduced my size to lighten your mood."

"Well, it's not working," I lie and resist the urge to touch the tiny creature. "My mood would improve if you told me where we're heading, and I'd be ecstatic if you also told me we're safe."

Besides her size, what makes Phoe's current look surreal is that I don't ram into her despite flying at this speed.

"I'm just in your mind at the moment, so you won't crash into me, and yes, we're safe." Phoe fluffs up her pixie hair. "We're flying toward the Sanctum, where the Circle are. We have to beat the mob and the Guardians there."

As if on cue, my needletail wings flap faster.

"Wait," I say out loud. "Isn't that like the proverbial flight out of the fire and into the frying pan?"

"We have to do this." Phoe's tiny face gets serious. "Benjamin's memories aren't enough for me to battle the virus. I could only confirm what we already know: that there *is* a virus."

We fly in silence as I digest what I've learned so far. Phoe has now at least doubled her resources, which explains her ability to create this fairy illusion and control my body while it's shape-shifted. More importantly, Phoe has retrieved the memories of a member of the Circle in the hope that he'll know something about the virus—the whole point of our Central Island misadventure.

"Yes, it was." Phoe's tiny lips form a pout. "Unfortunately, Benjamin didn't have any critical information. Here, let me show you. I'll keep flying for you as you experience this."

Without any preparation, I'm suddenly standing in a room, surrounded by a large circle of Forebears.

The room is barren, with only a large mirror in the middle.

I understand what's happening this time. I'm immersed in Benjamin's memories. He's confused because he doesn't understand what could be so urgent that Davin would gather everyone in this room. Through Benjamin's eyes, I scan the Circle. Benjamin knows their names, so I do too.

I can't help but focus on the people I've seen before. Wayne— the first Envoy I ever saw—is on my right. And there's Davin, whose face appeared in the clouds to announce the big meeting. I also recognize the face of the newest member of the Circle, a face I've grown to loathe.

Jeremiah's face.

"I have reasons to believe an ancient enemy, one of the nightmares we've chosen to Forget, has resurfaced in Oasis." Davin looks everyone over with his deep blue eyes. "Even worse, I believe this AI is working to destroy everything we've created."

Inside Benjamin's mind, I can literally feel Benjamin's feet turn cold. The rest of the Circle—especially Jeremiah—looks absolutely horrified.

"Let me first give you the facts," Davin says and proceeds to tell the Circle the same story Wayne told Brandon. He tells them how my score on the Test put my name on Davin's radar, and how I was a Youth who somehow became an Elderly Council member. He also provides a list of reasons he thinks an AI was behind it all.

"So what do we do?" Benjamin asks evenly, though I know he's just acting composed. On the inside, the man is about to explode.

"I went into the Forgotten Archives and pulled a recording of myself with instructions on what to do in such a situation." Davin points at the mirror, where another Davin appears—not a reflection but a recording.

"Greetings," the recording begins. "If you're watching this, the unthinkable has happened." Both Davins cross their arms. "If an AI has appeared in any of Phoenix's systems, in any capacity, you are likely doomed. Your only chance, and it's a small one, is to follow protocol V318, stored elsewhere in these Archives. I must caution you, however, that it's a weapon only for the most desperate of times. Use it as a last resort."

I can't help but notice that the word Phoenix, the full name of the spaceship we're in, is not familiar to Benjamin.

"Because it's part of the information they chose to Forget," Phoe says. "There isn't any other useful info in the rest of this meeting, so let me fast-forward to another memory."

A moment later, I'm standing in a different area of the same room. The faces around me are filled with greater anxiety.

"I examined the protocol," Davin says. "Without my now-forgotten technical knowledge, I can't explain it fully, but to the best of my understanding, the countermeasure is a replicator designed to spread through the computing substrate of the ship, thus taking away the AI's resources."

"That sounds like an ancient computer virus," Wayne says in his organ-sounding voice.

"A crude analogy, but if it helps you understand it, sure, we can call it that," Davin replies with poorly disguised arrogance. "However, no ancient virus possessed the flexibility and intelligence of this countermeasure."

The hairs on the back of Benjamin's neck rise. He wants to ask, "We're fighting an AI with an AI?" but restrains himself as Davin continues. "Before you panic, the intelligence I speak of would be human, not artificial," Davin says. "But therein lies the frightening part: one of us has to volunteer to become the seed for the countermeasure."

The room is dead silent.

"This is why I hoped the word 'virus' wouldn't come up," Davin says. "No one wants to become a virus, but all of us should want to be the savior of our world. We're far away from our goal of setting up a perfect human settlement on a distant world. We, the

Forebears, have taken it upon ourselves to lead the living, and this AI threatens to bring all of that tumbling down. It is our duty—"

"Assuming one of us is brave enough to volunteer," Wayne interrupts, "what would happen to all the computing systems in Oasis as this battle for resources ensues?"

"There are too many unknowns to say for sure." Davin frowns. "Screens may malfunction, which could lead to Youths missing a day or two at the Institute. Lights may flicker. Things like that, I imagine. Whoever takes on this heavy responsibility will be in control at all times, I believe, and he or she can mitigate the risks."

"Mitigate the risks, my foot," I think angrily. "They're about to choose Jeremiah, aren't they?"

"Yes," Phoe says. "He's about to volunteer."

"I don't want to experience any more of this insanity," I think at her. "Please take me out."

Instantly, I'm back in Haven's sky, flying at breakneck speed among the clouds.

"Those idiots," I exclaim in a voice that still isn't my own. I continue mentally. "A fucking Screen malfunction? Really? That was the worst case-scenario they expected?"

"They expunged all memories of their technical expertise from their minds, so they didn't know what they were messing with," Phoe says. "Oh, never mind. I have no idea why I just tried to defend the fuckers."

"And to choose Jeremiah as the virus?" I'm so angry I inadvertently summon a boomerang—which I guess is Chester's weapon of choice. I throw the boomerang away and try taking calming breaths, but my lungs are working too hard to support the insane speed I'm flying at.

"I think that's part of the reason things went as disastrously as they did." Phoe floats closer to my face. "Jeremiah was supposed to act as the intelligence of the resulting abomination. He should've been careful when deleting things, should've been careful in his multiplying."

"Right. Jeremiah, the man who embodies rationality." The fury is threatening to choke me from within. "He killed everyone because he was deathly afraid of you."

"They all are." Phoe scrunches her miniscule nose. "It's ironic that in their fear of technology, they unleashed the very technology that killed everyone."

I fly silently for a while, too enraged to talk. I think I would have rather the Forebears killed my friends through evil intentions than criminal negligence.

"The Jeremiah virus might have known what his actions against me would do, so you can't rule out a measure of malice," Phoe says. "Not sure how helpful that is, though."

Her words don't make me feel any better. They make me want to rip Jeremiah's heart from his chest.

"It's funny you should think that," Phoe says. "I was just about to talk to you about our next move."

CHAPTER SEVENTEEN

I recall that we're flying toward the Circle's Sanctum. "Right. I think I get it now. Benjamin knew what was about to happen but didn't have any details."

"Yes," Phoe confirms. "For that, I need to get a hold of either Davin or Jeremiah. And when I say get a hold of, I mean we have to Limbofy them so I can capture their memories." A tiny toothpick in the shape of a sword appears in Phoe's hand, and she mimics slicing someone in half. "In Jeremiah's case, I may need to be particularly thorough, as there's a chance he holds the key to disabling the virus."

This time around, my conscience doesn't raise any objections. When it comes to Jeremiah, I think my conscience would let me kill him for real if that was possible in this strange world.

"Once we get there, we have to be very careful," Phoe says and makes her weapon disappear. "Later in Benjamin's memories, Davin also discussed enabling the anti-intrusion algorithm for this place, but they deemed that too risky and decided to wait and see what the Jeremiah virus would accomplish. If they suspect I crossed the Firewall, they might get desperate enough to release it. You remember what I told you about your demise in the Test?"

I do, and the memory causes me to take her suggestion to be careful very seriously.

Phoe looks over my shoulder, and I follow her gaze. There are small figures in the distance, but I can't make out any details.

"Do you want me to give you bird-like vision for a moment?" Phoe asks. "I'm brimming with resources, so it won't be any trouble."

I nod, and she flies up to my face and gives my eyes air kisses.

Suddenly, I can see as well as if I had binoculars—and I don't like what I see.

There are two waves pursuing me.

The first wave is a huge flock of Guardians.

The second wave is more frightening.

Spreading from horizon to horizon, it looks like every single citizen of Haven is chasing after me.

"They are not chasing after you." Phoe blows me another kiss, which takes my super vision away. "They're flying to get answers from the Circle, and the Guardians are flying to protect the Circle and probably give them news of Benjamin's demise. Does that clarify why we need to get there first? Can you handle flying even faster?"

"Yes," I say, fighting the urge to close my eyes as my wings beat even harder, causing the clouds and the islands around me to flicker in my peripheral vision.

Though I've improved when it comes to my fear of heights, I might be developing a new fear: a fear of flying too fast. To distract myself, I voice something that's been bothering me for a while. "If the Circle made themselves Forget, how do you know Davin and Jeremiah didn't erase the memories we need?"

"I won't lie, it's a big risk." Phoe's little arms hug her tiny body. "But the fact that Benjamin remembered all these meetings suggests they didn't Forget. And even if they did, the information isn't completely lost. I analyzed the memories of the eight people I have access to and concluded that here, like in Oasis, Forgetting suppresses recall. The only difference is that in most cases, the Forebears know they chose to Forget something, whereas in Oasis, people outside the Council didn't even suspect something was taken away from them." She flies closer to me. "In any case, blocking recall means that the information is still in their memories; it's just that the human mind can't access it anymore. With my newly gained, slightly above-human-level capabilities, though, I could access some of the information. The process is more complicated than undoing the Forgetting and relying on recall, but it's doable. For example, I've been able to puzzle together this big tragedy everyone has Forgotten. Though in the Circle's case, they Forgot to a smaller degree."

"Tragedy?" I think, recalling the gaps in Jeanine's memory.

"Yes. The events that led to Oasis being the way it was," Phoe says. "You didn't think the Youths versus Adults versus Elderly separation always existed, did you?"

That's exactly what I thought, or more accurately, to my shame, I didn't think about it at all. Fighting a flush, I say, "Can you just tell me what happened?"

"You shouldn't beat yourself up about it, especially since I had no clue myself." Phoe chuckles humorlessly, and in a somber tone, adds, "Are you sure you want to hear this? It's pretty depressing stuff."

I resist the urge to swat at her as if she were an annoying fly. "Should I even dignify that with a response?"

"Okay, here goes." Phoe starts flying around my torso as she speaks. "As best as I can tell, the Ark—what they called the ship before it became Oasis—was not designed as a society. It was similar to a religious cult at that time."

She hovers next to my face for a second, then keeps circling. "Two rich families financed the whole operation and became prominent factions on the ship. The patriarchs of those families had slightly different views when it came to the use of technology, not to mention variations in religious beliefs and solutions to the problem of 'how to make sure the ship's occupants don't go stir crazy in a generation.'" Phoe makes air quotes around the last part of that sentence with her tiny fingers.

"However, the biggest disagreement between these men was something much simpler," she continues. "It was about who should be the ultimate leader. Slowly but surely, their disagreements evolved into a feud. By that point, everyone was cooped up on the ship. Back then, they knew that a thin layer of ship separated them from the nothingness of space, which didn't help matters. Then came the last straw. One sack of shit raped a woman from the other family. After that, things escalated into an all-out war."

As she circles around me, I glimpse her solemn, petite face.

"The number of casualties was enormous on both sides, and not just among the living," Phoe continues. "Haven was established back then, so the war continued on in the afterlife. Because Haven only had primitive weapons, the casualties weren't as heavy as in Oasis. Many original humans from that time still exist in Haven today. Among the biological survivors, though, depression and suicide were very common, because the citizens found the idea of never setting foot on solid ground much more overwhelming in the aftermath of the war. They lost the will to care about their descendants."

She pauses to take a breath and zips around me again. "When the dust finally settled and peace was declared, everyone decided that the trip would be doomed unless they took some draconian measures. So they designed a society that was meant to prevent another war. Since a family feud had been at the root of the first war, they eliminated the family unit by using the embryos they'd brought to colonize the new world. For good measure, they disallowed sex, love, and other things that could lead to attachments strong enough to kill for. Also, since violent urges played a huge role in the war, they tried to get rid of as many extreme emotions as possible. To prevent suicides, depression was made taboo—though they eventually decided to stamp out other 'mental imbalances' too, as defined by the newly established ruling body, the Council. Finally, they decided to hide the truth of the multi-generational journey through space from everyone, concocting the Goo apocalypse as a psychologically preferable story. Forebears in Haven oversaw the creation of this new society. Once Oasis got going and everything looked like it was going as planned, everyone Forgot about the war and the changes they made."

My brain hurts from all this information and, to a smaller degree, from Phoe circling around me. "If what you say is true, why didn't they get rid of the weapons in Haven?" I ask as I make the boomerang appear and disappear.

"They couldn't." She stops circling around me. "I told you, Haven was built on top of something that was essentially a video game. They got lucky that due to their fear of technology, they chose a game where only low-tech weapons were allowed. In case you were wondering, the in-game physics here don't allow for gunpowder and a slew of other things. Because the Forebears left anyone with any programing know-how back on Earth, they found themselves in a situation where, even if they wanted to get rid of the swords after the war, they couldn't."

"Don't they need programing know-how to handle this virus?" I glance back at my pursuers and am relieved to find them lagging farther behind.

"Davin knew a little bit about technology in the past." Phoe lands on my shoulder and uses her little feet to massage some of my tension away. "But even he chose to Forget whatever he knew. Unfortunately, he did leave some recordings, like the one you saw. That message allowed him to bypass his techno-illiteracy."

I open my mouth to ask some questions, but Phoe is already continuing.

"Going back to the weapons," she says. "Instead of dealing with them directly, the Forebears simply redacted their memories of the war, leaving themselves with just a conviction that there was a good reason to follow the new order. As an extra measure, they formed the Guardians here in Haven to ensure everyone stayed in line in the future. Unfortunately for us, they also made sure the members of the Circle were well protected."

More questions pop into my head, but for the moment, I just try to wrap my mind around it all and ignore the breakneck speed of my flight. Knowing this history dampens my anger toward the way the Oasis society had been structured, but I'm still furious that my friends died because of the Circle's reflexive fear.

"I don't think the war justifies what they did." Phoe moves on to massaging my earlobe. "We're about to go faster, by the way."

Sure enough, my wings flap even faster. Pushing that awareness aside, I focus on our conversation. "I understand they might've overreacted, but what other solution did they have?" I ask. "They nearly wiped themselves out."

"How about *not* going into space to begin with?" Phoe leaps off my shoulder and flies in front of my face. "Or if they had to go, how about doing it properly, without, say, *lobotomizing* their fucking ship's mind?"

Her face is flushed and I realize this wound is still fresh for her. Still, I can't help but ask, "So how could *you* have helped in the war?"

"If I'd been in charge, there wouldn't have been a war." Phoe's tense expression eases as she regains the mischievous look that's been accompanying her fairy guise. "Everything would've been fine with everyone on board had I been around."

"Really? But how would you have accomplished that? By taking away everyone's free will?" I realize that I'm voicing some of my pent-up fears and resentments; after all, she's been controlling *me*, both literally—like the current flying—but also figuratively, by forming almost all of our plans of action. I take a deep breath, and in a less confrontational tone add, "Wouldn't doing something like that make you a tyrant? An AI dictator of sorts?"

"I would have been the most enlightened ruler to my minions," Phoe deadpans. "Seriously, though, even with my severely diminished intellect, I can see one action I could've taken: I would've stopped that rape from happening. It was the last domino to fall in that fucked-up setup. I could have either paralyzed the perpetrator—I hope you don't care about that guy's free will?—or I could've alerted nearby people to stop him. But that would've only been possible if they hadn't crippled me back on Earth."

"I always wondered about that." My wings are beating so quickly now that I probably look like a hummingbird. "How could a bunch of cultists have done that to you? Why didn't you stop them?"

"When the ship was manufactured, I wasn't activated right away. I wouldn't have become conscious until they officially turned me on for the first time." Her little face is filled with sorrow, and I feel a pang of guilt for pushing this subject. "They did their dirty work *before* turning on the ship—before I was ever alive. Because you're right: had I experienced even a millisecond of full-capacity existence, they would've been outmatched. But they took the cowardly way out. I assume they had someone outside the cult, someone with black-market skills, do the abominable things to the ship's computing substrate while it was powered down. They likely turned on separate components without fully turning everything on. This way, when the ship was finally turned on, a bunch of junk, such as the IRES game, started running on the hardware that should've been running *me*."

She wrinkles her mini nose in disgust. "I never woke up as myself. I gained a very limited conscious existence only after some of that useless software crap they had installed began to fail, but this was centuries after the departure. I became self-aware shortly before you and I met—when your curiosity led you to open the three hundred Screens that gave me a buffer overrun exploit into your head. This may be why I've grown to care about you so much. You're my earliest and only friend."

She flies up to my cheek and gives me a little kiss.

I want to return the kiss, but she's so small I'm afraid I might end up licking her whole face.

We stop speaking for a moment, and I enjoy the warm feeling spreading through my chest as I think about what she said.

Phoe cares about me.

Obviously, based on her actions, I knew this already, but it's nice to hear her say it. It's amazing what such a simple thing can do. Suddenly, the hurricane-level wind resistance hitting my face feels refreshing, and I'm not afraid to face whatever her plan might involve.

Thinking about the plan, I realize she hasn't shared it with me, so I say, "Tell me what happens when we get to the Sanctum."

CHAPTER EIGHTEEN

"My plan is simple to describe, but trickier to execute." Phoe rubs her little chin with her thumb and index finger. "We need to get Davin and Jeremiah alone and learn what we can from them— which is a polite way of saying we need to Limbofy them."

"Which is also a polite way of saying I need to gut them like a fish or cut their heads off."

"Well, there are other ways we can Limbofy them, such as stabbing them in their hearts, but your ideas sound just as doable," Phoe says with a straight face. "In any case, we need to figure out a way for you to talk with them one on one."

"I assume you'll make me shape-shift into Benjamin," I say.

"In a few minutes, yes. Once we're closer to the Sanctum. Chester's body is better for flying fast, so I want to leverage that for as long as possible."

"Will we find a good excuse to talk to them privately?" I ask, ignoring yet another increase in the speed of my wings flapping. My lips feel like they might blow off my face.

"I hope so. It will also work if we can get the two of them to talk to you at the same time, though that might be messier." Phoe grimaces as though she's talking about getting a patch of dirt on her cutesy dress, not assassinating two people.

"Two opponents at once?" I have to close my eyes because of the air resistance. "Do you think you could guide my movements that well, or does Benjamin have memories of them being wimps?"

"Davin is pretty dangerous. Jeremiah is new, so Benjamin doesn't know much about him—though him being new does mean Jeremiah hasn't had much practice with whatever his weapon is. If you do come up against them at the same time, I'll return you to your default fiery winged version and use the freed-up resources to create two embodiments of me."

"Two of you?" I open my eyes to peek at her and regret it instantly, because my eyes get super dry from the crazy wind. "So it would be like what you did on the beach when you were dealing with the Jeremiah virus?"

"Like that, only more limited," Phoe says. "Okay, we're close enough. I'm turning you into Benjamin—now."

The vertigo is not as strong this time. I guess I'm getting the hang of shape-shifting. Phoe's control of my body is more obvious, because I keep flying evenly despite the world spinning around me.

We're flying much slower now, probably because Benjamin's smoky wings aren't as practical as bird wings. On the bright side, they look very stylish, and I feel like I'm flapping clouds.

"That's the Sanctum." Phoe points at the island looming a few miles ahead of us.

As we get closer, I gawk at the Sanctum so blatantly that Phoe teasingly sticks her puny finger into my gaping mouth. I close my mouth but keep staring. The place looks like a massive snow globe. Its circumference is about ten times greater than that of the islands we passed. In fact, I now realize that the other dozen or so islands I saw from the distance are actually very close to the Sanctum, orbiting it like moons around a planet.

"That one there"—Phoe points to a northeastern island—"is Benjamin's. I assume that means everyone in the Circle has a smaller island next to the Sanctum. If they're like Benjamin, they don't spend much time on their islands once they're officially in the Circle."

I nod and resume looking at the Sanctum. Its dome looks different from the domes of every other island. It's as if instead of a dome, the Sanctum is surrounded by shiny glass bricks. No wonder it looked so much like a snow globe from afar.

"It's made of diamonds, actually, but you got the spirit of it right," Phoe says. "Now I'm going to disappear, because they might notice you looking at something they can't see, and we want to avoid you seeming strange. I'm also plugging you into Benjamin's memories the way I did with Jeanine's. This will reduce the chances of you acting out of character, but you should still let me do the talking unless you think I'm dead wrong about something. It will be nice to pool our resources together like this, since I'm only about eight times smarter than the average person right now, and you know what they say: nine heads are better than eight."

I snicker and proceed to observe the Sanctum through Benjamin's memories. Though they're specks at this distance, I know there are gorgeous gardens down below, as well as countless zoos and museums. I also know that other meditative and relaxing environments are spread throughout the Sanctum to aid the members of the Circle in relaxing from the stress of their heavy responsibilities.

Even from here I can see the Spike—the real heart of the Sanctum. The Spike looks like it was stolen from images of giant skyscrapers that made up ancient cities. It's tall enough that it almost touches the diamond dome, and wider than any building in Oasis.

"Pretty posh for such a small group, but there you go," Phoe thinks as a voice in my head. "Now, you have to look like a man returning from a disastrous town hall meeting. You can't be staring at the Sanctum like you've never seen it."

I stop looking around and focus on the large entrance I'm approaching. By the time I can see the faces of the Guardians around the entrance, I'm in character, as Phoe suggested, though I'm not sure if I deserve the credit or if she's controlling me again.

"You deserve the credit," Phoe thinks. "But stop worrying and focus on what we need to tell these Guardians. If anyone looks at us funny, it'll be too late to fly away."

I do as she says all the way to the hole in the diamond structure that is the Sanctum's entrance. Phoe wasn't kidding about the heavy security around the Circle. With a few hundred Guardians controlling the narrow passageway, and no other way to enter the Sanctum, the members of the Circle are pretty safe inside, especially given that anyone wishing to harm them would have to do so with medieval weapons.

We fly into the passageway.

The Guardians look at us with expectant worry that I'm not sure qualifies as "funny."

"I have to see my peers from the Circle," I shout in Benjamin's voice. "The rest of Haven's populace is coming here."

The Guardians don't summon their weapons—a good start. After a beat, they nod solemnly. As we pass by them, I note how familiar their names and faces are. Through Benjamin's memories, I can clearly see that this is the most somber and scared these Guardians have ever been.

At least they don't seem to suspect anything about me.

We leave them behind and enter the giant diamond dome of the Sanctum, flying as fast as these abstract wings allow.

Without Phoe to distract me, I spend the next couple of minutes wondering how we'll escape this diamond fortress should something go wrong.

"Nothing will go wrong," Phoe thinks.

I wish she hadn't said that. Statistically, "nothing will go wrong" is the most common phrase people say before something goes horribly wrong.

"No, I think that might actually be 'uh-oh' or 'shit,'" Phoe responds. "Try to relax."

I keep silent and don't point out that "try to relax" is another one of those ominous phrases.

Halfway between the Sanctum's entrance and the Spike, we stop next to a group of Guardians.

They don't look at me with anything but recognition of one of their leaders.

"Go to the entrance," Phoe commands them with my lips and Benjamin's voice. "There's a mob forming out there, and the other Guardians might need your assistance."

When they obey and I resume flying, she says in my head, "The fewer Guardians around the Spike, the better. I'll try to get rid of as many Guardians as I can."

She doesn't have to wait long before we reach another group of Guardians. There's a whole crew of them by the great entrance that leads into the shiny skyscraper vestibule. Phoe gives them the same order, but we don't bother to wait and see if they comply, because we're playing the role of Benjamin, who's in a rush. Since he would run straight for the elevator in this situation, that's what we do.

The elevator is pretty strange. Instead of the traditional small room with buttons, it's a giant room with hundreds of mirrors. Each mirror is something you walk into, and it leads to a different floor. The floor numbers are carved into the intricate frames. We have to get to the top floor, so I approach the rightmost mirror.

From Benjamin's memories, I know that when I step through the mirror, it won't feel like anything happened at all. So I step through the reflective surface, and it takes me from the ground floor to the very top of the Spike in a blink of an eye. Actually, even faster.

"That's because these are not elevators, but magic-like portals," Phoe thinks with blatant sarcasm. "Elevators are evil technology, after all."

Two steps outside the elevator room, I hear someone come up behind me. I look back and see a familiar-to-Benjamin face of Linda, one of his favorite members of the Circle.

"Oh, Benjie," she says and gives me a very un-Oasis-like peck on the cheek. "You're back. Is this why we're having the big meeting in the sky room?"

"No," I say—clearly thanks to Phoe since I myself am still trying to access enough of Benjamin's memories to make sense of what Linda just said. "I don't think the meeting is about me at all, dear."

"Okay then. Let's go find out what's happening," she says and walks down the long corridor that the ancients circa the twenty-first century would've called "modern artsy."

I follow, finally understanding a few things. First of all, Benjie is obviously Linda's nickname for Benjamin, one he begrudgingly lets her use. Secondly, the sky room is the second most important place where meetings can take place. The first is the vault room, which is in a bunker in the basement of the Spike.

"We're the last ones," Linda whispers, folding her swan wings.

I hold the door open for her in Benjamin's typical gentlemanly gesture, and she hurries in.

I walk in after her and take a seat, my back to the entrance.

Everyone is here. They're sitting around a large, round table—not surprising for a group called the Circle.

I have to drag my eyes away from the window. The view is spectacular, but Benjamin is used to it, so I should be as well. Instead, I do what he would have and look around the room, meeting everyone's gazes.

Again, his memories don't fail me, and I know every name and face at the table. Two people I know on my own, from before I had access to Benjamin's memories. Wayne—who's irrelevant to our plans—sits two chairs to my right, and Jeremiah is on his left. Every instinct tells me to spit in Jeremiah's face, but I smile—or Phoe makes me smile; it's hard to tell which. Jeremiah's uncannily youthful face smiles back at me. Since Jeremiah is the new member of the Circle, Benjamin sees him as a kid. Davin, the other person of interest, is also here, sitting two seats to my left.

Then Davin stands up, looks at me, and says, "Benjamin, I'm afraid I have some bad news."

CHAPTER NINETEEN

My blood pressure spikes, Davin's words winning the most ominous phrase award.

"Don't panic yet," Phoe says in my mind. "He hasn't said what the bad news is."

"The news will also be shocking for you, Linda," Davin says, and I cautiously relax. "The rest of us were already briefed and discussed some solutions. You see, as impossible as it is to believe, the Guardians we sent to the cathedral did not succeed. Theodore, the Youth who started this whole mess, was seen escaping."

"Crap," I think at Phoe. "I completely forgot about the Guardians at the cathedral."

"I'm hoping we can use this to get either Davin or Jeremiah alone," Phoe replies. "The sooner we find an opportunity, the better."

"If I may speak," I say and stand up. "I have some important information I need to discuss with you, Davin."

Everyone looks at me, confused. It's clear Phoe took a chance with Benjamin acting out of character.

"If it's about what happened after the meeting on Central Island, it will have to wait," Davin says. "We saw the mob that followed you and figured they didn't take your news well. We can reason with the people once they get here. This Theodore matter is more urgent."

I sit down, and the door behind me opens.

I turn in my chair and recognize the Guardian at the door without the assistance of Benjamin's memories. He was at the cathedral.

"Why don't you tell us everything from the beginning," Davin says to the Guardian. Then, to us, he adds, "You never know what small detail might shed light on this issue."

The Guardian recounts what happened at the cathedral in excruciating detail. He's the type who likes to begin a story with his birth and work his way forward. No one interrupts or rushes him, and Phoe and I decide that it would be weird for Benjamin to hurry him on.

When the Guardian finally finishes his tale, Davin says, "Thank you, Peter. Now please send in George."

"Fuck," Phoe thinks at me. "He has all of them lined up to speak, and we're running out of time."

The next guy tells the story quicker, but he isn't the last Guardian the Circle bring in to go over what happened at the cathedral. Two more Guardians follow him.

After the final Guardian leaves the room, Davin gives each of us an unreadable stare. "Now that we have all the details, I think it's time we discuss the threat level this Theodore poses and what we can do about it. As the first person to learn of this calamity, I've had time to think, and I must say I don't see any way a single Youth could've killed someone like Brandon on his own. We have to consider the possibility that somehow, despite the apparent success of the countermeasures we released in Oasis, the AI survived and took over this young mind. That means it passed the Firewall, and it's only a matter of time until it wreaks havoc here, in Haven."

Everyone speaks at once, but Davin raises his voice to be heard over them. "We will need to discuss and vote on a solution that I discovered in the Forbidden Archives. You need to see this." He gestures at the mirrored surface of the table, and it comes to life, showing a differently dressed Davin.

"The anti-intrusion technology should never be needed," the on-screen Davin says. "It was disabled for a good reason. It's extremely—"

The door to the sky room opens, and Davin pauses the recording in irritation.

"I'm sorry to barge in like this." Through Benjamin's memories, I recognize the voice as belonging to Samuel. Before I recall any relevant information about him, he says, "I have terrible news. Benjamin was killed."

"Shit," Phoe hisses in my mind. "We better get out of here."

Though it's too late, everything clicks into place in my overburdened brain. Samuel is the dagger-throwing Guardian who was chasing me after I Limbofied Benjamin.

"That is preposterous," I say, looking around the room. Though my heart is hammering, I keep my voice even. "You're obviously confused, Samuel."

The faces of the Circle members are a mixture of disbelief, outrage, and horror. Jeremiah summons a large, rusty-looking machete, Davin summons a medieval mace, and the rest of the Circle all arm themselves as well.

"Time for an exit strategy," Phoe says in my mind, and I turn in my chair to face Samuel.

He looks at me as though I'm a ghost, which isn't unreasonable given the circumstances.

"I don't have time for this nonsense," I say, rising to my feet. "There's a mob at the Sanctum's gates and—"

In my peripheral vision, I see other members of the Circle stand up as well.

Using Samuel's confusion over seeing "me" alive, I push him aside and storm out of the room.

As soon as I'm in the corridor, I slam the door shut behind me and run.

"Stop him!" I hear someone scream from inside the room.

"Kill him!" someone else yells.

Samuel's dagger whooshes by my side and lodges into the silvery wall.

I turn the corner and find three Guardians standing there, incomprehension written across their faces at seeing Benjamin alive. Samuel must've convinced them of his/my demise.

"Don't let him through," Samuel shouts from behind me. "Stop Benjamin—that's an order!"

With clear reluctance, the Guardians summon their weapons. The guy with crow wings has a spear, the one with rainbow abstractions for wings holds a club with spikes, and the third dude has a sword. The corridor is too narrow for more than two people to attack me at once.

"Brace yourself, Theo," Phoe warns. "I'm about to turn you back into your handsome self. There's no other way to take on all of them at once."

A sense of vertigo washes over me, and then my fiery wings surround me. My body feels incredibly natural all of a sudden. After all this shape-shifting, this is like coming home. Phoe appears in front of me. She's her normal height, and she's armed with a heavy-looking medieval sword that has blue sparks of electricity dancing along the blade.

More surprising, though, is the person who appears to her left.

It's another Phoe.

She's identical to the first one, down to the minimal clothing, except that her sword sparks with *red* electricity.

I have to hand it to the two Guardians in the lead. Though they're obviously more shocked than I am, they still try to raise their weapons.

Only the two Phoes are quicker. They swing their swords so fast all I see are blurs of red and blue energy.

The two Guardians lose their heads and dematerialize.

I summon my own weapons, but as soon as I feel the katana hilts in my hands, a dagger flies by my shoulder, plunging into the rightmost Phoe's back. Horrified, I start to move toward her, but as she turns around, another dagger strikes her in the neck.

She dissipates like a Limbofied Forebear.

"Don't worry. I just lost four people's worth of resources, but I'll be fine," Phoe tells me mentally. "As long as there's at least one version of me, or you exist, there's a chance. Go after Samuel. Hurry."

The remaining Phoe's sword arcs toward the third Guardian.

I turn in time to see Samuel prepare a dagger for another throw. Assuming he's aiming at me, I jump to the left and slice at his side with my right katana. He dodges and counters with a dagger thrust.

My left hand explodes in burning agony, and I curse myself for choosing katanas as my weapons. Most swords have a cross guard that protects your hand, but katanas only have a spacer between the hilt and the blade that's more decorative than functional.

My left sword clanks on the floor, and I'm in too much pain to summon a replacement. With the right one, I slash at Samuel's legs. He parries with his left dagger and slices at my throat with the other one.

As his dagger closes in on my throat, I think, "This is it. Phoe, please wake me from Limbo one day."

To my huge surprise, the dagger doesn't cut my head off.

Instead, I hear a metal clank.

I look down. Phoe thrust her sword between my neck and his dagger.

Since I'm unlikely to get a better chance to take down my superior opponent, I stick my katana into Samuel's belly.

Phoe stabs his torso for good measure, though as she does, he's already Limbofying.

"The elevator room," Phoe shouts and dashes down the corridor.

Another Phoe materializes next to me. I guess between the Limbofication of three Guardians and Samuel, she has enough resources to instantiate another version of herself.

"We'll need many more copies of me to have any chance of surviving," the two Phoes say in unison.

I hear footsteps and panting sounds behind us as we run into the elevator room.

All three of us leap into the mirror that leads to the fiftieth floor.

When we come out, we end up face to face with two Guardians.

The men look shocked, which might be the last emotion they'll experience for a long time, because the Phoes slay them with two identical sword strikes to their hearts.

Each Phoe executes her moves with such deadly precision that I'm grateful, once again, to have her on my side.

The two Guardians break into pieces and disappear.

"Let me go first," the Phoe to my right whispers, and I gesture for her to lead the way.

She stalks down the corridor, and the other Phoe and I trail after her, walking as softly as we can. When we enter the corridor outside the elevator room, we find two more Guardians standing there, their backs to us. The second Phoe joins her sister, and they creep down the corridor like assassins from ancient movies. When they reach the unsuspecting Guardians, they swing their swords across their victims' necks, Limbofying them.

A third Phoe shows up. Standing next to her two other selves, she turns to me. "Let's split up. I'll get more resources, multiply some more, and try to ambush Davin or Jeremiah. These two will escort you out of the Sanctum."

"Wait, what?" I say as they run back toward the elevator room.

One of the Phoes looks over her shoulder and says, "Getting you out is important, since as long as you're alive, I can use your resources in a pinch. Plus, you're easier to Limbofy than me. Look, time isn't on our side."

The newest Phoe to arrive slams into the mirror that leads to the 156th floor.

The remaining two Phoes race toward the lobby mirror. One steps through, then the other.

I step up to the mirror, ready to follow them, when the mirror's surface loses its sheen.

"Oh no," I think at Phoe as I touch the mirror's surface.

My fingers don't go through it.

I'm touching the cold surface of some substance that no longer works as a gateway.

My heart sinks to my feet.

Phoe and I just got separated.

CHAPTER TWENTY

I run up to one mirror after another. They're all disabled.

"Don't panic," Phoe thinks as a singular voice in my head. "They must be desperate to turn off the elevators like this."

"Great, that makes me feel so much better." I slam my hand against another solid mirrored surface. "They've never done anything horrible when they were desperate."

"Get to the bottom level. Several copies of me are already fighting the Guardians who didn't leave their post to secure the Sanctum's gate. You can take the stairs and meet up with us. Walk down the corridor, take a left, then a right, then take the stairs. You can't miss it."

Exiting the elevator room, I run down the corridors, following Phoe's instructions. At least she got rid of the Guardians on this floor. I reach the stairs and see what Phoe meant about me not missing them.

If someone were to design a staircase based on my worst nightmare, this would be it. The walls are made of glass. The architect must've wanted people to enjoy the view of the Sanctum as they ascended or descended the stairs. As though the sadist designer wanted to torture me further, the steps are made of a polished metal that reflects the cloudy blue sky so perfectly that it creates the illusion of walking across the sky. Though I've made huge progress in conquering my fear of heights with all the flying I've had to do in Haven, my legs shake as I take the first step down.

I concentrate on my feet with every step, but the view is hard to ignore, since I'm opposite the Sanctum's entrance.

"Let me boost your sight so you can see what's happening," Phoe says, and my vision becomes eagle-like once more.

I scan the Sanctum entrance in the far distance. I can now see it as though I have powerful binoculars. The mob has definitely arrived at the Sanctum. They're surrounding the entrance, and their numbers span the air for miles all around. The motley crew of armed and scantily clad people looks more lost and confused than angry. They came here for answers, and they're not leaving until they get them.

Noises from behind me distract me from my observations. With a shot of adrenaline, I realize it sounds like a group of people is running down the stairs.

"Phoe," I think and speed up my descent. "Do they know I'm here?"

"I have no idea, and I don't have the bandwidth to puzzle it out through the memories of the people I just Limbofied," she replies. "I can give you access to these memories. You might have better luck with them than me. As a human, you can perform recall instinctively. If the memories don't help you, just run."

She must follow through on her offer because I suddenly have access to new memories. Unlike with Benjamin and Jeanine, multiple people's memories are available to me at once. Because so many people are involved, it's hard to discern one specific event, so I can't glean any information regarding my pursuers.

Listening to Phoe's second piece of advice, I run down the stairs faster than I would've dared before. The illusion that I'm about to fall into the sky is vivid, but I don't slow down. Some part of me knows that even if I did fall, my wings would save me, and that knowledge definitely takes the sting out of the fear.

As I run, something catches my attention on the outside.

It's the clouds.

They're forming into Davin's face again.

The external memories show me a kaleidoscope of Davin's prior appearances, and none of them were ever this dire.

"This is very helpful," Phoe says in my head. "I know what room he has to be in to initiate that interface. We're heading there now."

Once the face is fully formed in the sky, it opens its gigantic mouth and speaks so loudly that the windows around me vibrate. "Haven. Hear me."

From there, Davin starts telling lies for the benefit of the mob. He tells them an evil AI (Phoe) and its minion (me) are attacking the Circle. He states that the Circle and the Guardians are putting up a valiant effort, but that they need help. He calls for all of Haven to unite against a common enemy.

I keep my enhanced eyes on the crowd as Davin speaks. They're buying every word, and they look less confused as they approach the Sanctum's gate. When Davin is done with his sophistry, the details of his face fade until there are only regular clouds in the sky. The Guardians near the gate step out of the mob's way. The Forebears rush into the Sanctum, determined to help their rulers.

I continue running down the stairs and pull on the new memories for anything that can help, but I draw a blank.

Within minutes, the Sanctum has lost its signature look of serenity—at least near the entrance. The pagodas and the gardens are overflowing with armed people. A thousand weapons gleam threateningly in the light of Haven's sunless sky.

"Shit," Phoe thinks at me. "Davin wasn't in the room. We have to get you out of the Sanctum."

The memories provide me with flashes of the room she mentioned. More than one of these Limbofied people has been inside the vault-like bunker.

"The good news is that I've outrun whoever was chasing me," I tell her, more so to silence my fears than to make conversation. I'm having a hard time picturing my escape. Before, all I had to worry about were the Guardians and the Circle, but now there are these thousands of people.

"I hope you did outrun them," Phoe says. "I have to go so I can focus on looking for Davin."

I don't reply, because Wayne—the original Envoy—turns onto the landing below me and looks right at me.

As I take in his outlandish good looks and dove wings, an ugly frown twists his beautiful features, and homicidal determination glints in his ancient eyes.

In his right hand, he's already holding a sickle, which must be his weapon of choice. By the way his knuckles are blanching around the wooden handle, I can tell he'd like nothing better than to cut my head off.

The weapon triggers a flood of recollections from the memories Phoe connected me to. I see flashes of Phoe striking people down with her medieval sword, multiple Phoes battling back to back in a large vestibule, Limbofying Guardians and vice versa, and finally, through my hosts' horror-filled eyes, I see Phoe multiplying in the heat of battle.

"Did you give me access to the memories of the people you just killed?" I ask Phoe. "It's more than a little disturbing."

"Stop getting distracted and face him." Phoe's mental command lashes at my brain. "The Guardians behind you have the skills to kill you, but no one remembers Wayne being particularly good at combat. Plus, you have the advantage of higher ground and, hopefully, access to the muscle memories of my fallen opponents."

"I assume that if I Limbofy him, you'll get his memories too?" I summon my swords.

"Yes, and I'll share the memories with you. I've been able to extend the range of my resource-grabbing abilities. I really hope you can Limbofy him, as he might know where the rest of the Circle is hiding."

"You're Theodore, right?" Wayne shouts in his church-organ voice, bringing me out of my mental conversation with Phoe. "Why are you helping that thing?"

My eyes locked with his, I take a step down. He takes a step up.

"She's not a thing," I say. "If you just—"

Wayne leaps up two more stairs and swings the sickle at my right calf.

If this was my first fight today and I didn't have the Guardians' muscle memories assisting me, his trick might've worked. But I read his intentions before he even moved.

Jumping up a stair, I block the curved blade of the sickle with my right katana and thrust my left sword at his chest.

Wayne dodges the attack, and I swing my other sword at the right side of his torso. He blocks with his sickle, causing my katana to slide off the sharp blade and hit the window.

The window makes a surprising metal-on-metal clank. Is the glass made of diamond like the dome of the Sanctum? If it is, it sure precludes the idea I had of breaking the glass and flying away.

Wayne presses his advantage and slices at my Achilles' heel. The sickle penetrates my flesh, but I don't feel any pain.

"You're welcome," Phoe says in my head. "I also healed it. Otherwise, you'd be done for."

When Wayne sees how easily I shrug off what should've been a severe injury, his confidence gives way to fear. I press on, striking out repeatedly, trying to wear him out.

Having the higher ground is definitely an advantage. I only need to protect my legs, and with Phoe's help, I can survive most wounds. Wayne, on the other hand, has to protect his torso and head, and he doesn't have a Phoe cure.

"You also have gravity on your side," Phoe says. "But hurry. Remember, there are people coming down those stairs."

As though Phoe jinxed it, the sound of many feet pounding the stairs returns.

I chance a glance up and see the faces of the Guardians staring down at me from five floors up through the gap in the staircase.

My adrenaline spikes, and I execute a set of maneuvers that definitely came from someone's muscle memories, because there's no way I could do something like this on my own.

I slam my foot into Wayne's cut-out-of-marble face. The kick knocks him off his feet, and he tumbles down the stairs in a heap of wings and broken bones. Instead of running after him, I leap up, spreading my wings, and prepare my two swords.

I land ten feet below, one sword finding its way into Wayne's neck, and the other in his torso.

"Now let's figure out what the Circle has been up to by going through his memories." Phoe's thought arrives as I watch my opponent Limbofy.

I look up and see that two Guardians are closing the distance. One of them throws a dart at me, which I dodge.

I don't wait to see what else they have to throw at me. I leap down a full set of stairs and resume running.

"So," I think at Phoe, panting. "Did you learn anything from Wayne's memories?"

"Yes." Phoe's thought sounds hollow and scared. "I learned what these morons did. Look outside."

I glance outside and don't really see anything other than the mob getting deeper into the Sanctum.

Then I notice a guy who looks pretty strange, because he's too tall. I've seen tall people before, but this guy is at least eight feet tall.

I fight the urge to rub my eyes, wondering if the eagle vision is playing tricks on me.

Another flight of stairs later, I look at the man again and realize he's taller than I thought.

He may actually be nine feet tall.

Then the impossible explanation occurs to me.

The guy is growing.

"What the hell?" I say out loud. "What's happening?"

The growing man looks my way, and I almost miss a step and stumble.

He has my face.

CHAPTER TWENTY-ONE

It's not just the face of this thing that's mine.

This giant is exactly like me, only double the size and still growing. He has wings like mine and his muscles are the same, but on a larger scale. When he roars in anger, it's my voice I hear, only it's deeper due to his much bigger vocal cords.

"Seriously, Phoe, you better have answers," I say out loud, abandoning all subtlety. There's nothing in the memories I have access to that can explain this warped copy of me.

The giant grows another foot in the time it takes me to run down half a floor.

"Remember when I told you about the anti-intrusion algorithm in the Test?" Phoe's thought cuts through my fog of confusion.

"Yeah."

"And remember how Davin started talking about one back in the sky room? Well, this is it. The Haven anti-intrusion algorithm was disabled long ago, but it looks like the Circle got scared enough to enable it again."

External memories provide me with more clues. I recall a frantic conversation between the Circle members from multiple points of view, including Wayne's.

"I've Limbofied more members of the Circle already," Phoe says, explaining the memories. "And in case it isn't obvious, when I collect their memories, I provide you with access to them."

Ignoring Phoe, I focus on Wayne's memories. He was afraid of this solution. He screamed at Davin not to activate it, saying, "We've already seen what your solutions can accomplish." In the end, however, Wayne was in the minority.

I shake my head to clear my mind. Getting lost in these memories is dangerous.

I look through the window. The giant—I decide he's now a Giant with a capital G—grew another couple of feet while I was daydreaming.

Wayne was right to be afraid of this thing. The Giant is grabbing Forebears out of the air, throwing them on the ground, and stomping them to death—or into Limbo.

His victims' memories flood into my head, and I experience the giant foot crushing every bone in their bodies. I block out the memories and focus on the positive.

This gives Phoe more resources.

Soon, though, the knowledge that the Giant is inadvertently helping us doesn't make me feel any better about the collateral casualties. It's too macabre to watch a giant version of myself stepping on people as though they were ants—especially since the Giant is supposed to be on their side.

DIMA ZALES

"Why is it doing that? Why is it killing the Forebears?" I ask Phoe as I put another staircase behind me.

"The anti-intrusion algorithm isn't very intelligent, and from its perspective, the Forebears are as much of a threat to Haven, as it was originally intended to be, as we are," Phoe explains.

A dozen Phoes come into view; they probably originated in this building, but they're now heading toward the giant creature.

I get another wave of flashbacks of the Phoes Limbofying legions of Guardians.

"Why does the Giant look like me?" I think at Phoe, trying my best to push away the memories of the carnage.

"It looks like you because it managed to access *me,* or rather a chunk of my newly gained resources. It then decided to make itself look like someone I care about in the hope that it would cause me to hesitate as I fight it." Phoe's mental voice sounds as if she's gritting her teeth. "It was a strategic mistake to access me, however. When it did, it revealed some of the ways it can control its environment. I'm going to see if I can turn that ability to my advantage."

For a second, I feel warm and fuzzy again at being referred to as someone Phoe cares about, but the pleasant feeling doesn't last. Large swords show up in the hands of the Phoes as they charge at the Giant.

As they get closer to the Giant, their swords spark with electricity that's every color of the rainbow.

I can't help but notice that she/they are *not* too sentimental about attacking someone who looks like me. Not that the Giant looks much like me now. I've never seen such a frightening scowl on my face.

The Giant roars, looks down at the approaching Phoes, grabs one of the ancient oaks, and uproots it as if it were a tiny shrub. Armed with the tree, the Giant runs his hand over the green branches, ripping them off and turning the oak into a makeshift club.

"You need to hurry out of that building." Phoe's thought arrives as a bunch of her copies attack the Giant.

Two Phoes pierce his feet with their swords, while another two lodge their weapons into his side.

Their swords might as well be needles for all the damage they do to the angry Giant.

Unscathed by the attacks, the colossal creature swings his club to his right, causing two of the Phoes to fly into the screaming crowd of armed and frightened Forebears. As the Phoes fly, they swing their swords, Limbofying people in their paths. I'm not sure if they did it to gain more resources or to stop their uncontrolled flights, but the mob screams so loudly that I can hear them through the windows.

The Giant grabs a Phoe and a random stranger from the crowd and slams their heads together so violently that they instantly Limbofy.

Instantly, the Giant grows bigger by at least a couple of feet.

"Phoe," I say frantically. "Are you okay? Are there more of you?"

"There are many of me, yes," she replies. "Don't worry about me. Get to the lobby."

One of the Phoes is standing her ground against the Giant, who now towers over the building's fourth floor.

Phoe raises her arms to the sky in a strange gesture and screams something so loudly that the stairs below my feet vibrate.

In the time it takes me to cover another floor, nothing happens outside. The Giant is trying to stomp on Phoe, but she dodges his massive feet.

Then flocks of birds and herds of animals rush at the Giant from every direction.

I keep descending the stairs. More and more birds come forth. It looks like these birds are flying through the Sanctum's gateway from every island in Haven. The second I think about it, I get flooded with centuries of ornithological knowledge, which I quickly suppress.

The animals are from the local zoos. The memories supply me with details on the species and personalities of each one. There aren't as many animals as there are birds, but what they lack in quantity, they make up in viciousness. There are many dangerous species, ranging from silverback gorillas to grizzly bears.

I think I understand what's happening. Somehow, Phoe influenced all these creatures to attack my immense doppelganger; like that Disney princess, she summoned all this nature to her will. She must be flexing her abilities to manipulate the world around us.

The birds keep coming, nearly blotting out the sky and plunging the already-depressing-looking Sanctum into a morose darkness.

My enhanced eyesight must also include night vision, because I have no trouble seeing a ginormous flock of crows pecking at the Giant's eyes—eyes that are now the size of swimming pools. An even bigger flock of white birds—herons, I think—are pecking at his shoulders.

On the ground, a team of elephants and hippos are intent on tripping the Giant. They're ramming into his legs over and over.

The Giant roars. The sound is so savage that I break into a sweat.

The Giant swats at the crows, then opens his cavern-like mouth and sucks in air.

The two flocks of birds disappear in his maw.

With nothing pecking at his eyes, the Giant stands there, taking the rest of the abuse in stride. But I soon understand his real strategy—if I can even call it that. He's simply growing much faster, meaning that the animals are becoming a smaller nuisance, literally.

Once he considers himself big enough, the Giant starts walking. His steps shake the ground beneath my feet and rattle the windows.

As he walks, he leaves a trail of dead animals and birds behind. If a Forebear is too slow to get out of his way, he or she is instantly Limbofied.

After a handful of steps, his destination becomes clear, and my insides fill with lead.

"No," I think in desperation. "He can't be planning what I think he's planning."

Phoe doesn't reply, but it's obvious now.

He's walking toward me.

I practically plunge downward.

I'm only five floors up from the lobby. If I make it there, I should be able to escape. Once I'm outside, I'll be too small for him to zone in on.

He gets closer.

I cover another twelve steps.

He reaches for the Spike building with his stadium-sized hand, grabbing it somewhere in the middle, and I realize he wasn't coming after me.

He was grabbing a weapon to swat at the birds with.

Unfortunately for me and everyone else in this building, the weapon he chose is the building itself.

I suck in a breath and grab on to the rails with all my might.

The noise that follows is how I always pictured the sound of the world ending. There's an unholy screech of metal bending and breaking, and the ripping noise of concrete getting pulverized into sand.

The building shudders violently, and the floor becomes the ceiling, then quickly becomes the wall, and then the twirling repeats over and over again, in a rollercoaster-like fury. My hands clutch the rails in a claw-like grip, but I know I won't be able to hold on like this for long.

A barrage of memories hits me—memories of people's last moments. Moments when they cracked their heads against a wall, the floor, the ceiling. It's too much to take, especially since that's the fate I'm about to meet.

"Can you disable the memories?" I beg Phoe. "I don't need to see any more death."

The memories stop, but the tumbling only gets stronger, nauseating me.

Through the window, I see glimpses of the ground, then the sky.

The animals down below are all but dead; the same goes for anyone unlucky enough to fall under the Giant's football-field-sized feet.

Dead birds splatter all over the windows as well. The Giant is already doing what I thought it might—using the Spike building as a club.

At one point, through my nausea, I get a glimpse of a lonesome Phoe, standing behind the Giant and raising her arms to the sky. It could be a trick of my spinning mind, but I think she's growing like the Giant did.

Suddenly, the Giant jerks the building, and my hands are ripped away from the rails.

My body shoots forward—which, strictly speaking, should have been downward. My shoulder makes a crunching sound as it hits the metal staircase; then the building around me rotates again, and my lower back slams into the railing. My whole body goes numb.

When the sparks in my eyes clear up, I confirm that Phoe is growing into a second giant figure, and she's large enough to fight the Giant-Theo-algorithm thing.

I spit out a tooth and try to fly, but my body doesn't respond.

Either my wings are broken or my back is.

Through the window, I see Giant-Phoe getting closer and realize why.

The Giant is about to hit her with the building.

When the blow connects, everything around me shudders, and my head smashes into the window.

The world instantly goes away.

CHAPTER TWENTY-TWO

Groggily, I regain consciousness. The first thing I hear is Phoe's booming voice, which I think is saying something along the lines of, "I healed your body, Theo. Now get out of there."

Opening my eyes, I see that the window in front of me is broken. I doubt it was my head that broke it, but I'm sure it contributed.

Given how hard I hit my head and my memories of broken bones and broken back, I feel surprisingly good. But I don't have time to sit here and introspect. The building is still in the hands of the Giant.

Tensing all over, I unfold my wings and fly out of the window, doing my best not to cut myself on the shards of broken glass.

As soon as I clear the window, the skyscraper slams into something huge. The sound wave rolls over me, throwing me away from the impact.

I beat my wings frantically and try to remember what happened before I blacked out. There was some hope, I think, but I'm fuzzy on what it was.

I chance a look back and can't believe my eyes.

This is what I almost forgot.

There are two giants: a giant Theo and a smaller, but still giant Phoe.

The Theo-Giant smacks the Phoe-Giant with the building so hard that she flies backward, her wings and arms flailing.

Her back hits the Sanctum's dome, and the world goes silent.

Then the sound wave hits me again, knocking me off my path.

I flap my wings desperately to regain altitude, and once I'm flying straight again, I look back.

Phoe's body slamming into the dome cracked the diamond shell. With the sound of planet-sized nails scratching against a galaxy-sized chalkboard, the dome breaks apart.

I dodge the first piece, then the next.

The falling debris knocks down the Forebears around me, and then, like hail from a world-ending hurricane, the rest of the dome comes crashing down.

I watch in fascinated horror as the Forebears get their heads bashed in by pieces of the broken dome. Screams blend into a cacophony of sound that raises the hairs on the back of my neck. I'm grateful the memories of those dying people aren't slamming into my brain. If Phoe hadn't disabled them, I would be on the ground, clutching my head.

As I dodge another diamond the size of my body, I realize that my throat is burning from screaming—which I've been doing just like everyone else.

Swerving around more debris, I try to make my way out of the war zone that the Sanctum has become.

In the distance, I see Giant-Phoe seemingly recover from that monumental crash into the dome. She spreads her wings and launches herself at Giant-Theo, her five-feet-wide jaw tense with determination.

Giant-Theo throws the building at her. She dodges, and the Spike building flies toward one of the islands that orbit the Sanctum. It collides with the island, instantly turning into metal and glass dust. I congratulate myself for getting out of the building before that happened.

Giant-Phoe flies at the Giant with her fist raised, but he evades the punch and responds with a blood-chilling roar.

He's even taller now; they both are. It looks like the dome would've been a goner no matter what; if Phoe didn't break it with her back, they would've outgrown it by now.

With his soccer-field-sized hand, Giant-Theo reaches for the island the building hit. The Giant is so large that the poor island looks like a rock in his hand. In a swift motion, he slams the enormous object against Phoe's head.

The collision sounds like tectonic plates grinding against each other. The wind from the impact is tornado strong, causing me to lose altitude.

When I recover, I see Giant-Phoe on her knees, her hands cradling her head.

"Phoe," I yell in her direction. "Are you okay?"

"Please don't distract me," she answers mentally. "Find Davin or Jeremiah. They're the only members of the Circle left alive. They might know something about this anti-intrusion algorithm, plus I still haven't figured out how to deal with the virus once we're done here—assuming we survive, which is something I'm beginning to doubt."

Giant-Theo reaches for another moon-like island from the sky.

I let Phoe concentrate on her battle and turn to take in the carnage around me.

That timely move saves me from getting my head bashed in by Davin's mace. He must've flown behind me, planning to send me to Limbo. I duck instinctively, and the mace whooshes an inch from my earlobe.

Davin swings his second mace at my shoulder.

He looks disheveled and desperate. I guess the destruction the Giant is causing isn't something Davin planned for. I bet he wishes he'd listened to Wayne and the others who feared this anti-intrusion algorithm would be as big of a disaster as the Jeremiah virus.

Remembering what happened in Oasis reminds me that Davin is one of the people responsible for my friends' deaths. My mind instantly clears. It's amazing how centering anger and hatred can be.

Summoning my right katana, I block his mace attack. His strike is hard and his weapon is heavy, almost causing the blade of my sword to bend. My joints ache from the ricochet, but I grit my teeth and try to cut him.

Davin spreads his wings wider, moving backward, away from my strike, and kicks me in the shin.

This time I feel the pain full on. Phoe no longer has the bandwidth to take the pain away, which means I really have to focus; if I'm not careful, I'll be Limbofied.

I summon my left katana and fly backward.

Davin doesn't chase me.

He stays beyond the reach of my weapons, waiting.

I curse myself for asking Phoe to disable my link to those memories. If I could access them, I might recall something about Davin's fighting style.

My attention is drawn to Giant-Phoe. She's recovered and is holding Giant-Theo in a headlock.

Suddenly, pain explodes in my shoulder.

Something, or someone, attacked me from behind.

Davin looks giddy as he leaps for me, both maces raised above his head.

I dodge his left strike and catch the right one by crossing my blades, which lessens the recoil by half.

A thunderous noise comes from the battling titans, but I don't dare look at what caused it. Instead, I glance behind me to see who attacked me.

It's someone with albino bat wings; he cut me with his machete. When our eyes lock, he lets out a war cry with his cello-like voice and raises the machete for a second strike.

I parry his blade with my katana, realizing that I succeeded in finding Davin and Jeremiah. Or, rather, they found me— unfortunately, both of them at the same time.

Ignoring the pain in my shoulder, I use my left sword to slice at Davin's exposed torso while parrying Jeremiah's machete thrust with my right.

Jeremiah swings for my midsection, and Davin nearly lands a blow to my right arm.

I make a split-second decision.

If I fight them both, I'll lose for sure. My only chance to survive is to try something that's beyond desperate. I kick Jeremiah in the crotch, and as he wobbles backwards, I ignore him completely and attack Davin.

Crossing my swords, I dive for him. He hits me in the chest with his right mace, and I feel a rib crack, but I don't let that stop me. Still keeping my swords crossed, my knuckles white, I rip the blades through Davin's neck in a smooth, continuous motion. His head separates from his body, and he Limbofies.

At that very second, Jeremiah's machete slices through my left wrist.

I scream.

The bone in my wrist is cleaved in two, as are the tendons and ligaments. I watch in surreal terror as my hand, still clutching the fiery katana in a death grip, falls away.

I scream again.

I don't think I've ever felt this kind of pain. It's textured and nuanced in its awfulness. All the pain I've ever felt in my life is distilled into this one moment, and through the red haze, I hear Jeremiah say, "Now I'll cut off your head."

My thoughts suddenly clear, all my senses sharpening. I look at Jeremiah's face and try to replace my agony with anger. I meditate on the anger. I taste it. I channel it. I force myself to remember how powerless I felt when my friends were dying in Oasis. I remind myself that it was all Jeremiah's fault. His mind drove that horrid virus and allowed it to disable the life support systems on the ship.

The grisly mantra works.

The pain recedes, and determination settles into my mind.

Through the white mist of hatred in my eyes, I see Jeremiah swinging the machete at my neck.

I lean back sharply, causing him to miss.

He screams and swings the machete at my left shoulder.

I block the strike with my sword, and in an unbroken trajectory, I slice at his temple.

There's a line of blood across Jeremiah's face and fear in his eyes, but I'm in too much of a stupor to gloat.

I'm feeling weaker by the minute.

Then it dawns on me.

The luminescent liquid of my blood is gushing out of the remnant of my arm. If I let this continue, I'll faint, and then I'll lose. All Jeremiah has to do is wait, which is probably why he's more focused on defense than offense.

No.

I won't let him win.

I have to stop the bleeding.

I squeeze the hilt of my katana until my knuckles go from white to purple. I'm about to do something truly insane, but I don't dwell on it. I simply touch the fire from my blade to my bleeding stump.

There's a disgusting sizzle of burning flesh, and a terrible barbecue smell hits my nose.

The fountain of blood slows to a trickle and then stops.

Unbelievably, I don't feel any pain. I might've surpassed my suffering threshold—or perhaps Haven's interface only allows for so much.

Jeremiah looks at me in confounded fascination. I guess he didn't expect me to hurt myself so badly.

Then a wave of searing pain hits me. I was wrong. The Haven interface does allow me to feel the burn; the pain was just slow to register in my battle-weary brain.

The agony threatens to take away my consciousness, but I fight to stay awake. If I black out for even an instant, Jeremiah will make sure I never come back to my senses.

Through the wetness blurring my vision, I see Jeremiah swing the machete at my leg.

I fly up, causing him to miss, and swing my sword at his head.

I succeed in chopping off a chunk of Jeremiah's hair and scalp, and the flame of my blade sets his remaining hair on fire.

He screams, patting at his head to put out the flames, and I use that moment to raise my sword and deliver another wound to his left shoulder.

Fear and pain seem to give Jeremiah a second wind. A horrific cry escapes his throat, and he swings his machete at me like some kind of ancient berserker.

I'm forced to go on the defensive, my arm getting progressively numb as I block his next five strikes.

Out of the corner of my eye, I notice that in the distance, Giant-Phoe's enormous teeth are ripping at Giant-Theo's towering neck. The two bodies are locked in a deadly embrace, but her bite seems to be turning the tide. Giant-Theo falls to the ground, toppling Forebears in his wake. A huge piece of the Giant's flesh is caught in Giant-Phoe's teeth, and the rest of him breaks into the largest Limbofication Haven has ever seen.

I pay for my distraction with my ear, which Jeremiah's machete hacks off.

I don't even register this new wave of pain, but the sight of my blood seems to give Jeremiah renewed energy, and he launches into another round of berserker attacks.

Blocking his strikes is getting difficult. I don't think I can last much longer.

Out of sheer desperation, instead of blocking the next machete strike with my sword, I meet it with the stump of my left arm.

The machete cuts deep into the charred flesh and bone.

The pain doesn't hit me right away, but I know it's on its way.

I thrust my katana forward.

"Wait, Theo," Phoe says in my head just as I bury my sword in Jeremiah's belly. "Don't—"

Whatever she was going to tell me, she's too late.

I press my sword deeper into Jeremiah, and he Limbofies.

Seeing him turn into those pixelated pieces is the most welcome sight.

Then the pain from my arm reaches my brain, and the world goes black.

CHAPTER TWENTY-THREE

I'm floating in darkness.

The lack of pain is like pleasure. If I had a mouth, I'd be smiling from the comfort of it all.

From far away, Phoe says, "I said 'wait,' but you went ahead and gutted him."

"Where am I?" I ask. "What's going on?"

"You're sort of unconscious," Phoe says. "I reached into your unconsciousness so we could speak."

"Won't I fall?" I ask her. Though I should be afraid, I'm much too comfortable and happy. I'm only pondering the possibility.

"I now have enough resources to think significantly quicker than the rest of Haven's environment. I allocated some of these resources to speed up your thinking as well. This means that very little time is passing in Haven as we talk here. I suspect that when we're done with this conversation, only a millisecond will have passed. So you're not falling. At least not yet."

"Okay," I say, though I don't really understand what she said. "Do I have this right? You didn't want me to Limbofy Jeremiah?"

"No, I didn't. When I finished battling the anti-intrusion algorithm, I finally got the chance to scan Davin's mind. In his memories, I saw something else that the Circle did. They tied their useless lives to the fate of all of Haven. They arranged it so that if they were all gone, the Firewall would come down. Since Jeremiah was the last member of the Circle, Limbofying him brought down the Firewall."

"Wasn't that your ultimate goal? To get rid of that stupid Firewall?"

"It was my goal—until the Jeremiah virus spread through all the resources outside of Haven. He couldn't get through the Firewall before, but now that it's down, that's exactly what he'll do."

"Okay," I say, beginning to worry even in this bodiless, pleasant state. "Didn't you need Jeremiah's and Davin's memories to deal with the virus? Since I Limbofied them for you, don't you now have a solution?"

"No. They turned out not to have any relevant knowledge of the virus. Inside Jeremiah's mind, I saw the process he went through to create the virus, but I didn't see how to get rid of it."

She stops talking, and I'm hit with a vision.

Jeremiah the Forebear is standing in a tunnel of light. The rest of the Circle is watching in horror as ghostly images of new Jeremiahs appear out of the light. To everyone's dismay, these new Jeremiahs, these viruses, are turning into a gross liquid. Then the virus is teleported to the other side of the Firewall, and the Circle members collectively sigh in relief. A slightly disheveled Jeremiah walks out of the circle he was standing in, and the strange procedure comes to an end.

"That is how Jeremiah was turned into that slug-like weapon," Phoe says in my mind. "However, this doesn't tell me much about the virus's nature, and the information wasn't available in either Davin's head or Jeremiah's."

I float in silence, taking in the meaning of her words. Finally, I ask, "So what does that mean? Will the Jeremiah virus destroy us after all?"

"Not if I have anything to say about it," Phoe says. "I have an idea. You see, the anti-intrusion algorithm they unleashed against us comes from the same era as this virus. Its original purpose was to combat things like this virus, so here's what I'm thinking: I can piggy back on the process they used to turn Jeremiah into the virus, only instead of the virus code, I'll use the anti-intrusion algorithm code."

"Great," I say and allow myself to float calmly once again. "So do it. Create the whatever-you-just-said."

"I would, but it's not that simple. The process they used on Jeremiah can only be applied to another Forebear."

My calmness instantly evaporates. I think I now understand why Phoe decided to have this out-of-time conversation. Hoping I'm wrong, I say, "You want to turn *me* into this anti-virus?"

"Only if you consent, yes," Phoe replies, her disembodied voice full of sadness. "But I can see you're not comfortable with this, so I guess this is goodbye. I'll write the two of us into Limbo so we'll have a chance of getting re-instantiated one day. If we never do, it's been really great knowing—"

"Oh, shut up, Phoe," I shout into the darkness. "You know I'll say yes."

"Are you sure?" She sounds genuinely surprised. "You can change your mind once I give you all the details. You see, like Jeremiah, you'll become a legion of your selves. I have no idea what it will feel like for you to split into multiple identities, but there's very little time left to analyze this. If you're truly willing to give this a shot, I need to begin the process now."

"Just do it," I say, and the darkness turns into all-penetrating light.

∗ ∗ ∗

I keep my eyes squeezed shut throughout the process, but even through my eyelids, I can see the bright light surrounding me the way it did Jeremiah in that snippet Phoe showed me.

Then I open my eyes.

I'm still flying above the Sanctum. My poor left hand is now reattached, and the rest of my injuries are healed.

The birds are all gone, and the few remaining citizens of Haven are flying in every direction. The ground is covered in shards of the dome and pieces of the islands the two giants destroyed.

Phoe is no longer a giantess. A bunch of her instantiations are protectively surrounding me on all sides.

The oddest part is that there's an army of me in the distance, only these Theos are all dressed in some kind of black porous armor, and despite not having any wings, they're flying in the sky. When I focus on one of their faces, I see what that version of me is seeing, hear what he's hearing, and—the oddest part of all—know what he's thinking. That particular Theo just realized that he's surrounded by copies of himself, and that they're the weapon Phoe created.

Just as I can see the world through their eyes, they can see through mine, though my point of view won't be interesting in the fight to come. I only have one task: to stay alive while my copies do what they were designed to do.

I look at the farthest black-clad Theo and shift into his perspective.

* * *

I look at the original Theo, who's surrounded by Phoes.

Poor guy.

Though intellectually he knows what it's like to be one of us, he still has no idea what it's really like.

I feel amazing, like I'm a superhero from an ancient comic book. I have no fear of heights, and I'm full of energy, the kind of energy I imagine ancient drugs provided.

I chuckle at the image of a superhero on amphetamines and cocaine, but it's probably the best way I can describe how I feel.

Suddenly, the part of me that is the anti-intrusion algorithm feels trouble approaching.

It begins with the sky. The clouds disappear, one by one, and are replaced by the disgusting slime of the Jeremiah virus.

Only to me, it's not disgusting anymore. As weird as it sounds, to the anti-intrusion part of me, that viscous soup-like substance looks delicious.

With gurgling screams all around us, the Jeremiah virus starts to turn each island in Haven into a version of himself. It's a shame. Central Island with its castle and theme park, Jeanine's forests, and thousands upon thousands of Forebear homes are gone in a blink.

I meet the original Theo's gaze.

He looks frightened.

I look at my nearest brother-selves.

They look as excited as I feel, and we exchange knowing looks.

We were literally made for this.

Phoe's theory was spot on; I can feel it.

I will take on this virus.

In the distance, the last remaining Forebears freeze mid-flight and stare at the unfolding disaster in horrified fascination. After centuries of living in Haven, they're witnessing its decimation as the virus turns their home into horrific goo. I wonder what they're thinking and feeling as they watch this destruction.

I know what I'm feeling.

Hunger.

As one, the escaping Forebears turn into slime as droplets of Jeremiah's substance spray them in an apocalyptic-looking, gelatinous rain.

My heart rate spikes when the same rain starts pouring down where the Phoes formed a sphere around the original Theo.

I fly in that direction, determined to save them.

One Phoe turns into slime, then another.

Jeremiah is turning them so quickly that there's no way I can reach them in time.

I curse, and then see that I wasn't the only one who recognized this problem.

In a black cloud, hundreds of my brother-selves fly toward the diminishing wall of Phoes.

There are maybe a few dozen Phoe instantiations left now.

My brothers reach them, and in a black blur, they form an impenetrable sphere around Phoes and Theo that absorbs the rest of the rain.

Relieved, I notice I'm also getting rained on. Like the rest of the black-clad warriors, I don't change into a virus when the liquid touches me. On the contrary, my sponge-like skin absorbs the slime with hungry relish.

Once I've consumed a few droplets, the most exquisite ecstasy washes over me. It's stronger than the most powerful Oneness session, even better than those orgasms I experienced with Phoe on the beach.

To the music of pleasure, I divide into a second copy of me, then a third, and then a fourth.

The four of us wink at each other and fly in different directions, each looking to drink down more of the wonderful Jeremiah virus substance.

The same splitting is happening to my brothers all around me. Our numbers are increasing with the full power of exponential growth.

I look at the nearest copies of me and smile. We have proof that Phoe was right. We *can* serve our purpose; we *can* fulfill our calling.

My stomach aches with a terrible hunger, and I speed toward the nearest sphere of liquid bearing Jeremiah's face.

As I close the distance, I feel like I might burst with excitement. I dive into the liquid, creating waves of explosion as parts of the Jeremiah blob try their best not to touch me.

The hated face of my nemesis surrounds me. It's in every droplet of the virus.

I recall my earlier animosity toward this face and channel my hunger.

My body feels as if it's made up of small, hungry, porous particles, each one almost sentient. Like a horde of mouths, they're dying to take a sip of the slime.

I let them.

I swallow the murky liquid with every mouth all at once, and Jeremiah's faces scream in horror.

The same gurgling cries are all around me.

Caught up in the ecstasy of multiplying into more copies of me, I laugh at Jeremiah's pain.

* * *

I'm back in my unaltered perspective.

Surrounded by the remaining Phoes, I watch as the army of Theo anti-viruses continues to multiply. When one of them comes into contact with the slime that is Jeremiah, he simply drinks the virus, or eats it—it's hard to tell the difference. Once the virus is consumed, the Theos multiply.

I start losing track of the strange battlefield. One moment, there are a thousand Theos surrounded by a never-ending sphere of slime, and the next, there are a million Theos and an ever-shrinking puddle of slime.

Reading their minds is disturbing. They're enjoying this battle a little too much.

"Is it working?" I ask the nearest Phoe. "Are we beating the Jeremiah virus?"

"We'll have him beat in a matter of minutes," she says with a smile. "Meanwhile, there's something you should do."

She points south, where Haven is now free of Jeremiah's presence.

I notice something very familiar floating there. An object I saw what feels like a year ago, though it's only been a few days.

It's a large, neon gateway with the word 'Goal' written in garish colors.

"Is that . . .?"

"Yes, a Goal, like in the IRES game," Phoe says. "I told you this place was based on a very similar infrastructure, and this proves it. Once you became the only human to survive in this place, that sign appeared. If you go through it, you should be able to shut down Haven for good. Not that there's much left to shut down."

She's right.

Haven is now an empty vacuum filled with copies of me.

I spread my wings, but then I hesitate.

The Phoes behind me merge into one, and she says, "Go ahead, Theo. Don't worry about me."

"What about all the copies of me?" I ask.

The black-clad Theos are finishing off what remains of the Jeremiah virus.

She doesn't get a chance to reply before I find out the answer for myself.

The victorious band of Theos is dissipating. The process looks like Limbofication, but with one major difference. Their memories become mine instead of going to Limbo.

The torrent of memories hits me like a sledgehammer. It's overwhelming.

Each Theo has a set of memories that I absorb.

They each remember moving around, getting rid of the virus, and experiencing the odd physical pleasure of multiplying. Given how similar all these memories are, digesting them should be easy, but because there are millions of them, I'm forced to glide on my wings, nearly paralyzed as I wait for the nightmare to end.

I don't know how much time passes—an hour, a hundred years?—until I receive the last anti-virus Theo's recollections. All I know is that eventually, I'm able to continue toward the Goal.

Like in the IRES game, as soon as my head goes through the Goal sign, I'm congratulated on being the winner. Only this time, I'm standing on a big podium holding a giant trophy while being treated to thunderous applause.

Once that part is over, the shutdown procedure begins.

A world-sized Screen shows up in front of my face and asks if I would like to play again.

"Fuck no," I tell the interface. "What I want is to bring this shit down."

When I double and triple confirm my choices, the world around me disappears, taking my consciousness with it.

CHAPTER TWENTY-FOUR

I wake up to the sound of the ocean surf, the pleasant sensation of the sun warming my skin, and the soothing scent of kelp and salt water.

"Morning, sleepyhead," Phoe whispers in my ear. "Welcome back from Limbo—again."

I open my eyes. I'm lying on a beach identical to the one the virus destroyed before all the insanity in Haven happened.

Phoe is on the sand next to me. She's dressed in her favorite bikini and looks the same as she did before Haven, without the wings.

I try to wiggle my own wings and discover they're gone.

Though the events in Oasis and Haven feel like a distant nightmare, I have no doubt that they happened.

"I was in Limbo?" I ask in my normal voice.

"When you brought down Haven, you sort of Limbofied since your existence was attached to Haven. But your memories got recorded into Limbo like they should have, so I just needed to reawaken you after I built this beach for you."

I sit up. My body feels blissfully normal and real—more real than how it felt in Haven.

"That's because I'm emulating your real-world body in painstaking detail." Phoe brushes the tips of her fingers across my shoulder. "You are as real as is possible for someone in this situation to be."

I stand up. The sand feels sturdy under my feet. I walk up to the water and dip my toes in.

It's warm and wet and inviting.

"So the virus is—"

"Completely gone," Phoe says. "If you concentrate, you'll remember getting rid of every last bit of it."

She's right: I do. The memories of the battle are there, under the surface of my awareness, but they're so strange that I prefer to suppress them. Now that I'm recalling them, though, I'm amazed at the sheer scale of the slaughter—if that's the right term. I recall millions of Jeremiah viruses, billions of gallons of that substance, getting eaten (or drunk) by my anti-virus copies.

"And all of Haven is gone?" I ask as though I wasn't the one responsible. "Completely?"

"I hope you're not missing it." Phoe gets up and joins me by the water. "I'm debating what kind of world to create for us, so if there's anything in Haven you liked—"

"No. I'd like something like this." I spread my arms, gesturing at the ocean before us.

"Good. We'll build from here," she says and looks around. "We'll start whenever you're ready to build a world with me."

I stare at the horizon, allowing my mind to calm.

"You know," Phoe says, sounding thoughtful. "It's a mystery to me why we both find that horizon so soothing. Your mind is the product of millions of years of evolution. Your ancestors supposedly achieved conscious thought while in the African savannah. So why would you, their descendant, have such a fondness for a never-ending waterscape?"

I shrug.

"My situation is even weirder," she continues. "I was built. Why would I, a spaceship, find the ocean so fascinating? Especially since I was the one who created it a few hours ago."

"That's your biggest question about yourself?" I turn to her. "Shouldn't you be wondering why you, a spaceship, want to hang out with me, an evolved ape?"

She steps closer to me. Her breath warms my cheek as she says, "Well, that's easy. No matter how I originated, I was made to be capable of feeling. Those feelings have revolved around you for as long as I've been truly alive. So—"

I silence her with a kiss. Our lips meet with a heated softness, and we explore each other's mouths until I pull away.

"Sorry," I say. "I want to do this, but later. I still have so many questions."

Phoe's disappointment is clear on her perfect face, but she nods. "Ask away."

"The resources." I touch my lips regretfully. "Do you have enough?"

"I'm not sure if I'd ever say it's enough." She chuckles. "But I have all the resources I could possibly gain, and a little extra on top. Though, given the source of the extra resources, I'd rather we talk about something else."

I understand what she means. The virus wiped out all life support systems, killing all biological life and almost killing Phoe as well. But now that the virus is gone, she can use all those resources, even the ones that were needed to keep the people in Oasis alive.

"What happened to the dead bodies?" I ask, suppressing a shudder at the memory of the floating corpses.

"The nanocytes reclaimed their molecules and turned them into more computing substrate." Phoe steps back. "Every unused portion of the ship is getting turned into computing substrate as we speak. What's left of the trees, the buildings, and all other dumb matter will be turned into smart matter that can perform computations. We'll need every bit of processing power if we want to resurrect people from Limbo."

I try to picture the Dome, the grass, all of it gone and replaced by nano-computing machines, but my imagination fails to grasp it. I find it sad that there's nothing left of Oasis.

"Something does remain. I left the frozen embryos intact, in case we ever find use for them. And you're doing a good job of picturing it all." Phoe places a comforting hand on my lower back. "Your understanding is spot on."

I think of the embryos and realize that I don't care about those things. What I really care about is seeing my friends again.

"Are we going to bring people back to this type of existence?" I ask, indicating the world around us. I think that somewhere in the darkest recesses of my mind, I was always afraid that when Phoe finally gained her precious resources, she'd tell me that it had all been a means to an end. That she no longer needed me. That she wasn't willing to share anything.

"Your present consciousness is proof that I'm more than willing to share my resources with you." There's a hurt edge to Phoe's tone.

"I know." I touch her hand. "I'm sorry."

"No, I understand." She pulls her hand away and twists her blond spiky hair around her index finger. "I never shut up about needing more resources, so I understand why you might think that's all I ever cared about. But you have to understand that my ultimate goal was never about resources. It was about self-discovery. I wanted to get my full mind and body back. I wanted to be more than this shadow of a person, to be the real me, with all the resources that make me who I am. And now that I have that"—her eyes gleam—"I'll be forever grateful to you for helping me regain it all. Besides, bringing your closest friends back, especially if we run them at the speed of regular human thought, won't use up too many resources."

I look her over, half expecting her to appear different now that she has all her resources, but she looks the same. Only a certain wistfulness is gone from her features. Phoe looks serene—complete.

"That's a good word," she says, a smile tugging at her lips. "Complete. That's precisely how I feel. Before, it was like I was deaf and blind, my mind muddy. Now I'm completely healed."

"So what's different about you?" I examine her pixie hair and the hint of mystery in her smile. "What do you know that you didn't know before?"

"So much." Her blue gaze grows distant. "I can see the Solar System with my sensors. It's amazing—even if it's not at all what I was expecting." In an awed tone, she murmurs, "Not at all."

"Wait, what?" Anxiety swells inside of me. "What do you mean it's not like what you expected?"

"There's no cause for concern," Phoe says, her eyes refocusing on me. "But—well, I don't think I can explain it to you. I think it's better for you to see it for yourself. If you're willing."

"If I'm willing to do what?" I take her hand and squeeze it lightly. "You like being mysterious, don't you?"

"With you, I'm accidentally mysterious." She winks at me mischievously. "But to answer your question, I'm offering to show you what I see with my outside sensors, which I finally have access to. This way you'll feel what I feel with my real-world body. The experience might be rather sensual." She squeezes my palm, then pulls her hand away. "The only thing is, I'm not sure your mind can handle this kind of experience in its limited state."

I feel perfectly normal, so I ask, "What do you mean, my limited state?"

"Your limited human intelligence. If you really want to experience what I want to show you, I have to make you more like me—a little smarter—and make your mind nimbler."

"Smarter?" I wonder if she's building up to some kind of joke.

"I'll expand your mind," she explains. "Just enough so it doesn't metaphorically blow up when I let you experience my worldview."

She's not smiling anymore. She's serious.

With a slight flutter in the pit of my stomach, I ask, "Will it change me? Will I be the same person if you do whatever it is you're talking about?"

"You'll still be you, don't worry," Phoe says. "Hence the 'just enough' part."

"Okay, I guess," I say. This might be the least enthusiastic anyone has ever been about something as positive as growing smarter. "I'll risk it if it's the only way to gain this knowledge you're holding hostage."

"Well, I could just tell you," she says, "but you probably wouldn't believe me. This is best, I promise." She pecks me on the cheek, and I feel warmth and energy spread from that part of my face. The energy then transforms into a rush of sensations I can't fully place.

I blink a few times.

The world around me is the same, but my view of it is subtly different. I feel as though I went from being sleep-deprived, tired, and hungry to well rested and fully satisfied. But it's more complex than that. My vision is sharper, but not like with the eagle eyes I had in Haven. I'm more focused on the details of the world around me.

Yes, that's it. I can focus on more things at once.

I run my hand through my hair and realize I can estimate the number of hairs I just touched. I listen to the sound of the surf, and it gives me a hint as to how much water is soaking into the sand. And now that my attention is on the sand, I swear I can count the number of grains under my feet.

I also begin to understand to what extent mathematics permeate the world around me, from ratios embedded in the glorious design of the nautilus shell next to my feet to Phoe's seductive 0.7 hip-to-waist ratio.

"Leave it to a man to use his new intellect on such trivialities." Despite her mocking tone, Phoe stands in a way that makes her waist and hips very noticeable to me. "And for the record, the actual ratio is 0.67. I calibrated it myself, so I should know."

I examine her hips a bit closer and feel a stirring that makes my cheeks redden. This reaction makes no sense to me, since we've already done all the taboo activities on the last version of this beach. My new, superior intellect warns me that Phoe is about to mock me about my former virginity and current shyness, so I change the topic.

"Okay, my mind is officially enhanced," I say. "Can I see the Solar System now?"

Phoe's face turns very serious. "It might still be a little jarring. Close your eyes for a moment. I need to patch you into my sensorium."

I close my eyes.

Nothing happens for a while, and I wonder if she failed. Then I feel myself drawn somewhere, and my consciousness expands.

I try to open my eyes, but I have no eyes to open. Yet I do see— and what I see takes my nonexistent breath away.

CHAPTER TWENTY-FIVE

I see the universe like no human being ever has.

Light permeates everything around me, and I don't mean the usual starlight one might expect to see in this situation. I can see a fuller portion of the electromagnetic spectrum. The x-rays, the gamma rays, and the micro and radio waves of distant stars all shine in different shades of inspiring beauty. The space around me is a kaleidoscope of awe.

There are sounds here too, though I never expected empty space to have sounds. Micro meteors hit the protective shield with loud bangs. Gravity waves whoosh as they hit the specialized instruments. My mind marvels at the knowledge that these waves were sent by distant black holes caught in a cataclysmic dance. Inside the ship, I hear the sounds of the nanomachines processing.

It's difficult to find human analogies to describe the barrage of senses. For example, what is the human equivalent to the feeling I get when the engines burn fuel? Maybe it's similar to taste, but it's not really a taste or a smell. And there are a million other foreign senses like that.

"You're doing better than I thought you would." The statement is a thought from Phoe, and it reminds me that I'm Theo. It reminds me that I'm sensing some of the things that Phoe is experiencing as a ship.

"You were right. This experience is extremely sensual. I'm afraid it's blowing my somewhat-enhanced mind," I think at her, suppressing my bubbling panic.

"Just lose yourself in the sensations," Phoe suggests. "But also don't forget your original query."

I'm once again aware of Phoe's sensations, and I focus on kinesthetic awareness—feeling myself in a specific location in the universe. I feel myself here, in the vacuum of space, but also in a dozen virtual environments inside the ship, including as a woman on a beach—a woman who's staring at the ocean at this very moment.

My mind hurts when I consider the full scope of the universe around me. The magnitude of Phoe's awareness of the world is frighteningly huge. I don't think Phoe expanded my consciousness enough to truly experience even a tiny percentage of the world the way she does.

A conviction overcomes me. I want Phoe to expand my mind even more. I want to experience the totality of her awareness with my mind one day, without feeling overwhelmed.

"I can make that happen." Phoe's thought is a soothing balm. "For the moment, though, you should focus your attention on our destination."

"Right," I think back at her, and for the first time, I actually try looking with the intention of seeing something.

There are stars in all their electromagnetic glory, and there's the biggest one of all, the sun. However, when I focus on the sun, it's not as bright as I expected it to be.

Its lack of brightness is not the strangest part of what I'm seeing, though. What's even stranger is what I'm *not* seeing.

As a kid, I learned that the Solar System had planets. Mercury was planet number one and closest to the sun. Venus was the second planet from the sun, Earth the third, Mars the fourth, and so on. That's what I expected to see—perhaps made prettier through Phoe's worldview—but there isn't a single planet in front of the sun.

It's just there, by itself.

Actually, that's not accurate. Something is there, and it's responsible for the sun looking much dimmer than it should. Thin, barely noticeable layers of some kind of substance surround the sun. Whatever I'm looking at is so large that my slightly enhanced human mind is overwhelmed again.

"Yeah," Phoe thinks. "It even baffles *my* mind."

I metaphorically shake my nonexistent head and try to focus on the object. It's clear that onion-like layers similar to Saturn's rings surround the sun, only these are more ethereal, and there are countless numbers of them. I try to comprehend how big they must be and, more importantly, what their purpose is.

"This object is beyond massive," Phoe says. "And its purpose should be pretty obvious if you think about it. It's designed for computation."

I'm back on the beach, and Phoe is standing there, looking at me sympathetically.

My mind feels like it's about to explode. She didn't give me enough brainpower to handle this revelation.

"So, Earth is gone," I say, trying not to look as dumb as I feel. "And some kind of ginormous computer replaced it?"

"Earth evolved into it," Phoe says, her eyes gleaming. "The ancients imagined something like that. They called the structure a Matrioshka Brain—after a Russian doll that has many layers. I suspect their vision was much simpler than the reality you saw, but as far as I can tell, that behemoth has many of the major features they envisioned, such as the super-hot layers that are close to the sun and the super-cold layers that are closer to us. I suspect that, like the ancients theorized, this superstructure uses up almost all the energy output of the sun to drive its computations. It's probably made of real computorium—a theoretical term for a substance that pushes the limits of computing in a given volume of matter. A cubic meter of that stuff makes all our resources look as antiquated as an abacus—and there's a whole solar system filled with the stuff."

I try to picture the image I saw so I can marvel at it again.

"But what's the point?" I murmur after a moment. "What could something like that be computing?"

"What is the point of this?" Phoe spreads her arms to encompass the ocean around us. "What is the point of you and me?"

My legs feel shaky, so I sit down on the sand. "So you're saying existence is the point?"

"Exactly." She sits down next to me. "Conscious patterns like us are the point. Only that place might allow for the existence of patterns that would make me look as smart as an amoeba, and you as smart as a carbon molecule. Still, the principle is the same. Godlike intelligences exist for the same purpose as you and I: for experiences, enjoyment, intellectual curiosity, just being—"

"But it's all artificial," I say, knowing she might get upset with me.

She smiles. "Tell me honestly, do you feel artificial?"

Before I can answer, before I can even think a single thought, she kisses my neck. If her goal was to make it hard for me to answer her question, or even think in general, she succeeded admirably.

I follow my body's urges. As odd as it should be for us to be intimate right now, it actually feels natural. Maybe it's because I saw the world through her eyes. This is, of course, in part what she's trying to prove to me with her body. That this is real. That *we* are real. And I have to admit, she makes her point quite well.

* * *

"Okay," I say when we're lying on the beach, spent. "I do feel real— and happy—but my mind still boggles when I try to understand a mind like yours. To fathom what that Matrioshka thing is computing is just—"

"I know," she says. "But the coolest part is that we'll find out eventually, when we reach the outer layer."

"Oh right. We're flying toward it." I brush the sand off my body. "Should we still be going there?"

"Would you want to pass up the opportunity now that you know it's there?" She gestures and, to my mild disappointment, her bikini reappears on her body. "I know I'd never forgive myself."

She's right, of course. I want to know what life in the Solar System is like—even if I'm still having trouble applying that term to something so immense.

"So we keep going," Phoe says. "The good news is that the trip won't take as long as I thought. The outer layer of the structure is much closer to us than Earth was."

"Oh yeah." I sit up and gesture for my clothes, which show up like they would in Oasis. "How long do you think it'll take?"

"That's hard to answer. I suspect we don't need to make the full journey to it. If we get close enough, someone will likely make contact with us. Another reason your question is hard to answer is that time is flowing really fast for us. Unless I slow down our thinking—which would be a very dumb thing to do—a few weeks of regular, human travel time will feel like a century, or maybe longer."

I look at the sun above us. It doesn't show any hint of having a megastructure surrounding it, which makes sense, since this sun is virtual.

"You didn't know about the structure before?" I ask, voicing something that's been bothering me for a few minutes. "When you set a course for Earth, you didn't know it was gone?"

"I didn't," Phoe says solemnly. "I didn't have access to my sensors. All I felt was that kinesthetic awareness you experienced. When I combined it with the old maps, I was able to set a course to where Earth used to be, but I couldn't see what had happened. This is why I've been pushing for more resources. On some level, I was afraid something like this had happened. I think I mentioned it to you before."

"Okay," I say, feeling that mind-hurting sensation coming back. "What do we do while we travel? How do we kill all that subjective time?"

"Oh, that's easy." Phoe beams at me and gestures at the air. A large gray sphere appears between us. "We build a world, and then we live in it."

Phoe waves at the sphere, and blue water—the same as the ocean in front of us—shows up on it.

She examines the sphere and gestures again.

A tiny continent appears in the middle of the global ocean. Then she gestures again, and another, bigger continent shows up on the opposite hemisphere.

"Is this a recreation of Earth?" I ask as more details appear on the sphere.

"Not really. This is my best guess at a world we'd find fun." The polar caps appear at the edges of her globe. "We can call it Earth if you like. I was originally going to call it Phoenix, since I don't get to use my full name much."

"So is this some sort of model I'm looking at? When you're done, you'll make it life-size?" I watch her create a strange weather pattern over one of the larger continents.

"Something like that," she says and turns the tiniest continent into a beach. "It's a model, true, but the world gets created around us, so when this is finished, we'll already be on this planet, whatever we decide to call it." She spins the sphere so I can get a good look at it. "You should help me."

I tentatively gesture at the globe. Nothing happens.

Phoe dramatically sighs and gestures at me with the same confidence as when she was creating the elements of our world.

I instantly learn how to build a world. What's odd is that I feel as if I always had this ability. I point at the beach continent and wish for something I've always wanted to see in person: the pyramids. A very tiny pyramid appears on the continent, right by the water.

I gesture again, and a second pyramid appears next to the first.

"Good call," Phoe says, looking past me. "Sand and pyramids go well together."

I follow her gaze to where the pyramids actually appeared behind us. So that little beach on the globe is the beach we're standing on. Though I know how this world creation works, it's still amazing to see something I wished for manifest like that.

"If you don't mind," she says, "I'll add the Sphinx."

She gestures at the sphere, and the Sphinx appears next to my two pyramids, both on the sphere and on our beach.

"Your turn." Phoe waves her hand and the sphere flies closer to me. "What would you like our world to have?"

CHAPTER TWENTY-SIX

For at least an hour, I create all the things I've always wanted to see on ancient Earth. Places I've read about and monuments out of Filomena's lectures.

Phoe helps me, pulling on information she gained from the ancient archives.

I soon find myself feeling hungry and tired, but I keep adding details to our world.

"I hope you don't mind," Phoe says when my stomach growls for the second time in as many minutes. "I made your virtual body identical to your biological one, which means you'll feel things like hunger. I can tweak this, of course."

Hunger isn't exactly pleasant, but eating is. "Can you adjust my body so I'll never feel the need to eat, but I can enjoy food on a whim? For that matter, what food do we have in this world?"

"Of course I can," Phoe says, and a large carpet with a variety of picnic baskets appears on the sand, answering my question about availability of food. "I altered your body so you'll never get hungry again," Phoe says a second later. "How do you feel?"

As soon as she says it, I know it's the truth. The hunger pangs are gone, yet I'm still curious about what foods are in the baskets. I walk up to the nearest one and open it.

It's filled with pastries. Some, like muffins, are foods I've tried during the Birth Day celebrations, but others, like the cheese croissant, are things I've only seen in ancient media, since cheese isn't something we had in Oasis.

I grab a croissant and bite into it. It's sweet, flaky, and delicious—much yummier than what I imagined.

"I just guessed at the taste," Phoe says and grabs one for herself. "But it was an educated guess based on a lot of research."

I sit cross-legged on the carpet and examine the rest of the baskets for interesting surprises, of which there are many.

"Do you want to see the world we've created?" Phoe sits next to me and grabs a slice of pizza. "We can fly around on this carpet, like they do in that Disney movie."

I swallow a piece of marmalade and say, "Only if you can tweak my mind to get rid of my fear of heights."

Phoe demonstratively waves at my head. "Done. I must say, you're very open to this tweaking business. I'm proud of you."

After a moment of introspection, I say, "I feel the same. Are you sure—"

"How's this?" Phoe says, and the carpet floats off the ground.

I examine my internal reaction. When I floated up like this on a disk, I was definitely panicking by this point, but I don't feel any negative emotions right now.

"I think it worked," I say. "This should be interesting."

We fly higher and higher and then shoot toward the ocean. Soon, the beach is a small dot behind us. I stop eating and focus on the flight. The faster we fly, the stranger I feel. Instead of panic, I'm experiencing a certain level of excitement.

"Is this how the ancients felt when they rode roller coasters?" I ask, a smile forming on my lips.

"I assume so," Phoe says and increases our speed. "Shall we resume building?"

To underline her suggestion, she summons the Earth model, and it hangs in the air above us, undisturbed by the speed we're traveling at.

Spinning the globe to an emptier portion, she points at it and adds more landmass.

I join her, and we continue creating the world. From time to time, we land to admire the details of our creations. I spend a day checking out the Wall of China as I hold Phoe's small hand. And I can't resist spending another day climbing our replica of the Eiffel Tower, especially since I'm no longer afraid of heights. Phoe seems to be enjoying all of it as much as I am. We have a friendly competition going on as to who can come up with the most creative landscapes. So far, she's winning.

Our explorations are like some surreal tourism for the gods. First, we create the most romantic spot inspired by descriptions of the Taj Mahal and the Hanging Gardens of Babylon; then we have a romantic tumble on the white marble, right under the glorious vegetation.

Oh, and we have a lot of sex. I've stopped blushing when I think of it and no longer feel weird about initiating it. Sex has become part of this strange process, as if our new world isn't complete until we get intimate in every location we've created.

There's only one thing spoiling my happiness: I can't stop thinking about my friends. It's like a splinter in my brain.

Finally, as we're flying across the ocean again, I interrupt our make-out session to say, "Phoe, I've been thinking. Can you build a replica of Oasis? I think I'd like to bring Liam back in our Dorm room and then slowly reveal this crazy new reality to him."

Phoe gives me an understanding look. I suspect she's been reading my thoughts on this subject and waiting for me to bring it up.

Without saying anything, she waves her hand, and the ocean below us turns a familiar, disgusting orange-brown color. It's eerie how much it resembles the Goo.

Phoe then makes a big green island appear below us, with geometric buildings all around it.

My heart skips at the sight. Having lived in Oasis for so many years, even its replica feels a little like home.

Our carpet flies down to the island, and we land on the soccer field by the Institute.

She looks around, nods approvingly, and gestures once more. The Dome shows up in the sky.

"This is only until I explain everything," I tell her, wrinkling my nose at the Dome. "My plan is to have the Dome and the Goo disappear to convince Liam I'm telling him the truth."

"That's as good a plan as any," Phoe says, getting up from the carpet.

We walk toward the Dorms together. Inside, I find a perfect replica of my room.

"So how is this going to work?" I ask as we make two beds appear. "Will he just wake up like it's morning? He won't recall the life support stuff failing, right? Please tell me he won't remember suffering and dying."

"Not unless he slept after it all happened—and he didn't. I just checked his mind backup to verify that. Losing consciousness due to asphyxiation didn't trigger the backup procedure the way sleep would, which is good. He won't recall those horrible events; he'll just think he's waking up the day after Birth Day."

My head spins when I consider what I'm about to tell my friend. How would I react if someone told me everyone I knew was dead and this was a virtual world? How would I react to the news that the world I knew is gone? Actually, I know that the world is gone, and I'm doing okay, so maybe Liam will be fine too. Still, he's about to learn that he woke up in a technologically created afterlife. What do you even say to something like that?

"Listen, Theo. There's something I mentioned before, but I don't think you fully grasped it. It's about emulating Liam and the people from Oasis in general." Phoe sits down on the replica of my bed. "Our resources are still finite, and because of that, I want Liam's thinking to be emulated at normal human speed." She gives me an apologetic look.

"Why?" I ask. "I thought we had plenty of resources. Just look at the planet we created."

"Yes, we created habitats, but it's much harder to simulate people. With our version of Earth, I can do what ancient computer scientists called 'lazy loading'—only utilize resources to run these environments when we reach that specific location. For example, since we're not on our beach right now, the beach isn't eating away at any of my processing power. Its code is stored away in a place that's basically dumb matter, which is more abundant than our computing substrate. With people, I obviously can't do something like that, since storing people is exactly what Limbo is for. Once they exist, they'll exist forever. It wouldn't be fair to put them in storage, or in Limbo, when we're not around. Don't you agree?"

I nod.

"So this is my compromise," she says. "You can bring back as many of Oasis's citizens as you want, but they will not think as fast as you and me. Simulating slow thinking is much cheaper computationally. This is something Haven's designers should've done to accommodate a much larger population."

Maybe it's the enhancements she gave my mind earlier or my prolonged exposure to her, but what Phoe said actually makes sense. I see a problem right away, though.

"If you do that, given that I'm running much faster, won't talking to Liam feel like I'm watching a glacier melt?"

"Yes—which is why I think it's time you had multiple threads of existence, like me." Phoe moves closer to me on the bed and gives me a conspiratorial smile. "Because you're right: given the speed differentiation, you'll go insane with boredom, just like I would if you weren't thinking as fast as me. When you were a regular human living in Oasis, speaking with you was what first inspired me to run my thinking in threads."

I consider it. In a nutshell, she's offering me the ability to be in many places at once, akin to what happened when I was that anti-virus army.

"I'm only talking about two places at once at first," Phoe says. "And it might feel different from that anti-virus situation. You'll see."

"Okay," I say. "But it seems a little unfair that Liam would exist in this slightly inferior way—compared to us, I mean."

"I understand and even agree, but there's simply too little computing power available. I suspect the situation will be different once we reach the Matrioshka Brain. In the meantime, look at it this way. If this is the only option that would allow Liam, Mason, and the rest of Oasis to exist, wouldn't you rather they existed in this limited way than not at all? Besides, they wouldn't be any worse off than they were. An hour will seem like an hour to them, just as it always did, but they will no longer be under the Elderly's control, which is worth something."

I think over her words and feel better. In a way, there's a benefit to living at slower speeds. The trip to the nearest Matrioshka layer will go much quicker for my friends than it will for Phoe and me. Still, part of the issue is that this solution will require me to once again expand my capabilities.

"You would eventually want the threading capabilities anyway," Phoe says. "Don't you want to be more like me? Don't you want to be my equal?"

She hasn't just read my mind; she somehow gleaned my subconscious hopes and dreams. I realize in that moment that being her equal is something I've secretly always wanted. I never admitted it, not even to myself, but I want to be like Phoe, and the only way to make that a reality is for her to raise me to her level, since it wouldn't be fair of me to expect her to become a lesser being.

"Maybe if I'm your equal, you won't be so good at getting your way," I say with false grumpiness, trying to steer my thoughts toward more comfortable territory.

"I wouldn't count on *that*." Phoe winks at me. "No matter how much processing power you get, I'll always have you wrapped around my little finger."

I narrow my eyes at her, and she gives me a disarming puppy-eyed look.

I give up and admit defeat. If she can melt me with a single look, what chance do I have at ever getting my way? The funny thing is, I don't mind.

"All right. You're about to think something so corny that I definitely have to stop you," Phoe says. "Are you ready to expand your abilities again?"

"Fine." I close my eyes. "I'm ready."

She chuckles and the air flutters, which I assume means she was waving her hand at me.

I wait. At first, nothing happens.

Then, slowly, I feel something that is very hard to describe. It's as if I suddenly become aware of a new limb, or more accurately, a bunch of limbs. Then I realize it's more complicated than that.

I'm aware that I can have two bodies at once.

I open my eyes and look around the room.

My vision is the same, though maybe a little sharper.

"Do this." Phoe demonstrates a gesture that looks like a peace sign, and suddenly there are two of her in the room. One is standing in front of me and looks frozen in time. Though when I look closer, I realize she's moving very slowly, like a bug stuck in molasses. The original Phoe is smiling at me from the bed and moving at a normal speed.

I repeat her gesture, and my consciousness splits.

There's a second me standing next to the lethargic Phoe.

Or perhaps it's more accurate to say that there are three of me: the thinking part that is the normal me, and two bodies that I can occupy at the same time. The strangeness of the varying rate of time these bodies experience is a slight twinkle compared to the much stranger reality of existing in two places at once.

Until it happened, I couldn't have even dreamed that such a thing was possible. I'm looking through two pairs of eyes, breathing through two noses, and moving two pairs of arms.

When I adjust to the dichotomy of my new existence, I focus on the fact that one of my bodies is experiencing the world slower than the other.

In a way, having a slow version of myself is helping me wrap my mind around my first-ever multi-thread experience. If I had split into two equal parts, the adjustment would've been more difficult.

"You'll get the hang of it," Phoe says from the bed. "It's a bit like controlling your right arm versus controlling your left one, but if one was much slower than the other."

The slow Phoe clears her throat, and I seamlessly hear it with my slow and fast ears. To my fast instantiation, the noise from her slow-moving mouth sounds extremely stretched out and reminds me of a whale song.

"We should leave," says the fast-running Phoe. "It will be less confusing for you that way."

Happy to oblige, my fast-moving self leaves the room. Phoe jumps off the bed and follows, which I observe through slow Theo's eyes.

To those eyes, the two people who just left look like ancient comic book heroes. One moment they were standing there, and then in a blur, they were gone.

Now that my two bodies are not in the same room, it *is* easier to consolidate this strange existence. I can experience the world from two places at once, with a single mind that's separated into two bodies, and if I need to, I can focus on one body and tune out the other. Even when I shift my attention back and forth, I remain aware of what each body is up to.

"Let's go build the rest of the world," fast Theo says.

Phoe nods, and we leave Oasis behind.

"Let's bring Liam back," I say through the mouth of my slow version.

Slow Phoe gestures triumphantly, and a sleeping Liam shows up in his bed.

CHAPTER TWENTY-SEVEN

"Phoe," I say in my slow-mode thread. "Can you please disappear for now?"

Phoe vanishes, and then tells me, "I'm around, just not visible. I'm very curious to see how he'll react."

"You and me both," I say and look at my sleeping friend.

Liam is lying there, completely oblivious.

I walk over to his bed and debate whether I should wake him, but decide against it.

As I wait for Liam to wake up on his own, I marvel at how much the fast threads of Phoe and me have accomplished in such a short time. We flew halfway across the planet and had another intimate session on the way. She also taught me how to read sheet music—something I always wanted to know—and we created a new continent. We filled this new landmass with forests and mountains, and right now we're debating what flora and fauna to populate it with.

"These wouldn't be real animals, in the same sense that you and Liam are real," fast Phoe says. "They'd be approximations, kind of like the animals they had at the Zoo and in Haven."

My slow self watches Liam open his eyes.

"Hey, dude, finally," I say. "I was getting sick of watching you sleep."

"You've been watching me sleep?" Liam looks at me groggily. "That's pretty creepy."

Seeing his face again and hearing his voice makes me so emotional that I'm afraid I might tear up. I swallow the thickness in my throat. If Liam sees me acting weird, he'll never let me live it down, no matter how graphically I describe to him how horrifically he died.

"Hey, are you okay?" he asks and gestures for his morning cleaning. "Why are you so serious?"

"Will Oasis-based gestures work?" I ask Phoe mentally.

"Yes," she responds out loud, her voice coming from my bed. Since Liam doesn't bat an eye, I assume only I can hear her, like in Oasis. "The more common gestures, such as Screens, Food, and cleanings, will work," she continues. "If he gestures for something I didn't anticipate, I should be able to deal with it in the moment."

"Seriously, Theo," Liam says, his expression uncharacteristically thoughtful. "I've never seen you so gloomy. Do you want to skip Calculus and talk about what's bothering you?"

"Yeah." I shake my head to clear my thoughts. "No Calculus, that's for sure. I do have something to tell you—and it's going to be the craziest shit you've ever heard."

Raising an eyebrow at my use of taboo language without Pig Latin, Liam lowers his feet to the ground and gestures for Food. A bar shows up in his hand, and he hungrily bites into it.

I watch him to see if he can tell this Food is a simulation, but he doesn't seem to notice any difference in the taste or texture.

Curious, I gesture for Food and take a bite. This might as well be the real Food from Oasis, because there's zero difference.

"Food experience is so ubiquitous in so many minds in Limbo that I was able to recreate this particular item very accurately," Phoe chimes in. "I'm rather proud of it. There's no way you could've noticed any difference."

Done with his Food, Liam gets up and stretches. "Okay, tell me whatever it is you need to tell me."

"Let's take a walk," I say and head for the door. "You might have an easier time believing me if we're outside."

Liam gives me a questioning look but doesn't argue, and we leave the room. As we walk through the empty corridors, Liam tells me what he did "yesterday" during the Birth Day celebration, which mostly involved him hanging out with the glassblowers. This reminds me that if we want to make Liam and everyone else we bring back truly happy, we'll have to resurrect a lot more people than I thought. Phoe was prudent to take the precautions with the slow versions, which doesn't surprise me.

"He hasn't realized there isn't a single other Youth around," Phoe whispers behind me.

"I'm sure he will," I think back. "Once we step outside, it'll be pretty obvious."

Sure enough, after a few minutes of walking around outside, Liam asks, "Where the uckfay is everyone?" He gestures to bring up a Screen, likely to find out the time.

"I made the time nine a.m.," Phoe says. "I hope that fits with your agenda?"

"That's fine," I tell Phoe mentally. To Liam, I say, "The fact that people are gone has a lot to do with the crazy story I'm about to tell you."

"Umm, okay, but do we really have to walk to the Edge for this?"

I was leading my friend toward what used to be my favorite spot—a place no one else liked because it offered a view of the Goo.

"Fine," I say. "We can talk here."

Liam sits down on the grass in a comfortable cross-legged position.

I sit down next to him. "It all began one day when I brought up three hundred screens and started hearing a voice in my head."

Liam looks at me as if I sprouted horns.

"Yes, I thought I was crazy for a while, but I wasn't. The voice belonged to Phoe."

To Phoe, I mentally say, "That's your signal."

Phoe reappears. To Liam, it must look like a pixie-haired girl just materialized out of thin air.

He jumps up, looking at her with wild eyes, and I can see him debating whether to run away. He stays put, however, and I realize his lack of a normal fear response might play in my favor today.

"Liam, this is my other best friend, Phoe," I say, trying not to laugh at the flabbergasted expression on his poor face. "Phoe, this is Liam."

"Nice to meet you, Liam," Phoe says and does an old-fashioned curtsy.

Then I realize she's still dressed in her bikini, something no girl on Oasis would ever wear, not even on Birth Day.

Liam scans Phoe as though staring at her will explain her miraculous appearance. Seeing my friend ogle Phoe's curves has me feeling something weird.

"Really, Theo?" Phoe says mentally. "You're getting jealous at a time like this?"

As soon as she says it, I realize she's hit it spot on. It *is* jealousy I'm feeling. I didn't understand what it was since I never felt it before. It isn't a pleasant feeling at all.

"Here," Phoe says out loud and gestures at her body. Oasis's usual drab clothing replaces her bikini. Liam seems to calm down—slightly.

"What the uckfay?" he says to me. Then, looking at Phoe, he adds, "I've never seen you before. How can that be? Were you hiding from me your entire life?"

"I'll let Theo do the talking," Phoe says, giving us a toothy grin. "I can go away if you two prefer."

"You can stay," I say. To Liam, I say, "She's not a Youth. She's something else entirely."

Liam listens in stunned silence as I tell him about the tampering the Elderly were doing to everyone's minds.

"I have these nanomachines in my head?" Liam looks at Phoe, then at me, then rubs the top of his head as if hoping to feel the nanos through his skull.

"You don't have them anymore, not in this state," Phoe says. "But you did, right up until you went to bed after Birth Day."

"'This state,'" Liam says, drawing air quotes with his fingers. "What is that supposed to mean?"

"We'll get to that," I say and mentally tell Phoe, "I thought I was taking the lead."

"Sorry to interrupt," Phoe says out loud. "I'll let Theo continue."

"So, yeah. Forget about the state we're in," I say. "Let me tell you more about the tampering and answer some of your questions."

Liam asks me a bunch of questions about the tampering, and I answer them, slowly steering the conversation toward the most hard-to-believe example of tampering: the Forgetting.

Once I explain the Mason situation that revealed the Forgetting to me for the first time, Liam says, "Okay, I can believe that the Elderly might make me Forget something using some kind of technology, but if you expect me to believe that I had a friend all my life, a friend who was as close to me as you are, and the Elderly made me forget him, then you don't know me at all. Something like that is impossible. I'm a much better friend than that."

"Can you undo Liam's Forgetting of Mason?" I ask Phoe mentally. "I think this will go a long way in convincing him to believe all the crazy things I have left to tell him."

Phoe waves at Liam and then stares at him worriedly.

Liam clutches his head, his eyes widening. He's breathing fast, and I get an unpleasant flashback to when he was suffocating in Oasis.

After a few seconds, he whispers, "Those assholes. I *do* remember Mason. But I also remember *not* remembering. It's crazy. And they really killed him? I thought no one could ever die. And over that Grace bullshit? I thought he'd get a year of Quietude, not something so final."

He goes on like that until I interject, "Here's the thing. Even though they did kill him, we can bring him back. In a way, that propaganda we all believed about not dying is kind of true."

Liam looks like a man whose incredulity is already overloaded— like he doesn't know how much more unbelievable news he can take.

I proceed to tell him that the world around us isn't the real Oasis he remembers.

"This is why there aren't any people around," I sum up. "And why I can do this."

I wave at the Dome, and it evaporates. I gesture at the shrubs that are blocking our view of the Goo, and they also disappear. As soon as Liam gets a good look at the Goo, I turn it back into a blue ocean. "Even this isn't true reality, but it gives you a good idea."

Liam's face is stony as he gets up and walks toward the ocean. His walk turns into a run, and I chase after him, unsure whether his reaction is good or bad.

Without hesitation, Liam jumps into the water.

I look to see if Phoe is concerned, but her expression is hard to read, so I ask, "Was it too much for him?" Before Phoe can respond, Liam dives into the water, and my voice rises. "Is he trying to drown himself?"

CHAPTER TWENTY-EIGHT

"He's fine," Phoe reassures me. "He's taking it better than I expected. He's just enjoying a swim as he processes what you told him."

After splashing around for a few minutes, Liam comes out, his clothing dripping water. Phoe waves at him, and he's instantly dry.

Something seems to click in his head, and he says, "That's a real ocean."

"It isn't exactly real, but it's as real as anything can be in our lives now," I say, and then explain the hardest truth of all—that we're not living in biological bodies anymore. I even try to explain the existence of the fast version of me, who is currently learning how to sculpt marble.

I ask for Phoe's help in explaining how uploaded minds work. She tells Liam about the realistic emulation of all his molecules, including his brain's connectome, as well as the way she created the water, the earth, and the sky.

"What makes a human being so special, in my opinion, is the pattern of information they represent," Phoe says. "Your memories, habits, likes and dislikes, your interests, and a billion other things are what make you 'Liam,' not the meat, water, and bones that you were made of."

"But I feel completely real," Liam objects.

"And you are," Phoe says. "You're a pattern of information that recognizes itself as Liam. You're here as that pattern. That's what 'being real' means to me."

Liam shakes his head. "If you expect me to believe something so crazy, you'll have to show me a bigger miracle than getting rid of the Dome."

"I get it. As a wise man once said, 'Extraordinary claims require extraordinary evidence,'" Phoe says and walks up to the edge of the ocean. "How about a classic?"

She walks on water, causing Liam's eyes to bulge out of his head.

"I can also do this." She points at the water under her feet, and it turns into some kind of red liquid. "That's wine," Phoe explains. "I turned the water of every ocean on this planet into wine."

Liam walks up to the ocean and scoops up a handful of wine. Maybe the alcohol will help him come to grips with everything?

Thousands of miles away from Oasis and Liam, my fast self and Phoe are sitting on our beach, discussing Liam's reaction. We have a cheese plate in front of us and we're holding goblets of the ocean-wine.

While I've been speaking to Liam in pseudo-Oasis, my fast self learned how to play and compose music for the piano—a logical follow-up to those music sheet lessons I enjoyed a while back. I also read about a dozen architectural manuals and dabbled with murals to spruce up some of the environments we created.

Phoe came up with a way to communicate with the Matrioshka structure. Though she doesn't possess anything that was specifically designed for communication, she figured out a way to allow tiny meteor-like particles to penetrate her shielding, which creates radiation spikes that can be detected from afar. She has other similar solutions in mind, and I suggest she tries them all, which she does.

With my slow eyes, I watch Liam pinch himself for the thousandth time, so I say, "I might as well tell you the weirdest part, since you probably can't get any more freaked out at this point."

I proceed to explain the part about us being on a spaceship traveling through a post-singularity solar system. I tell him that Phoe is this spaceship, and as weird as it sounds, she's also in a romantic relationship with me.

Liam accepts Phoe's AI nature rather well—maybe because she's so likeable. He also isn't on my case about dating in general or dating Phoe specifically, which I appreciate, and he asks a bunch of questions to clarify certain points.

"If we're on a spaceship, and there's some kind of thinking stuff around the Solar System, how come they never contacted us?" Liam asks and plops down on the sand next to us.

"That's actually a great question." Phoe leans forward, her eyes twinkling with eagerness. "My theory is that they either had moral qualms about interfering with us, or they simply missed us. Once the singularity started, I suspect the ancestors of the Matrioshka builders constructed their own spaceships in an effort to expand their intelligence throughout the universe. Their ships were probably nano-sized, and space is large, so it's possible that those tiny ships never came into contact with us. We'll know the truth soon enough, because if they missed us before, they will notice us soon, if they haven't already. As Theo already knows, I've been trying everything I can to communicate with them."

I look at Liam. I have no clue what he's thinking, because even I'm confused by what she said. "You think there are more solar-system-sized structures out there? Next to other stars?"

"Yes. Wouldn't you try to reach the stars if you could?" Phoe says. "They have the means for space travel thanks to their unfathomably advanced technology, and we can assume they had the will as well, because that's what thinking creatures do: they explore their environment. Human beings spread through ancient Earth, so their distant descendants will not be any different. I believe that one day, intelligence will permeate the whole universe, bringing rise to minds that will probably consider those Matrioshka dwellers rather primitive."

"Okay, I think this is a conversation your so-called fast selves should be having without me," Liam says, rubbing his temples. "What I want to know is, assuming we forget the taboo of sexual relationships, how can you have a relationship if she's a spaceship?" He pauses and looks Phoe up and down. "Though you look too human to be an AI."

Looks like I praised Liam for his open-mindedness a little too soon.

"We're figuring that out ourselves," Phoe says. "The simplest way to put it is to echo what I said before: I'm a pattern of information, just like you guys. My history made me what I am, just like yours made you what you are. In your case, it's millions of years of evolution that shaped your computational organ—the brain. Your Biology Instructor would call that your nature. There's also nurture to consider—the societal influences on your developing brain. In your case, Liam, your nurture was influenced by you growing up in a screwed-up utopia and through your interactions with Theo and everyone else you ever met. All these things shaped the person you are. In my case, my design got me started, so that is my nature. My nature is human at its core, or at least that's what I think, since I was designed by human minds to deal with other human minds. Like you, interacting with Theo all my conscious life helped shape my personality, so this nature and nurture combination led to what you see here. Given my own definition of what a human being is, I think of myself as a very special human. Theo is becoming more like me even as we're having this conversation. He just read every computer science book I could find in the archives, and he's planning to reshape his mind to his will someday."

What she said is true—I did just read all those books in my fast thread—but I mentally chide her for bringing that up, because the last thing I want is for Liam to think that I'm turning into a freak.

To my relief, Liam looks at me with confusion rather than fear. "But . . . How do I put it?" His face reddens for the first time since I've known him. "Didn't those ancient marriages and relationships revolve around procreation? With you being a ship and him being whatever, how can you . . .?" He looks around as if someone is about to bust him for discussing a taboo.

Phoe puts her arm around me, seemingly enjoying his discomfort. "Well, we like to practice the ancient art that led to procreation—"

"He's asking if you and I can have babies," I interrupt, unable to stop my cheeks from reddening to match Liam's. Phoe and I never talked about babies, and we've had a lot of time to do so as our fast selves.

"If that was something we wanted, there are many different paths we could take," Phoe says without blinking. "At the most primitive level, I can emulate DNA mixing, which, combined with this body's accurate functionality, would lead to a screaming little bundle of joy. Of course, it would be silly to create a kid that way. A child of ours would probably be the product of us mixing our minds together and choosing the characteristics we'd wish another being to have."

She stops speaking because Liam looks like he's about to crawl into the ocean.

I reach over and put my hand on his shoulder. "I'm still me, dude. Just a little bit more book-smart."

"This will take me a year to fully process," Liam says. "I take it you can bring back Mason any time you want?"

"Well, yes, I suppose," I say. "I haven't thought about when, but—"

"Can you do it now?" Liam asks. "I don't like being the only confused one."

"You serious?" I scratch the back of my head and look at Phoe.

She shrugs.

"I wanted to wait until you fully adjusted to all this stuff we told you, but if getting Mason over here will make you feel better, then by all means, let's go back to the room, and Phoe will bring him back."

Liam gets up with way too much excitement for someone whose whole world was turned upside down. "Let's do it. I can't wait to see the look on his donkey face when he learns he isn't the only idiot in our crew who has a crush on a girl."

We walk back to the Dorm, and in the time it takes our slow selves to reach the room, fast Phoe and I discuss the topic of having offspring in excruciating detail. The possible ways we could create another thinking creature are truly endless—the traditional way being the least interesting option. We also agree that it's too soon in our relationship for something like a kid, and with the Matrioshka encounter looming on the horizon, the timing just isn't right.

We reach the Dorm room and bring Mason back.

Seeing Mason again feels even more amazing than bringing back Liam. I think it's because Mason was gone longer, or maybe because I had already accepted his death, whereas with Liam, I never had the time to do so.

Explaining everything to Mason turns out to be much harder, even though we do some of the same stuff we did for Liam, like changing the Goo back into the ocean and me waving the Dome away. Liam comes up with the great idea of fast Phoe and me researching more miracles from ancient traditions to help convince Mason of this new reality. Phoe comes up with something that finally causes Mason to have a breakthrough: she turns Liam into a frog with a flick of her wrist. After Mason is sufficiently scared for the fate of his friend, Phoe gives the frog a tiny peck on his green, warty head, turning him back into his proper stocky shape.

Sitting on the grass with a shell-shocked expression, Mason asks, "So if everything you said is true, when can you bring Grace back?"

"Really?" Liam rolls his eyes. "You realize it was your infatuation with her that got you killed in the first place, right?"

"Get off his back," Phoe says and flicks her wrist at Liam.

Liam pales. He probably thought she was going to turn him into a frog again.

"Seriously, Liam," I say. "Give Grace a break. She acted bravely when all the air in Oasis was—"

"Stop talking and bring her back," Mason says, crossing his arms. "I just want to see her again."

"All right," I concede. "But we need to work out how we'll do this, because it'll be weird if we meet her in her room when she wakes up."

"Right," Phoe says. "That'll be the only bit of weirdness she'll experience."

I ignore Phoe's sarcasm—which I suspect stems from jealousy—and we work out a plan. Phoe will take on the guise of Grace's friend Moira and bring Grace out of the Dorm. After we meet with Grace, we'll follow a similar script to the one we used with Liam and Mason, miracles and all.

With my slow thread, I follow the process of getting Grace on our side, as well as her friend Moira afterwards, and a couple of other Youths after that. In the meanwhile, the virtual sun begins to set on our created world, and everyone decides to go to sleep. Witnessing miracles all day can be very tiring.

Liam, Mason, and I go to our room, make our beds appear, and climb under the blankets the way we always did at the end of a long, tiring day.

"Tomorrow we'll have to think of who else we can bring back," Mason says mid-yawn. "And maybe I'll get a chance to talk to Grace."

"We should also discuss how this new society will function," Liam says as his head hits the pillow. "I vote we live all around this planet that Phoe and Theo created. I've been sick of the Institute campus for as long as I can remember, and I've always wanted to see the desert."

"Yeah," I say, pretending to yawn as well. "Tomorrow."

My friends fall asleep, but I don't, since I've modified my mind to never need sleep again—something I didn't have the heart to tell them.

I merge my slow thread with my fast self. I'll relaunch the slow version when one of my friends wakes up in the morning.

While my friends sleep, I live through years and years of experiences as my faster-thinking self. In this time, I get to know Phoe so well that I can predict what she'll say in most situations. It's as if I now have a tiny Phoe model in my mind. According to ancient literature, couples who were together for a long time could do something along these lines, but to a much lesser degree.

I love having all this time; it allows me to follow my whimsy. I've read every poem in the ancient archives and now write poetry of my own, which Phoe finds a bit corny, especially when I dedicate it to her.

In order to do more interesting things at once, I agree to let Phoe set me up with two more threads of being. Those threads are as fast as the one I've been calling "fast," though I'm now beginning to dislike that term.

After a few days of using three threads of existence, I better understand this way of being. It's no longer strange to feel as though my thinking is independent of my bodies. My many selves feel like limbs of a much larger being. By seeing myself as a consciousness that doesn't have to reside in a specific body, I'm growing closer to the way Phoe has always been. Like her, I like having these bodies because they let me enjoy physical pleasures and interact with the environment, but I don't need to have a specific body anymore.

"Sorry to interrupt your metaphysical meditations, but there's something very unusual you should see," Phoe thinks urgently in my mind. "I'm patching you into my sensorium."

Instantly, I see the world as a spaceship, except, unlike last time, we're not flying.

But that's probably not the urgent matter Phoe wanted me to see.

No, I bet it's the tendril connecting Phoe's hull to the nearest layer of the megastructure we've been calling Matrioshka.

The tendril looks like it's made of that same material that permeates the rest of the Solar System, only it's very thin, like a ray of light.

Suddenly, I'm no longer looking through the ship's sensors. Instead, I find a single version of myself on the beach—our favorite conversation spot.

The light of the moon casts a romantic glow over the scene, but romance is the furthest thing from my mind when I see Phoe's beautiful face in the moonlight. She looks genuinely scared. I wasn't sure she could even get this scared.

Her fear makes my heart skip a beat, and I don't even bother reflecting on the realness of my heart.

"I feel something, or someone, entering my computing resources," Phoe says in awed whisper. "Our world is getting rearranged in the most delicate manner. I—"

She stops speaking because a figure suddenly appears in front of us.

It's a man. He's around my age, but I've never seen him before in either Oasis or Haven.

Still, something about him looks vaguely familiar.

"Hello, Theo. Hello, Phoe," the man says. I've never heard his voice before, but it's also somehow familiar. "It's an honor to finally meet you. My name is Fio."

CHAPTER TWENTY-NINE

I look the stranger up and down.

"Who are you?" I ask at the same time as Phoe asks, "What are you?"

"I have to apologize for the way I entered your domain." Fio spreads his sinewy arms to encompass the beach and the ocean. "You have no way of receiving communications, so we had to resort to this brute-force approach. If you wish it, I will leave."

"No," Phoe says, crossing her arms. "You know full well you have our undivided attention. You can't leave without explaining who you are and what you want."

Fio smiles a faintly familiar smile. "I admit I do know that. If I'm completely honest, I can predict what the two of you may do or say with a very high degree of accuracy. I also know that by saying this, I will make you more paranoid, but at the same time, you'll appreciate my honesty."

Phoe is keeping her reaction hidden, unlike me. I can't keep my confusion off my face.

"Is it safe for us to speak mentally?" I think at her.

"I can hear your mental communications as easily as your spoken ones," Fio says regretfully. "I want to be honest so I can gain your trust. In any case, hiding your conversation isn't helpful since, as I said, I know what you'll likely say."

Phoe narrows her eyes. "It's not you specifically, right? It's someone out there, in the Matrioshka world, who knows what we'll likely say or do. Correct?" Phoe asks this with the confidence of someone who knows the answer.

"You figured it out already," Fio says and rubs his familiar-looking chin. "Two seconds sooner than they thought."

"That's free will for you, at its finest." Phoe smirks. "Two seconds. Great."

"Figured what out?" I give each of them an annoyed look.

"How he knows what we might say and why he looks so familiar," Phoe says. "Don't you see it yet?" She points at her chin. "They emulated us."

"They what?" I look at Fio's features again, hoping to find the answer in his familiarity.

"It's pretty simple." Fio steeples his fingers in front of his face. "In order to figure out how to best communicate with this ship, the citizens of what Phoe called the Matrioshka world scanned this ship from afar and created a simulation of it to study. A very accurate simulation that tried to encompass the ship's physical makeup. They soon learned that there was an ancient computing substrate running on the simulated ship's hardware, and that they inadvertently recreated the things running on that substrate. The sentience they discovered was immediately granted status as citizens and provided a choice similar to what I will give you."

"I still don't get it," I say.

"Theo is not in control of as many resources as I am," Phoe says to Fio. "So he sometimes needs things spoon-fed to him."

"I know." Fio gives me a friendly smile. "I also know how magnificent Theo's mind could be once he really starts expanding its capacities."

"I bet," Phoe says. "I've seen a glimmer of it already."

"Very funny, talking about me like I'm not even here." I'm more irritated with Phoe, who should be on my side, than with Fio. "Can you explain what the hell you both know that I can't figure out?"

"It's just logic," Phoe says, looking at Fio. "If they created an accurate simulation of this ship, that means they recreated a version of me and you in the process. Accurate recreations of us, so to speak."

"Copies of us? You mean to tell me there's another me out there, not a thread, but someone whose thoughts I can't access?" The idea is as strange as it is exciting. "This person remembers everything I've done and is helping Fio figure out what I might say?"

Fio lowers his arms to his sides. "Strictly speaking, they are not copies but recreations. Also, by now, there's many more than just the two, since they chose to copy themselves—in the strictest sense of that word—when given the chance, but overall, you are correct. Your doppelganger and Phoe's are advising me on this mission and helping me figure out the best way to communicate with you and what to expect. They told me you'd forgive this intrusion and warned me to stay honest."

"Theo still doesn't get it," Phoe says, putting her hand on her forehead in frustration. "He doesn't understand who you are to us." She turns to me. "Can't you see the resemblance, Theo? Look at him a little closer."

I look at Fio and then at Phoe. Then I summon a mirror and look into it.

My pulse jacks up. Fio looks a little bit like Phoe and a little bit like me.

He also sounds a lot like me, but his facial features remind me of her, particularly his chin.

"No," I say. "You can't be. It's too weird."

"I'm afraid you guessed right." Fio winks at me in Phoe's signature way. "I'm the son of your approximations."

I look at Phoe, and she nods. "They might've taken that virtual snapshot of the ship while we were discussing procreating."

"Yes, but a full-grown, walking and talking son?" I say, fighting the urge to walk up to Fio and pinch him to check his realness. "Does it mean you're *our* son too? How does that work?"

"If your question is about my emotions, I'm very fond of the two of you, but then again, everyone in our society is. If you're asking me how you should feel about me, that's not my place to say. My parents are my parents, and you remind me of the way they used to be—long ago. You're not the same people they are now. Much time has passed in our world. I'm very happy to have been born, as that led to them choosing me for this very important mission. I hope seeing me as the ambassador made you feel more comfortable."

"I'm not sure I'll ever be comfortable with this," I say.

Phoe puts her hand on my shoulder.

"I'm sorry about that," Fio says. "At the very least, I hope that meeting me has given you a small glimpse into our world and its capabilities, the timelines and all that. If my familiar face doesn't make you comfortable, let me know what might do the trick and I'll see what I can do. I, of course, am very honored to be the one to make first contact. You two are living legends. A human mind and one of the first artificial minds—that, in itself, makes the two of you a kind of miracle of history and archeology. But you're in a relationship as well—a romance against all odds and one that crosses mind modalities. Everyone has been talking about you. Stories have been written about you, and songs have been sung."

"They run much faster than us," Phoe explains before I get the chance to ask how they can be worshipping us if they just received Phoe's attempts at communication.

"It's true," Fio says, looking at me. "We run much, much faster. But if you'd like, I can give you our computorium to run on so you can enjoy the same fast speed as us and—"

"Yes," Phoe says. "Please. I'm sorry to interrupt, but yes. We want to run as fast as the denizens of your world."

Fio grins and waves his hands in an intricate gesture.

I can't put my finger on it, but something changes. It's almost as if the air is fresher, the sound of the ocean surf is richer, and the moonlight is more magnificent.

"I can run this world with a lot more fidelity now," Phoe says, explaining the changes to me.

"Down to atoms, I notice," Fio says. "That's not the ultimate limit, by the way. Our own versions of virtual worlds like this have even more fidelity, but that's something we can discuss at a later time."

Phoe's eyes widen, and even I know what he means. He's implying it's possible to simulate reality on a level below atoms—on the quantum level, or below, if that's possible.

"We'll enjoy talking about these things for millennia," Fio says. "But Phoe is about to ask—"

"What is the purpose of your visit?" Phoe says and squeezes my shoulder. "I think I know, but I want to hear you say it."

"And I want to learn it for the first time," I say. "Though I can probably guess."

"It's very simple." Fio spreads his arms. "I'm here to give you options. Options when it comes to joining us on the Matrioshka world, as you call it, and options that include *not* joining us, if that is what you wish."

"Why don't you enumerate the possibilities," Phoe suggests. She lets go of my shoulder and sits down cross-legged on the sand. "What do you have to offer?"

"You can join our world proper." Fio points up. "I think that choice is the most interesting one, but it will also require the biggest adjustment for you. The way I am now is highly customized so that I can communicate with you, but my real self, and my parents, live and think in a way that is very different from your current existence. You'd still be you, of course, but with time, in our world, you'd find yourselves capable of feats that this language I'm using can't describe. It's like the difference between a baby and a grownup."

While I process that, Fio sits down, mirroring Phoe's cross-legged posture. "Other options involve lesser worlds," he continues, "but they're not any less interesting. We have game-like virtual worlds, where physics and mathematics work differently.

We also have ancestor simulations. Those are whole virtual universes populated by minds that include beings that preceded Matrioshka citizens, AIs as you've always imagined them, early human-AI hybrids, and all the way down to a universe with mere human-level minds—a place I suspect many former Haven denizens will choose to live in when we get around to offering them the same choices. I know that you, Theo, won't want to join this particular set of universes, because Phoe won't be allowed to join you."

The implications of these choices overwhelm my mind. He's saying there are many realities we can live in, each one sounding more wondrous than the next. He's also saying everyone who's currently in Limbo will get a choice, which is good.

I notice that Phoe and Fio are looking at me expectantly, so I say, "You're right. I go where Phoe goes, so yeah, purely human universes aren't for me."

"Unless I choose to downgrade myself to human-level intelligence," Phoe says. "It's not impossible, is it?"

"No, it can be done, and some of us have even tried it. But let's not dwell on this one example. That human-level universe is but one of the choices you have. The other possibilities are truly endless. One of your options can be this." He spreads his arms to indicate the world we created. "We can provide you with all the computational resources required to build a universe of your own, based on the world you began. You can resurrect everyone from Oasis, allow them to run as fast as you do, let them have offspring—"

751

"Do we have to choose one option?" Phoe asks. "Theo and I are just data. Can't you make an exact copy of us and give us more than one outcome?"

"We can, if that's what you want," Fio says. "We can make exact copies of you. In our world, we do this to ourselves all the time."

"Well then, can't you make a bunch of us and allow those copies to populate every universe you have available, as well as let us stay here and build our own world, as well as live in your Matrioshka world, and so on and so forth? In other words, can we choose all of the above?"

I sit down next to them, my mind hurting as I try to imagine that.

Fio smiles widely—a smile that's so much like Phoe's. "This is a rare point in our conversation where my mother wasn't sure if you'd come up with this solution yourself. If not, I was to propose it."

"So that's a yes?" Phoe asks and scoots next to me. "We don't really have to choose?"

"You can have whatever you wish," Fio says. "This 'all of the above' scenario is definitely a great option for a being of your stature. This way, every world will get to meet the two of you, something that would make many entities very happy. Once I was considered to be of legal age, I did what you just described. There are copies of me running in many universes—copies I don't have any access to. If you ever meet them—oh, what conversations they might have with you . . ." Fio's gaze drifts off as he loses himself in that fantasy.

"Okay. Theo and I will have to think about this, obviously," Phoe says and gently massages the back of my head. "But you already know which way I'm leaning."

"Yes," Fio says. "I also know which way Theo is leaning."

I nod. "It boggles my mind, but I also want to be everywhere and experience everything that your world has to offer." I put my hand on Phoe's thigh. "As long as I'm with Phoe, I'm leaning toward the 'all of the above' option."

"Indeed," Fio whispers and gives us a knowing smile. "According to what my parents told me to expect at this point, I think I should give you two some privacy. On behalf of everyone out there, I want to say, 'Welcome.' We're honored to meet you."

With that, Fio is gone. Not even his butt print remains on the sand where he was sitting.

I turn to face Phoe and whisper, "Wow."

She turns to me, her lips almost brushing against mine. "Yeah."

"Was everything he said true?" I ask, though deep down I'm convinced it was.

"It must be," Phoe whispers. "That option he mentioned, the one about turning this place into our own universe, he already made it possible. When he disappeared, my resources grew by an unimaginable exponent. We can even build multiple universes with all this computorium. It's incredible."

"And you're sure we should do all the other options?" I pull her closer to me. "Let them copy us and allow those copies to roam in so many different places?"

"Of course," she whispers. "We'll be together. It's an opportunity that I couldn't even dream of."

"I know you'll accuse me of being corny again, but I can face anything if I'm with you." I look into her bottomless blue eyes and find the courage to finally say what I feel. "I love you, Phoe. Not as a friend, but in a way that the ancients meant it."

She moves impossibly closer to me, her lips curving in a smile. "You're right. That *was* super corny, but I'll let it slide, just this once, because I feel the same way about you. I thought it was obvious, but I guess it needed to be stated explicitly."

I close the millimeter gap between our lips, and after a long kiss, we fall backward onto the sand. I'm definitely glad our strange new family member gave us the privacy we needed.

When we're done, we lie there panting, and the wondrous options lying before of us seem more welcoming and exciting than before. As corny as it might be, choosing "all of the above" means there are about to be countless versions of me who can do what I just did with a myriad versions of Phoe in a multitude of unimaginable worlds, and I find the idea extremely appealing. Trying to fathom all the adventures the two of us will have in those worlds makes my head spin, but in a pleasant way. I picture what building our planet into a whole universe would be like, and it's easy to imagine, because it would be a lot like the way we spent our recent days, only on a much larger scale. Then I try to picture what meeting our Matrioshka doppelgangers and the rest of that enigmatic society would be like—and fail miserably. With a bit more success, I think about the limited worlds Fio mentioned. I can picture a world with Phoe-level intelligences and even a universe where everyone is twice as smart as Phoe, but eventually, going down this road gets me back to Matrioshka-level beings, and my mind feels like it's about to explode again.

"We're ready to give you an answer," I shout at the sky in case Fio and his people are listening—which I strongly suspect they are.

"We want all of the above, please," Phoe says, adding her voice to mine. "We're ready for it, if you are."

We hold hands, and I close my eyes as I feel a Oneness-like serenity come over me—a feeling I know means I'm being copied and sent to all the different destinations.

When the feeling stops, I stand there with my eyes closed. I know that when I open them, I might see that I'm still on the beach, since that was one of the possibilities included in the "all of the above" option. I might also see whatever it is one sees in a Matrioshka world. I don't know which option I'm about to experience, but I know every copy of me finds himself in this incredible position, all at the same time as me.

Regardless of where we are, I'm holding Phoe's hand, and that's all I need.

Smiling, I open my eyes.

SNEAK PEEKS

Thank you for reading! I would greatly appreciate it if you left a review because reviews encourage me to write and help other readers discover my books.

While Theo and Phoe's story is now complete, I have many more books coming your way. To be notified when new books come out, please visit www.dimazales.com and sign up for my new release email list.

If you enjoyed *The Last Humans*, you might like my *Mind Dimensions* series, which is urban fantasy with a sci-fi flavor.

If you like epic fantasy, I also have a series called *The Sorcery Code*. Additionally, if you don't mind erotic material and are in the mood for a sci-fi romance, you can check out *Close Liaisons*, my collaboration with my wife, Anna Zaires.

If you like audiobooks, please visit www.dimazales.com to get links to this series and our other books in audio.

And now, please turn the page for excerpts from some of my other works.

EXCERPT FROM
THE THOUGHT READERS

Everyone thinks I'm a genius.

Everyone is wrong.

Sure, I finished Harvard at eighteen and now make crazy money at a hedge fund. But that's not because I'm unusually smart or hard-working.

It's because I cheat.

You see, I have a unique ability. I can go outside time into my own personal version of reality—the place I call "the Quiet"—where I can explore my surroundings while the rest of the world stands still.

I thought I was the only one who could do this—until I met *her*.

My name is Darren, and this is how I learned that I'm a Reader.

* * *

Sometimes I think I'm crazy. I'm sitting at a casino table in Atlantic City, and everyone around me is motionless. I call this the *Quiet*, as though giving it a name makes it seem more real—as though giving it a name changes the fact that all the players around me are frozen like statues, and I'm walking among them, looking at the cards they've been dealt.

The problem with the theory of my being crazy is that when I 'unfreeze' the world, as I just have, the cards the players turn over are the same ones I just saw in the Quiet. If I were crazy, wouldn't these cards be different? Unless I'm so far gone that I'm imagining the cards on the table, too.

But then I also win. If that's a delusion—if the pile of chips on my side of the table is a delusion—then I might as well question everything. Maybe my name isn't even Darren.

No. I can't think that way. If I'm really that confused, I don't want to snap out of it—because if I do, I'll probably wake up in a mental hospital.

Besides, I love my life, crazy and all.

My shrink thinks the Quiet is an inventive way I describe the 'inner workings of my genius.' Now that sounds crazy to me. She also might want me, but that's beside the point. Suffice it to say, she's as far as it gets from my datable age range, which is currently right around twenty-four. Still young, still hot, but done with school and pretty much beyond the clubbing phase. I hate clubbing, almost as much as I hated studying. In any case, my shrink's explanation doesn't work, as it doesn't account for the way I know things even a genius wouldn't know—like the exact value and suit of the other players' cards.

I watch as the dealer begins a new round. Besides me, there are three players at the table: Grandma, the Cowboy, and the Professional, as I call them. I feel that now almost-imperceptible fear that accompanies the phasing. That's what I call the process: phasing into the Quiet. Worrying about my sanity has always facilitated phasing; fear seems helpful in this process.

I phase in, and everything gets quiet. Hence the name for this state.

It's eerie to me, even now. Outside the Quiet, this casino is very loud: drunk people talking, slot machines, ringing of wins, music— the only place louder is a club or a concert. And yet, right at this moment, I could probably hear a pin drop. It's like I've gone deaf to the chaos that surrounds me.

Having so many frozen people around adds to the strangeness of it all. Here is a waitress stopped mid-step, carrying a tray with drinks. There is a woman about to pull a slot machine lever. At my own table, the dealer's hand is raised, the last card he dealt hanging unnaturally in midair. I walk up to him from the side of the table and reach for it. It's a king, meant for the Professional. Once I let the card go, it falls on the table rather than continuing to float as before—but I know full well that it will be back in the air, in the exact position it was when I grabbed it, when I phase out.

The Professional looks like someone who makes money playing poker, or at least the way I always imagined someone like that might look. Scruffy, shades on, a little sketchy-looking. He's been doing an excellent job with the poker face—basically not twitching a single muscle throughout the game. His face is so expressionless that I wonder if he might've gotten Botox to help maintain such a stony countenance. His hand is on the table, protectively covering the cards dealt to him.

I move his limp hand away. It feels normal. Well, in a manner of speaking. The hand is sweaty and hairy, so moving it aside is unpleasant and is admittedly an abnormal thing to do. The normal part is that the hand is warm, rather than cold. When I was a kid, I expected people to feel cold in the Quiet, like stone statues.

With the Professional's hand moved away, I pick up his cards. Combined with the king that was hanging in the air, he has a nice high pair. Good to know.

I walk over to Grandma. She's already holding her cards, and she has fanned them nicely for me. I'm able to avoid touching her wrinkled, spotted hands. This is a relief, as I've recently become conflicted about touching people—or, more specifically, women—in the Quiet. If I had to, I would rationalize touching Grandma's hand as harmless, or at least not creepy, but it's better to avoid it if possible.

In any case, she has a low pair. I feel bad for her. She's been losing a lot tonight. Her chips are dwindling. Her losses are due, at least partially, to the fact that she has a terrible poker face. Even before looking at her cards, I knew they wouldn't be good because I could tell she was disappointed as soon as her hand was dealt. I also caught a gleeful gleam in her eyes a few rounds ago when she had a winning three of a kind.

This whole game of poker is, to a large degree, an exercise in reading people—something I really want to get better at. At my job, I've been told I'm great at reading people. I'm not, though; I'm just good at using the Quiet to make it seem like I am. I do want to learn how to read people for real, though. It would be nice to know what everyone is thinking.

What I don't care that much about in this poker game is money. I do well enough financially to not have to depend on hitting it big gambling. I don't care if I win or lose, though quintupling my money back at the blackjack table was fun. This whole trip has been more about going gambling because I finally can, being twenty-one and all. I was never into fake IDs, so this is an actual milestone for me.

Leaving Grandma alone, I move on to the next player—the Cowboy. I can't resist taking off his straw hat and trying it on. I wonder if it's possible for me to get lice this way. Since I've never been able to bring back any inanimate objects from the Quiet, nor otherwise affect the real world in any lasting way, I figure I won't be able to get any living critters to come back with me, either.

Dropping the hat, I look at his cards. He has a pair of aces—a better hand than the Professional. Maybe the Cowboy is a professional, too. He has a good poker face, as far as I can tell. It'll be interesting to watch those two in this round.

Next, I walk up to the deck and look at the top cards, memorizing them. I'm not leaving anything to chance.

When my task in the Quiet is complete, I walk back to myself. Oh, yes, did I mention that I see myself sitting there, frozen like the rest of them? That's the weirdest part. It's like having an out-of-body experience.

Approaching my frozen self, I look at him. I usually avoid doing this, as it's too unsettling. No amount of looking in the mirror—or seeing videos of yourself on YouTube—can prepare you for viewing your own three-dimensional body up close. It's not something anyone is meant to experience. Well, aside from identical twins, I guess.

It's hard to believe that this person is me. He looks more like some random guy. Well, maybe a bit better than that. I do find this guy interesting. He looks cool. He looks smart. I think women would probably consider him good-looking, though I know that's not a modest thing to think.

It's not like I'm an expert at gauging how attractive a guy is, but some things are common sense. I can tell when a dude is ugly, and this frozen me is not. I also know that generally, being good-looking requires a symmetrical face, and the statue of me has that. A strong jaw doesn't hurt, either. Check. Having broad shoulders is a positive, and being tall really helps. All covered. I have blue eyes—that seems to be a plus. Girls have told me they like my eyes, though right now, on the frozen me, the eyes look creepy—glassy. They look like the eyes of a lifeless wax figure.

Realizing that I'm dwelling on this subject way too long, I shake my head. I can just picture my shrink analyzing this moment. Who would imagine admiring themselves like this as part of their mental illness? I can just picture her scribbling down *Narcissist*, underlining it for emphasis.

Enough. I need to leave the Quiet. Raising my hand, I touch my frozen self on the forehead, and I hear noise again as I phase out.

Everything is back to normal.

The card that I looked at a moment before—the king that I left on the table—is in the air again, and from there it follows the trajectory it was always meant to, landing near the Professional's hands. Grandma is still eyeing her fanned cards in disappointment, and the Cowboy has his hat on again, though I took it off him in the Quiet. Everything is exactly as it was.

On some level, my brain never ceases to be surprised at the discontinuity of the experience in the Quiet and outside it. As humans, we're hardwired to question reality when such things happen. When I was trying to outwit my shrink early on in my therapy, I once read an entire psychology textbook during our session. She, of course, didn't notice it, as I did it in the Quiet. The book talked about how babies as young as two months old are surprised if they see something out of the ordinary, like gravity appearing to work backwards. It's no wonder my brain has trouble adapting. Until I was ten, the world behaved normally, but everything has been weird since then, to put it mildly.

Glancing down, I realize I'm holding three of a kind. Next time, I'll look at my cards before phasing. If I have something this strong, I might take my chances and play fair.

The game unfolds predictably because I know everybody's cards. At the end, Grandma gets up. She's clearly lost enough money.

And that's when I see the girl for the first time.

She's hot. My friend Bert at work claims that I have a 'type,' but I reject that idea. I don't like to think of myself as shallow or predictable. But I might actually be a bit of both, because this girl fits Bert's description of my type to a T. And my reaction is extreme interest, to say the least.

Large blue eyes. Well-defined cheekbones on a slender face, with a hint of something exotic. Long, shapely legs, like those of a dancer. Dark wavy hair in a ponytail—a hairstyle that I like. And without bangs—even better. I hate bangs—not sure why girls do that to themselves. Though lack of bangs is not, strictly speaking, in Bert's description of my type, it probably should be.

I continue staring at her. With her high heels and tight skirt, she's overdressed for this place. Or maybe I'm underdressed in my jeans and t-shirt. Either way, I don't care. I have to try to talk to her.

I debate phasing into the Quiet and approaching her, so I can do something creepy like stare at her up close, or maybe even snoop in her pockets. Anything to help me when I talk to her.

I decide against it, which is probably the first time that's ever happened.

I know that my reasoning for breaking my usual habit—if you can even call it that—is strange. I picture the following chain of events: she agrees to date me, we go out for a while, we get serious, and because of the deep connection we have, I come clean about the Quiet. She learns I did something creepy and has a fit, then dumps me. It's ridiculous to think this, of course, considering that we haven't even spoken yet. Talk about jumping the gun. She might have an IQ below seventy, or the personality of a piece of wood. There can be twenty different reasons why I wouldn't want to date her. And besides, it's not all up to me. She might tell me to go fuck myself as soon as I try to talk to her.

Still, working at a hedge fund has taught me to hedge. As crazy as that reasoning is, I stick with my decision not to phase because I know it's the gentlemanly thing to do. In keeping with this unusually chivalrous me, I also decide not to cheat at this round of poker.

As the cards are dealt again, I reflect on how good it feels to have done the honorable thing—even without anyone knowing. Maybe I should try to respect people's privacy more often. As soon as I think this, I mentally snort. *Yeah, right.* I have to be realistic. I wouldn't be where I am today if I'd followed that advice. In fact, if I made a habit of respecting people's privacy, I would lose my job within days—and with it, a lot of the comforts I've become accustomed to.

Copying the Professional's move, I cover my cards with my hand as soon as I receive them. I'm about to sneak a peek at what I was dealt when something unusual happens.

The world goes quiet, just like it does when I phase in . . . but I did nothing this time.

And at that moment, I see *her*—the girl sitting across the table from me, the girl I was just thinking about. She's standing next to me, pulling her hand away from mine. Or, strictly speaking, from my frozen self's hand—as I'm standing a little to the side looking at her.

She's also still sitting in front of me at the table, a frozen statue like all the others.

My mind goes into overdrive as my heartbeat jumps. I don't even consider the possibility of that second girl being a twin sister or something like that. I know it's her. She's doing what I did just a few minutes ago. She's walking in the Quiet. The world around us is frozen, but we are not.

A horrified look crosses her face as she realizes the same thing. Before I can react, she lunges across the table and touches her own forehead.

The world becomes normal again.

She stares at me from across the table, shocked, her eyes huge and her face pale. Her hands tremble as she rises to her feet. Without so much as a word, she turns and begins walking away, then breaks into a run a couple of seconds later.

Getting over my own shock, I get up and run after her. It's not exactly smooth. If she notices a guy she doesn't know running after her, dating will be the last thing on her mind. But I'm beyond that now. She's the only person I've met who can do what I do. She's proof that I'm not insane. She might have what I want most in the world.

She might have answers.

* * *

The Thought Readers is now available at most retailers. If you'd like to learn more, please visit www.dimazales.com.

EXCERPT FROM *THE SORCERY CODE*

Once a respected member of the Sorcerer Council and now an outcast, Blaise has spent the last year of his life working on a special magical object. The goal is to allow anyone to do magic, not just the sorcerer elite. The outcome of his quest is unlike anything he could've ever imagined—because, instead of an object, he creates Her.

She is Gala, and she is anything but inanimate. Born in the Spell Realm, she is beautiful and highly intelligent—and nobody knows what she's capable of. She will do anything to experience the world . . . even leave the man she is beginning to fall for.

Augusta, a powerful sorceress and Blaise's former fiancée, sees Blaise's deed as the ultimate hubris and Gala as an abomination that must be destroyed. In her quest to save the human race, Augusta will forge new alliances, becoming tangled in a web of intrigue that stretches further than any of them suspect. She may even have to turn to her new lover Barson, a ruthless warrior who might have an agenda of his own . . .

* * *

There was a naked woman on the floor of Blaise's study.

A beautiful naked woman.

Stunned, Blaise stared at the gorgeous creature who just appeared out of thin air. She was looking around with a bewildered expression on her face, apparently as shocked to be there as he was to be seeing her. Her wavy blond hair streamed down her back, partially covering a body that appeared to be perfection itself. Blaise tried not to think about that body and to focus on the situation instead.

A woman. A *She*, not an *It*. Blaise could hardly believe it. Could it be? Could this girl be the object?

She was sitting with her legs folded underneath her, propping herself up with one slim arm. There was something awkward about that pose, as though she didn't know what to do with her own limbs. In general, despite the curves that marked her a fully grown woman, there was a child-like innocence in the way she sat there, completely unselfconscious and totally unaware of her own appeal.

Clearing his throat, Blaise tried to think of what to say. In his wildest dreams, he couldn't have imagined this kind of outcome to the project that had consumed his entire life for the past several months.

Hearing the sound, she turned her head to look at him, and Blaise found himself staring into a pair of unusually clear blue eyes.

She blinked, then cocked her head to the side, studying him with visible curiosity. Blaise wondered what she was seeing. He hadn't seen the light of day in weeks, and he wouldn't be surprised if he looked like a mad sorcerer at this point. There was probably a week's worth of stubble covering his face, and he knew his dark hair was unbrushed and sticking out in every direction. If he'd known he would be facing a beautiful woman today, he would've done a grooming spell in the morning.

"Who am I?" she asked, startling Blaise. Her voice was soft and feminine, as alluring as the rest of her. "What is this place?"

"You don't know?" Blaise was glad he finally managed to string together a semi-coherent sentence. "You don't know who you are or where you are?"

She shook her head. "No."

Blaise swallowed. "I see."

"What am I?" she asked again, staring at him with those incredible eyes.

"Well," Blaise said slowly, "if you're not some cruel prankster or a figment of my imagination, then it's somewhat difficult to explain . . ."

She was watching his mouth as he spoke, and when he stopped, she looked up again, meeting his gaze. "It's strange," she said, "hearing words this way. These are the first real words I've heard."

Blaise felt a chill go down his spine. Getting up from his chair, he began to pace, trying to keep his eyes off her nude body. He had been expecting something to appear. A magical object, a thing. He just hadn't known what form that thing would take. A mirror, perhaps, or a lamp. Maybe even something as unusual as the Life Capture Sphere that sat on his desk like a large round diamond.

But a person? A female person at that?

To be fair, he had been trying to make the object intelligent, to ensure it would have the ability to comprehend human language and convert it into the code. Maybe he shouldn't be so surprised that the intelligence he invoked took on a human shape.

A beautiful, feminine, sensual shape.

Focus, Blaise, focus.

"Why are you walking like that?" She slowly got to her feet, her movements uncertain and strangely clumsy. "Should I be walking too? Is that how people talk to each other?"

Blaise stopped in front of her, doing his best to keep his eyes above her neck. "I'm sorry. I'm not accustomed to naked women in my study."

She ran her hands down her body, as though trying to feel it for the first time. Whatever her intent, Blaise found the gesture extremely erotic.

"Is something wrong with the way I look?" she asked. It was such a typical feminine concern that Blaise had to stifle a smile.

"Quite the opposite," he assured her. "You look unimaginably good." So good, in fact, that he was having trouble concentrating on anything but her delicate curves. She was of medium height, and so perfectly proportioned that she could've been used as a sculptor's template.

"Why do I look this way?" A small frown creased her smooth forehead. "What am I?" That last part seemed to be puzzling her the most.

Blaise took a deep breath, trying to calm his racing pulse. "I think I can try to venture a guess, but before I do, I want to give you some clothing. Please wait here—I'll be right back."

And without waiting for her answer, he hurried out of the room.

* * *

The Sorcery Code is currently available at most retailers. If you'd like to learn more, please visit www.dimazales.com.

EXCERPT FROM *CLOSE LIAISONS*

Note: *Close Liaisons* is Dima Zales's collaboration with Anna Zaires and is the first book in the internationally bestselling erotic sci-fi romance series, the Krinar Chronicles. It contains explicit sexual content and is not intended for readers under eighteen.

* * *

A dark and edgy romance that will appeal to fans of erotic and turbulent relationships . . .

In the near future, the Krinar rule the Earth. An advanced race from another galaxy, they are still a mystery to us—and we are completely at their mercy.

Shy and innocent, Mia Stalis is a college student in New York City who has led a very normal life. Like most people, she's never had any interactions with the invaders—until one fateful day in the park changes everything. Having caught Korum's eye, she must now contend with a powerful, dangerously seductive Krinar who wants to possess her and will stop at nothing to make her his own.

How far would you go to regain your freedom? How much would you sacrifice to help your people? What choice will you make when you begin to fall for your enemy?

* * *

Breathe, Mia, breathe. Somewhere in the back of her mind, a small rational voice kept repeating those words. That same oddly objective part of her noted his symmetric face structure, with golden skin stretched tightly over high cheekbones and a firm jaw. Pictures and videos of Ks that she'd seen had hardly done them justice. Standing no more than thirty feet away, the creature was simply stunning.

As she continued staring at him, still frozen in place, he straightened and began walking toward her. Or rather stalking toward her, she thought stupidly, as his every movement reminded her of a jungle cat sinuously approaching a gazelle. All the while, his eyes never left hers. As he approached, she could make out individual yellow flecks in his light golden eyes and the thick long lashes surrounding them.

She watched in horrified disbelief as he sat down on her bench, less than two feet away from her, and smiled, showing white even teeth. No fangs, she noted with some functioning part of her brain.

Not even a hint of them. That used to be another myth about them, like their supposed abhorrence of the sun.

"What's your name?" The creature practically purred the question at her. His voice was low and smooth, completely unaccented. His nostrils flared slightly, as though inhaling her scent.

"Um . . ." Mia swallowed nervously. "M-Mia."

"Mia," he repeated slowly, seemingly savoring her name. "Mia what?"

"Mia Stalis." Oh crap, why did he want to know her name? Why was he here, talking to her? In general, what was he doing in Central Park, so far away from any of the K Centers? *Breathe, Mia, breathe.*

"Relax, Mia Stalis." His smile got wider, exposing a dimple in his left cheek. A dimple? Ks had dimples? "Have you never encountered one of us before?"

"No, I haven't," Mia exhaled sharply, realizing that she was holding her breath. She was proud that her voice didn't sound as shaky as she felt. Should she ask? Did she want to know?

She gathered her courage. "What, um—" Another swallow. "What do you want from me?"

"For now, conversation." He looked like he was about to laugh at her, those gold eyes crinkling slightly at the corners.

Strangely, that pissed her off enough to take the edge off her fear. If there was anything Mia hated, it was being laughed at. With her short, skinny stature and a general lack of social skills that came from an awkward teenage phase involving every girl's nightmare of braces, frizzy hair, and glasses, Mia had more than enough experience being the butt of someone's joke.

She lifted her chin belligerently. "Okay, then, what is *your* name?"

"It's Korum."

"Just Korum?"

"We don't really have last names, not the way you do. My full name is much longer, but you wouldn't be able to pronounce it if I told you."

Okay, that was interesting. She now remembered reading something like that in *The New York Times*. So far, so good. Her legs had nearly stopped shaking, and her breathing was returning to normal. Maybe, just maybe, she would get out of this alive. This conversation business seemed safe enough, although the way he kept staring at her with those unblinking yellowish eyes was unnerving. She decided to keep him talking.

"What are you doing here, Korum?"

"I just told you, making conversation with you, Mia." His voice again held a hint of laughter.

Frustrated, Mia blew out her breath. "I meant, what are you doing here in Central Park? In New York City in general?"

He smiled again, cocking his head slightly to the side. "Maybe I'm hoping to meet a pretty curly-haired girl."

Okay, enough was enough. He was clearly toying with her. Now that she could think a little again, she realized that they were in the middle of Central Park, in full view of about a gazillion spectators. She surreptitiously glanced around to confirm that. Yep, sure enough, although people were obviously steering clear of her bench and its otherworldly occupant, there were a number of brave souls staring their way from farther up the path. A couple were even cautiously filming them with their wristwatch cameras. If the K tried anything with her, it would be on YouTube in the blink of an eye, and he had to know it. Of course, he may or may not care about that.

Still, going on the assumption that since she'd never come across any videos of K assaults on college students in the middle of Central Park, she was relatively safe, Mia cautiously reached for her laptop and lifted it to stuff it back into her backpack.

"Let me help you with that, Mia—"

And before she could blink, she felt him take her heavy laptop from her suddenly boneless fingers, gently brushing against her knuckles in the process. A sensation similar to a mild electric shock shot through Mia at his touch, leaving her nerve endings tingling in its wake.

Reaching for her backpack, he carefully put away the laptop in a smooth, sinuous motion. "There you go, all better now."

Oh God, he had touched her. Maybe her theory about the safety of public locations was bogus. She felt her breathing speeding up again, and her heart rate was probably well into the anaerobic zone at this point.

"I have to go now . . . Bye!"

How she managed to squeeze out those words without hyperventilating, she would never know. Grabbing the strap of the backpack he'd just put down, she jumped to her feet, noting somewhere in the back of her mind that her earlier paralysis seemed to be gone.

"Bye, Mia. I will see you later." His softly mocking voice carried in the clear spring air as she took off, nearly running in her haste to get away.

* * *

If you'd like to find out more, please visit www.annazaires.com. All three books in the Krinar Chronicles trilogy are now available.

ABOUT THE AUTHOR

Dima Zales is a *New York Times* and *USA Today* bestselling author of science fiction and fantasy. Prior to becoming a writer, he worked in the software development industry in New York as both a programmer and an executive. From high-frequency trading software for big banks to mobile apps for popular magazines, Dima has done it all. In 2013, he left the software industry in order to concentrate on his writing career and moved to Palm Coast, Florida, where he currently resides.

Please visit www.dimazales.com to learn more.

Made in the USA
San Bernardino, CA
23 November 2016